THE KNIGHTS OF ALANA

The Complete Trilogy

AARON HODGES

Edited by Genevieve Lerner
Proofread by Sara Houston
Illustration by Christian Bentulan
Map by Michael Hodges

ABOUT THE AUTHOR

Aaron Hodges was born in 1989 in the small town of Whakatane, New Zealand. He studied for five years at the University of Auckland, completing a Bachelors of Science in Biology and Geography, and a Masters of Environmental Engineering. After working as an environmental consultant for two years, he grew tired of office work and decided to quit his job in 2014 and see the world. One year later, he published his first novel - Stormwielder.

FOLLOW AARON HODGES...

And receive TWO FREE novels and a short story!

https://aaronhodgesauthor.com/newsletter

Book 4: Dreams of Fury

The Alfurian Chronicles

Book 1: Defiant

Book 2: Guardian

Book 3: Conquest

The Swords of Heaven and Hell

Book 1: Darkstrider

The Four Circles

Book 1: Help! My Wizard Mentor Had A Heart Attack And Now I'm Being Chased By A Horde Of Giant Spiders!

The Untamed Isles

The Path Awakens

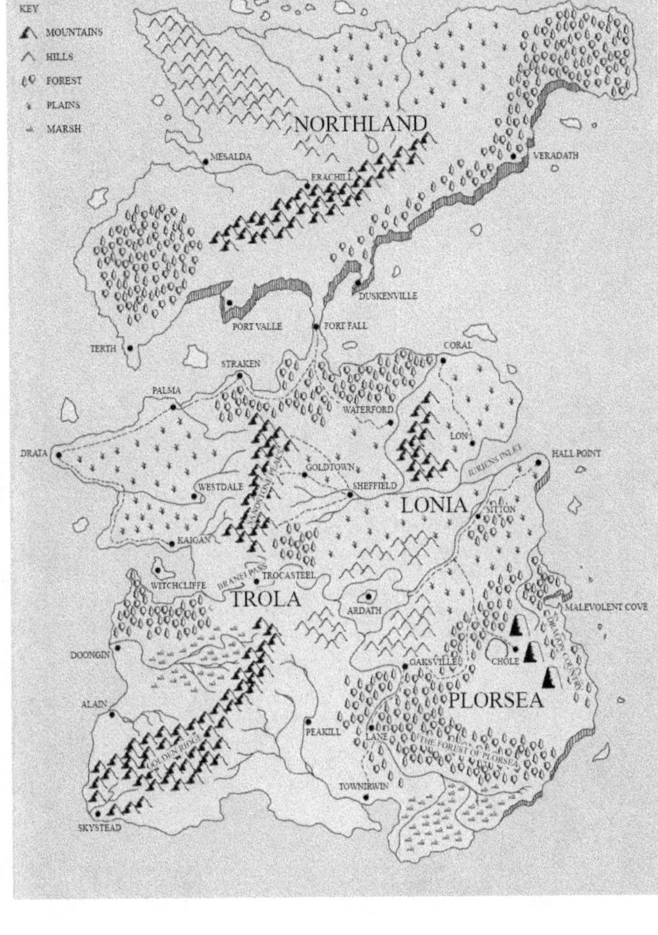

KEY
MOUNTAINS
HILLS
FOREST
PLAINS
MARSH
NORTHLAND
MESALDA
ERACHILL
VERADATH
DUSKENVILLE
TERTH
PORT VALLE
FORT FALL
STRAKEN
CORAL
PALMA
WATERFORD
LON
DRATA
GOLDTOWN
HALL POINT
WESTDALE
SHEFFIELD
LONIA
SITTON
KAIGAN
WITCHCLIFFE
BRANEI PASS
TROCASTEEL
TROLA
ARDATH
MALEVOLENT COVE
DOONGIN
OAKSVILLE
CHOLE
ALAIN
PLORSEA
PEAKILL
LANE
GOLDEN RIDGE
THE FOREST OF PLORSEA
TOWNIRWIN
SKYSTEAD

New York Times Bestselling Author
AARON HODGES
DAUGHTER OF FATE
THE KNIGHTS OF ALANA : BOOK ONE

PROLOGUE

Ikar's heart quickened as his horse rounded a curve in the mountainside, revealing a town nestled on the edge of the fiord below. The setting sun shone on the crystal blue waters, where several ships bobbed at anchor, shielded from the open ocean by the enclosing arms of Golden Ridge. Barely a cloud could be seen in the sky and the slopes ahead were a parched-brown, strewn with gravel except where the thin line of the trail wound its way down towards the village.

Studying the quiet seaside settlement, Ikar wondered how a place so beautiful could breed such treason.

"We have arrived," he announced, twisting in his saddle.

His armour creaked, confining his movement, and though the heavy steel had long been a part of him, he felt a moment's longing to hurl it from him. The journey through the mountains had taken over a week, and in all that time he had removed his armour only to sleep. It was forbidden for a Knight of Alana to remove his helmet in public, least an unbeliever learn their identity.

But with the summer sun beating down upon them, the faith of even the most devout of Knights had been tested. The Saviour had granted them her strength though, and none had given in to temptation.

Only Merak, an Elder of the Order of Alana, was permitted to go without his helmet. He edged his horse past Ikar to study the landscape.

"The Saviour has blessed us." His voice was soft, for he was far older than the rest of their party. He was one of the first of their Order, born in the days before magic left the world. His days as a Knight were long past, but an Elder had been needed for this quest, and he had volunteered. "We have arrived in time to thwart another of their profane ceremonies."

"You are sure?" Ikar asked, edging his horse alongside the Elder.

The shuffling of hooves on gravel came from behind them as the other Knights pressed forward, eager to see an end to their quest. Word had reached their Castle weeks ago, brought to them by a devout farmer who had stumbled upon the ritual while tending his goats. They'd been fortunate; this was old country and there were few believers in the Saviour. Ikar shuddered to think how long the evil here had been left unchecked.

Ikar tightened his grip on the reins. How anyone could commit such blasphemy was beyond him. For a thousand years, the Three Nations had suffered beneath the yolk of the False Gods. Only thirty years ago had they finally been liberated, when the divine Alana had slain the Gods and purged the world of their magic.

Before that fateful day, Magickers had roamed the Three Nations at will. Granted powers beyond imagining by the False Gods, they had wielded their magic without thought of consequence. Those not cursed with power had been reduced to nothing, slaves to the will of Magickers.

After the death of magic, many had despaired, so accustomed had they been to the rule of the Gods. Thousands had suffered as the rulers of the Three Nations sought to survive without the crutch of magic. Amidst the chaos, the Order of Alana had been born. The first Elders had shown the lost the way, revealing a new path—the *true* path—for humanity, one of independence and freewill.

But there were those who still longed for the past, who wished to restore the power of the False Gods. They gathered in the shadows, joining their minds, seeking out old secrets. Perhaps they even knew the truth, that with the solstice approaching, the old powers were rising.

The thought filled Ikar with rage, but with an effort of will he pressed it down. A Knight must always remain in control, for they were blessed with the strength of the Saviour, and had sworn to wield it only in service to the Order. The Elders had plans for the ones below, designs that would ensure their false Gods would be forever bound in the darkness.

"I am sure," Merak finally answered Ikar's question. He turned and addressed two of their Knights. "There is a ship at the pier. You will go ahead and convince the captain to grant us passage."

"We will not fail you, Elder," the Knights answered, their voices made metallic by their helmets.

Ikar shivered as the Elder's eyes fell on him. "Ikar."

He inclined his head. "Yes, Elder."

"They say you are descended from Alan the Great, who fought the False Gods on the walls of Fort Fall."

"It is true, sir," Ikar replied, his heart pounding hard in his chest.

"Then in the name of your ancestor, I ask you to lead our Knights against the enemy."

Merak pointed down the path towards the town, and Ikar saw now the ruins of a temple rising from the slope of the mountain. The three spires of the False Gods had begun to crumble. Only one now stood. Ikar took it as a sign and smiled.

"May Alana bless our swords."

Pela let out a long breath as she topped the stone stairs and stepped onto the ramparts of Skystead. She had finished her chores early—mopping up the floors of the dining room, hanging out the linens for drying, refilling the stable troughs—and had departed before their guests in the upstairs rooms had awoken. Despite spending all of her seventeen years growing up in the town's only inn, Pela preferred her own company, and had little desire to stammer through pleasantries with the strangers.

They were leaving today anyway, heading out on the ship that had come into port the night before. Hearing the shouts of the captain from below, Pela stepped up to the edge of the crenellations. The wall fell sharply into deep water beneath where she stood, but away to her right were the main gates of the town. They opened out onto the stone docks, where sailors carrying wares darted frantically to and fro. With high tide only two hours away, they would need to be quick if they wanted to depart this morning.

Pela thought they would probably make it. The captain

looked like an experienced hand. With no other travellers in sight, the inn would be peaceful tonight—though her mother, Kryssa, would be worried at the lack of business.

Thinking of her mother, Pela sighed. No doubt Kryssa would be searching for her by now, to drag Pela to their weekly meditation at the temple.

As though summoned by her thoughts, a distant voice echoed from the town. "Pela!"

Pela slid off the crenellation and ducked down, hoping her mother had not spotted her. The walls stood some thirty feet high and the two-storey roofs of the town were well below her. Most of the buildings in Skystead were built of stone and stood side by side with no space between them, except where the narrow alleyways crisscrossed the larger avenues. Below the streets were a maze, but for the agile, the flat rooftops often offered faster passage around the town.

But Pela's mother, who turned her nose at such notions, would be in the alleys below. She would not spot Pela on her remote perch.

"Pela, I know you're up there!" Her mother's voice rang from the stone walls, sounding as though she were directly below.

Cursing, Pela stood and looked into the alley behind the wall. Kryssa stood with hands on hips, a furious scowl etched across her face. In many ways, she was Pela's twin, though Kryssa was outspoken where Pela was quiet. Her mother wore the platinum hair that marked them both as outsiders in a tidy braid. The sight made Pela wish she'd at least run a brush over her head that morning. Their sun-kissed skin, narrow noses, and sharp cheekbones proved their relation. Only their eyes were different: her mother's a brilliant silver, while Pela's were a hazel-green she was told had come from her long-deceased father.

"What do you want?" Pela called down.

"You know what, young lady," Kryssa hissed, her voice quieter now.

"I told you, I don't want to go anymore," Pela groaned. "All those people…can't I just meditate up here?"

Kryssa tapped her foot on the tiled road. "You still live under my roof, young lady. Until you turn eighteen, you'll do as I say."

"Or what?" Eighteen was still months away.

"Would you like to clean out the barn tonight?"

Pela suppressed a groan. "Fine!" she relented. "I'll meet you there."

Before her mother could call her back, she darted along the ramparts to one of the taller buildings. Here, the drop to the rooftop was only five feet. She leapt before her mind could dwell on the fall, her boots thumping down hard. A voice called up from the alley, but Pela was already gone, leaving her mother behind.

She took the circular route across the town towards the mountain path, her good mood restored. She was in no rush to beat her mother to Temple. If she took enough time, meditation might already be underway when she arrived, and she would not have to bother herself with any clumsy conversations.

Mountain peaks loomed overhead as she wandered the rooftops. Skystead straddled a narrow patch of land where Golden Ridge met the deep fiords of the coast. They were as far south as anywhere in Plorsea, and it was a long boat ride and a longer walk to anything else resembling civilisation. Only once in her seventeen years had Pela made the trip to Townirwin, the nearest settlement, and that had been so long ago she barely remembered it.

Her gaze roamed the skyline as she neared the mountain gate. A winding road led up the steep slope, where a dozen workers could already be seen making their way to work. High above, beyond sight of town, the coffee plantations that were Skystead's lifeblood awaited. Even further up, the road led eventually to the nation of Trola. But no one ventured there now, not since the Trolan King had closed their borders under penalty of death.

But Pela's destination was nowhere near so far. Three hundred feet above the town, a second path branched from the main road, leading along the stark slopes to where a cluster of ruins clung to the mountainside.

Once three spires had risen above the walls of granite and marble, but only the jagged remnants of one remained now. The outer walls were mostly solid, though small sections had begun to crumble, the mortar rotted away. Summer storms had taken their toll, smashing in the roof in several places, leaving the insides exposed to the elements. One day, it was said, the whole thing would be washed away, and all that remained of the Three Gods would vanish from Skystead.

The temple had been abandoned for over thirty years, but only in recent times had the ruins become a source of controversy. There were those who said now that the Three Gods had been evil, that the gift of their magic had been a poisoned chalice, that they had enslaved humanity to some unknown purpose.

For Pela's mother and others who still knew their history, the Three Gods remained the true saviours of the Three Nations.

Coming to the edge of town, Pela found a narrow staircase and returned to ground level. There was no sign of her mother at the gates, but far above she spotted Kryssa at the fork in the road. Despite the distance, Pela could sense the anger radiating from her mother's distant figure. Her cheeks warmed, and feeling slightly abashed, she hurried up the winding path.

Within minutes her calves were burning. The mountainside was steep here, rising sharply from the fiord up to the peaks three thousand feet above. There were exactly 1,555 steps from the town to the temple—Pela had counted them many times before—and in the burning summer sun, her tunic was quickly soaked with sweat. The undulating mountains of Golden Ridge stretched away to the north in an unbroken line, dividing the lands of Plorsea from Trola to the west.

It took half an hour to make the crossroad, and another ten minutes to reach the ruins. The mountainside was quiet as she approached; her mother and the others must have already begun their meditation. Her shame returning, Pela darted through the doorway. Darkness engulfed her and she let out a sigh, relieved to be out of the sun.

Inside, cursory efforts had been made at repairs, though rays of light still filtered through cracks in the ceiling. Whispers carried down the corridor, drawing Pela deeper into the ruin. The temperature dropped as she followed the familiar path towards the central chambers. Rubble lay strewn across the granite tiles hazardous in the dark, but Pela had explored these corridors as a child, and could have negotiated the temple blindfolded.

The whispers grew louder as Pela turned a corner and found herself at the entrance to the main chamber. At least two dozen villagers were already present. Many had taken up positions on the faded emerald and sapphire carpets, their eyes closed, and legs crossed as they sought the inner calm taught by the Gods. Several others still stood near the entrance speaking quietly. An old man, his face wrinkled and hair grey with age, saw her and offered a greeting.

"Welcome, Pela," he murmured, "it is good to see you. How are you?"

Pela's heart beat faster as he held out both hands, palms up. She took them in hers and smiled, though internally she was struggling desperately to recall his name. The awkward silence stretched out as he looked at her with kind eyes.

She opened her mouth, garbled something nonsensical, then blurted out: "*Thank you!*"

Her cheeks grew hot and she darted past him before he could ask anything else. Internally, she cursed her bumbling tongue. Slipping between the seated meditators, she approached the altar and lit a stick of incense to honour the Goddess Antonia, setting it alongside those already left by others.

As she turned away, she caught the scent of rose petals and earth in her nose. Instantly, her mind was whisked away to a forest grove, lit by sun and filled with the chattering of squirrels and the whispers of branches in the breeze. She clung to the image, but inevitably the realm of the Earth Goddess faded, leaving her standing once more before the altar.

Letting out a long sigh, Pela searched for her mother. Finding Kryssa seated cross-legged nearby, she sat beside her. Kryssa cast a sidelong glance in her direction and Pela quickly lowered her eyes. She didn't know why her mother dragged her here every week.

Everyone knew the Three Gods were dead.

Hearing her mother's breathing deepen, Pela looked back up. Her mother had begun to meditate, but Pela's heart was still racing from the climb. Silence had fallen over the room, the last of the meditators taking their places on the carpet. Coffee incense burned on the altar at the front of the room, where candles illuminated a mural that took up the entire wall. It depicted the Three Gods—Jurrien, Antonia, and Darius—united together against the Dark Magicker Archon, who had twice tried to conquer the Three Nations.

In the end, the Three Gods had destroyed him utterly, but in doing so they had retreated from the world. Their temples had been abandoned then, the citizens of the Three Nations turning to other pursuits.

But the gift of their magic had remained, and in the Gods' absence, Magickers had thrived, and many had abused their power. Eventually the Tsar had risen, uniting the Three Nations beneath his tyranny and vowing to sponge all magic from the land.

Some legends claimed the Gods had tried to cast him down, others that they'd supported him. Only one thing was agreed upon—that it had been Alana, the Tsar's daughter, who had destroyed the Three Gods.

And magic with them.

The world had changed in the thirty years since. Now it was the warrior who ruled, the power of the sword worshiped above all else. And a new cult had been born with the death of the Gods—the Order of Alana. They worshipped her as their Saviour, believed her sacrifice had cast off the shackles of the Gods, beckoning in a new era of enlightenment.

Only a few, like Pela's mother and her departed grandmother, remained faithful to the Three Gods. It was partly in respect for her grandmother that Pela came at all. Selina had been a ferocious woman, well known around the village for her sharp knives and sharper tongue. Even approaching ninety, she had still visited the temple for the weekly meditation. In the end, only death had stopped her.

Pela had asked her once why she bothered. After all, Selina had been alive during the days of magic. She knew better than anyone that the Gods were truly gone. But the old woman had only smiled.

Antonia saved my life once. She and her brothers may be gone, but what they did for us should never be forgotten.

Smiling at the memory, Pela's mind drifted to the days before her grandmother's passing. They had often gone to visit her uncle after temple, who would greet them with honey cakes and ginger ale. The best roof-builder in Skystead, he was a giant of a man and not really her uncle, though that was all Pela had ever known him as. There were those in the village who said he had been a warrior once, but Pela had only ever known him as a kindly man with greying hair and smile lines on his cheeks.

She had not seen him since her grandmother's funeral. Kryssa had insisted that Pela keep away, though she had never offered any explanation. That had been almost five years ago now. It saddened Pela to think of him alone in the big house he had shared with her grandmother. As a child, they had all lived in the inn, running it together, but those days were long ago now. All Pela could recall from those days was the faded image of them all gathered around the fireplace on a cold winter night.

Realising she'd become side-tracked from her meditation, Pela dragged her thoughts back to the present, concentrating instead on her own body. Eyes closed, she centred herself, focusing on the slow in-out of her breath, on the distant thudding of her heart, the pulsing of blood in her ears. Nearby, she heard the faint whisper of another's breath, the rustling of cloth, the faint *tap-tapping* of some rodent hidden in the walls. Her mind examined each of them in turn before releasing them. Slowly, her consciousness sank, and she reached for her inner cal—

Bang.

Pela startled out of her trance as noise erupted from the rear of the chamber. Angered at the intrusion, she swung around in time to witness armed men swarming inside. All wore heavy suits of plate mail armour and full-faced helmets. They spread out around the door, barring the only exit.

Her eyes were drawn to the centre of their breastplates, where each had been adorned with a flaming red sword. A chill slid down Pela's spine as she recognised the symbol.

The Knights of Alana.

"On your feet!" a Knight boomed.

⚜ 2 ⚜

"**O**n your feet!" The Knight's voice echoed strangely from behind his visor, giving it a metallic quality, as though the man within was not entirely human.

Crouched on her knees, Pela found herself frozen, unable to so much as cry out as the Knights advanced. The summer solstice was only a few weeks away and most of the congregation had gathered to begin preparations for the sacred day of the Goddess Antonia. Pela was near the back of the chamber, furthest from the Knights, but those at the front scrambled over one another in their desperation to escape the shining blades. With over forty meditators present, it was chaos.

Pela's heart hammered hard in her chest as her mind raced, struggling to understand where the Knights had come from. The nearest Castle was in Townirwin, a journey of many days by ship, and a week over land. How had they come upon the temple so suddenly? And what were they here for?

Death.

She shuddered. No, those were just rumours. Otherwise, the Plorsean King would have outlawed the Order of Alana, regardless of who they worshipped.

But why then were they here, with naked steel in hand? What other purpose but murder would have brought them?

"*Silence!*" the Knight roared over the screaming, "By order of the Crown!"

The command went unheeded. With a start, Pela realised she was the only one still on her knees. The crowd was pushing towards the altar, putting her at risk of being trampled. She had just scrambled to her feet when a vice-like hand gripped her by the wrist.

"*Pela!*" her mother hissed, suddenly beside her.

Kryssa pulled her towards the rear of the chamber. Stumbling after her mother, Pela glanced back as another scream came from behind them, and tripped over a tear in the carpet.

"Quickly!" her mother snapped, dragging her bodily behind the altar.

"There's no way out," Pela moaned.

"There is," Kryssa replied.

Pela shook her head, knowing her mother was wrong. Behind the altar they were hidden from the Knights, but there was nowhere left to go. The rear wall was made of brick and held up by stone pillars.

Still Pela's mother pulled at her arm, and she relented, allowing Kryssa to pull her into the corner where a pillar had fallen against the wall.

"Quickly, you must find your uncle!" Kryssa gasped, pushing Pela towards the broken pillar. She said something else, but her words were drowned out by the screaming.

"*How?*" Pela yelled, anger lending her strength. Her mother never explained, only told.

A gurgling cry rattled from the walls. Pela looked back and saw an older villager stumbling away from the Knights. Blood spurted from his throat and he went down clutching the wound with both hands.

Pela stared, unable to tear her eyes away. She had never seen someone die before; let alone someone she knew. It was the old man who had greeted her at the temple door. She remembered him now—it was Fervil, the village baker. He had given her a sticky cream bun once, when she was young, as a reward for safely delivering some bread to her grandmother.

Now his lifeblood was soaking into the dusty carpet of the ruined temple, and Pela could not begin to understand why.

"Pela!" Kryssa shrieked, shaking her. With an effort of will Pela focused on her mother's face. "Inside!"

"Inside what?" Pela gasped. Nothing made sense anymore.

Her mother pointed at the wall beneath the pillar, and finally she saw. Where the pillar had come to rest, the wall had cracked and crumbled away. Higher up, the break was barely noticeable, but at the base it widened enough that Pela might be able to fit.

"Go!" Kryssa moaned, her eyes flicking toward the Knights. Most of the congregation had already been subdued, and the few remaining villagers were pressed against the altar. They had only seconds before the Knights saw them.

"What about you?" Pela asked.

"Don't worry about me," her mother hissed. "Get out. Take the back trails down the mountain. Find your uncle!"

Pela swallowed, heart suddenly in her throat, but Kryssa didn't give her an opportunity to argue. She gripped Pela by the shoulders and pushed her into the crack. The pressure did not relent until Pela crawled into the darkness beyond the candle-lit hall. Then an angry voice shouted out and her mother's hands vanished.

Blood thundering in her ears, Pela continued forward. She glanced back only once, in time to see a pair of thick leather boots appear alongside her mother's moccasins, then she was through the other side and on her feet, racing through the shadows of the temple.

In her panic, Pela didn't think about where she ran, only that she needed to escape the men who had taken her mother. Then a stray pile of rubble caught her foot and she went crashing to the ground. Pain flared as her elbow struck the ground and she cursed, the sound shockingly loud in the dark corridors.

Reason came rushing back and Pela clamped a hand over her mouth to keep from crying out again. The hackles on the back of her neck rose as a voice called from somewhere ahead, followed by the heavy thump of leather boots.

They're coming!

Struggling to calm her racing heart, Pela scrambled to her feet and went back the way she'd come. Her eyes strained against the dark, trying to place where she was. She needed somewhere to hide, or the Knights would surely find her.

Finally, she recognised a mosaic of the Three Gods. Half of it was gone—only the face of Darius, the God of Light, remained complete—but she now knew where she was. She scanned her memories, thinking back to long ago when she had explored the temple as a youth. There were a thousand hiding places for a child, but few for a girl almost fully grown.

Only one was near, though it would test her courage.

She turned left, then right, and ducked into a narrow doorway. A long rectangular room stretched away from her, a massive fireplace taking up most of the far wall. Once it had been a kitchen, with a stove large enough to feed a hundred meditators, but now all that remained of the stove was a rusted ruin in the empty fireplace.

Stepping over the twisted iron, Pela moved into cavernous space beyond and looked up. The chimney was so long it could have fit two of her lying down, but it was narrow. If she was careful, she could wedge herself in place above the level of the room, out of sight.

If she could climb that high.

Don't think—do!

It was something her grandmother used to say, and Pela drew inspiration from the words now. Taking care to be quiet, she jammed her hands into the cracks left between the bricks by the crumbling mortar and tried to haul herself up.

Pain flared in her hand as it slipped free. Pela gasped as she slammed into the ground. A voiced echoed from the corridor, closer now.

Covered in black ash, Pela scrambled up and tried again. This time a clump of soot fell in her face, but she managed to wedge her feet into a crack and hold herself in place. She sucked in a breath, and soot rushed up her nose.

Her eyes watered as a sneeze built, until she could hold it no longer. Quickly she released a hand hold and pinched her nose. She was just in time, and only the tiniest of squeaks came out.

Even so, she held her breath, listening for the telltale crunch of boots on rubble. Suspended just out of sight of the room below, her arms shook…but she dared not move, lest she give herself away. A minute ticked by, then another, until finally she was convinced the Knight had gone another way.

Letting out a breath, Pela shifted so her feet were beneath her, and started to climb. She did not look down, though in the darkness she could not have told how high she was. The chimney had once extended far above the temple's roof, but age had toppled it along with the three spires. Light streamed through the narrow gap a dozen feet above, showing her the way, and there were no more accidents.

Clambering onto the rooftop, Pela crouched amongst the rubble of the ruined chimney and squinted against the sudden brightness. The roof had been painted white and reflected the sun, though thankfully the fallen spires covered much of it. She searched for sign of the Knights, but there was no one in sight.

A shout carried to her on the ocean breeze, sending a tingle of premonition down her spine. Her heart began to race again. Crouching low, she crept across the broken stone, silent as a cat. She had to skirt several places where fallen rock had caved in the temple roof. Long minutes passed before she reached the front of the temple. Voices carried up from below. Craning her head, she peeked down at the speakers.

Dust billowed up from the two dozen men and horses gathered below, and she quickly ducked back out of sight. Rolling on her back, she gasped, struggling to control her panic. If they had seen her…

Her blood went cold. *Had* they seen her? Even now they might be drawing their swords and scrambling up the lead drainage pipes…

Pela scrunched her eyes closed and sucked in a breath.

Listen.

Slowly she exhaled, focusing on the action and not the

fear. The wind whistled through the nooks and crannies of the ruin. She strained her ears, seeking out sounds of pursuit. Voices rose from below, raised in anger but directed elsewhere, not at the hidden watcher on the roof.

Her heartbeat slowed. They had not seen her.

Pela had only caught a glimpse of what was going on, but it was all she'd needed. The villagers had their hands bound behind their backs and were roped together in a line. She'd had no time to count but it looked like everyone inside had been subdued. Now the Knights were mounting up in preparation to depart.

What do I do? Pela shrieked in the silence of her mind.

Her mother must be below, but there was no way to reach her, no way to free her from the armoured Knights and their terrible greatswords. At the thought, she saw again the image of Fervil choking on his own blood, his fingers unable to stem the terrible bleeding…

Stop it.

Pela forced herself to breathe, pushing back the onset of panic. She couldn't afford that luxury. Kryssa was in trouble and she was the only one who knew!

"Ready men?" A voice carried up to her. "Let's ride!"

The sharp *crack* of a dozen whips followed as the Knights set their horses on the narrow trail. Several villagers cried out, but from where Pela lay, she could not see who or why. Angry curses and more *cracks* followed, and a woman wailed. Pela prayed to the Three Gods it was not her mother. Finally, the clip-clop of hooves on stone faded away.

Cautiously, Pela lifted her head and watched the Knights move off, their captives strung out between them. She waited several minutes before pulling herself up, wanting to be sure no one had remained to keep watch. A dust cloud clung to the mountainside where the Knights rode, their captives in tow. They were already a quarter of the way down the mountainside. Beyond, the deep blue waters of the harbour waited.

Her heart fluttered as she thought of the ship waiting there. That must be how they intended to escape, though what they intended for the prisoners…

Pela tore her thoughts away from torture and death. High tide was still an hour away; the ship would not depart until the currents turned. The Knights couldn't move quickly with the prisoners in tow. If Pela ran, she might beat them to Skystead. Balling her hands into fists, she focused on her mother's last words:

Find your uncle!

∗ 3 ∗

Rivulets of sweat trickled down Ikar's forehead as the sun beat down on the mountain trail. Outside the refuge of the old temple, there was no escaping it, and the heavy armour made the heat all the worse. He fought the temptation to remove his visor, calling on his ancestors for strength.

He had not lied to Merak, it was well known his family had descended from Alan the Great, who had died over a century ago in the war of the Gods. But of the man's children, Ikar was descended from the lesser line, and his family had done little of note since. Nothing but…

Ikar shook his head, determined to leave the past in the past. His family might have once sinned, but he had been born on the day the Gods fell, and had never known any power but his own strength. He had been raised in Lonia, the poorest of the Three Nations, though their king had designs to change that fate. Ikar had served as the man's bodyguard for a time, and later for his daughter, only departing their household a year ago, when his faith had called for his service.

And so he had joined the Knights of Alana, and been sent as a missionary into Plorsea. The Order was still young here, its growth hindered by antagonism towards Lonia, where the cult had been born. Though few still worshiped the False Gods, they had been equally reluctant to embrace the Saviour. Townirwin, where he had settled, was one of the few towns to boast a Castle—the fortresses of the Order.

Anger stirred in Ikar's chest as he inspected the villagers they had captured. They stumbled along the path, hands bound, barely able to keep upright. His fellow Knights rode alongside them, brandishing their riding crops at those who slowed the progression. The sight made him sick. Such weak, selfish creatures they were, to beg the False Gods to save them.

Did they not realise their prayers endangered all the Three Nations? That their belief fed strength back to the False Gods, so that they might one day threaten the world once more? The Order would not allow it, though the cowardly King of Plorsea had forbidden interference.

Ikar snorted. As far as he was concerned, Braidon was a weak and ineffective king, though the man's tolerance for the False Gods and their followers bordered on outright blasphemy. It still surprised Ikar that Lonia had made a pact with such a man—had even offered him their princess's hand in marriage in order to buy peace.

Sucking in a stifling breath, Ikar forced his thoughts from politics. He tried to judge their progress down the mountainside, but the town was still far below and several of the prisoners were already flagging. He cursed. They needed to be away on the high tide, before the townsfolk might learn of their presence and attempted a rescue. He had no doubt his two dozen Knights could fend them off, but there had already been enough bloodshed.

Ahead, a young boy stumbled on the uneven ground and fell. Ikar cursed and rode closer. The boy struggled to right himself with his hands tied behind his back, but only succeeded in toppling himself face-first into the ground. When he saw the Knight looming overhead, he screamed.

"Stupid boy!" Ikar growled, lifting his crop.

"Stop!" Another prisoner, a woman, darted between Ikar and the boy.

"Get out of my way, woman," Ikar snapped. He flicked the crop at her, but she leaned back, and the blow missed by a hair's breadth.

The woman sneered. "Such a brave man," she said, her voice rich with sarcasm, "that you must beat women and children to show your power."

Angered, Ikar prepared to strike the woman down. She did not shrink away. Her silver eyes flashed in the midday sun as she watched him. There was not an inch of give in those eyes, and Ikar hesitated, then lowered his crop.

"Get him up," he grunted.

With her own hands still bound, the woman could do little to help the boy, but eventually she got him on his feet. Taking him under her wing, she moved off down the track without a backwards glance at Ikar.

He edged his horse after her, equal parts disturbed and fascinated. The other villagers had shown little defiance since the bloodshed in the temple. The baker's death had robbed the rest of their courage, and now the rest marched wilfully to their fate.

"Ikar."

Ikar looked around as Merak called his name and found the Elder riding several horses back. He had removed his helmet once more, but sweat still beaded his forehead, drenching the greying hair that hung in tangles around his face. Dragging on his reins, Ikar waited for Merak to catch him before setting off again.

"What was that, with the woman?" Merak questioned.

Ikar shrugged. "She was right. They might be blasphemers and traitors, but we should not sink to their level. We are Knights of Alana; we must uphold our own honour."

"Ay," Merak mused, "but I do not like how these peasants defy us. It should not have taken a death to subdue such creatures."

"Hard country, the mountains," Ikar replied. "In Lonia, they breed strong warriors."

"Even so, it would serve them well to be reminded of their place. I will take five to the town square and conduct a cleansing. Shall I include the witch who challenged you?"

Ikar looked ahead to where the woman walked alongside the boy, turning over the man's offer in his mind. It would be just, to repay her earlier defiance. Yet their orders were to return with as many prisoners as possible, for the Elders needed candidates for their Great Sacrifice.

He shook his head. "No," he replied. "She is strong, we may need her for the solstice."

Merak laughed. "You are right, brother." He offered a grim smile. "I will take the weak and cowardly. They will not be needed."

Ikar shuddered as the Elder moved away. There was something about Merak that set his teeth on edge, a cruelty that went beyond the bounds of what was needed to preserve the natural order. Watching the man inspect the prisoners, Ikar was reminded of a wolf circling its prey.

As they neared the town, Merak cut five prisoners from the line, all men. "Make for the ship and load the prisoners," the Elder ordered. "I will join you within the hour. If I am postponed, do not wait. The candidates must be brought before the Order without delay."

With that, Merak moved off, taking five Knights along with the prisoners. Ikar waited until they disappeared down the broad avenue through the centre of town before shaking himself into action.

"Let's go!" he bellowed.

The prisoners stood staring after Merak. They had not been told what the Elder intended, but from their defeated looks, several had guessed. Ikar scanned their ranks, catching the eyes of the woman from earlier staring back at him. Her gaze was strangely unnerving, and he quickly looked away.

"I said get moving!" he screamed.

Several of his Knights brandished their crops, and the group moved off, making for the port.

＄ 4 ＄

Devon sat back on the slate roof and let out a long breath. Taking a rag from his belt, he wiped the sweat from his face. The familiar ache had begun in the centre of his back, and his knee had been troubling him for close to an hour now. He would need to stop soon, but he was determined to continue for as long as possible. Already the longest day of the year was just weeks away, and he was not yet half finished with the repairs.

He should have started sooner, but as always, he had put the needs of the village first, had dedicated too much time to other projects. Now he would need to rush to get the holes in his own villa fixed before the autumn rains arrived.

Selina would have shaken her head and cursed him for a fool. The thought of his former business partner brought a smile to Devon's face. Her loss still hurt, though Selina had been so old at the end she could barely make it up the steps to the temple.

A shiver went through him at the thought. How long before the same weakness claimed him? He already felt its approach. Once, he would have finished retiling his entire roof in the span of a week; now he would need to enlist help if he was to avoid being bogged down in the winter.

Devon cursed and straightened. He wasn't dead yet, and he'd be damned if he allowed despair to rule him. He might be approaching fifty-five, but he was still the strongest man in the village. Just last month he'd carried the Lifting Stone further than any other challenger, and he was yet to meet the man who could best him in battle.

That thought brought another pang of sadness. Fifteen long years had passed since his last campaign. It had ended in such disaster that even now he regretted accepting the call. At the time, Selina had railed against him, had begged him not to go, but Devon had left anyway, marching to the aid of his old friend, Braidon.

How he wished he could take that decision back. He had lost everything because of it: friends and family and his own honour. But Braidon had been desperate—and if Devon was honest, he had longed to experience the thrill of battle one last time.

But with the wisdom of age, Devon could see now what he had never accepted as a young man. He did not have the courage to live as an ordinary man, to toil day in and day out to add something to the world. Selina had recognised it in him, when they had stood on the plains of Trola and fought the Tsar and his armies. But her advice had helped him little then, and it was too late to admit it now.

Sitting back on the roof, Devon found himself wondering after the king. He had not heard from Braidon for many years now. He supposed with the peace treaty signed between Lonia and Plorsea, Braidon had little need for old warriors.

Devon shook himself from his reverie and reached for

his hammer. If he pressed on for another hour, he might just keep to schedule. If the rains came late…

"*Uncle!*"

Devon started as a scream came from below. Sitting up, he saw a young girl race into his courtyard. Tangled platinum hair bounced around her face as she stumbled to a stop, her hazel-green eyes whipping about in search of somebody. She had not noticed him sitting on the roof.

A broad grin stretched Devon's cheeks as he recognised his niece. Pela had taken to calling him "Uncle" when she was just a child, though they had no direct relation. If anything, he was more like her grandfather. Years ago, when he and Selina had run the Firestone Tavern in Ardath, the old woman had adopted an urchin from the streets. He recalled with a mixture of regret and fondness the night she'd returned with Kryssa, and changed their lives forever.

But Kryssa had not spoken to Devon since Selina's death, nor allowed her daughter, Pela, to visit him. He could hardly blame her, after his failure…but the absence had hurt. Seeing Pela now brought a smile to his face, and sitting up, he waved a hand.

"Morning, missy. Where have you been hiding?" he shouted down.

"Temple…Knights…Mum…Uncle!" Pela gasped, her voice echoing incoherently from the walls of the courtyard.

Devon frowned. Her words made little sense, but there was no mistaking her urgency. A spark of worry lit in his stomach, and he levered himself up. He strode across the roof, taking care to step lightly on the slate tiles, and clambered down the ladder to join her in the courtyard.

"What's that, missy?" he asked when he was on the ground.

Still struggling to catch her breath, Pela straightened.

"They have Mum!"

"What?" Devon asked, his chest tightening. "Who?"

"They have her—the Knights of Alana!"

"Slow down, missy," Devon said, though there was a roaring in his ears now.

Pela's words made no sense. Skystead did not have any of the cult's ridiculous Castles, and was about as remote as a village could get in Plorsea. There was nothing to bring them here. And they wouldn't want anything with Kryssa, not unless…

"It's true!" Pela panted. "We were at Temple—"

"*What?*" Devon boomed, worry giving way to anger. "I told your mother to stop with that nonsense years ago. What was she thinking?"

Pela paled in the face of his rage. Her mouth hung open, but no more words came out. Devon groaned, running a hand through his thinning hair.

"When did this happen?" he asked, trying to keep his voice calm. Pela was…sixteen? A woman grown, but inexperienced in the world and its dangers. He tried to reassure her: "Don't worry, we'll get this sorted."

"*They killed Fervil!*"

Devon knelt and placed a hand on her shoulder. "Listen to me, Pela," he said, face to face with the girl now. "I promise you; we're going to get your mother back. Okay?"

Pela nodded, her head bobbing up and down like it was on a chain. Her eyes were still wild, but at Devon's words she sucked in a great, shuddering breath, and seemed to calm a little.

"Okay," she whispered.

"Good," Devon rumbled. "Now, when did this happen, and where have they taken Kryssa?"

"Half an hour ago," Pela replied. There was still a

quiver to her voice, but the panic was fading. "I think they're heading for a ship at the port. High tide is soon!"

"How did you get away?"

"Mum sent me through a crack in the wall. She said to find you. *We have to help her!*"

"We will," Devon said, rising. "Did you see how many there were?"

The girl hesitated before replying, "A dozen, maybe two dozen."

Devon cursed inwardly. Even in his prime, a dozen would have been too many for him. The ache in his back seemed to redouble, dragging on his confidence. Slowed by age and old injuries, he wouldn't stand a chance against those odds.

But neither could he simply allow them to leave with Kryssa. Whatever they were here for, whatever their intentions for the prisoners, he doubted they were good. He had never liked the Order of Alana, though he had known the woman herself a long time ago. Perhaps that was why, for the Order and its Knights resembled little of what Alana had stood for at the end.

But despite his reservations, the cult had flourished over the last thirty years, finding fertile soil in a world suddenly without magic. The God's sudden absence had left a power void in the Three Nations, and the Order had taken full advantage.

"Uncle!" Pela shrieked, dragging him back to the present. There were tears in her eyes and she looked ready to crumble. "What are we going to do?"

Devon forced a smile. Striding across the courtyard, he hefted the sledgehammer he'd been using to break the old roof tiles, then looked at Pela.

"Let's go."

❧ 5 ☙

Caledan let out a groan as he lowered himself onto the tavern bench. The four days at sea had been the longest of his life, made all the worse by the sudden squall that had struck yesterday. The pounding rain would have been a relief after the relentless sun, if not for the surging waves that had made his already knotted belly convulse until he was throwing up bile.

Now he could not wait to wash away the taste of salt and vomit. Sucking down a long draught of his ale, he wondered again what had possessed him to make such a trip. By all logic, he should never have accepted the ship captain's commission. Work might have been scarce for a sellsword in recent years, but there was always need for men of Caledan's calibre and he'd had no need for the coin.

But something in the captain's tale had awoken his curiosity. The man had claimed a ship full of Baronians had almost set upon his ship on the journey from Lon. Baronians were tribes of nomads who roamed the Three Nations, preying on whomever was unlucky enough to fall within their power. But their presence alone had not been enough to pique Caledan's interest. It was the Captain's claim of magic, of a ship with an unnatural ability to sail against the wind, that had captured Caledan's imagination.

He still wasn't sure of the story's truth, but it had been enough to buy Caledan's protection for a few days. Such a power might have advanced his own goals. But the Baronian vessel had never appeared, though with Caledan brought down by seasickness, that might have been for the best.

They had made port in Skystead last night and Caledan had promptly retired his commission, telling the captain he'd rather walk back to Townirwin than set foot on the *Red Seagull* again. The man had been enraged, but Caledan had little sympathy for him.

After all, he knew better than most that life was full of disappointments.

The captain must have been sailing under lucky stars though, for two Knights of Alana had ridden up before Caledan had even left the port and requested passage.

Seated at a table in front of the tavern, Caledan glimpsed another group of Knights riding past. The sight brought a frown to his face, and he wondered whether a new Castle had been opened in the sleepy village. He doubted it; Skystead was a long way from anywhere that mattered.

The tavern opened out onto the northern edge of the town square. From his vantage point, Caledan could see the quiet stalls of the bazaar directly opposite. A slate roof protected its occupants from the elements, but with the sun approaching its midday position, most of the stalls were already packing up for the day. On the eastern side of the plaza was the town hall, its front lined with granite pillars.

Gargoyles stretched out from its roof, overhanging the square. The other buildings bordering the plaza were mostly eating houses and taverns, already beginning to fill with noon approaching.

Caledan expected the Knights to turn at the bazaar and head for the docks, but instead they cantered up to the town hall and all but one dismounted. He noticed now that only five of the party were Knights. The rest were plain-clothed men, their hands bound behind their backs. They stumbled to a stop behind the Knights, eyes fixed to the ground.

Sipping his ale, Caledan watched in fascination as a Knight took rope from his saddlebags and flung it over one of the gargoyles. A crowd began to gather as the Knight tied a noose.

"What's going on here?" an onlooker shouted.

The Knights ignored the question, but one of the prisoners looked up. Seeming to notice the crowd for the first time, he came alive. "Help us!" he shouted, tugging at his bindings. "They attacked—"

He broke off as a Knight bounded forward and slammed a mailed fist into his head. The man went down with a *thump*, unable to break his fall with his hands bound. When he tried to recover, the Knight drove a boot into his stomach. The rattle of iron striking flesh whispered through the square, silencing the crowd.

Arms resting against his table, Caledan said nothing. Several of the townsfolk had not lost their courage though, and the whispers soon began again.

"That's *Zenner*…who are you…where…what right…?"

The crowd had recognised the prisoners as their own people. But before they could gather their courage, the Knight who remained mounted edged his horse forward. Unlike the others, he did not wear a helmet, and his cape was dark red, while the rest wore white. He drew his sword and waved it at the crowd.

"Back!" The man's voice boomed across the square. His horse reared, its cry echoing its master's. "Or suffer the wrath of Alana!"

As one, the villagers retreated, though the agitated whispers did not cease.

Sword still in hand, the man turned his horse on the spot. "My name is Merak, Elder of the Townirwin Castle! We come before you today in the name of the Saviour, to cleanse from these lands those who would undo her saintly work."

Amidst the villagers, a man stepped forward in defiance of the Elder. "Why are these men bound? What do they stand accused of?"

"They were found in the ruins above your town, sending their blessings to the False Gods!" Merak bellowed.

"Ay, and what of it?" The villager didn't back down. "Skystead does not belong to your Order. In whose name do you deny these men their freedom?"

"In the name of the Crown!" Merak snapped, his irritation showing. He pointed his blade at the villager. "Now get back, or you will suffer the same fate as these sorry blasphemers."

"Be damned—"

Merak's sword flashed down before the man could finish, severing his throat. Blood sprayed across the dusty cobbles. Caledan watched with detached curiosity as the villager staggered back, clutching his throat in a desperate attempt to stem the bleeding. He'd seen many such wounds in his lifetime; the man was already dead. Within seconds the villager crumpled to the ground and lay still.

The crowd drew back, their anger turning to sudden

fear. Silence fell across the plaza as they stared at the Elder. Blood still dripped from Merak's blade. He sneered down at them.

"Blasphemers must be cleansed from our lands, lest the False Gods return and bind us once more with their magic."

Caledan watched on, bemused by the performance. There were over a hundred villagers in the plaza now, against the Elder and his five Knights, but not one lifted a hand as the killer turned his horse towards the prisoners. He dropped a hand to his sword hilt. He was tempted to interfere, if for no other reason than to irk the Elder's arrogance.

But there was no profit to be made upsetting the Order of Alana. Caledan had learned to trust his instincts long ago; he recognised a rising power when he saw one. Just like Lonia before it, the cult would grow until it touched every aspect of Plorsea's governance. If the Elder was to be believed, they already had the ear of the crown.

Not that corrupting King Braidon would have been difficult.

Caledan waved for a server to bring him another pint of ale. But the man had been distracted by the altercation and had abandoned his post. Swearing, Caledan returned his attention to the Knights. At least there was entertainment, even if his drink was empty.

Merak had dismounted now. He stood before the crowd, arms raised. "Bring the first to be cleansed!"

Two of his men grabbed a prisoner and dragged him forward until he stood before the dangling rope. At a gesture from their leader, the Knights looped the noose around the captive's neck. The man cried out as the fibres tightened around his throat and tried to fight back, but his armoured assailants held him tight. After a moment he slumped in their grip, defeated.

"Please…don't do this…stop!" The villagers were growing restless again.

"Silence!" Merak's voice boomed out. "Darkness has infected your town, but we have come to deliver you! We bring the blessings of Alana."

No one spoke as the Elder approached the prisoner in the noose.

"What is your name, traitor?"

"Ze…Zenner."

"Zenner, you stand accused of blasphemy against the Saviour, and worship of the False Gods. How do you plead?"

The man's mouth opened and closed, but he couldn't seem to find the words. Caledan felt for him. There were no laws outlawing belief in the Three Gods, though Caledan knew that in Lonia their worshipers were now hunted. Such foulness had not reached Plorsea though, certainly not a small town like Skystead. At least, not until now.

"Will you repent, blasphemer, and surrender yourself to the mercy of Alana?"

"I…I…please?"

The man still seemed to think he could reason with his captor, but Caledan recognised the eyes of a fanatic. It was no surprise; Elders were generally zealots of the highest order.

"No?" Merak asked. When the man still did not answer, he nodded to his followers.

The two Knights took hold of the rope. The prisoner's eyes widened and he cried out, "Wait—"

Before he could say more, the noose snapped tight around his throat and he was dragged into the air. He kicked out wildly as the rope swayed, but he could find no purchase in the empty air, no relief from the fiery grasp of the noose. The villagers screamed, but with their comrade lying dead on the ground before them, none were bold enough to intervene.

Caledan watched on, slightly bored by the lack of a fight. He had expected at least a few townsfolk to try and save the man. Instead, they stood and did nothing as the prisoner's eyes rolled back into his skull and his struggles grew feebler.

Finally, the man stilled, and Merak nodded for the Knights to cut him down. As though choosing a chicken at the market, the Elder moved down the line of prisoners and stopped in front of a white-haired man.

"You, what is your name?"

The old man stared calmly back at his accuser. Unlike the others, there was no fear in his eyes. He smiled at the question.

"May the Three Gods bless you, brother."

"Blasphemy!" Merak screamed. Face flushed, he raised his blade.

"I wouldn't do that if I were you, sonny."

The Elder froze as a voice boomed across the square. Frowning, he turned and sought out the speaker. Caledan did the same, scanning the crowd before settling on a figure standing in the shadows of an alley. A whisper went through the plaza as he stepped into the sunlight. Age lined the man's face and his beard was grey, but he strode towards the Knights as though he owned the world. He carried a sledge-hammer in one massive fist.

"Who's this now?" Caledan mused.

"That's Devon," the tavern's server answered, appearing finally with a fresh jug of ale. "They say he fought for the king, back in his day."

"Interesting." Caledan nodded his thanks and handed over a shilling for the drink.

Caledan studied the giant as he advanced on the Knights. Could it be true? Devon was a name carved into the legends of the Three Nations. The Trolans knew him as the "Butcher of Kalgan," the Lonians as the "Consort of Alana," while most Plorseans were divided between "King Killer" and "Liberator." All agreed he'd played a part in the fall of the Empire so many decades ago.

But surely this couldn't be the same man?

6

P ela stood transfixed as her uncle strode through the crowd, seemingly unconcerned by the armed men awaiting him. Gone was the gentle giant of her childhood; in his place was a man of ice, a face that promised death. The crowd parted before him, swept aside by his rage, leaving the Elder, Merak, standing alone.

Yet Devon too was alone, and armed only with the sledgehammer he'd taken from his home. Merak seemed to realise this too, and with a start he came alive. Lifting his blade, he pointed it at the advancing hammerman.

"This is none of your business, greybeard," he cried. "I suggest you depart, before I have you join your fellows!"

The man's voice rang with power, and many in the square found themselves stepping back from the Elder. But Devon continued as though he hadn't heard the man. Teeth bared, the Elder flourished his blade again, then apparently thought better of it, and turned it on his prisoner.

"Stop!" he snapped.

"Kill him, and your body will be the next to strike the

stones," Devon rumbled, coming to a stop several feet from the Elder.

Merak's lips drew back in a sneer. "Such blasphemy cannot go unpunished. Swanson, Cidar, take him!"

Two Knights advanced, drawing broadswords from their sheaths. Stepping around their leader, they approached Devon with broad grins on their faces, already anticipating an easy victory.

Pela clenched and unclenched her fists, still frozen on the edge of the square, where they had first noticed the commotion on their way to the docks. She longed to go to her uncle's aid, but she had no weapon, not even a rock to throw—and anyway, she knew nothing of the warrior's arts.

Did her uncle even know? Or was this all an act?

"This village is under the king's rule," Devon said, his voice low, though every soul in the plaza heard his words. "You have no authority here. Leave now in peace, or die."

The Knights paused, glancing back at their leader, suddenly uncertain. Though they wore full-faced helmets, from the way they moved Pela guessed they were young, confident in their abilities and used to being feared. In their plate mail armour they seemed to Pela untouchable, and she couldn't begin to think how her uncle could threaten them.

"*I said, take the bastard!*" Merak shrieked.

The Knights jumped, shocked out of their hesitation, and continued. "Put down the hammer, old man," one shouted, his voice rattling from inside his helmet.

"So be it," Devon murmured.

He surged forward, the construction hammer already in motion. One of the Knights had drawn slightly ahead. He cried out, taken unawares by Devon's charge, and raised his broadsword to defend himself, but Devon's hammer swept below his guard. A crash echoed loudly across the square as it struck.

Pela gaped as the Knight staggered back, his breastplate caved in by the blow. The sword slipped from his fingers and he toppled backwards, slamming into the cobblestones with a shriek of twisting metal. His helmet was knocked loose. Seeing his pale face, a scream built in Pela's throat. His eyes were wide open, staring into the sunlit sky, but there was no life there now. Where a second ago there had been a young man in his prime, now there was only death.

And still Devon was moving, stepping past the fallen Knight and charging the second. Shocked by his comrade's death, the man barely had time to lift his blade before Devon was on him. Steel shrieked as hammer struck sword, then again, before Devon's third blow found its mark. There was a sickening *squelch* as it struck the man's helmet, the steel giving way like putty. The man crumpled without a sound and lay still.

This cannot be happening.

Awed and disbelieving, Pela watched as her uncle stepped over the second body and stopped in front of Merak.

"Last chance," Devon said. He did not raise his voice, but a collective shiver went through the crowd at his words. "Leave, or die."

"*Be damned!*" Merak shrieked.

Before Devon could react, Merak plunged his sword through the neck of the prisoner he was holding. The old man's eyes widened as blood gushed from the wound. Pela slapped a hand to her mouth, shocked by the suddenness of Merak's brutality. Dragging back his blade, the Elder kicked the old man in the back, toppling him face-first to the stones.

"You shouldn't have done that," Devon murmured.

"Be damned!" Merak snarled, leaping at Devon.

His blade hissed for Devon's face, but her uncle's hammer leapt to meet it. A great *shriek* tore through the plaza as the weapons met, and Devon leapt back. Pela gaped as a chunk of metal fell from Devon's hammer. The greatsword had carved straight through the dense metal.

Devon flicked a glance at his weapon, but the rest remained intact, and he advanced again. The Elder snarled, but as Devon neared his opponent seemed to stumble, his face paling. With a roar, Devon charged and the Elder turned and fled.

"Kill the blasphemer!" Merak shrieked as he leapt for his horse. His foot jammed in a cobble and he would have fallen if he hadn't caught the reins and dragged himself up.

Devon was almost on him, but before he could drag the Elder from the saddle, the remaining Knights cut him off. They spread out to encircle the hammerman, broadswords at the ready.

Watching the scene unfold from the shadows, Pela's heart sank. Her uncle's speed and skill had taken the other men by surprise, but there would be no such luck with these three. They edged forward slowly with blades extended, eager to avenge their comrades' deaths.

Devon stood fixed in place, hammer clenched in both hands now, his face impassive. Only the slightest flicker of his amber eyes betrayed any emotion. Encircled, Devon could only keep two of his foes in sight at a time, and the third was readying himself for the attack.

Before Pela could call a warning, the Knight leapt forward with blade raised. But the rattle of his armour must have given him away, for Devon spun, hammer already in motion, and batted away the attack. The Knight scrambled back as Devon parried, and the blow struck empty air.

Then the other Knights were charging in, and Pela knew her uncle would be overwhelmed, cut down by sheer weight of numbers…

Before the men could attack again, a man dressed in a leather jerkin and tight-fitting pants leapt into the battle, silver sword in hand. He struck at the hilt of a Knight's weapon, deflecting the attack into the cobbles, and with a screech of tearing metal, the blade shattered. The Knight staggered back and stared at the now useless weapon. The newcomer's sword took him through the visor before he had a chance to recover.

Pela watched as the stranger and Devon faced off against the last two Knights. Though they appeared evenly matched, it was clear the balance had changed, and now it was the Knights who hesitated, confused by the new element posed by the plain-clothed swordsman.

Devon leapt at the Knight still facing him. The man staggered back, his confidence evaporating like water in the summer sun, and Devon barrelled into him. The power behind his blows rendered the Knight's armour worse than useless—even his non-fatal blows warped the steel, twisting it to incapacitate the man within. The Knight fell with a cry, and Devon spun in search of his last foe.

He was already dead. Blood seeped from where the knife had been driven through his gorget to pierce his throat. The swordsman retrieved the blade and wiped it clean, before returning it to a hidden sheath on his person.

Hooves thundered across the cobbles as Merak kicked his horse into a gallop. Devon roared but he could not catch the Elder on foot. He spun, scanning the fallen Knights, then the crowd, but whatever Devon was searching for he did not find it. Cursing again, he swung his hammer at the cobbles.

Stumbling across the square to join her uncle, Pela's eyes were drawn inexorably to the dead Knights. Their blood pooled amongst the stones, already turning black with the dust and the heat. A fly buzzed in her ear before darting towards the bodies. She swallowed and tore her gaze away.

It was soon caught by a fresh horror. The innocent old man lay dead where Merak had left him, his chest torn open, eyes staring blanking up into the cloudless sky. Beside him another villager lay dead. He sported no wounds, but the purple mark around his throat told the story of how he'd died.

A shudder swept through Pela and she fought to keep from throwing up. It was a full minute before she noticed the other prisoners standing nearby, arms still bound behind their backs.

"Where's my mum?" she gasped, racing to where they stood. "Where's Kryssa?"

The prisoners stared blankly back at her, as though not comprehending the words. The fear in their eyes was palpable, but in that moment, Pela didn't care about anything but her mother.

"Here, girl." The strange swordsman stepped around her and drew a dagger.

One of the prisoners cried out, while the other two whimpered, still in shock. But the stranger only cut free their bindings before stepping back. The newly freed men rubbed their wrists, hardly seeming to comprehend the sudden reversal in their fortunes. Their eyes kept darting to where Merak had vanished, as though expecting him to return at any moment to follow through with his threat.

Leather scuffed on stone as Devon approached. "Any of you lads know where they took the others?"

The men exchanged glances. "The docks," one said finally. "There was a ship they were meant to catch."

"Ay." Pela looked around as the strange swordsman spoke. "I arrived on it last night. The *Red Seagull*, it's called. It'll be gone by now."

Devon eyed the man before nodding. "Thank you for your help back there. Not sure I could have taken all three myself."

The swordsman laughed. "I suppose that depends whose legends you believe. If you're *mortal*, like the followers of the Three Gods claim, surely not. But these lads…" He gestured at the fallen Knights. "Not sure they'd have been so quick to tackle you, if they'd known they were going up against the Consort of Alana."

Devon's face darkened and he stepped towards the swordsman. At six feet tall, the stranger was by no means a small man, but he looked tiny in her uncle's shadow.

"So you know who I am," Devon rumbled. "And who might you be, sonny?"

$\mathbf{\mathcal{X}}$ 7 $\mathbf{\mathcal{X}}$

Devon stared down at the man who'd come to his aid. A dull throbbing came from the centre of his back and the ache behind his left knee had returned with vengeance, but he refused to show any hint of his pain. He drew in a breath, his heart still racing from the brief fight, and cursed again his aging body.

Exhaling, he studied the strange swordsman. His clothing was nondescript and the weapons he carried plain, but he had shown unusual skill earlier. It was no easy feat to defeat a man in armour with only a sword and dagger—let alone two. Yet Devon's unlikely benefactor had made it look easy.

He was sure the man was new in the village—Devon recognised all Skystead's citizens by sight if not by name. So how did this stranger know him? Had he come looking for a legend, or had he been told by someone, his arrival here coincidence?

"So you know who I am," Devon rumbled finally. "And who might you be, sonny?"

"Only a humble sellsword," the man said, spreading his hands in a gesture of peace and offering a half-bow. "I go by Caledan."

The name was familiar, but scanning his memories, Devon could not recall where he'd heard it mentioned. He swore silently; his recollection was not what it had been. So many friends, so many comrades, had been lost to the mists of time. Staring at the stranger though, he was sure they had never met.

"Might be I've heard of you," he said, "but I do not care to be reminded of my past."

It was true. Devon rarely spoke of his service as one of Braidon's King's Guard, and even less about the time before that. The Tsar had taken so much from him, he could hardly bear to think about the friends who had died in that battle. Even thirty years later, the memories still stung.

He knew his silence had allowed the rumours to spread, but so long as he'd been allowed to retreat from the world, he hadn't cared.

Only now the world had come for his family, and he was beginning to regret his absence.

"My apologies, hammerman," Caledan was saying. "I did not know."

Devon scowled. "Never mind that. What were you saying about the ship? Are you sure it's gone?"

The man shrugged. "They might have missed the tide, but I doubt it. Two Knights came last night and booked passage. They would not have allowed a late departure."

"Dammit," Devon muttered.

"They have Mum!" Pela cried, grabbing at his arm. "Devon, what are we going to do?"

Devon could see the girl was on the edge of panic again,

but time was slipping through his fingers, and with every passing second Kryssa got further and further away.

He knelt beside her and placed a hand on her shoulder. "Go to the house and wait."

"But——"

"Pela," Devon said patiently, "I'm going to get her back, I promise you. But I need you safe, okay?"

Eyes wide, she nodded, and Devon released her. As she moved away, Devon faced the crowd. He knew some of those present by name, and liked and respected most. They were farmers and fishermen, solid folk, men and women you could rely on to clear a landslide from the road or work through the night to extinguish a burning building. But what faced them now was a different kind of challenge, and Devon did not know how they would react.

One of the villagers caught his eye and shouted, "Devon, what do we do now?" More voices quickly joined in.

"Where have they taken them?

"The king must be told——"

"Damn the king, the man never cared about us——"

"*Quiet!*" Devon shouted over the chorus, bringing silence.

He drew in a lungful of air. If only it could be so simple as calling the king. But Ardath was many weeks' journey from Skystead and by then it might already be too late for Kryssa and the others. Whatever the Knights of Alana had planned, they would not want to be caught with the evidence of their crime.

"They have our people," he said finally, his voice soft now, but still powerful. "The king is far away; he cannot help us."

The villagers looked back at him, their eyes filling with

fear as they realised what he was asking. Devon tried to keep his own worries concealed. He could not go after the Knights alone—even in his prime, the two dozen who had raided the temple would have been too many. If they reached Townirwin, and the protection of their Castle, the odds would be even worse.

"I'm going after them," he said, his eyes travelling over the crowd, and when he spoke, he spoke to all of them. "Who will go with me?"

Devon's heart palpitated as the villagers stared back at him. Not one spoke, not even the three he had freed. Anger took him then, taking light in his fear for Kryssa, in his frustration at his failing body.

"Are you all such cowards?" he bellowed. "Are you sons and daughters of Skystead, or are you field mice, skulking in the grass before the cat? Are you truly such wretches, that you would allow evil to walk unchecked amongst you, to take your neighbours, your friends, your family, and you will do nothing?"

Still no one spoke, though few were those that could meet his eyes. A wave of despair swept over Devon and he turned away. These people weren't soldiers, used to the violence that had just played out in the plaza. Few would have seen a man die by the blade before today.

"I will."

The voice was so soft, so trembling, he almost missed it. Devon turned to find Pela still standing behind him. Her face was pale, but she met his eyes resolutely.

"I'll come with you, Devon," she continued. "I'll help you bring them home."

Devon stared at her, too stunned to reply. He had thought she'd left, gone home to wait for him. For a moment he was reminded of her father, on that fateful day…

"I'll come too," another voice piped from the crowd. A man stepped forward, wearing the plain-spun cloth of a coffee farmer. He looked nervous, his eyes flickering from Pela to Devon, before he nodded and drew himself up. "They won't get far."

"Me too."

This time it was a woman who spoke. She carried an axe slung over one shoulder and wore a knife on her belt. Sweat shone from her brow and she looked like she'd arrived in a rush. Devon recognised her as one of the trappers who made their living harvesting the pelts of mountain hares and marmots, though he had never spoken with her before.

The rest of the crowd shifted nervously, exchanging glances, but no one else volunteered. Pela had shamed them all, but not enough to move them to action. Devon let out a sigh, disappointed, but at least two was better than none.

"Very well," he murmured. "Begone then, the rest of you, if you will not help. But at least send word to the king, about what happened here."

Muttering to each other, the crowd departed, leaving Devon and Pela alone with their two volunteers. Devon recognised the man now as one of the captives—the one who had screamed when Caledan drew his knife to cut them free.

"My ship will carry you as far as Townirwin, Devon," a man announced, extricating himself from the departing crowd, "but I won't fight."

Devon's heart lifted as he recognised Tallow, a captain from Skystead's fishing fleet. His ship, the *Seadragon*, was small, but had a reputation for being well-kept, not that

Devon knew anything about boats. Smiling, he offered his hand in thanks, then noticed the sellsword still lurking nearby.

"What about you?" Devon asked, eyeing the man.

He still had no idea why the man had intervened in the fight with the Knights. Sellswords were notoriously obsessed with self-preservation. Involving himself in a conflict with the Order of Alana seemed out of character for such a character.

Caledan shrugged. "What's in it for me?"

"I don't have the gold to pay for a sellsword."

"I wasn't thinking of coin," Caledan answered quickly.

"What then?" Devon pressed. "Unless you're suggesting you'll work for free."

Caledan chuckled. "If even a fraction of the legends about you are true, then you have a friend I'd like to meet."

"Who?"

"The king."

Devon stared at the man, weighing his options. Remembering the speed with which Caledan had dispatched the Knights, he knew the man was no ordinary sellsword. With such skill, he might have commanded a small fortune in the service of a noble. An introduction with the king should not be hard to arrange, despite the years it had been since they had last spoken. But what did Caledan want with Braidon? He sensed the man would not say, but even so…

"Very well," Devon said.

He had no choice; he could not rescue Kryssa alone. Turning to the two who had volunteered, he ran a professional eye over them. Both were well-muscled, toned by the toils of their professions, but he doubted they'd ever killed before. Then he saw the look in the woman's eyes, and reappraised his initial thoughts. There was steel there, that much was sure.

"If you join us, are you ready to fight?" he asked the two finally.

They nodded, though the man had a nervous look about him. Even so, he stepped forward, as though eager to convince himself he could in fact do what Devon asked. "Whatever it takes," he said, then hesitated. "If…you really think we can bring them back?"

Devon realised that the man must have had someone taken by the Knights. It was as strong a motivation as any. He offered a grim smile and nodded.

"We'll get them back, sonny, don't you worry," he rumbled. "Now, let's get moving."

$\mathfrak{H}$ 8 $\mathfrak{K}$

Sitting on the railings of the *Seadragon*, Pela watched as the light faded from the world. Patterns of blue and white and grey swirled on the smooth waters of the southern sea, but there was no sign of the sun itself in the cloud-streaked sky. The ship rolled with every swell, though the waves were gentle, unbroken. Sea spray obscured the mountains of Skystead, and she strained her eyes for a last glimpse of home.

She could hardly bring herself to believe that the last twelve hours had been real. Any minute, Pela expected to wake and find herself warm and safe in her bed, her mother calling for her help with the daily chores.

But as darkness claimed the world, and Tallow's sailors scuttled across the deck lighting lanterns, she knew this was no dream. It was too real, too stark and unrelenting. Images flashed through Pela's mind as she recalled the baker dying on the temple floor, her mother's terrified face as she told Pela to run; then Devon in the plaza, standing in defiance against the Knights with their armour and their swords.

Another shock. She had always dismissed the rumours about her uncle, but now that she had seen him fight, she found herself wondering what else might be true. Had he truly served with the king, or fought the Tsar, or spoken with the Gods? Had he known Alana? Surely not, or the Knights of Alana would not have stood against him.

She shook her head, trying to clear the clutter from her mind. Her thoughts turned to Kryssa. Where did the setting sun find her mother tonight? How fast had the merchant's ship carried her away from Skystead?

By the time Pela and the others had gathered their supplies, high tide had long passed, and they'd been forced to wait out the day, only setting sail an hour before sunset. Unfortunately, the *Seadragon* was built for fishing and short voyages, not speed, and there was little chance they could catch the Knights before they reached Townirwin.

Stuck in the twenty-foot skiff without so much as a cabin or bathroom, it was going to be a long three days. Still, at least Pela did not suffer from seasickness. Her uncle and the swordsman who had come to his aid back in the plaza had already been laid low.

She could see Devon in the bow of the ship, his eyes on the distant shoreline, the lines on his forehead knitted in concentration. Or so it would have appeared to the casual observer. Pela knew he was only trying to keep the remnants of his supper in their rightful place. At the stern, Caledan crouched with head in hands, looking as pale as a ghost. He had already lost that fight.

Chuckling to herself, Pela wondered at how such fearsome warriors could be brought low by the power of the ocean. Tallow and his two crewmembers certainly didn't seem affected, nor did the quiet trapper, Genevieve. She sat on a barrel leaning against the single mast, running a whetstone down the blade of her hatchet. With every stroke, a shrill grinding carried across the deck, joining the gentle lapping of water on the bow and the creaking of the sails.

The woman had said little since coming aboard, other than offering her name. Pela already knew Genevieve as a regular at their inn, though they'd rarely spoken in the past. She thought the huntswoman might have been a friend of her mother. Perhaps that was why she'd volunteered.

Tobias the farmer, on the other hand, was difficult to avoid. Since boarding the *Seadragon*, he had darted from Devon to Caledan to Tallow, offering his assistance wherever he thought it needed. He carried a nervous energy about him, an eagerness to help that might have come from fear, or simply a need to be busy. He stood beside Tallow now, pointing at the emerging stars and discussing navigation with the sea captain.

Along with herself and Tallow's crew, there were eight of them aboard the *Seadragon*. Suddenly, Pela found herself wondering what she was doing there. She was sixteen years old. This morning, her biggest worry had been avoiding awkward conversations at Temple. Now she was winging her way across the southern sea on a rescue mission, upon which she could only be a burden.

Devon had his hammer, Caledan his sword. The others were at least adults, experienced in the hardships of life, ready for what awaited them at the end of this voyage.

But what could Pela offer? What had possessed her to volunteer back in the plaza? She had no place here, no skill with weapons that might save the day. She was terrified of confrontation, and pain, and the unknown, all of which she was likely to face in the coming days. If only she hadn't been so stubborn, she might have listened to Devon when he'd told her to go home, and remained safe in Skystead.

Pela shuddered as goosebumps ran down her neck. There was no going back now. And anyway, she was a woman grown. If there was danger to be faced, she would not run from it. Her mother needed her to be brave. She would not fail Kryssa now.

Leather scuffed on wood as Caledan staggered from the stern and drew his sword. Pela started as lantern light caught on the blade, but Caledan only held the weapon over his head. Standing on one foot, he closed his eyes. His breathing deepened and he stilled, perfectly balanced, in harmony with his weapon.

When he moved, the act was so sudden that Pela almost fell backwards over the railing in surprise. The silver blade flashed as Caledan lunged, skewering empty air. Then he was leaping and slashing, sword arcing sideways as though to deflect an invisible foe, his footsteps so soft they made no sound on the wooden deck.

A stillness fell over the *Seadragon* as all eyes turned on the swordsman. There was a pattern to his movements, a rhythmic beat that only he seemed able to hear. Caledan continued through the deadly dance, every twist and turn coupled with another jab or thrust. His sword flashed up, then down and back, spearing an invisible opponent. Spinning, he blocked high, then kicked out to his right, before turning to bring his sword down in a double-handed attack.

By now even Devon in his sickness had taken note of the impromptu performance. Silence hung over the ship as Caledan continued his deadly dance, sword rising and falling, his movements growing faster, until the silver blade was little more than a blur.

Suddenly the weapon slipped from Caledan's fingers. Pela cried out as it spun through the air, arcing to half the height of the mast before plunging down. Others echoed

Pela's fright, but Caledan was already diving, rolling across the deck and coming to his knees. His hand snapped out, plucking the blade from the air.

Releasing a long breath, Caledan rose to his feet. Surprise showed in his eyes as he saw the others watching. His jaw hardened, and spinning on his heel, he started back towards the stern.

"Wait!" Pela was on her feet before she could stop herself. Her cheeks warmed as everyone looked at her, but she knew what she needed to do. "Can you teach me that?" she asked in a rush.

Her mother had never let Pela learn the warrior's arts, never let her hold anything larger than a steak knife, for that matter. What use were such skills in a town like Skystead? Yet with her mother gone, Pela was now confronted by the world beyond their sleepy village. She no longer had the luxury of running from her fears.

"No!" Pela jumped as Devon's voice came from the bow. Swinging around, she watched the big man approach, his bulk emerging from the gloom. "Your mother forbade it."

Despite her nerves, Pela bristled. "Well she's not here now, is she?"

"I should never have let you come," Devon said, shaking his head. "I don't know what I was thinking. First thing when we make port, I'll find a ship to take you back."

A lump lodged in Pela's throat as she looked into her uncle's amber eyes. This was the opportunity she had wanted, a chance to take back her words in the plaza, to return to Skystead, and hide from the dangers of the world outside.

An image flickered into her mind, and she saw again the baker dying on the Temple floor, the Knight standing over him. The world had brought its evil to them. There could be no safety in Skystead now. The evil would return with renewed strength.

If she allowed it.

"*No!*" The word left her in a rush, carrying across the deck for all to hear.

Silence answered her cry. Devon stared down at her, the flickering light of the lanterns seeming to age him. In that moment, Pela realised his fear, that he would not be able to protect her, that he might fail, that she would die. Cold touched her then, the weight of what she was committing herself to pressing down on her shoulders. Yet still she refused to relent.

"Please, Uncle," she said. "There's nothing for me in Skystead, not without Mum."

Devon's shoulders slumped, and Pela knew she'd won. He waved a hand, already turning away. "Very well," he murmured, his words whispering in the night. "Though your mother will kill me for it."

Letting out a long breath, Pela closed her eyes, relieved she'd won the battle.

"You ever used a sword, girl?" Caledan asked.

Jumping at the swordsman's question, Pela spun to face him. In the heat of the moment, she'd forgotten what had started the argument with her uncle. Her mouth opened and closed, words abandoning her. Caledan raised an eyebrow, his eyes showing his disdain, and Pela cursed herself for a fool.

"Ummm…" she managed finally.

The man snorted and made to turn away. Gathering herself, Pela leapt into his path.

"Please!" she gasped. "They have my mother; I need to be able to help."

Caledan scowled. "I don't have time to teach a brat how

to hold a blade." He sidestepped her and started for the stern again.

"What are you afraid of?" Pela shouted at his departing back, anger giving her courage. "That you'll fail?"

The swordsman paused. Sword still in hand, he stood looking away from her. But there was a rage in the way he stood, in the rigidity of his stance, and Pela felt a sudden fear of the deadly man. She swallowed as he turned to face her.

"You may as well give in," Devon rumbled from the shadows. "If she has half her mother's will, she'll wear you down eventually."

Caledan's eyes flickered, but after a moment, the anger vanished from his eyes. "Very well, Devon," he said. "I'll teach your niece a few things." He flicked his sword into the air and caught it by the blade, then offered it to Pela, hilt first.

Taken aback by his sudden change in manner, Pela hesitated before tentatively accepting the blade. The sword itself was a plain thing, its leather hilt unadorned, the blade thick at the base and some thirty inches long, ending in a razor-sharp point. Testing its weight, she gave a practice swing—and cried out as the leather slipped from her grasp.

The blade *clanged* loudly as it struck the deck point first and lodged there. Laughter burst across the *Seadragon* as her so-called companions doubled over in mirth. Even the farmer Tobias wore a broad grin on his bearded cheeks.

Her face aglow, Pela stood frozen to the spot, horrified by her own clumsiness. She wanted to race home and bury her head beneath the sheets, but on the ship, there was nowhere to go, no place to hide from the shame.

Footsteps thumped on the wooden planks as her uncle

returned from the bow. His eyes swept the faces of their companions, silencing them with a glance. Gingerly, he reached down a massive hand and plucked the sword free, before offering it back to Pela. Cheeks still burning, she shook her head, but Devon was insistent, and finally she accepted the blade with a trembling hand.

"Your mother really is going to murder me, you know," he murmured. She frowned, but he was already turning. "Who are you to laugh?" he bellowed at the others. "Who of you would have done any better, at sixteen? Which of you could do better now?"

In the darkness, Pela could not see the faces of her fellows, but the silence was palpable. In other circumstances, it might have bolstered her confidence. Instead, her heart sank at the reminder that her mother's life now rested in the hands of untrained villagers. Pela's grip on the sword tightened as she realised her fellows were just as unprepared for this mission as herself.

"I thought as much," Devon continued, his tone turning gentle. "Well, we have three days before we reach Townirwin. I suggest you take heed of my niece, and ready yourselves. The Knights will not surrender their prize without a fight."

"Will you teach us, Devon?" Tobias asked.

Devon eyed the farmer for a long moment, then shook his head. "Not tonight," he said softly, his voice sad. Before anyone could press him, he returned to his spot at the bow, and sat staring out at the dark shore.

Swallowing, Pela looked from Devon to Caledan. Movement came from around them as Tobias and Genevieve stepped closer. Tallow and one of his sailors also approached, arms crossed.

"So, where do we begin?" the captain asked.

This time when Caledan smiled, it was genuine. He gestured to Pela, then waited until everyone was paying attention, before pointing at the ground. "With your feet."

Devon's spirits were low as he sat listening to the clashing of swords. Twice already he'd heard Caledan cursing his new students. Plagued by doubt, Devon wondered whether he'd been wrong not to come alone. What difference could a few inexperienced villagers make, courageous though they might be?

And how could he hope to protect his niece where they were going? He should have refused her back in the plaza, rather than entertain this fantasy of a rescue mission. Timid as she was, he hadn't expected her to come this far. But Pela had surprised him. Perhaps there was more of her parents in the girl than even she realised.

His hammer lay beside him and he picked it up. Gripping the haft tight in one hand, Devon swore to himself he would not allow anything to happen to her. He owed Kryssa that, after everything they'd been through.

Holding the old hammer, Devon's gaze was drawn to the chunk Merak's blade had torn from the steel head. He shivered; that too gave him pause. It should not have been possible. Perhaps there had been an imperfection in the metal, though he knew the hammer well. An old friend had made it for him back in Ardath, after his ancestor's hammer had been destroyed by the Tsar. But then it *had* been made for construction, more than war.

He spent another few minutes inspecting the weapon, but he could see no other damage. Finally, he set it aside and returned his eyes to the night's sky.

After an hour, Caledan ended his impromptu training session with an explosion of curses, and silence returned to the *Seadragon*. Silhouettes flickered in the lantern light as the others made themselves comfortable for the night.

Devon was about to do the same when Pela appeared at the railing.

"What are you still doing awake, missy?" he asked gently.

"You don't want me here." She said the words matter-of-factly, a sad smile on her lips.

He sighed. "No, but then I rarely get what I want."

"I never knew you were a warrior," she murmured, taking a seat beside him. "Mum never wanted me to learn how to use a sword."

"No," Devon replied, "she…didn't believe in violence."

Pela snorted. "Could have fooled me…" She trailed off, looking to Devon for a response, but he said nothing, and she went on. "It isn't just her though. *You* don't want me to learn. Why?"

"I don't want to see you hurt," he replied, obfuscating. "Where we're going…I can't protect you."

"Who asked you to?"

"I can't fail your mother, not again."

"Again?" Pela's voice rose an octave.

Devon cursed his loose tongue. The girl was astute. "I only meant…I failed to rescue her."

"No…" Pela gripped the cuff of his shirt, her hand dwarfed by his own. "You know something, Devon…what is it? Why don't you or Mum want me to learn how to fight? Why did she push you away after my grandmother passed?"

"Pela…" Devon trailed off, struggling for the words. "I can't, I promised your mother…"

"I might not even *have* a mother anymore," his niece snapped, struggling to her feet. "What are you keeping from me?"

Devon lowered his eyes. "Your mother…she's…Selina and I raised her," he said, remembering the scrawny ten-year-old who had first shown up on the doorstep of the Firestone.

It had been Selina who had invited her in. Devon had been reluctant to be dragged into the role of a caregiver, but eventually the fiery youth had wormed her way into his heart. How she had grown, these last thirty years. Tears stung his eyes as the years flashed by, and he recalled her marriage to Derryn, the arrival of Pela. They had all moved to Skystead not long before the birth, in search of a safe place to raise a child.

They should have found peace there.

Would have, if not for Devon's weakness.

"I wanted to protect her from the world, but I failed. I couldn't save him," he whispered.

"Save who?"

"Your father," Devon grunted. He rubbed his cheek, trying to conceal his tears, trying to decide how much to tell her. "He fought alongside me many times…your father."

"*What?*" Pela gasped.

"This was before you were born, before we moved to Skystead, when we lived in Ardath."

Pela was on her feet. "Mum…how…she never!"

"Breath, Pela," Devon murmured, placing a hand on her shoulder. She nodded, her eyes as wide as saucepans, and he swallowed. Guilt weighed heavily on his chest as he went on, "We…he and I were both members of the King's Guard, the most elite of his soldiers. But when your mother became pregnant…we retired and moved to Skystead. Except, not long before your birth, the king sent for me, begged for my help with the war. I could have refused him, *should* have refused him, but…that was ever my weakness."

He hung his head, no longer bothering to conceal his tears, as the memories of that time rushed through his mind. Pela sat beside him, silent now, and he dared not meet her gaze.

"I would have gone alone," Devon whispered, "but… your mother wouldn't hear of it. She asked your father to go with me, though he didn't want to leave the two of you." He balled his hands into fists and squeezed his eyes closed. "I should have protected him. I failed."

"My father…" Pela croaked. "You saw him die?"

"Ay." His voice barely rose above a whisper. "In the foothills north of Lake Ardath, the enemy came upon us. No one knew they were so close. The army was far ahead of us; the king was unprotected but for twenty of his guard. Derryn and I stood at the centre and defied the Lonians until reinforcements could reach us. But when the last enemy was slain and I looked for him, he…he was already gone."

He hung his head, unable to even look at his niece. If not for him, she would have grown up knowing her father.

If not for him, Kryssa would have enjoyed many more years with her love…

"How could you keep this from me?" Pela hissed. He looked up at the anger in her voice. "I thought he was killed by Baronians!"

"Your mother wanted to protect you—"

Pela laughed harshly. "Well the two of you have done a great job of that, haven't you?" Her shoulders slumped suddenly. A shudder swept through her and the tears returned. "If you'd taught me to be a warrior like my father, I might have saved her. I might have done *something*, anything but run away."

Devon realised then what had driven his niece to join this ill-fated quest—she was ashamed. Ashamed that she'd frozen, ashamed she hadn't fought back when the Knights came, that she'd run away. Gingerly, he placed a hand on her head.

"To run when there is no hope of victory is not cowardice, Pela."

"*You* would not have run."

"Perhaps not, but even I could not have won that fight. Not even in my youth could I have defeated so many alone. If you'd fought, even if I'd taught you to use a blade, you would have only thrown away your life. That was why your mother never wanted you to learn in the first place."

Pela frowned. "What do you mean?"

"She was afraid of losing you, that you might follow in your…father's footsteps, and become a soldier."

"I…" Pela swallowed, averting her eyes. "Why would she think that? I never wanted anything like that…"

"Ay, but would it have been different if you'd known the truth? Maybe you wanted more than what Skystead can offer."

"Even so…" she murmured. "She should have told me, should have given me the choice."

Devon eyed his niece closely. She had always been a timid child, when Kryssa had brought her on their weekly visits after Temple. There had been little of her parents' fire in Pela then; now he wondered if she possessed that flame after all. Back in Skystead, while Pela had been packing for the journey, he'd retrieved some things from Kryssa's basement. With weapons in short supply in Skystead, he'd intended to arm the villagers. Now though…

"She didn't want you to die young, never knowing your family," he said, his voice little more than a whisper. The blood drained from Pela's face at his words, and he went on, "She wanted more for you than to lose your life fighting someone else's war. But…maybe you're right. Maybe it should have been your choice."

Reaching into the worn canvas sack he had brought, Devon rummaged around until he found what he was looking for. He drew it out and unwrapped the silk cloth Kryssa had bound it in all those years ago. The light of the nearby lantern revealed a polished leather sheath and a hilt inlaid with gold wire.

"This was your father's," he said, offering it to Pela. "If you intend to fight, he would have wanted you to have the best."

❧ 10 ❧

Ikar stood at the railings of the *Red Seagull* and breathed in the fresh ocean breeze, savouring its coolness in the humid air. The prisoners were all locked in the hold, but with the sailors scuttering about the deck, the Knights were still forced to wear their suffocating helmets. Along with the heavy plate mail and the thick woollen padding beneath, it would make for a long journey.

The sun remained low on the horizon, but already he could feel the sweat beading his forehead. Cursing, Ikar checked if anyone was watching, but the crew were occupied and most of his fellow Knights still slept. Quickly, he ducked into the shadows alongside the captain's cabin and removed his helmet. He wiped his face with a cloth from his belt, before replacing it on his head.

"Uncomfortable, Ikar?"

Ikar spun around at Merak's voice. The Elder leaned against the railing where just moments before Ikar had stood. With the prisoners secure, Merak had removed the rest of his armour and now wore the swathing red robes of the Elders. At first glance the man seemed relaxed, but as Ikar approached, he glimpsed a hint of irritation in the man's eye.

"It is nothing," Ikar replied, thinking of the Elder's return in Skystead. The ship had been preparing to depart when Merak had come galloping into the port and leapt aboard. The fear in the Elder's eyes had been palpable, but Ikar was tactful enough not to mention it. "I persevere in the name of our saviour."

Merak smiled grimly. "As do we all." His sapphire eyes flickered in Ikar's direction. "Tell me, Knight, would you give your life for our cause?"

"Of course," Ikar answered without hesitation, before adding, "as my brothers in Skystead did before me."

He watched the Elder for his reaction. Merak claimed his party had been set upon by a mob in the town square. His fellow Knights had been slaughtered and the blasphemers freed, the Elder himself barely escaping with his life.

Yet when Ikar had volunteered to lead the rest of their company back into Skystead, Merak had refused, instead ordering the *Red Seagull* to set sail.

The memory burned at Ikar. It shamed him that they had fled, allowing their brothers to go unavenged. Worse, they had given the followers of the False Gods a victory. It would make the blasphemers bold. Skystead must be purged, its infection scourged before it could spread to other settlements, lest all the Order's work come to naught.

"Ay," Merak smirked. "Perhaps one day Alana will call on you to make that sacrifice."

Ikar bowed his head. "I can only pray."

"For now though, our preparations must continue, despite the loss of our brothers. Thirty years have passed since Alana made her sacrifice, and the solstice approaches.

The power of the False Gods grows stronger with each passing day; candidates to renew her sacrifice must be found."

The Elder's words sent an icy fear racing through Ikar, raising the hackles on his neck. The False Gods could not be allowed to return. His people had fought too hard to free themselves from the yolk of magic, to be returned to the shackles of the past.

"What do you require of me?" he asked.

"Take the blasphemers their supper," Merak replied. He gestured at a pair of pails. "The ship's cook prepared them some food. Speak with them, discover if any might be worthy of our needs."

Ikar's shoulders fell at the menial nature of the assignment, but nodding, he turned his back on the Elder and retrieved the pails. Within, a murky liquid resemblant of stagnant water slopped back and forth and split over the edge of one bucket. He cursed as the muck stained his leggings. Thinking he heard laughter, he glanced back at Merak, but the Elder had already moved on to other tasks.

Muttering under his breath, Ikar staggered to the ladder leading into the hold. The stench of vomit and rotting fish swamped him as he carried the first bucket down, and it was a relief when he returned above-deck for the second. Cursing Merak, he gulped down several mouthfuls of fresh air before stumbling down the ladder a second time.

The prisoners had been relegated to a section in the bow, where the rocking of the ship was worst. It was a pitiful act of retribution for their fallen brothers, though Ikar had to admit it was effective. He doubted many of their prisoners would be interested in the food he'd brought. Placing the buckets on the shifting boards, he folded his arms and waited for them to take notice.

"What do you want, Knight?"

Ikar scowled as the woman who had defied him on the mountainside rose to her feet. She seemed to be one of the few who had not succumbed to seasickness, though her face was pale and he guessed she was not far from joining the others. The boy she had helped earlier crouched at her feet, but she stepped forward, as though to separate her fate from his.

"To feed you," Ikar snapped, sliding a bucket forward with the toe of his boot.

The woman fixed him with a glare. "Are we to eat like dogs then?" she asked, one eyebrow arched.

It took Ikar a moment to realise what she meant. With their hands still bound behind their backs, the prisoners wouldn't even be able to lift the buckets, never mind spoon the broth into their mouths. He was about to reach for his knife to cut them loose, when he caught the defiance in the woman's eyes. Scowling, he released the hilt of his knife.

"Do as you please, witch," he snapped. "If it were up to me, you would all have been cleansed with your fellows in the town square."

The woman paled. "I have a name," she said. "As did those your Elder took."

Ikar's retort died on his lips as he heard the woman's sorrow. He hesitated, his anger quenched as though plunged into ice water. Swallowing, he stepped towards her and placed a hand on her shoulder.

"I am sorry," he said, though he could not have said why, "I should not have spoken so harshly. What is your name?"

"Kryssa," the woman murmured.

"Fear not, Kryssa, you shall all have the chance to repent before the end," Ikar reassured her.

Her eyes flashed silver as she looked up at him. "Repent?" she asked. "And for what do any of us have to repent?"

A long sigh whispered between Ikar's lips and he took a step back. "You were caught worshipping in a temple of the False Gods, committing blasphemy against the apostle Alana."

"Do our beliefs threaten you so much, oh Knight?"

"Your Gods would threaten us all!" Ikar snapped.

"And yet we lived peacefully beneath their rule for centuries," Kryssa replied.

"Peace?" Ikar asked, disbelieving. "Were you not taught of the scourge of Archon? Or the devastation wrought by the Tsar? Or the countless other atrocities committed by their Magickers, down through the centuries?"

"The Gods gave us power, and the free will to use it," the woman replied. "It is not upon them what we chose to do with it. And what of the good that was done? The Magickers who healed the sick? And those who stood against the dark? Do they count for naught?"

"We never had free will, only servitude," he retorted. "Against the forces of magic, what power did we mortals have? What hope, when a single Magicker could slay hundreds? No, the only freedom your Gods offered was for the powerful, to those they deemed worthy of their gift. The rest of us were doomed, enslaved by their power."

"Us?" the woman asked. "You speak as though you were there—yet you sound no older than me, sir Knight. How do you know what the Gods desired?"

"It is there for any with open eyes to see."

"Ay, the truth is there," Kryssa whispered. "Who is it that enslaves us now? Who has hunted us down, who seeks to take our freedom from us?"

"Your beliefs endanger us all!"

"How?" Kryssa asked, her eyes aglow in the darkness.

Ikar swallowed. "You would restore the Gods to life." Somehow, his words suddenly seemed hollow, as though he were a fool to speak them.

Kryssa laughed, the sound harsh and mocking. "The Gods are dead, you fool," she replied. "We all know that, and do not seek to change it, however much some might wish it. We go to Temple in honour of their memory. And to meditate, to find our own harmony, and seek the true paths for our lives."

"Lies," Ikar whispered, backing away from the woman.

Her eyes followed him, accusing. "Look around, oh Knight," she replied, gesturing behind her. Huddled on the ground, the other prisoners watched him, terror written across their faces. "Where is the danger here? The threat? Do you not see? We are just a scapegoat, a false evil for your Order to strike down."

"Stop!" Ikar roared. Steel hissed on leather as he drew his sword and pointed it at her. "No more of your false-hoods, witch!"

Kryssa's face wilted at the sight of the blade. Shaking her head, she took a step back, a pall of fear coming over her. Ikar scowled and stepped after her, unsure whether the change was an act. Her mouth opened, but he darted forward, resting the tip of his blade against her breast.

"Not another word from you."

She nodded, the fear no act now. A sense of power surged through Ikar then. Savouring in her acquiescence, he looked around, ensuring the others saw his strength, knew the Knights of Alana were not to be defied.

"You are all worse than the sorriest wretch," he said vehemently. "Less than the lowest beggar on the streets of

Lon. You asked if you are animals to us, woman? I say you are worse! Vermin who would drown us all in your filth."

As he spoke, he kicked at her legs. Kryssa cried out as his heavy boot connected with her shins, and crumpled to her knees. With one foot, he pushed the bucket of slop closer. She looked up at him with horror written across her face.

"Please," she whispered.

"Eat," he growled. When she did not move, he drove his boot down into the woman's back, forcing her head down into the bucket. She cried out, but her shrieks were cut off by gurgling. Ikar's eyes swept the other prisoners, so that when he spoke, they knew his words were for all of them, "Like the vermin you are."

11

Caledan was already awake when the first hints of sunlight touched the horizon. The gentle rocking of the ship had kept his stomach roiling all night, and no amount of practice with his blade had helped to settle it. Whatever food he'd eaten before embarking on the *Seadragon* was long gone, and he was beginning to wonder if joining Devon had been the right choice.

"Of course it is," he muttered to himself, though the words meant little for his nausea. Only the fact his stomach was empty kept him from vomiting again.

"What is?"

He jumped as Devon appeared at the railing beside him. For such a big man, he moved with an unnatural quiet, even on the tiny ship. The rest of the crew were just beginning to stir, and Caledan let out a long sigh at the thought of spending another day trapped with the foolish villagers.

"Nothing," he murmured.

The hammerman leaned his arms against the railing and fixed his amber eyes on the distant coast. Overnight, the shoreline had changed. They had left behind the towering cliffs and peaks of Golden Ridge, and now the land had given way to marshland, its myriad of twisting streams and dense mangroves all but impassable by foot. The tide was out, exposing close to a mile of mudflats upon which great crocodiles basked.

Caledan's gaze drifted from the mud to the waters around the ship, as he considered what might happen should they capsize. The crocodiles were larger than any man, with massive jaws lined with dagger-like teeth. He had seen a man caught by the arm once. The witless fool had been dragged into the water before he could do anything more than scream. Caledan and the other bystanders could do nothing but watch as the man was torn apart.

A great splash drew his eyes back to the shore, where a trail of mud now led into the ocean. There was no sign of the croc though, and shuddering, Caledan turned his attention back to Devon.

"I was only wondering, what is our plan once we arrive in Townirwin?"

The big man shrugged. "Find wherever the Knights are keeping our people, and take them back." Devon grinned. "Kill whoever gets in my way."

"Sounds promising, if a little light on the details," Caledan commented.

Devon chuckled. "I never was one for planning," he replied. "Although...at this time of year, the tax collectors should be making their rounds. Bound to be a few of the King's Guard in town for their protection. I'll see if we can't enlist them to our noble cause."

"When was the last time you visited Townirwin?"

"Five...no, it must be closer to ten years now. How the years fly." Devon sighed, running a hand through his thinning hair. "There will be those in the Guard that remember me, though."

"Of that I have no doubt," Caledan replied, then hesitated. Much had changed since the war with Lonia had ended. "However, you may…find the people of Townirwin less than receptive to your cause."

"Oh?" Devon asked, raising an eyebrow.

"The Knights of Alana are well-liked there. It would be foolish to denounce them, without proof of their crime."

"What more proof could we need than catching them red-handed with our people?" Devon snapped, his brow hardening.

Caledan held up his hands. "Easy, man. I only meant we would be wise to keep our heads low, until your daughter and the others are safe."

"She's not my daughter…" the old hammerman said, though his thoughts were obviously elsewhere. "At least… you might be right though. We cannot risk the Knights… disposing of the evidence before we can free our people." He glanced at Caledan. "But we can trust the King's Guard."

Trying not to roll his eyes, Caledan nodded. Devon was a fool if he believed he could trust anyone associated with Braidon. Though of course, the two had fought alongside each other, early in the civil war. Last night, lying awake in the darkness, Caledan had heard the story about Pela's father.

"Whatever you say," Caledan replied, keeping the doubt from his voice. He nodded at the hammer lying at Devon's feet. "Were you planning on finding a new weapon?"

Devon chuckled. Hefting the hammer, he turned it in his hands. Light shone from the corner that had been carved away by Merak's sword. "This will do, whatever its flaws. Truth be told, no weapon has ever been able to replace *kanker*, the warhammer I inherited from my ancestor."

"They say it was cursed?" Caledan asked, recalling the legends.

"Cursed? No, only spelled by a Magicker named Alastair. It protected me from magic, so long as I was holding it. Allowed me to stand against all manner of Magickers and demons. Now…"

"Now a man, and women, must stand behind their own strength," Caledan muttered. "The strong rule, and the weak make do with the scraps that we leave."

The lines in Devon's face deepened as he looked down at Caledan. "Ay," he replied sadly, "and we are all the lesser for it." Letting out a long breath, he looked out over the ocean. "So, what were you doing in Skystead in the first place? The town is no place for a sellsword."

"Perhaps it was fate that brought me there, to help with your cause."

Or to bring me closer to my goal, he thought silently, careful to keep the excitement from his face.

Devon chuckled. "I've seen Gods and demons and dragons, but I've never believed in fate. A man, or indeed a woman, forges their own path in this world."

"Then perhaps it was intuition," Caledan replied with a grin. There was at least truth in that. He had learned long ago to trust his instincts. They had rarely led him astray, though he'd had his doubts when he set foot in the backwaters of Skystead. "I was following a story. The captain who hired me claimed there were Baronians in these waters, that they possessed some new magic that allowed them to sail against the winds."

"And how did that turn out?"

"After three days of misery, I decided the story wasn't worth pursuing."

"Lucky for us, I guess," Devon grunted. He flicked a glance at Caledan, his eyes hardening. "Though your story seems a little too convenient. You'd best not cross me, sonny. It won't end well."

Unable to help himself, Caledan smirked at the hammerman. "You think you could take me, old man?"

Devon's face darkened and he straightened. Caledan's hand dropped to his sword hilt, but when he looked into the hammerman's amber eyes, the blood froze in his veins. In that instant, it seemed as though death itself stared back at him, and Caledan knew the old warrior would not hesitate. The second he tried to draw the blade, his life would end. It took an effort of will for Caledan to release his sword hilt.

"Good decision," Devon said, his voice barely rising above a whisper.

With that, he turned and wandered away. Caledan stood staring after him, the hairs on his neck still standing on end. Slowly the coils that had wrapped themselves around his stomach loosened, though the ice in his veins took longer to melt. Finally he let out a breath he had not realised he'd been holding.

"We'll see," he muttered to himself, trying and failing to draw strength from the words.

Out on the mudflats, one of the crocodiles slid down the bank into the ocean, without so much as a splash.

           ❧   12   ❧

P ela rolled her shoulders, trying to loosen the ache that
      had taken root in the muscles of her neck. For two
days now, Caledan had pushed her and the others hard,
drilling them in the basic attacks, stances, and parries of
sword fighting. It was hard work, and the poorly-weighted
blades they'd managed to scavenge from Skystead's decrepit
dungeon made the work all the harder.

She hadn't touched the blade Devon had given her yet.
She could hardly even bring herself to believe it had truly
been her father's at all. All her life, she had grown up
believing he'd been killed on the road by Baronians. To
suddenly learn that had been a lie, that he had died
defending their king from enemy soldiers…

Pain flared in her arm as Tobias's sword slipped beneath
her guard and struck her wrist. Cursing, she leapt backwards out of range. The clumsy farmer tripped over his
own legs chasing after her, and she struck back, her
sheathed sword tapping him lightly on the side of the head.

"Enough!" Caledan shouted at them.

Breathing hard, Pela lowered her sword and spun around. Caledan sat on a barrel leaning against the mast, equal measures of anger and frustration writ across his face. Since accepting them as students, his expression had hardly changed, and Pela wondered whether he regretted taking her on. So far, neither herself nor anyone else had shown much sign of improvement, though at least Genevieve had started with some basic knowledge of how to wield a blade.

But Caledan was not a man to accept defeat. He would either turn them all into something resembling warriors, or toss them overboard to hide his failure. His hard attitude had turned them all against him, even the unfathomably cheerful Tobias, and if it came to it, they might be the ones to throw him overboard.

Not that it seemed to matter to Caledan. With a weapon in hand, the man was cold, bordering on cruel, and when they took turns sparring with him, he did not pull his blows. Wielding an old fire poker one-handed, he'd given Pela more than bruises when she'd been careless enough to lower her guard. None of them had even managed to touch him yet.

The heavy footsteps of her uncle approached from the bow where he had been napping all afternoon. Tomorrow they would finally reach Townirwin, but she could see the worry in his eyes, the fear that they would be too late. For herself, Pela had tried not to think about what would happen when they got there.

Rubbing his eyes, Devon yawned and gestured her to join him. She glanced at Caledan for permission, and the swordsman waved a hand, dismissing them for a break. Pela retrieved a jug of water and wandered over to Devon.

"I haven't seen you with your father's sword yet," he said without preamble.

Pela quickly looked away. "No…" She trailed off, her throat contracting. She glanced at her bag where she had stashed the blade. It remained out of sight, but she could sense it there, a presence in her mind. "I…what if I'm not worthy?"

"Worthy?" her uncle pressed.

Lowering her eyes, Pela fought back tears. "I'm no good, Uncle!" The words went from her in a rush. "I keep dropping my sword, tripping over my own feet, flinching when someone swings at me. How can I use my father's sword when I'm so *useless?*" She kicked the side of the ship to emphasise her last words.

To her surprise, Devon chuckled. Pela swung on him, shame giving way to anger. "What are you laughing at?" she snapped.

Devon smiled. "Do you think your father, or myself, were any different when we first began?"

Pela blinked. "I…what are you talking about? I'm *terrible!*"

"A man my size, you wouldn't believe the trouble I had keeping my feet under me in my first year as a recruit," Devon said. "I didn't know your father when he was younger, but I have no doubt he was the same. The warrior's arts require skill, and *practice*—you cannot become a master like Caledan overnight."

"Oh." Pela blinked, feeling suddenly foolish for her worries. She glanced at her pack again, and the sword within. "Still, though…I should wait, until I get better."

"Or you could use it now," Devon replied. "If you want to be a good swordswoman, you need a better blade than that thing you're currently calling a sword."

Pela sighed. "Fine." She strode across the deck, dragged the blade from her bag and carried it back to Devon.

"Why don't you draw it for me?" Devon asked.

There was the slightest of sheens to Devon's eyes when she looked at him. Pela remembered then that the last time this sword had gone to battle, her father had been carrying it, marching at Devon's side. Swallowing, she did as her uncle bid.

Light caught on the blade as it emerged, so that for a moment it seemed to be sheathed in flames. Then she turned it in her hand, and the fire died, and there was only the silver sword of her father. She sucked in a breath, struggling with a sudden wave of emotion.

My father.

He had carried this weapon into battle, had saved the *king* with it, had died with it in hand…

She didn't want you to die young, never knowing your family.

Pela lowered the blade quickly as Devon's warning came back to her. She let out a breath, the pride dying in her throat, replaced by a sudden terror. Was that to be her fate, now that she had embraced Derryn's legacy?

No, this is not my life. I only want my mother back.

But then she remembered Devon, back in the plaza, as he had carved through the Knights like death itself. She remembered the screams of the young men as they had fallen. They hadn't expected to die either—how could they? The villagers had removed their armour to bury them, revealing their youthful faces, barely older than herself.

A trembling began in her knees as she stared at the blade. What was she doing? Who did she think she was, holding the sword of a King's Guard, believing she could be a hero?

"How did you do it?" she asked suddenly, her voice several pitches above normal.

Devon frowned, one silver-streaked eyebrow lifting above the other. "Do what?"

"Win!" she gasped. "Defeat all those Knights! There were so many of them, but you won and they died or ran. How?"

Letting out a long sigh, Devon leaned one elbow against the railing. "You've been training with Caledan for three days now, little one. How do you think I did it?"

"How should I know?" Pela snapped.

"Think."

Pela tried to quell her racing heart. They were nearing Townirwin now, and still she knew nothing. How could she help her uncle, her mother, when she couldn't even beat the coffee farmer? It wasn't possible. But then, Devon had been able to do the impossible. Despite his age, despite being outnumbered, he'd crushed the Knights and caused their Elder to flee in…

"Fear?" Pela asked, the blood still pounding in her ears.

"Fear." Devon nodded in agreement. "It is a warrior's greatest weapon—and greatest weakness."

"What do you mean?"

"In small doses, it gives us caution, keeps us alive," Devon replied. "But when left unchecked…"

"Like that Elder…" Pela finished for him.

"Ay. He saw me kill two of his men in as many seconds. Never mind that they were taken by surprise—he panicked. His fear spread to the others, and they hesitated. If they had gone for the kill then, I could not have beaten them all. They might have won before Caledan intervened."

"But how did you know that would happen?" Pela pressed. "What if he'd sent all of them against you from the start?"

Devon shrugged. "Then I would be dead."

A cold hand gripped Pela's belly. "Then why were *you* not afraid?"

A sad smile touched Devon's lips. "I have lived for a long time, little one, far longer than I ever expected. Most of my friends are waiting for me on the other side. What do I have to fear from death?"

Pela shivered, but before she could respond, a call came from Caledan.

"Back to it!"

Swallowing, Pela looked from her uncle to the swordsman. Devon's explanation had done little to quell her own concerns. He might not fear death, but she did, and she had little doubt it would find her if she continued down this path. Even so, she nodded her thanks and returned to stand beside Tobias and Genevieve.

"A new sword, Pela?" Caledan commented, nodding to the blade in her hand.

Pela blinked. She'd forgotten she still carried her father's blade. After a moment she nodded, and Caledan smiled grimly.

"Very well then," he said. "Let's see whether it helps, shall we?"

He gestured her forward. After a moment's hesitation, Pela nodded and looked around for the scabbard to sheath the blade while they fought.

"Leave it," Caledan ordered. "Ready?"

Pela lifted her father's sword and nodded, sliding one foot behind her in an attempt at a fighting stance. Caledan strode forward, eyes hard, and hefted his iron poker.

"Defend yourse—"

"Sails to starboard!" a voice called down, interrupting Caledan before he could launch his first attack.

Pela had bunched herself up in preparation to spring,

and almost tripped over her own legs trying to spin around in search of the new ship. She had assumed her mother's captors would have already made port, but what if they had been delayed?

Squinting at the horizon, she couldn't see any sign of another ship. She tried to recall which direction was starboard, but wherever she looked there was nothing but empty ocean. The ship, if it existed, hadn't come into view for the rest of them yet, only for the man in the rigging.

"There's nothing out there," Caledan murmured, moving to the right-hand railing of the ship. "Who would be mad enough to sail out of sight of land?"

"No one with good intentions on their mind," the captain replied. He rushed past the villagers and grabbed the tiller. "Hope your people are ready for a fight, Devon!"

"Fight?" Tobias asked, the colour fleeing his face.

Pela's heart started to race as a black dot appeared on the horizon. Beside her, Caledan cursed, then glanced at the sails.

"The breeze is coming from the north," he muttered. "They'll never catch us sailing from the south."

"It's flying a black flag!" the man in the crow's nest called down.

"You'd better pray to whatever Gods you worship you're right," Tallow replied, before turning to his men. "Sails at full tilt, lads! Let's outrun those Baronian bastards!"

$\mathfrak{X}$ 13 $\mathfrak{X}$

Caledan watched in silence as the black dot grew larger. The Baronian ship had changed direction to cut off the *Seadragon's* escape and was no longer sailing directly against the wind, but it was still moving far too quickly for his liking. Already it had halved the distance between them.

So the captain was right, Caledan thought, and cursed out loud.

Tallow's shouts were becoming more desperate. As the gap between the two vessels narrowed, the Baronian crew came into view. Most stood waiting at the railings, swords and axes in hand and grins on their faces. Behind them, several crew members scurried around the deck, but it appeared there was little that needed doing. Only one of the ship's three masts had a sail up, and that hung loose in the wind, seeming to only be for show. Sunlight reflected from the other two empty masts, and Caledan realised with a start that they were made of steel.

His frown deepened as a puff of black smoke bellowed from the top of one of the masts.

They're not masts at all, he realised, *they're smokestacks.*

Though what they were for, he could not have guessed.

"What in the damn *hell?*" the captain muttered beside him.

Wood creaked as Devon appeared alongside them. "We're not going to escape them."

"Impossible," Tallow snapped, then shouted another string of orders to his men.

The *Seadragon* surged forward as another span was added to the sails, though Caledan could see by now it would not matter. Whatever magic the Baronians were working, they were faster, with or without the wind. Clad in their black-leather armour, their fighters packed the deck, waiting in grim silence for their prey to come within reach. They outnumbered Caledan and the others ten to one.

"Well, folks, I hope you've been paying attention to Caledan!" Devon bellowed, turning to address the villagers and Tallow's crew. "Ready those weapons, you're going to need them. Pela, to me."

The girl rushed forward, still gripping her father's blade. Caledan watched as Devon kneeled in front of her, wondering what he would do. Despite his best efforts, neither Pela nor the others were ready to go up against battle-hardened warriors like the Baronians. They would be cut down in moments.

Then again, against so many, Caledan doubted even he would last much longer. Studying the oncoming ship, he searched for another way to strike.

"Your mother wanted a better life for you than this," Devon was saying to Pela, his voice barely audible over the shouts of the sailors. "So did I, once upon a time. But such is fate. Are you ready to use that sword?"

There was open fear on the girl's face, but to her credit, she lifted her jaw and nodded.

"Good," Devon replied. "Your father would be proud to see you carry it."

Tears formed in the girl's eyes, quickly wiped away.

"You'd best stick close to us, girl," Caledan said, still watching the Baronian ship. "You're quick; use that. And remember, the Baronians are born killers."

"They're not all bad," Devon murmured. A grin crossed his bearded face. "I led one of their tribes once—albeit, only for a few weeks."

"Whoever was calling themselves Baronian back then, they're a different people now," Caledan snapped, irked by the old man's seemingly cheerful mood. "These ones will show you no mercy. If you see an opening, take it!"

Devon hefted his hammer. "Never said I wouldn't," he growled, and Caledan was reminded of their earlier disagreement. Then the hammerman turned back to his niece. "Caledan is right though, they're experienced warriors. Keep a tight hold of that sword, but stay back unless the fight comes to you. Caledan and I will lead the charge, see if we can't scare them off."

Pale-faced, Pela nodded and took her place alongside Genevieve and Tobias. The other sailors had retrieved long knives and were gathering around their captain. It seemed they'd given up trying to escape the oncoming ship.

Studying his companions, Caledan wondered whether they would hold. He'd been impressed with their resolve these last few days. He'd pressed them to breaking point, but they'd risen to every challenge he'd set, even timid Pela and nervous Tobias. He would not blame any one of them for fleeing at the first clash of battle, but he sensed they would stand strong.

Caledan loosened his sword in its scabbard, then transferred the poker he still carried to his left hand. He did not have a shield, and he would need every advantage he could get in the coming fight.

"Damnit, how is this possible?" the captain growled as he came to stand alongside them. A big man himself, he had armed himself with an axe. "They barely have any sail out."

"We can worry about that if we survive," Caledan snapped. "Are your men ready?"

Tallow answered with a string of vulgarities that would have made even the hardest veteran blush.

"If we keep on this heading, they're going to take us side-on," Devon observed.

"Did you have a better idea?" Tallow asked.

"Ram them," Devon replied.

"What?!" the captain exploded. "This is a *fishing* ship, we have no ram, we'd be torn apart."

Devon shrugged. "Do they know that?"

"You want to play chicken with the Baronians?"

"They want your ship and whatever goods we have on board. We're no good to them on the bottom of the ocean. They'll turn away. Trust me."

"Trust you?" Tallow asked with a scowl.

He stood staring at Devon, expecting an answer, but the big man just grinned. Letting out another string of curses, the captain gave in and leapt to the tiller. The ship turned slowly as he swung them away from the coast.

Caledan's stomach roiled, reminding him uncomfortably of his seasickness. It had improved over the last few days and he'd managed to eat a little, but he was still weaker than he would have liked.

"There's too many!" one of the sailors shouted.

"They've got to board us first!" Devon bellowed back. "So long as they're over there, we're safe. If they throw hooks, cut the ropes. If they jump aboard, kill 'em!"

Silence settled over the ship as they watched the gap narrow. The two vessels were rushing headlong at one another now. Running with the wind, the *Seadragon* had picked up speed. Overhead, the mast and rigging creaked and the sails went *crack*, and Caledan wondered for a moment whether they might tear themselves apart before they ever reached the Baronian ship.

The gap was hardly a hundred feet wide when the enemy ship swung violently to the left, its speed slowing abruptly. Onboard, the Baronians stumbled over one another, thrown off-balance by their sudden change in the direction. The *Seadragon* surged onwards. For a moment it looked as though they might sweep past into open sea, that the Baronians would be swamped. They were close to Townirwin now, if they kept going at this pace, they might reach port before…

Sunlight glinted on metal as a hook shot from the Baronian ship, a black line trailing out behind it. They must have fired it from a bow, for it flew far further than Caledan would have believed, clunking down onto the deck of the *Seadragon*. Before anyone could react, it snapped backwards, and the steel hook sank deep into the wood of the railings. The deck lurched beneath their feet as the line went taut, throwing half of them from their feet.

"Up!" Devon bellowed as the *Seadragon* pitched wildly. Overhead, the sails went slack as the line dragged them around so that they sat headlong into the wind. "At 'em!"

Caledan rushed to join the old man. On the other ship, the Baronians jeered as another line grabbed hold of the

Seadragon, dragging them closer. Caledan hacked at the first cord, but his blade sprang back, the line untouched. He stared at it in shock, realising the rope was made of steel. There would be no cutting themselves free.

Grimly, he turned to face the Baronians, sword and iron poker in hand. Only a few feet separated the two ships now, and roaring, a giant of a man sprang over the railings and leapt at them. His shoulder slammed into Devon, staggering him. An axe shone in the sunlight as the Baronian lifted it above his head.

Surging forwards, Caledan drove his blade low, catching the man unawares. The Baronian staggered as Caledan's sword pierced his chest, but as he fell, two more jumped to take his place. This time they came at Caledan, giving Devon a chance to recover.

Caledan caught the tip of a spear with his sword, then spun, reversing his blade and driving it into the stomach of his attacker. The man staggered back, and Caledan roared, his blade rising to block the second's sword—but he was already dead, his skull crushed by a blow from Devon's hammer.

Nodding his thanks, Devon bellowed a war cry and vaulted onto the railing of the *Seadragon*. A horde of Baronians awaited on the other ship, but most had not yet been able to cross to the wallowing fishing ship. Devon's laughter washed over them.

"Come on then, cowards!" he roared. "Come and get me!"

Angry screams answered his challenge as the Baronians surged forward, each desperate for a chance against the grey-haired warrior. Caledan joined Devon on the railing. A Baronian spear shot right by his shoulder. Caledan's blade flashed out and the Baronian on the opposite railing fell back into the crowd of black-garbed enemy.

An axe flew at Caledan's face, but he wrenched himself back. Balanced precariously on the edge, he felt the breath of the weapon sweep past, then straightened and skewered the wielder. Beside him, Devon's silver beard was drenched with sweat and his face seemed a shade paler, but his hammer still rose and fell with devastating power.

Aboard the Baronian vessel, three faced them now across the narrow gap. More could have come, boarding the *Seadragon* from other vantage points, but the enemy was focused now on destroying the old man who had dared to call them cowards.

Caledan readied himself to face his next foe, but the ship pitched wildly beneath him as a rogue wave struck. His arms windmilled as he struggled to keep upright, while alongside him Devon dropped to his knees and gripped the railing tight. On the other vessel, the Baronians weren't so quick, and two toppled forward into the sea. Their screams were silenced as the ships slammed back together.

Regaining his feet, Devon's hammer claimed the third. Before others could take their place, Devon leapt across the gap to the other ship. Caledan stared in shock, unable to believe the old hammerman had just boarded the Baronian vessel.

"Back!" Devon boomed, his voice ringing out over the black-garbed men.

The Baronians were as shocked as Caledan, for they obeyed, taking a collective step away from the madman and his hammer. It gave Devon the space he needed to speak.

"My name is Devon, great-grandson of Alan!" he roared. "Are you not Baronians, that you do not know me?"

Caledan gaped at the man. He'd thought Devon was

joking earlier. Had the man actually lived amongst the Baronians? He seemed to recall some obscure legend from around the time of the fall of the Tsar, but so much folk law and legend was attached to that time, one could never know truth from fiction.

Aboard the Baronian ship, the black-garbed warriors wavered.

Then a man at the front raised an axe and shouted. "To hell with history!" he shrieked. "We are Baronian, and we take what we want!"

A roar of agreement came from the others, and Caledan tensed, preparing to join the old man, but another voice rose to silence the enemy cheers.

"Hold!"

It was more of a croak than a bellow, but the speaker must have held great authority over the enemy, for every soul aboard the Baronian ship froze in their tracks. Movement came from the rear of their ship as a man appeared on the upper deck. Leaning on the railings, he squinted down at them.

"Is that truly you, Devon?" he called.

Devon stared back. "Ay, Julian, though I had not expected to find you in such company."

The old Baronian chuckled. "Times change. After your escape in Lon all those years ago, the blame eventually found its way back to me. The Tsar confiscated everything I ever owned."

"I'm surprised he didn't kill you," Devon retorted.

"In his mercy, he spared me. I *did* betray you to him, after all."

"Ay, you did," Devon rumbled. "Do you intend to finish the job this time?"

The Baronian named as Julian stared at them for a long

while. "No," he said finally. "I did you a great wrong, Devon. I have regretted that day for a long time. Let today be my penance."

He made a gesture with his hands, and the Baronians retreated, giving Caledan enough breathing room to appreciate their discipline. The black-garbed fighters were renowned for their ferocity, but this was something different.

"Thank you, Julian, though I forgave you a long time ago."

"Go in peace, Devon," Julian said, "though should we ever meet again, I cannot promise the same mercy."

"Fair enough." Devon started to turn away, then paused. "What are you doing all the way out here, anyway? I thought the Baronian hunting grounds were to the north"

Julian chuckled. "I might ask the same thing of you, old man."

"I'm looking for a friend. She was taken by the Knights of Alana."

"They're a day ahead of you," Julian replied. "We saw their ship, though they were too heavily armed for my people."

"So that's all you're up to, pirating the southern seas?"

A chuckle came from the old Baronian. "Don't press your luck, hammerman," he replied. "My purpose is my own. Now get off my ship and out of my waters, before I change my mind."

Devon nodded and returned to the *Seadragon*. Hammers were retrieved and the hooks torn from the railings. The Baronians wound them in with great wheels, then smoke erupted from the ships chimneys and they were powering away, leaving Caledan and the others standing aboard the *Seadragon* wondering what exactly had just happened.

⚜ 14 ⚜

The wailing rose above the clanging of bells as Braidon followed the procession down the streets of Lon. Mourners filled every alleyway, spilling out into the broad avenue and hampering those at the front who carried the body of the Lonian King.

It seemed as though the whole country had come to farewell their fallen leader. And no wonder; for over a century, Lonia had been ruled by council. But upon the fall of the Empire and the death of the Gods, the Lonians had called for a new kind of leader. Elections had been held, and Ashoka had become king. He had quickly set about rebuilding the impoverished nation, endearing himself to the people.

That had been twenty-five years ago, when Braidon himself had just been coming into his own as King of Plorsea. Seeking to take advantage of Braidon's youth, Ashoka had marched on the southern nation, provoking a ten-year-long war that had left thousands on either side dead.

It had taken a marriage pact between Braidon and the young Lonian princess, Marianne, to bring an end to the conflict. She walked hand in hand with him now, and he gave her fingers a reassuring squeeze as they continued after her father's coffin. Her blue eyes shone with unspilt tears and the ocean breeze blowing up the street whipped her auburn hair about her face, but she smiled and nodded her thanks.

Plorsean soldiers marched to either side of them, King's Guard to his left, the Queen's Guard on her right, their ranks marked by gold or silver streaks on their scarlet cloaks. Catching the eye of his captain of the guard, Rylle, Braidon offered the slightest of nods. The Plorsean crown weighed heavily on his head, and Braidon was glad of the man's presence. While there was now uneasy peace between the two nations, an undercurrent of hate still tainted the relationship, leftover from the Tsar's tyranny.

Braidon might have helped end the Tsar's reign, but he was also the man's son, an unforgivable fact for many here. There would be those in the crowd who still wished for Braidon's death, despite his marriage to their beloved princess—or perhaps because of it.

The crowds, if anything, grew thicker as the procession left the cobbled streets and entered the port. The mourners wore all style of colours: red and white and blue and yellow, and a dozen others, creating a jumbled rainbow that covered the wooden docks as far as Braidon could see. They pressed forward, each desperate for a glimpse of the fallen king. A group of Knights, their Order more populous here than in Plorsea, spread out to form a barrier between the procession and the crowd.

Braidon felt a touch of admiration for his former rival. Though he had loathed Ashoka during the war, it was apparent his people had loved and respected him above all others. He was the man who had raised them up, lifting them from the darkness left by Braidon's father.

Though of course, there was only so much one man could do, even a king. Looking out over the crowd was a study in inequality. The royal family and their retainers were richly garbed in expensive silks and jewellery—even the king's body had been adorned with enough gold to feed a small town. Many of the onlookers, though, were lucky to have even thread-worn tunics to protect their fair skin from the harsh sun. More still sported sunken cheeks and withered limbs, as though food were a privilege they rarely enjoyed.

Such starvation was a strange sight in the capital of a farming nation, and Braidon wondered briefly where the food from their crops and livestock had gone. His eyes roamed, spotting child beggars amongst the crowd, some even clutching babies of their own. There were amputees as well, men and women with limbs cut short below the joint, their gaunt frames looking as though they lacked the muscle to even stand.

Yet the eyes of all were filled with tears, and as the procession reached the edge of the docks, a great silence fell over the crowd. Braidon returned his gaze to the body of Ashoka. The Lonian soldiers were carrying him aboard an old ship. Sunlight had warped the wooden boards of the deck and everything of worth had been stripped clean. Even the masts had been taken, cut short to be used for other designs.

The soldiers lowered the Lonian king onto a bed of thatch in the centre of the vessel, then retreated to the docks.

Braidon tightened his hand around Marianne's. "Are

you okay?" he whispered as the crowd began to sing, a mournful tune that was little better than the wailing of earlier.

Marianne nodded, a smile crossing her face. Two soldiers cut free the lines tying the ship in place, and with the soft creaking of timber, it drifted out into the harbour. No other vessel sailed the waters of Jurrien's Inlet today, and the king's ship encountered no obstacles. Soon it was a hundred yards offshore, and the eyes of the crowd turned to Marianne.

Releasing Braidon's hand, she stepped up to the edge of the docks. A longbow was pressed into her hands, its steel arms shining in the noonday sun. Despite the sombre atmosphere, Braidon's curiosity was piqued by the weapon. He edged sideways for a better view. His own men used bows of yew or oak, but the Lonian weapon had somehow been crafted entirely from steel.

An attendant passed an arrow to the queen and a burning brazier was already set in place. Braidon wondered how anyone could be expected to draw a bow of steel, let alone his wife. While she wore a slim rapier on her waist and had practiced archery as a child, she'd shown no interest in such activities since moving to Ardath. Petite as she was…

Marianne dipped the arrow into a brazier until it caught light, then nocked it to her bow. Her stance shifted slightly, turning side-on. Braidon thought he glimpsed a smirk on her lips as she glanced back at him. Then she drew smoothly, tiny wheels on the arms of the bow turning to assist the movement, and released.

A hush fell over the crowd as the arrow rose, arcing out over the waters of the harbour. Not a single man or woman breathed as they waited to see where it would fall. For a moment it seemed the wind might catch it and hurl it away…then gravity took hold and it fell smoothly to land amongst her father's pyre.

The wood caught with a great *whoosh*. Flames spread with unnatural speed across the wooden deck, as though some accelerant had been used, until the entire ship was ablaze. Thick black smoke spewed from the doomed vessel, filling the harbour. A gust of wind carried it over the crowd, making Braidon's eyes water and his throat burn.

He looked away, and several ships docked at the end of the wharf caught his attention. They were unmistakably war galleys. That in itself was of little interest, for the Lonian coastline was often plagued by pirating Baronians. But there was something different about the galleys. Each sported two large masts, but there were also several smaller masts at the stern and bow. Braidon realised with a start they were made of steel.

Braidon was tempted to take a closer look, but Marianne reappeared beside him before he had a chance. He made a note to ask his emissaries to investigate later, and forced his attention back to his duties.

"You did well," he said, putting an arm around his wife's waist.

She raised an eyebrow at him. "Did you expect anything else?"

A smile crossed Braidon's lips at the fire in her eyes. "My love, you could conquer the world if you desired it."

With that, he turned his gaze back to the harbour. Sadness touched his heart as he watched his rival burn. Ashoka had been a bitter enemy, but he had been a known quality. Who would the Lonians raise as their next king?

Marianne might have taken the title once, but she was Plorsean now, and would never be accepted.

Whoever it was, Braidon prayed they would honour the pact between the two nations.

❧ 15 ❧

D evon groaned as the sharp light of day dragged him from his sleep. There was a pounding in his temples and an ache in his spine that reminded him of the months he'd spent on the march as a youth. Only now, he was suffering from what amounted to little more than a skirmish.

He hadn't felt it in the heat of the moment. Facing the Baronians with hammer in hand, it had been as though the clock had been wound back, as though he were a young man again, able to overcome whatever his enemies hurled at him.

It hadn't taken long for that sensation to fade. Even amidst the rush of battle, he had noticed the dulling of his reactions, the diminishing of his strength. If not for Caledan, he might have been killed in the first seconds, when the charging Baronian had knocked him from his feet.

No, you are Devon. You would have beaten him.

He shivered. Those were the words of a younger man, one convinced of his own immortality. Devon no longer had any such disillusions. Whatever Pela and the villagers and even the Baronians might think of him, he was just a man—an old man, at that. And today he was paying for his defiance.

At least he'd had a proper bed in which to sleep. They'd reached Townirwin before sunset and Devon had settled them all in an inn for the night. He'd slipped a few extra shillings to the innkeeper to keep their presence quiet. There was no point forewarning the Knights of their presence.

The clashing of steel came from outside. Devon rose from his bed and crossed to the window. Down in the courtyard, Pela was already up and running through a drill with Caledan. Their swords rang with each blow as they worked their way back and forwards across the smooth tiles.

Devon sighed, saddened by the sight. Once, he'd held hopes the world might move on from such pursuits, that a new generation might grow up in a world without war. For a while it had seemed his dream might come true, after the fall of the Tsar and the liberation of the Three Nations. Then Lonia had marched south, forcing Plorsean farmers from their lands, and the wars had begun again.

An awful fatigue touched him in a moment of premonition. The world had come full circle. All his long life he'd been a warrior, fighting to keep the darkness in check. But it had all been for naught. Evil had returned to the land, and now his niece would pick up the sword and continue the charade.

The thought left a bitter taste on Devon's tongue, and silently he cursed the king he had served so faithfully. He had trusted Braidon to bring peace to the land; instead, his friend had allowed the Knights of Alana to spread like a disease, infecting Plorsea with their hatred.

He let out a heavy sigh, then threw off his melancholy and dressed himself. Heading downstairs to the tavern, he was greeted by the sweet aroma of honeyed oats and roasting coffee. He smiled. At least the seaside port was near enough to Skystead to stock the bitter drink; it was rare elsewhere. The plant preferred high altitudes and did not fare well in the harsh winters further north. Only the plateaus above Skystead were suitable for the coffee plantations. Devon had disliked its taste when he first arrived in the small town, but he had become accustomed to it through the years.

After ordering himself a mug and a bowl of oats, he sat down for his meal. It wasn't long before Pela and Caledan joined him. The double doors to the courtyard squealed as they pushed their way inside—Pela still red-faced and puffing, Caledan with just a hint of perspiration on his forehead. There was no sign yet of Tobias or Genevieve, while Tallow and his crew had opted to sleep on the *Seadragon.*

Devon waved to the innkeeper for a round of food as they sat down opposite him. Pela grinned when a mug of coffee was placed before her, but Caledan wrinkled his nose.

"How can you drink that mud-water?" he asked.

Devon chuckled. "It grows on you."

Caledan snorted. There was silence as they broke their fast, before the swordsman leaned back in his chair and raised his eyebrows at Devon.

"So, what's the plan?" he asked. "Ready to storm the Castle?"

"Not quite," Devon replied, keeping the irritation from his voice. The swordsman's confidence irked him, and while the aching in his bones had settled slightly, he was in no mood for jokes.

"Oh yes, you wanted to speak with the King's Guard

first," Caledan replied, eyeing him across the table. "I'm still not sure that's such a great idea."

"We'll find out soon enough," Devon retorted. "I'm heading to the barracks after we finish up here."

Caledan sighed. "Very well. In that case, I'll make some inquiries around town. If we're going to go up against the Knights, we'd better at least be sure the prisoners are in the Castle."

"Thank you," Devon said with genuine gratitude. He had never been a subtle man and if he started asking questions in Townirwin, it wouldn't take long for word to get back to the Knights. "And thank you for your aid on the *Seadragon*," he added as an afterthought.

A smile crossed the sellsword's face. "A good thing you didn't die, or the lot of us would have ended up as croc food. Don't think the old Baronian would have spared us over your dead body."

Devon's melancholy deepened. "He was a good man once," he murmured. "A coward, but then who could blame him, the way the Tsar waged his wars?"

"He betrayed you, man," Caledan replied. "If he'd done the same to me, I'd have gutted the pig."

"And then yesterday you would have died," Devon commented, drawing himself to his feet. "Better to forgive, if you want the opinion of an old man. Dead men can't help you."

"They also can't stick a sword through your back," Caledan snapped, his eyes flashing.

Devon waved a hand. "I'll see you later," he said, then turned to Pela. "You coming, missy?"

Pela jumped, looking around in confusion before realising he was talking to her. Nodding, she quickly spooned down the last of her gruel, gulped a mouthful of coffee, and raced out the door after him.

"Where did you say we were going?" she gasped as they started through the muddy streets.

Devon smiled. "The guard barracks. The King's Guards occupy a dorm there—during tax collection, at least."

As far as he knew, Pela had only been to Townirwin once, and then she'd been little more than a child. Swampy backwater as it was, the town was four times the size of Skystead and all the more exciting for it. It was well past sunup now and the streets were already crowded. Wagons rumbled up the main avenue from the port, winding their way over the narrow bridges that spanned the multitude of canals upon which the settlement had been built. Townirwin was the only port on the western coast of Plorsea that connected with the Gods Road, and most would be bringing their goods farther inland.

The town grew busier as they left the main avenue and continued through a network of unsavoury canals and narrow alleyways. Unlike in Skystead, there was no dedicated marketplace here, and merchant stalls appeared at regular intervals through the settlement, the sellers shouting their wares at the tops of their lungs. Pela spent the entire journey looking around with wide eyes, an equal measure of amazement and fear written across her face.

"Relax, missy," Devon rumbled, "we're almost there."

Pela shook herself. "What was it like, fighting for the King's Guard?"

Devon smiled. "Tough. Long days on the march, longer nights without sleep. Especially during the war with Lonia."

"Then why did you keep going back?"

His smile faltered. "I..." He sighed, glancing at his

niece. "It was all that and worse, but…there is nothing so thrilling as marching to battle."

"You fight because you enjoy it?" Pela twisted her lips, and Devon knew what she was thinking.

"Yes, and no," he sighed. "It is difficult to explain. It was always awful, in the moment. But afterwards, when I returned home and resumed real life…You miss the excitement, miss the comradery. When at war, you know you're alive, that every moment must be cherished. Later…" He shrugged. "Later…everything else seems ordinary."

"I'm not sure I understand," his niece replied, frown still in place.

Devon thumped her on the shoulder and laughed. "I hope you never do."

"What about my father, was it the same for him?"

A smile touched Devon's lips. "Derryn was a good man and a canny fighter. But he wasn't like the rest of us. A King's Guard is usually ice or fire—cold-blooded killers or berserkers that nothing but death will stop. Derryn though, he was like water, cool in the heat of battle, yet razor quick as well, adaptable. And no, he never enjoyed it. He was there because his king needed him, and afterwards, when he retired, he had no desire to return…" Devon trailed off at that, words abandoning him.

"But he went back anyway."

"Ay," Devon croaked. "If ever there was a time I should have spurned the call, it was that day."

"But you didn't," Pela murmured.

"No, and that decision will haunt me to my dying day."

He drew to a stop in front of an old stone building. They were beyond the canals now and the air was fresher, the stench of stagnant water behind them. Solid and nondescript, the only sign the building was anything different from its neighbours was the king's emblem carved into the stone above the door. Townirwin was hardly large enough to require a full contingent of guards, but its position between the Gods Road and the coast afforded the settlement certain privileges.

It had not always been so—a century ago, the lower reaches of the Lane River had been deep enough to allow ships passage. But over the decades, sand bars had formed throughout the delta, making the way impassable to all but the most experienced captains. Most now made port in Townirwin and sent their goods overland the rest of the way, to Ardath and beyond.

The change had enriched Townirwin fortunes, and Devon wondered if that was what had brought his old friend so far south. Could the Baronians be planning a raid on the town?

"This is it?" Pela asked.

Devon shook himself, drawing himself back to the present. "This is it," he confirmed, and thumped a massive fist against the heavy wooden door.

A few minutes passed before a *clang* came from inside the building. With a squeal of hinges, it opened towards them, forcing them back a step. Beyond, a man in the gold and scarlet tunic and polished chainmail of the King's Guard stood watching them. His eyebrows lifted in surprise as he looked them up and down.

"Well met, Aldyn," Devon rumbled, a grin splitting his bearded cheeks.

"Devon?" the Guard said, blinking. "What in the Three Nations are you doing here?"

❧ 16 ❧

"So this is the daughter of Derryn and Kryssa?" asked Aldyn as they sat in the courtyard of the barracks. "She must be quite the prodigy with a sword!"

Pela's cheeks grew hot and lowering her eyes, she fiddled with the hilt of her father's sword. Anger and embarrassment warred within her, but she said nothing. How had she not have known about her father? How could her mother have kept it from her? It was galling to hear such admiration in a stranger's voice, and know next to nothing about how her father had earned it.

And worse still to know she had none of his talent.

"Her name is Pela," Devon answered for her, "and Kryssa chose not to teach her the warrior's arts."

"You can't be serious?" Aldryn cried. Pela's uncle shot him a dark look, and he quickly masked his shock. "A wise choice." He nodded solemnly, then blinked. "Err, then… why is she wearing Derryn's sword?"

Devon sighed. "My fault, though it couldn't be helped. Kryssa's been taken. We're here to get her back."

"What?!" Aldyn leapt to his feet and spun around, as though her mother's kidnappers might be hiding somewhere in the courtyard. "By who?"

"The Knights of Alana," Devon rumbled. "They came to Skystead and attacked the old temple, took everyone they found there. One of their Elders, Merak I think his name was, took five of their captives to the town square where he planned to execute them. I stopped him. But the rest were brought here, including Kryssa. I don't know why."

"Oh." While Devon spoke, Aldyn had sunk back into his chair. There was now a wan look to his face. "That's...bad."

"Agreed," Devon grunted, then paused, eyeing his former comrade. "Though I sense you know more about this than we do."

Aldyn shook his head. "You've been away in that backwater awhile, haven't you?"

Pela would have bristled at the casual way he dismissed Skystead as a backwater...if it hadn't been true. As it was, the man's tone sent a chill down her spine.

"The war almost bankrupted Plorsea," Aldyn was saying. "Braidon had to raise taxes just to keep the Gods Roads in order, but even that wasn't enough to keep every town and village properly armed against thieves and the resurgent Baronian tribes."

"You mean there aren't enough guards here to protect the town?" Devon asked.

"Not exactly..." Aldyn murmured. "The queen had an idea, a few years back. She believes in the Saviour, you see, like many Lonians. Goes to Castle every week. And she saw all these armed Knights, this force that wasn't being used. She suggested they could take some of the responsibilities from the city guards..."

"*What?*" Pela shrieked, leaping to her feet.

Aldyn held up his hands in entreaty. "Myself and many others argued against it, but Townirwin was one of the first places they were trialled. We've had a lot of trade with Lonia over the years, so the people here were already more comfortable with the Order and their Knights. And for all appearances, they've done a good job, kept the peace, so to speak."

"They murdered our baker!" Taking a step closer to the King's Guard, Pela pointed a trembling finger at his chest. "They kidnapped my mother!" She slumped back to her chair, suddenly lost, the hope slipping from her in a rush.

"How could Braidon let this happen?" Devon groaned.

"Like I said, Devon, you've been gone a long time. But you were there when magic died. You know how it was, the hopelessness, the fear. People have been looking for something to believe in for a long time. If it hadn't been for the civil war, the Order might have appeared here sooner. As it is, their talk of free will and power for all, it's proven popular."

"I refuse to believe cold-blooded murder has become popular with our people," Devon snapped. He rose and began to pace.

"There have been rumours of a more sinister faction within the Order. There are some who believe Alana's 'sacrifice' must be repeated every year—"

"*Nonsense!*" Devon bellowed. "I was there. Alana died because…"

Fists clenched, he trailed off, and Pela remembered that other rumour about her uncle. What had Caledan called him, back in Skystead? *The Consort of Alana…*

"Regardless, they're only rumours. Nothing ever came of them."

"Until now!" Pela interrupted.

"Until now," Aldyn agreed, though there was a hesitant note to his voice.

"What?" Devon growled.

"We'll need proof," the King's Guard replied. "If you want the king to believe…"

"Surely Braidon must see the truth about these Knights."

"Braidon does not see half as much as he should," Aldyn replied.

"Then we'll bring him his evidence," Pela growled, enraged that the king who professed to protect them would ignore such evil amongst his people.

"Ay," Devon agreed. "Let's search their damned Castle and find the prisoners. They might control the streets, but surely they don't have the authority to refuse the King's Guard."

"They don't," Aldyn replied, "only…"

Devon gave the man a despairing look, as though to say "what now?" while Pela's heart sank.

"Yesterday a Raptor sighting was reported on the Gods Road. A group of Knights came calling for our help. It's… been a while since the men and women here saw any action. Most of our contingent went with them."

Raptors were a ferocious creature leftover from the time of Archon. They had been driven almost to extinction during the Tsar's reign, but with the death of magic, they had become…hazardous to hunt, let alone kill.

"*Dammit!*" Devon slammed his fist into the table. It creaked beneath the blow, and Pela scrambled back in case it collapsed. "When are they back?"

"A week, if they find its tracks. Sooner if it left no sign, but who knows?"

"That's too long," Pela whispered. "My mum…"

"No, we can't afford to wait," Devon agreed.

"How many Knights were in the group that took Kryssa?" Aldyn asked.

"Two dozen, minus a few we killed."

Aldyn swore bitterly. "Twenty Knights went with the King's Guard, but the Castle barracks have forty. We'd still be badly outnumbered."

Devon let off a string of profanity that made Pela blush. "How did Braidon let things come to this?"

"The treasury vaults are almost empty," Aldyn said, shrugging. "Even the King's Guard have missed our pay a few times. Maybe if the border opens with Trola one day, things will get better. Or maybe relations will improve with Lonia, now they're to have a new king. Either way, Braidon has larger concerns than a few religious zealots in the far south."

"Damnit, the girl's father once saved his life. He *cannot* let this continue. Can you get him a message to the capital?"

Aldyn sighed. "I could, but he's not even in the country. He went to Lon for Ashoka's funeral. You won't want to wait that long."

"No," Devon rumbled. "So we're going to rescue them tonight."

"That's more like the Devon I remember," Aldyn laughed, a grin crossing his face. "Mind if I join you? I wouldn't mind putting a few of those bastards back in their place!"

$\approx$ I 7 $\approx$

Exhaustion weighed heavily on Ikar as he made his way along the corridors of the Townirwin Castle. The *Red Seagull* had arrived late at the docks, and they had unloaded the prisoners under cover of darkness, ensuring there were no witnesses. There was no need to add to the rumours already swirling about the Order.

By the time the prisoners were secure, the night had been old and Ikar had barely snatched a few hours sleep before being called to the pantheon. Now he would have to hurry if he was not to keep them waiting. At least now he could forgo his armour in favour of a tunic and breeches— only the devout were allowed within the Castle walls, so there was no risk of an outsider learning his face.

The hallways narrowed as Ikar neared his destination, an old design from darker days when the keep had been the last bastion of safety for Townirwin.

But those times were long since passed. The fortifica- tions had been a dilapidated ruin when the Knights of Alana had taken possession. The first brothers to occupy the

Castle had reinforced the crumbling mortar and repaired much of the damage, but even after five years, it could not compare to the glorious citadels held by the Order in Lonia.

Turning the final corner, Ikar slowed as he approached the towering double doors leading to the inner chambers. Beyond the iron-studded wood, Merak and his counterparts awaited Ikar's report on the undertaking in Skystead. Ikar had not yet decided how much to say. He was still angered by Merak's refusal to avenge their fallen brothers, but it was a dangerous course to criticise an Elder.

The doors had been left unguarded—none in the Order would dare invade the inner sanctum without permission—and Ikar pressed a shoulder to the heavy oak, pushing them open. The hinges moved with barely a whisper and Ikar stepped inside.

Within was the pantheon—the holy centre of each Castle. Only the most loyal followers of the Order were allowed entrance here—Knights and parishioners who had spent at least five years with the Order. It was here the Elders conducted their cleansings, though Ikar had never witnessed one in the year since his arrival in Townirwin. It was said by many that the Plorseans would not accept such rituals. They would soon find out, for there could be only one fate for the foul blasphemers they had taken from Skystead.

To either side of Ikar, the pantheon opened out into a circular chamber, its high roof held up by thick arches of wood. In Lon, they would have been stone, but here in the south such material was scarce—it had cost a small fortune just to repair the crumbling walls. Thirty feet above, the arches converged in a dome, its cheap plaster concealed by a great painting of the genesis of their Order: Alana towering over the world, three shadows knelt at her feet, begging for their lives. The artist had captured the righteous fury in Alana's eyes as Ikar had always imagined it, and there could be no doubt what fate awaited the fallen Gods.

The whisper of voices drew Ikar's gaze down. Pews lined the pantheon, except where a fine woollen rug let up to a raised dais at the end of the chamber. The three Elders awaited him there, seated on three golden thrones that would have made the Plorsean King weep with jealousy.

Ikar's cheeks grew hot as he found their eyes on him and he quickly strode the length of the chamber and stopped before the dais.

Placing a fist to his chest, Ikar bowed. "Your Excellencies."

"Welcome, Ikar," Merak said, his voice echoing through the hall. "Thank you for joining us. We know your duties kept you late last night. We will not keep you long."

Ikar struggled to conceal a grimace. No sooner had they made port than Merak had bid them farewell, leaving Ikar and the other Knights to oversee the disembarking of the prisoners. No doubt the Elder had enjoyed a full night's sleep while the rest of them laboured.

"It is nothing, Your Excellency," Ikar said, keeping the irritation from his voice. "It was my honour to ensure the blasphemous were safely locked away."

"I'm sure," the second Elder, Servo, murmured. He wore dark blue robes and was the youngest of the three, barely thirty. It was said he had performed some great task on behalf of the Order as a young man, and been honoured in return, though none could say what it had been. His hazel eyes were soft as he looked down at Ikar. "Though no doubt sleep would also have been welcome after such a journey. Merak tells us you captured the peasants in the midst of worshiping the False Gods?"

"Ay, that is what it appeared, though…one claims they were simply meditating," Ikar replied, remembering Kryssa's words.

"They were in the temple of the False Gods?" Servo asked.

"Yes."

"Then the blasphemers lie!" the third and oldest Elder, Putar, bellowed. His hair and beard were long and greying, and his stomach strained against emerald robes as he rose from his throne. Halfway to his feet, he seemed to think better of it and sat once more. He continued in a calmer voice. "And afterwards, it was you who led the prisoners to the port?"

"Yes." Ikar's flicked in Merak's direction. "The esteemed Elder placed me in charge until his return."

"So you did not witness the events in the town square?" Servo asked, his voice low, eyes narrowed.

"No." Ikar bowed his head. "Though I wish I could have stood alongside my brothers."

"You would not have made a difference," Merak snapped, anger in his voice.

"Is that why *you* did not fight with your fellows, brother Merak?" Servo asked pointedly, a smirk on his lips.

Merak scowled. "There were too many. Had I not carried warning to the ship, they might have freed the prisoners. Then we would have had nothing to offer for the Great Sacrifice."

Ikar raised an eyebrow. His orders had been to depart should Merak not return. The ship had been about to depart when Merak had finally appeared—the Elder had not *saved* anything. But he kept his lips tight shut, unwilling to brave the Elder's wrath.

A dry, rasping laughter came from Putar. "You assume

any of your prisoners are worthy of such an honour, Merak," he said. "You stained our Order with your cowardice."

"Ha!" Merak snapped. "Easy to claim for one as old as you. When did you last go questing beyond the dining hall, Putar?"

"Enough, brothers," Servo interrupted as the two Elders started to their feet. "This is unseemly."

Tension hung in the air, before Merak and Putar both sank back into their thrones. Ikar swallowed, aware that disagreements between the Elders were rarely witnessed, and did his best to go unnoticed.

"My apologies, Ikar," Servo continued. "I trust you shall not repeat any of what you have seen here."

Ikar bowed his head. "Never."

"Ikar has shown great loyalty," Merak proclaimed. "Is that all you have to report from our journey?"

Catching the Elder's eyes on him, Ikar knew he'd been right to keep quiet earlier. "It is, Elders, and thank you for your praise," he said, then hesitated. "Though I would ask one favour of you?"

"What would you have of us, young Knight?" Putar asked, his eyes shining as he glanced at Merak.

"Grant me permission to gather my brothers and return to Skystead," Ikar said, looking each of them in the eye. "Allow me to avenge our fallen comrades."

The smile fell from Putar's lips. Merak's face darkened, while Servo only sighed. "Alas, we cannot act so openly. The king still will not condone violence against the blasphemers, though they threaten all our existence."

"They murdered our brothers!" Ikar exclaimed. "How can you let them go unpunished?"

"Patience, sir Knight," Servo replied. "Their penance

may be deferred, but their crimes are not forgotten. Justice will find them, sooner than you might think."

"How?" Ikar pressed, still angered by their dismissal.

"You forget yourself, Ikar," Servo admonished.

Ikar swallowed, aware he had pushed them further than was wise. "My apologies, Your Excellencies," he murmured. "I only wish to see justice."

"And you will, brother," Putar replied. "For now though, we must bide our time, and honour the king's wishes." The Elder's tone was bitter.

"Yes," Servo continued. "To that end, a cleansing must be held with all haste. While the blasphemers still breathe, their lifeforce feeds strength to the False Gods. We will take that strength for ourselves, before the king discovers their presence. Though we have time, I would act tonight, before Braidon returns from Ashoka's funeral in Lon."

"*What?*" Ikar gasped, his heart suddenly racing.

"You had not heard?" Servo frowned. "My apologies, Ikar. The Lonian king is dead."

"How?"

"His heart failed him. His shadow council rules until a new ruler can be elected, since his only daughter is no longer eligible."

Grief washed through Ikar. He and Asoka had been close, when Ikar had served as his guard. And his daughter...His anger flared as he recalled her marriage to the Plorsean king.

"Marianne would have made a great queen. There is no way to free her from the marriage pact?"

The Elders exchanged glances. "You ask ideas above your station, Ikar," Servo said finally. "Though we understand your grief for Ashoka, the leadership of Lonia is none of your concern—nor ours. Though it should be enough for you that Marianne's marriage has brought peace, and allowed our Order to expand into Plorsea."

"Very well," Ikar grated, struggling to keep his anger in check.

Even as a youth, Marianne had sat in on Ashoka's councils, and as a young woman had often spent afternoons debating with her father. Intelligent beyond her years and skilled with bow and rapier, she had been born to rule. It galled Ikar to hear her birth right could be stripped away so easily, all because her father had pawned her off to buy peace. It was the one decision Ashoka had made that Ikar could never understand.

"Now, we must continue preparations for the Great Sacrifice," Servo was saying. "Half our Order has already gone ahead to make our preparations. We must decide if any of these prisoners of yours are worthy. There must be three, strong of will and soul, to aid the Saviour in her eternal battle with the False Gods. Are there any you would deem suitable?"

Shaking his head, Ikar tore his mind from memories of Marianne and faced the Elders. Quickly he cast his thoughts over the prisoners. They had taken eighteen in total, though only a few were memorable. The rest were timid, unworthy creatures by any manner of definition.

Then Kryssa's face appeared in his mind, standing strong. Recalling the anger she had elicited from him, he felt a pang of shame. Rarely had he been so cruel, had he so misused his power. Something about her insolence had worn away his self-control. But even after, hair drenched and half-drowned, there had been a glint of defiance in the woman's eye. He swallowed, and looked up at the Elders.

"There is one…"

❧ 18 ☙

The hammer weighed heavily on Devon's back as he stood in the shadows across from the gates of the Castle. It was nearing midnight, and overhead, dark clouds covered the moon and stars. The streets were pitch-black except where the occasional lantern cast back the darkness. The Castle itself stood in the centre of Townirwin, its stone walls rising from a raised mound of earth and encircled by a canal. Shadows flickered atop the ramparts—Knights completing their patrol.

The hoot of an owl sounded from overhead, but otherwise the night was still—until the faintest whisper of footsteps carried to Devon's ears. He tensed, lifting a hand to silence his companions, and peered out into the darkness.

A figure appeared on the street, walking with purpose towards the Castle. The light of a nearby lantern cast his shadow far across the cobbles, but the figure showed no sign he'd noticed Devon and the others. The shadows on the ramparts flickered, darting towards the tower atop the gates.

"Hoy!" a Knight called as the newcomer came to a stop before the gates. "Who goes there?"

"Open up!" the figure replied. A torch was held up atop the walls, revealing Aldyn standing beneath the gates. A scowl wrinkling his forehead, he called again, "I need to speak with the Elders!"

"They're busy! Come back in the morning, scoundrel." The Knight's irritation was obvious.

"I don't care if they're fast asleep!" Aldyn snapped. "I am a lieutenant of the King's Guard, and the Elders will see me, *now*, or the king will hear of it!"

Muttering came from atop the wall, but the gates remained closed.

Aldyn wasn't having any of it. "If you don't open these gates right now, I'll have you hung for insubordination, and to hell with your Elders!" he bellowed.

There was still a moment's hesitation, before the Knight disappeared from sight. Devon held his breath, praying the Knight had bought his friend's act. Then a great groan came from the timbers of the gate and they swung open.

"You stay there," the Knight started, but Aldyn darted forward before he could finish. The Knight's voice rose: "Hey, what are you doing!"

"*Go!*" Devon hissed.

A string of curses erupted from within the Castle walls as Devon raced out into the open. The patter of boots on stone came from behind him as Caledan, Pela and the others followed. They sprinted across the cobbled plaza to where the drawbridge and gates still stood open. At any second, Devon expected a shout to come from the walls, as some unseen Knight spotted their approach. But the only sound was the cursing coming from beyond the gates.

Devon held his breath as the walls loomed. If they were spotted, the Knights would have plenty of time to sound the alarm. With some twenty Knights inside, plus whatever followers had attached themselves to the Order, Devon and the others would quickly be overwhelmed if they were discovered. The rescue attempt would be over before it started.

"Hey what—?" a man was shouting as Devon slipped through the open gates.

Glimpsing Aldyn standing nearby with sword in hand, Devon started towards him, before he noticed the blood on his friend's blade. He slowed, then saw the bodies of the two Knights slumped on the cobbles at Aldyn's feet.

"Quick," the King's Guard whispered, sheathing his sword, "help me with them!"

Devon swore and laid his hammer against the wall and grabbed the feet of the nearest Knight. Together with Aldyn, they dragged him into the garden that ran the length of the small courtyard. Tossing him behind the bushes, they returned for the second.

Only then did Devon take the time to examine their surroundings.

They were in a circular courtyard situated directly between the gates and the castle keep. Solid stone surrounded them, but for the oaken double doors that led into the keep. The gardens in which they'd dumped the bodies lined the walls, twisted trees and vines climbing upwards to the guard tower above the gates.

Aldyn crept to the doors of the keep and pushed them open. Light spilled from within, illuminating the six of them in the courtyard. Devon took a moment to check on his companions. Caledan was his usual composed self, as was Aldyn. Tobias's eyes darted around in his face and he looked like he might bolt at any moment, though so far, he had remained resolute. Genevieve caught his eye and flashed him a quick grin.

Turning his gaze on his niece, Devon wondered whether or not he should ask her to guard the gates. After all, they would need a way out, if they succeeded in rescuing the prisoners. Pela's face was pale and her eyes stared straight ahead, no doubt lost in some terrified imagining of what was to come. She shouldn't be here, wasn't ready for something like this. And yet…he knew she wouldn't listen if he told her to hide.

"The place looks pretty awake for this late at night," Caledan was saying.

Devon shook himself free of his reservations and nodded. A dozen lanterns were burning within the entrance hall and he could hear the distant humming of voices. What were the Knights up to?

"Many of their rituals take place at night," Aldyn murmured.

"That would have been useful to know earlier," Devon muttered, raising an eyebrow, but Aldyn only shrugged.

"It didn't cross my mind until now. It's not like you would have waited," he replied.

"We'd best get moving then, before someone notices the missing men," Devon snapped.

"Where will they be keeping my mum and the others?" Pela asked.

There was a tremor in her voice, but when Devon glanced at her, she met his gaze and gave the slightest of nods. Devon's heart swelled. Her father would have been proud, though he'd never wanted this life for his daughter. Her mother, though…

He shook himself free of the thought. Kryssa could

curse him to the end of her days for endangering her daughter…so long as she lived.

"Close to the pantheon," Aldyn answered. "I've been inside a few times. The cells are there."

"Lead the way, Aldyn," Devon said.

They fell in behind the King's Guard. Devon brought up the rear, swinging the doors closed behind them. They had an hour before the next change of watch—Aldyn knew their schedules well—but that did not guarantee they would remain undiscovered.

"The Knights like to throw banquets for us common soldiers sometimes," Aldyn was saying. "They even make allowances for us to see them without their helmets." He chuckled. "I suppose it would be difficult for them to eat otherwise."

Devon nodded but said nothing, concentrating on the way ahead. The corridor was lit by lanterns and after the dark outside, the brightness hurt his eyes. Fortunately, the hallways remained empty, though voices still drifted on the air. They moved quickly, aware that a group of armed men and women could not go undetected for long, while Aldyn continued his story.

"I think the banquets were thrown to recruit new Knights. Certainly a few of the King's Guard have changed colours over the last few years. Can't say I liked 'em. They were the sort who fight because they enjoy death. Guess it fits well with the Order's whole freewill thing."

"I don't see how," Pela muttered.

"You don't?" Aldyn asked. "Imagine it: a world where everyone did whatever they liked. No laws or rules. The strong would take whatever they wanted. Say what you will about the king, his laws protect those who cannot defend themselves, prevent chaos."

Caledan snorted. "Some job he's doing."

Aldyn flashed him a grimace. "You should walk a mile in a man's shoes before you judge, sellsword," he replied. "If not for Braidon, the Lonian King would have taken half our land and put the rest of us to the sword."

"And he set out new trade routes with Northland," Tobias cut in. "Our farm would have gone broke when the Trolans closed their borders, if not for that."

"Is this really the time to be talking about politics?" Devon growled, gesturing ahead.

Just then, the whispers lifted a notch in pitch. The company slowed.

"We're close," Aldyn hissed, "just around this corner, I think. The voices must be coming from the pantheon."

Devon looked at the others. "It looks like this is going to come to a fight," he said, looking from Tobias to Genevieve to Pela. "If anyone still wants to back out…"

Tobias swallowed and shook his head, while his niece only gripped the hilt of her sword tighter. Genevieve smiled. "We go on."

Devon nodded, and prayed to the memory of Antonia that they weren't too late. "Keep close," he said softly. "Whatever's waiting for us, we get in and get out as quickly as possible."

The others nodded, their faces a mixture of fear and determination, and Devon's chest swelled. The villagers had no business being here, no experience with war and death, but in that instant he knew they would not break. Gathering himself, he turned the corner to the pantheon.

He'd expected guards to be posted outside the Order's innermost sanctuary, but the corridor was empty. Devon started towards the massive oaken doors. Blood thudded in his ears as he glimpsed the murals on the walls, depicting scenes of heroism and war, of evil magic-doers and dark creatures from the north. Amidst them all, a single woman stood tall with sword in hand.

There was no doubt she was a representation of Alana. But while Devon's memory had blurred through the years, even now he knew the image bore little resemblance to reality. The woman in the mural was tall and blonde, her skin unblemished and eyes cold, almost a Goddess herself in her perfection. Alana, for all that he had loved her, had been far from perfect.

"Ready for this, big man?" Caledan whispered as they approached the doors.

The mural stretched up over the entrance to the pantheon, where a final depiction of Alana stood with flaming sword in hand. Devon shuddered, tearing his thoughts from the past. Beyond the wooden panels, the whispers of prayer had risen to a fever pitch.

For a moment, Devon couldn't help but compare their quest to the Knight's attack on the temple above Skystead. How different were they now, to have come to this place of worship with weapons in hand? Yet it was not hatred that had drawn them here, but love. They had not come for blood, only to bring their people home. He nodded to the sellsword and pressed a hand to the door.

"Go quietly," Aldyn said. "They might not realise we're intruders."

Devon checked one last time that the others were ready, then gave the door a push. It swung open with barely a squeak, and together they slipped inside. The roar of voices struck as the door swung closed behind them. Bewildered, Devon reached for his hammer, shocked at the madness within the pantheon.

Towering columns lined the room and rows of pews cluttered the chamber, but few of the congregation were using them. Aldyn had told them only twenty Knights remained in the Castle. There were far more people than that present. They packed the pantheon, standing and sitting and on their knees with hands raised to the sky, as though calling upon some divine power.

A man stood on the raised platform opposite where they had entered. He wore robes of fine green silk and a crown of silver wire, while a heavy gold necklace hung around his neck. Raising a jewelled sceptre skywards, his voice boomed out across the chamber, though Devon could make no sense of his words. The worshipers seemed to understand though, for their voices joined with his, until it seemed the noise might shake the very walls.

Two men sat in silence behind the speaker in the wings of the dais. One was a young man, unknown to Devon, but it was clear from his robes and throne that he was an Elder. The other man was Merak. He wore a broad grin as he watched the proceedings, though in the heat of the thousand candles lighting the pantheon, his face glistened with sweat.

A great *boom* came from a door to the side of the dais, and a Knight in full plate mail appeared, leading a prisoner. Her arms were tied behind her back and a hood had been pulled. She staggered as the Knight shoved her, and her scream rang out over the cries of the audience. The Knight grabbed her by the scruff of the neck before she could fall and dragged her in front of the speaker.

"The solstice approaches!" the man holding the sceptre boomed, returning to a language Devon understood. He was the oldest of the three Elders on the stage, and his voice cracked before he managed to continue, "Thirty years have passed since the Saviour freed our lands, but the power of the False Gods is rising. The profane cannot be allowed to proliferate, lest the tyranny of magic be restored. Today we cleanse their blasphemy from our shores."

He raised the sceptre above his head as the Knight forced the prisoner to her knees. A hundred voices roared their agreement. Devon winced and glanced around, but amidst the madness, the zealots had not taken note of the intruders. He started down the centre of the pantheon towards the speaker.

A sick feeling touched Devon's stomach as he looked out over the crowd and finally noticed the second prisoner. Her crumpled figure lay at the foot of the dais where she had fallen, arms still bound, feet sprawled at odd angles against the stone. The silken hood covering her face was stained red.

Rage touched Devon as he looked at the Elder standing atop the stage. His eyes were drawn to the sceptre, and this time he saw the blood dripping from the heavy gold. The jewels studding the awful instrument shone in the candle-light, almost seeming to take on a life of their own. Devon picked up his pace.

Around him the voices rose higher. Those present wore the fine silks of the rich, and he was surprised to see many sporting knives or even swords on their belts. He had spotted five Knights in their plate mail up on the dais behind the Elders. Others stood lookout at the edges of the chamber, though they had become engrossed by the exhibi-tion on the stage.

The first worshipers finally took note of Devon as he passed beneath the centre of the dome. They fell silent, turning to one another in question, unsure of these new arrivals or their purpose.

Atop the dais, the Elder was speaking again, but his voice died when his eyes fell on Devon. The sceptre in his hand lowered half an inch as a frown creased his forehead.

"Who dares interrupt our sacred ceremony?" he shouted.

Devon grimaced and drew his hammer from its sheath. "My name is Devon of Skystead!" he bellowed. "And we have come to restore our people to their homes!"

The Elder scowled. "What madness is this?"

Behind the man, his fellows rose from their thrones. Fear showed on Merak's face as he pointed a finger at Devon. "He led the mob in Skystead!" he screamed. "Kill him!"

Pela and the others grew close around Devon. They had come to a stop at the foot of the dais, though the Elders and their protectors stood several feet from the edge. Whispers came from the pews as some of the worshipers stood and drew swords.

Locking eyes with Merak, Devon let his laughter boom out over the pantheon. "What mob?" he called. "Is that what you told them? There was only one of me, coward."

"He lies!" Merak screamed. His face a mottled red, Merak grabbed the arm of a Knight and shoved him in the direction of the intruders. "*I said, kill them!*"

Finally the Knight obeyed, drawing a broadsword and advancing. Blood pounded in Devon's temples as he leapt the three feet to the dais. He deflected a wild swing of the Knight's blade as the others followed him, then charged. He slammed into the man's plate mail armour, and pain lanced through his shoulder, but the Knight staggered backwards, off-balance. Surging forward, Devon drove his hammer into the man's chest.

A great *crash* echoed through the hall as the Knight tumbled from the dais. Devon spun, seeking out Merak, but the other Knights on the stage were already advancing. A curse slipped from his lips, before Caledan surged past.

"The prisoner!" a voice bellowed from somewhere, while behind them the worshipers screamed.

Devon risked a glance back. Chaos had erupted across the pantheon, as some tried to flee the melee on the dais, while others charged forward with weapons drawn. They lashed about them in their desperation to reach the stage, showing little concern for their fellow believers. Several fell bleeding or dead to the floor. Horror touched Devon, until he recalled that just moments before these people had been cheering for the deaths of innocent women.

A man reached the edge of the dais and tried to climb up, but Genevieve darted forward and speared him through the throat. He fell back with a cry, and she looked back, catching Devon's eye.

"Go!" she cried. "We'll hold them."

As though to emphasis her point, Tobias swung his sword at a second attacker, almost decapitating the man. He glanced back, his face more sombre than Devon had ever seen it, and offered a nod before returning to the battle.

Devon's heart lurched as he realised he'd lost sight of Pela, but before he could look for her, a voice called him back.

"Drop your weapon, hammerman!"

He spun, finding Merak standing nearby. Two more Knights had fallen to Caledan's blade. A third was battling furiously with the sellsword, but he seemed to have more skill than his fellows, and neither was giving an inch. The other Elders had vanished, leaving Merak alone on the stage, but he had claimed the sceptre and now held it high above his head.

"Why?" Devon growled, starting forward.

"Or she dies," Merak hissed, pointing the golden sceptre at the prisoner lying crouched at his feet.

🐾 19 🐾

The breath *whooshed* from Pela's lungs as she slammed into the ground. She groaned and curled into a ball as her blade went skittering between a Knight's legs. Shouts erupted overhead as Caledan leapt past and engaged the Knights.

Gasping for breath, Pela dragged herself to her knees and swore beneath her breath. What had happened? One moment she'd been facing the charging Knights, her throat clogged with terror and blood pounding in her ears, the next, a heavy blow had struck her in the legs, sending her tumbling. But only Caledan had been…

"Bastard!" Pela hissed as she realised he'd tripped her.

The sellsword spun, driving his blade through a Knight's gorget, but he still managed to flash her a smile. Teeth bared, Pela reached for her scabbard, before remembering she'd dropped her father's sword yet again.

Swearing, she darted past Caledan, who was battling furiously with the remaining two Knights. Her eyes swept the dais, finding her blade lying near one of the golden thrones. Heart racing, she scanned the shadows beyond, searching for the other Elders. The dais was empty; it appeared they had fled, leaving Merak to stand alone against the intruders.

Pela recovered her sword and turned back towards the fight. She scanned the chamber. Caledan was still battling with the two Knights. They appeared to be getting the better of him, until he ducked a blow and darted forward suddenly, his blade stabbing low. His opponent staggered back clutching his groin. Blood pumped between his fingers and within moments, he collapsed to the ground.

A roaring sounded in Pela's ears as Caledan launched himself at the last Knight. She couldn't tear her eyes away from the dying man. Even in his armour she could feel his pain, sense his terror as his life's blood fled from him. It had happened so quickly, the shift between life and death.

Her legs began to shake as she turned away, and she saw Genevieve, Aldyn, and Tobias battling furiously with the congregation. In the chaos, the pews had been shoved up against the dais, blocking the worshiper's passage everywhere but the centre of the chamber. Her friends stood there with swords in hand, defying those below. From their vantage point atop the dais, they had managed to keep the zealots from gaining a foothold. But the horde below were too many; they couldn't possibly hope to hold them off forever.

As she watched, Aldyn went down, a gash opening on his calf. Her heart lurched, but he was up again in a second, his blade flashing down to skewer the swordsman that had struck him.

The trembling spread until Pela's entire body was shaking. Fists clenched, she shrank backwards until she struck one of the thrones. Before she could stop herself, she darted behind it. Her father's blade slipped from her fingers as she leaned against the cold steel and slid to the ground. Screams came from behind her and she drew her legs up to her chest.

"No, no, no," she whispered, scrunching her eyes closed in an effort to deny the death creeping towards her.

"Drop your weapon, hammerman!" Merak boomed suddenly.

Pela flinched. It sounded as though the Elder was almost directly behind her. She sat frozen as her uncle's angry retort rumbled through the hall.

"Why?"

"Or she dies," came Merak's hiss.

The roaring in Pela's ears rose to a thunder as she leaned out from behind the throne and saw the Elder poised over his prisoner. He held the golden sceptre in one hand, ready to strike the helpless woman dead. Several feet away, Devon stared him down, teeth bared and hammer clutched tightly in both hands. The rest of the room had stilled with the priest's words.

Pela swallowed as she met her uncle's eyes. There was a flicker of recognition, before they returned to Merak. Ever so slowly, he relaxed, lowering the hammer to his side. He held up one hand.

"Easy there, sonny," he murmured.

"I said put it down!"

The *thud* as Devon's hammer struck the ground echoed loudly in the chamber.

No, no, no!

His eyes flickered to her again. Pela shook her head. She couldn't do it. If she tried, she would die. There was no doubt in her mind anymore; she had no business being here.

Unable to face her uncle's disappointment, she lowered her gaze.

Her eyes caught on her father's sword. It lay at her feet, its silver blade glistening in the candlelight. A lump lodged in her throat. What would her father think if he could see her now? Her uncle, her friends, they were all relying on her, needed her. All sound drained away as she realised that if she failed, they would all die. The zealots below would tear them apart.

"Very good." The Elder's voice dripped malice now.

A sob came from the woman at his feet. Pela's heart lurched. Had that…been her mother's voice? She craned her head, trying for a better view, but there was nothing she could see to identify the woman. Then she saw Devon, still watching her. His amber eyes shone with a quiet confidence.

Unconsciously, Pela gripped her father's sword tight in one hand. Before she could think about what she was doing, she was on her feet. The throne still hid her from the crowd below, but as soon as she stepped from its shadow, she would be revealed. She could not hesitate, not even for a second. Releasing a shuddering breath, she leapt.

The sword slid into the Elder's back with surprising ease, as though it were not flesh and bone she had stabbed, but soft mud or a melon. Even after all her time practicing with Caledan, she was not prepared for the reality.

A terrible scream erupted from Merak and he staggered away, tearing the blade from his back. The sceptre struck the ground with a sharp *crack*, followed by a flash of light as it split in half.

Pela hardly noticed. She stood frozen, staring down at the bloody sword clutched in her hand. The Elder made it two steps before he collapsed to the floor of the dais. His cries echoed pitifully around the room, growing weaker as he pawed at the floor. Then Devon was beside Pela, drawing her into a hug.

"Well done, missy," he whispered in her ear, and then released her.

A roar came from the worshipers as they charged. Aldyn and Tobias were there to meet them, but they could not hold them back this time. Enraged, the men and women below hurled themselves at the swordsmen.

"Where do we go?" Pela choked.

"Here!" Genevieve's voice called from the side of the stage.

Pela spun, finding her in the shadows from where the prisoner had been led. A door stood open beside her. Caledan had already dispatched the last Knight and was racing towards her. No longer able to think rationally, Pela sprinted after him, bloody sword still clasped in her hand. Behind her, Devon scooped the prisoner up over his shoulder and followed.

Another roar came from the crowd at the sight of their prey escaping. Pela glanced back as they surged forward. A man hurled himself at Tobias and was run through, but the farmer's blade lodged in his ribcage and was torn away. Tobias stumbled back as two more followed the dead man over the edge of the dais. Seeing them in the wings, he ran towards them. Blade still in hand, Aldyn fought on with a cold ferocity Pela would not have expected from the light-hearted soldier.

"Come on!" Devon bellowed as he reached the door and glanced back.

Aldyn started towards them, but as he lowered his sword, a zealot scrambled onto the stage. Throwing himself forward, his hand whipped out and caught Aldyn by the ankle. The King's Guard cried out and went down.

Cursing, Devon handed the prisoner to Genevieve and stepped towards his friend, but now that there was no one to stand against them, the crowd swarmed up onto the dais. Scrambling to his knees, Aldyn looked from the horde to Devon.

"*Go!*" he screamed, launching himself to his feet.

His sword speared down, killing the man that had toppled him, then skewered a second. But the worshipers were all around him now, and a sword flashed out, catching him in the side.

Aldyn screamed and tore himself away. Dragging free his blade, he brought it down in a double handed blow on another zealot. The man's skull split with a horrifying *crack*.

Then a woman leapt on him, driving a dagger deep into Aldyn's chest, and he went down. The crowd swept forward and Aldyn disappeared from view.

"*No!*" Pela shrieked. She leapt at the door, but Caledan caught her by the waist and hauled her back. "Bastard!"

Turning, she tried to attack him with her blade, but he slapped her hand down and the sword clattered to the ground. Pela screamed again, slamming a fist into his cheek. Curses erupted through the room as Caledan tossed her aside. Scrambling across the floor, Pela swept up her blade and swung on Caledan.

Boom.

Darkness engulfed the room as Devon swung the door closed. "Enough!" he bellowed. "Tobias, you have the lantern."

Something heavy struck the door as the farmer scrambled in his bag, then a moment later a spark appeared in the pitch-black. Pela strained her eyes as it brightened, revealing first Tobias, then Devon and Genevieve and the woman they had rescued, then finally Caledan. She bared her teeth and was about to launch herself at him again, when Tobias gave a cry and fell to his knees beside the prisoner.

"Marce!" he cried, engulfing her in his arms. "You're alive!"

Pela lowered her sword as the two hugged. Someone had freed the woman of her bonds in the chaos of their flight. The two held each other now as though nothing else existed. Then another *thud* came from the door to the pantheon. They all spun to face it, and watched a large crack spread through the wood. It was made of heavy oak and secured by a locking bar, but even that would not last long beneath the weight of the crowd beyond.

Pela's sorrow for Aldyn turned to sudden fear as she realised they'd lost their guide. Without Aldyn, how would they find their way out again? Was there even another way out of this room?

"What's happening out there?"

Pela spun as another voice came from the darkness behind them. They'd forgotten the Elders! They must have fled this way, and yet…straining her eyes, Pela approached the shadows at the rear of the chamber. The darkness resolved itself, revealing the bars of a cell. Her heart began to race as she realised they'd found the cells Aldyn had mentioned. This must be the rest of the prisoners from Skystead.

"Mum!" She darted to the cell door.

Movement came from beyond the bars as the occupants exchanged glances. Tobias approached with the torch, illuminating their faces. Pela's heart pounded in her chest as she searched for her mother…and did not find her.

No, no, no…

She checked again, eyes sweeping the gathered faces, but none of them were Kryssa.

Pela scrunched her eyes closed. A scream built in her throat as she realised the truth. She wanted desperately to run back out into the pantheon, to the prisoner who had been murdered before they arrived, to tear the bag from her head and hold her close.

But she could do none of those things. They were too late. They had failed. Sobbing, she sank to her knees and ground her fists into the stone.

A rhythmic thumping was coming from the door. It echoed the pounding of her heart, of some song she could not quite remember.

"Get up, girl." It was Caledan. He placed a hand on her shoulder. "We have to go."

Tears streamed down Pela's face as she looked up at him, her rage from a moment earlier forgotten. "They killed her."

"They'll kill us too, if you don't get up," he growled, dragging her to her feet.

Pela staggered as he released her. Her sword hung loosely in her hand and she looked at it, wondering what was the point. Blood stained its tip, reminding her of the man she'd killed. She hadn't even stopped to process that yet. Hands shaking, she tried to sheathe the blade. It took two attempts before she succeeded. By then Devon had the prison cell open, its lock smashed to pieces by his hammer.

"This way," Caledan was saying, gesturing to a passageway leading into darkness, though without their guide they had no way of knowing the way out.

"Come on." Devon was beside her now. He squeezed her shoulder. "You did a good job back there. If not for you we'd all be dead. Now we need to keep it together until we can get these people to safety."

Looking at him, Pela wanted to throw herself into his

arms. She could see Devon was close to tears himself. But he was right; these people needed them. They had no one else. Straightening her shoulders, Pela swallowed back her grief and nodded, not trusting herself to speak.

There was an open gate of iron in the passageway leading away from the cell. They stumbled through, single-file, and then Genevieve gripped it in both hands and swung it shut behind her with so much force the locking bar jumped back out. She gave it another shove to click it in properly, then checked the lock was secure, before joining them.

They went slowly after that, Caledan and Pela taking the lead. They must have been in a disused section of the Castle, for the passageways were unlit. Every so often they would come to an intersection, and Pela and Caledan would creep forward to check for anyone coming. Shouts echoed from distant passageways, but there was no sign of pursuit.

"The front gates are no good," Devon said at one point. "Aldyn mentioned a canal gate. It'll have to do—if we can find it."

But no one knew which direction to take, and they continued to stumble blindly through the Castle, lost. The sounds of the chase grew steadily closer. Pela's fear came rushing back, growing with every scrape and echo in the dark corridors.

They were approaching their fourth intersection, when a sudden cough whispered from the corridors ahead. Pela froze, glancing sidelong at Caledan. Several feet behind her, he held up a hand to wait. Then the whisper of footsteps came to them, and Caledan nodded. He was too far away, she would have to do it.

Don't think, do!

As quietly as she could, Pela drew her sword. The blade

shook in her hands as she stepped up to the intersection. Afraid her ragged breathing would give her away, Pela settled into the familiar rhythm of her meditation.

In, out, in, out.

The footsteps approached. Drawing on her calm centre, she gathered her courage into a ball and then leapt from her hiding place, her sword coming up to find her foe.

The beady-eyed Elder from the pantheon squawked and jumped in the air, his robes fluttering as he tried to turn away. For a moment, Pela was so shocked she just stood there, but the man tripped over his own feet and crashed to the floor. Then a wave of rage swept through her. This was the man who had first held the sceptre, the one who had wielded it to kill…

Grief choked her and she raised her father's blade to strike.

"Please!" the Elder wailed, raising his hands in front of his face. "Don't kill me. I'll give you whatever you want!"

Pela's rage was all but suffocating now. *"You killed my mother,"* she hissed.

"Pleeeease," the man cried again. "I have coin, I can make you richer than you ever dreamed!"

"Pela, wait!" Caledan hissed, catching her by the arm. "He might be useful."

"Yes, I—"

"Never!" Teeth bared, Pela strained against Caledan until Devon stepped between them.

"He's not worth it, niece," Devon murmured. "Look at him, he's a grub."

The anger went from Pela as quickly as it had come, and she slumped in Caledan's grip. She stared down at the pathetic excuse for a man, who had so bravely slain her helpless mother. "Take him," she choked.

Caledan released her and dragged the man up. "Which way to the canal gate?" he growled, drawing a dagger. "And do not lie to me, for your life depends on it."

The Elder blubbered and stammered, but eventually he managed to get out the words. "That way!"

"Show us."

They continued, Pela walking with the prisoners now, her eyes fixed on the Elder's back. Again and again she saw the body on the ground in the pantheon, her grief turning to rage, then regret.

If only they'd been a little bit sooner, if only they hadn't delayed…

"Here!" the priest announced suddenly.

Pela's head snapped up, surprised to find herself outside. Like the front entrance, there was a courtyard before the gates, but here it was tiny—and for the moment unguarded. Used to bring goods by gondola from the port, she hoped no one would have thought to look for them here yet.

"Get them open," Caledan snapped.

Two of the villagers started working on the locking bar while the others edged forward, casting furtive glances back the way they'd come. Thunder boomed overhead and Pela glanced up. The sky was black, the moon and stars concealed, but the rain had not yet reached them. A shout echoed from the keep, but Pela could see no one in the corridor behind them.

The gates swung open with a sharp creak. She stepped towards them, then hesitated. Blood pounded in Pela's ears as she set her sights on the Elder. She tightened her grip on her sword.

"Don't," Devon murmured, blocking her path.

Tears blurred Pela's vision as she looked at her uncle. "Why?" she croaked. "He killed my mother."

"Ay," Devon rumbled, the lines of his face deepening, "but this isn't what she would have wanted, nor your father."

"He deserves it!" A brilliant light flashed across the sky, followed by the *crack* of thunder. As though the heavens had opened up, rain began to bucket down around them.

"He is unarmed!" Devon shouted through the downpour. "Did your parents raise you to kill a man in cold blood?"

"No—"

"Kill him, and you become no better than the evil you seek to destroy, Pela," Devon said, his face haggard as water ran in rivulets down his face. "Trust me. There are many things I regret in my life. Do not follow in my footsteps. Be better. Be the woman your parents would have wanted you to become."

The fight went from Pela in a rush, her anger racing away like water over a cascade. She lowered her sword.

"Mum's gone," Pela croaked.

Devon nodded, and she threw herself into his arms and buried her head in his chest.

$\mathfrak{R}$ 20 $\mathfrak{R}$

The mood was sombre amongst the rescuers as they
returned to the inn. They had succeeded beyond
anything Caledan had expected, but the sense of loss Devon
and Pela carried about themselves was palpable. Not only
had the kindly Aldyn been butchered where he stood, but
they had failed to achieve the one thing they'd set out to do:
rescue the girl's mother.

Only Tobias seemed to have thrown off the melancholy. He had walked the whole way back arm-in-arm with
a young woman that could only be his wife. Caledan had
to admit, the farmer had surprised him back in the
pantheon. He might have been jovial during training, but
when it had come to the battle, Tobias had been all business. The man might never have Caledan's skill, but he'd
shown his worth.

His thoughts turned then to the huntress. Genevieve too
had shown her worth. He searched the crowded inn and
found her seated alone in the corner with a jug of ale.
Taking his mug, he strolled across to join her.

"Not in the mood to celebrate?" he asked as he sat down.

"Not really." Her eyes flickered but she did not look up. Reaching for the jug, she gulped down a mouthful of the amber liquid.

Caledan raised an eyebrow. "Wha—"

"Not in the mood for conversation either," she snapped, and this time she did look at him. Tears spilt down her cheeks. "*If* you don't mind."

A strained silence stretched out between them, before Caledan nodded.

"Fine," he said, raising the glass. "Mind if I keep you company?"

"You're not my type."

Caledan snorted, drink still extended. He was surprised at her sudden show of emotion—after seeing little of the sort during their voyage from Skystead. But she was still better company than Devon. The hammerman had hardly spoken on the way back, and now sat alone in the middle of the inn, quietly nursing his drink. Caledan's attempts at conversation had been met with a cold stare, and he had quickly stopped trying.

Genevieve eyed him for a long moment, before taking up her jug and clinking it against his glass. They drank deeply and then sat there in silence, watching as the other villagers exchanged stories.

"What will you do now?" Caledan asked finally.

Nose in her jug, Genevieve glanced at him. "I will go wherever Devon does," she answered, as though that explained everything. "What about you?"

Caledan's stomach contracted at the thought and a grin crossed his cheeks. She was right: the rescue mission was over, whether they had lost the woman or not. He had hardly given a thought to his request. To finally come before the king…though now that the time was finally here, he wondered if the hammerman would honour his word.

He considered approaching Devon for reassurance, but one look at the man banished the idea. Stoney-eyed and rigid, now was not the time to pick a fight with the giant warrior.

Cursing into his mug, Caledan waved for another jug. "Tomorrow I'll ask Devon to honour our agreement," he replied finally.

"If there is a tomorrow," Genevieve muttered.

"What's that?" Caledan asked, his head coming up.

Genevieve raised an eyebrow. "You don't think this is going to get back to the Order?" She gestured at the general revelry taking place in the dining hall. "How long before those Knights come looking for revenge?"

A curse burst from Caledan. Why hadn't he thought of that? There'd been a dozen Knights left alive in the Castle, and plenty more of their followers. He started to rise when a tap came on his shoulder. Caledan spun and was reaching for his sword, when he realised it was only Tobias.

"May we sit?" the farmer asked.

His wife was with him, and they pulled up chairs before either could respond. Cursing, Caledan sank back into his seat. His heartbeat eased. Outside, rain still lashed at the windows and the occasional boom of thunder shook the walls. Few would dare venture out in such weather. Word was unlikely to reach the Knights until morning. By then the villagers would be long gone on the *Seadragon*.

"Marce," Tobias said, introducing his wife.

Despite her recent travails, the woman had a cheerful look, though the smile lines on her cheeks suggested this was her usual state of mind. Idly, Caledan found himself wondering why. How much joy could exist in the life of a farmer? To toil day in and day out on the land with never an ounce of excitement—just the thought of it made him shudder.

"I can't thank you enough," Marce was saying. "I know you suffered greatly to save us. He must have been a brave man, Aldyn. Did you know him long?"

Caledan snorted. "A few hours."

Her smile faltered and she exchanged a glance with Tobias. The farmer gave the slightest shake of his head. Caledan almost rolled his eyes. Was he meant to grieve every ally who fell in battle? What he'd said was true—he'd barely known Aldyn long enough to learn his name, let alone *know* him. Why should he grieve a stranger, when there was so much to celebrate?

Like his coming meeting with King Braidon…

"I'm just so sorry about Kryssa and Ariane," Marce was saying, her eyes traveling across the table to Devon. "I knew Selina quite well. We often had coffee together, though the hammerman—I mean Devon—never joined us. He must be devastated to have lost his daughter."

Caledan grunted, but Genevieve came to her feet so suddenly her chair toppled to the ground. Marce's mouth fell open and Tobias rose, but before anything could be said, a crash came from the entrance to the inn. The doors swung open and the winds carried the swirling rain inside, drawing curses from the nearest patrons. They fell silent as an armoured Knight stepped into the room.

The silence spread as others noticed the newcomer. Cursing, Caledan leapt to his feet and reached for his sword.

"Where is the hammerman?" the Knight bellowed.

"Here," Devon growled, striding past Caledan with hammer in hand.

There was a dangerous look in the man's eyes, and Caledan realised with a start he'd been waiting for this. The floorboards creaked as Devon came to a stop several feet from the Knight.

Two more Knights shouldered their way inside. Caledan wondered how many more were waiting without, but three were more than enough of a concern for the moment. Loosening his blade in its scabbard, Caledan edged forward. Genevieve and Tobias followed just a step behind him. The rest of the villagers from Skystead watched on, fear written across their faces.

"Can I help you lads?" the innkeeper asked in a hard voice. He stepped out from behind the bar, a club gripped tightly in one hand. But the weapon was for dealing with unruly drunks, not armoured men, and the Knights took no notice.

"No," Devon growled, hefting his hammer, "but I can—"

"Easy!" Caledan interrupted, darting forward before the hammerman dragged them all into a fight they could not win. Stepping in front of Devon, he flashed the man a glance before facing the Knights. "I think you'd best be going, lads."

The first of the Knights stepped forward. "He desecrated our sacred pantheon!" he snapped, his voice echoing strangely from the helmet. "He killed our Elder! We won't be going anywhere without the old man's head on a pike."

Under different circumstances, Caledan might have been offended the Knights had not recognised him back in the Castle. Just now though, he would take every advantage he could to defuse the situation.

"But how can that be?" He spread his hands. "The man

has been in this tavern all night, with myself and these good folk from Skystead."

"Lies!" the Knight screamed, though he did not draw his sword. "He was seen with the traitor from the King's Guard. Him and all these others—"

"—came from Skystead," Caledan interrupted. His voice took on a hard edge. "Now, let us be reasonable. We've all lost people this night. No doubt we could keep fighting until there's no one left standing." A yelp came from the innkeeper at his words. "But we all know the truth about what happened in Skystead, and here. Should that truth get out…"

"We are the authority in Townirwin," the Knight hissed. Then his eyes flickered around the room, taking in Devon, Genevieve and Tobias. Several of the former prisoners had also armed themselves. The sight seemed to give him pause.

"The others can stay," he growled at last. "We already took what we needed for the Great Sacrifice."

"You're monsters!" Pela shrieked.

Caledan cursed inwardly as the girl came marching forward, sword in hand.

"You murdered my mother in your foul pantheon. How can you believe your Great Sacrifice is anything but evil?"

The Knight seemed taken aback. "Because it is *necessary*," he said, then smiled. "But…that was only a cleansing! Fear not child, for your mother died free of her evil." He laughed. "The Great Sacrifice is to burn away the tendrils of the False Gods, to keep them from this world. It does not take place until the solstice. The Saviour has blessed the woman Kryssa as one of the three."

Silence answered the Knight's words as every eye in the tavern turned on him. Caledan felt as though he'd been struck a great blow. Was the man speaking the truth? Could Pela's mother truly be alive?

"What did you say?" Devon whispered.

"Do you know her, hammerman?" the Knight sneered.

"If you lay a hand on her—" Devon bellowed, starting forward, but Caledan leapt between them.

"Easy, Devon!" Caledan hissed. The hammerman's eyes were wild, but he stopped when Caledan placed a hand on his chest. Letting out a sigh, Caledan looked at the Knight. "What do you mean, she was 'blessed'?"

"That is none of your concern," the Knight snapped. "She is beyond your reach now. Now hand over the old man, it is time he paid for his crimes this night."

"No." Caledan released Devon and stepped towards the Knights. "Believe me, lads, I'm the only thing keeping you alive right now."

The Knights laughed. "You think we're afraid of a greybeard?"

"Do you know his name?" Caledan asked mildly.

"What do we care for the bastard's name?" the leader snapped.

Caledan smiled. "It might interest you," he murmured, "to know that this is Devon. I believe he has a place in your legends."

A stillness came over the Knights. They stood staring at Devon, and while the helmets hid their faces, Caledan knew he'd struck a nerve. It was said that Devon had known Alana, had been there at the end even, when she had sacrificed herself to banish the Gods. And he was not known as the Consort of Alana for nothing…

"It's not possible," the leader replied.

"I'd be more than happy to resolve any doubts you have, sonny," Devon growled.

Caledan raised a hand. "It's true," he replied. "Look at him. How else could an old man have carved through your Knights?" He adapted a reverent tone. "You should be honoured, that the Consort of Alana deigned visit your Castle." He might have laughed, if not for the seriousness of the situation.

"Then where is *kanker*?" the Knight argued, gesturing at the construction hammer in Devon's hand. "You can't expect us to believe *that* is the hammer of heroes?"

"It was destroyed," Devon rumbled. "Or do you not know your own history?"

"What are you playing at, swordsman?" the Knight asked. "What part do you play in this?"

Caledan smiled. "My ambitions are my own," he said, "but if you think to go against us, you should know my name as well: *Caledan.*" Armour rattled as the three retreated a step. Caledan followed them, his eyes hard now, glad that his reputation still preceded him. "I take it you have heard of me?"

"What is a man of your standing doing with such rogues!" the leader gasped.

"I think we're done here," Caledan said.

The Knights were standing in the doorway by now. It was obvious they were young men, despite their armour and greatswords—their inexperience betrayed them. They believed in the legends, though the tales of his exploits had grown greatly with time. Caledan sneered as they shrank before him.

"Go back to your Elders—what's left of them—and tell them what happened here. Tell them Skystead is under the protection of Devon and Caledan. If they seek retribution for what happened tonight, there will be a reckoning, whether they come alone or with an army."

He stood staring at the three of them. Still, they hesitated. Caledan dropped a hand to his sword hilt. With a rattle of metal, they turned tail and fled into the darkness. Shouts came from outside, made nearly inaudible by the swirling rain, but after a long moment they heard the tramping of departing boots.

Shaking his head, Caledan walked back to his table and took a seat. Silence hung over the room as he reached for his drink. The mug was almost empty, and he poured himself another drink before taking a swig. He shivered as a cold breeze blew through the open doors, damp with rain, and cursed.

"For the Gods' sake," he snapped, "someone close the door!"

$$\text{❧} \quad 21 \quad \text{❧}$$

Sitting in the saddle with the rain pouring down around him, Ikar had rarely been so miserable. They had ridden through the afternoon and late into the night, and the storm had not relented in all that time. Eventually it had forced them to make camp in a grove of trees, but the sparse shelter hardly spared them from the wet, and as the rains continued Ikar had found himself cursing Merak for choosing him.

Even when the morning broke, the rain had continued unabated. Ikar had saddled their horses in silence and they'd set off once more.

His only consolation was that he did not suffer alone. On the packhorse, Kryssa sat with her hands bound to the saddle. Despite the miserable conditions, the woman had not complained, had not said a word so far in fact. He wondered if she knew what they had chosen her for, where they were headed.

The light grew around them as they continued down the Gods Road, and finally it seemed the rain might ease. The thunder faded away and the fog clinging to the damp ground dissipated, revealing the way ahead. Ikar breathed a sigh of relief. The road to Lane was well-travelled, but it could still be treacherous in such conditions.

As the last of the fog lifted, he glanced at his companion. He was surprised that the Elders had agreed with his suggestion, even more so that they'd granted him the honour of escorting her to Lane. Though looking at her now, Ikar couldn't help but wonder if his assessment of her had been wrong. Her head bobbed with each trod of her horse and her eyes were closed, as though asleep in the saddle.

Ikar's frown deepened as he noticed her blue lips, and the pallid colour of her skin. Edging his horse closer, he called out to her: "Kryssa, are you okay?"

The woman gave no answer. His heart began to race, and he leapt from his saddle and rushed across the road to the packhorse. Tugging at the knots of her bindings, he shivered at the icy touch of her skin.

"Damnit, witch" he muttered beneath his breath, cursing his stupidity. He had given her an oilskin jacket to fend off the rain, but she was freezing without anything thicker to protect her. "Don't you dare die!"

"Okay."

The last knot had just come free when Kryssa sat up straight in the saddle and kicked out with her boot. The blow caught Ikar square in the chest and sent him staggering back. In the heavy armour, he almost lost his balance, but some quick footwork kept him from falling. The thunder of hooves sounded in his ears as he swung around.

Swearing loudly, he leapt for his horse and hauled himself up. He was barely in the saddle before the horse set off at a gallop. The beast had been bred for war, a monster to a man of lesser size than Ikar, and they quickly ate up the distance.

Weighed down by their supplies and not built for speed, Kryssa's mount could not outrun him. He almost smiled, before anger at her defiance burned away his mirth. Crouching lower in the saddle, he watched as Kryssa glanced back at him, expecting to see fear in the woman's eyes. She smiled.

"Witch," he muttered.

A moment later he pulled alongside her. He snatched at the reins, dragging the horse to the side of the road. Unable to continue its headlong flight, the packhorse slowed. When they were almost at a stop, Ikar reached for Kryssa, but the woman was faster still. She leapt between the horses with a snarl and smashed into his chest. Entangled, the two of them toppled from the saddle and struck the ground with a *crash*.

Kryssa was up in an instant, but she hesitated for half a second, her eyes darting from Ikar's sword to the open fields. Before she could flee, he caught her by the ankle and hauled. Screaming, she slammed to the ground. Her fist smashed at his visor and she cried out again, but unarmed, there was nothing she could do to hurt him in his armour. Within a few minutes, Ikar had her hands bound behind her back once more.

Stumbling to his feet, he looked around for their horses, and discovered they'd vanished.

"*Damnit!*" He drew back an iron boot and slammed it into Kryssa's side.

She cried out as the blow sent her rolling through the mud. Enraged, he readied himself for another blow, then noticed her silver eyes watching him. There was no fear there—only unbridled rage. In a rush, he recalled his mission, and let out a long breath.

"You're a pain in the ass, you know," he growled.

Sitting up in the mud, she blew a strand of hair from her face and cackled. "My mother used to say the same." Her eyes shone. "So why don't you free me, and save yourself the trouble?"

Ignoring her words, Ikar pulled the woman to her feet. "That way," he said, pointing down the Gods Road. No doubt the horses had continued the way they'd been heading.

"I've been wondering," Kryssa said conversationally as they started off. "Did my…friend catch up with your Knights in Skystead?"

"Your friend?" Ikar asked. He searched the trees alongside the road for signs of their mounts while they walked. "What are you talking about?"

"Devon; he was a friend of my mother's. He would have been…irritated when he discovered you took me. I thought he might have caught up with that Elder and his Knights when they went into town."

Ikar blinked. "You can't mean *the* Devon, the Consort of Alana?"

Kryssa chuckled. "The way my mother told it, they barely exchanged more than a few steamy looks," she replied. "But yes, that Devon."

"I…" Ikar struggled to find the words to reply.

Devon was also a descendant of Alan the Great, though of a different line from Ikar—a line of warriors. While Ikar's parents and grandparents had been tarnished by magic, Devon's family had wielded *kanker*, the hammer of heroes. That is, until it had been destroyed in the final battle against the Tsar.

Ikar could hardly believe his distant cousin still lived. As a child, Devon had been a legend, but by the time Ikar had grown to manhood, the man had vanished from the world.

"I thought so," Kryssa surmised, Ikar unable to keep the truth from his face. "You should *really* let me go."

For a moment, Ikar felt fear. Then excitement touched him as he realised what this meant. Devon's line had always carried the glory of their shared ancestor, but now it was Devon who stood on the wrong side of history. If he fought the Knights now, his legend would forever be stained. He would become the Traitor.

And if Ikar was the one to slay him…

"Finally, I know what the Saviour intends for me," he said, a grim smile touching his cheeks. "I too am descended from Alan the Great. I look forward to meeting my long-lost cousin. But if he stands against the Order, I shall meet him with weapon in hand."

As though summoned by his words, the pounding of hooves came from the road behind them. Spinning around, Ikar grabbed Kryssa by the arm and pulled her close as a horseman came into view. But after a second he relaxed, recognising the amour of the Order, though the rider wore no helmet.

A few minutes later Putar rode up, pale-faced and sweating. His horse gasped and coughed, its eyes rolling in its skull, as though it had galloped all the way from Townirwin. Ikar frowned as the Elder practically tumbled from the saddle.

"Thank the Saviour!" he gasped, grasping at Ikar's chest. "We feared they might have already caught you."

"Who?" Ikar frowned, struggling to hold Putar upright. The man's blubbering was unbecoming of an Elder at any time, let alone in front of a non-believer.

Putar seemed to realise this as well, and straightened. A frown touched his brow as he looked around. "Where are your horses."

"Lost," Ikar said. "The woman…is devious."

"Yes, and her family is hateful. Merak is dead, the Castle in chaos. The Consort wants his daughter back."

Kryssa threw back her head and laughed. "Told you," she smirked, before continuing in a wistful tone, "Though… I am not his daughter."

"And what is the will of the Elders?" Ikar growled, flashing a scowl at the woman.

"This news changes everything." Ikar shuddered, but after a moment, he drew himself up. "The Great Sacrifice cannot be disrupted, there is too much at stake. The power is needed. The woman has been chosen, and must be brought with all haste before her destiny."

"And where in the Three Nations would *that* be?" Kryssa asked, her voice like acid.

❧ 22 ❧

Devon sat at the bar, fist clenched around the iron tankard, and stared into the amber ale. His vision swirled, made fuzzy by the strong drink the bartender had served him through the night. The others had retired long ago, but Devon remained, sitting through the night in silent vigil. Now, finally, sunlight had begun to seep through the shutters, burning at his swollen eyes.

All of him ached, his bones, his joints, his every muscle. Death had been a constant presence for most of his life, always close—but now he felt as though he had one foot in the grave. The prodigious strength he'd once relied on was failing, now, when he needed it the most.

He closed his eyes and his head swam. Devon cursed himself for a fool. If not for Caledan's quick thinking, he and everyone else in the tavern would have been killed. Drowned by loss and caught in the grips of an awesome rage, he hadn't cared, but now he saw the futility.

She's still alive.

A groan rattled up from his chest and he slammed a fist into the bar top.

"Enough of that, my friend," the bartender remarked, appearing from the kitchen. "You're lucky I didn't throw the lot of you out last night after that hubbub with the Knights."

"Fortunate my gold speaks louder than your conscience," Devon snapped.

The man had wanted them gone, though the storm had been raging outside and many of the former prisoners were in poor conditions. Another gold libra from Devon's purse had bought them peace for the night, though it was an exorbitant price for such accommodations.

"True that," the innkeeper replied easily. He obviously had no qualms about the deal. "Speaking of which, you want to break your fast?"

Devon's stomach swirled, but he knew the food would do him good. "One minute."

Rising from the stool, he staggered outside to the water trough where the horses drank. He fell to his knees beside it and plunged his head into the icy water. Gasping and spluttering, he stood and returned to his seat. The icy wakeup cleared his head somewhat, but it did nothing for the despair.

"I'll take some sausage and eggs," he rumbled, still dripping water.

The innkeeper nodded and vanished into the kitchen. Devon laid his hands on the bar top and rested his head in his arms. There was a pounding in his forehead and he still wasn't sure he'd be able to stomach food, but at least it might help with the hangover.

"Devon?"

Devon lifted his head as a tentative voice came from

behind him. He was surprised to find Tobias and his wife Marce standing across from him with sheepish looks on their faces.

"What is it, Tobias?" Devon asked.

Tobias cleared his throat, glancing at Marce as though for reassurance, before the words tumbled from him in a rush. "I'm going back to Skystead," he said quickly. "We… ah, I'm sorry about Kryssa, Devon. I'll never forget what you did for us, but…I'm only a farmer. I can't go on with you. I'm taking Marce back to the *Seadragon*. She's setting sail in an hour for Skystead. I'm sorry."

An awful weariness rose within Devon as he stared at the farmer. Finally he nodded. Without saying a word he turned away and reached for his mug. Realising it was empty, he cursed and bellowed for the innkeeper.

"Sorry, Devon." Tobias repeated, sadness in his voice. Footsteps followed as the couple departed.

Scrunching his eyes closed, Devon fought back the urge to scream at the man, to name him a coward. Tobias was right; he was out of his depth here. Devon could not expect him, or anyone else from Skystead, to continue. After suffering so much loss, they deserved to hold their loved ones tight, to return to their homes in peace.

How he longed to do the same, to return to Skystead and live out the last of his days in the quiet of the fiords. But how could he give up now, when Kryssa was still out there? How could he rest, so long as the Knights had her?

Yet he did not know where they had taken her. There was just one main road out of Townirwin, but the Knights could have taken any of a dozen smaller trails, or even set sail again on the southern seas. There was no telling where they would go now. It would take precious time to discover their path, and every moment Devon wasted, Kryssa drew further away.

And the solstice drew closer.

One by one, he watched as the villagers filed out of the inn. They all stopped to thank him, for risking his life to see them safely home, but not one offered to continue. In the end, when the last had disappeared through the double doors, Devon slumped in his stool and fought to keep himself from crumbling.

"Good morning," Pela announced cheerfully, appearing from the corridor leading to the rooms upstairs. Wandering across the tavern, she frowned. "You look awful."

Devon scowled, but before he could reply, the innkeeper reappeared with his plate of sausages and eggs. He replaced Devon's empty mug of ale with coffee, then took Pela's order and returned to the kitchen. Contemplating the plate, Devon breathed in the scent of fresh herbs in the sausages and pepper on the eggs, and fought the urge to throw up. Instead, he picked up his knife and fork and began to eat.

"So what's the plan?" Pela asked, drumming her fingers on the wooden bench.

Her eyes were alight. Devon could understand her excitement—last night they'd thought her mother was dead. Discovering she was still alive had restored Pela's hope. If only Devon could find the same strength of spirit.

"I don't know," he grunted, not wanting to have the conversation but knowing Pela would persist until he answered. "They could have taken Kryssa anywhere."

"Caledan already left for the marketplace, to ask around," Pela replied easily. "He says we should be gone by noon, before the Order changes its mind."

There was an expectation in her eyes as she watched him. Devon knew that look. She believed he could do anything, defeat anyone that stood in their way. His aches redoubled as he closed his eyes.

"What does it matter, girl?" he snapped. "Look around! The others are all gone. They've abandoned us. We're all alone now. How do you hope to get your mother away from the Knights, with just the three of us?"

"Four," Genevieve said quietly, emerging from the corridor and joining them at the bar. "And we don't need the others."

"Yes!" Pela added. "We just need courage! Like Enala and Eric when they stood against Archon."

Devon snorted. "Don't believe everything you hear, girl," he roared. "I met them both; they had far more than just courage on their side. They were the most powerful Magickers of a generation."

"It doesn't matter!" Pela insisted. "You saw what those people were doing in the Castle. They're monsters, someone has to stop them!"

Ay, Devon thought wearily, *but why does it have to be me?*

Out loud, he only grunted: "Maybe."

"Please, Devon," Pela whispered, and for a second he saw a flash of terror behind her eyes. "I can't do this without you. You're a hero."

Devon smiled despite himself. "I've never been a hero, little one," he murmured. "And last night, you were the hero. You saved us all."

His niece looked away. "I...I froze though—I could barely move. I don't even know how I...killed him." She swallowed at the final words.

"You did more than anyone could have expected," Devon said gently, placing a hand on her shoulder.

"Please, Devon," Pela murmured, "We need you."

He sighed. "I know," he said. "I just hope…that I don't let you down."

Pela grinned. "You could never let me down, Uncle."

At that moment the innkeeper emerged with a plate of beans in sauce and eggs, along with several pieces of toasted bread. Pela dug into the food without another word. Devon made a half-hearted effort to finish his own plate. In his mind, he sent up a silent prayer to the long-dead Gods that she was right.

＊ 23 ＊

Braidon groaned as sunlight filtered in through the windows of the cabin, dragging him from the depths of sleep. Squeezing his eyes tightly shut he rolled over and reached for Marianne, only to discover the sheets empty. He groaned again; it must be later than he thought if his wife had already risen.

The ship rocked gently back and forth as he sat up. The cabin was empty but he could hear the sounds of the crew overhead as they moved about the deck, readying the oars to continue their passage upriver. Idly, Braidon wondered if it wouldn't be better to turn back—after all, there was a reason ships rarely sailed through the lower reaches of the Lane.

But a storm had come over them in the night, and the river delta had been the only safe birth they could reach before it broke. With the summer upon them, rain was scarce but for the great storms that came rolling in from the southern ocean, and it hadn't been long before Braidon had been thanking the dead Gods for the safety of the Lane.

Of course, he hadn't been so foolish as to thank them out loud. In their eight years of marriage, he had rarely had cause to argue with his wife, but the Three Gods and the Order of Alana had often been points of dispute. It was a strange thing, to be arguing about his sister and her relationship with the Gods, thirty years after her death.

In the end, Braidon had granted the Knights some influence in far-flung settlements of Plorsea on Marianne's urging. It had been a canny solution to the nation's struggles. The Knights had brought peace and order to many towns, without costing the crown a copper austral. Though he was loathe to admit it to his wife.

Chuckling, he threw off the duvet and dressed himself. What would his sister think if she could see him now? As a youth, he could never have imagined the title of king would entail so much tedious administration. Anything that broke the monotony was a welcome distraction.

He was not excited about returning to Ardath, and if the captain successfully negotiated the delta, they would arrive several days ahead of schedule. The thought filled Braidon with a longing to abandon his crown and flee. In his worst moments, he found himself dreaming of the old days, when he had travelled with Devon and Alana and Kellian—though they had been dangerous times, with his father hunting them.

Perhaps his life would seem less monotonous, if anything he did actually made a difference. Yet no matter how long he spent in negotiations or how hard he worked, Plorsea continued its slow slide into poverty.

Braidon shielded his eyes as he opened the door of their cabin and stepped out into the sunlight. Sailors raced to and fro across the deck of the galley, trimming sails and slotting oars into place in preparation to set off. With the shallow sandbars dotting the delta, the going would be slow the first few leagues, and a watch would need to be kept, ensuring they did not run aground.

The King's Guards standing outside the cabin saluted as Braidon emerged, but he gestured them to stand down. They grinned. Rylle and Salver were old hands and had served with him in the civil war; they were practically family, and knew well such formalities annoyed him.

"Where is my wife?" he asked a little sharply.

His head ached and he wondered what time he'd gotten to sleep the night before. The storm had raged long through the night, and while the river had sheltered them from much of its wrath, it had not stopped the ship from rocking wildly with each gust.

"At the stern, sir," Rylle replied.

They followed him as he crossed to the stairs and climbed to the upper deck. There the captain stood at the tiller, his eyes on the bow where a man stood with rope and anchor. As they drifted, the man tossed the anchor overboard, letting the rope run between his fingers, before quickly dragging it back up. Beside him, a second man waved a red flag, and the captain adjusted their heading, presumably to avoid a shallow patch.

Braidon found his wife at the stern staring back the way they'd come. She had a distant look about her, but as he approached she turned and smiled.

"My husband," she said, stepping forward and embracing him. "Finally awake, I see."

She lifted her face and he bent to kiss her. "You should have woken me," he replied as they broke apart. A grin touched his lips as he held her close. "I would have enjoyed your company."

Marianne smiled but did not reply. Turning, she leaned

against the railings again. "The storm has broken," she said. "The captain says we'll reach Lane by nightfall."

"That's…excellent," Braidon replied with a sigh.

His wife laughed. "You almost sound sincere."

"I tried." A smile broke across Braidon's face. "Though it will be good to see Calybe again."

Calybe was their son. He was only five, too young for such a journey. Marianne had wanted to bring him, to show him the city she'd grown up in, but with the uneasy tensions with Lonia and the growing presence of Baronians, Braidon had refused.

A distant look came over his wife's face again. Frowning, he stepped up and placed an arm around her waist. "Are you okay?"

Marianne nodded. "I'm okay, only…I will miss him." Her voice cracked, and Braidon was surprised to see tears in her eyes. "I would have liked to have been there, at the end."

"I know," Braidon murmured, squeezing her shoulder. "And I'm sorry we didn't bring Calybe. Things will be better soon. Next year, we'll take him down the Jurrien. The last of the dark forest should have been burnt from Sitton by then. It'll be safe."

"Will it?" There was an edge to his wife's voice now. "Or will a new threat conspire to keep us at home?"

Braidon raised his eyebrows, but a shout from the helm drew his attention back to the captain. The man was gesturing wildly at them—no, *behind them*. Spinning, Braidon looked out over the waters of the Lane. They were a murky brown here, impenetrable but for the strange pink dolphins that were sometimes seen in the deeper channels. Islands of mud and mangroves split the river into a multitude of channels; a ship could get lost under the command of a lesser skipper.

But it was not their course that upset the captain. He was pointing behind them, directly off the stern, and Braidon felt a tingle of fear as he saw the sails of a ship emerge from a nearby channel. Trumpets sounded from the lower deck as it turned to follow them. A black flag flew from its mast.

Baronians.

Braidon cursed. What was a pirate ship doing in these waters? They must have taken refuge during the storm as well, and thought they'd stumbled upon easy pickings. His hand dropped to the sword on his belt, but after a second he released it again. There were civilians onboard, accountants and negotiators who had joined him to speak with the Lonian council. Not to mention Marianne.

No, best they outrun the Baronian scum. The barbarians had no oars, not even a sail out; they couldn't hope to catch the king's galley. He would send a squadron to hunt them down once they reached Lane.

"Outrun them, Captain!" he shouted, joining the man at the tiller.

"At the oars!" the man bellowed. "Count of three!"

"Marianne, get below." Braidon said urgently, then: "Where are your guards?"

"I'll find them." She darted down the stairs to the main deck.

Braidon was relieved to see several of the Queen's Guard waiting for her at the bottom. He followed them as they made a beeline through the chaos below and disappeared into their quarters. Only then did he turn his attention back to the Baronian ship. A frown touched his forehead.

"Captain, they're gaining. What are you doing?"

The captain glanced back at the chasing ship, a panicked look on his face. "I've no idea, Your Highness," he gasped. He bellowed down to the oarsmen below. "Double count!"

Striding to the stern railing, Braidon watched the oncoming vessel. Now he noticed the smoke hanging about the vessel, heard the distant clanging of steel. It surged upstream—despite the currents—as though propelled by some unseen source. He shivered. What magic was this?

"Sir?"

The King's Guard were forming up behind him. He had twenty of his own men aboard, plus ten of the queen's, but he trusted them not to leave her side. Against them, a horde of men and woman stood atop the decks of the enemy ship. They were armed with axes and short swords for the most part, though many were spotted with rust.

Braidon's heart quickened as he realised it would come to a fight. They were badly outnumbered, but he had seen Baronians fight before—they were brave warriors, yet undisciplined and poorly trained. He was confident the King's Guard would see them off.

"Captain, bring us around!" he shouted. There was no point risking running aground when they could not hope to escape. "Let's show these scum some Plorsean steel!"

Braidon was touched by a sense of deja vu as the ship swung out into the current. Decades had passed since he'd fought alongside Devon. Yet as they raced down the river, Braidon found himself recalling the day a Baronian tribe had hailed the hammerman their leader. That had been before the Gods had died with his…sister, when magic still flowed through Braidon's veins. He'd used that power to create an illusion, to make Devon seem some giant sent by the Gods themselves.

It was strange, how illusion became truth in the eyes of men. The hammerman was spoken of with reverence now, Devon himself almost a myth to those who had come later. Standing at the rails, Braidon's mind wandered to the old warrior. He hoped Devon had finally found peace in Skystead. The man had never been the same after Alana's death. Braidon guessed they had that much in common.

The shouts and taunting of the Baronians carried to Braidon's ears as the gap between the vessels narrowed. Then a sharp *crack* came from the other ship, and a line arched across the waters and slammed down into the galley. Another followed before the first could be cut loose. The ship lurched beneath Braidon's feet as the lines snapped tight.

Then the ships were side by side and the Baronians were leaping to the railings of the galley. Bellowing a war cry, Braidon met them with steel in hand. The King's Guard raced after him, and the screams of the dying engulfed the royal ship. Braidon's sword rose and fell, striking down the poorly-armed warriors left and right, but there were more than enough to replace them, and the black tide continued unabated.

A giant of a man leapt forward, his axe sweeping down. Braidon spun to the side and the axe buried itself in the wooden railing. Driving his sword up, Braidon sought to impale the Baronian, but the black-garbed warrior released his axe and threw himself back, and the king's blow went wide. Before Braidon could swing again, his foe snatched up the axe and dragged it free.

Across the ship, the Baronians attacked with a berserker rage that surprised even Braidon. His men met them with tightly controlled fury, enraged that these savages dared challenge their strength. The red and gold of the King's Guard was an honour reserved for only the bravest soldiers, and not one of them gave an inch. But the black-garbed warriors were taking their toll, and bit by bit the Guard was forced back by the greater weight of numbers.

Braidon cursed as the axeman came at him again. This time his foe slipped in the blood that ran thick beneath their feet, and the king dispatched him with a thrust to the groin. The axeman staggered back, his eyes showing fear, and collapsed against the railing. A great *crack* came from the wood as it gave way beneath his weight and the damage dealt by the axe. He disappeared over the side, followed by a great splash as he struck the water.

Steel rang out behind Braidon, and he spun in time to see a massive Baronian almost decapitate one of his guards with a swing of a broadsword. Ice spread through Braidon's veins as the man turned and saw him standing there. The Baronian had cut a path of blood through Braidon's men and now he stood alone, the rest of his Guard pushed back by the tide of black-garbed warriors.

He glanced to the right, where his men still held strong. Beyond, the Queen's Guard stood in a ring around their cabin, and he breathed a sigh of relief that at least his wife was safe. Spinning to face the giant, he retreated slowly towards his Guard, aware that to turn his back on such a man would mean certain death.

Roaring, the giant swung his blade in an arc that would have cut Braidon in two—had he not thrown himself to the floor. A great *thud* rang out as the blade struck the railing, sending another piece tumbling into the river. Braidon staggered to his feet and stabbed out clumsily with his blade, but the Baronian swatted the blow aside.

Off-balance, Braidon drove his shoulder into the giant's midriff. A groan came from the giant and they toppled backwards. Braidon threw out an arm to catch the railing…

…but the railing was not there. He cried out as he found himself falling. His arms windmilled, searching for anything that might break his fall, but there was only empty air. He twisted in time to see the river come racing up to meet him, and with a great splash, he vanished beneath the swirling currents of the Lane.

On the banks, alerted by the screams of the dying and the scent of blood on the air, the crocodiles went sliding into the water…

❧ 24 ❧

Pela and her companions reached Lane late in the afternoon, two days after setting out from Townirwin. By then the city was alive with the news, and even with sunset approaching, the streets were clogged with people and wagons.

King Braidon was dead and no one knew what that meant. What would become of Plorsea now? With the king's son not even passed his fifth birthday, who would lead their armies, who would keep them safe? And what of Lonia? Would their war-faring neighbour turn its sights south?

Tens of thousands inhabited Lane, for it sat on one of the main trading routes through Plorsea. But if war came, the city would be one of the first to fall, for its walls were in disrepair and most of its buildings constructed of wood. Many stood five or six stories tall; a fire within the city would be terrible to behold.

Struggling through the crowds, Pela and the others tried to make sense of the news. Some claimed the king had been slain by rogue Lonians, others that it had been the Baronians, and still more that a great storm had swept his ship to the bottom of the ocean, that his sister had reclaimed his soul, or he had somehow suffered the wrath of the Three Gods.

The only thing for certain was that Braidon was gone, and the world had forever changed.

Devon led the way through the twisting streets. He had denied the news at first, but as it was repeated by each passing stranger, his face had darkened and he'd picked up his pace. It was even worse for Caledan. Pela knew of his agreement with Devon—that her uncle was to give him an audience with the king—but no one knew what he'd wanted from the man. Now he walked with shoulders slumped and eyes fixed straight ahead, as though he no longer had a purpose in the world.

Pela didn't know where Devon was taking them, but within a few blocks she was lost. The buildings here were far larger than in Skystead or even Townirwin, and the streets were unpaved. Rainwater pooled in the grooves left by the passage of wagons through the mud, and the stench of sewage wafted from nearby alleyways.

Pela could not have imagined a fouler place. Townirwin had been chaotic, but at least the canals had flushed away the occupants' waste with each outgoing tide. Turning to Caledan, she tried to draw him out of his stupor, to bring life back to the sellsword.

"Why would they create such massive buildings from wood?" she asked.

The sellsword did not so much as glance in her direction, though she was sure he'd heard her. She swallowed, preparing to try again, but Genevieve answered in his stead.

"Lane was never meant to grow so large," she said.

"Once, Sitton was the main hub for trade between Lonia and Plorsea. But it was destroyed during Archon's second coming, and eventually turned back to forest. Even then, the Jurrien River was still used to ferry goods. Then the Gods fell, and the dark creatures within Sitton Forest revealed themselves. Now none pass that way. The Lane River became the new trade route, turning Lane from quiet back-water to bustling city."

"But why didn't they at least build in stone?"

Genevieve shrugged, gesturing into the darkness ahead. "Beyond the banks of the Lane lies the Forest of Plorsea. Though much diminished now, the forest supplied the orig-inal timber for the city. Those who came after have only added to them, building upon what the founders left. And so they rise, up and up, until their weight grows too great for the foundations."

A shiver ran down Pela's spine as she looked at the wooden structures. Many were lopsided, leaning against their neighbours as though the merest breeze might knock them down. She swallowed as the wind went howling down the street. She could have sworn some of the buildings began to sway.

"How can he be dead?" Caledan snarled so suddenly that Pela jumped. The sellsword's face was like thunder and he looked ready to lay into the first person that crossed him. "*How?*"

"We're about to find out," Devon muttered.

The hammerman had come to a stop in front of one of the few stone buildings in the city. Built of worn red sand-stone, it rose only two storeys from the muddy street, and was separated from its neighbours by an alley on either side. Bars protected the windows facing the road and two men stood guard outside its door, watching them with undisguised suspicion.

"Hey!" one shouted as Devon approached. He hefted a spear and pointed it at Devon's chest. "Stay back!"

Coming to an abrupt halt, Devon lifted his hands in a gesture of peace. "Easy," he said, "we're friends, boys."

"We're rather short of those tonight," the second man growled. He stepped towards them and gestured with his spear. "Why don't you get out of here, ruffians?"

Devon's face darkened. "I've come a long way," he rumbled, "and I'm in no mood for a fight."

"Then you'd better piss off, hadn't you?" the guard snapped.

Lowering his hands, Devon fixed the guard with a glare. Almost unwittingly, the man retreated a step. Devon advanced on him, and he fumbled with the spear, trying to bring it around.

"Easy, sonny," Devon murmured. "I do not lie, I am…*was* a friend of the King." He placed a hand on the guard's shoulder and nodded to the door. "Whoever's left of the King's Guard, tell them Devon is at the door."

The guard hesitated, glancing at his comrade in askance. Then, his courage seemed to snap, and almost dropping his spear, he darted to the door and disappeared inside.

Devon grinned at the second guard. "New recruit?"

The man glared back at him, spear still held at the ready. "Your story better check out, old man."

Devon lifted one grey-streaked eyebrow. "There's no need for compliments. Don't see me calling you a piss-riddled biscuit, now do ya?"

"What did you say to me?" the guard grated, his face turning a mottled-red. "I'll—"

"Devon!" A voice shouted as the door opened with a crash. The guard swung around at the interruption, but the speaker was already advancing through the mud, a weary grin on his face. He wore the familiar uniform of the King's Guard. "Didn't think we'd ever see you again in these parts!"

Pela breathed a sigh of relief as the men embraced. The second guard retreated to his post without a word. His face still showed rage, but it was impotent now. Laughing, the King's Guard took a step back and appraised Devon, before turning his eyes to Pela and the others.

"You've brought quite the company, old friend," he said, his voice losing some of its shine. He looked back at Devon. "You've arrived at a bad time."

"So I hear, Rylle," he replied, grimly.

Rylle nodded. "You'd better come inside."

They bundled inside and a third guard slammed and bolted the door behind them. Though it was still light outside, it was dark within. Rylle ushered the group down the corridor. Silence permeated the house as they filed through the building, though Pela sensed there were unseen eyes watching them.

Rylle led them down several corridors, before they suddenly found themselves back outside. Several lanterns had already been lit, casting light over a courtyard stacked with crates and sacks of cloth. Taking one from its bracket, Rylle continued until the lanternlight caught on water.

Pela blinked as she came to a stop beside Devon. It took several seconds for her to understand what she was seeing. Amidst the tall buildings, she hadn't noticed how close their journey through the city had brought them to the river, but the villa had been built right on the banks of the Lane. The courtyard led right out onto its own private jetty.

There was only one ship at the docks, though it was larger than any Pela had ever seen. With a raised fore and aft deck and twin masks, it was four times the size of the little fishing vessel that had brought them from Skystead. A dozen men stood watch onboard and spaced along the jetty.

"So it did not sink," Devon murmured, looking from the ship to Rylle. "What happened?"

"Baronians," Rylle replied. "They came upon us in the delta of the Lane. At first we thought to outrun them, but they had some magic that propelled them through the current without need of sails or oars. We fought them off, eventually, but the king was dragged overboard by one of the thugs."

"Then he could have survived?"

"The water was infested with crocs," Rylle replied, his voice thick. "Nobody that went in came out alive, though we looked for him."

Pela's stomach tightened as she remembered the Baronians that had attacked the *Seadragon*. Surely it couldn't have been the same crew, and yet…

"Devon…" she started, but her uncle waved a hand.

"I know," he said, slumping onto one of the barrels strewn around the courtyard. He pressed a hand to his forehead. "I know."

"Devon?" Rylle said, his voice raising an octave. "What do you know?"

"The Baronians were led by a man called Julian," her uncle whispered. "They set upon us a week ago, but I knew him from my days serving beneath the Tsar. He spared us. I…I should have put an end to him then and there…"

Rylle sat down hard beside him. "You could not have known," he croaked. "It was we who failed him, myself and the rest of the Guard. Braidon relied on us to protect him. In all these years…"

"What of the queen, and his son?" Devon croaked. "Did the boy…?"

"They're safe," Rylle replied quickly. "The queen was aboard, but her guard kept the Baronians from her. Once we fought them off and freed the ship, we made for Lane with all haste."

"Thank the Gods."

Rylle flinched. "Don't let the queen hear you speaking of such things," he murmured. "She's in no mood for blasphemy."

"Since when did it become blasphemy to speak of the Three Gods?" Devon replied, his voice hardening. He rose from his seat. "Though that is what brought us here."

"What has happened?" Rylle did not move. His face suggested he could guess what was coming.

"The Knights of Alana sacked the old temple above Skystead," Devon began.

"That's not so bad—" Rylle tried to say, but Devon cut him off.

"They killed several of the villagers they found there and took the rest hostage. We followed them to Townirwin and freed most of them, though Aldyn lost his life in the effort. But…they brought Kryssa here, for some Great Sacrifice they have planned for the solstice."

"Oh…" Rylle whispered, his face losing its colour. "Devon, I'm…" he trailed off, and sat staring up at Devon, as though waiting to hear it was all some joke. Finally his eyes slid closed and he wavered in place.

"*Gods!*" He said the word like a curse. "I warned Braidon not to trust them."

"We must act quickly," Devon continued, "before they realise I'm here. If they find out, Kryssa—"

"They're already gone," Rylle said.

Pela's heart lurched in her chest. "*What?*" she croaked.

The King's Guard frowned at Pela, before his eyes darted back to her uncle. "I'm sorry, Devon. I know how much Kryssa meant to you. But you're too late, the Order and their Knights are already gone."

"What do you mean, 'gone'?" Devon growled.

"Whatever this ceremony of theirs is, they're not holding it in Lane. The entire Castle is empty—the Knights and their followers all set off into the Forest this morning. From what I've heard, it's the same all over Plorsea."

No, no, no. Pela shook her head.

This couldn't be happening, not again. Every time they got close, her mother slipped through their fingers. The solstice was less than a week away now. Heart in her throat, she looked at Devon.

"We need to go after them," Devon said quickly. "How many of the King's Guard can you spare?"

"None," Rylle replied. He looked up at Devon, his eyes hollow. "The King's Guard leave at first light."

"*Leave?*" Devon yelled.

"The rest of the Guard is already on its way from Ardath," Rylle continued. "Birds were sent as soon as we made port. We're going to track down the Baronian who killed the king, and make them pay."

Fists clenched, Devon stood towering over Rylle. For a moment, it seemed he would grab the man and shake him, but in the end he only shook his head. "Rylle, I loved him as much as you," he whispered, "but he's gone, and killing a few Baronians won't bring him back. But there's a chance we can still save Kryssa."

"That's not my decision to make, Devon."

"Then whose is it?" Devon bellowed.

"It's mine, Devon," a woman spoke from behind them.

Pela spun towards the voice. Her sapphire eyes alive with grief, a woman threaded her way through the court-yard towards them. A rapier hung from her belt, though she was even shorter than Pela and of a lighter build. She wore a silken dress, all black, its edges seeming to merge with the growing dark, and her auburn hair was tied back at the nape.

A sinking feeling weighed on Pela's stomach as she realised who the woman was, though Devon asked the question all the same:

"And who might you be, missy?"

"The queen," Marianne replied. "It is so good to finally meet you, Devon."

❧ 25 ❧

Devon sat in the dark, staring into the flickering light of a single candle. Pain was his constant companion now, an ache that started in his shoulder and radiated through his entire body. He still had not recovered from the battle in the Castle, and he found himself yearning for the old days, when he could fight all day and drink all night, then get up and do it all again the next day.

A smile touched his lips. Maybe it had never been that easy. But he was damned sure he'd never ached for three days straight after a fight.

A *bang* came from the door of the quarters the queen had offered them. He looked up as Caledan staggered inside. Crossing the room, the sellsword smiled down at him —then stumbled sideways into the table. His hands slammed onto the tabletop as he tried to steady himself, almost knocking the candle from its stand. Finally he managed to slump into the chair across from Devon.

Devon smelt spirits on the sellsword's breath as he laid his head on the table.

"All this time," Caledan muttered into the wood, slurring his words. "All these years, for nothin'!"

"I'm sorry," Devon grunted. "Don't know what you wanted from the king, but…" He trailed off as the warrior looked up suddenly.

Squinting, Caledan narrowed his eyes. "It's typical, life." His head bobbed up and down. "Should have known better. Learnt nothing all these years. Typical!"

Devon watched as the man put his head back on the table. He'd seen Caledan drink a time or two, but had never seen him even tipsy—let alone drunk to the point of falling down. Caledan was normally so controlled, calm even in the heat of battle. Whatever he'd needed from the king, it must have been important.

"What did you want from him?" Devon asked softly. "I swear, if it is within my power…"

"I don't think so!" Caledan chuckled.

Sitting up suddenly, he jerked back in the chair, his head lolling. He leered at Devon, then reached into his coat and drew out a flask. Devon cursed and tried to snatch it from his hands, but the warrior still managed to take a swig before he could take it.

Devon returned to his chair as the sellsword cackled again. "Good stuff, that."

A sniff of the flask confirmed his words. Devon's eyes watered as he found himself staring at the candle again. Silently, he wondered what Selina would think of him now. It seemed everything in his life had fallen apart after her death. He'd fought with Kryssa not long after the funeral; though he couldn't remember over what now. It hadn't been important—Kryssa had never forgiven Devon for his part in her husband's death. She'd only been looking for an excuse to cut him from her life.

That had stung, but Devon could accept it, so long as Kryssa and her daughter were safe. But then Pela had come running into his courtyard, upheaving his world yet again. And now Braidon was dead, and it seemed no matter what Devon did, things would never be right again.

The queen had listened in silence to their story, but not even Pela's pleas could move the woman from her course. She would sail south with the king's fleet in the morning, five ships to scour the River Lane and the southern coast until they found Julian and his Baronians. They were welcome to join the hunt, but Marianne would not spare any soldiers until the king's killers were brought to justice.

So Devon would be left to search the Forest of Plorsea alone. A forest teeming with Knights who wanted him dead. The task would be the death of him, and yet he had to try. But he would not bring Pela with him, not this time, when death was almost certain. He would send her back with the queen in the morning. She might hate him forever, but at least Pela would be safe with the King's Guard.

Remembering his friend brought Devon full circle, and he raised the flask. "To the king," he said, and drank.

The liquor burned its way down his throat and he had to choke back a cough.

"To the king!" Caledan bellowed, raising an invisible glass. "May the miserable bastard rot at the bottom of the river!"

Devon frowned at the sellsword. "You never did say what you wanted from Braidon," he said quietly.

"I wanted to watch the light fade from his eyes," Caledan hiccupped. "For him to die by my sword. But the bastard Baronians beat me to it."

For a full ten seconds, Devon sat staring at the man.

Blood throbbed in his temples as he rose to his feet, fists clenched hard against the table.

"Ruined my life, you see," Caledan continued, unaware of Devon's rage in his drunken state. "Destroyed our family. Or at least, his sister did. Just had to die, and take the Gods with her, didn't she? The Gods and their bastard magic."

Now it was the sellsword who sat staring into the candlelight. Devon slumped back into his chair, the anger falling from him like water over stone.

"My father borrowed every shilling he could to pay for the healer, but when the man's magic failed, he fled," Caledan continued. "I can barely remember her face now. I *wish* I couldn't remember my father's. Bastard drank himself into a stupor for most of my childhood." His eyes flickered up, though he didn't seem to see Devon. "That's why I wanted it to be *me*. I wanted him to suffer like I suffered. I wanted the *witch* to know."

Sitting there in silence, Devon wondered how he could have been so blind. Madness shone from the sellsword's eyes, borne of the pain he had suffered as a youth, of the hatred that had driven him for all his adult life. It made little sense, the blame he placed at Braidon's feet, but who else could a child blame but the king?

"It wasn't Braidon's fault, you know," Devon murmured, though he sensed it was hopeless to argue.

Caledan cackled. "Oh I know." Now his voice took on a steely tone. "But an eye for an eye, as the Knights say, and nothing cuts quite so close as family."

A chill raised the hackles on Devon's neck.

"I wanted *her* family to suffer, as mine suffered," Caledan spat bitterly. "To die, knowing it was justice."

"Braidon was a good man," Devon said. "What would murdering him have achieved?"

"Why should her family get to live," Caledan roared, coming to his feet, "when mine is all gone?" He finished, his words a misery.

"And what about Plorsea?" Devon asked, mustering all the calm he could manage. "You've seen what his death has brought, the chaos. Is this what you wanted, for the sake of revenge?"

"What do I care for Plorsea?" Caledan retorted. Anger seemed to have sobered him somewhat. "What has *Plorsea* ever done for me? The only person you can rely on in this life is yourself, hammerman. Or haven't you figured that out yet?"

Devon laughed. "Quite the opposite. I wouldn't be here if I'd stood alone all these years." Faces flickered through his mind—Kellian and Merydith and Alana, and so many more now lost to him—and he continued in a softer voice. "I learned long ago that no matter how long I trained, or how hard I fought, there will always be someone better. Magic or no."

"There is *no one* better than me," Caledan hissed, drawing his sword and holding it aloft.

"Is that so?" Devon asked quietly. He rose and advanced on Caledan, until the sword pressed against his chest. His hammer lay at the foot of the table, but Devon had no need for it.

"What are you doing?" Caledan growled.

"I owe you a debt, don't I?" Devon murmured. "You helped me rescue the villagers. I could not have done it without you. If you wanted to hurt Alana, to hurt the ones she loved, you never needed to kill Braidon."

"What are you talking about, old man?" the sellsword slurred.

"Alana died to protect me," Devon whispered. "That is a

truth the Knights refuse to heed. She gave her life for mine. If you wish to hurt her, you only need kill me."

Caledan stared at him, his face contorting with agony. The tip of his sword trembled, and the razor-sharp blade sliced through Devon's tunic. Eyes wild, Caledan bared his teeth, an almost inhuman growl rumbling from his chest. Then he stepped back and pointed at Devon's hammer.

"Pick it up!" he shouted.

"No," Devon said, moving forward until the sword rested on his chest again. "I'll not fight you."

"Do it!" Caledan screamed. "Let us see who's the better fighter!"

"No," Devon rumbled, his voice echoing through the room. "If you want your revenge, *take it*!"

Caledan pressed down with his sword until blood began to flow. Devon said nothing, only stared at the sellsword, waiting to see what he would do. The strong spirits burned in his stomach and he had no idea why he'd challenged the young warrior. It was madness, and any second now he expected Caledan to skewer him.

What then for Kryssa? There would be no one left to rescue her from the Knights, no one to free her from their clutches. He could not afford to die here, so why had he handed his life over to a madman? Fists clenched, he waited for Caledan to strike the killing blow.

But with an awful scream, Caledan spun and hurled his sword away. Sparks flashed as it struck the bricks of the fireplace. He stumbled away from Devon and crumpled onto the sofa lying in the corner.

Standing by the table, Devon watched him for a long time, until the soft whisper of his snores filled the room and he was sure the swordsman was asleep. Then he retrieved Caledan's sword and returned it to its scabbard.

After a moment's hesitation, he leaned the sword against the sofa.

He hesitated again before departing for his own bed, staring down at the sellsword. The man had had his chance for revenge. Devon could not understand why he'd refused to take it, but he was relieved. Despite his aging body, he'd realised in that moment he was still needed. He could not allow despair to conquer him now, not so long as he still breathed. Only when he lay cold in his grave would he finally rest.

———

The next morning, Devon was woken by a groan and a curse. He looked up to see Caledan stagger into the room. For half a second his heart began to race…and then he recalled he was sharing the room with the sellsword. The man's eyes were red and his face pale; it looked like he was suffering. Stumbling past Devon, he made for his bed before apparently deciding better of it.

He reached the window just in time to hurl the contents of his stomach out into the street. Somewhere outside a voice shouted out, but Caledan was already sinking onto his bed.

"Don't think that'll help our relationship with the door guards," Devon remarked. "Better?"

Caledan shook his head. "I'm never drinking again."

"I've rarely seen a man in such a state."

Caledan shrugged. "The king is dead."

Devon eyed him closely, but the sellsword did not seem to recall the conversation from the night before.

"I suppose you'll be leaving us then?" he asked.

Caledan looked up. "Why?"

"The king is dead," Devon said, repeating the obvious.

"Yes…" the warrior trailed off, his face taking on a pained look. "But…the Knights still have Pela's mother."

"Ay, but I can't afford you," Devon said softly.

Caledan shrugged, his eyes distant. "It can't all have been for nothing," he murmured, almost to himself. Then he shook himself. "You can't rescue the woman without me."

"I'm not sure we can rescue her *with* you."

"Even so." Caledan gave a pained grin. "I have a reputation to uphold. I cannot go abandoning a quest half-done."

Devon eyed the man, remembering his rage the night before. Finally he sighed. "Very well." He glanced out the window. The first hint of light now lit the world. "We'll take the first ferry across the Lane. But first I need to talk with Pela. She won't be continuing with us."

"Good luck with that," Caledan remarked.

"I wish I'd never let her come this far," Devon murmured. "But it can't go on, not now, when so much is at stake."

"Did you have a plan for how to rescue the woman from a hundred of the bastards?" Caledan grunted.

"Ay," Devon replied. "I have a few ideas."

26

Caledan's head pounded with each step as he descended the stairwell and stepped out into the backyard of the villa. His stomach swirled and he wanted more than anything to return to his bed and sleep. Silently, he cursed his weakness of the night before, for letting grief sweep away his self-control. After watching his father drink himself to death, he rarely tasted anything stronger than ale.

But the king's death had shocked him, cutting him adrift. He had no purpose now, no dreams, nothing to aspire to. For so long, he'd dreamt of slaying the king. But always Braidon had been protected, surrounded by his Guard. Only the most loyal soldiers could join the King's Guard, and Caledan had never been the soldier type. He fought for himself—or whoever could pay the most.

So why had he agreed to continue with Devon's foolish quest? After all, his skills would be in high demand in the coming days, as vultures circled the flailing country. Nobles and merchants alike would offer good gold for his sword. Instead, he'd agreed to help a man who could pay nothing.

Yet his time as a sellsword had only ever been a means to an end. Now that that end no longer existed…what was the point? But neither could he simply retire. Sure, he had coin enough to buy a farm, but what joy would he find eking out an existence on the land? He was a warrior, and he would sooner lie down in a ditch by the Gods Road than surrender to such an existence.

So he would ride with Devon for now—at least until a better opportunity presented itself. Whatever he'd told Devon, he didn't intend to see out his quest until the end. Storming a Castle was one thing; only a madman with a death wish would go up against the full might of the Order.

Caledan grimaced as the clouds parted overhead and the sunlight lit the courtyard. Spotting Devon standing at the docks, he started towards him. The hammerman wore a grim smile, but it fell from his face when he turned and saw Caledan approaching. Their eyes met, and Caledan hesitated.

If you want your revenge, take it!

A frown touched Caledan's forehead. The words were spoken in Devon's voice, but he could not recall the old warrior saying them. Dismissing them, he crossed the court-yard to where the rest of the King's Guard were gathering.

Two dozen remained of the garrison in Lane, along with those men and women who'd survived the Baronian attack. All were garbed for war, their red and gold armour gleaming in the morning sun.

"Caledan!" Pela shouted behind him before he could join the Guard.

The young woman came storming across the courtyard, her face twisted in a fiery rage, and drew to a stop in front of him.

"You can't let him do this!"

Caledan sighed, the pain in his forehead redoubling. The crunch of footsteps saved him from answering as Devon appeared alongside him.

"This discussion is over, missy," Devon rumbled. "You're going back."

"No." Pela's sword flashed into her hand. She pointed it at Devon, her eyes shining. "You can't!"

Devon lifted a finger and moved the point of the sword away.

"I can," he said quietly, crouching beside her. "I told you at the start; I should never have brought you. In that forest, I can't protect you—"

"And who will protect *you*?" Pela snapped. "Or did you forget I saved you in Townirwin?"

"I did not forget," Devon murmured, crouching beside her, "and you have my thanks. But…"

"You don't think we can win, do you?" Pela croaked.

The hammerman closed his eyes and his head bowed. "I…I won't give up, Pela."

"You need me."

"Maybe we do," Devon whispered, and for a moment hope showed on Pela's face. "But Kryssa would not want you to trade your life for hers."

"I won't go," Pela grated. "I'll follow you."

"I know," Devon replied, coming to his feet. "That's why I told Rylle to look out for you. You'll be on the queen's ship, nowhere near the battle, should they find the Baronians. They'll take you home."

"You're passing me off to the King's Guard," Pela hissed.

"Yes," Devon sighed, and Rylle stepped up beside him.

"You can't—"

"I can," Devon cut her off. "You're going, Pela—if I have to chain you to the mast myself, you're going."

Pela's eyes darkened. "I'll never forgive you for this," she hissed, then turned on her heel and stomped down the pier to the queen's ship.

Genevieve appeared from the shadows at the edge of the courtyard. She raised an eyebrow at Devon, but the old warrior only shook his head. "It's for the best," he murmured, then looked at Rylle. "You'll look after her?"

"She's the daughter of Derryn and Kryssa," Rylle replied, as though that was all that needed to be said.

"Thank you," Devon said. His eyes flickered to Genevieve. "Are you sure you're up for this? Going against the whole Order is more than any of us bargained for back in Skystead."

Smiling, Genevieve stepped around the hammerman and crossed the courtyard to where a line of horses waited for them. She swung herself into the saddle of a white gelding and took up the reins of the pack horse.

"Let's get moving," she said shortly, "before we miss the ferry."

A smile flickered on Devon's face and he followed suit. Struggling to keep the last remnants of his supper in his stomach, Caledan hauled himself onto the last horse and followed his companions out the side gate of the villa. Glancing back, he caught a glimpse of Pela on the deck of the queen's ship. She stood with sword in hand, hacking and slashing at invisible enemies—or perhaps at Devon—and Caledan felt a touch of sadness at their departure.

Despite his initial reservations, he'd liked the girl. Terrified as she might have been, Pela had shown more courage over the last few weeks than many adults Caledan had known throughout his thirty-three years. But he supposed the old warrior was right—chances were, none of them would survive an encounter with the entire Order of Alana.

Which raised the question again: why was he following Devon on this suicide mission?

27

Pela shrieked as she lashed out with her sword, skewering an imaginary enemy and then spinning in time to deflect a second. A sharp hiss followed each swipe of the blade, her breath coming in short gasps. The deck of the ship rocked gently beneath her as the oars rose and fell, propelling them ever downriver.

She barely noticed. The queen's ship was crowded, but she had managed to find some space at the bow where she could practice the drills Caledan had taught her. Not that they mattered now. She cursed and speared an imaginary heart.

After everything they'd been through, how could Devon have done this? He needed her! Pela had not forgotten the despair in his eyes back in Townirwin, how close he had come to giving up on her mother. Now he had lost faith in himself; he was defeated before he'd even begun.

Shouting again, Pela brought her blade down in an overhead slash that would have beheaded anyone standing in her path, then stepped back and sucked in a breath.

What was she going to do? The queen was taking her back to Skystead, to the sleepy little town she had always called home. But what was left for her there now, without her mother or grandmother or Devon? How would she support herself?

Her eyes dropped to the sword in her hand and a shiver ran down her spine. He'd hid it well, but Caledan was no pauper. He had spent his life fighting other men's wars and grown rich doing it. Remembering the rush as her blade sliced through the Elder's back, Pela felt a tremor of excitement, but it was quickly doused by the icy hand of reality.

Most of her life had been spent in fear of one thing or another; how could she think that would change now? She could never be a sellsword, nor a soldier like her father. Her courage would fail. Maybe that was why Devon had sent her away. Had he seen her terror, and given her an escape?

I am not a coward.

Swallowing, Pela brushed a tear from her eye and clung to the thought. She had killed a man, had helped save her fellow villagers against all odds. And still Devon had packed her up and shipped her off as though she were a child in need of protection.

Angrily she sheathed her sword and moved to the railing. Four other ships carved their way downriver alongside them: the King's Guard that had come from Ardath. Men and women packed their decks, red and gold armour shining in the morning sun as they scanned the way ahead for a sign of the Baronians. The survivors of the attack had warned how the black ship had suddenly come upon them, as if out of nowhere. There would be no surprise attacks this time.

Only a few King's Guard remained onboard with Pela,

including Rylle. The rest wore the silver and red of the Queen's Guard, her personal order.

Pela had spent the first few hours exploring the vessel. But while it was the largest ship she'd ever seen, there was little of interest to discover. Only the catapult bolted to the aft deck had perked her interest, though it was covered by a canvas and did not look to have seen any use for a long while. Otherwise, there were the usual sacks of cloth and rope and barrels of whatever supplies the queen had seen fit to stock for the journey, and Pela had soon returned to her sword practice.

Sailing downriver with the oars pounding to the count of five, they were already nearing the delta of the Lane. Pela was glad she would at least be able to see the end of the vicious Baronians. Once the fleet reached open ocean, they would split in two and scour the coast. No matter what magic propelled the Baronian ship, they could not simply vanish.

"What are you doing up here, little one?"

Pela started and spun around, her eyes widening to find the queen standing behind her. Her mouth dropped open, before she remembered her manners and snapped it closed again, biting her tongue. She swore, then slapped a hand to her mouth in horror.

The queen only smiled and joined her at the railings. "I have never been to Skystead, though I hear it is beautiful," she commented. "Do you have those…beasts there?" She nodded to one of the great crocodiles basking on the banks of the Lane.

A shudder ran down Pela's spine. "Sometimes," she murmured, "but mostly the water is deep and too cold in the fiord. They only appear after a storm, when they've been washed from the marshes or the delta."

"They killed my husband," the queen murmured. "I was in my cabin when it happened. I did not see, but they say when he fell overboard…" She shook her head, and for a second the mask of royalty cracked. Her eyes shone in the morning sun. "They say the water was red with blood."

"I'm sorry," Pela whispered. Tentatively, she placed a hand on the woman's shoulder, unsure how to comfort a queen.

Marianne shrugged and looked away. "We'll have the bastards who did it soon," she said, a smile touching her lips. "We'll make them pay for taking him from me."

"I hope so," Pela replied. Sadness tinged her voice as she thought of her mother, all alone with an entirely different set of monsters.

"Devon will find your mother," the queen said, as though reading her mind. "My husband always spoke highly of him, though the hammerman retired his commission long before we were married."

"And what about the people who took her?" Pela asked, a little too sharply.

The queen's eyes flickered closed. "I am so sorry," she whispered. "In Lonia, there have been those who claim to follow the path of Alana, who have committed such acts. I did not think they had reached my adopted nation. Trust me, whatever radicals have taken her will face the queen's justice."

"Thank you," Pela whispered, though she wished the queen had cared enough to send some of the King's Guard with Devon.

The fleet had close to four hundred soldiers between them; against no more than fifty Baronian warriors, it would be a slaughter when they tracked them down. Though when the fleet divided, Pela supposed those odds would narrow.

"You are most welcome, young Pela," the queen replied, embracing her. Then she smiled and gestured at the sword on Pela's belt. "Do you wish to become a warrior yourself someday, like Devon and your father?"

Pela's jaw tightened and she looked away. "I don't know," she murmured. "Maybe I will when we reach Skystead, but then…if my mother never returns, there is nothing for me there."

"Perhaps you should consider returning to the capital with my people?" Marianne offered. "I'm going to need brave women and men around me if we're to keep Plorsea from tearing itself apart."

"You would really want me?" Pela stammered, her vision blurring as she fought back sudden tears.

The queen smiled, but just then a shout carried across the water from the leading ship. They swung around as a dark vessel emerged from the mangroves ahead. Pela's heart clenched as she recognised the black flag atop the strange masts. It raced upriver towards them, hugging the starboard bank.

"What are they doing here?" Pela gasped.

"Trying to get past us," the queen replied.

Pela saw that it was true. The fleet had been negotiating the deeper waters to port and been caught unawares. If they did not act quickly, the Baronians would shoot past and escape upriver. But the first of the Plorsean ships was already turning to cut them off. The King's Guard were bulkier and slower to respond than the Baronians', and Pela held her breath.

At the last moment it became clear the Baronians would not make it. Julian must have realised it too, for the ship turned sharply, abandoning any attempt to escape and angling towards their pursuers. Unable to manoeuvre as quickly, the King's Guard turned to meet them and found themselves floundering in the surging currents. The captain bellowed orders and the men struggled to withdraw their oars…

The Baronian prow slammed into the wallowing ship with a crash of breaking timber. Oars shattered and men were hurled overboard by the power of the collision, disappearing beneath the murky currents. Pela gasped as screams drifted across the open water, followed by the cheering of Baronian voices.

The black ship surged on, struggling to escape the tangles of the King's Guard.

"*No,*" Pela whispered. They were going to escape.

She looked around for the queen, but her guard was already shepherding her below deck to her cabin. Pela cursed and returned her gaze to the entangled ships. A line rose from the Plorsean vessel, clanking down onto the enemy ship. A second followed, then a third, and suddenly the Baronians were no longer pulling away, but being dragged back towards the floundering King's Guard.

"Yes!" Pela punched the air as the ships crashed together.

A roar came from the King's Guard as they surged over the railings onto the pirate ship. The Baronians met them with bellows of their own, and the forces came together in a clash of steel on steel.

With the two ships locked together, the remaining vessels of the King's Guard powered closer and hurled lines of their own. Wood splinted as the ships converged, surrounding the Baronians on all sides. Only the queen's ship hung back.

Outnumbered and outmatched, the Baronian black slowly gave way to the red and gold. Though they fought like demons, there was no hope for them now. One by one they fell, until only a small ring of armoured fighters remained in the centre of the ship.

Movement came from within the circle as one of the Baronians leapt onto a barrel. Pela recognised Julian, his fists and mouth open as he shouted his defiance. Then one of the King's Guard hurled an axe. The heavy blade embedded itself in Julian's chest and he toppled backwards without a sound.

After that, the remaining Baronians fell quickly, and a heavy silence returned to the river. The five ships bobbed gently together, the four vessels of the King's Guard locked to the black one. Their oars unmanned, they drifted slowly downstream, their progress mirrored by the queen's galley.

"Long live the king!" As one, the King's Guard lifted their swords to the sky.

Pela smiled and was about to answer their cry, when shouting broke out behind her.

"No, what are you doing?!"

Devon, Caledan, and Genevieve took the river road for the first day, following the directions of strangers who had seen the Knights depart. No one recalled seeing a woman of Kryssa's description though, and Devon was beginning to doubt that Kryssa had ever reached Lane. It mattered little now though—his path had been chosen; he would not retreat from it now.

Older and more disused than the Gods Road, the track they followed was overgrown and washed out in places, and they had to take care that their horses did not to slip from the banks into the river. They were far above the delta here and the currents were quick, still muddy from the storm of several days past.

Not long after they'd started out, the fleet had drifted past, oars beating the water in their haste to catch the Baronians. Devon had waved and looked for Pela, but if she was watching she had not made herself known.

Now he wondered if he'd done the right thing, sending her away, but it was too late to change his mind now. At least if they did somehow rescue Kryssa, she was less likely to kill him offhand for endangering her daughter.

Devon was surprised though to find himself with companions on this final quest. Glancing sidelong at Caledan and Genevieve, he wondered again at their motivations. Caledan still had not said anything of the night before, and Devon hadn't pressed the matter. The king was dead and there was no need to revisit that pain—for either of them.

Watching Caledan ride, Devon felt conflicted. He respected Caledan's skill—and was grateful for his aid—but there was a darkness to him as well. To be willing to kill the king and plunge Plorsea into chaos…

Devon shook his head, turning his attention to the huntress. If anything, Genevieve's continued devotion was even more perplexing. When they'd first set off from Skystead, he'd thought her motivations the same as Tobias's and his own. Yet there had been no one for Genevieve amongst the villagers they'd rescued, no loved one to embrace.

With a start, Devon realised what he'd missed. In the rush of discovering Kryssa was alive, he'd forgotten the dead women on the floor of the pantheon. Touched by guilt, he looked sidelong at Genevieve. He'd been too consumed by his own grief in Townirwin to notice her state of mind, and he wondered who that unknown woman had been to the huntswoman. Devon wasn't game to ask now.

They continued downriver for several hours. The passage so many men and horses had churned the track to mud, but as they struggled to free their horses for the third time, Genevieve reassured them it was a good sign. Such a large group travelling on these backroads could only be the Knights. They would not go unnoticed; tracking them might yet prove easier than Devon had expected. And where the Knights went, surely they would find Kryssa.

"Have you thought of a better plan yet?" Caledan asked as the sun passed noon and began its descent towards the west.

"No," Devon sighed. "It's the only way."

"We don't even know they'll have her," Caledan put in.

"That's a gamble I'm going to have to take," Devon replied.

Caledan nodded and dropped the subject, but on the other horse Genevieve shook her head. "It's suicide."

Devon chuckled. "I'll admit, I'm open to other ideas."

They rode on in silence for a while, until the path veered suddenly inland. At the bend, a smaller track led down to where a wharf stuck out into the river. Water raced past beneath the wooden struts, but there was no sign of the crocodiles below. Bootprints led up from the wharf to join the churned-up mess the Knights had left.

"Looks like more joined them here," Genevieve commented.

"If things go to plan, numbers aren't going to matter," Devon answered.

"Easy for you to say," Caledan said. "You're not going to have them on your trail."

Devon grunted but did not reply. They plodded inland, the great trees of the Plorsean Forest rising up to swallow them. They were lucky the main body of Knights was ahead; the track was badly overgrown, and their passage had crushed many of the young saplings that had taken root in the open earth.

Even so, by the time night fell Devon was puffing hard and cursing the Knights for leading them so far off the Gods Roads. The sun had dropped early beneath the canopy, but they'd pressed on at pace, eager to close the gap before the last shadows faded beneath the trees. Finally, they made camp in a small glade not far from the track.

Against Caledan's warnings, Devon lit a fire before sitting back on a tree stump to enjoy the warmth.

"What makes you do it, Devon?" Caledan asked after they'd finished a sparse dinner of dried beef and onions.

"Do what?" Devon asked as Genevieve leaned in.

"All this." Caledan gestured around the clearing, as though that explained his question. When Devon only raised an eyebrow, he sighed and elaborated. "Play the hero. What do you get out of it? You know you're more than likely going to fail, so why put yourself at risk?"

Devon stared into the flames. "Because Kryssa needs me," he whispered.

Caledan snorted. "You're not even related."

"No," Devon answered quietly. "I never let her call me 'Father', when she was young. I never understood why Selina brought her into our house. Life was hard enough as it was."

He looked up at them then, taking them in. Genevieve still sat slightly apart, her eyes distant, as though she were lost in some other time. The sellsword stared back at him though.

"Then why didn't you leave?" he asked. "That was, what, twenty years ago? You had your youth, your strength…you could have done anything, gone anywhere."

"I still have my strength, sonny," Devon replied, then shook his head. "And I'm glad I didn't leave. What Selina and Kryssa gave me, no amount of strength or coin can buy. They were—*are*—my family."

Caledan looked away sharply, and Devon knew he was thinking of his own family, torn apart by the death of magic. He swallowed, wondering what words of comfort he could offer the man. Yet Caledan did not know that Devon knew about his past—nor of his secret quest to kill the king. After a moment's hesitation, Devon decided to remain silent.

"I never had a family," Caledan replied finally. "When I was young, I learned to rely on myself. I need no one else," he finished, his voice taking on a sharp tone.

"I won't argue with you," Devon murmured.

"Do you think the others made it safely to Skystead?" Genevieve interrupted.

Devon smiled and nodded his thanks for the change of subject. "I hope so. Tallow is a fine captain."

Caledan laughed. "Poor Tobias, returning to that farm in the mountains. How will he cope after having a taste of the good life?"

"I don't know that he thought of this as the good life," Devon commented mildly.

"Ha!" Caledan straightened. "Don't tell me you weren't bored in that village, Devon. A man like you, you used to be a hero! People worshiped you. I don't know how you turned your back on that life."

Devon shrugged. "I've never been a hero," he replied. "I am merely a man who was better than average with a warhammer. It saddens me now, knowing that is the legacy I leave: as a man that excelled at violence. There is nothing heroic about that."

"The villagers we freed would disagree."

"Ay, I suppose that's true," Devon replied. "They look at us and see warriors, men to walk the mountains with, who guard the nation against evil. But that's not really the truth, is it? We are only men, just like them, only we're afraid to live an ordinary life, to earn an honest living toiling in the earth, to build something rather than tear down the works of our betters. The life they live in Skystead, that takes real courage, sonny."

"What rubbish are you talking, old man?" Caledan snapped, quick to anger now. "Have your advanced years finally addled your mind?"

Devon chuckled. "Maybe," he said, "or maybe I'm just the wiser for them. Tell me, Caledan, which is more noble? The man who spends his life growing crops to feed his family and others—or the man who comes with a sword and takes those crops for himself?"

"The farmer, of course," Caledan retorted. "There is no honour in theft."

"Devon said nothing of theft," Genevieve said with a smile. Caledan glared at her, but Devon gestured for her to go on. "Is that not what a conquering army does? Takes from those they have defeated?"

"That's different."

"How?" Genevieve pressed.

"A soldier takes no coin from those they fight. The crown pays their wage."

"Ay, but where does the crown's coin come from, when they go to war?" Genevieve laughed.

Caledan swore and exploded to his feet. "That still does not explain how the farmer is braver than the warrior!"

"Do you not fear such a life then?" Devon asked quietly, though he knew the answer. He'd seen it in the man's eyes the night before, with his talk of having nothing left to live for.

A stillness came over the sellsword. When he said nothing, Devon continued:

"I know I did, once. There was a time when I feared just the thought of such a life. The idea of rising each morning, to etch out an existence in the same menial job, day after day…it filled me with dread."

"And now?" Caledan croaked, his eyes wide, like a deer caught in an open field.

Devon made to reply, but at that moment there came a *crack* from outside the circle of firelight. He was on his feet in an instant, hammer in hand, searching the darkness for signs of movement.

"I'd stop talking with him now, if I were you," a voice spoke from the shadows, raising the hairs on the back of Devon's neck. "Devon's spent far too much time drinking with Selina."

A figure stepped into the firelight. Braidon's clothes were torn and mud-stained, and his beard was matted with grime, but the king wore a ragged grin on his lips as he staggered across to the fire and slumped onto a log beside them.

"Lovely evening," he said conversationally, holding his hands out to the flames. "What brings you to this part of the woods, Devon? Last I heard, you were happily retired in Skystead."

❧   29   ❧

For Braidon, the seconds after his fall were a blur, as he had first tried to fend off the berserker who'd gone over the side with him—and then escape the croc that had torn the man in two. Blood had stained the river red, the waters churning with the ravenous creatures. Desperate, Braidon had swum faster than he ever had before, making for the shallows.

Miraculously, he had made it. Perhaps the crocodiles had been occupied by easier prey, or perhaps he'd just been lucky. But his luck had run out once he'd hauled himself ashore and looked around. Locked together in battle, the two ships had been caught in the currents and were already drifting out of sight. By the time he'd called out, they'd been far away, already disappearing into one of a myriad of channels.

He had waited for long minutes, knowing his ship would return—if his King's Guards managed to see off the Baronians. But as the waters grew still, Braidon had sensed unseen eyes watching him. Marshland bordered the lower reaches of the Lane and he'd still stood in knee-deep water. With the thick mud beneath his feet, there would be no opportunity to manoeuvre should the crocs seek fresh prey.

Remembering the ferocity of the Baronians, Braidon had sent up a prayer to the Gods that Marianne was safe. After a moment's hesitation, he'd added Alana to the prayer, though even in his desperation had failed to keep a grim smile from his face. Not in a million years would his ten-year-old self have guessed his sister would become a deity worshiped by thousands.

Fear of the crocodiles and the return of the Baronians had eventually forced Braidon away from the river. He had trekked inland until coming to solid ground, then followed the first trail he could find leading north. Lane was the nearest settlement of any size, though on foot and on poor roads the journey could take as long as three days.

That had been two days ago. By now the world must think him dead, and Braidon feared for what might have transpired in his absence. Had Marianne survived? Was his son safe? And what of the Lonians? They would take advantage of any Plorsean weakness they could exploit.

Then there was the matter of the Baronian ship. Its design reminded him of the strange vessels he'd seen at the docks in Lon. He wondered if the Lonians had had a hand in the attack, and what this new power was they possessed. In a world without magic, it posed a threat he did not know how to counter. And if the Lonians were bold enough to act against him, even under the guise of Baronians…he feared what that meant for Plorsea, and for his family.

But finding Devon here, in his darkest hour, gave Braidon hope that all might not be lost. Surely it was a sign. He didn't care if it came from the Three Gods or his sister, only that he could return to Ardath with the hero beside him. It might even give Lonia second thoughts about attacking Plorsea, with their faith in the Knights of Alana and Devon's place in those tales.

Holding his hands out to the fire, Braidon couldn't help but grin at the shock written across his friend's face.

"You look like you've seen a ghost, old friend," Braidon announced finally, after Devon had not said anything for a long moment.

Stepping quickly across the clearing, Devon hauled him up and engulfed him in a bear hug. "Good to see you," he bellowed, then in a softer voice that only Braidon could hear: "*Say nothing of your name.*"

Frowning, Braidon stepped back as Devon gestured to his companions. "This is Caledan and Genevieve," he said, indicating each in turn before pointing at Braidon. "This is Brenden. He fought with me in the Plorsean army, for a time."

Braidon shook each of their hands. "Nice to meet you," he said, then sank back onto the log. "Don't suppose you've got any food? I'm starving."

"What happened to your gear?" Caledan asked, his tone unwelcoming. Braidon had lost everything but his sword in the fall.

"You heard the news?" Devon asked before Braidon could respond. "The king is dead."

"Here," Genevieve added, holding out a strip of dried beef.

Braidon took it with a grin. "Cheers," he said, then looked at Devon. "This morning. I heard Baronians were involved."

"Baronians? In Plorsea? Now how would such bandits have crept into our great nation?" Devon asked, his voice heavy with sarcasm.

"If I remember correctly, you led a band of them once, didn't you?" Braidon replied, trying not to respond to the man's baiting. "Regardless, do you know what's to be done about them?"

"The queen is leading an expedition to hunt them down," Devon answered.

"*The queen!*" Braidon gasped, before swallowing back his shock and continuing in a more measured tone. "Surely that would be the job of the King's Guard."

"They're going with her. Five ships in all. We saw them sail past us."

"Well, I hope they catch the bastards," Braidon muttered.

"I doubt they'll have much trouble, once they track 'em down," Devon said, "but the Baronians are not our biggest problem just now."

"Oh?" Braidon asked. "So it was not the king's death that brought you out of retirement?"

Devon smiled grimly. "No," he replied. "It was the Knights of Alana."

Braidon snorted. "What have those fanatics done now?"

"They came to Skystead and attacked the temple, took Kryssa. I believe they plan to sacrifice her at the midsummer solstice."

"Wha…what?" Braidon gaped. "This…you're joking, right? Who's Kryssa?"

It was the wrong thing to say.

Devon's face darkened. "Kryssa is the child Selina adopted, when we still lived in Ardath. You have met her in fact, many times. But then I would not expect—" He cut himself off, and Braidon realised he could not finish the sentence without giving his identity away.

"I'm so sorry," he whispered, knowing it was not

enough. Still reeling from the last few days, he had forgotten the name for half a moment, though he did not expect Devon to take his word for it. "When did this happen?

"We have been hunting the Knights who took her for weeks," Genevieve said when Devon did not answer.

"Been a while since the two of you saw each other," Caledan murmured. "How did you say you met again?"

Braidon's heart quickened beneath the man's hawkish gaze. Sweat trickled down his neck as the moment drew out. He didn't know why Devon wanted to keep his identity secret, but Caledan had the look of a killer about him. Braidon knew a man he did not want to cross when he saw one.

"Brenden fought with me in some border skirmishes," Devon answered finally.

"I'm sorry, Devon," Braidon repeated. "Do you know where these Knights are heading?"

"Somewhere in the forest," Genevieve answered.

"The Forest of Plorsea? It spans for leagues in all directions from here. And the deeper you go, the more dangerous it becomes."

"We'll find them," Genevieve replied with feeling. "I've been following their tracks, from one group at least. More have joined them since we left Lane. There must be hundreds in the forest."

"*Hundreds?*" Braidon exclaimed, looking from her to Devon. "You can't be serious? With the king…dead, the queen needs people she can trust to keep the peace. We cannot afford for you to throw your life away on some hopeless quest!"

"The queen can take care of herself," Devon replied, his eyes shining. "My…Kryssa needs me."

"You're just one man, Devon," Braidon whispered. "Not even you can defeat so many."

"It doesn't matter."

Braidon knuckled his forehead and turned to the others. "What about the two of you? Surely you can't be going along with this?"

Caledan shrugged and Genevieve gave a quiet grin. "The old man has a plan."

"A plan!" Braidon burst out, swinging on Devon. "*Now* you have a plan?"

Devon shrugged and looked away. Braidon swallowed. Devon had always had a presence about him, an unyielding strength that made people believe he could move mountains. But in the flickering firelight, Braidon could see the lines on his face, the bags under his eyes, and for a second he wondered how long his friend had for this world.

Then the hammerman blinked, and the image vanished, his familiar confidence returning.

"Please, Devon," Braidon said. He needed to get back to Ardath and his son, to take command of the situation. But even more, he needed his old friend at his side, to stand against this new darkness. "Plorsea needs you."

"Kryssa has a daughter," Devon rumbled. "Her name is Pela. I promised I would not return without her mother. She needs me more, sonny."

"What is one woman, one girl, to the fate of a nation?"

"What is a nation, if it cannot protect the innocent?" Devon countered.

"*Everything!*" Braidon snapped, leaping to his feet. Breath hissed between his teeth as he inhaled, then he realised Caledan was watching. Slowly he sank back to his seat. "If the king is dead, the Lonians will come. It's only a matter of time," he explained. "We're not ready. We need a hero like you, or Plorsea will be lost."

"And what of it?" Caledan growled. "What is Plorsea but a name? What does it matter if we are ruled from Lon? They can't be any worse than the fool we had until two days ago."

Braidon glanced at Devon, expecting his friend to disagree, but the hammerman only raised an eyebrow. It was left to the huntress to come to his defence.

"Thousands will die," she murmured.

"And others will find their fortune," Caledan replied. "It's how I made mine."

Braidon looked at Devon. "You truly believe this woman is worth sacrificing a nation for, Devon?"

"What's the point of saving Plorsea, if I can't save my family?" Devon replied.

The breath caught in Braidon's throat and he had to look away. His mind raced back to the day they'd lost Alana. The Tsar had been defeated, his armies sundered, but for Devon and Braidon there had been no joy, no celebration. The price had been too high. Braidon had lost his sister, Devon his love.

"We could use an extra sword," Devon murmured.

Braidon's head whipped around, his eyes catching in Devon's amber gaze. He remembered another time then, long ago, when Devon had stood aboard the *Songbird* and defied a demon to protect Braidon and Alana. And again in Fort Fall, against the Tsar's Stalkers, and in the throne room against their father himself. Again and again, down through the decades, this man had been there for Braidon, had laid his life on the line for the Three Nations.

Now he was asking Braidon to do the same for him.

Looking into his eyes, Braidon glimpsed again Devon's

pain, the exhaustion he tried so hard to disguise. Age had caught up with him, diminished his once-great strength. He had no right to be wandering these country roads on a quest to rescue a kidnapped woman, no right to stand against the Knights of Alana. Yet he would, because he was Devon.

And Braidon could not deny him.

"Okay, Devon," he said. The decision was surprisingly easy to make. "What's the plan?"

❦ 30 ❦

"We'll reach the Cove tomorrow," Putar declared as they dismounted.

"If we survive the night," Ikar grunted.

They had recovered their horses not long after Putar's appearance, and from there had veered from the Gods Road onto the backtrails of the Forest of Plorsea. A ferryman had helped them across the Lane the same day, and they'd spent another two days within the forest before moving out onto Chole's volcanic plateau.

It had not been until this morning though that they had left Plorsea behind, and ventured into the uncharted jungles of Dragon Country. Ikar had pushed them hard, eager to leave the forest behind. Putar had assured him the Red Dragons would not touch them, but Ikar was far from convinced. The beasts were vicious, hateful creatures and would attack at the slightest provocation. He would be glad to reach the end of their journey.

Even more so to bid farewell to the Elder. The last few days on the road had diminished Putar. The man needed

Ikar's aid just to climb into the saddle each morning, and spent most of his time complaining of one discomfort or another. He seemed to blame Kryssa for his situation, and as his mood grew fouler each day, Ikar was forced to place himself between the Elder and their captive.

He untied her from the saddle now, though he left her hands bound, and helped her to dismount. She staggered as her feet touched the ground, cramped from the long hours in the saddle, but she recovered without Ikar's aid. He quickly withdrew the hand he'd extended to help her, but not before Kryssa noticed.

"Thank you, oh Knight," she said, a smile twisting her lips, "but I am quite alright. Perhaps the fat man has need of your assistance?"

"Blasphemous witch!" Putar cursed. He swung from the saddle with a little too much violence and his foot caught in the stirrup, toppling him face-first into the mud.

Ikar snorted as the Elder thrashed in the mud. By the time Putar finally sat up, he was covered from head to toe, and Ikar was glad for the helmet concealing his face. He did not think the Elder would appreciate his amusement. Kryssa's mirth had enraged him enough.

Dragging himself to his feet, he tore the riding crop from his saddle and advanced on Kryssa. Ikar stepped between them and raised a hand.

"We cannot touch her," he said quietly, though there was steel in his voice. "Were those not your orders?"

Putar's face went a mottled purple. "Ay, they were *my* orders. And now I command you to step aside, Knight. The witch must pay for her disrespect."

Ikar remained in place for several seconds longer than was proper, but finally he stepped aside. Whatever his personal thoughts, he had no right to defy an Elder, though in truth he had come to enjoy the woman's company far more than Putar's on this journey. Despite her predicament, Kryssa remained surprisingly light-hearted throughout the long days, although that was perhaps only to deflect their suspicions from her own schemes.

She had made another two escape attempts since the first, frustrating Ikar to the point of violence. He had been forced to knock her from the saddle at almost full gallop the last time. The hard mountain earth had been unforgiving, and a dozen scratches and bruises now marked her arms and legs.

"Is it disrespectful to point out the obvious, fat man?" Kryssa laughed, her head tilted to one side.

"Witch!" Putar bellowed, his teeth bared. "You dare to laugh at an Elder of the Order!"

Kryssa snorted. "Only when they fall on their—"

She broke off as Putar whipped her across the face with his cane. Her hands still bound, Kryssa toppled backwards into the mud, a cry on her lips. Ikar gasped and took half a step forward, but Putar flashed him a warning glare, and he stilled once more.

The cane still in hand, he advanced on the woman. Still on her back, Kryssa glared up at him, her sapphire eyes defiant. Snorting, she spat a bloody glob of saliva at his feet.

"Is that the best you can do?"

Snarling, Putar lashed out with his boot, catching her in the stomach. The blow lifted her from the ground and sent her rolling across the clearing. Nearby, the horses snickered, made nervous by the woman's cries. Ikar swallowed and looked away, disgusted by this new level of cruelty from Putar.

Air whistled between Kryssa's teeth as she struggled to her knees. "Coward."

The cane descended again. Ikar winced and closed his eyes to the *crack* of wood on flesh. Again and again it came, punctuated each time by a scream from Putar. Clenching his fists, Ikar struggled to control his rage. Putar's malice had revealed him for what he was: a cruel, vile man, obsessed with his own power. His prior virtue had only ever been a deception.

A scream rent the clearing and finally Ikar could take it no more. Spinning, he reached for his sword…

…and froze when he saw Kryssa half crouched in the mud, Putar now lying motionless at her feet. Eyes wide, she stared back at him, as though waiting to see how he would react.

"What have you done?" Steel hissed on leather he drew his blade and advanced on the woman.

She did not move, not even when he stretched out his sword and rested the point against her throat. A fresh bruise was already beginning to darken on her cheek where Putar had struck her.

Ikar's eyes darted to the Elder, but it took only a glance to confirm he was dead. Putar's neck was bent at an unnatural angle, and his open eyes stared back at Ikar, unblinking. He swallowed. Kryssa's hands were still bound before her— how had she killed him? A shudder raced down his spine as he tensed, readying himself to strike her down.

"Do it," she hissed, eyes aflame. "Go on!"

Shocked by the venom in her voice, Ikar took a step back. Unperturbed, Kryssa rose and advanced until his blade touched her throat once more.

"Please," she whispered. "Or let me go. I refuse to be your sacrifice, to feed whatever hatred burns in your Order."

For a moment, Ikar was prepared to do it, such was her

desperation. All it would take was one thrust, and her suffering would end. Then he looked into her eyes…

"I can't," he croaked.

"You must!" she snapped. "I murdered your precious Elder."

He glanced again at the body lying by his feet. Even in death, Putar's face had a hateful look about it. Slowly Ikar shook his head.

"He was no Elder," he murmured. "He defiled the title with his malice. You are chosen by the Saviour, if he died by your hand, it must be her will."

Kryssa stood unmoving for a long time, her eyes transfixed on Ikar, as though somehow her gaze could pierce the steel confines of his helmet.

"So be it," she said suddenly, her words as sharp as razors. "But know this, from now on you are my enemy, and I will not hesitate to kill you."

Ikar opened his mouth to laugh, then he saw again Putar's body, and the laughter died on his lips. A shudder raced up his spine, lifting the hackles on his neck.

"So be it," he agreed.

That night, Ikar did not rest, only sat watching the woman in her sleeping sack, and when the first light of the morning found them, they were already well on their way.

Pela sat crouched amongst a cluster of barrels, arms wrapped tightly around her chest. In her mind, she could still hear the screams of the dying men, rising like banshees above the crackling of flames. She could still see the burning ships, still smell the stench of roasting flesh.

A shudder rippled through her body and she struggled to keep from crying. She couldn't afford so much as whimper, lest they hear and find her. Closing her eyes, she prayed to the Three Gods for deliverance, for rescue, to be anywhere but the queen's ship.

She still could not process what had happened. One second, the King's Guard had been celebrating their victory, their cheers rising up from the defeated Baronian vessel. The next, someone had been screaming, and Pela had spun in time to see a melee break out on the queen's ship, to glimpse the catapult crouched like a spider on the stern deck.

Then with an awful *crack*, the weapon had released,

hurling a burning barrel high overhead. Up and up it had risen, until it reached the peak of its arc, and went tumbling back down. Down into the cluster of ships it had fallen, and with an awful *boom*, exploded.

Almost in slow motion, the Baronian vessel had lifted from the water, as though propelled upwards by the hand of the Gods. Men had been hurled screaming into the air as flames blossomed, then suddenly the five ships were gone, vanished amidst the flaming tempest now burning upon the waters of the Lane.

Pela had hurled herself to the deck as pieces of wood and debris rained down. A wave had swept across the queen's ship and for a moment she'd thought they would all burn. Clenching her eyes closed, she had waited for death to find her.

But somehow, Pela had been spared, and the heat had gone racing away, to be replaced by plumes of smoke that went billowing across the river. The clashing of steel had rung out across the deck of the queen's ship, but amidst the putrid fumes Pela could not see who was fighting.

Stumbling through the chaos, she'd searched for the queen, but the woman had vanished, and Pela had searched for a hiding place of her own. With the screams of the dying and the roaring of flames all around, she'd stumbled into the pile of barrels at the stern—and had crawled between them.

Only when she was deep in the depths of the pile, did Pela realise the barrels were the same kind the catapult had hurled at the Baronian ship. Crouching low, she cracked the top off one, revealing a strange black powder within. An acrid stench touched her nostrils and she quickly replaced the lid, the hackles lifting on her neck.

If one barrel could do so much damage, what would a dozen do? But silence had fallen across the queen's ship now and there was no time left to search for a new hiding place. She held her breath, waiting to find out who had won.

"There's men in the water!" a voice called out.

A soft *thud* followed, then another, before a second voice replied, "Not for long."

Pela choked back a sob as she realised the men were firing on any of the King's Guard who had survived. Stuffing her fist into her mouth, Pela scrunched her eyes closed and waited for the nightmare to end.

Except it never did. As the hours crept by, Pela found herself dozing, made drowsy by the heat beneath the canvas covering the barrels. Eventually someone spoke nearby her hiding place, snapping her awake.

"Anyone seen the girl?" a man's voice carried on the breeze.

"Not since the attack," another replied. "Probably jumped ship.

Someone cursed. "Then she's croc food. I wonder who the third sacrifice will be now."

"The Elders will find one. Maybe the Consort, or one of his companions. I hear they're riding straight for the Cove."

The first speaker laughed. "More fool on them," he said, then after a moment had passed: "Have you ever seen such a sight?"

"The flames?" came the reply, the speaker's voice touched by awe. "Never."

"That black powder…"

"Not even the cursed Magickers could have done so well," another added. "Truly, the engineers have outdone themselves. When all of Lonia's ships possess the black powder and steam engines, no force in the Three Nations will be able to stand against us."

"Praise be Alana!" the other exclaimed. "Her sacrifice finally bears fruit for our people."

"Her sacrifice, and all those who have followed," another chuckled. "The solstice approaches. How long until we reach the Cove?"

An icy chill spread through Pela's stomach as she listened. Their words revealed them as members of the Order, but how had the infiltrated the queen's ship? And where was the queen? Pela had not seen or even heard her since the explosion. Had she been caught in the melee?

The men had spoken of the Elders finding a third sacrifice. A cold breeze touched her neck as she realised the first must be her mother, the second the queen.

She was to have been the third.

Suddenly Pela was unable to catch her breath.

They planned to murder me!

Pela gripped the top of a nearby barrel, struggling to keep quiet, and only the tiniest of squeaks slipped from her lips. She felt as though she were suffocating. Then another thought struck her:

They know about Devon!

They knew her uncle was coming. She shuddered, the blood pounding in her ears as true panic took hold. What was she going to do? She was trapped aboard this ship, going who-knew-where! The rowers had taken to the oars not long after the battle; they could be anywhere by now.

I must warn Devon!

But she couldn't even help herself.

No, she hissed in the silence of her mind. *You are a fighter.*

Her hand dropped to the hilt of her father's sword. Derryn had fought for the king himself, had saved the man's life. How could she do anything less? If she could get the queen away from wherever they were keeping her and over the side, Pela thought they could make it to the riverbank before anyone noticed. It was already growing dark, and it did not sound as though there were many men left onboard. And those that remained were relaxed, thinking the day won.

"Tomorrow night, I expect. I'll not be sad to see this ship burn. Tired of rowing."

The other laughed. "Can't stand a little hard work?"

"Not when a bit of coal will do it for me."

"Soon enough," came the reply. "Come on then, the girl's gone. Let's put our backs into it. The harder we row, the faster we're there. Then we can finally burn this archaic heap of timber."

"Ain't that the truth."

The voices retreated, and Pela crawled to the edge of the stack of barrels. She poked her head out from the canvas and saw the red light staining the horizon. The yellow orb of the sun was just visible through the wiry branches of the mangroves. The speakers were just disappearing beneath the deck to the oar banks. Pela had only been down there once and was in no hurry to return. It stank of rotting fish and sweating bodies, the air stifling in the summer heat.

Silently, she crept from her hiding place. The aft was raised, with a single flight of stairs leading down to the rest of the ship. Beside the stairs, a railing prevented anyone from accidentally falling from the upper to lower deck. Pela crept forward until she was positioned behind the railings and peeked over the edge.

Directly below her, two men stood with their arms folded, guarding the door to the main cabin positioned beneath the aft deck. She cursed silently to herself. That had to be where they were keeping the queen.

Pela loosened her sword in its scabbard, then thought better of it. Both guards wore plate mail armour and carried heavy broadswords on their belts. She wouldn't stand a chance if it came to a fight.

I should never have brought you.

She shrank as Devon's words whispered in her mind. Retreating to her hiding place, Pela crouched in the shadows and hugged her knees to her chest. Her uncle had been right. She should never have come. What chance did she stand against full-grown men, when they'd already cut down the best of the King's Guard? She should just do as the men thought she had and jump overboard. She could swim to shore and head for Lane, and report the attack to…

Who?

There was no one left. The King's Guard were all gone, slaughtered to a man. The queen was held hostage and Devon was walking into a trap. If she fled, she would be giving up her one chance to do something, to fight back against the Order and their Knights.

Pela sucked in a breath, thinking again about the guards outside the queen's door. They were well-armed, but relaxed, confident of their victory. Their barrels of magic powder had won the day with them hardly having to lift a hand.

Remembering the awful explosion, Pela shuddered. Then an idea came to her. How much did the Order truly know about this magic powder of theirs? It was obviously dangerous. What would they do if anything happened to their supply?

She couldn't risk a fire. Pela had seen the damage done by a single barrel; there wouldn't be much left of the queen's ship if a dozen took light. But if she made them *think* something had happened …

Studying the barrels, she tried to estimate their weight, but dismissed the idea. They must weigh eighty pounds each; there was no way she could lift them. But she might be able to knock one over. Putting her shoulder to the closest, she heaved with all her strength.

The barrel rocked on its base and started to tip, but she let go before it could fall. She sucked in a breath, wondering if she was truly game. Angrily, she shook her head. If she hesitated, she was lost. She shoved the barrel again until it tipped, teetered on the edge of its base, and then toppled to the deck with a *crash*.

"What was that?" a voice shouted from below.

Pela retreated as the barrel rolled across the tilting deck. Clearing her throat, she shouted in her deepest voice: "Fire!"

Panicked shouts followed, then the *thump* of boots on the stairwell. Pela reached the railing just before the guards reached the aft deck, and vaulted over the top. Lowering herself down, she landed softly on the main deck. There was a slight overhang and she quickly stepped beneath it so she could not be seen from above.

The cabin door was closed and Pela cursed under her breath. She hadn't thought about a lock…but it was too late to turn back now. Casting aside the last of her caution, she gripped the handle and turned.

Her heart skipped a beat as it opened with a click. She quickly stepped inside, swinging the door gently shut behind her. Within, the cabin was dark and warmer than outside, but at her entrance she sensed movement. A glow appeared in the corner.

The queen blinked, holding out the lantern and sitting

up in bed. A frown crossed her delicate features as she saw Pela standing in the doorway.

"Pela?" she murmured, and Pela could tell she was struggling to wake.

"Dim the light!" Pela hissed, glancing at the glass windows. "Before they see!"

❈ 32 ❈

Crouched on the hard earth, Caledan's muscles were beginning to cramp by the time the Knights had finally ridden into view.

Devon had spotted the group the day before, while they'd been riding up into the foothills of Mount Chole and its two unnamed shadow peaks. They'd been a long way off amongst the mountain tussock, but there was no mistaking the shining armour and long white capes.

The Knights might have only been late to the gathering, but Caledan thought it more likely the men were hunting them. If that was the case, they had not sent enough men. He'd counted half a dozen—against Devon and Caledan alone they would have struggled. With Genevieve and the man Brenden adding their swords, the Knights might still have the numbers, but not the advantage.

Caledan glanced across the track, trying to spot where Genevieve and Brenden had hidden themselves amongst the trees. The forest was sparse here in the foothills, little more than a few wiry mountain beeches. Even so, his companions were well concealed, but Caledan was patient, and eventually their movement gave them away.

The huntress was crouched in the shadows of a jagged boulder, sword in one hand, hatchet in the other, while Brenden hid behind a narrow tree trunk with sword in hand. Caledan eyed the man, then shook his head. Their new companion might have fought beside Devon, but he was obviously out of practice—no veteran would have wasted energy drawing his sword so soon.

Devon himself stood in the centre of the trail, hammer in hand. The pounding of horse's hooves slowed as the party galloped around the bend below and spotted him barring their passage. A voice carried up the mountain, ringing from the cliffs that rose at their back.

"Who goes there?"

"You know who!" Devon bellowed, raising his hammer. "Who are you, Knight, to follow me?"

The Knights drew up a few yards from Devon. "The queen asks you return to Lane," their leader answered. "The culprits of the attack on Skystead have been found, and the woman Kryssa freed."

For a moment, Caledan thought the hammerman would believe them. Their words seemed to stagger him, his hammer lowering half an inch. But finally he shook his head.

"I wish I could believe you," he croaked. "But you are Knights of Alana, not the Queen's Guard. Why would she send you?"

"My heart grieves for the hurt these radicals amongst my Order have dealt you, Devon," the Knight answered. "We come to make amends."

Devon shook his head. "You came for blood," he

murmured. "Is that not why your Order has come to these lands?"

"My brothers come on pilgrimage, to witness a ritual to the Saviour, to commemorate her sacrifice," came the Knight's response. "None of us wish for more bloodshed."

"Then throw down your swords and remove your helms."

"We cannot," the Knight answered, his voice taking on a harder edge.

Devon hefted his hammer. "Then blood it shall be."

The Knights exchanged glances, then as though suddenly realising they were wasting their time, they drew their blades. Caledan tensed as the hiss of steel whispered up the trail.

"You will not grant me the honour of a duel?" Devon asked.

The leader chuckled. "No, Consort. I'm going to ride you into the ground like the animal you are." He lifted his sword and his horse reared. With a scream, he charged towards Devon.

Caledan braced himself, but the old warrior's words rang in his ears—*wait for my signal*—and he forced himself to still. The Knights closed in rapidly, the steel-shod hooves of their horses tearing up the trail and filling the air with dust. The damp of the river lands was far behind them now and in the shadow of the mountains, the earth was hard.

Bellowing in the face of his attackers, Devon drew back his arm and hurled his hammer. His aim was true, and the heavy weapon struck the leading horse in the chest with a sickening *thud*. The beast screamed and crashed to the ground, hurling its rider from the saddle. Behind, the other horses reared, toppling several of their riders, while others furiously tried to regain control.

"Now!" Devon shouted. Charging forward, he swept up his hammer and launched himself at the nearest Knight.

Shouting a war cry, Caledan leapt from the trees. A Knight was just coming to his feet and died without ever drawing his sword. Leaping past the dead man, Caledan glimpsed Brenden engaged with a second, and Genevieve burying her hatchet in the helmet of a third.

Another man came at Caledan, sword raised and shield in hand. Cursing, Caledan parried the blow and riposted, but the man blocked the attack with his shield and then thrust forward. The shield caught Caledan in the wrist, almost jarring the blade from his hand. He retreated, and his feet became entangled in the dead man.

Glimpsing an opportunity, the Knight attacked again, and only a desperate flick of Caledan's blade saved him from being impaled. Even then, he felt a slash of pain from his arm as the broadsword nicked him.

He leapt back, clearing the dead man, and blocked another flurry of blows from the Knight. Then he grinned. The man was good, but Caledan had his number now. Every time the Knight attacked, his shoulder dropped, exposed the joint in his armour at the throat. As the man lunged again, Caledan's blade speared through his gorget, hard enough to sever his spine.

Blood spurted from the wound and the man fell. Caledan twisted his sword to free it, but the jagged tear in the man's armour caught the blade, dragging the weapon from his hand.

Caledan leapt for the man's fallen sword as a horse screamed behind him. Lifting the unfamiliar blade, he turned to see a horseman barrelling down on him. The broadsword was heavy in Caledan's hands, sluggish as he tried to raise it. The Knight's sword swept down…

…A shriek erupted from overhead as Brenden appeared in front of Caledan, his long sword leaping to deflect the Knight's attack, then spearing up through the Knight's armpit, where the joints in his armour were weakest. The horse's momentum carried the Knight past, tearing the blade from Brenden's grip, but after a few paces the Knight topped from the saddle with a *crash*.

Caledan looked around for the other foes, but Devon had already toppled the final man. The Knight's steel plate armour had been caved in and blood now stained Devon's warhammer.

Caledan shuddered at the sight. With the sword, one had to seek the weak points in an opponent's armour—the throat or groin or armpits. Devon had no such concerns. It didn't matter where he struck: one blow from his hammer and a man would be crushed within his own armour.

A groan came from the road beyond Devon, where the first Knight had fallen. His horse had landed on him in its death throes, but protected by his armour, he had survived mostly intact. The little good it had done him—he was still trapped beneath the beast.

Devon strolled over and crouched beside him.

"Help me," the Knight croaked.

"Oh I will," Devon replied. "Right after we've had a little talk."

❦ 33 ❦

Devon groaned as he lowered himself onto a tree stump. The Knight of Alana lay on the road beside him, arms bound tightly behind his back. They had stripped him of his weapons and armour; without them he was a Knight no longer, only a man, and there was little sign of the defiance he'd shown earlier.

The Knight flinched as Devon tossed his hammer down beside the man's head. They were alone on the road now—Devon had sent the others for firewood and to check their backtrail for signs of further pursuit. He hadn't wanted to risk their hostage giving away the king's identity to Caledan.

Not for the first time in the last few days, Devon sent up thanks to the Three Gods that Caledan had only ever glimpsed Braidon from afar before their meeting in the forest. But then, few would have recognised Braidon without his crown or armour.

"So…" Devon said softly. "You came to kill me."

"Capture." The Knight spat on the dusty ground. "Our Elders have plans for you, Consort."

Devon chuckled. "Do they? What do those fools want from me?"

"Blasphemy!" the Knight snarled. "The Saviour would—"

He broke off as Devon leapt to his feet and planted his boot on the man's chest. "Do not seek to lecture me on the woman I loved, Knight," he grated.

"Loved?" The man sneered. "Hollow words, when you spit in the face of her sacrifice."

Devon could only shake his head at the fervour in the man's eyes, the absolute belief in his own truth. He was young, not even in his twenties. He had never lived with magic, yet the Order had taught him to fear it, to hate the Gods that had died with Alana. They said nothing of the miracles the Gods and their magic had performed, the peace and prosperity they had once brought to the Three Nations.

Letting out a long sigh, Devon sank back onto his stump. "I honour her memory by doing as she once did for me— giving my life to protect the ones I love. How do *you* honour her?"

The man's eyes shone. "By following the preaching of the Elders, by renewing her Great Sacrifice, by burning the scourge of the False Gods from our land wherever I find it."

"The Three Gods are dead, sonny," Devon sighed. "They're not coming back, however much some may pray for it."

"Blasphemy!"

Devon waved a hand. He wasn't getting anywhere with this line of questioning. "And what is this Great Sacrifice of yours? Where have they taken Kryssa?"

The man blanked. "Knowledge of the Great Sacrifice is not for non-believers."

"How about we make an exception, given my prior relationship with your Saviour?"

The man opened his mouth, but before he could refuse, Devon picked up his hammer and twirled it in his hand. "Keep in mind, I'm only asking nicely this once."

The Knight swallowed. "I believe in the power of the Saviour."

"Alana's not going to help you now."

"The Saviour does not protect, only grants us the free will to live our lives."

Devon chuckled. "Then you'd better get talking."

The Knight swallowed, his eyes flicking from Devon's face to the hammer. "You wouldn't kill an unarmed man."

"You're right," Devon rumbled. He drew a knife from his bag and moved behind the knight, cutting his bindings loose. The Knight sat up, looking confused. Devon tossed him his sword. "Get up. Let's see how you fare against an old man."

The man paled as he looked at the sword, but he made no move to pick it up.

Devon smiled. "I thought as much," he said, crouching alongside the man. "Listen up, sonny. I'm not going to kill you, not unless you piss me off." He nodded at the trees. "Now Caledan, he's not so forgiving. I sent him out to look for firewood, to give us some time to talk. But when he returns, he plans to string you up by your neck."

Colour fled the Knight's face. He began to shake, his hands clenching into fists, though his lips remained tight shut.

"How old are you?" Devon asked.

The man swallowed. "Sev…seventeen."

"A young age to die, whoever your Gods," Devon

commented. "You seem like a good kid. Misguided maybe, but you still have time to learn."

The young Knight swallowed. "What do you want to know?"

Devon gave a cold smile. "What is the Great Sacrifice?"

"It's…a renewal of Alana's sacrifice. We…it has been performed every decade since her death, to keep the powers of the False Gods apart from this world."

"And where will this sacrifice be performed?"

"This year…the Elders wanted a demonstration of our strength. They…the sacrifice will be held in Malevolent Cove," he whispered. "Where the Goddess Antonia was struck down, where the False Gods first revealed their mortality."

A cold breeze slid down Devon's spine. Malevolent Cove was only a day's march from where they sat, assuming they survived the journey. Once they crossed the plateau, they would be entering Dragon Country. A party of armoured Knights would be troubled by even one of the beasts—the four of them wouldn't stand a chance. Even the greatest of Magickers had feared the creatures, in the times before magic was lost.

And then there was Malevolent Cove itself.

Legends told that the Old King Thomas had lost himself to darkness there, succumbing to the call of his magic and unleashing a demon upon the Three Nations.

And Devon's ancestor, his great, great Grandfather Alastair, had been slain on its black sands.

A shudder swept through Devon at the thought, but summoning his courage, he continued with his questions. "How many Knights will there be?"

"It is the thirtieth anniversary," the Knight replied as though that answered Devon's question. When Devon only glared at him, he went on: "They will come from all over Plorsea *and* Lonia. Hundreds of Knights, and more still of our followers."

A lead weight settled in Devon's stomach. It was too many. Even with a distraction, how could they possibly hope to free Kryssa and escape?

To say nothing of the beasts that would hunt them in the wilderness of Dragon Country.

For half a moment, Devon wondered if Braidon had been right. The threat of the Order could not be ignored any longer; if hundreds were willing to gather for this sacrifice, what else might be at risk? How many more innocents would be persecuted, if the Knights were not stopped? Only the king could gather an army great enough to crush this insurrection once and for all.

But what then of Kryssa?

Silently, Devon imagined telling Pela he had failed, that he had turned his back on her mother. He could almost see the judgement in her eyes, the accusation, a mirror of the day he had returned to Skystead with Derryn's body. Kryssa had met him on the pier, the light in her eyes turning from joy to despair, and finally to rage.

You were meant to keep him safe!

Devon shuddered. No, whatever the odds, he could not go back now. Kryssa and Pela were family, and he could not let them down, not again.

Standing, he held out his hand to the Knight. "Give me the sword."

"You're…you're not going to kill me, are you?"

"I gave you my word," he replied.

"Even so…"

Devon's eyes flashed. "My word is iron," he snapped. "Now give me the blade, before I change my mind."

The Knight flinched and tossed the sword on the ground. He scrambled backwards as Devon retrieved the weapon.

"Go!" Devon snarled, pointing the blade at the man's chest. "Return to Lane and tell your masters of your failure. Or go home, I do not care. But do not come this way again, for if I see you, I'll not hesitate to strike you down, armed or no."

The Knight swallowed. "My armour, it's sacred—"

"*Go!*" Devon bellowed.

He went.

Genevieve appeared from the nearby bushes a few minutes later. From the pointed look she flashed him, she'd been listening, but she said nothing when the others returned carrying an armful of firewood each.

"You let the bastard go?" Caledan asked.

Devon shrugged. "He told me what I needed to know."

"Oh?" Braidon questioned. "So where are we going?"

Devon drew in a deep breath. "Malevolent Cove."

34

Ikar breathed a sigh of relief as they cleared the last of the trees and emerged into the open. Ahead, campfires lit the night and the stench of smoke was heavy in the air. They had ridden hard all through the day and into the night to reach the safety of the Cove. Shouts carried through the darkness as figures moved in the shadows, and Ikar raised an empty hand.

"Hello, brothers," he hailed them, "well met."

"Who goes there?" came the response.

"Ikar." He grinned as the shadows slowed. "The Elders are expecting me."

A torch was lit and several Knights strode forward, the flames reflecting from their metallic helmets. Ikar shuddered —in the dark, his fellow Knights no longer seemed human. There was no expression to read in their steel faces, no warning as to their attentions, and for a moment Ikar saw what others must see when they looked upon him.

His hand was halfway to his helmet before he caught himself. Swallowing, he gestured at Kryssa. She sat on the packhorse, her eyes on the ground. Despite her threats, she had made no further attempt to escape since killing Putar. It seemed as though she'd finally come to accept her fate. Sadness touched him.

"Ay, you are just in time. We'll send for them," one of the Knights replied.

A brief discussion was held and then they ran off, clambering down a ditch laden with spikes before disappearing through the gates of a wooden palisade. Ikar was surprised at the span of the fortifications—the Elders must have been planning this for some time.

"Come," one of the Knights said, gesturing them forward. "We have made the dragons fear us, but there are other creatures in these woods. It's not safe to stand here in the dark."

Ikar nodded. Taking up the reins to Kryssa's horse, he followed the Knights inside. The gate groaned as it closed behind them, sealing them within. Dismounting, Ikar moved to Kryssa and freed her hands from the saddle. With his help she stepped down. After a moment's hesitation, he untied her hands as well.

She rubbed her wrists and frowned at him, a puzzled look in her eyes, but Ikar only shrugged. A young boy appeared, bowed to Ikar and the other Knights, and then took the reins of their horses and disappeared into the darkness.

Ikar watched him go, and then turned to survey the rest of the camp. The smell of smoke was stronger here, and he saw that the ground was covered in soot. Fire must have been used to clear the trees. The Red Dragons would not be pleased, and he glanced over his shoulder nervously.

It was then he noticed the great catapults lining the interior of the palisade. Barrels lay stacked alongside them and men stood nearby, their eyes on the starry sky. Ikar swallowed, recognising what they were. He wondered how the Order had gotten hold of the black powder. But it gave him at least a small measure of confidence that the Red Dragons could be handled.

The rest of the site was similar to the military encampments of the Lonian army. Rows of canvas tents stretched away from the gates, with a single avenue leading deeper into the camp. At this late hour there were few members of the Order awake, but those he saw wore the armour of Knights. He noticed with distaste that most carried large crossbows on their belts. They were the weapons of cowards, though he supposed they were needed to keep the beasts at bay.

A distant banging could be heard, as of hammers striking wood, along with the faint crashing of waves on a sandy shore. Ikar found himself wondering about the Cove, and what waited for him on the infamous shore. It was said his ancestor Alastair had died there, though few knew of the association. The man was despised by the Order for his magic and his service to the Gods.

The association shamed Ikar as much as his family's other secret—that they had inherited the man's magic, at least until the Gods had fallen. He prayed to the Saviour that tonight he would finally help put that past behind him. It was the reason he had joined the Order in the first place, to purge the darkness from the world, to make amends for his family's past evils.

Now, remembering the Elder's sick joy at Kryssa's pain, and his own treatment of her on the ship from Skystead, Ikar found himself wondering…

No, he thought, clenching his fists tight. *The False Gods must be kept from this world.*

He looked up and caught Kryssa staring at him. Warmth touched his cheeks, though she could not see beneath his helmet. The whisper of a sigh from her, and she turned away, casting her eyes over the camp.

The thud of hooves announced the approach of a new group of men. Ikar edged closer to Kryssa as Servo rode up, surrounded by a large party of Knights. He was surprised to see the Elder here. The man had been intending to remain in Lane, when Ikar had departed. How had he come here so quickly?

"Ikar," the Elder announced, "well met." His eyes flickered to Kryssa and his voice took on a hard edge. "Where is Putar?"

"He caught up with us on the road to Lane. But...we were set upon by a Raptor," he lied. "The Elder...died well."

Servo stared at him for a long while. Ikar held his gaze, and finally the Elder nodded. "His wisdom will be missed," he said, then smiled, and Ikar sensed the fabrication had not gone unnoticed. "You did well to defeat such a beast, without even a scratch to your armour, Knight. I thank you for delivering the woman safely."

Inclining his head, Ikar spoke without thinking: "What is to become of Kryssa now?"

A stillness came over Servo. Without speaking, he dismounted and strode to where Ikar stood. "As you know, Knight, the *woman* is to be one of the three for our Great Sacrifice," he said dangerously. "Is that a problem?"

"No," Ikar replied, though his heart was racing now. "And what of the others?"

"We already have the first," Servo said, his voice growing light once more. "Fate has conspired to deny us a third. But fear not, the Saviour plays to her own tune. The third comes."

"Who?"

"Our scouts report the Consort and his companions are within a day's ride from our camp. They have evaded our forces until now, but they cannot remain free forever. If our people do not find them, the dragons will."

"Devon is close?" Ikar asked, a weight lifting from his shoulders. Surely this was a sign from the Saviour. "Good. I will put an end to him."

"*No*," Servo shot back. "He must be taken with the others. If the Saviour wills it, her Consort will join her in the heavens."

Ikar clenched his fists, though his armour revealed no other sign of his anger. For a long moment he stood staring at the Elder, struggling to push down his rage, to gather the will to agree. Finally he bowed his head in acquiescence.

"Very well," he rumbled, his voice betraying him despite his best efforts. "If it pleases you, my Elder, I will wait here. I would ensure my cousin receives an appropriate greeting." He glanced at Kryssa, feeling the need to say something, to bid the woman farewell, but the words died on his tongue. "I trust you will see the woman safely to her cage."

With that he turned away, but not before he caught a last glimpse of Kryssa. She wore a look of disappointment on her face, as though she had expected more from him. Shame burned his throat, though he knew…knew in his heart he was doing the right thing.

Head bowed, Ikar marched slowly back to the gates to wait for his rival.

❦ 35 ❦

The humid air clung to Braidon's skin as he hacked at the dense forest, moisture dripping down his back and making him long for the icy air of the mountains. The heavy armour they had taken from the Knights only made it worse, and he wondered how the men stood to wear the plate mail all day long.

They had left the volcanic plateau last night, dropping down into the jungles of Dragon Country, where the air was stifling, so thick it felt like he was breathing sludge. Even with his horse doing most of the work, Braidon had been sweating, and they had left their mounts in a clearing half an hour before. The creatures could not go quietly through the forest, and as they neared the Cove, they could not risk detection. Only Devon had kept his mount, riding on ahead down the broad trail left by the Knights.

Braidon just hoped the horses would still be there when they returned. They would be needed once Kryssa was freed. But even given free rein to roam, the horses would stand little chance if they were discovered by a Red Dragon.

But then, nor did they, whatever their accumulated skills with the blade.

Thinking of the great creatures, Braidon felt a pang of longing, as he recalled the powers he'd once commanded as a child. Though it had developed late, he'd feared and appreciated his magic in equal measures. Since the day Alana had died and magic was sponged from the world, it had been as though a part of him was missing, stolen away along with his sister.

Ahead of him, Caledan released a branch, which whipped back and struck Braidon in the face. The blow snapped him from memories of the past, and he cursed. Caledan glanced back and grinned.

"Better pay more attention," he whispered.

"Ay," Braidon snapped. "And I don't need you reminding me of it." He shouldered past Caledan and settled himself in behind Genevieve. "What's a sellsword like you doing here anyway?" he asked over his shoulder. "Gold's not much good if you're dead."

"I'm still trying to work that one out myself," Caledan replied.

Braidon raised an eyebrow. "Better figure it out quickly."

In the front, Genevieve gave a throaty chuckle. "Caledan's just embarrassed to admit he has a conscience."

"You wound me, woman," Caledan replied, then chuckled. "I thought I'd have figured it out by now, but…" He shrugged. "Maybe you're right. Or maybe I'm just curious to see if the old man can pull it off."

Braidon grunted. "I've seen Devon win when he had no right to—but I think even he might have bitten off too much this time."

He raised his sword and was about to slice through a

vine Genevieve had missed, when a hand gripped him by the shoulder.

"*Wait*," Caledan hissed.

"What?" Braidon asked, shrugging him off. "I don't see—"

"Listen," Genevieve said.

Braidon lowered his sword and frowned. Turning on the spot, he scanned the forest, listening for what Caledan had heard, but: "There's nothing."

"Ay," Caledan replied. "Not a sound."

Braidon's heart lurched, then began to race. They were right. A moment earlier the forest had been alive, a cacophony of hissing cicadas and squawking parrots, but now there was…nothing.

The Knights? Braidon mouthed, but Genevieve shook her head.

Scanning the undergrowth again, Braidon sought signs of pursuit. Raptors were known to lurk here; the monstrous creatures could stalk through the undergrowth with hardly a whisper, and tear a man's head from his shoulders before he knew what had struck him. He swallowed, the hackles raising on his neck as he imagined some dark monster watching them from the shadows.

"*Down!*" Genevieve shouted suddenly.

They threw themselves into the mud a second before the canopy exploded inwards with the shriek of breaking wood. Something red and massive crashed down through the branches, knocking a giant ficus tree sideways and ripping its great buttressed roots from the soft earth. The ground shook as the creature landed not twenty feet from where they crouched. Silence fell as it exhaled, the heat of its breath washing over them. The only sound was the slow creaking of the ficus as it continued to topple, followed by a muffled *thud* as it slammed into the earth.

Humans...

The dragon's voice sounded in his mind like iron on a chalkboard. Braidon wanted to slap his hands over his ears in a desperate attempt to block it out, but he remained frozen to the spot. Scarlet scales rippled in the sunlight streaming through the newly created hole in the canopy. The dragon took a step towards them. Horns twisted up above its massive head, tearing through vines as though they were made of paper. Claws the size of swords flashed out, ripping apart the trunk of another tree. It crumpled before the beast's power.

Filthy wretches, trespassing in our land.

There was no doubt it had seen them, and cursing, Braidon hurled himself to his feet and drew his sword. Almost instinctively, he reached for the power that had once been his, before remembering once again it had died with his sister.

Laughter roared in his mind, so loud he had to clench his teeth to keep from crying out.

You think to defy me, human?

Caledan and Genevieve joined Braidon, swords and daggers in hand. There was open fear on the woman's face, but she showed no hint of panic. In contrast, Caledan remained his usual impassive self. Braidon was impressed with the man's calm in the face of almost certain death. For himself, he had to grip his blade in two hands to keep the tip from shaking.

There was nothing they could do against this creature. Only blades that had been enchanted in the days of magic could pierce a dragon's thick hide. Its great black eyes were vulnerable, but the creature stood twenty feet high and they had no bow to even attempt such a shot.

Once, Magickers had hunted down any dragon that crossed the boundaries of Dragon Country, but now the creatures were almost unstoppable, only ever defeated by sheer numbers.

And there were just the three of them.

Braidon let out a long breath and sheathed his sword. He faced the beast with empty hands.

"No," he said, trying to keep the tremor from his voice. "We come to make an alliance."

"*What?*" Caledan exclaimed, while in their minds the dragon's laughter sounded again.

You have mistaken me for my long-extinct cousins, human.

"You need us," Braidon replied, ignoring its taunts.

We need for no one, the dragon snarled.

It stepped forward, nostrils flaring, and another wave of heat washed over them. Braidon shuddered as its jaws opened a fraction, revealing the red-hot glow deep in its throat.

"Then why do the Knights of Alana trespass in your lands?" Braidon asked.

A rumble sounded in the dragon's chest and a tendril of flame escaped its jaws, incinerating a nearby sapling.

The Knights shall pay for their impudence.

"No," Braidon replied. "There are too many, even for your great powers."

The dragon bared its teeth. Braidon gagged at the putrid stench of its breath, but this time it did not reply.

"The Knights are our enemies as well," Caledan added, finally understanding Braidon's plan. "We seek to drive them from our lands, and yours."

The giant eyes of the dragon studied them. *Then why do you wear their armour?*

"To deceive them," Braidon answered. "To sneak into their camp and take back what they stole from us."

And how does this aid my peoples?

Braidon swallowed and glanced at his companions. It all came down to this. Whatever resentment Caledan carried for the Plorsean King, Braidon would have to take his chances. The dragon would kill them all if he did not act. H pulled the helmet from his head and tossed it aside.

"Do you not know me, dragon?" he asked.

Caledan stared at him in confusion, but the Red Dragon's eyes narrowed to slits. It stepped closer, the long neck bending down to inspect him, the slits of its nostrils widening to breathe in his scent.

*King…*its voice sounded in their minds. It bared its teeth. *Or is it Tsar? Yes I know you, pup. Your father enslaved us! Tell me, why should I not roast you where you stand?*

Braidon flicked a glance at Caledan. The man stood beside him, eyes hard and jaw clenched, sword trembling at his side, but Braidon could not be distracted now.

"Because it was my sister and I who freed you!" he called. "And because I am your only chance. Help me, and I will bring my armies against the Knights. I will drive them from your lands."

The Knights have great weapons, King, the Red Dragon replied. *Perhaps yours is the wrong side to choose.*

"And if you choose the Knights, what then?" Braidon shot back. "At least my people have always respected the boundaries of your lands."

The Red Dragon bared its teeth. *We would have new boundaries.*

Braidon's heart palpitated. He sensed the eyes of his

companions on him, but there was no going back now. "So be it," Braidon whispered, knowing it was a betrayal of his people, "but the Red Dragons must pledge a new oath, to honour my rule and all my line that comes after."

Our Golden cousins once made such an oath, the Red Dragon snarled. *To their doom.*

"And how long will your people survive against these new weapons?" Braidon asked, taking a gamble. He shuddered to think what type of weapon the Knights had, that even the Red Dragons feared them.

The Red Dragon growled and clawed at the ground, tearing up roots and great chunks of earth. Lifting its head, it howled. The sound tore at their ears, echoing up through the canopies and the skies beyond. From the distance, there came an answering cry, then another and another. Braidon shuddered, looking again at the Red Dragon, but its eyes were opaque now, its mind elsewhere. Then it blinked, the awful intelligence returning.

Very well, King, it rumbled in his mind. *We swear, though know this, our price is the land from here to the Lane.*

Braidon's stomach tied itself into knots, but he inclined his head. "So be it."

I am Ingytus. Call when you have need, and I shall answer.

With a roar, the dragon bounded into the air, a single beat of its wings carrying it free of the canopy. An icy sweat dripped down Braidon's back as he watched it disappear into the sky beyond. Then he sucked in a breath and turned to face his companions, aware he had only traded one enemy for another.

Caledan stared back at him with ice in his eyes.

"Draw your sword, *Braidon.*"

❧ 36 ❧

"Draw your sword, Braidon," Caledan repeated, thrusting his blade at the man's chest.

Brenden—Braidon—leapt back and raised his empty hands. "I'm not going to fight you, Caledan."

"Then die!" Caledan screamed, and made a wild swipe at the king's head. Braidon ducked and his blade took a branch from a tree.

Caledan's heart was pounding in his chest and he wanted nothing more than to see the king's blood soaking the leaf-strewn earth. Devon had betrayed him—though how the man had known what Caledan intended, he could not guess—and now he would die, too. But not before Caledan finally had his revenge.

"Caledan, stop!" Genevieve tried to get his attention, but when she darted towards him, he spun, his boot flashing out to catch her in the stomach. She crumpled to the ground clutching her midriff, and turning, he advanced once more on Braidon.

Crying out, the king tripped and crashed to the ground. Caledan leapt after him, his sword aiming for the man's back, but Braidon rolled and Caledan's blade sank deep into the dirt. Tearing it free, Caledan stalked after his foe.

Now Braidon scrambled to his feet and drew his sword. "Let's not do this," he hissed. "You'll draw the Knights down on all of us."

"Let them come!" Caledan roared, directing an attack at Braidon's head. The king blocked it smoothly and retreated. Caledan followed with a roar: *"Fight me!"*

"Why?" Braidon gasped as Caledan's blade slid beneath his guard and slashed his plate mail.

A shrill scraping sound rent the air, then Braidon's mailed fist swept around, catching Caledan in the helmet and sending him staggering back. His ears rang, but snarling, he recovered his feet and started towards the king once more.

"You destroyed my life!" he shrieked, emphasising each word with a wild swing of his blade. He made no effort to defend himself, only attacked with relentless fury. "You took *everything* from me!"

"What are you talking about?" Braidon snapped, parrying each blow.

"You will pay for what your sister did!" Caledan bellowed. "For leaving my mother to die!"

Braidon's eyes still showed his confusion. Steel rang out as their blades met again, then he spun on his heel and struck Caledan with his elbow. Caledan stumbled back, and the king held out his hands for peace.

"I'm sorry!" he gasped. "Whatever Alana did to your mother, I'm sorry! But I cannot change it."

"No, but you can pay for it with your life!"

Braidon leapt away. "And the rest of Plorsea with it?"

"Plorsea be damned!" Caledan cursed.

The king parried another blow, but Caledan lashed out with a boot, catching him in the chest and toppling him with a crash of metal. He swung his sword again, but Braidon raised an arm and the blade went shrieking off his heavy wrist guards. Rolling clumsily, the king came to his feet.

"And what about Devon?" Genevieve interrupted. She was up again, a massive dagger in hand. "You swore you'd help him."

Caledan glanced at her. "He lied to me," he gasped. "I'll kill him next." He raised his sword to strike at the king again.

"And what about Kryssa?" Braidon shouted. "What about Pela? You might not care for me or Devon, but they have done nothing to harm you!"

An image of Pela flashed into Caledan's mind, back on the *Seadragon,* when she'd first asked for his help. She'd dropped her sword, made a fool of herself, almost run in the face of his laughter, but in the end she had picked it up and tried again.

Angrily, he bared his teeth. "We're all alone in this world," Caledan hissed. "Best the girl learn that now."

"No, Caledan," Braidon replied. "We're not. We have friends, family. You said Alana left your mother to die—will you do the same now to Pela?"

"It's not the same!"

"It is!" Braidon bellowed. "Can you not see it? If you kill me, if you murder Devon, Kryssa dies! *Pela's mother dies!* And what will you achieve? It won't bring your mother back, only destroy more innocent lives."

"I..."

"Caledan," Genevieve whispered, edging forward. "Please, don't do this. We need you, Kryssa needs you. Please help us bring her home."

Caledan glanced from the woman to the king and sucked in a breath. His entire life he had waited for this moment, to have the king standing before him with nothing but blades between them. He had trained and saved and brokered deals, all to this one end. Now fate had finally brought them together...

"I swore on my mother's life," he croaked. "I have waited so long..."

"Then wait a little longer," Braidon hissed. "Until we've rescued Kryssa. Then, if you still wish to fight, I'll happily oblige you."

Caledan looked up. "Why should I believe you?" he whispered. "You have lied to me for days."

"Because it's the right thing to do," Braidon snapped. "Because you have no other choice."

"Fine," Caledan hissed, sheathing his sword in a rush. "But the second we're free..."

"We fight to the death," Braidon replied wearily.

Caledan let out a long breath. In the distance, shouts whispered through the trees. Together the three of them turned towards the sound.

"Better put your helmets back on, boys," Genevieve said lightly. "We're Knights of Alana now, nothing more. Think you can do that?"

"Sure," Caledan muttered.

Braidon had just settled the helmet back on his head when the cracking of forest litter announced the arrival of mounted Knights. They rode into the clearing with swords drawn, all wearing the familiar armour of their Order. Now though, heavy crossbows also dangled from their saddles.

Caledan narrowed his eyes at the sight. The Knights usually scorned such weapons, preferring the test of hand-to-hand combat. As they neared, he realised these bows were different from any he had ever seen. The wooden bow arm was gone, replaced by smooth steel and a winch to reset the wire string. Caledan couldn't help but remember the dragon's words.

The Knights have great weapons.

Were these what it had spoken of? Caledan shuddered to think of the damage the bolt from such a crossbow might do. It didn't bear thinking about, and raising a hand, Caledan hailed the Knights.

"Hoy, lads!" Caledan shouted. "Well met."

"Well met indeed," the Knight in the lead said. They had slowed upon seeing their armour, though the group still eyed the broken trees cautiously, as though expecting a dragon to appear at any moment. "You're well off the regular path. What are you doing out here?"

"Dragon spooked the horses," Caledan replied. "Lost the path, and the stupid beasts."

"Lucky you didn't lose your lives," the Knight replied. "We saw it fly off, big bugger. Still, a few of shots from these and they turn tail quick enough." He patted the crossbow in emphasis.

"Where are you from?" another asked, kicking his horse forward. His eyes bored into Caledan, and he sensed the man's suspicion.

"New recruits from Goldtown," Caledan answered, naming a Lonian town far up in the Sandstone Peaks.

"Long ride," the Knight grunted.

"Ay, we'll be glad to reach the Cove."

The first Knight snorted. "I'll bet." He turned his horse on the spot. "Well, I don't think your horses are coming back. You can walk with us though. We'll see you safely to camp. Wouldn't want any brothers eaten by those red buggers."

"Thank you," Caledan said, with feeling this time. "One encounter was more than enough."

❧ 37 ❧

Devon walked slowly down the beaten path, savouring the tranquillity of the forest, the quiet chirping of birds and the whisper of wind in the branches overhead. Unfortunately, the breeze did not reach the undergrowth, and taking a rag from his pocket, Devon wiped the sweat from his forehead. The warhammer hung heavy on his back, and he found himself doubting whether he still had the strength to wield it.

His misgivings grew with each twist and turn of the path. Once it might have been only a deer trail, but the passage of Knights had carved a broad passage through the jungle. He scanned the undergrowth as he walked, though alone he would stand little chance against even a Raptor, let alone a dragon. He wondered how the Knights had grown so bold, to venture into a place like this.

Because if the Knights of Alana no longer feared the Red Dragons…

Devon squared his shoulders and pushed away the defeatist thoughts. He could not afford them now, not when he was about to walk into an enemy stronghold and demand Kryssa's release.

A shudder ran down Devon's spine as he imagined Kryssa bound and chained, readied for the slaughter on the solstice—tomorrow.

What foul minds had created such a ritual: this *Great Sacrifice*? The Order claimed it was in honour of Alana's own sacrifice, but Devon had been there, had witnessed her final moments.

And it had not been for the Gods, or magic, or even the Tsar that she had sacrificed herself.

It had been to save Devon's own life, to shield him from her former lover, his rival Quinn.

Even thirty years later, the memory scorched him. He felt an awful sadness that her final moments had been so twisted by the Order, that deceitful men now ruled in her name, manipulating thousands into believing such an awful lie.

There was a bitter taste in Devon's mouth as he continued through the jungle. He could have prevented this long ago, had he paid attention, spoken out against the rising Order. But after Alana's death he had been tired of the world, of leading, of fighting other men's wars. So he had retreated, and the Order had taken full advantage of his absence.

Now their vile beliefs were ingrained in the Order's followers, its Knights so fanatical they could attack innocents at worship and believe they were heroes for doing so. It made Devon sick to his stomach and he longed to put an end to them.

But after all this time, he was only one man, well past his prime. His name no longer had the power to turn back armies, to send fear down the spines of his foes. He was just Devon, the roof-layer, the tavern keeper.

It would have to be enough.

Voices carried through the forest as he rounded a bend, drawing him back to the present. He sighed and marched on until the trees gave way to open ground. Ash stained the earth black beneath his boots, crushed into the earth by the passage of men and horses. A wooden palisade and trench barred his path and he drew to a stop.

Shouts came from behind the wall, followed by the squeal of hinges as the wooden gates were dragged open. A Knight strode forward, flanked on either side by others. He came to a stop several feet from where Devon stood and crossed his arms.

"So, you are Devon," he said, his voice echoing within the helmet.

The Knight stood shoulder to shoulder with Devon, and in the steel-plated armour he made an imposing sight. Devon had fought many large men in his life, and had defeated them all, but the sight of the Knight now gave him pause. There was something familiar about the man, something that called to him, though he did not recognise the voice.

Finally Devon grinned. "I am," he replied. "And who might you be, sonny?"

Laughter rumbled from the Knight's helmet. "My name is Ikar," he said. "Well met, cousin."

"Cousin?" Devon frowned. "Can't say I'm aware of any family in these parts."

"Our lines separated after Alan," Ikar replied. "Followed different paths. Yours claimed the hammer of heroes, while mine…"

He trailed off, and recovering from his surprise, Devon

grimaced. "Remained." He took a step closer. "Tell me, cousin. If my family followed the warrior's path, what of yours? Were they Magickers, like our great, great grandfather, Alastair?"

A stillness came over Ikar at his words, while behind him the other Knights shifted nervously and glanced at the giant. Devon laughed, knowing he'd struck a nerve. "That is quite the career change, from Magicker to Knight."

"Silence!" Ikar snarled. He reached for his sword, but something gave him pause, and with an effort of will he released the hilt. "I am here to make amends for my family's past, to reclaim the legacy of Alan the Great."

"You're here to kill me then?"

"No," Ikar said shortly, and Devon sensed what he said next was not his desire. "I'm to take you before the Elders."

"And why would I allow that?" Devon rumbled.

"You don't have much choice." Ikar shrugged, gesturing to the men behind him. "But, for the sake of avoiding further bloodshed, I'm told you care for the woman, Kryssa."

Devon bared his teeth. "Ay," he growled. "If you've har—"

"The woman is safe," Ikar interrupted, raising his hands in a gesture of peace. "Or she was last night, when I delivered her into the custody of the Elders. But if you wish to see her, you must come with me."

For a long while, Devon stared at the Knight, though he could decipher little of the man's intentions behind the steel visor. Like so many of his brethren, he spoke with the fervour of the devout, and yet...he seemed different, as though touched by the slightest of doubts, and finally Devon nodded.

"Very well," he murmured. "Take me to my...to

Kryssa."

Ikar inclined his head, and turning, he marched through the gates without a backwards glance. The other Knights fell in around Devon as he followed the man into the camp. Beyond the palisade, they marched down a great avenue of canvas tents. Men and women raced amongst the tents, most dressed in ordinary clothing rather than the armour of Knights, and Devon wondered where so many worshipers of the Order had come from. Surely there weren't so many in all of Plorsea?

Devon walked with his fists clenched tight at his side, aware he was truly in the dragon's den now. He could sense the Knights watching him from beyond the dark slits of their visors, but kept his eyes fixed straight ahead, determined not to show his fear. Focusing his mind, he breathed deeply, concentrating on the action rather than his surroundings, and his heartbeat slowed.

The meditation helped to calm him, and by the time they reached the cliffs, his mind was focused, fixed on the task ahead. He prayed the others had managed to infiltrate the camp and were even now seeking out Kryssa's prison. If all went to plan, Devon's distraction would allow them the opportunity to free her, and they would escape unnoticed before the Knights noticed her absence.

"Our ancestor died here, you know," Devon said, making conversation as they started down the narrow trail that had been carved into the granite cliffs. Unlike the path in the forest, the steps appeared to have been there for centuries.

"Alan the Great died at Fort Fall."

"Ay, and his father-in-law, Alastair, died on this beach, betrayed by one of Archon's minions."

"An evil man betrayed by an evil man," Ikar replied

shortly.

But Devon was hardly paying attention to the man's words now. His eyes had been drawn down into the Cove, across the black sands and jagged fingers of rock, to where a great project was underway.

Men and women bustled to and fro across the beach, disappearing into a massive wooden structure that stretched almost to the tops of the cliffs. From his vantage point, Devon could just see over the top of the outer wall, where row upon row of benches spiralled down to a wooden platform in the centre. It was almost an amphitheatre, stretching from the cliffs all the way down to the ocean, where in place of a fourth wall, a makeshift dock extended out beyond the waves.

Devon could only shake his head at the undertaking. The Knights had built a great stadium in which to conduct their cruel ritual, to make an exhibition of Kryssa's sacrifice —or perhaps a threat to those that opposed them.

As they neared the beach, Devon finally turned his attention to the warships floating in the bay. Most were anchored far out beyond the barrier reefs, their passengers using the rowboats now lining the shore to make landfall. The green flag of Lonia flew from most, outnumbering the red of Plorsea three to one.

Only one ship had sailed close, almost to the docks of the amphitheatre itself.

Sand crunched beneath Devon's boots as he stepped down onto the black sands of Malevolent Cove. How different it must be now, from when his ancestor had died here. A powerful Magicker, Alastair had sacrificed everything to protect the Three Nations, abandoning even his wife and his daughter to answer the call of the Gods. His very existence spat in the face of everything the Knights of

Alana believed in. No wonder Ikar wanted to sponge his lineage from history.

Looking out over the murky waters of the bay, Devon wondered if he too had come there to die, if this dark shore would be his doom. He could almost accept it, if it meant Kryssa would live.

Ikar led him along the sand and through a tunnel into the amphitheatre. Within, the structure groaned and creaked, and Devon wondered how long such a creation could last. The Knights were well-armed, but surely the Red Dragons would not stand this interference. If the stadium caught light, everyone within would be consumed in minutes.

He shuddered, but after a few minutes they passed safely back into the open, onto the wooden stage at the centre. Attendants raced past hauling sand and spreading it over the platform. Whispers came from overhead and Devon was surprised to see the stands above were already beginning to fill. The sun was dropping fast towards the horizon, lighting the sky aflame, and Devon realised with a start midnight was only a few hours away.

The solstice was approaching.

The Knights led him out onto the docks. At the end, steps led down to the water, where a rowboat bobbed. Devon's heart dropped into his stomach. If they were holding Kryssa on the ship, how would Braidon and the others reach her in time?

But there was no going back now. He closed his eyes, and prayed his old friend would find a way.

They boarded the boat and the tiny vessel surged forward as several Knights took up the oars. The ship itself was not far, just a hundred yards off the pier. Its open deck was easily visible from the amphitheatre, and Devon was touched by a premonition: that this ship would somehow form part of the spectacle.

He swallowed, his gaze turning to the men standing at the railings of the ship. He recognised the face of one of the Elders from Townirwin, but the rest of the men were unknown to him, though all wore the red, green and blue robes of Elders.

A rope ladder was tossed down to them. Ikar went up first, then gestured for Devon to follow. Oars splashed below as the remaining Knights turned the boat back to shore, robbing Devon of his only escape route. He might be able to swim the distance to shore, but he would make an easy target for the heavy crossbows of the Knights.

Reaching the deck, Devon swung over the railings and found himself surrounded. Ikar stood closest, his armour shining in the noon sun, along with a dozen other Knights. Beyond, the Elders stood watching him in a half-circle. The one from Townirwin stepped up beside Ikar, his eyes aglow.

"Welcome, Consort of Alana," he whispered.

Devon couldn't help but chuckle. "You did not welcome me the last time I stepped foot in one of your Castles."

A frown touched the Elder's forehead, but he continued unperturbed. "I am called Servo, and we did not know you then," he replied. "Now we know you come before us by the Saviour's will."

"I've come to free…Kryssa," Devon snapped, his good humour evaporating. "Alana has nothing to do with it."

"The Saviour has proclaimed that Kryssa must join her in the struggle against the Gods," the Elder replied.

Devon's heart beat faster. "If you've hurt her…" His hammer leapt into his hands and he took a step towards the Elders.

Ikar moved to intercept him, his silent helmet vacant of

emotion, while the Elders took a collective step back.

"The woman lives," Servo replied. Of all of them, only he had not retreated. "The Great Sacrifice is to be completed on the birth of the solstice."

Devon lowered his hammer half an inch. "I wish to see her."

"She's otherwise occupied," another of the Elders said with a laugh. Devon fixed him with a glare and he fell suddenly silent.

"You will not take her," Devon growled, his voice rumbling across the broken waters, carrying even to the distant shore. Then he bowed his head. "Free her, and I will take her place."

Whispers spread across the deck of the ship as the men exchanged glances, building until finally Servo's voice rose above the others. "Silence!"

Devon looked up as the Elder approached. Their eyes locked and a shudder slid down Devon's spine at the passion in the man's eyes.

"You would sacrifice your life for the Saviour?" he murmured, coming close.

For a moment, Devon considered striking him down. The man's insanity was a plague that would sweep across his nation. But then there would be no bargaining, no saving Kryssa, no walking away. His shoulders slumped. "I would."

Abruptly, Servo turned away, re-joining the Elders. "We have our third!" he proclaimed, turning back to Devon. "The three will join the Saviour at midnight!"

"What?" Devon hissed, his hammer coming up. "That is not the deal I offered!"

"The Saviour's will is clear," Servo continued, ignoring him now.

Snarling, Devon advanced until Ikar blocked his path

again. He glared into the metal mask. "Out of the way, cousin," he snarled. "Or you'll be the first to die."

Quick as lightning, Ikar drew his sword. Devon leapt back, readying his hammer to attack.

"No!" Servo screamed as the two warriors faced off against one another. "It cannot be this way!"

His words gave Ikar pause, but Devon roared his anger and charged. The Knight's sword leapt to meet him and sparks burst from their weapons as they clashed. They sprang apart once more as the Elder continued to scream.

"I'll kill you all before you harm my daughter!" Devon bellowed.

A woman's laughter carried down from the upper deck before he could launch another attack. He paused, a frown creasing his forehead as he searched for the source. Then he staggered, almost losing his grip on his hammer, as he saw the woman standing atop the stairwell.

An amused smile on her lips, the Queen of Plorsea slowly descended to the main deck. The rattle of armour came from Ikar as he dropped to his knees before the woman.

"My queen!" he cried, clearly as stunned as Devon to see her there.

"Marianne," Devon whispered, a pit opening in his stomach. "What are you doing here?"

Ignoring him, she turned to Servo. "My dear Elders," she murmured. "Would you deny us all the battle of the ages? Let the men fight, let all of our people see it."

"But my Queen, what of the Great Sacrifice?" Servo howled.

Marianne only laughed. Her eyes flashed as she set them on Devon once more. "My dear Elder, there will be blood enough for all by the time these two have finished."

❦ 38 ❦

Standing at the edge of the cliff looking down into Malevolent Cove, Braidon wondered how he could have been so foolish. It had all been there for him to see, but he had walked blindly into a catastrophe of his own making.

Maybe it was the memory of his sister that had misled him, a desire to see her memory live on. Yet now, looking down upon the packed amphitheatre and knowing what was to come, he felt ashamed that he had allowed her name to become so sullied.

"I have failed my people," he whispered.

"You did that a long time ago," Caledan snapped.

Genevieve placed a hand on his shoulder. "You haven't failed yet, Braidon."

Braidon gestured at the bay. Only one warship had entered, but a dozen others bobbed at anchor out beyond the dangerous reefs. Most flew green flags, only a few the red of Plorsea. "Those are Lonian warships. And they're using the same devices as the Baronian ship that attacked us. They've been working together all along. If our army isn't roused, they could sail right up to Lake Ardath and take the capital."

Caledan snorted. "Ardath won't fall so easily."

"Just now, I think we need to worry about how we're going to find Kryssa in all this," Genevieve murmured.

"They'll have her somewhere down there, I'm guessing." Braidon nodded at the amphitheatre. "If this is for the Great Sacrifice they've all been talking about, they'll…make a spectacle of it."

Genevieve's jaw tightened. "It'll be dark soon. We'd better get down the cliffs before we lose the light." She set off without looking back.

Braidon followed after a moment's hesitation, Caledan a step behind.

"You don't think it's time to call the dragons?" the sellsword asked as they picked their way down towards the beach.

"No," Braidon replied shortly, "we wait until we find Kryssa. All hell's going to break loose once the Red Dragons become involved."

"Fair enough," Caledan chuckled.

"Keep it down," Genevieve hissed. "There's men on the beach."

They descended the last dozen feet in silence. The whisper of voices inside the amphitheatre rose in pitch as they stepped onto the sand, then became a roar. They swung around in time to see a line of fire leap along the rim of the stadium. Braidon held his breath as the flames raced outwards, waiting for the whole structure to catch alight, but they did not spread beyond the rim. Finally he caught the dim glint of steel amidst the flames, and realised a line of torches had been placed around the top of the stadium.

"I don't think light is going to be a problem," Caledan muttered. "Though how we're going to escape…"

"Let's figure that out once we've found her," Genevieve snapped, taking the lead.

In their armour they had passed unnoticed, but Braidon was more than aware how flimsy their disguise would become under questioning. They knew little about the particulars of the Knights and their Order. The beach was crowded with worshipers and other Knights, but Genevieve cut across the cliff before they reached the bottom, leading them through the faint shadows towards the rear of the amphitheatre.

As they neared, Braidon saw that the structure had been built right into the granite cliffs. The wooden outer walls blocked their path. They stood there for a moment trying to find a door or some other entranceway, but the shadows revealed nothing. Below, men and women were beginning to file through the tunnel into the amphitheatre. It appeared to be the only entrance.

"What now?" Caledan hissed.

"Maybe we should try the front door," Braidon suggested, nodding to the tunnel.

The *crack* of splintering wood came from behind them, and they spun in time to see Genevieve lining up a second blow. Her boot slammed into the wall of the amphitheatre, and the wood gave way, revealing the pitch-black beyond.

"What are you doing?" Braidon gasped.

"Those people down there are spectators," she replied. "I'm not going to sit around and watch while they hang Kryssa. Come on, help me with this."

"That's—"

Before Braidon could finish his objection, Caledan joined the huntress and they managed to tear another plank from the wall. Braidon swore and checked on the crowd below, but between their hushed whispers and the roar of the ocean, the commotion had gone unnoticed.

Joining the others, Braidon saw the wooden boards that made up the amphitheatre's walls had been cut haphazardly and hammered together to fill in the gaps. He'd rarely seen such poor construction outside the slums of Lane, though he supposed the Knights did not need the place to last. The thought of all the worshipers now perched above them gave Braidon pause, but Genevieve and Caledan had already disappeared into the darkness, and taking a deep breath, he followed them through the jagged hole, into the hollows of the outer wall.

Within, not even the great torches above the stadium could penetrate, and they found themselves in the pitch black. Braidon fumbled around for his flint, but Genevieve beat him to it. Sparks flashed and then a tongue of flame cast back the darkness. Half-a-hundred support beams packed the open space like the trees of a forest, while above the roof zigzagged downwards. They were directly beneath the stands of the amphitheatre.

They spread out, searching for an exit that would lead into the main areas of the amphitheatre. This section appeared completely unused, its floor littered with discarded pieces of wood and construction materials. Threading his way through the support beams, Braidon was beginning to think they would have to return to the beach and attempt the tunnel after all, when a call came from Caledan across the space.

Braidon and Genevieve stumbled to join him. A tiny crack, no wider than a fingertip, allowed a sliver of light to pierce the darkness. It was a door, though the shadows crisscrossing the light indicated it had been boarded up from the other side.

Caledan put his eye to the crack, then withdrew once more. He looked at them, his jaw clenched. "There's a guard."

Braidon loosed his sword in its scabbard. The time for caution had run out; if they didn't find Kryssa soon, they would be too late. Devon could only distract the Elders for so long.

"Are you ready?" he asked, glancing at Genevieve and Caledan. Once they went through, there would be no turning back.

They both nodded and Caledan stepped aside, clearing the way for Braidon. He launched himself forward, aiming a kick at the thread of light. The door gave way with a *crash*, and they rushed through with swords drawn.

＊ 39 ＊

"Hurry up," the guard growled, shoving Pela in the back.

She cried and almost tripped over the final step before the door above was yanked open. Her eyes watered as the light struck her and she blinked, unable to shield her face with her arms bound behind her. Before she could continue up, rough hands grasped her arms and hauled her the rest of the way.

The breath hissed between Pela's teeth as the guard tossed her to the deck. Gasping, she struggled to sit up. The flickering of firelight in the distance lit the deck of the queen's ship, blinding her until her eyes adjusted.

"*Pela!*" a woman shrieked. "No!"

Pela gasped and swung around, recognising Kryssa's voice. After all this time, she'd begun to think she would never see her mother again. Hope swelled in her heart, only to wither and die as she found Kryssa edged by two guards, her arms similarly bound. Tears stung Pela's eyes as she took in her mother's dishevelled hair and bruised face. Gritting her teeth, she tried to fight back, but the guard only grabbed her and dragged her across the deck to join her mother.

"What are you doing here?" Kryssa croaked, her face a mask of grief.

"I invited her."

The two of them looked around as the queen stepped from her cabin out into the twilight. She strode across to join them, a smile on her perfect lips.

"You witch!" Pela screamed, struggling in the grasp of the guard. "I trusted you!"

Marianne sighed. "I am sorry, young Pela," she replied. "Truly I am. Had the Baronians not failed so spectacularly, we would not have needed you. My dear husband was meant to be our sacrifice against the Light, but alas, the fool had to go and die too soon. We had to make…last minute adjustments."

"*No!*" Kryssa shouted. Tearing free of the guards, she charged at the queen, but a fist caught her in the stomach, doubling her over. She crumpled to the deck, her breath coming in half-shrieked gasps.

Teeth bared, Pela threw herself at the man that had attacked her mother, but he was twice her size and her hands were still bound. His iron fist caught Pela in the face and sent her crashing down alongside Kryssa.

"If we're quite done?" Marianne murmured, wandering closer. "Mother and daughter—has there ever been a bond so strong?"

"May the Three Gods curse you," Kryssa snarled.

The queen chuckled and leaned in close. "My dear, you and I both know those sorry creatures are dead," she whispered, before saying in a louder voice, "Even now, at the end, you cling to your cursed deities. Get them up."

Men raced forward and hauled them to their feet. Kryssa seemed to shrink into her captive's arms as she stared at the queen. "Please," she whispered. "Do what you want with me, but leave my daughter—"

"Your daughter is twice the heathen you are, witch," an Elder snapped, stepping forward. Pela started as she realised she recognised him from Townirwin. "She killed an Elder in cold blood. She'll burn at your side for her crimes against the Order, as our sacrifice against the Light God. As you will burn against the God of the Sky."

"Please..." Kryssa tried again, but the Elder back-handed her across the cheek.

"Speak no more, witch!"

Kryssa's face hardened, her eyes taking a dangerous glint. "By the Three Gods, I'll see the both of you dead," she hissed.

The Elder raised his hand again, but something about Kryssa seemed to give him pause, and after a second he smirked and stepped back, though now Pela thought she glimpsed fear on his face.

The queen stepped between them. "Enough of this," she announced gaily. "We're about to find out who our sacrifice against the Earth is to be!" She pointed off the bow of the ship.

Pela followed her arm and finally saw the source of the firelight. A thousand torches burned around the rim of a massive structure stretching out from the cliffs of a cove. She had never heard of its like anywhere in Plorsea. Where in the Three Nations had the queen brought them?

Then her gaze was drawn to the two figures standing on the great stage of the theatre. A lump lodged in her throat as she saw the massive man with warhammer in hand. It had to be Devon. Blood pounded in her ears and she barely heard her mother's scream.

"What is he doing here?"

"Devon?" Marianne chuckled. Arms folded, she stepped between them. "Why, he's here to save you, of course. I told him if he could defeat Ikar, he could take your place in the flames."

"*No…*" Kryssa whispered, her silver eyes wide.

"He *must* know we intend to betray him, but the man refuses to give up. Of course, we didn't leave him much choice."

"You witch," Pela gasped. "*Devon!*" She screamed his name until one of her captors thumped her in the head, but it made no difference. He could not hear her over the waves crashing on the black shore.

Pela sagged in her captor's arms. Looking from her mother to Devon, she struggled to find the strength that had carried her this far, but it had abandoned her. Across the narrow waters, Devon stood out stark against the burning torches, his aged face cast in shadows. Against him stood a mammoth of a man, larger even than Devon in his plate mail armour. As she watched, he drew a broadsword from his back and saluted.

"May your legend end with courage, cousin!" his voice boomed out across the waters.

"And may yours end in flame," the queen said to the two of them.

She gestured to the guards, who dragged them to the mast and bound them there, back to back. The Elder and his guards departed, followed by the rest of the Knights, until only Marianne remained with them on the deck of her ship.

The clash of weapons echoed from the cliffs as the battle in the stadium began. Wood creaked as the ship rocked at anchor. Pela strained against her bonds, glaring at the queen, but it made no difference.

Smiling sadly, Marianne wandered across to them. "I am sorry, you know," she murmured. "But you really are the best sacrifices I could have asked for."

"You don't even believe!" Kryssa shrieked, her jaw snapping closed as though to tear out the queen's throat.

"No," Marianne shook her head, "but the Elders, they discovered long ago there was a power in death. They just lack the…creativity to use it efficiently."

"You're insane," Pela said.

"We'll soon find out, I suppose," the queen responded. She reached into her pocket, and withdrew two necklaces of polished metal, though not of any kind Pela had ever seen. Runes had been carved into the dark steel. "I'm afraid you will not live to find out though. Here, would you be so good as to wear these?"

She fastened the steel to their necks, despite their protestations. Bound tightly to the mast, there was nothing either of them could do to resist. An icy cold slid down Pela's spine as the clasp clicked shut, though the metal was warm from the queen's pocket.

"There!" Marianne said, stepping back. "Now we match." She held up her arm, revealing a similar band around her wrist.

"What are they?" Kryssa grated.

"Oh don't worry, they can't harm you," Marianne replied easily. "They're just a prototype, based on a little something we took from the Tsar's records."

"So what do they do?" Pela snapped.

But the queen was already turning away, one hand raised in farewell. "Farewell!" she laughed. "I do hope you enjoy the show."

Then she was gone, disappearing over the side into the rowboat, leaving the two women alone aboard the ship.

40

Defeat my Knight, and I will set your family free.

Devon's heart thumped in time with the pounding waves as he watched Ikar. All around the stadium, the stands were packed with the followers of the Order. Their jeers and taunts rained down upon him, but Devon hardly heard. There was an ache in his chest as though he'd been impaled, as though the queen had already struck him a mortal blow and he was simply living out the last motions of his life.

And perhaps that was the truth. Somehow, he had convinced himself that this plan could work, that he could march into the centre of the Knights of Alana and cause a commotion, a distraction of some sort that would give his friends the opportunity to free Kryssa.

How foolish he'd been.

Marianne, the queen who had stood beside Braidon all these years, was behind everything.

And he had delivered Pela right into her hands.

Roaring, Devon threw himself suddenly forward,

swinging his hammer with all his might. In his heart, he knew this battle had no meaning, that ultimately Marianne would betray him as she had everyone else. But in that moment, he did not care. So great was his rage and desperation that his exhaustion, his age, all were forgotten in the face of this foe that dared stand against him.

But for all that, Ikar was faster still. He twisted from the path of Devon's hammer and lashed out with his fist. Devon's ears rang as the blow struck him in the side of the head and he staggered back, holding up his hammer to deflect a riposte.

But Ikar did not follow, and cursing, Devon began to circle the swordsman. The slits in Ikar's visor followed him, and Devon found himself wondering at the man hidden within. This was no green recruit like the Knights they had defeated on the plateau; Ikar was a man grown, as skilled as any opponent Devon had faced in his long years.

The stage had been covered in sand from the cove and raked clean, clearing it of obstacles that might trip an unsuspecting boot. The crowd had fallen silent now, but each time their weapons clashed, it seemed as though the very earth shook with their screams. They knew this battle could not last long, that with warhammer and broadsword, a single blow could end the fight. No one wanted to miss that final blow.

Devon adjusted his grip on his hammer and stilled. Ikar mimicked the movement, the tip of his sword lifting half an inch, and Devon attacked. The broadsword leapt to meet him, and steel rang out as the weapons smashed together. But using his prodigious strength, Devon dragged on the haft of his hammer, redirecting his attack for Ikar's helm.

Ikar cried out, his head whipping back, but he could not completely avoid the blow. There came a great shriek of metal as Devon's hammer ricocheted from Ikar's helmet. Then his foe's sword lashed out, slashing Devon across the chest, and he was forced to retreat before it impaled him.

Cursing, Ikar staggered on the black sands. Devon's blow had warped his helmet and visor, making it difficult for the Knight to see. Devon started forward and then hesitated, his eyes flicking out to where the queen's ship still bobbed at anchor. His stomach twisted as he finally saw Kryssa and Pela, bound now to the masts of the ship. Movement came from the end of the docks as the queen climbed from her rowboat and turned to watch him, a smile on her lips. Her eyes were mocking, as though begging him to strike Ikar down, so that she might betray him one final time.

Turning back to his opponent, he lowered his hammer. "You'd best remove it."

"I can't!" Ikar snapped. "I am a Knight of Alana. We are forbidden from revealing ourselves to those outside our Order."

"So be it," Devon chuckled, "if you're that eager to die…"

"Wait!" Ikar snarled, then cursed. He tore the helmet loose and hurled it away.

The breath caught in Devon's throat as he saw the Knight's face for the first time. He could have been looking into a mirror of his younger self. Anger and confusion reflected from the man's amber eyes as he lifted his sword once more, preparing himself for the battle to come. Devon swallowed, reminded of his own fervour as a youth, when he had marched against Trola beneath the flag of the Tsar.

He lowered his hammer. "I don't want this," Devon murmured. "There's no need for us to fight."

"Ah, but there is," Ikar said. He unclipped the straps of his breastplate, and it toppled to the ground with a *thump*.

He continued to remove the rest of his armour. Stepping clear, he grimaced and gestured at the pile. "It's no use against a warhammer, is it?"

"No…" Devon replied, his voice sad. He lifted his hammer as Ikar started towards him.

"No," Ikar agreed, his sword coming up.

Unencumbered now, he moved with the speed of a scorpion, his blade flashing out to catch Devon on the arm. A curse tore from Devon's lips as he tried to counter, but the Knight danced clear and the warhammer struck the sand with a dull crash. He jumped back as Ikar attacked again, and this time managed to deflect the blade on the head of his hammer.

Ikar twisted and lashed out with his boot, striking Devon a blow to the calf. He staggered and lashed out wildly, coming within an inch of crushing his cousin's arm. Ikar leapt clear and Devon made to follow, but there was a burning in his chest and he almost staggered. Breath ragged, he recovered and forced a grin, but the disdain in Ikar's eyes told Devon the man had seen.

"It is a shame we could not have met sooner, cousin," Ikar puffed. Rolling his shoulder, he gave a practice swing. "I would have liked to fight you in your prime. It is sad to see you now, your stamina spent, your strength worn away by the passage of time."

Devon's heart palpitated in his chest as he struggled to regain his breath. "You know nothing," he breathed at last, "or you would not follow the queen's evil. Alan and Alana both would be rolling in their graves to know what you have done."

"And what of your deeds, Devon?" Ikar asked as they circled one another again. "You served the Tsar for years, allowed his avarice to drive Lonia into poverty. What would

Alan have thought of his ancestor wielding *kanker* against his home nation?"

"I never fought against Lonia," Devon snapped. "Not for the Tsar."

"No," Ikar replied, "but you did for Braidon. You served in his guard, fought beside him, protected him from our swords."

"Braidon did not seek war with Lonia," Devon growled. "It was *your* king who started the war…or had you forgotten that?"

"Ashoka only ever took what was rightfully ours!" Ikar thundered.

Devon shook his head. "We could argue over the past all day," Devon said. He pointed his hammer out to the ship bobbing at anchor. "But Braidon never sentenced innocent women to death."

"He may as well have," Ikar snarled, and then he was on the attack, his sword slashing for Devon's face.

Sparks flashed as Devon caught the blow on the head of his hammer. The crowd roared their approval as the fight resumed, a flurry of violence from the Knight driving Devon backwards. But he held on, knowing Ikar could not keep up such a pace, though his arms burned with the weight of his hammer and his mouth was parched.

Finally there was a break in the attack, and digging deep, Devon countered. Unleashing every drop of rage he had left, he forced Ikar backwards across the sands, hammering again and again at his defences. But Ikar avoided each blow with apparent ease, twisting to dodge each whistling swing of the hammer, his sword rising to deflect the occasional attack that came close.

The shriek of steel meeting steel echoed from the cliffs, and the crowd roared again. Their screams drowned out the howling of the wind and the crashing of waves, even the beating of Devon's heart, until all there was in front of Devon was the rush of battle. Adrenalin fed strength back to Devon's limbs and to his surprise, he found his exhaustion falling away. For the first time in years, he felt almost young, his strength renewed, age forgotten.

Ikar cursed and screamed, trying to regain the initiative, but Devon's relentless assault forced him ever back. Sweat appeared on his forehead, and Devon saw the first traces of doubt enter his enemy's eyes. Still he kept on, thoughts of Pela and Kryssa aboard the queen's ship driving him on. He had to keep up the spectacle, distract the Knights from their prisoners long enough for Braidon and the others to reach them. There was no doubt in his mind Marianne would betray him. His life was already forfeit—all he could do now was buy the others time to escape.

But Ikar would not submit and as the battle drew out, Devon felt the familiar pain return. His movements slowed, and with every blow his strength lessened. Slowly Ikar forced himself back into the fight, pressing Devon to defend himself, to duck and weave as Ikar's blade sought his flesh. Blood dripped from the wound on his chest and Devon found himself regretting his earlier mercy.

Slowly Ikar forced Devon to a standstill, then back one step, and another.

Devon gasped as the broadsword sliced at his head. He leapt back, and the tip cut through the collar of his shirt, narrowly missing his throat. Blood thundered in his ears as he sucked in a breath. All the pain of his body came rushing back in an instant, the burning in his arms, the ache in his shoulder, the agony of his knees. He sagged where he stood, almost falling.

His foe saw it and grimaced, but he did not back away.

He had seen Devon's strength now, had learned to respect it. He would not allow the old warrior another chance to recover. Devon raised his hammer just in time to deflect his next attack, though the power in the blow sent him reeling back.

Steel rang out again as he blocked a second blow, then used the weight of his hammer to force Ikar's sword into the sand. The weapon struck the wooden stage beneath with a *thud* and became lodged there.

Seeing his chance, Devon lashed out with a fist, striking Ikar full in the side of the face. The punch shocked the man off-balance and he lost his grip on his sword. He leapt to the side as Devon attacked, seeking to end Ikar's threat.

"Devon!"

Ice slid down Devon's spine as Marianne's voice carried across the stadium. Filled by a sense of premonition, he spun towards her. She still stood on the docks, arms crossed. A smile crossed her lips as their eyes met.

"Time's up," she shouted.

Before Devon could cry out, a flaming arrow rose into the sky. It flashed upwards like a shooting star through the night, higher and higher, before gravity finally took hold and it began its slow descent towards the ocean.

Except it was not the ocean it was aimed at. Down it spiralled, down towards the deck of the queen's ship, where Kryssa and Pela still stood bound to the masts. Pela opened her mouth in a silent scream as it struck, before an audible *whoosh* carried across the waters, and flames leapt from the decks, stealing them both from view.

41

The breath caught in Caledan's throat as he glimpsed the flaming arrow soaring out over the waters. He followed its path to the ship bobbing in the cove. His gaze took in two figures bound to the masts, silver hair flying in the wild wind.

"Pela!"

Before he could comprehend how she had come to be there, the arrow struck the deck and flames engulfed the ship.

"*No!*" Genevieve staggered past, one hand outstretched towards the flames.

Cursing, Caledan grabbed her and dragged her back. They had searched the entire amphitheatre without success and returned to the shadows of the tunnel—empty now, as the rest of the Order had filled the stands. But just fifty feet away, Devon was down on one knee, his eyes on the flaming ship.

"It's not over yet," he hissed, dragging Genevieve towards the beach. "Come on, there's rowboats on the shore. If we're quick…" He trailed off as Genevieve came alive in his arms.

She threw him off and sprinted towards the beach. He made to follow her, and then noticed Braidon's absence. He swung around and found Braidon still standing frozen at the edge of the arena. A curse left his tongue he stepped towards the king. If the Knight that had defeated Devon noticed him, it would bring the entire weight of the Order down on them. They would never escape, not unless…

"Braidon," he hissed. "It's now or never—call the bloody dragons, or Pela and Kryssa are dead!"

But the king did not respond. Another roar came from the crowd outside, and beyond the king, Devon surged back to his feet and hurled himself at the Knight. But Devon's opponent had the old man's number now, and he deflected the attack almost effortlessly, then smashed Devon with a right cross that hurled him from his feet.

Caledan winced, bracing himself for the end, but instead Ikar turned and addressed someone Caledan could not see. "The sacrifice was meant to wait until the duel was ended."

A woman moved forward, striding across the sand until she stood before the two men, and finally Caledan realised why Braidon had frozen. The queen stood for a moment looking at the towering Knight, then around at the stadium. She raised her arms, and silence fell over the amphitheatre.

"Is this not the Saviour's will?" she called to the fanatics in the stands. "To see her champion crush the defender of the False Gods? To burn the blasphemous believers from our lands?" Her hand flung out to point to the burning ship. A dark band shone on her wrist. "With the Great Sacrifice, our freedom is assured!"

The crowd roared, and after a moment's hesitation, Ikar

dropped to one knee before the queen.

"*Braidon,*" Caledan hissed. Heart pounding in his chest, he darted forward and grabbed at him, but the king shrugged him off. "Call the dragons!" he tried one last time.

"Marianne," he croaked, his voice barely a whisper. Caledan shrank into the shadows of the tunnel as the king entered the stadium, his voice roaring up into the stands. "*Traitor!*"

Leaving behind the safety of the entrance tunnel, Braidon advanced on the queen. Her eyes had widened at his shout and her face had lost all of its colour. But she recovered her composure quickly, gesturing her guards forward. They spread out to encircle the king.

"Take him, alive!"

A groan tore from Caledan as the guards surged forward. Braidon swayed on his feet, his face a mask of agony, but his sword leapt to meet the first of his challengers. It speared through the guard's throat and the man collapsed, choking, to the ground. Braidon continued on without slowing, his voice ringing from the stands.

"How could you?" he bellowed, his voice taut with rage. "After everything we shared? After everything I did for you?"

He swayed as a blade flashed at his face, then surged forward, his short sword plunging under the guard's sword arm and deep into his armpit. It sank to the hilt and lodged there, tearing from Braidon's hands.

Drawing his dagger, the king staggered on, but the guards were all around him now. They swarmed him, pinning his arms to his side and bearing him to the ground. In seconds they had Braidon's hands behind his back. They dragged him forward and shoved him to his knees in front of the queen.

"Oh, now my night is complete," her voice whispered across the sands to where Caledan stood.

He couldn't bear to watch any longer. His life's goal had been robbed from him yet again. He might have still run out into the stadium and stolen the king's life himself, but his other mission called to him now. There was still a chance they could save Pela and Kryssa. However small, he had to take it. Turning, he sprinted from the tunnel out onto the beach.

There was no sign of Genevieve and he prayed she was already in the water. Out in the coves, flames leapt across the deck of the ship, but the masts did not seem to be burning yet. Praying the smoke had not already killed them, Caledan hurled himself into the nearest rowboat.

Waves surged around the vessel, almost upending him. He cursed as water flooded over the side, and struck out again, desperate to pass beyond the breakers. The light of the burning ship flickered on the waters, turning them to a living, churning mirror. Just below the surface, he glimpsed the twisted reefs waiting to tear his boat to pieces. He still wore the heavy armour of the Knights. It would drag him straight to the bottom.

Teeth clenched, he heaved again on the oars, and the boat crashed through another wave. He twisted on the bench, saw he was closer, just twenty yards away now. The flames were everywhere and he strained his eyes, searching the heavy smoke for sign of Pela or Kryssa. He redoubled his efforts as the crackling of burning wood rose above the screams from the stadium.

He was still ten yards away when the fire reached the aft of the ship. They crawled up the stairwell, creeping along the railings and catching on a pile of canvas stacked in the centre of the deck. Caledan gritted his teeth, eyes fixed on the rope ladder. The flames still had not reached it. If he could just—

With an almighty *boom*, the rear of the ship suddenly lifted from the water, hurled skyward by a massive column of flames. They spread upwards and outwards in a violent wave of orange, consuming wood and cloth and steel alike. Caledan watched in horror as the entire ship disintegrated before his eyes.

Then the shockwave struck, a roiling, boiling blast of energy that lifted the rowboat beneath him and hurled it shoreward as though it weighed no more than a box of kindling. Caledan tried desperately to turn it, to direct it, but the oars were torn from his hands. He threw himself down and clung to the boat, breath searing in his throat, and prayed to whatever Gods remained to protect him.

The rowboat struck the shore with such force that Caledan was hurled bodily onto the rocky sands. The impact sent an eruption of sand up in every direction and he felt the armour buckle around him, twisting and tearing. Breath hissed between his teeth as his lungs emptied, and he felt the sword torn from his belt and hurled away into the darkness.

Pain swamped him as he lay there on the beach, waiting for death to come, for the swirling flames that had engulfed the queen's ship to reach the shore and consume him, or for the ocean to rise and suck him into its murky depths.

But a minute passed and the roaring of the inferno lessened, and finally he groaned and lifted himself to his hands and knees. The armour creaked and squalled, moving sluggishly, and in a rush of claustrophobia Caledan tore off the helmet and hurled it away. He dragged the dagger from his belt and cut the straps of his breastplate and grieves, until he stood again in pants and tunic, free of the cursed steel.

When Caledan finally took note of his surroundings, he was surprised to find himself at the other end of the beach, two hundred yards from the amphitheatre. A sharp cramp tore through his calf as he stepped towards the stadium. Cursing, he sank to one knee and gripped his leg, and clenched his teeth until the pain ceased.

The crackling of flames drew his gaze offshore. There was nothing left of the queen's ship, and now the waters of Malevolent Cove were aflame with burning debris. Scorched pieces of wreckage lay strewn across the cove. Caledan had never witnessed such a blast, though the great tales told of Magickers who had commanded similar violence.

He closed his eyes, recalling Pela's bravery on their journey. She had faced down Baronians and Knights in her quest to save her mother, but in the end, it had all been for nothing. A wave of grief struck Caledan. He'd failed Pela, had failed them both.

Another cry echoed form the amphitheatre. Caledan wondered whether the queen had struck down Braidon too, if she had robbed him of that last piece of meaning in his retched life. Staggering to his feet again, he found his sword sticking from the sand nearby. He claimed it, and then looked from the amphitheatre to the cliffs.

There was no one watching the path now. He could walk from the Cove without a backwards glance, leave behind Devon and Braidon and Pela and never look back, could go and find a new path, a new purpose.

Then he remembered Devon's words, the night Braidon had joined them.

What's the point of saving Plorsea, if I can't save my family?

Sword tight in one scorched hand, Caledan limped towards the shadow of the amphitheatre.

42

Braidon stared up at his wife, grief and shock tearing him apart in equal measures. Two members of the Queen's Guard held him tight, but the fight had left him now. He was still struggling to comprehend what he was seeing: that the sweet young woman he'd first met in Lon, that the woman he loved, who had borne his son and slept beside him all these years, had betrayed him.

"Why?" he croaked finally.

Marianne's smile faltered. "Why?" she hissed, stepping closer and raising her fist. "Because I'm not some trophy for you and my father to trade!"

Held tight by her men, Braidon couldn't avoid the blow. It struck him hard across the cheek and he heard something go *crack*. He reeled back, but the guards' grips did not loosen. Tasting blood in his mouth, he spat on the black sands.

Cursing, Marianne retreated a step, holding her wrist. "Damnit," she said, her eyes flickering in the direction of the cove. "They still live."

"I thought you *wanted* to marry!" Braidon snapped.

His wife's lips twisted in a sneer. "Are you really so blind?" she snapped. "I was barely a woman; why would I want an old man like you?"

"You lied…"

"Oh, you poor thing," Marianne snarled. "Yes, I played my part well, obeyed my father's command and brought peace for our nation. But I have *always* loathed you, Braidon. Every second, every time I lay with you, I longed to drive my blade through your heart. How I wept, when I thought my Baronians had robbed me of that chance, how I laughed when they burned."

Braidon shook his head. "We have a *son.*"

"Perhaps there is a Saviour, after all," Marianne continued, her eyes aglow. "For my prayers have been answered: I *finally* have you in my power. Now you will die, dear husband, knowing who it was that killed you. If only I could have done the same with my father, but only poison can slay the snake."

Marianne drew a slender rapier from her belt and held it up to the light. "There is power in death, in our life-force," she murmured, turning her eyes on Braidon. "The greater the sacrifice, the more power spilt. *That* is why I wanted Devon here, why his daughter and granddaughter burn. Only the fiercest, the bravest would do." She glanced again at the bracelet on her wrist, a frown touching her forehead.

"What are you talking about?" Braidon snapped, regaining some of his fight. He strained against the guards, but they pinned his arms behind his back and forced him face-first into the sand. Teeth bared, he spoke into the ground. "If I'd known…"

"You didn't *want* to know, husband," Marianne snapped.

"You only wanted to believe that this beautiful young woman could love you."

Braidon flinched as the cold point of her rapier touched his neck.

"I'm sorry," he croaked, scrunching his eyes closed.

"Oh yes, tell me—"

Boom!

The roaring struck a second before the concussion wave. Braidon cried out as burning air swept through the amphitheatre, hurling sand at his face and staggering grown men. Caught off-balance, the queen and her guard were thrown sideways.

There wouldn't be another chance, and Braidon grasped it with both hands. Leaping up, he slammed his shoulder into the nearest guard, hurling the man from his feet. His sword skittered across the sand and Braidon dove for it. Scrambling back up, he spun in time to slam the blade through a guard's unprotected groin.

The guard went down with a groan and Braidon leapt at the queen—but the giant warrior that Devon had been fighting stepped between them. Unfazed by the explosion out in the cove, he lifted his sword.

"Put it down," he said quietly. "My queen is not done with you."

"But I'm done with her," Braidon snapped.

He launched himself at Ikar, but the big man was faster still, and Braidon's strength was failing. His broadsword swept Braidon's blade aside, then his fist slammed into Braidon's stomach, driving the air from his lungs. Choking, Braidon sank to his knees, the sword slipping from his fingers. A kick from Ikar's boot sent it out of reach.

"No," Braidon gasped.

"Yes," Marianne growled, stepping around the giant.

Looking up at his wife, Braidon saw again that day on the river, how he had done everything he could to protect her from the Baronians. But she had been on their side all along, had even been behind her father's death, if her words were to be believed. Hatred rose in Braidon's chest and he struggled back to his feet.

Ikar held out a hand to bar his approach, but Marianne waved him aside and walked forward until they stood face to face.

"I loved you," he whispered.

"You always were a fool."

Before Braidon could react, Marianne lanced her slender sword out, stabbing him through the chest. He gasped and staggered back, clutching at the blade, but Marianne yanked it back, slicing his fingers. The strength went from Braidon's legs as blood blossomed. He sank to his knees, struggling to slow the bleeding.

Sand crunched as his wife approached. She crouched in front of him, her eyes aglow, drinking in his suffering.

"I'm glad you didn't die in that river," she whispered. Gripping him by the chin, she forced him to look at her. "I want to see you suffer, like I have suffered all these years."

Groaning, Braidon tried to push her hands away, but his bloody hands slipped from her wrist. An icy cold had begun in his fingertips and was already spreading up his arms. His legs were numb, and he knew if he did not stop the bleeding soon…

His vision blurring, he stared past the queen, taking in the flames still leaping from the top of the amphitheatre, the roaring inferno in the cove. There was nothing left of the queen's ship or Kryssa and Pela. Sadness touched him as he realised he had failed even that small task.

Sadness gave way to anger as he looked up at his wife.

"Oh yes, *fight*, it makes this all the sweeter," Marianne mocked, her voice a whisper. "I need no bracelet for this—I know the words. When the life slips from your body, it will flow into mine, as the Elders do it. Who would have thought dark magic could be so joyful."

His entire body numb now, Braidon struggled to understand her, but he could make no sense of her words.

"How it must hurt, to die such a failure," the queen continued. "Knowing you have brought nothing but death and destruction to your people. How you have failed so utterly, that your entire life was meaningless. You could not save your beloved sister, nor Plorsea, not even a single innocent woman."

A groan tore from Braidon as he struggled to break away from her iron grasp, his will to live slipping away with each passing moment.

"Yes, I can feel the life leaving you..." Marianne's eyes were aglow now, lit by some unknown force.

"He hasn't failed yet," a woman's voice spoke from behind the queen.

The darkness was beckoning. Braidon squinted, trying to make out the speaker.

"How?" the queen growled.

She shoved Braidon back and stood. He lay on the sand and clutched weakly at his wound, slowing the bleeding as best he could.

"I said I would kill you," the woman's voice came again, strangely familiar.

"You won't get close!" Marianne screamed. "Kill her, Ikar."

Braidon's head flopped to the side as the giant strode forward.

"Put down that sword," the giant said, his voice strangely muted.

"So, this is you, Ikar," the woman replied, her voice strangely muted. "Step aside," she continued sadly. "Or only one of us will leave this place alive."

"You know that I cannot."

"Then defend yourself!"

❦ 43 ❦

Pela watched, horrified, as the flaming arrow struck the deck. She strained against her bonds, tearing the skin from her wrists, but nothing she did seemed to make a difference. The necklace Marianne had placed around her neck seemed to tighten and her flesh crawled, though she still knew nothing of its dark purpose.

"Be brave, my daughter," Kryssa croaked behind her.

Watching the flames crawl across the ship towards them, a sob tore from Pela. Already the smoke was billowing around them, robbing her of breath. Choking, she clutched at her mother's fingers, terror wrapping its icy hands around her chest.

"Please mum," she gasped, "I don't want to die!"

Her mother's hand tightened around her own. "I love you so much, Pela."

Hearing despair in her mother's voice, Pela slumped against her bindings. How had it come to this? She thought back over the past few weeks, everything she had faced, the fears she had overcome. There was so much she wanted to tell her mother: about the fight with the Baronians, the rescue in the Castle, how she had learned to use her father's sword.

The blade lay discarded on the deck now, tossed aside along with the rest of their belongings. If only she could reach it, they might free themselves.

"I love you too, mum," she whispered.

The crackling of the fire crept closer, its heat washing over them. She coughed, the acrid fumes burning her throat, and her vision swum. Each breath was a struggle now.

Then movement came from the railings, and like a messenger from the Gods themselves, Genevieve appeared through the flames. She staggered across the deck, scooping up Pela's sword as she went, and fell to her knees beside the mast. The blade sliced easily through the ropes, and Pela slumped to the deck as she found herself finally free

"Gen!" Kryssa cried, hugging the woman tightly. "What are you doing here?"

"No time," Genevieve coughed. She grasped Pela by the collar and dragged her up, then pulled them towards the railing. "Into the boat, before the fire…"

She trailed off as they reached the railing and saw the rowboat had drifted from the ladder. The flames crackled behind them, spreading quickly across the ship now. Pela's hackles rose as she looked at the aft deck, and saw the inferno had almost reached the store of black powder.

"*Jump, now!*" she screamed, and before either woman could react, she grabbed them by the collars and dragged them over the railing.

They cried out as the waves came rushing up to meet them. The icy water swallowed Pela up and she gasped, kicking back towards the light. She broke the surface and swung around, finding her mother and Genevieve bobbing close by.

"Get awa—"

An awful *boom* drowned out her words as the burning ship turned suddenly to a column of flame. Pela opened her mouth to scream, but a wave of water caught them up before the words could leave her mouth, and then the world had turned to madness…

Sometime later, Pela woke to her mother shaking her. She opened her eyes, and found herself dangling from the side of the makeshift dock. The wave must have deposited her there, for the water was a good four feet below them. She tried to move and groaned—her entire body ached as though she'd just finished training with Caledan. Gritting her teeth, Pela managed to drag herself to her knees.

"Stay here," Kryssa was saying, her eyes on the amphitheatre.

Pela followed her gaze and saw the queen standing on the black sands, flanked by the massive Knight, Ikar. Devon lay nearby, dead or unconscious, while a third unknown man stood before the queen. As they watched, she darted forward, her slender rapier piercing his chest.

Kryssa started down the docks towards the theatre. There was no sign of Genevieve and Pela prayed she'd reached the shore safely. But just now, Kryssa was her greatest concern. She recognised the look in her mother's eyes. Kryssa intended to honour the promise she'd made on the queen's ship. Derryn's blade glinted in her hand—she must have taken it after Genevieve freed them—but as far as Pela knew, she didn't even know how to use it.

Fighting through the pain, Pela came to her feet and started after her mother. The roar of the crowd buffeted her as she approached, almost a physical force in itself, seeking to force her back. She kept on, unable to hear the words that passed between the queen and Kryssa, but determined to intervene.

Then Kryssa dropped into a fighting stance, squaring off against the giant of a man who had defeated Devon. Pela stumbled to a stop, horrified. The giant was twice her mother's size—a single swing of his broadsword would cleave her in two. Pela's eyes caught on a short sword lying discarded on the black sands; she swept it up and raced to join her mother.

Kryssa glanced back, her eyes widening. "Stay back!" she cried. "This is between me and Ikar."

Pela lifted her blade. "Not a chance."

Her mother flashed a look that had once sent terror shooting down Pela's spine. She smiled back—and ignored her. She hadn't come all this way just to run now.

Ikar lifted his broadsword and gestured them forward. "It doesn't matter how many—"

Kryssa attacked before he could finish, her blade lancing for his unprotected head. Ikar's blade barely rose in time to parry her attack; then he was retreating before the force of her fury. He had discarded his armour during the battle with Devon, and now Kryssa's blade found his flesh again and again, opening cuts across his arms and chest.

For a moment, Pela stood frozen, shocked at her mother's sudden violence—and skill. Apparently, she had kept more than just her father's past from Pela. But such revelations would have to wait for later, and gathering herself, Pela edged sideways the way Caledan had taught her, seeking an opening. Kryssa had forced Ikar backwards across the stadium, and she had to rush to catch them.

Above, jeers rained down from the crowd, as though this was all some great show for them. A deep hatred rose in

Pela's throat as she saw the grins on their faces, their open mouths as they shouted for their deaths.

Ikar was slower now than during his fight with Devon. Pela watched him closely, and glimpsing an opening, she darted in, her sword spearing for the giant's face. His eyes flickered in surprise, and a gauntleted arm lifted to deflect her attack. Sparks flashed as the power behind Pela's blow tore open the only armour he still wore, shattering his wrist.

Crying out, Ikar went reeling back. Pela attacked again, but the giant recovered faster than she had expected, and his broadsword swept around in a wild arc aimed at her chest. Too slow, Pela threw up her arm, but there was no way she could deflect the sword…

A dark figure slammed into her before the blow could fall, dragging her from the path of the blade. Breath hissed between Pela's lips as her rescuer's weight slammed down on her back. She groaned, thinking it was the queen and trying to free her blade, before Genevieve's voice hissed in her ear: "Stay down; your mum and I will handle this."

The weight vanished as Genevieve launched herself back into the battle, hatchet in one hand, hunting knife in the other. With Kryssa at her side, they forced the Knight back. The crowd was silent now, and the crackling of flames out in the cove rose above the whisper of the wind. Kryssa ducked as a violent swing of Ikar's blade swept for her head. Genevieve darted in, her hunting knife opening a cut on their foe's face.

Still on the ground, Pela watched as the two battled the giant to a standstill. Her mother's every movement, every swing of her sword, was smooth and practiced, her body telegraphing nothing of her attacks until the blade leapt to do her bidding. Ikar was struggling now, his blood dripping from a dozen wounds.

"Yield!" Kryssa screamed as they forced him back another step. "I have no wish to kill you, Ikar."

Ikar grimaced. Retreating a step, he held up a hand. Pela's heart beat faster, but the Knight was not surrendering. Even so, Kryssa and Genevieve paused, offering him respite.

"Where did you learn such skill?" he asked.

Kryssa smiled. "I was a member of the King's Guard for many years, alongside my husband."

Pela's heart thundered in her ears. She stared at her mother, mouth hanging open. "*What?*"

"I'm sorry, my daughter," Kryssa whispered, and Pela saw that her eyes were shining. "After I lost Derryn, I couldn't..."

"Devon told me..." Pela croaked.

"I should never have kept this part of our lives from you," Kryssa said, swallowing visibly. "But...after Derryn... I couldn't have you following in our footsteps. So I forbade Devon and my mother from speaking of our past, and hung up my sword for good."

"How could you keep this from me?"

"Do not hate me, daughter," Kryssa replied, then turned back to Ikar.

Without warning, she hurled herself forward. Sparks flashed as the two came together again, and all Pela could do was stare, still struggling to comprehend this new revelation. Her father she had never known, but her mother...she had been there for all of Pela's life, had prevented her from even touching a sword, and she had been lying the entire time...

In the centre of the amphitheatre, Genevieve and Kryssa fought on. Ikar had regained his breath and now fought like a man possessed, while beyond the queen stood watching in silence. Most of her guards lay dead on the sand, but Knights still stood in the shadows around the arena.

A roar came from the crowd as Ikar's fist caught Genevieve in the chin, staggering her. The Knight advanced with sword raised, but Kryssa leapt to her defence, forcing him back. Twisting to avoid her blow, Ikar brought his sword around, seeking to cut her in two. Kryssa's sword slammed down, catching his blade near the hilt and deflecting the attack into the ground. But the shock of the impact knocked the weapon from Kryssa's fingers, hurling it across the sand.

Ikar roared and raised his sword, but Kryssa flung herself back and his next blow cut only air. Empty-handed, Kryssa retreated, Ikar chasing after her. Behind them, Genevieve snatched up a sword and tossed it at Kryssa, but the giant swept up his great sword, knocking it aside.

"Damn you!" Genevieve screamed, hurling herself at the Knight's exposed back.

He spun to meet her and grinned, for though brave, Genevieve did not have Kryssa's skill. Wielding the broadsword like it weighed nothing, he knocked aside Genevieve's attack, then kicked out with his boot. The blow caught Genevieve square in the chest and she doubled over. Before she could recover, a second blow from Ikar's fist knocked her out cold.

"*No!*" Pela screamed.

Scrambling for the hilt of her sword, Pela raced in. But her cry had given her away, and Ikar turned to meet her. He batted aside her attack as he had Genevieve's, then lashed out with a meaty fist, sending Pela crashing to the sand alongside her friend.

Gasping, she tried to scramble away, but Ikar grabbed

her by the scruff of the neck. Hauling her up, he spun and found Kryssa several feet away, sword in hand once more.

Her face twisted with fear as she saw Pela in Ikar's grip. "Let her go."

"I cannot," Ikar said, his breath coming in great puffs. "The Saviour calls out for her death. The False Gods must be defeated."

"They were never evil, Ikar," Kryssa whispered, holding out a hand in entreaty. "Your ancestor fought alongside them to banish a great darkness from this world. Alan would never condone what you do here today."

Ikar's face twisted as though in pain. "He lived in a simpler time, but my people cannot return to the yolk of the False Gods. I must preserve our freedom. I cannot allow their evil back into this world."

"And is my daughter evil?" Kryssa asked. "Am I?"

"I don't know!" he cried, swinging away, then back. "But your very belief threatens my world!" His jaw tightened and he raised his broadsword.

"*Wait!*" Kryssa screamed, desperation showing in her eyes. Lines stretched her face as she lowered her blade. "Please, spare my daughter. She is no threat to you. She does not even believe."

"But you do," Ikar said.

"Yes." She tossed aside her sword. "So kill me instead."

"*No!*" Pela screamed, thrashing in Ikar's grip, though it made no difference to the giant.

Ikar stared at Kryssa for a long moment, then with a jerk of his arm, he tossed Pela aside. She flew several feet and slammed into the sand, winding her for the second time in as many moments. Coughing and spluttering, she struggled to pull herself up, to go to her mother's aid. But strength abandoned her, and she collapsed back to the black sand. In despair, she looked at the giant, expecting to see the sword poised above her mother's head.

But Ikar still stood fixed in place, his hulking shoulders looming in the shadows. As she watched, the broadsword slid from his hands and struck the earth with a *thud*. Pela stared, seeing now that a blade protruded from the giant's chest. Sand crunched as a silhouette strode forward, and with a violent yank, plucked the short sword free.

A whisper hissed from Ikar's lips as he swayed, then toppled to the ground. His last, dying breath hissed across the sands, and then he was still.

Caledan strode past him, bloody sword in hand, and pulled Pela to her feet. "I think we'd be going," he said, as a great roar came from the crowd.

Stunned, Pela could only nod her agreement. A second later, Kryssa engulfed them both in a hug. "*Thank the Gods.*"

Then she was gone, darting across the sand to where Genevieve lay. The huntswoman was just sitting up, a confused look on her face, but she smiled when she saw Kryssa.

"Gen!" Kryssa gasped, falling to her knees beside the huntress.

Pela smiled as they embraced, then her mouth dropped as Genevieve pulled her mother into a kiss. Kryssa did not pull away, only pulled the huntswoman closer, kissing her back. They broke apart quickly and looked around with sheepish grins on their lips, but only Pela seemed to have noticed. Kryssa met her eye and mouthed silently:

I'll tell you later.

After everything else her mother had kept from her, this was nothing. Pela would have laughed had they not been surrounded by enemies. Instead, all she could do was smile as her mother helped Genevieve up. Devon was back on his feet and lifting his fallen comrade into his arms. Pela had started towards them, when a wild shriek brought them up short.

"*Stop!*"

Marianne's voice rang with power, and to Pela's shock, her legs suddenly became trapped, as though she were moored in quicksand. Unbalanced, she crashed to the sand. Her head whipped around, finding the others similarly frozen.

The queen herself was crouched beside the fallen Ikar, but now she rose and started towards them.

"Not quite the death I wanted." Her words hissed across the sands. "But it's a start."

$$\mathscr{X} \quad 44 \quad \mathscr{X}$$

Devon ached as though he'd been in a brawl with death itself. The darkness swirled, pulling him back down, but he fought against it—though he no longer knew why. There was a desperate desire in him to lie down, to close his eyes and bid farewell to the world.

But Kryssa's cries and Pela's voice and Braidon's dying groans called to him, and he fought back, if only for a short while longer. He could not fall, not now, not while his family was in danger. Stumbling to his feet, he lifted Braidon into his arms.

All around him, the followers of the Order were on their feet. Many were already streaming from the stands down the stairs towards the arena. The other Knights, silent spectators until now, were moving forward as well. They would be on them in moments, and there were only two ways out of the amphitheatre. He turned towards the tunnel, but several Knights had already reached it and he no longer had the strength to fight them.

The docks then. The queen had left her rowboat there, though it might not have survived the explosion. They would have to risk it. Devon started towards the wooden structure, only for the queen's voice to draw him up short.

"Stop."

His legs shook, drawing him to a stop. He looked back and found himself trapped in the burning rage of the queen's sapphire eyes. A groan tore from his battered body as her will pounded him, commanding him to stay, and despite himself he could not look away. Braidon groaned in his arms, but the king was too weak to stand or even speak by now.

The queen rose from beside Ikar's body. "Not quite the death I wanted, but it's a start."

Blood stained her hands and Devon shuddered, looking at his fallen relative. She had had her sacrifice after all. Power shone from her eyes, commanding them, and somehow Devon knew she had stolen it from Ikar, that the Knight's death had empowered her with something they could not understand.

"Devon," Braidon croaked, his eyes flickering open. "Leave me. It's my life she wants."

"Not happening," he whispered.

Devon looked at the queen again. She walked slowly towards them, rapier in hand, and Devon knew if he did not act now, they would all be lost. Defeated, broken, he looked around, saw the fear in Pela's eyes, saw Kryssa in Genevieve's embrace, and Caledan standing tall, yet unable to move.

Drawing in a breath, he centred himself, and reached deep within for an extra ounce of strength, for something to fight back with. The passage of years had eaten away at him, corroding his strength, but within he was still the same Devon that had stood against the Tsar, who had fought demons and monsters and Magickers and won. Now, at the end, his will did not fail him. It rose slowly, but unrelenting, an iron core to his soul.

"Caledan!" he boomed, his voice ringing out across the stadium.

The sellsword's head whipped around, dragged away from the queen's call by the steel in Devon's voice. "Guard him with your life," Devon said, and passed the king to the sellsword.

A hint of a grin touched Caledan's cheeks as he accepted the burden.

"Stop!"

The queen's will washed over them again, staggering the others, but Devon had lived sixty years and faced far worse than the likes of Marianne. He staggered, weathering the storm, and found Kryssa next. He placed a hand on her shoulder, and she looked around, her eyes shining with tears.

"Devon," she whispered. "I'm sorry."

"No," he said, embracing her. "I am sorry, my…daughter. I wish I could do it all again, could do it right, but I cannot. I can only say that you are my daughter, now and always, and that I love you."

"No…" Kryssa gasped, her eyes widening as she realised this was farewell.

"Look after the girl," Devon rumbled, before turning to Genevieve. A smile split his bearded cheeks. "And you look after my daughter, huntress."

Genevieve replied with a sad smile and a slight nod of her head, and Devon moved on, drawing Pela to her feet. "I should have never sent you away," he whispered. "Thank you for saving my daughter."

"Devon…" she whispered as he pushed her towards the others. "Thank you."

"Go," he replied, offering one last farewell, then turned to the queen. "Run!"

Her face a mask of rage, Marianne screamed after them. Reclaiming his hammer, Devon stood guard against her, withering the force of her will. The last of his strength was fading now, consumed by the effort of facing the queen as surely as if he had fought the woman herself. He staggered and dropped to one knee, but he only had to hold her a few seconds longer…

A snarl hissed from Marianne's lips, and pointing the rapier, she stalked towards him. "Out of my way, fool!" she spat, the blade trembling in her hand.

The sword slashed out and Devon came to his feet. But his reactions were slowed, his strength spent, and the sword plunged through his thigh. He cried out and fell back. The queen tore her rapier loose and attacked again. Devon brought his hammer up, but the queen's rapier flashed red, and its blade sliced through the head of his weapon, just as Merak's had all that time ago in Skystead.

Devon staggered away, but he knew it was hopeless now, and her next blow took him in the shoulder. Pain lanced down his arm and the broken hammer slipped from his fingers. Still he backed away, still he blocked her path. Clutching his arm, he glanced back and saw the others were at the end of the dock, where to his relief the rowboat still bobbed. Across the floor of the arena, the crowd had now gathered behind their queen. They stood waiting for the final blow to be struck.

"Let's see how a legend dies," Marianne snarled.

"Go ahead," Devon whispered, a smile on his lips. "I'm ready."

"So be it," the queen replied, and rammed her rapier into Devon's chest so hard it sank to the hilt.

❧ 45 ❧

Pela had just jumped into the rowboat when a roar came from the crowd behind her. She turned back in time to see the queen lunge forward. Devon made no attempt to defend himself as her blade plunged home. Only then did he stagger. He collapsed to the black sands as the queen tore the blade loose.

"*No!*" Pela screamed, scrambling for the docks, but the others grasped her and held her back.

Still on the wharf, Caledan cast off the mooring rope and leapt aboard, just as the queen's voice carried to them: "Stop!"

But whatever power she'd had over them had vanished now, and they turned away. Caledan took up one oar, Genevieve the other, and together they struck out across the cove. Remembering the necklace at her throat, Pela tore it lose and hurled it into the ocean. Her mother did the same and they exchanged a look. Finally they understood their purpose—however the Queen had taken power from Ikar's death…they had been meant to share that same fate.

Burning rubble still lay scattered across the waters, and Pela shuddered at the thought of what might have been.

"Pela, jump in the front and watch for reefs," Caledan gasped. His face was wan and Pela wondered what he'd been through to get there, but she obeyed.

Flames still lit the waters, allowing her to spot the corals and redirect their course, and they passed slowly through the surging waves. The light of the amphitheatre fell further behind, but as Pela glanced back she saw rowboats pushing off the beach in pursuit.

And ahead, the fleet of warships anchored beyond the breakers still awaited. Already torches were being lit on those barring the mouth of the cove, as signals passed from the amphitheatre. Her heart sank. Devon had only bought them a few more moments of life. There was no way they could escape so many. Soon they would follow him on the dark path.

Caledan cursed; he'd seen them as well. "So much for the damn dragons," he muttered.

On the floor of the rowboat, Braidon's eyes flickered open and a word slipped from his lips: *"Ingytus!"*

His eyes closed again before Pela could ask what it meant, but a second later, a voice sounded in all of their heads:

Fool of a King, the voice rumbled, and Pela saw an image in her mind of a great beast lifting off. *If you die, my kin will wage such war against your people, the Gods themselves will tremble in their graves.*

Pela shook her head and the image vanished. A frown touched her forehead as she looked at the others. Her mother looked just as confused, but Caledan and Genevieve had both grown pale.

An almighty roar sounded through the night, and movement flickered across the stars. Pela glimpsed red scales glittering in the firelight. A hushed silence fell suddenly over the cove; even the watchers in the arena did not so much as whisper. All eyes were lifted to the sky, waiting to see what would come next.

A light appeared, a candle before the half-moon in the sky, but in seconds it grew—becoming an inferno that went rushing down to crash upon the waters of the cove. The rowboats giving chase were caught in its light, and then swallowed up by the awful flames. Screamed rent the air as men leapt, burning, into the dark waters.

The shadow passed overhead, rushing out towards the warships in the mouth of the cove. The sailors aboard began to shout at one another, racing about in the torchlight, dragging weapons from their foxholes. Several leapt overboard, in their panic, and a *clanking* noise rattled through the darkness.

The rain of fire fell again, engulfing the first of the warships in its orange glow. In seconds the entire vessel was aflame, its crew incinerated or hurled overboard into the saving waters. An explosion rocked the night as another store of black powder caught light, tearing the ship asunder.

Pela's heart soared as she saw their chance. With the dragon, they might just escape. She clutched a hand to her mouth as the waters around them burned, its light revealing the great beast in the sky.

But the flames had also revealed the beast to the soldiers aboard the other warships, and the *twang* of crossbows followed. An awful scream came from the creature as bolts flashed in the darkness, piercing its great hide.

It twisted again, dark wings beating the air, and another warship was consumed. The shrieks of burning men joined the chorus of terror ringing from the shore.

"There's a gap!" Pela shrieked, pointing to the space left by the sinking ships.

Teeth bared, Caledan and Genevieve rowed on. The light of the flames grew and Pela held her breath, praying the other warships did not see them. But the men aboard were preoccupied with their own survival, their weapons trained on the dragon as it swept down for a third time.

Crack.

Pela saw the catapult on the rear of the warship a second before it fired. She shrieked a warning. The dragon was far too close, almost upon them. The burning barrel rose to meet it, but at the last moment it banked, and Pela breathed a sigh as she realised it would miss.

Boom.

A flash of light burst across the night sky as the barrel exploded, banishing the stars and moon and blinding them but for the dark shadow of the dragon.

Crying out, Pela tripped and fell to the floor of the rowboat. Shadows and light danced across her vision, but through it she saw the fire raining down around them, flickering out as it disappeared beneath the waves. She stared at the sky, straining to see through the chaos, seeking out the dragon.

Then she saw it.

Wings folded in two, it tumbled through the sky towards them. The explosion had torn a great hole in the beast's chest, but still it lived, its screams echoing from the cliffs around them. Pela watched it fall, her hope turning to sudden despair. They had only seconds…

With a great crash, it struck the water alongside the boat. A wave rose from the ocean and rushed towards them, catching their tiny rowboat and hurling it sideways. Pela screamed, clutching desperately to the side of the boat.

But the wave was too great, and suddenly the boat was overturning. Pela's hands were torn free by the violence of the ocean, and then they were all falling, toppling forward into the darkness.

And the waters of Malevolent Cove rose up to greet them all.

EPILOGUE

Pela groaned as she licked her lips, trying desperately to dampen her parched skin. The noonday sun beat down, unrelenting in the cloudless sky, while gentle waves lapped at her heels. She could hardly recall how long they had floated on the scorched piece of the ship's hull, only that her whole body ached, that her skull felt as though it was about to crack open.

Genevieve lay draped across the other side of the flotsam, eyes closed and head resting on the wooden boards. She hadn't spoken for hours. The only sign of life was her iron grip on their life preserver.

Pela swallowed – even that simple action agony now – and squinted against the brilliance of the sun. The ocean rose and fell beneath them, the great swells unbroken but still a threat. Already Pela had lost her grip once, when the tip of one wave had washed over them, dragging her from the makeshift raft. Fortunately, she'd still had the strength to regain the wooden boards.

She didn't now.

There was no sign of the shore. Pela lowered her head back down, feeling the gentle rocking of the ocean beneath her, a gentle lullaby that called her to sleep. She resisted, though she could hardly recall why now. Surely it would be better, to finally give herself to the darkness, to release the fragile piece of wood, allow the depths to claim her?

After all, what was the point of going on? The queen had won. Despite their victory over Ikar, despite her uncle's sacrifice, it had all been for nothing. Her mother was gone, Caledan and the king as well. Her uncle was dead, and she and Genevieve would not be long in following him.

As though bidden by the thought, Genevieve's hand slipped from the hull and she began to slide into the water. Pela's hand snapped out and caught the woman by the wrist. Genevieve groaned, but her eyes did not open. Gasping, Pela clung to her. With the last of her strength, she delivered a hard slap to Genevieve's face.

"Wake up!" Pela screamed, though it came out more as a croak.

Genevieve groaned, her head lifting half an inch. Emerald eyes stained red with exhaustion stared out from beneath a mop of tangled black hair.

"What?" Genevieve groaned.

Pela swallowed, fighting the fear that clogged her throat. "Don't leave me."

Genevieve stared at her a moment longer, then nodded her acceptance. Laying her head back down, her eyes slid closed. "I'm sorry. I wish…" she trailed off.

Greif stung Pela's eyes, though there was no moisture left for tears. "I know," she replied. "Do you think…?"

"If they survived, the queen has them," Genevieve replied, her voice thick with despair.

Pela looked away. "Maybe the dragons saved them."

"There was only one, and its dead."

"You said Braidon made a bargain with the whole clan."

"I suppose," Genevieve murmured, "though you saw the weapons the Knights had. They killed the beast easily."

"But not without cost," Pela said with a shudder.

The sight of burning men had been seared into her mind. Before the beast's death, dragon fire had consumed most of the rowboats in the cove, as well as several of the Order's warships. But Genevieve was right. In the end, it had mattered little. The Knights were too powerful, their inventions deadly to dragon and human alike.

After their rowboat had capsized, Pela had been lost in the chaotic water. With darkness and dragon fire all around, she had thrashed amidst the debris, screaming her mother's name. At one point she'd thought a response had come from amidst the ruin, but the currents in the mouth of the Cove were too strong, and she'd been swept out into the ocean beyond.

Only then had she discovered Genevieve, clinging to a piece of debris. Together they had kicked out for the direction they hoped was the shore, but the surging waters off the west coast were too strong, and they'd made no progress. Eventually their strength, worn down by the battles of the day, had been depleted, and they'd surrendered to the might of the ocean.

So they had lain there all night, resting as best they could, the currents taking them where they would. When the sun had finally appeared on the distant horizon, there had been no land in sight, not even another ship.

Now Pela no longer knew how many hours they had drifted – only that her body screamed out for water, that her skin was cracked and flacking, her strength close to an end. Soon…

She shook herself, looking to Genevieve. The huntress was fading again, her breath little more than a dull wheeze between her nostrils. Pela had to do something to keep her friend awake, or Genevieve would slip beneath the waves. The thought of being all alone in the giant ocean, alone with the depths, the infinite darkness waiting below…

"Gen!" Pela gasped, then: "That's what my mother called you, right?"

The huntress groaned. Salt coated her eyelashes, dusting her face as they cracked open. "What?"

Pela sighed. "I'm trying to say…to ask…you're dating my mother!"

"Am I?" Genevieve whispered. Her voice was so faint she might have already been a ghost.

Pela raised an eyebrow. "It certainly looked that way, back in the cove," she said, trying to lift the woman from her despair.

"Sorry." A rasping noise that might have been laughter came from the huntress. "Probably wasn't the best way for you to find out your mother…" she trailed off.

"Likes women?" Pela laughed despite herself. "I can't say it was the biggest surprise of the day, with everything else that happened."

"Your mother is quite remarkable," Genevieve said, seeming to perk up somewhat. "I don't think I quite understood how much I cared for her, until the Knights took her from us."

Pela swallowed. That day still haunted her, the terror of their invasion, the bloodshed that had stained the temple floor. She had seen worse in the past few weeks, but that had been the day her innocence had been lost, when she'd first seen the darkness in their world.

"I don't remember ever seeing you at the old temple?"

A smile touched Genevieve's face, but her lips cracked at the movement. She wiped away a drip of blood before she spoke: "Whatever happened to the Gods, I've never felt the need to visit some old ruins to remember them."

"Oh?"

Genevieve's head lifted a fraction more. "Whatever remains of the Olds Gods is all around us, even now. In the mountains and oceans and forests of the Three Nations, in its people, in every good deed, and every man and woman who stands against the darkness."

The breath went from Genevieve in a rush as she finished, and laying back down, she smiled at Pela. Pela stared back, surprised by her words. It was the longest sentence she'd ever heard from Genevieve.

Finally she smiled. "I don't suppose that means Jurrien has a ship winging its way towards us, even now?" she teased. Jurrien had been the Storm God of Lonia, who's powers had once guided sailors safely through these waters.

Rasping laughter came from Genevieve's throat, but it died as the huntress suddenly lifted her head. The raft rocked beneath them as she pushed herself up, eyes on a spot over Pela's shoulder.

"What is it?" Pela asked.

The piece of hull turned slowly in the water, and finally Pela saw what Genevieve had glimpsed. A ship surged towards them through the waters, its high decks packed with men and women who ran scurrying about their business. A *boom* carried across the dark waters as it rose on a swell and then dropped down the other side. It looked as though it would miss them, then a voice called down from the crows nest, and with a creaking of ropes and clothe, the ship began to turn.

Only then did Pela notice the black sails hanging from

its masts, the pitch-black armour worn by the crew, the flag fapping from the stern. Her heart dropped as she realised who the ship belonged too.

"Baronians," Genevieve whispered.

———

HERE ENDS BOOK ONE
OF
THE KNIGHTS OF ALANA
The adventure continues with…
Queen of Vengeance

New York Times Bestselling Author
AARON HODGES
QUEEN OF VENGEANCE
THE KNIGHTS OF ALANA : BOOK TWO

PROLOGUE

Senator Isybelle strode through the narrow corridors of Lon's citadel, her heels tapping loudly on the granite floors. A breeze blew through the broad windows, carrying with it the tang of the ocean and relief from the summer heat. Red sandstone walls stretched up to the high ceilings, where spiders were busy spinning fresh cobwebs.

Muttering beneath her breath, Isybelle made a mental note to have the slaves flogged. It was enough that their ugly sandstone buildings could never compete with rival Ardath's marble palaces. There was no need to highlight Lon's poverty with uncleanliness.

A drip of perspiration slid down Isybelle's neck as she took another corner. She cursed again. Thirty years ago, she and other senators would have been followed through the citadel by slaves waving fern fronds. But King Ashoka had done away with those luxuries, claiming the Lonian crown could not afford the extravagance. Their resources had been thrown into new industries instead, seeking to transform the nation's future.

They had succeeded beyond all expectations, but Isybelle would never forgive the insult to her heritage. It was enough that the populace had lifted Ashoka, a minor noble, to the office of king. Too much that he expected his betters to impoverish themselves for his plans.

The council had tolerated him for long enough, suffering their loss of pride in silence. Until today. Now, finally, Lonia would see a return to nobility.

Ahead, armed men lined the corridor, spears held perpendicular to the floor, ready to defend the council with their lives. At her appearance, the spears rose as one and struck the tiles. A great *boom* of steel on stone echoed from the walls, announcing her arrival to those within.

The slightest hint of a smile touched Isybelle's lips as she strode the length of the corridor, her gaze fixed straight ahead. It was beneath her station to look upon fighting men —and any who caught her eye would be whipped. That was as it had been for all of her sixty years, even during those dark days when the council had existed only to serve the Tsar.

Hinges squealed as the doors to the council chamber were pushed open, and she again cursed the slaves for their negligence. An example must be made of their failure. For the first time in a generation, the Lonian council would be restored to its true glory. No infraction, however minor, could be allowed to mar this day.

Inside the chamber, a dozen men and women stood at Isybelle's appearance, their chairs scuffing gently as they were pushed back. They watched as she strode the length of the table to where her chair awaited, a slave at its side.

There she paused, savouring the moment. Long had the council waited for this day, plotting and scheming to regain their former power. Ashoka may have been incorruptible, but he'd also lacked the intelligence of his betters. In the end, he had been easily manipulated, had even married off his only daughter to buy peace for his people.

Marianne. She had played her role well as Queen of Plorsea, remaining at King Braidon's side for close to a decade. Ever dutiful to family and nation, she had accepted the arranged marriage with good grace, though she'd loathed the man from the start. That anger had driven a wedge between the girl and her father, growing into a hatred the council had been all too happy to exploit. They had only needed to wait for the right moment.

That moment had come just days ago, on the thirtieth anniversary of the Order of Alana's founding. Marianne's faith had made her predictable, and the Order's Great Sacrifice had provided the perfect spectacle to dispose of King Braidon. The carrier pigeon had arrived just last night —on the shores of Malevolent Cove, Marianne had cast down her husband and taken the Plorsean crown for herself. With Ashoka already dead, there was no one left to stand against the council.

"Let us be seated," Isybelle said finally.

"Yes, take a seat."

Isybelle froze as a voice spoke from behind her, though there had been no one there a moment ago. She made to turn, but found her body unwilling to respond to her commands. Her muscles spasmed, and against her will, Isybelle lowered herself into the mahogany chair.

"Very good," the voice came again. A woman stepped around Isybelle and approached the council table.

Isybelle's confusion turned to shock as she recognised Marianne, King Ashoka's daughter. She was not a large woman, barely five-foot-four. A floor-length black dress clung to her figure, and a fine golden crown twisted through the locks of her auburn hair. She wandered the length of the room to where the heavy wooden doors still stood open. Marianne swung them closed and dropped the locking bar into place, before facing the council.

A gasp stole from Isybelle as she found herself able to move again. She slumped in the chair, taking a second to gather herself, while the Plorsean queen sat at the other end of the table. Answering exhalations came from the other senators as they looked uncertainly from Marianne to Isybelle.

Silently, Isybelle tried to understand what was happening. Why was Marianne here, rather than taking her place on the Plorsean throne, as intended? And what strange power had she used against them?

"Thank you for seeing me on such short notice, my good senators," Marianne said quietly, her sapphire eyes boring into Isybelle from across the table. "It seems all did not go to plan in Malevolent Cove."

"No," Isybelle rasped, deciding it best to speak with the woman. Marianne would need careful handling, if Isybelle read the situation right. "But the result is the same. Your father is gone, dead for his treachery against you and our nation. Your husband, too. You are Queen of Plorsea, as we planned."

"Ay," Marianne said, leaning forward, "but for how long? My husband did not die on that beach."

"He could not have survived the reefs," Isybelle countered. Regaining her cool, she flicked a piece of dust from her sleeve, and added: "Or the dragon fire."

"We found no body," Marianne hissed.

"Ha! As far as anyone who matters is concerned, Braidon is dead. His King's Guard has been slaughtered to a man. What threat can he pose? Do not worry yourself about it, girl."

"*Queen*," Marianne answered.

"Queen of Plorsea," Isybelle said, inclining her head with a smile. "A title you have more than earned, my dear."

"And of Lonia," Marianne added.

Isybelle's smile faltered. "Perhaps you do not understand," she said, straightening in her chair. "The people, they will not accept—"

"They will accept what they are told," Marianne interrupted.

"Even so…surely you cannot hope to rule Lonia from all the way in Ardath," Isybelle ground out the words. "It is better if the council—"

"This council's duty is to follow, not to rule," Marianne said dismissively. "You exist to administer our great nation, no more. Do not forget yourself, Senator."

Isybelle sat in silence, staring at the young queen. Marianne still wore the arrogant smile on her lips, as though the whole room—indeed, the whole world—belonged to her. Remembering her father, little more than a pig farmer before the people raised him up, Isybelle's anger took hold. She shot to her feet.

"It is *you* who forget yourself, girl," she snapped, slamming her palms into the tabletop. "You are only what we have made you. Step out of line, and the council will replace you with someone who knows their place."

The young queen did not move from her seat, though the smile left her face. "What do you mean when you say you 'made me'?"

"It was *we* who put you where you are now, girl," Isybelle said. A whisper came from the other senators, but enraged, she spoke over the top of them. "*We* who made you queen to that sorry excuse for a king. If not for us, you would be *nothing*."

"Is that so?" Marianne asked, rising as well now. Her eyes flashed dangerously.

The anger went from Isybelle in a rush. Why had she said that? Their efforts to convince Ashoka to sue for peace had been a secret the council had kept for a decade. She had given it away with nigh a thought. The other senators stared at her from their seats, aghast.

But what could the girl do about it? There were two dozen soldiers outside, loyal only to the council. She opened her mouth to call them.

"I always suspected this council had a hand in my father's decision," Marianne said quietly, walking around the table towards her. "I was never anything but a pawn in your games, was I? No matter that I was barely a woman; you put me in the bed of a man I loathed, made me bear his child. It was just a game for you, a subversion, to regain your former power."

"No...I..." Despite herself, Isybelle retreated from the fury in the queen's eyes. She tripped over her chair, sending it crashing to the stone. The sound broke the spell and she shouted, "Guards!"

"They cannot hear you," Marianne said. "You are alone, Isybelle."

Isybelle sneered at the woman, waiting for the guards to come bursting into the room. Her words could not be true, and yet...no sound came from beyond the oaken doors. Fear touched her then, and she turned to the other senators.

They stared back at her, faces pale with fear. Not one of them moved to help her.

"You cannot do this!" she gasped, turning back to the queen and drawing herself up. "I forbid it! There are still more of us here than you. If you do not—"

She broke off, suddenly unable to finish the sentence. It was as though an invisible fist had gripped her by the throat, choking off her words, her breath. Isybelle fumbled at her neck, but there was nothing there, no hand to free.

"You always scoffed at the Elders and their Order," Marianne commented. "Even as a child, I remember your disdain for them. But there is power in religion, even *real* power, it seems. It just took a few bright minds to discover it."

Despite her fear, anger flared in Isybelle's chest, that her associates had so abandoned her. Her mouth opened and closed, trying to form words, but no sound came out.

"What's that?" Marianne murmured, leaning close.

The pressure relented slightly, and Isybelle spat: "It was your precious Elder's idea!"

Marianne reeled back at that, her eyes widening, and the pressure vanished from Isybelle's throat. She gasped, straining to fill her lungs as she fell to her knees.

"What?" Marianne hissed, crouching alongside her.

Isybelle suppressed a smirk. "You did not know?" She felt the balance in the room swinging back towards her. The Elders and her fellow senators be damned, she would not be hung out to dry. Looking into the queen's eyes, she offered a sigh of empathy. "I am sorry, my dear. The plan was as much the Elders' as our own, a way to open Plorsea to the Order."

Rocking back on her heels, the queen stared at Isybelle,

as though contemplating the truth of her words. "Yet it is you who would take my birthright."

"Lonia is yours!" The words left Isybelle in a rush. Though they tasted of bile, better she survived today, that she might fix this mistake on another. She straightened, brushing the creases from her satin surcoat, refusing to let the woman steal her dignity.

"I was not asking your permission," Marianne replied, her voice turning cold once more.

Isybelle faltered, taken aback by the abrupt change in her foe. "I…then what do you want of us?"

"My father is dead, my husband in the wind. Both have suffered for their hand in my fate," Marianne surmised. Her sapphire eyes turned on the council. The senator shrunk in their seats, unable to meet her gaze. "But here this council sits, thinking to rule Lonia in my stead."

"But the Elders!"

"The Elders will have their reward," Marianne snarled. "As for this council…it only seems fear its leader suffer for their crimes."

Fear wrapped its icy coils around Isybelle's gut as the queen pulled a dagger from the folds of her dress. She stumbled back. It couldn't end like this, not after all her years of planning, after suffering the indignities of poverty. This was meant to be her day of reckoning, when the council regained its power, and Lonia its nobility.

But to Isybelle's surprise, Marianne offered her the knife. Glancing from the blade to the queen, Isybelle sensed a trap and shook her head. Marianne only smiled, and as though possessed by a will of its own, Isybelle's hand took the weapon.

Marianne faced the room. The other senators sat transfixed, and Isybelle cursed their cowardice. She had done everything for them, lifted them to the heights of power, disposed of King Ashoka – and now not one lifted a finger to aid her. If she survived, they would suffer for this betrayal.

"Councillor Isybelle has confessed to the murder of King Ashoka," the queen declared, flashing Isybelle a conspiring smile. It had been Marianne herself who had arranged her father's death. "In her shame, she has taken her own life, to spare this council the horror of executing one of their own."

"*No!*" Isybelle cried, lifting a hand to beg for her life.

The dagger glinted in her slender fist and Isybelle saw her chance. Marianne's back was to her. One thrust was all it would take to free them of the madwoman. Isybelle took one trembling step. The queen looked back and their eyes met.

"Try it," Marianne said.

"*Die!*" Isybelle screamed.

Staggering forward, she raised the dagger, but a sudden, awful pain tore through her abdomen. Horror touched Isybelle as she found the dagger embedded in her own stomach. In shock she tore the blade loose and let it fall. She clutched at the wound, but blood still pulsed between her fingers. The strength fled her and she sank to the ugly sandstone floor.

Pressure touched her shoulder. She swayed, surprised to find the queen beside her. The woman's sapphire eyes smiled.

"Ah, you might have been a manipulative witch, but you had *strength*, Isabelle," Marianne whispered. "Now die, and your hateful soul with you."

The queen's touch vanished, and Isybelle slumped on her side. Voices whispered in the room as Marianne took her seat at the head of the council, but Isybelle saw no more than that. Darkness swirled across her vision and her consciousness drifted, fell away. Her last thought was of the council, of Marianne, of the Elders of Alana, and how they would all pay…

❧ I ☙

Ocean water stung the burns on Kryssa's arms as she hauled herself onto the beach. Darkness clung to the night sky, the stars concealed by cloud. She could hardly see, was at the end of her strength, but she could not rest yet. A shout called her back into the crashing waves. She splashed through the breakers and caught Braidon by the shoulder, a second before he slipped from the arms of Caledan. The king's weight almost dragged him from her arms. She staggered, then righted herself before another wave could strike.

Caledan bent in two, gasping, but they were not safe yet. The currents had dragged them out of Malevolent Cove, but the distant glow of dragon fire still lit the horizon. Kryssa scanned the waters for Pela or Genevieve, but there was no sign of her daughter or the huntress. A tightness clutched her chest and she struggled to breathe.

"Pela!" she screamed into the darkness. "Gen!"

There was no reply and she struggled to control her panic. This could not be happening, not again. She had already lost Devon tonight, just minutes after their reunion, after he'd spoken the words she'd longed to hear all her life.

My daughter!

But the queen had killed him, as she had tried to kill Kryssa and Pela and Braidon. Kryssa had already promised the woman would pay—now she would dedicate her life to that cause.

But thoughts of revenge could wait—danger still threatened now. Clinging to Braidon with one hand, she grabbed Caledan by the shirt and dragged him back to his feet. She hardly knew the man, but her father had trusted him and so would she.

"Help me!" she shouted above the roar of breaking waves, gesturing at Braidon. "Before his bloody wife catches up with us."

Pale-faced and hollow-eyed, Caledan took hold of Braidon's other arm. The king was badly wounded, his skin cold to the touch. He had not spoken since they'd gone into the water, but as they dragged him onto the sand, a groan whispered from his lips.

Kryssa let out a sigh; he lived! She could not have born it if this had all been for nothing.

Not that she understood what exactly *was* happening.

What had Braidon, the King of Plorsea, been doing here in the first place? The others, Devon and Pela and Genevieve, had come to rescue her from the Knights of Alana, but Braidon…Kryssa had served on his King's Guard, long ago. She knew the man, and could not understand what had brought him to the black shores of Malevolent Cove.

Stumbling up the beach, they entered the treeline and carried the king several yards into the forest. There they lowered him gently to the ground. Kryssa knelt to inspect his wound.

"I'll cover our tracks," Caledan said, and vanished.

"Firewood!" she called after him.

Kryssa wondered too what the sellsword's place in all this was. She'd barely caught his name, back in the amphitheatre, but he had saved Pela from the sword of Ikar. With his help, and her father's sacrifice, they had almost escaped. But nothing could have saved them from the dragon that had fallen from the sky, capsizing their boat in its death throes. She shuddered, knowing that more of the creatures lurked in this forest.

Caledan was back within minutes, a stack of firewood in hand. He set to work lighting a small fire, using a husk of bark and dry stick to spark the wood shavings to light.

"Any sign of the Knights or the bloody Dragons?" Kryssa asked as she pulled up Braidon's shirt.

It was still too dark to see how much damage the queen had done, and she sat back, waiting for him to build up the fire.

"Dragons are on our side," Caledan said as he added a broken branch to the crackling flame. "No Knights."

Kryssa raised an eyebrow, but in the burning glow she could finally see their patient. Praying the trees would conceal the light from prying eyes, she leaned in close to inspect Braidon's wound. The king had begun to shiver, and if shock took hold, nothing they did was likely to save him. He needed to dry off, needed warmth.

With Caledan's help, they stripped Braidon of his wet clothing and laid him down close to the fire. Kryssa had seen her fair share of wounds as a King's Guard and knew a thing or two about treatment in the field, but she feared Braidon's injuries might be beyond her.

The queen had stabbed him with her rapier, leaving a small circular wound. At first inspection it did not appear serious, but who knew how much internal damage had been done. She had obviously missed his heart, but if a lung had been pierced…Braidon might drown in his own blood, and there would be nothing Kryssa could do to save him.

Placing an ear to his chest, she listened for the rattle of liquid. Braidon was barely breathing—only the slightest rise and fall of his chest revealed he lived. She closed her eyes, allowing the crackling of the fire to fade away, disengaging from the stench of smoke, the rustling of branches over-head. Concentrating on the erratic thud of Braidon's heart, the whisper of his breath, she allowed her own self to drift away.

After a few minutes, she sat back up.

"What do you think?" Caledan asked, his forehead creased.

"She has poor aim," Kryssa commented. "Thank the Gods, he might live if we can stop the bleeding and keep him warm."

She unfastened the sword from her waist and drew the blade, then paused. In the race to flee the amphitheatre she had picked it up without thinking, but now she saw it was her husband's blade. Pela had been wielding it, but had lost it in the battle with Ikar. Kryssa's eyes flickered closed. One day, she resolved to give it back to her daughter.

Then she swallowed her grief and took up Braidon's jacket. Cutting it into strips, she did her best to bind his chest tight.

"We'll need to find something to help fight infections," she said, sitting back on the damp earth. Her eyes slid closed as a wave of weariness swept her. "In the morning."

Caledan still stood staring down at the king. His brown

eyes shone in the firelight, his black hair plastered to his scalp. Kryssa was sure she'd never seen him before, yet back in the arena he had slain Ikar with hardly a thought. Not even Devon had managed such a feat. The man was a killer, and in different circumstances she might have been cautious of him. But her father's trust did not...*had* not, come easily.

"Are you okay?" she asked into the silence.

The swordsman shook himself and offered a strained smile. "Well enough." He seated himself across the fire from her. "The name's Caledan, by the way," he murmured. "Since we weren't formally introduced back there. It's nice to finally meet you, Kryssa. You certainly don't disappoint. I didn't think anyone could stand against that giant of a Knight, after he defeated Devon."

"His name was Ikar," Kryssa replied, remembering the Knight's face at the end.

A lump lodged in her throat and she swallowed. Ikar had been many things, both kind and cruel when it took him, noble in his own way, determined to stand against what he saw as evil. Over the weeks he had held her prisoner, he had revealed his humanity in a million small gestures. But in the end, Ikar had been as much a prisoner to the Order's beliefs as she had been. And he had died for them.

"Yet you were the one who killed him," Kryssa added after a pause. "Thank you for that. I...couldn't risk my daughter's life."

She and Ikar had fought each other, but in the end the Knight had beaten her by threatening Pela's life. She'd had no choice but to surrender, though in the end it did not seem to have mattered...

A shudder ran down Kryssa's spine as she remembered the cove aflame, the waves raging across jagged reefs, the desperate fight to reach the shore, the panic as she realised Pela was missing, that Genevieve had vanished. She had lost everything in that dark place.

"I did very little," Caledan said, his eyes on the fire. "I'm…sorry I could not do more. After we went in the water…I thought I'd lost all of you." He paused, then nodded at the king. "Everyone but that deadweight, at least."

"It was brave, carrying him all that way," Kryssa offered.

"I would not have done it, if not for Devon," Caledan replied. "But…I could not ignore his last wish."

Kryssa looked away, her vision blurring. Exhaustion weighed on her shoulders and she closed her eyes. A shiver raised goosebumps on her arms, though it was hot in front of the fire.

How could she have allowed this to happen?

It was meant to be *her*. She had given herself up for dead days ago, when her last escape attempt had ended in failure and left the Elder Putar dead. She had begged Ikar to kill her, rather than continue as a pawn in the Order's game.

But he had refused, and now Devon was dead in Kryssa's place—her daughter and Genevieve as well, for all she knew.

A desperate guilt twisted her abdomen and she bent in two, the salt-soaked contents of her stomach rushing up. Groaning, she vomited into the dirt alongside the fire. The first traces of panic tugged at her. She was alone, had lost everything. For a moment she was back on the streets of her childhood, fleeing guards and dogs and slavers—always running, never safe.

Not until the day Selina and Devon had taken her in.

Sucking in a lungful of air, Kryssa sought her calm centre the way Selina had shown her, so many decades ago. She concentrated on her breath, on the slow in-out of air through her nostrils, the swelling of her chest. Blood thumped in her ears, slowing with each inhalation. A peaceful darkness rose in her mind, an empty void of calm.

Kryssa exhaled and opened her eyes.

Caledan still sat nearby, a concerned look on his face. "Are you okay?"

As Kryssa made to reply, a sharp *crack* came from the nearby trees. In an instant they were both on their feet, swords in hand. Kryssa dragged a burning brand from the fire with her left hand, and Caledan did the same. Holding the torches aloft, they scanned the shadows for beast or man.

For a second there was nothing—then the firelight caught the glimmer of blood-red scales. A giant ficus tree groaned as a taloned foot pressed against it, then toppled slowly sideways. A scream built in Kryssa's throat as it struck the earth with a muffled *thud,* but there was no time to panic, no time to do anything but stare as the Red Dragon clambered into the clearing.

It rose before them, one great blue eye watching them with frightening intelligence. The ruined remnants of its other eye still dripped blood where the crossbow bolt had struck it. Kryssa's gaze swept the rest of the creature, noticing the torn and broken scales. She swallowed, realising the beast had encountered the weapons of the Knights— though clearly not the explosives that had torn its brethren from the sky.

The Knights have slain Ingytus. The dragon's words rattled in Kryssa's skull so loudly she had to clench her jaw to keep herself from screaming. *Others died on the sands of Malevolent Cove. You will burn for their deaths.*

Caledan stepped between Kryssa and the beast, sword in hand, though he could not hope to harm the creature. "Stay back, beast," he snarled. "You made a pact, you and your kin. We stand with the king."

The king lies dying! the dragon roared.

"He is not dead yet!"

Ingytus was a fool to side with such feeble creatures; the pact is void!

"The pact stands!" Caledan shot back. His sword shimmered in the firelight as he pointed it at the dragon's breast, and Kryssa wondered at his nerve. "You are bound to it, so long as Braidon draws breath."

The dragon reared up on its hind legs, teeth bared. The heat of its breath swept through the clearing, causing the fire to flicker dangerously. Kryssa braced herself, preparing for death. She could hardly believe it could end like this, after everything she had survived.

But the dragon fire did not come, and with an awful howl, the dragon sank back to the earth.

The pact must be fulfilled. Its voice hammered at Kryssa's senses. *The king must drive these Knights from our land, or we will bring our grief to your towns and cities. Betray us at your peril, humans.*

"Braidon will complete his side of the bargain, when he recovers," Caledan replied quickly.

The great eye stared at them, and the dragon's jaws opened and closed, as though their soft flesh were between its teeth.

So be it, finally came the reply, *but should your feeble king perish…*

The dragon left the threat unfinished. It moved off

silently through the trees, obviously as desperate as they were to remain undetected by the Knights.

When it had vanished, Kryssa slumped to the ground alongside Braidon. Quickly she checked his pulse. It was weak and unsteady, though at least some colour had returned to his cheeks. Sitting back on her haunches, she looked at Caledan.

"We'd better make sure he lives," she murmured.

"Agreed," the swordsman said grimly.

❧   2   ❧

The next week dragged by at a crawl for Caledan. With the Knights and their followers sweeping up and down the coast, they had been forced to move their camp further inland. After that, the monotony soon set in. Kryssa had returned several times to scour the beaches herself, seeking signs of Pela or the huntress Genevieve, but finally she was forced to abandon the search. If their friends lived, they'd either been taken by the Order or swept elsewhere by the erratic currents of the western coast.

Caledan had given them both up for dead the first morning after the solstice, when he'd returned to the beach and looked upon the devastation left by the dragon. Burnt timbers and bodies lay scattered across the sand, washed up during the night. He could not imagine how either Pela or Genevieve could have survived the deadly waters.

Kryssa must have known it too, for she grew silent as the week progressed. Any sense of levity fell from her as she faced the cold reality of her daughter's loss. Caledan felt for her, but there was little he could say. Already he felt trapped by his friendship with Devon, by the hammerman's final words. He remembered now why he had avoided such connections—all they ever brought was pain and loss, the sacrifice of his own ambitions for the sake of others.

What madness had possessed Caledan that he'd returned to the amphitheatre rather than flee? He'd thought to help his friends, to rescue Devon and Genevieve from the clutches of the queen. But he had failed utterly. Instead, he had become minder for the ruin that was Braidon.

The fallen king might have survived the battle in Malevolent Cove, but his spirit had been destroyed by his wife's betrayal. He had woken on the first day, but had hardly moved from his bed of ferns since.

Caledan had taken to avoiding their camp during the day, preferring to range along the volcanic range in search of supplies. Kryssa had shown him a few plants that could be used to prevent infection, and he'd managed to kill a fat pigeon once with a stone. Mostly they ate berries and fruit, though Kryssa sometimes went out in the early mornings, often returning with a hare or marmot.

The sun was getting low on the horizon now and Caledan was returning to the camp, a fresh bundle of firewood tied to his back. They were encamped near a spring on the steeps of Mount Chole, still within the treeline but where the undergrowth started to thin. He wondered if Braidon would be any better this night.

As a sellsword, Caledan had spent most of his life around fighting men, but he knew little of the treatment of wounds. Braidon was lucky his King's Guard were trained in the basics of first aid, though Caledan had been surprised to learn Kryssa had once served amongst their ranks. Truly she was her father's daughter.

All the more confusing then that Kryssa had refused to

teach Pela the warrior's arts—or even tell the girl about her heritage. Thinking of the naïve girl he'd first met in Skystead, Caledan wondered how Kryssa could have kept so much from her only daughter.

Then again, after seeing Kryssa's embrace with Genevieve in the amphitheatre, it was clear the woman had kept more than just the warrior's arts from Pela. A smile touched his lips as he wondered what else Pela might have missed in her youthful innocence. It quickly vanished as he remembered the girl's likely fate.

Drawing in a breath, Caledan paused on the mountainside to take stock of his surroundings. There had been no sign of the Knights or their followers for several days now, and a set of tracks he'd found heading west suggested they'd left the area. Above him, a gravel slope stretched up towards the rocky sides of the volcano, atop which a sprinkling of snow still showed from last winter.

Here and there, steam rose from hollows on the mountainside, the earth around them stained scarlet and yellow and orange. Caledan did his best to avoid those areas during his scouting, though he knew the inhabitants of nearby Chole had taken to mining the precious minerals found in the volcanic range.

Spotting a familiar landmark, Caledan entered the trees on the slope below him. He was close to camp now, and he slowly made his way into the denser forest. Away from the high slopes, the air quickly heated up, the humidity making the sweat bead on his forehead. At least with sunset nearing, the worst of the day's heat was behind him.

Voices came from the trees ahead, and pushing aside a heavy branch, he stepped into the camp.

"I don't know how she could do—" Braidon was saying, but he broke off as Caledan appeared.

Crossing the clearing, Caledan added his firewood to the stack near the fire. "Still moaning about your wife?" he asked, turning to face the king.

Braidon's face darkened, his jaw taking on a hard edge. "I loved her," he grated.

"Ay, and she made a clown out of you," Caledan replied. "Not a difficult thing to do."

The king said nothing, but his eyes shone at Caledan's words and he quickly looked away. "I was such a fool," he whispered. "Devon should have left me to die there."

The past week had helped heal the king's wounds and he could now walk short distances. But still Braidon clung to despair and self-pity, hardly lifting a finger to help while Kryssa and Caledan cooked the meals and tidied the camp. All he did was sit and complain and rage against his wife. His self-defeat made a mockery of Devon's sacrifice.

"Perhaps he should have," Caledan agreed. "I would have."

"And what is she doing now?" Braidon continued, hardly seeming to hear Caledan's words. "It's been a week. Even now she might be planning some fresh evil for Plorsea. My nation has suffered enough!"

"On that we can agree!" Caledan snorted. "Who knows, maybe she's doing a better job of it than you. The Gods know, it wouldn't be hard."

Finally his words enacted a response from Braidon. The king's head snapped up and he locked eyes with Caledan. "I did my best," he hissed. "I didn't see anyone else volunteering."

"A dimwit could have seen the Order sought power in Plorsea."

"Power, yes," Braidon replied. "But *human sacrifice*? How could I have known that?"

"I don't know," Caledan mocked, "maybe if you weren't *sleeping* with one of them, for what, eight years? *Surely* you must have noticed something when your wife started butchering the hired help?"

Braidon staggered to his feet and pointed a finger at Caledan. "How dare you speak—"

"I dare!" Caledan roared, tired of the king's self-loathing. "I dare because you do not deserve to be king. You never did, pathetic excuse for a man that you are. It was you who got us into this mess—and now you sit here wallowing, expecting us to clean it up for you, for the rest of us to save you like Devon did, and your sister before him. Well, guess what, they're all gone. There's no one left to do your dirty work for you—"

Caledan broke off as the king roared and staggered at him. Dragging his sword from its scabbard, Braidon swung it at Caledan's head, but his injuries made the king slow and Caledan leaned back, allowing the blade to cut empty air. His own blade leapt to his hand and he parried a second cut.

"Stop!" Kryssa screamed. "Or by the Gods, I'll cut you both down." She started towards them, then paused. Her hands were empty. Her scabbard and sword lay on the other side of the firepit.

"Die, *bastard!*" Braidon roared, swinging at Caledan again.

The sellsword parried, then lashed out with his boot, catching Braidon's insole and sending him crashing to the dirt. The sword spun from the king's grasp, but he scrambled across the ground and swept it back up.

"What are you waiting for? Fight back!" Braidon spat, lashing out with the blade.

Caledan knocked aside the blow and retreated. The king

might have been weak, but his sword was no less dangerous and a single lucky blow could prove fatal.

"Why bother?" he retorted. "A child could defeat you."

Screaming, Braidon hurled himself forward. Caledan's sword flashed up, catching the king's blade close to the hilt and jarring it from the man's hand. Sparks flashed as it struck a rock and spun towards the fire. Caledan readied another retort—but Braidon charged emptyhanded, slamming into Caledan's midriff.

Caught unawares, the breath left Caledan's lungs in a rush. He staggered back, his foot catching on a stray root. They both fell, striking the ground together and rolling. Braidon came up on top, pinning Caledan down. The king's fist caught the sellsword in the temple and drove his head backwards into the earth.

A bright light flashed across Caledan's vision. Anger flared in his chest and he bared his teeth. The king reared back, readying another blow, but Caledan rolled to the side. His greater weight was enough to throw the weakened Braidon off-balance, toppling him sideways. A glancing blow careered off Caledan's shoulder, then he was free.

They reared up together, but Caledan was far quicker, and he hammered a left cross into the king's jaw. A punch from Braidon was easily deflected, then Caledan slammed a fist into his opponent's midriff. Braidon doubled over and collapsed to the dirt, his breath coming in strained gasps.

Rising to his feet, Caledan recovered his weapon. Leaves crunched behind him and he spun, the blade coming up to point at Kryssa. She held Braidon's sword in one hand now, but made no move to attack.

Caledan looked back at the king. Braidon had managed to recover his breath but he remained crouching in the dirt. Their eyes met and Caledan saw the defeat in the king's blue eyes. Marianne had ruined him, cast him off and left him with nothing, not even his pride.

"Kill me," Braidon croaked. "Isn't that what you came here to do?"

It was true. Caledan had spent half his life planning Braidon's demise, plotting to get close enough to drive a sword through his heart. His sister had robbed the world of magic and so doomed Caledan's mother to a painful death, when a healer might have saved her. It was only right that Alana's family should die as well.

Caledan gripped the hilt of his sword so tight he felt the leather digging into his skin. The tip trembled as he pointed it at Braidon's throat. He had longed for this day, to finally face this man in single combat and defeat him, to take his revenge against the woman who had stolen everything from him.

The king did not move. He crouched helpless in the mud, defeated, begging for his death. In that moment, Caledan felt nothing but loathing for the pitiful creature before him. Braidon was no longer a king, not even a man. He had fallen into a pit he would never climb back out of. It would be a mercy to kill him now.

A mercy.

Caledan shuddered, lowering his sword. "You disgust me," he spat. "Pathetic creature, begging in the mud for me to end your misery. Well, you don't get to escape so easily. You broke this nation; you can damn well stick around to fix it."

Sheathing his sword, he turned away. His eyes roamed the campsite, sharing a glance with Kryssa. He held her gaze for a long moment, realising that he could help her no longer. If he stayed with the broken king, Caledan *would* kill him. He could do no more in this forest. Kryssa could take care of herself, and he would not waste any more energy on Braidon, no matter what Devon had asked of him.

"I'm leaving," he said shortly.

"What will you do?" Kryssa asked.

Caledan started away, but he paused at the treeline, pondering the question. Finally he shook his head. "I don't know," he murmured, glancing back. "Something productive, I hope."

❧ 3 ❧

Darkness surrounded Pela, thick and suffocating, lit only by the flickering glow of a distant lantern. It seemed an age had passed since she'd last seen the sun, since she'd tasted fresh air and felt the wind on her cheeks. Overhead, the weight of a mountain pressed down on her, a thousand tonnes of rock and dirt and death that would be her tomb.

How long had she toiled now? She no longer knew, only that her arms ached and that each day she grew weaker, the flesh shrivelling from her bones, her spirit fading. The steel collar, inset with a single black gem, pressed tightly at her throat, a constant reminder of her fate.

Pela had been elated when she'd first seen the ship on the horizon. For a day she had drifted with Genevieve, clinging to the plank of wood that was their only hope. The hot sun had beaten down on them and the saltwater had drained away their strength, but finally hope had been at hand.

Only when the ship neared had they seen the black sails,

the dark-garbed men and women crowding the decks. The Baronians had hauled them from the ocean and locked them away in the bowels of the vessel. There with a half-dozen other unfortunate souls, they had been condemned, sailed upriver to Sheffield and sold as slaves. The practice was forbidden in Plorsea, and legal only for condemned criminals in Lonia. But the Lonian overseers who'd bought them had not cared about their innocence.

They had been taken from Sheffield to the mines and separated there. Pela had not seen Genevieve since, and now she no longer had the strength to worry for her friend. She had been placed in a chain gang with a dozen other unfortunate souls—some the criminals the Lonians believed them to be, others like her, taken by slavers to toil beneath the earth. It didn't matter which—those who tried to proclaim their innocence were beaten mercilessly by their captors.

Watched by an overseer, they were fed once a day, a meal of watery gruel that could scarce be considered food. At night—though there was no telling night from day in their filthy holes—they were left chained together, to sleep as best they could in the cold dirt.

The rest of the time they worked, hours upon hours uncounted, smashing the slick black rock from the walls and loading up carts, dragging them towards the surface—but never quite reaching it. When the light was but a pinprick in the distance, another crew of slaves, those trusted by the overseers, took over the barrows, loading them onto carts on a steel track and pushing them to the open air.

How Pela longed to join them. Each trip she stole a full minute to stare at that tiny light, allowing herself to dream of freedom, of returning to the outside world.

It was a hopeless dream, and soon the cruel overseer

would shout and she would stagger back into the awful depths, return to the darkness and the creeping death that stole closer each day. She could feel herself wasting away, her will devoured by cold and starvation.

Her arms burned as she swung the pickaxe, but she lacked the strength to aim the tool now, and the blow missed, skittering off the paler rock she had come to know as limestone. Sparks flashed and her heart lurched. She held her breath, waiting to see if she had doomed them all. The other slaves had told her the black rock was flammable, and talked of stray sparks setting entire tunnels alight, but no fire followed, and Pela breathed a sigh of relief.

A curse came from behind her and Pela turned in time to catch the overseer's whip across her breasts. The leather tore through cloth and skin and she cried out, falling back and dropping her pick.

"Stupid witch!" the overseer screamed, lashing out again. Fire encircled Pela's wrist as the whip wrapped around her forearm. "Careless!"

Another blow followed. All Pela could do was curl into a ball and endure. Hot blood trickled across her stomach and tears beaded her eyes, but she was so dehydrated they did not fall. The overseer continued to scream, raining down blows she hardly felt, until he abruptly changed tact. His boot caught Pela in the stomach and hurled her into the wall.

The breath hissed in Pela's throat as she gasped, unable to draw breath. The overseer loomed, mining pick in hand. He tossed it at her with a sneer, and the wooden haft struck her in the forehead. Stars flashed across her vision as he snarled:

"Do that again, and I'll kill you myself."

Then he was gone, moving on to some other victim.

Connected to the other slaves, the chain at her ankle tugged, a not-so-subtle hint for her to get up. All would suffer if they failed to meet the overseer's quota.

Pela crawled to her knees, wondering how much longer she could endure. The movement stirred the thick dust covering the ground and she coughed, her lungs choking in the darkness. Always the air was stale and thick with poison, so that it seemed she were breathing inside of a chimney. She could not catch her breath, no matter how hard she tried.

"Here," a kindly voice whispered.

A leather waterskin appeared in front of Pela's eyes. She straightened slowly and glanced at the speaker. It was Siden, the kindly old man who worked one chain link down, Pela's only friend in this awful place. She nodded her thanks and accepted the skin, though she took only a sip. Siden needed the water as much as her and there would be no more today, once the skin ran dry.

"You must be more careful, youngling," he whispered.

Pela nodded, though her eyes flickered closed and she swayed on her feet, barely able to keep herself upright. A hand, surprisingly firm for Siden's advanced years, gripped her by the shoulder.

"I...can barely lift it," she croaked, opening her eyes to stare at the pickaxe.

Before Siden could respond, she bent and picked it up. It was not heavy—no heavier than the sword she'd once owned. That seemed another life now, the day Devon had given Pela her father's blade. She thought herself weak then, but now she was no more than skin and bone. Even so, she gripped the pickaxe tight and forced her attention to their task.

Thick veins of black criss-crossed the tunnel walls, softer

than the surrounding rock. It shone in the light of the distant lantern. Pela had learned from her fellow slaves that it burned far hotter than any wood, though she was lucky enough not to have witnessed it personally. Coal, they called it, just one of the many dangers in the death-trap that were the mines.

The fumes were another threat. There was a constant stench of rotten eggs in the tunnels, most times almost unnoticeable, but occasionally the fumes grew so strong men had been known to lose consciousness. Then the overseer would retreat up the tunnel, ordering the slaves to remain until the weakest fell, and only then allowing them to flee.

At first the constant dangers had filled Pela with terror. Eventually though, exhaustion and hunger had lessoned their sting, wearing at her until she no longer cared for her approaching death. She could not even muster fear for the overseer and his whip. Nothing could prevent the beatings, for she was so tired mistakes were a certainty. She simply endured.

Pela lifted the pick above her head and was about to strike again, when a voice called down the tunnel. Lowering the tool, she looked up, seeking daylight but seeing only darkness. Then the flickering glow of a lantern appeared around a bend in the tunnel, followed by two figures.

"Overseer Harrison!" a woman's voice echoed through the gloom. "It's your lucky day!"

"Ay?" the overseer's harsh voice called back.

Taking the opportunity to rest, Pela put down the pickaxe and pressed up against the wall. Chains rattled as the other slaves did the same. The overseer strode past to meet the newcomers, shaking hands with the woman. There was a slightly perplexed look on his bearded face and dirt streaked his forehead—not even the overseers could escape the filth of the tunnels.

"The Order has accepted your request," the woman explained. "Their Knights are seeking fresh blood, to spread the Saviour's word to Plorsea. You are to leave immediately for your initiation. Ruebyn is here to replace you."

A young man not much older than Pela's seventeen years stepped forward and extended his hand. The overseer stared at him for half a second longer than was polite before accepting the offer. Pela could see her own thoughts mirrored in the man's beady eyes. The boy was far too young for a position of authority.

"Congratulations," Ruebyn said. "To be Knighted is a great honour. Our new queen will be glad to have your sword."

The overseer snorted. "The Knights are soldiers of the Saviour, not some traitor who thinks to rule us from Ardath."

Pela frowned, confused by the man's words. She had thought Marianne was popular in Lonia.

The boy seemed similarly confused. He glanced uncertainly at his superior, then back at Harrison. "Marianne is one of our own. The Elders and the Lonian council have both given her their blessing..."

"She is tainted," the overseer said dismissively. "Plorsean scum, we should have never made peace with them. Never mind, I will be glad to show them the true path of the Saviour."

"Yes," the woman said, stepping between them. "I thank you for your service, Harrison. You have yielded great boons for our mine." She held out her hand, and after a moment's hesitation, the overseer passed over his whip. The woman promptly deposited the cruel weapon into the boy's hands. "I can only hope young Ruebyn continues your legacy."

Pale-faced, Ruebyn looked from the whip to his superior. "Thank you, ma'am, I…I will not let you down!"

"They're yours now," she said, gesturing to Pela and the other slaves. There were twelve on their chain, the usual arrangement for each overseer. "Be sure you keep them in line. Never forget, they are criminals, and must be treated as such. Do not give them an inch, least they hang you with it." Then she was gone, their former overseer following her up the tunnel in silence.

Pela watched them go, surprised by the sudden turn of events. For a second, she felt uplifted, relieved to be free of the man who had so cruelly tortured her for all these uncounted days. As the last echoes of their footsteps faded, she looked at the young man who now controlled her life.

Ruebyn shifted nervously on his feet, his eyes flicking from the whip to his slaves. His Adam's apple bobbed up and down, and Pela realised he had no idea what he was doing. She felt a touch of empathy for him. Maybe this was his first time separated from his family, his first time away from the safety of his own home. Attempting a smile, she took a step towards him.

The whip slashed out, catching her across the face. Gasping, Pela staggered back, clutching her cheek. Hot blood seeped between her fingers—then her feet lost their footing on the uneven rocks. She crashed to the ground as the boy's voice echoed from the cavern walls, several pitches above normal:

"Stay away from me!"

Wincing, Pela pushed herself up on her elbow, her head spinning. The cut to her cheek was not deep, but like all the others it would most likely become infected. She watched the boy, expecting a fresh beating to follow, but he did not move. Eyes wide, he stared at her as though not sure what he'd just done.

A sudden anger took her, a rage she had thought long lost. It rose from the dark depths of her soul until her entire body was shaking. Pushing herself to her feet, she sneered at the boy, swaying where she stood. Her past life was a distant memory now, the fears that had once controlled her fled in the face of her exhaustion. All she could think of was the injustice of the world, that even this useless, inexperienced boy should have power over her.

"What, have you never beaten a woman before?" she hissed.

The boy gaped as though she had struck him. His eyes were wide, flicking from her to the other slaves, but they shrank back, even sweet Siden. He could not help her, no one could. She had spoken the words; there was no taking them back.

"What, are you stupid or something?" she spat when still the boy said nothing.

Raising a fist, Pela staggered at him. To her surprise, Ruebyn retreated, lifting the whip in front of him as though it were a shield. His cowardice fuelled her rage and shrieking, Pela leapt at him—but there was no strength in her legs, and instead she found herself falling. The ground rose to meet her. Light flashed across her vision as she struck.

Her sight spinning, Pela stared at the ceiling, her fury vanished as quickly as it had appeared. Darkness pressed in on her, and she could no longer tell whether it was reality or her own personal nightmare.

A face appeared through the fogs: old Siden. His forehead was creased and his lips moved, but Pela heard no sound. She sensed movement around her, felt hands grasping at her arms and legs and tried to fight them off, but her body refused to obey. A groan whispered from her lips, what remained of the shriek she had intended.

Finally, she could fight no more. Her eyes slid closed, and she sank into the kind embrace of unconsciousness.

❦ 4 ❦

Braidon sat in the darkness, listening to the slow trickling of the creek as it wound its way past the camp. He had sat there for most of the night, trapped in his ruined body as much as he was stuck in Dragon Country. Thoughts of Marianne brought an equal measure of grief and anger, but Braidon knew he was not strong enough to face her.

Once, he might have summoned the will to oppose her, to gather his followers and restore his crown, to drive Marianne and the Order of Alana from his lands. But now he was lost, his confidence eroded by a decade of failures, by his wife's betrayal, by his own folly.

And she had their son, Calybe. He was only five. Braidon shuddered to think what the woman he'd seen in Malevolent Cove would do to the boy.

He swallowed. How had it come to this? Thirty years ago, after the Tsar's death and the departure of the Gods, the Three Nations had finally been free. His reign as king should have beckoned in a new era of prosperity for Plorsea.

Instead, Trola had shuttered its borders to the outside world, ceasing all trade. Until then, Plorsea had flourished on trade between the Three Nations, situated as it was on the main trade route between Lonia and Trola. The sudden absence of the western nation had plunged Braidon's lands into crisis.

Then King Ashoka had led the Lonian army south, forcing Plorsean farmers from their land and igniting a decade-long war that had almost destroyed both nations. By the time of Braidon's marriage to the Lonian princess Marianne, both countries had been eager for peace.

Knowing Ashoka to be a kind man, if a ruthless one, Braidon had never questioned Marianne's devotion. Now he found his anger stirring at the realisation he'd been played a fool. Not even the so-called peace had been genuine. Lonia had spent the last eight years developing new weapons of war, deadly steel crossbows and terrifying explosive powder, and ships that could sail without wind or oars.

If it came to war, Plorsea would be badly outmatched. But Marianne was a shrewd woman—he knew that, at least, had not been an act. She had played her cards well, disposing of her father and husband within weeks of each other. She would be queen of both nations, without a single soldier lifting a sword.

He cursed beneath his breath.

"Can't sleep?"

Braidon was surprised to find Kryssa sitting up. Her silver eyes shone in the darkness, almost supernatural in their luminosity, and he shuddered. This was the woman he had given up his crown for, who he had crossed half the nation to save. Devon had sacrificed his last breath to see her safe, to protect his daughter.

Now Braidon was failing her, failing them all. He hung his head.

"Caledan was right," he murmured. "I'm a fool. Marianne has the Knights and her Queen's Guard behind her, and a power I cannot explain. I cannot stop her."

"Perhaps you're right," Kryssa said. Throwing off the blanket she had woven together from fern fronds, she stood. "Perhaps I should leave you here for the dragons to find."

Fear twisted Braidon's stomach into knots. "Please don't," he croaked. He was not strong enough to walk a hundred paces, let alone climb the mountain paths back to Plorsea.

"Then give me a reason to stay!" Kryssa snapped, her lips curling back in a sneer. "Show me what my father saw in you, why he died rather than leave you in your wife's tender care. Show me the man who stood against the Tsar."

Braidon lowered his eyes. "He is gone."

"Then we are all doomed," Kryssa murmured. She strode from the campsite.

He watched as the darkness swallowed her up, unable to summon the will to call her back. Then he placed his head in his hands and sobbed. All these years, he had done his best to rule Plorsea, to bring prosperity to his people. He had hated it, had loathed the bureaucracy, despaired as setback after setback saw his hope wither and die.

For the last eight years, Marianne and later their son had been his sole consolation, the only light in the darkness.

But that too had been a lie. He had nothing left to give. He was undone, broken.

I believe in you, brother.

Braidon shivered as the ghost whispered in his mind. They were his sister Alana's words, rising from the faded memories of his past. He had been a frightened child, terrified of the power that lurked within him. Magic had been a dangerous force, and those who feared it were destined to be controlled *by* it—their souls consumed, their bodies becoming host to the darkness within.

Alana had sheltered Braidon for most of his childhood, protecting him from their father's rages. Yet isolated from the world, Braidon's growth had been stunted. Only when they'd been separated had he finally flourished, overcoming his fears and mastering his magic. And finally Alana had seen the truth, that he too could be strong.

But as he'd told Kryssa, that was a long time ago. He was no longer that man. His magic was gone, his best years behind him. Perhaps Marianne was the future now, Plorsea destined to fall beneath her rule.

Braidon's mind turned back to the night of the solstice, to the great amphitheatre on the shores of Malevolent Cove. The followers of the Order had gathered in their hundreds for the Great Sacrifice, had watched as their queen attempted to burn Kryssa and Pela alive, had howled for Devon's death as the hammerman fought their champion.

Anger stirred in Braidon's stomach. If that was to be Marianne's way, Plorsea would never follow. Perhaps some of his people had been in the crowd, but many more had come from Lonia. It had been their ships that had bobbed off the coast, their Knights who had brought hatred to his land.

Their queen who had betrayed him.

He let out a long breath. Marianne thought she had

defeated him, that she could betray him and he would submit without hardly a whimper. His thoughts spun. All those years of his life, wasted by the woman's treachery. Looking back, he saw now that she had been behind all his failures, that she had pulled his strings, had manipulated him all along.

Perhaps she had not chosen their marriage, but she had made a choice every day since. She had played her own game, taken her revenge, plotted her conquest.

Clenching his fists, Braidon staggered to his feet. The fight with Caledan had robbed him of the little strength he had regained, but rage gave him power. He stumbled to the stream and splashed water in his face. The cold woke him, tore him from the stupor that had gripped him since that night in the cove.

Perhaps there was no longer magic lurking within, waiting to pray upon his fear, but the emotion was no less treacherous. And he had succumbed to it, had allowed his terror to rule him.

No longer.

Braidon recalled the hatred in Marianne's eyes as she had looked upon him in Malevolent Cove. There'd been no love there, no trace of compassion. He must be the same. In that moment, Braidon's love for her died, plunged into the fiery embrace of his fury, forged into a new weapon, a hatred that would give him the strength to rise again.

He was Braidon, son of the Tsar, brother of Alana, last descendant of a line of kings stretching all the way back to the birth of the Gods.

Never again would he be defeated by despair.

A branch cracked at the edge of the clearing and he turned to see Kryssa step back into the camp, a fresh bundle of firewood in her arms. She raised an eyebrow when she saw him standing by the creek.

"Gotten over yourself then?" she asked.

"Ay." Braidon smiled. "I think it's time we took the war to my wife."

❧ 5 ❦

Pela's escape into unconsciousness did not last long. Pain soon dragged her back to reality, back to the pounding in her skull and the burning in her lungs. Tasting blood, she turned her head and spat on the floor. No one moved to help her, but she heard voices nearby.

"What's wrong with her, slave?" It was the new overseer, his voice bordering on panic. "How am I meant to do my job with only eleven of you?"

"Master, she is just a girl, and starving." Siden replied, his voice soft, beseeching. "Your predecessor saw fit to halve our rations. The girl is starving."

"I'm sure the man had good reason," the boy said.

"It was a bold decision, no doubt," Siden said, omitting his agreement. "But you are our master now."

"I am!" Ruebyn yelled. "And I want her to work!"

"She is so weak, she can barely hold a pickaxe," Siden explained patiently, "and that was before the…accident."

"She was strong enough to defy me," Ruebyn muttered,

then: "If she will not work…then she must be replaced. I cannot have a slave that won't pull their weight."

"A wise decision, Master," Siden murmured. "Her replacement would only take a few months to arrive. Your output would suffer, but no doubt it would be worth the lesson for any others who seek to avoid their duty."

There was a long pause. "What?"

Siden cleared his throat. "There is a…shortage of labour, Master."

The silence resumed. Pela did not move. Ruebyn had not noticed her awakening, and she savoured the chance to rest. For half a moment she wondered whether she might crawl away and escape, but then the chain tugged at her ankle again, chafing on her skin, and the hope shrivelled away.

"I can't fall behind the quota," he said uncertainly. "My family are relying on me to prove our worth to the queen and the Order."

"Then…perhaps there is another way?" came Siden's voice.

A strained pause followed, then: "Yes?"

Pela cracked open her eyes and found the two standing a little way up the tunnel.

Siden bowed his head. "Master, I would not presume to speak for you, but perhaps full rations could be restored. With food, we would work all the harder."

The boy's Adam's apple bobbed up and down. Wandering to one of the barrows, he took a slate tablet from a hook on the side and inspected the marks. He flicked over the contents, then looked back at the old slave.

"You currently supply ten barrows of coal per day between the twelve of you." He frowned. "Strange, according to the records I studied, that's less than expected.

I thought Harrison had been performing well…I suppose the savings on food were important though, with the famine and all." The boy seemed to be muttering to himself now. "Even so…if my output increased to fifteen barrows…it might be worth the risk."

A collective whisper went through Pela's fellow slaves, though she could not tell whether it was of excitement or vexation. Either way, Siden nodded his assent.

"You will not regret this, Master!" he exclaimed.

Ruebyn's eyes widened, as though just realising he'd been talking out loud, but Siden was already shuffling towards Pela. It was too late to take back the words without Ruebyn looking foolish.

Pela sat up slowly as her friend approached, keeping her eyes averted from the overseer. She'd been beyond stupid earlier, and feeling more alert for her rest, she suddenly feared his coming retribution. There was plenty an overseer could do in this place to make her life hell, without condemning her to wherever failed slaves were sent.

Siden knelt and helped her up, but the crunch of stones announced the overseer's approach. As Pela stood, she found his hazel eyes on her. She lowered her gaze, though not before glimpsing his expression. Jaw hard and lips pursed tightly together, he looked a confused mixture of angry, confused and afraid.

"You spoke against me," he said quietly. "According to the rulebook of Itorn, that is a crime worth twenty lashes, slave."

Unable to muster the strength to resist his authority, Pela nodded dumbly. Her heart thudded weakly against her chest. Twenty lashes…in her current state, it would kill her. Most times their last overseer had attacked in sudden fits of rage, but the punishments had ended just as quickly.

"But I struck you out of turn," Ruebyn went on. "A lesser offense, but a mistake no less. I am prepared to defer your punishment—on the presumption of your good behaviour?"

He spoke in an official tone, as though recalling the words from an old textbook, and Pela found herself wondering where this boy had come from. She inspected him more closely, her eyes long since adjusted to the dim light.

His boots were of dark leather and his clothes a fine silk, though already the pervasive dust had left its marks. Pela felt a moment's shame for the hessian rags she wore, the fabric torn in so many places that there were more holes than stars in the sky. The rough fabric chafed her sensitive skin, adding to her long list of pains.

Angrily Pela pushed aside her humiliation. Ruebyn's hair had been trimmed short in the style of the military, and she recalled the awe in his voice earlier, when he'd congratulated Overseer Harrison on his promotion. Pela doubted the boy had ever seen the Knights in action, let alone a battle, or he might not have been so excited at the thought of becoming a divine soldier.

Then she noticed the frown on Ruebyn's face and realised a full minute had passed without her speaking.

"Of course!" she all but shouted, her cheeks warming. "Master!"

The word still tripped on her tongue and she had to swallow hard to keep the bitterness from her face. The boy did not seem to notice, only offered a curt nod.

"Very well, back to work then, slave," he ordered.

"My name's Pela," she muttered without thinking, then froze, mortified.

Ruebyn stared at her a second, taken aback. Then he

straightened, pulling himself up to all of his five feet and nine inches. "Do not mistake my actions for kindness, *slave*," he said officiously. "Whatever despicable crimes you have committed, you forfeited your right to a name. You are a slave and will answer to whatever I decide to call you. Do you understand?"

Pela wanted to scream at him, to tell him she was not a criminal, but one look in the boy's eyes told her Ruebyn would not listen. He had made his mind up about them the second he'd stepped foot in these tunnels. Denying her guilt would only reinforce his own beliefs. Never mind that many of her fellow slaves came from foreign villages in Northland, taken from their homes by Baronian raiders and brought here for sale.

Holding back tears, Pela nodded her assent.

"Then get back to work, *slave*," Ruebyn repeated. "There will be a second meal this evening, but I will brook no slacking until it arrives."

Pela went.

Stumbling across the uneven ground, she joined Siden at the coalface. Wordlessly he handed her the pickaxe. Stifling a sob, she took it and stepped past him before he saw the shimmering in her eyes. It scared her, how much this place had robbed her of hope, of spirit, of humanity. She was nothing now, just a body to be used until she could do no more, then discarded.

Angrily she hefted the pickaxe and swung it at the rock. The rest had restored some of her strength and this time it struck true. Imagining the black vein was Ruebyn, she struck again, and a block of coal tumbled clear. Siden picked it up and carried it to the barrow while Pela continued to vent her anger against the stone.

But in her half-starved state not even her rage could last.

Slowly she faded into the dim trance that was their work, the pick rising and falling with rhythmic slowness, the pause for breath, the gathering strength, then through the whole process again. It was almost meditative, and she often found herself slipping into the trance she had once practiced in her mother's temple, fading into the darkness of *nothing*.

In that state, time passed quickly, her body working almost of its own accord, and before she knew it a bell was ringing. Shaking her head, she came back to herself—and groaned. Her arms had picked up a fresh collection of bruises from stray rocks and poor blows of the pickaxe, and a familiar ache had begun in her shoulder blades.

For a moment, Pela was confused. The bell was not usually rung until it was time to sleep. The other slaves were shuffling towards the collection of rocks where they took their meal. The chain tugged at her ankle and only then did she recall that they were to be given a second meal. She swallowed, the steel collar pressing at her throat, and tears sprang to her eyes.

She quickly wiped them away, annoyed at the display of emotion, and joined her fellow slaves. The familiar pot of broth sat between the stones. Taking up the ladle, Siden dished it out into bowls. A greasy layer had congealed on the surface of the broth and it carried the faint odour of something rotten. In another life, Pela would have turned away in disgust, but now her stomach rumbled and she gratefully accepted the bowl from her friend.

Sipping at the gruel, Pela shivered. The stuff tasted of mould and old leather, but she had grown used to it long ago. It was hot food she longed for, for soup to warm the ice that had seeped into her core. She ate quickly, aware they could be ordered back to work at any moment, though

Ruebyn was still speaking with the man who had brought the pot.

She sat up straighter as he turned away. He carried a second bundle beneath his arm as he wandered across to the circle of stones and he took a seat alongside Siden. The other slaves stared as he placed the bundle on his knees and unwrapped it.

The rich scent of roasted meat and freshly baked bread wafted across to where Pela sat. Her eyes widened as Ruebyn lifted the sandwich to his mouth. The bread gave a sharp *crunch* as he bit into it. She spied fresh salad alongside pieces of browned beef. Her mouth started to water.

Their last overseer had always taken his meal further up the tunnel, out of sight. Ruebyn obviously hadn't given a second thought to where he ate. He bit into the sandwich again, then took a book from his jacket and began to read, though it must have been difficult in the faint light.

As though suddenly realising he was being watched, Ruebyn head jerked up, his eyes locking with hers. A frown creased his forehead, then he glanced at the pot of gruel. Pela could have sworn his cheeks turned red—before his brow hardened again.

"What are you staring at, slave?" he snapped.

Pela jumped. "Sorry!" she gasped, burying her eyes in her empty bowl.

Siden chuckled and took up the pot to give her the last scraps from the bottom. The other slaves grumbled, but on the back of the second meal, offered no other complaints. Pela nodded her thanks, though with the scent of fresh food in her nostrils, she could hardly stomach the sight of her own food.

"Eat up," Siden murmured, seating himself beside her. "Who knows how long it will last?"

Pela glanced at their new overseer again, but his attention was back on the book. "He's lucky none of us tried to jump him for it," she muttered, indicating the sandwich.

"It might even be worth it," Siden said lightly.

Chuckling for the first time in days, Pela spooned the last few scraps into her mouth and tried to ignore the taste. They had only a few more minutes before Ruebyn stood up suddenly, rewrapping the last of his sandwich in the paper parcel before clearing his throat.

"Right!" he called. "Shall we get back to it, then?"

She almost snorted at his phrasing, as if they had a choice—or that he would in any way be sharing in their toil. Not unless they counted using the whip he now kept strapped to his belt.

Instead, Pela discreetly rolled her eyes at Siden and stood. Chains rattled as the slaves returned to their stations. Pela thought they moved with slightly more vigour now, and was surprised to find herself feeling stronger than she had in in weeks.

Picking up the axe, she was just taking aim when the boy spoke from directly behind her.

"Slave!"

She jumped, a yelp slipping from her lips, and fumbled at the pickaxe—only just managing to catch it before it fell. Turning, she eyed him warily.

"Yes?"

He hesitated, looking around indiscreetly, as though afraid someone might be watching them. But Siden and the other slaves were working further down the tunnel and their attention was on their work. He stepped in close, staring down at her.

Pela shuddered, terrified she had done something wrong. She flinched as he stretched out a hand, but the boy only touched it to her cheek, where his whip had broken the skin.

"I'm sorry…there are rules…the guidebook of Itorn," he said beneath his breath.

Pela only caught snatches of what he was saying. Before she could put them together in her mind, he shoved something into her hands. Then he was walking away, leaving her standing there in shock. She stared at the scrunched up parcel he had given her, struggling to find the courage to open it. The faint scent of bread still clung to the wrapping and she drew in a deep breath, savouring the smell. Finally she pulled open the paper, revealing the leftover portion of sandwich within.

Tears burst from Pela eyes and she sank to her knees, unable to bear the strangeness of it all a second longer.

❧   6   ❧

nother week passed before Braidon could walk any significant distance, but Kryssa was pleased with his progress. His attitude had changed since the sellsword's departure, and while a dense silence still hung over the camp, the king no longer lay in the grips of despair. Each morning Braidon would rise early to push himself through a sequence of drills and exercises that Kryssa recognised from her training in the King's Guard.

By the time Kryssa herself rose, he would have a hot cup of bush tea prepared. They had found a grove of bamboo earlier in the week and by cutting the shoots into pieces, they were able to fill the interior hollows with water and heat them over the flames. Kryssa had been cynical at first, for while Genevieve had taught her some bush craft, this was something different. But the water inside had kept the shoots from burning—at least for a few uses—and there were herbs aplenty for tea.

As the week progressed, they began to spar in the evenings, though only with sticks from the pile of firewood.

Braidon was clumsy and out of practice, slowed by his injuries, but Kryssa was impressed by his determination. There was a steely look to his eyes now, a cold resolve to recover, and she couldn't help but remember his words the night of Caledan's departure.

It's time we took the war to my wife.

It was a bold sentiment, but Kryssa could see no practical way of achieving his ends. Braidon might still live, but he had been isolated from his followers, while Marianne must have had time by now to consolidate her power in the capital.

And the queen could not have achieved her coup alone. Who else in Ardath had plotted against Braidon? To trust anyone would risk betrayal and capture. And Kryssa had no intention of ever surrendering her freedom again.

But nor could she stand by and do nothing. Pela and Gen were still missing. Kryssa could only assume the Knights had caught them. She could not bring herself to consider any other possibilities. That meant a confrontation must come, sooner or later. But first they needed to build their strength, study the ground ahead. Kryssa needed to know what had befallen her daughter and Gen, and Braidon needed to find allies.

"What about the army?" Kryssa asked as they sat by the fire on the tenth night since Caledan had departed.

Braidon sat whittling a stick on the other side of the fire. He looked up, his eyes widening. They had hardly spoken throughout the long days, and while Kryssa had been happy for the peace, it was past time they made plans.

After a moment, the king sighed. "The army was disbanded," he grunted. "Turned into local militia after the peace treaty was signed. We couldn't afford the expense of a standing army."

"Seems I missed a lot while I was in Skystead," Kryssa commented, unable to keep the anger from her voice. She was beginning to see the source of some of Caledan's frustrations.

"You disagree," Braidon stated.

"Of course."

"You think Plorsea should have been prepared for another war?" he asked. When she only stared blankly at him, he chuckled and went on. "Then I might ask why you never taught your daughter to fight? Devon told me, before…"

"Because I feared she would follow on her father's path, or my own," Kryssa murmured.

Braidon's eyes took on a distant look. "Ay, and perhaps I hoped Plorsea could finally leave its violence behind," he said. Then he blinked, and his face hardened as he came back to himself. "But I was naïve. Strive for peace, but prepare for war…that was something my father said once, I remember."

Kryssa shuddered at the mention of the Tsar, and quickly changed the topic. "The past is set. We must work with what we have. Is there anyone you trust in Ardath?"

"Only my King's Guard. No doubt Marianne has them under watch though." He paused. "And I fear what she will do with our son."

"Surely she would not harm her own child?" Kryssa said, shocked.

Braidon sat staring into the fire, but his head jerked up at her question. "How should I know?" he snapped. "She could be capable of anything, after what we saw in Malevolent Cove!"

"Then what is your plan?" Kryssa hissed. "Because there is far more than just your own son at stake here!"

The anger went from Braidon in a rush. "I don't know," he said. "I don't even know *what* she did that night. Where did her power come from, that she could hold us with only her voice?"

A shudder passed through Kryssa as she recalled the strange compulsion the queen had cast. Then she remembered Devon's voice, ringing with a strength all of his own, cutting through her words like a knife. "And how did my father free us?"

"That's easy," Braidon chuckled. "Devon always had a knack for doing the impossible!"

"Perhaps…" Kryssa replied, "or perhaps that is also where our answers lie."

Braidon did not seem to hear her. "Magic has been gone for thirty years," he murmured. "Why would it return now?"

"Yours has not reappeared?"

"No," Braidon grunted. "Though it would not help us anyway. I only ever possessed the power of illusion, to trick the watcher's eye and ear. It would not stop Marianne—and it died with the Gods."

"What about dark magic?" Kryssa asked after a moment's thought.

"Demons and their ilk perished not long after the Gods. Their power is dark and twisted, but they still needed true magic to feed it. They could not survive without the Gods." He paused for a long while, then added, "So if even a demon could not find power, where did Marianne get it?"

"From Ikar," Kryssa whispered, remembering the queen's words.

There is power in death.

"The Knight? But he was just a mortal. There were

once Magickers who could transfer magic between themselves…"

"No, not his magic, his *life*," Kryssa interrupted. "Marianne told us there was power in death. She even made Pela and I wear some necklace when we were to be sacrificed—an experiment, she said. But we didn't die. It was only when Ikar…"

"*Not quite the death I wanted,*" Braidon quoted his wife. "You can't think…?"

"I think Ikar was stronger than all of us," Kryssa replied. "He defeated us, had the will to stick to his convictions, despite all the evidence of the Order's corruption. They were always talking about needing a powerful sacrifice, someone worthy. Why?"

"It makes sense…in a sick kind of way," the king murmured. "The stronger the man—or woman—the stronger the power that would be taken from them."

"But not strong enough to stop my father…"

"Yes…" Braidon trailed off, his eyes returning to the fire. "Though he could barely move for the effort of holding Marianne off. I wonder…"

"What?"

The king shook his head, a frown creasing his forehead. "I'm not sure, but it feels like the answer is there. I just cannot quite fit the pieces together."

Kryssa sighed. "Either way, there is still the problem of the Knights, and the Lonian army. We need to know what we're facing."

"You're right." Braidon swore and lifted his shirt, taking a moment to inspect the wound. There was still a scab over the wound, and the flesh around it was a bright pink. "I could take weeks yet to heal. We can't afford to wait that long."

"I could go…" Kryssa started dubiously.

"No," Braidon interrupted, "Chole is the closest city to us, but it would still take five days to reach on foot. Too long for you to return if things are urgent. We'll have to go together."

Kryssa raised an eyebrow. "Are you sure?"

"No," Braidon chuckled, "but it's not like I can make things any worse."

❧ 7 ☙

Pela slammed the point of her pickaxe into the seam of coal, then paused to sniff the air, checking for the tell-tale whiff of sulphur. In the last week with two meals a day, her strength had returned, and she and the other slaves had dug deeper than ever before. But the progress had brought unexpected consequences, and they had encountered several pockets of the gas that Ruebyn called "methane."

During their first encounter, the stench had been so strong Pela's head had been spinning before she could even put down her axe. Unlike their previous overseer, Ruebyn had reacted instantly. His screams had echoed loudly from the rock, ordering them up the tunnel. Pela might have thought he'd been over-reacting, if not for the sheer terror in this voice.

Later, he had explained that the gas was far more flammable than the coal they mined. The thought sent chills down Pela's spine, and now she was more careful than ever. With her energy returned, so too had her will to live, and her terror of meeting an untimely death.

Fortunately, Ruebyn—if nothing else—was well-read on the subject of mining. He spoke often of his tutors back in Lon—famous engineers who had worked on behalf of the crown for the better part of a decade. Though the slaves rarely responded, the boy liked to talk, and Pela came to learn he was the third son of some noble family. They had sent him here to complete an indenture, to raise their worth in the eyes of the powerful who ruled Lonia.

For herself, Pela had kept her head down since their first confrontation, unwilling to risk anything that might be considered insubordination. Despite his secret act of kindness, Ruebyn had proven unfailingly proscriptive in his role as overseer, administering punishments for any transgression noted down in his precious manual.

Letting out her breath, Pela decided the rock was safe, and swung her pick again. This time it sank deep, breaking through the soft stone, and a piece of coal toppled loose. Hefting it in her arms, she carried it to the barrow and carefully added it to the load. It was only half-full, but she paused there a moment to catch her breath.

Siden joined her, a weary smile on his dusty face. "You are looking better, young Pela," he murmured, adding a large rock to her barrow.

Despite her exhaustion, Pela returned the smile. "Thanks to you," she said. "I still can't believe your nerve, convincing him to give us more food."

"A stroke of genius, I'll admit," Siden chuckled, but it faltered, turning to a hacking cough. He bent in two, eyes watering.

This time it was Pela's turn to offer her water. He accepted it with a trembling hand and took a swig.

"You're sick," Pela said, noticing the pallid colour of his skin, the purple tinge to his lips.

Returning the waterskin, Siden waved a hand as though to dismiss her words. "I'm old, it is not a new sensation," he murmured. "Come though, we had best return to our work, before the good master comes calling."

Eyeing him closely, Pela nodded, though now that her mind was working again, she realised Siden had not been well for a while. In her half-starved state she had not noticed his coughing fits, but in the last week they had come regularly, as though the cloying dust were permanently lodged in his lungs. Even while sitting, there was a wheezing to his breath, a rattling from the depths of his chest.

Lost in thought, Pela lifted her pickaxe and resumed her work. Alone again, the walls pressed in, the gloom reminding her of their fate should the tunnel collapse. She shivered, forcing her mind away from the fear, and sought instead the peaceful quiet of meditation. It helped to focus her thoughts elsewhere, to keep them from returning to all the multitude of ways she might meet her doom—burning alive, crushed beneath tonnes of rock, trapped amidst rubble, unable to move, her air slowly running out…

Pela cursed and shook herself. Her heart thudded painfully in her chest. The *clack* of steel picks on rock echoed in the darkness, a constant reminder of their doom. She sucked in a breath, concentrating her mind on the action, on the swelling of her chest, the whisper as she exhaled again.

Her heart slowed, and she continued the exercise. Each swing of her pick was matched with an exhalation, her arms operating almost by instinct, lifting, striking, again and again to the rhythm of her breath. She hardly felt the pain in her shoulders or the ache in the small of her back any longer. Her fear receded as she centred herself, and she reached for that quiet place her mother had shown her, that peaceful void where the rest of the world would fade away.

Pela longed for that escape, to leave behind the harsh realities of the world, if only for a short while. She had been practicing over the last week, but amidst the peril and pain, she had been unable to reach it. Something always contrived to bring her back. This time though, Pela sensed she was close…

It came slowly, a dim darkness that rose around her, until it seemed she floated alone on a pool of nothingness. Distantly, she sensed her body still at work—some small part of her mind directing her through the monotonous routine —but her mind was free. A sense of peace touched her, one she had not experienced for the longest time. She drifted there in the nothingness for time uncounted, for it did not seem to matter amidst the void of her inner mind.

Slowly though, Pela came to sense she was not alone in the nothingness, that some other force drifted there, something *more*. She found herself searching the endless black, though she knew nothing could be here, in her most private of places. Dismissing the sensation, she focused back in on herself.

A light flickered into life, a whiteness that seemed to spring from nowhere. It burned in her mind's eye, a candle of warmth in the black. A strange joy filled Pela, though she could not have said why. The thing was hardly more than a spark, but she was drawn to it, as though it were a part of her—as though it *were* her. Amidst the absolute black, she stretched out a tendril of her mind to touch it…

Crack.

Pela gasped as a noise in the outside world dragged her from the trance. Staggering back, she stared at the rockface she'd been mining. Her pickaxe was embedded deep in the stone, almost to the hilt. Cracks radiated outwards from her tool, growing as she stood there with mouth hanging open.

"Run!" Siden's shout came from nearby.

Dust filled the tunnel and Pela turned to run, but the chain around her ankle snapped taut and she crashed to the ground. The rocks behind her cracked and popped and she scrambled back up, fear turning her bones to jelly. With the chain still trapping her leg, she could not run.

Turning, she found Siden collapsed on the ground nearby. She cursed, searching for help, but the other slaves were further up the tunnel, the chain snaking away around a bend in the rock. They were alone. Siden managed to find a knee, but his hand was clutched at his chest and he did not seem able to move any further.

Her heart thrashing wildly, Pela staggered towards him. The shriek of breaking rock came from the wall as the cracks grew. His face pale, Siden looked up and saw her coming.

"Get back!" he screamed, but even if Pela could not have left him behind had she wanted to.

Falling to her knees beside him, she threw her arm beneath his shoulder and hauled him up. A gasp tore from her lips as Pela was reminded how weak she still was. She swayed on her feet, willing herself to move. Siden was a deadweight at her side, his breath coming in ragged gasps.

Putting one foot in front of the other, she started up the tunnel. Rocks were falling from the ceiling now. One the size of her head slammed into the ground not two feet from where she stood. If it had struck her, she would have been dead without ever knowing it.

A roar came from behind them, followed by a *boom* as the wooden support beams lining the tunnel sheared in two, bringing down an entire section. Pela staggered on, sobbing in her desperation to escape, but unable to push her beaten body at more than a hobble. They made it around the bend and found the next slave's manacle empty—Ruebyn must have freed them and fled. Furthest down the tunnel, Pela and Siden had been left to fend for themselves.

Another crash came, followed by a rush of air and dust as another section of ceiling fell. A rock struck Pela in the back of her leg, knocking her from her feet. A scream tore from her lips. It turned to a choking cough as dust filled her lungs.

"Help us!" she screamed, but it was pitch black now, the lantern swallowed by stone, the dust obscuring even the distant lights ahead.

She tried to get up, but something hard struck her in the small of her back, driving her into the floor. Clawing at the stone, she tried to crawl, desperate to live, to escape the tomb of death closing around her. The roaring came from all around now, as though she were in the middle of a landslide, as though the entire mountain was about to fall on her.

Pain radiated from her spine, but below where she'd been struck, there was nothing. Horror rose in her throat at the thought she might be paralysed—then something sharp tore through the flesh of her thigh. A moan bubbled from her throat, where the iron collar suddenly felt warm.

Pela no longer had the strength to scream, no longer knew where Siden was, only that she had to get up. Forcing herself to her hands and knees, she crawled from the stone and dust and dark, unable to see even the tiniest speck of world, but knowing she had to go up, must follow the slope of the tunnel to safety.

Thunder filled the pitch-black, deafening her to all but the pounding of blood in her ears. She sensed rock still falling around her, felt the little stabs of pain as splinters of stone sliced her skin. In places she had to crawl just to find her way around the rubble filling the tunnel. At any moment she was sure the whole mine would collapse and bury her alive.

Then, just as Pela began to imagine that she must soon see light, that the rescuers must come for her, her foot snagged on something in the dark. She cursed, shaking her leg to free herself, and heard the telltale rattle of chains.

An awful sob rose in Pela's chest and slipped from her as a moan. In her panic she had left Siden behind, had forgotten about their shared fate and abandoned him to his death. She gripped the chain in both hand and slammed it into the ground, screaming her frustration, her guilt, her despair. It was hopeless; the steel would not yield.

She did not have the strength to return, to stagger back into the dust and dark and find her friend. There was nothing more she could do. Tears streaked her cheeks and weeping, Pela curled into a ball, to wait for the end.

The sound of breaking rock grew louder again, a creeping doom approaching through the black—until with a roar, the world came alive, and Pela knew no more.

❧ 8 ❧

Caledan slipped carefully through the press of bodies, towards the raised voices calling from the plaza. The crowd jostled around him, some doing their best to escape. Others moved forward with Caledan, perhaps drawn by a morbid sense of curiosity, though there could be little doubt as to what waited ahead.

The tall marble buildings of Ardath towered around him, their awnings worn and stained by the soot of decades, but otherwise no less grand for the passage of time. While the cobbled streets were in shadow, the narrow walls trapped the summer's heat, and the air was suffocating. Sweat dripped from Caledan's forehead, but just ahead the walls finally opened out, giving way to a plaza. A voice boomed out over the crowd, its meaning lost in the rumbling of a hundred other speakers, but Caledan didn't need to hear the words to know their intent.

He had seen it all over Plorsea on his journey from Dragon Country. In the small villages of Lane and Oaksville, the stories were all the same. The Knights of

Alana were riding in force, spreading the word of Alana, hunting the country for the blasphemous. Many of their followers had taken up the call, marching in the streets, informing on their neighbours, attacking the few Temples that remained in Plorsea, whatever they could to aid the cause.

Finally Caledan reached the open square. A brick path led around the boundary of the plaza, while in the centre, gardens had been planted in better times. Tall trees provided shade for the host of men and women drawn by the commotion, but the flowers had been trampled into the dirt by the crowd in their haste to find a view.

Caledan loosened his sword in its sheath as he stepped into the gardens. Stones crunched beneath his feet as he threaded his way between the watchers. A breeze rustled the leaves of a nearby tree. He let out a sigh as it touched his forehead, drawing away some of the heat.

Scanning his surroundings, Caledan noticed Knights stationed at intervals around the plaza. Though the heat must have been unbearable, all wore the familiar steel armour adorned with the flaming sword that was the symbol of their Order. Even their visors were down, concealing their true identities.

As Caledan watched, one of the Knights moved into the path of a spectator as he tried to leave the plaza, obviously having seen enough. A steel hand caught the man and held him tight while another Knight appeared. The captive's arms were bound behind his back as a crowd watched on, his pleas falling on deaf ears.

"Blasphemers! Traitors!"

A metallic shout drew Caledan's attention back to the centre of the plaza. There, three Knights stood with swords in hand, four prisoners on their knees before them. The prisoners' hands were similarly bound and their faces showed the purple bruises of their captivity.

The Knight in the centre raised his sword high and a roar came from the crowd. Many raised fists to the sky, though Caledan noticed even now others tried to retreat, realising too late what they had stepped into. Tightening his jaw, Caledan dropped his hand to his sword hilt, but after a moment he forced himself to release it. He was confident he could take the three Knights holding the men captive, but with their brothers lining the plaza, escape would be out of the question.

Caledan had not come to Ardath to throw his life away. He watched as the Knights stripped the clothes from the prisoners, until the four were left huddling naked on the ground. Without the use of their hands, they struggled to sit up, eyes wild as they searched the crowd for mercy.

"Darkness has crept into Plorsea!" the tallest of the Knights bellowed. "The Saviour calls for a cleansing, lest the scourge of the False Gods return to these lands."

Another roar came from the crowd. Caledan shuddered at the hatred on the faces around him. This was Braidon's doing, the result of his weakness, his failure to protect Plorsea from his own foolishness. How could he have been so blind, have ignored the darkness in the woman who lay beside him each night? If that was what love did to a man, Caledan was glad he had never felt its sting.

"The might of Alana must be renewed!" The Knight called. "The souls of the blasphemous will become her strength, when the faithful send them into her embrace. Will you do the Saviour's will?"

Caledan edged himself back and the crowd surged forward, eager to fill the gap he had left. The sound of the gathering was like thunder echoing from the stone walls.

Caledan glimpsed a man at the front of the pack lean down and scoop up a rock. He drew back his arm and Caledan quickly looked away, but he could not block out the distant *thwack* of stone striking flesh.

Picking up his pace, Caledan fought against the push of the crowd, even as more surged forward, eager to join the slaughter.

"Going somewhere, brother?"

Caledan swung around to find a Knight ahead. He swore silently and tried to side-step the man. The Knight followed, barring his path. Grinding his teeth, Caledan drew to a stop.

"Can I help you with something?"

"My brothers asked you to add your strength to the Saviour's cause."

"Maybe another day," Caledan said, offering a smile, even as a horrible scream rose above the shouts of the mob. "It's market day." He tried to get around the man again.

"I don't think so," the Knight snarled, dropping a hand to his sword.

Steel hissed against leather as he tried to draw the weapon. Realising the pretence was over, Caledan caught him by the wrist and forced the weapon back into its sheath. The Knight growled and swung out with his free hand. Caledan ducked, and still holding the man's arm, dragged him forward. The man staggered past, and twisting, Caledan launching a kick at his metallic back.

A cry rattled from the iron helmet, lost in the roar of the crowd, and the Knight flew headfirst into a tree. He crashed into the ground and started to thrash, unable to find his feet. Men and women retreated from him, trying to understand what had happened, but Caledan was already well away, turning a corner from the plaza. He weaved quickly through the narrow streets until he reached the broad avenue that ran from the main gates to the citadel.

There he slowed, merging with the crowds, and continued his way through the city. He glimpsed several more demonstrations, but these he ignored. His worst suspicions had been confirmed. With her power affirmed by whatever she'd gained during the Great Sacrifice, Marianne had set her Knights loose across Plorsea, even on the capital itself. Those who still believed in the Old Gods—or who defied the Order's power—were being slaughtered. Something had to be done, and if Braidon was too much a coward to right his wrongs…

Caledan shook his head. What was he thinking? Just a month ago, he'd wanted nothing more than to kill the king and have his revenge. Yet when he'd finally had Braidon in his power, Caledan had spared him. Why? Because a dead man had begged him to protect the king? Caledan owed Devon nothing.

So what was he doing here, thinking to save Plorsea from the mad queen? He wasn't a hero, taken to glory, or throwing his life away on a lost cause. There was no way he could stop Marianne—to even try would guarantee his death.

Recalling that strange power she had wielded back in the cove, Caledan felt a sudden urge to flee the city. He had grown up in a time without magic. Always before he'd had the skill to face down his enemies, to match them blade to blade and conquer. But when Marianne had *commanded* him, he'd been helpless before her power. If she'd asked it, he would have taken the dagger from his belt and plunged it into his own stomach.

Finally Caledan turned a corner and was greeted by the familiar sight of the Firestone Inn. The establishment was on the rougher side of the city, but the owner was a former sellsword Caledan had fought beside in a dozen skirmishes. He had hung up his sword after the civil war, purchasing the inn from a couple retiring from the city. Caledan was confident the man could be trusted.

The wooden steps squeaked as he made his way up, announcing his approach, and the bartender thrust open the double doors before Caledan reached them. He had been a giant of a warrior in his day, wielding a twin-headed axe with enough force to carve through plate mail. But his fighting days were long over; now his beard was grey and his stomach strained against the buttons of his tunic. Even so, a grin spread across his cheeks when he saw his guest.

"Caledan!" he bellowed. "Glad to see you're still alive, I've been hearing all sorts of rumours. Come in!"

Cursing silently, Caledan cast a glance in either direction, but the cobbled street was empty, and he quickly followed his friend inside.

"Thank you, Grif," he murmured, finding himself in the dimly-lit dining room. They were alone, but he did not say more until he crossed to the bar. "I'd appreciate it if you didn't spread the news around though."

Grif chuckled. "Got yourself embroiled in something messy, have you, sellsword?"

"You might say that," Caledan replied. Seating himself on a stool, he waved for a drink.

Taking two glasses from beneath the bar, Grif poured them each a measure of whiskey, then a second helping for good measure. He pushed the glass across the bar.

"If there's going to be trouble, I'd rather you didn't bring it to my doorstep," he said quietly. "Times are hard enough as it is."

"Agreed," Caledan muttered, "but don't worry, all going well, no one will know I'm here."

"Why *are* you here?" Grif asked. "Word is there's a bounty of your head, lad."

"World's coming to pieces, thought I should go where the action was," Caledan replied, then paused. "I saw some of the demonstrations on my way in."

Grif shuddered. "Ay. Large group of 'em rode in a couple weeks ago, joined with the little congregation in that Castle of theirs. Never caused us any trouble before now, but within a day there was talk of people being hauled away in the night. Then those Elders started giving talks around the city, claiming magic is making a return. That got a lot of folk scared."

"I can imagine," Caledan said.

After thirty years without the Gods and their gifts, people had grown used to the new world order. Magic had passed into memories, becoming a precautionary tale against the dangers of unconstrained power. Even those who still worshipped the Old Gods did so now only out of custom, knowing in their hearts those they prayed to were gone for good.

But the Order of Alana believed otherwise. The Elders had convinced their followers they must be ever vigilant against the Gods' return, had armed their Knights as their divine warriors. And now they were recruiting more followers, taking advantage of the power vacuum Braidon had left in his absence. But then, where was Marianne?

"What of the queen?" Caledan asked, his heart beating faster. Had he come to the wrong place?

"Off chasing King Braidon's killers. Last I heard, she'd had a great victory—though it came at great cost. Most of the King's Guard were lost. Can only hope she returns soon. Someone needs to take control of this mob."

"And you think Marianne is the one for the job?"

Grif frowned. "Seems she put an end to the Baronians that killed old Braidon," he said. When Caledan did not reply, he went on. "Anyway, she's the only one with the power to oppose them. There's plenty who don't like what's happening, but they're afraid of speaking out. Too many already gone missing, or been accused of this crime or another."

"And what of Lonia?"

"We were lucky. Seems their council has been busy worrying about who will rule them, now that Ashoka's dead. But I suspect whoever takes over will be eager to test their nettle against our new queen." He chuckled. "I think they'll be in for a surprise."

"You think?"

Grif only grinned. "Daughter of one king, husband to another. Must be something to her, right?"

Caledan shrugged and took another sip of his ale. Grif was right about one thing—Marianne was a worthy foe. She had played Braidon like a puppet, gathering her own followers around her, even finding a new power they had no way to match. And yet her own motives remained almost unknown.

"Dad!" a young voice burst into the dining room. Caledan turned in time to see a boy come racing across the wooden floor. "Dad, she's here!"

A lump lodged in Caledan's throat at his words. Grif stepped out from behind the bar and scooped the boy up in his arms, his laughter ringing from the walls.

"Who's that, son?" he asked, but Caledan already knew the answer.

"The queen!" the boy exclaimed. "She's returned! They're gathering in the grand plaza now, to hear her speak. Can we go?"

"No," Caledan said, his voice hard.

Grif swung around, a frown on his face, but one look at Caledan and the words on his lips died. Rising from his chair, Caledan placed a silver shilling on the counter.

"For the ale, and a room," he murmured.

Stepping around his friend, he headed for the door. At the last minute, he glanced back. Grif still stood beside the bar, his face tight with fear. He swallowed visibly, and Caledan felt a moment's compassion.

"If I don't return by the night, give the room away," he said. "I was never here."

Then he turned and stepped back through the double doors, out into the sunlight.

❧   *9*   ❧

Braidon was panting hard by the time they reached the treeline that marked the boundary of Dragon Country. The steep slope of Mount Chole stretched upwards from where he stood, all loose gravel and broken boulders. A trail wound away from them, little more than a goat track that zigzagged its way across the mountainside.

The summer sun beat down on the open scree, and Braidon wondered how he would survive such a climb. His entire body was already aching, the chest wound a constant presence, an angry throbbing that stole away his breath and left him gasping. He was in no condition to travel, let alone face whatever waited for them in Chole.

But there was no choice, and squaring his shoulders, Braidon stepped from the trees. Kryssa followed silently behind him. They had started out early, but Braidon's slow pace had already put them behind schedule. Noon was approaching and they still needed to cross the mountain range, or else face a night exposed on the open slopes.

Braidon had barely made it a dozen feet from the treeline when a sharp *crack* came from overhead. The hackles rose on his neck as a shadow fell across their path—then the Red Dragon slammed into the mountainside, sending gravel raining down around them. Braidon covered his head, wincing as a chunk of rock the size of his fist struck him. Above, the dragon turned, its amber eyes glaring down at them.

Where do you go, King?

Straightening, Braidon reached within for the will to face the creature. His weakness dragged at his confidence and his legs shook. Laughter sounded in his mind as the dragon took a step towards them, setting off a miniature landslide.

Does the mighty King seek to flee?

The beast's mockery fuelled Braidon's rage and he straightened. "I go to face our enemies, dragon!" he snarled, raising a fist. "I will hide in this forest no longer. Stay, if you wish, and hide behind your mother's skirts, but I will face my foes."

Heat washed over them as the dragon opened its enormous jaws and roared. The sound staggered Braidon and for one mortifying second, he thought his legs would give way. Then Kryssa caught him beneath the shoulder and he recovered. Together they faced down the dragon's rage.

You dare insult my people's courage?

Braidon bared his teeth. "What courage, dragon?" he shouted. "Have the Red Dragons ever shown anything but cowardice? When Archon threatened the world, where were your people? When my father came to enslave your fellows, where was the battle? Even when the lowly Knights of Alana trespass freely in your lands, you offer nigh on a whimper. No, do not talk to *me* of fleeing. At least I fight my battles."

Do you not see my scars, King? the dragon growled, its scales glittering in the noonday sun, highlighting the great tears. Its one good eye burned with untold rage. *Ingytus was not the only dragon to fight, though he was the first to fall.*

"Ay," Braidon replied, lifting his chin. "For the first time in an eon, I saw dragons fighting against the darkness. It was a glorious sight. I would see it again."

The dragon lowered its snout until the giant orb of its eye was just a few feet from them. *And what would you have of me, King?*

Braidon swallowed, hardly daring to speak the question. One memory shone bright in his mind, of a time long ago with his grandmother, when he had flown with the last Gold Dragon. But no one had ever ridden a Red. Even now he could sense the hatred radiating from the creature. Their species loathed humanity with an ancient potency. Only their desperation to be free of the Knights had given Braidon the opportunity to bargain with them. Even so, just to ask...

"Carry us to Chole," he said, before his courage failed him. The Red Dragon reared up on its hind legs with a roar, and this time Braidon saw the flames flickering deep in its throat. He continued quickly, "For I do not have the strength to cross the mountains."

The admission gave the beast pause. It stared at them a long moment, then lowered itself back to all fours. Teeth bared, its voice boomed into their minds.

The Knights have not all gone from our lands, it howled. *Some remain in our most sacred of places. A great work is underway there, a construct of stone and steel. We will not stand for it.*

Braidon bowed his head. "If I succeed in Chole, the Knights will fall. On that, you have my promise."

And what of our demand? The dragon growled. *We will settle only for Dragon Country no longer. You promised Ingytus all the lands south to the river Lane. Do you remain true to your word, King?*

A shiver lifted the hackles on Braidon's spine. He had not forgotten the promise, though it would prove costly to his people. But it had already been made, it would mean his life to go back on it now.

"Of course," Braidon said, inclining his head. "My word is sacred, and when I regain my crown your people shall have their reward."

Very well, King. The dragon flexed its claws, driving them deep into the rocky ground. *Then I will take you to Chole, though I will be forever tainted in the eyes of my people.*

"Thank you, dragon," Braidon whispered. "It shames me to ask this of you."

The great head turned away. *I am called Nidryt,* it rumbled, *and these Knights have lessened us all.*

"When did they first come here?" Braidon wondered out loud. The amphitheatre in the cove had not been built overnight.

A shiver went through the beast. *Five years past, they first appeared on our beaches. We made to drive them away, confident in our power, and many of their number died. But their weapons slew us in turn, and like our extinct cousins, my people have never been numerous.*

"I am sorry to have called you cowards," Braidon replied, ashamed despite himself.

A rumble came from the dragon's chest, laughter. *And I you, King. Now let us journey together to the Dying City.*

It stretched out a forearm. Braidon swallowed, sharing a glance with Kryssa. The woman had been unusually silent, and her face had gone unnaturally pale.

"Ladies first?" he offered.

She swallowed visibly. "This was your idea."

Braidon let out a long breath, fear and excitement

warring within. He remembered again his grandmother, Enala, and her joy sitting astride the Gold Dragon, Dahniul. It was a legacy of their family, an agreement stretching right back to King Thomas. But when Dahniul had fallen, that agreement had come to an end. Now Braidon had forged the pact anew, though with a species that would rather tear him apart than fight beside him.

He swallowed, and before his fear could stop him, climbed up onto the dragon's forearm. Weakened by his injury, he almost fell, but Kryssa's hand on his back kept him in place. The scales shook beneath him, and Braidon saw Nidryt turn his head to watch. Steadying himself, he climbed the rest of the way up the dragon's back, then grinned at Kryssa.

"Your turn!"

Kryssa swallowed visibly, her silver eyes wide. Braidon grinned. It was the first time he'd seen her frightened. He was enjoying the reversal.

"Come on, he won't bite," he said, holding out his hand.

A rumble came from Nidryt's chest and Kryssa raised an eyebrow. "I'm not sure he agrees."

Braidon chuckled. "Would you prefer to walk?"

Kryssa stood there so long Braidon thought she might do just that. But with a roll of her eyes, she leapt up quickly onto the extended forearm, then scrambled up behind him. Settling herself on the rippling scales, she looked around.

"Where do I ho—" Her question turned into a scream as the dragon leapt into the sky.

The great wings snapped open, beating the air, and Kryssa grabbed desperately at Braidon's waist. Braidon groaned as the movement disturbed his wound, but he could do nothing but hold the scales in front of him. They clung on desperately as the ground spiralled away, the soft laughter of the dragon whispering in their minds.

Wind buffeted them as Nidryt turned and made for the triple peaks. Mount Chole and its nameless siblings rose before them, jagged fingers of rock and snow, each stretching far higher than even a dragon could fly. Braidon gasped at the cold, but it did not seem to bother Nidryt. The dragon made for a pass between two of the peaks.

Braidon was not dressed for such temperatures, and he was soon shivering so violently he could hardly keep his grip on the dragon's back. Behind him, Kryssa was coping little better. Her eyes were closed and her grip on Braidon's waist was so tight he could hardly breathe. The sight restored some of his good humour though, that the woman had at least one weakness.

Behind them, the dense forest of Dragon Country stretched unbroken to the jagged western coast, but for a single blackened piece of land that the Knights had claimed as their own. He swallowed at the sight, reminded of his agreement with the dragons and the challenges awaiting him in Chole. If the Knights could wield such power here, what new terrors had they brought against his people?

A month had passed now since Braidon's apparent death. In his absence, what had become of Plorsea? He watched the approaching mountains, eager for a first glimpse of his nation. The volcanic peaks rose around them, their pale escarpments stretching up into the blue sky. Below, the earth was torn and broken, cliffs giving way to jagged slopes, and then to broad passes between the peaks. One side of the northernmost volcano had collapsed in ages past, exposing the great crater. Mounds of scarlet and yellow rock dotted the alien landscape within. Steam still seeped from the earth in places, a reminder of the violent potential of the silent mountain.

Then Braidon glimpsed movement within the crater. He leaned forward, then reeled at the sight of men and women below, swinging picks around the steaming vents, dragging carts down the jagged slope towards the faint outline of a road.

See how humanity encroaches upon our territory?

"They're Knights?" Braidon shouted over the howling wind.

No.

The dragon spoke no more, but Braidon continued to watch the people. Several looked up as they flew past, their tanned faces reflecting sudden fear. The dragon's appearance sent them racing down the slope towards the road, where several horses and wagons stood waiting. But Nidryt ignored them, and they were soon left far behind.

The volcanic range gave way to the open steeps of Chole, a vast expanse of patchy forest and sprawling grassland that stretched all the way to the Forest of Plorsea. In the time of Archon it had been desert, a deadly place filled with dark creatures that only the boldest of souls had dared to cross. Then had come the mortal Eric and his Sky magic, and the rains had been restored, returning life to the plateaus.

In his first few years as king, Braidon had feared that magic's departure would see the desert's return. But while the summer rains had dwindled, the grasslands survived, fed every spring by glacial melt that brought streams all across the plateau alive.

Though the soils were thin and unable to sustain the traditional farming styles of the north, a nomadic group had made the lands their home. Said to have descended from Baronians, the tribes followed the wild cattle as they grazed across the plains. Braidon had found an ally there during the Lonian war, when the tribes had helped to feed his army. Idly, he wondered if he might find aid there again.

That was a thought for another day. Ahead, Chole rose from the plains, a sprawling collection of stone buildings. Most stood only two storeys tall, with narrow streets that wound in every direction, creating a maze that could confuse even the staunchest local should his attention wander.

Tall walls bordered the city, dating back to the Great Wars, before even Archon had darkened the horizons of the Three Nations. They had never fallen, not even on Archon's first coming, when the Dark Magicker had marched his armies all the way to the city gates. Even so, his defeat had almost seen the death of the city. The terrible clashing of magic between Archon and the Gods had torn the earth asunder, giving birth to the volcanic range they had just crossed, and creating the century long drought that had given rise to the nickname "the Dying City."

It was such tales that had given birth to the Order of Alana. Not even Braidon could deny the danger of wild magic, and he could well understand the fear amongst many that one day it would rise again. The Order had harnessed that fear, giving it a power they now used for their own purposes.

Nidryt circled lower, keeping close to the mountains, unwilling to expose himself to anyone watching from the city. Beyond the buildings, the waters of Lake Chole shone red in the setting sun, the lifeblood of the city. Several streams threaded their way across the plains, dwindling now with the coming of summer, but still fed by the melting snow atop the volcanoes.

The city itself had prospered over the last few decades, its inhabitants seemingly impervious to the death of magic, or war, or even the threat of another drought. They were descended from those who had remained all those years ago, when so many others had fled the Dying City, and had inherited their stoicism. In the face of adversity, the citizens of Chole stood strong, and found another way.

Perhaps Braidon would find his own answers within its ancient walls.

Pela woke to a pressure on her chest. Groaning, she tried to lift her arms to push it off, but found them trapped by cold stone. Her eyes snapped open, but they revealed only darkness. Her panic building, she sucked in a breath and coughed as dust filled her lungs. Stars flashed across her vision as her head struck solid rock above her.

"No, no, no," she gasped, a lump of terror lodging in her throat.

Her heart raced as she shifted her legs, her hands, anything she could think of. She was met by solid stone in every direction. A moan tore from her lips and terrified she started to thrash. Her fists struck the walls of her prison, but made no difference. In the pitch black she could see nothing, but she sensed the weight of the mountain pressing down on her, entombing her in the tiny hollow.

"No, please, Gods, no!"

Tears streaked her face and she kicked out. Pain stabbed through her shin as it struck something hard. Rocks groaned and the pressure on her chest increased, forcing a whisper of air from her lungs. She struggled to inhale, but could not quite catch her breath.

"Help!"

The scream was little more than a whisper, its potency stolen by the pressure, by the creeping horror of her fate. Pela wanted desperately to fill her lungs, to shout until even the dead Gods must hear her, but instead she was reduced to whimpers that turned quickly into sobs. Here was an enemy she could not fight, an obstacle she could not over-come. All she could do was lie there in the darkness and wait for death to find her.

Minutes turned to what seemed hours. There was no telling the true passage of time. Eventually Pela's panic subsided, giving way to a strange peace. She could do nothing to change her fate, and so she accepted it. Her heart slowed and her breathing eased, though the constant pressure still made it a struggle to inhale.

Time continued onwards, and her mind drifted, returning to that fateful strike. Her pickaxe had sunk deep into the rock, shattering the tunnel wall—but how? Had there been a weakness, a rotten patch of rock? But she had smelt no gas. She supposed it did not matter now.

Regret touched her at leaving Siden behind. He had been kind to her, had stood up for her when the other slaves would have left Pela to her fate. He'd deserved better than to be left alone to die. The chain was still tight around her ankle, though surely it must have been shattered by the rock fall.

Clack, clack, clack.

The sound of stones shifting was constant, though the ones around Pela had ceased to move. Listening to the noise, Pela was reminded of her own creeping fate. She stared into the darkness, wondering whether she would feel it, when the rock finally came crashing down. Would she be crushed instantly, or would the stone shift just enough to steal away the last of her breath, so that she slowly suffocated, unable to quite inhale?

Clack, clack, clack.

Pela frowned. There was a rhythmic timing to the sound now, a constant tapping. And it was not that deep groaning of rocks under pressure, but something else, almost…steel on stone?

Her heart beat faster and she tried to twist amidst her prison. Still unable to move more than a few inches, she only managed to send a cramp burning up her leg. She folded against the rock, a cry tearing from her lips.

"Wh…s…ht."

Distant words carried through the darkness and Pela could have sobbed with relief.

"Help me!" she screamed as loudly as she could manage.

The distant clacking ceased suddenly and she heard muffled voices. Unable to understand the words, she called again, though it was quieter this time, her breath not recovered from the last. The sounds resumed, the *clack-clacking* seeming faster this time.

Pela waited amidst the darkness, listening as her rescuers came closer. Soon she recognised the sound of pickaxes on stone.

They're coming for me!

She would not have thought it possible. She hadn't thought Ruebyn would care about a couple of slaves buried in the tunnels, whatever small kindnesses he had offered them. But maybe she had misjudged him, maybe he truly cared…maybe she should tell him the truth. He might be the saviour she had prayed for, might free her if he knew Pela was not truly a criminal.

Suddenly the sounds were coming from directly above her. She called out, cry of pure desperation and relief, of salvation. A stone was lifted from above her head and a light appeared, burning in the darkness. Her eyes watered but she did not look away, such was her joy.

The rest of the rock was removed and then rough hands reached into her tomb. The shackle was removed from her ankle and she was lifted out. They carried her several feet up the tunnel, and then laid her down. A lantern was held close to her face and finally Pela was forced to close her eyes.

"How does she look?" She recognised Ruebyn's voice, somewhere overhead. He sounded concerned.

"Bruised," a voice answered from beside her head. She thought it was another of the slaves.

"How bad is it?"

Firm hands patted Pela down, pressing their way down her arms and then legs. She stirred and dragged in a great breath, but only managed to moan something incomprehensible. Her chest ached, but the fresh air restored some of her strength and her eyes flickered back open.

"Hey…" she muttered.

A slave was crouched beside her. He sat back at her voice, but spoke only to Ruebyn. "Nothing broken, I don't think," he said. "Bad gash on her leg, though."

Pela remembered the rock that had slashed her leg as she'd fled, forgotten in her stone tomb. Gritting her teeth, she forced herself to sit up. Her head spun as she squinted into the glare of the lantern. A long gash stretched down her calf muscle, though it was no longer bleeding.

Ruebyn shifted closer, his jaw clenched tight. "What happened down there, slave?"

Blinking, Pela looked up at him. "The roof fell in."

Irritation showed on the overseer's face. "*Why* did it fall in?" he snapped, gesturing down the tunnel. Below, two slaves were taking turns digging out the rubble, while a third pushed a barrow past where Pela lay. "We've lost a day of work, at least!"

Pela gaped at him. "You're upset because you lost time?"

Ruebyn was apoplectic. "*Why else?*" he screamed.

Rising unsteadily to her feet, Pela looked him in the eye. "Because two *people* were trapped in there?" she said, her voice rising in pitch. "*Because my friend might be dead?*" She shook a fist and would have continued, but in that moment her strength failed and she sank back to the ground.

A strained silence followed, punctuated only by the *clack-clacking* of pickaxes—though Pela sensed even her fellows' attention on the two of them. She had done it again, lost her temper and spoken out of turn. But how could she not? Trapped in this place, doomed to one terrible death or another, better to give in to her anger than her fear.

Ruebyn stared down at her, his face a carefully-kept mask. The whip hung from his belt and his hand twitched. Pela was sure he would strike her now, that she had finally pushed him too far, but instead his hand dropped back to his side.

"You've been through a lot," he said, "and you're injured. Go to see the doctor and have that wound treated. I want you back before the night's count. I trust you will not go missing."

Pela gaped at him, unable to believe what he was saying. Her mouth opened and closed, but in the end the only words she could get out were:

"What about Siden?"

Ruebyn blinked, flicking a glance at the rubble. It filled

the tunnel from floor to ceiling. A pile of support beams had been laid alongside the waiting barrow, and the slaves were using them to prop up the ceiling again as they dug back down into the earth. Staring at the pile, Pela could hardly believe she had survived.

"I doubt..." Ruebyn began, then shook his head. His voice took on a sad tone. "By my calculations, the coal vein is another thirty feet from here. With luck, we will find him before then. If not..." He shrugged and turned away.

Pela thought to argue, but as she staggered to her feet, pain tore through her leg and forced a cry from her. The fight went from her in a rush. Ruebyn was right, there was nothing she could do for Siden. Biting her tongue, she turned away.

Starting her long trek upwards, Pela wondered whether she would make it. There would be no asking for help now. A slave was only useful so long as they could work. Even with their shortage, the Lonians would not waste much time or resources restoring a failed slave like her to health.

Then excitement touched Pela as a sudden realisation touched her. She was going up. There was only one doctor's clinic, and while she had never seen it, she knew one thing.

It was on the surface!

Her pace increased, though it remained little more than a hobble. She lifted her eyes, already looking for the distant glow of sunlight—though she was still far beneath the earth.

For a moment, Pela's mind turned to the possibility of escape. She dismissed it just as quickly. She wouldn't make it a mile in her current condition, and the punishment for runaway slaves was severe. Her arms and legs would be shattered with hammers, then she would be left in the mountains for the Felines and other animals to find. Just the thought made her shudder.

She continued on, dreams of warm sunlight on her face giving her strength. The tunnel curved upwards in a spiral, winding its way towards the distant surface. In places she had to bend over just to make it past the lower sections of the roof, but she was undaunted. Her small stature was an advantage in these cramped places—she suspected it was one of the reasons she'd been sent into the deepest sections of the mine in the first place.

Finally the tunnel widened, converging with other passages. She was overtaken several times by slaves pushing heavy barrows of rock. They gave her strange looks as they passed, though nothing was said. Less lenient overseers would whip a slave caught speaking without permission.

Another slave, burdened with a barrow of coal, had just passed Pela when she finally staggered into the great chamber where the coal was transferred into carriages for the final journey to the surface. A crew of slaves quickly took the barrow from the newcomer and loaded its contents onto a larger carriage. It must have completed their load, for the six slaves then took hold of handles on the cart and started pushing it up the steel track.

A seventh man remained behind. Though his collar still marked him as a slave, he must have held some position of respect, for he stood with arms folded and made no move to join his fellows. He watched the other slaves disappear up the tunnel, but when he turned, his eyes caught on Pela.

"You!" he shouted, a frown touching his forehead. "What are you doing here?"

Pela's legs were shaking by then, and she stood there staring at him for a long moment, unable to summon the will to speak. She sucked in a mouthful of dusty air, longing for what waited above. Bliss.

"I…Overseer Ruebyn…sending me to the infirmary."

The man stood staring at her as though he could not believe what he'd just heard, then burst abruptly into laughter. "The infirmary!" he gasped between snorts. "Of course! Shall I grab you a fresh glass of ale while we're at it?"

Pela gaped at him. "I…it's the truth."

The man's mirth vanished, his face darkening. "Scuttle back to your master, girly," he growled. "I'll not be caught slacking 'cause of some disobedient runt. Get out of here!" He took a step towards her, fist raised.

"No!" Pela shouted, standing her ground despite her injuries. "I'm going to the surface!"

"My people's the only ones gets to visit the surface," he snapped, swinging at her.

She leapt back out of his reach and her injured leg almost gave way. Staggering sideways, Pela continued to retreat, though he was forcing her back towards the tunnel she had entered by. Her boot scuffed against a rock and she scooped it up.

"I have orders," she insisted.

"Disobedient runt—" He broke off as Pela's stone struck him in the nose.

As the man clutched at his face, Pela darted forward, seeking to escape past him. But his arms swung out wildly, catching her in the forehead and knocking her off-balance. She crashed to the ground, tearing open her wound. Hot blood ran into her boot. Before she could recover, the slave staggered across and drove his foot down into her back.

"Damn witch, I'll see you hung for that!"

Blood poured from his nostrils and his face was twisted with rage. He caught Pela by the tunic and dragged her up. She cried out as her weight came on her injured leg, trying to twist away, but he held her tight. He raised a fist.

"Marcus, what are you doing?" a woman shouted.

The hackles stood up on Pela's neck as she recognised Genevieve's voice. Sudden hope swelled in her chest as she saw the huntress approaching through the gloom. Genevieve's clothes were torn and streaked by dirt, but there were no bruises on her skin. She wore the collar of a slave, the single black gem shining amidst the cold iron, but at first glance she seemed to have had an easier time than Pela. Their eyes met, but for a moment Genevieve did not seem to recognise her.

Then the woman's eyes widened and her hand went to her mouth. "Pela?" she whispered.

Groaning, Pela pulled herself free of Marcus's grip, who had frozen at Genevieve's appearance.

"Gen?" she croaked. "Is it really you?"

Genevieve pushed Marcus aside and they embraced. A dam broke within Pela as they hugged, and she sobbed quietly into her friend's shoulder, hardly able to believe Genevieve was really there. The huntress held her tight for a long moment, as though not quite able to believe it either, and then stepped back, her eyes shining with unspilt tears.

"Oh Pela," she whispered. "What have they done to you?"

❧ 11 ❧

"People of Ardath!" Wearing an ankle-length dress of black satin, the queen stood on a dais that had been hastily set up outside the marble courthouse. Her voice boomed out over the square, carrying to the ears of every soul in the crowd. She held her arms out to either side of her, as though to embrace her audience. "I have returned from Lon with news."

Caledan watched from amongst the throng, one man among thousands. The great square was so packed he could hardly move—even the balconies and rooftops were filled to bursting. Men and women watched her with equal parts fear and hope in their eyes. Ardath was a city afraid. The peace of the last eight years had been shattered by Braidon's disappearance, and they didn't know where to turn. They all wanted to know whether Marianne could step into the shoes of ruler.

"It grieves me to come before you today, a month after my husband's cruel murder. I thank you for your love, and your patience during these hard times. We as a nation must come to terms with this horrible tragedy." Her head dipped almost imperceptibly, and Caledan realised then that Marianne was a terrific actress. There was no hint of the raw hatred that had shone from her face back in Malevolent Cove, when she'd looked upon Braidon.

"But we must also rejoice! For though they suffered terrible casualties, the King's Guard has brought justice to our king's murderers. On the river Lane they caught the Baronian thugs, and slew them to a man. Forever will we remember those brave souls who gave their lives to avenge our king!"

A whisper went through the crowd as many lowered their eyes, placing hands to their chests. It was a gesture of faith to the Old Gods. The Knights stationed at intervals around the square made no move to intervene, though Caledan did not doubt names would be noted.

"As for our brothers in Lonia," Marianne continued, clearing her throat, "the wisdom of King Braidon and my father has been proven true. The council of Lonia has elected me as their queen. From this day forth, Lonia and Plorsea shall be as one, united in cause and action. I pray the Saviour grants me the wisdom to continue the legacy of those who came before me."

Stunned silence answered Marianne's proclamation. With Braidon's death, many had been expecting their old enemy to attack. Leaderless and with their army all but disbanded, Plorsea made an easy target. Caledan couldn't understand it—why would the council surrender their sovereignty to a monarch seated in Ardath? After the last Tsar had driven them into poverty, it went against everything their people believed.

Then with a roar, the crowd erupted into cheers. Men and women around Caledan embraced, tears shining in their eyes as they realised this meant there would be no war. Braidon's last act had been to build a lasting peace. Perhaps Plorsea could strive again for its former glory, without the threat of violence looming on its borders.

"Alas, not all who live within our two nations are joyed by this new bond. Some seek to sow the seeds of dissent amongst our people. Just two weeks ago, a Castle in Town-irwin was attacked, and two of its Elders murdered. To these few, I say you shall not prevail. I have granted the Knights of Alana the power to hunt out these dissidents, asked their Elders to cleanse this evil from our lands. In the name of the Saviour, we *shall* have peace!"

At that, the queen threw out her hands. To Caledan, the air before her seemed to shimmer. Her long auburn hair caught in the sunlight and came to life, shining as though aflame. The black dress flickered and her face lit up. A sigh went through the crowd as they looked on her, as though she might be the Saviour herself reborn.

His mouth suddenly dry, Caledan's heart beat faster, and it seemed he was seeing the queen for the first time. How could he not have seen it before? Marianne was right; she *was* the person to lead Lonia and Plorsea—even Trola, should she wish it. Who could deny her beauty, her wisdom, her *power?* Had she not hunted down the foul Baronians that had slain the king?

He swallowed at the thought. Sweat dripped from his forehead to sting his eyes. He wiped it away, aware something was not quite right. Watching Marianne, he again felt that rush of love. She was descending the steps of the dais now, offering her hands to the crowd, her whispers of comfort carrying across the square.

Caledan shook his head. It was as though a fog had attached itself to his mind. He thought again of Braidon, summoning up the anger, his rage at the king's failure…and in a rush the haze fell away. Marianne was using that strange power again—not to command this time, but to confuse, to convince the crowd she was worthy of their love.

His heart quickened as he saw the queen making her way through the press of bodies. Her Queen's Guard came behind, but Marianne was almost unprotected. Convinced of her own power, she walked freely amongst the crowd, a smile crinkling the corners of her lips.

But her spell no longer touched Caledan. Without thinking, he threaded his way through the crowd towards her. This was his chance. He knew well enough from his years stalking Braidon he would never get another opportunity like this. One quick thrust of his dagger, and Plorsea would be freed from another tyrant. He could slip away in the ensuing chaos, leave the city before anyone was the wiser.

"May the Saviour bless your family."

Marianne's voice carried over the heads of the onlookers. She was just a few yards away, so close, but the crowd was dense around her—he could not approach. Taller than most, he craned his head to watch the queen's path, trying to predict where she would go. He prayed she would not turn back to the dais.

Taking a guess, Caledan maneuvered himself into the path he hoped she would take. He held his breath as she moved closer, her progress slowed by her admirers. She stopped to talk with a mother and her newborn baby, to shake a young boy's hand, to offer a quiet word of reassurance to a one-armed veteran.

It was quite the performance, made all the stronger by whatever spell she had cast. Even without her power Caledan might have been convinced, had he not witnessed her attempt to burn Kryssa and Pela alive.

Finally Marianne was just a few yards away. Her Guards followed close behind, but they would not be able to save her. Silently, Caledan drew the dagger from his belt and held it beneath his cloak, readying himself to spring.

The crowd parted and suddenly Marianne was standing before him. Her blue eyes shone as she looked at him and a smile touched her lips, granting warmth to her face, though he was sure it was not magic this time. He hesitated.

Then an image flashed into his mind, of the flaming arrow arcing above the waters of Malevolent Cove, of a ship burning, the scream of a falling dragon, Pela's last cry of terror. He had tried to find her in those churning waters, tried to protect her as he had before, but Braidon's weight had dragged him down into the depths of the sea. Now he was sure Pela and Genevieve were both dead. His jaw hardened into a scowl.

Marianne's eyes widened and he saw the recognition there, the realisation of what he intended to do. Her mouth opened, but he was too close for her Guards to save her, too strong to stop. His hand slipped from beneath the cloak, the dagger aimed at her heart.

"No."

Caledan gasped as his blade struck something hard and unyielding, as though an invisible suit of armour protected the queen. The impact jarred the dagger from his grip, and it clattered uselessly to the cobbles without ever touching the queen. He stared at it, unable to understand what had happened.

"Who are you?" The queen's voice was like ice. Around them the crowd went still, as though he and Marianne were the only ones left alive in the entire square.

A pressure gripped Caledan by the throat. He tried to cry out, but the invisible fingers grew tighter and he managed only a squawk. Eyes bulging, he stared down at the demure woman. He stretched out an arm and tried to strike her down, but she stood just out of reach, and he found his feet would not obey his commands.

Then a tremor went through her face, and he caught a hint of weariness in her eyes. The grip around his throat loosened, but she stepped away before he could swing again. Around them the crowd came alive. Roaring, they surged forward. Fear touched Caledan. They would tear him apart!

"Guards!" Marianne shouted, her voice cracking. "Take him!"

A Queen's Guard leapt forward and an iron fist struck Caledan in the forehead. Red flashed across his vision. Before he could recover, strong hands caught him by the arms and forced them behind his back. The sword was torn from his belt and his feet swept out from underneath him, slamming him face-first into the cobbles.

The last of the queen's power left Caledan then. He surged against the man holding him—almost managing to throw him off. The crowd roared and he saw them pressing against a wall of Queen's Guards, trying to reach him, to tear him apart for daring to attack their beloved queen. He bucked again, desperate to escape, but a second Guard drew back his boot. Still pinned beneath the first, Caledan could not avoid the blow.

Light exploded across his vision, and then he sank into the darkness.

$\maltese$ 12 $\maltese$

Pela stood staring at Genevieve, still not quite able to believe it was truly her. How long had it been since she'd last seen the huntress, since they had been separated, since these dark tunnels had become Pela's life? She could hardly keep the tears from falling.

Finally, Pela realised she had not answered her friend's question. "I'm fine," she whispered, surreptitiously wiping her eyes. "What…what about you?"

Genevieve face was a picture of shock, and Pela realised how she must look. She hadn't seen herself in a mirror for weeks, but bloodied and bruised and half-starved, covered in coal dust with the clothes rotting on her back, she must be a sight. Pela's cheeks grew warm, the collar pressing uncomfortably against her throat.

"Are you sure?" Genevieve asked, ignoring Pela's question.

Swallowing, Pela flicked a glance at the head-slave that had attacked her, then lowered her eyes. Despite the joy of their reunion, Genevieve could change nothing. If Pela spoke out, she would only have to face the repercussions later. She nodded quickly.

"I have to go to the infirmary," she said, gesturing at her leg. The wound had opened again and a trail of blood was congealing on her leg. "There was a cave-in."

"Then come with me," Genevieve replied quickly, casting an angry glare at Marcus. She must have a higher position amongst the slaves than him, for he shrank away from her. "I'm heading up myself. I was just dealing with a rat infestation in the latrines."

"There are latrines?" The words slipped from Pela before she could stop them. Genevieve's mouth fell open and Pela quickly went on. "I'm…much further down the tunnels."

A mask slipped over Genevieve's face and Pela knew the huntress was struggling to hide her pity. But in the end Genevieve said nothing, only let out a long breath, and gestured to the tunnel leading to the surface.

"Come on," she said softly. "I'll take you."

Pela nodded and the huntress took the lead. Despite the encounter with Marcus, Pela had at least rested from the long climb, and she managed a reasonable pace for the first hundred feet. Soon, however, the exhaustion returned, and they slowed. Genevieve filled the silence with her own story.

"When they found out I was a hunter, they put me to work bringing in meat to supplement their supplies," she explained as they walked. "There's plenty of game in these mountains—deer and goat, and marmot on bad days."

"Why didn't you run away?" Pela whispered, trying to preserve her breath.

"I'm always accompanied by a couple of their own hunters, though calling them that is generous. They couldn't catch a rabbit with a broken leg. No wonder they needed me."

"Lucky," Pela puffed, pausing to suck in a lungful of air. "You don't know what it's like…down here every day. We sleep where we work, eat and do our business. There's no escape, and only the dim lanterns for light." She looked up as she spoke, her heart beating faster at the glimmer of light amidst the black. It was daytime.

Genevieve lost some of her colour as Pela caught up. "I…only spent a couple of days down there," she said, and her voice cracked. "I cannot imagine…Pela, I promise I'm going to get us out of this. We'll find a way back to Kryssa, I swear."

Pela said nothing, only nodded. She knew the truth. It lurked behind the whites of Genevieve's eyes, whatever her reassurances. The huntress was brave and strong and determined, but she had no magic. She could not perform miracles, and not even Devon could have rescued them from this nightmare of a place.

"It's okay," Pela whispered, resting a hand on the woman's elbow. "This isn't your fault, Gen."

"I…" Genevieve's voice faded, but she swallowed and went on. "I won't give up. I'll protect you."

Pela chuckled, though the act made her chest ache. "That's what everyone says," she said, smiling despite herself, "but I'm not a girl anymore. I can look after myself. Protect yourself, Gen. It's all either of us can do now."

Silence fell between them and they continued their steady march up the tunnel, though Pela went more and more slowly. Her eyes began to water as the light grew brighter, but she could not look away. Sunlight speared through the tunnel, setting the swirling dust aflame. A weight seemed to lift from Pela's shoulders, as though the light itself were magic, possessed of a power of its own.

It also burned, and by the time they reached the surface, Pela's eyes were watering so badly she could barely see. Red dots danced across her vision and she held a hand against her face to shield her eyes—though as they emerged onto the mountainside, she realised it was a cloudy day.

A pain began in the back of Pela's skull and fingers of despair wrapped around her mind. After so long in the darkness, would her eyes ever readjust to the light? What was the point of going on if she could never see a blue sky again?

Even so, she forced herself to at least take one look at her surroundings. The stark red slopes of the Sandstone Mountains fell away beneath them, down to the river lands far below, where the plains of Lonia stretched all the way to the ocean. She could not see that far though, and within a few seconds the glare forced Pela to cover her eyes.

At least the air was fresh, the cool breeze carrying with it the scent of alpine grass and livestock. A roughshod town sat just below the entrance to the mine, which was little more than a black hole in the side of the mountain. Steel wheels squealed on their tracks as the slaves tramped past with their carriage, returning to the darkness. Pela heard them muttering as they passed, but did not open her eyes.

"This way," Genevieve said gently, taking her hand. "Come on, I'll lead you. It's not far."

Pela swallowed, horrified at her own weakness, but there was nothing she could do but allow the huntress to lead her. The slope was broken and she staggered several times, her feet tripped by unseen obstacles. Genevieve caught her each time, hauling her back up, and after a few minutes Pela sensed they were inside a building.

It was still bright when she opened her eyes, but with the door closed she could manage in the gloom. The room itself was sparsely furnished but for a dozen stretchers, many of them occupied by the sick or injured—though none of the patients sported the collar of a slave.

Movement came from the other end of the room as a man entered from another door and paused beside one of the stretchers. He held a notepad in one hand and mumbled to himself as he made marks on the paper. He did not notice them until Genevieve loudly cleared her throat.

"Oh!" the man exclaimed, jumping half a foot in the air and spinning towards them. "I didn't see you there! How can I help you?"

Pela said nothing, only stood staring in disbelief at the man. She had not recognised his clothing in the gloom, but now that he faced them, the fiery sword on his robes was clearly visible. It marked him as an Elder of the Order, as one of the men who'd kidnapped Pela's mother, who had seen her life torn apart and her freedom taken.

Pela's rage flickered into life, and she fought the urge to launch herself at the man. It would be so easy, here alone but for the sick and the injured. And he was old, his face lined and hair long and white. His kindly eyes did not fool her, not after everything she'd seen these last few months. He could not stop her, not once her hands were around his frail neck…

"Elder Lewis, I have a new charge for you," Genevieve said, gesturing to Pela. "She was caught in a collapsed tunnel. Her overseer wanted you to patch her up."

"A slave!" Lewis exclaimed, striding forward. His face registered surprise. "Are you sure…which overseer was this?"

"Overseer Ruebyn," Pela snapped.

She took a step towards the man, but before she could make any more untoward threats, Genevieve snatched her by the arm and dragged her back. They shared a glance, and while the huntress said nothing, Pela caught the warning in her eyes.

Behave!

Grinding her teeth, Pela nodded. Genevieve gave her arm a final squeeze, then turned to face the Elder again.

"Special circumstances, you understand," she said, flashing the man a smile. "She has a nasty gash, but I'm sure your talents will have her back to work in no time."

Still frowning, the Elder wandered closer. "Yes, yes," he murmured, his eyes sweeping Pela up and down. "Your leg, I see. Nasty indeed. You can walk though? Of course—otherwise you would not be here, no?" He chuckled at his own joke, then gestured to a bench that ran along one wall. "Jump up there then, so I can take a look."

Pela looked from the Elder to Genevieve, not quite sure what to make of it all, but her friend only shrugged.

"I'd best be going," she said, offering Lewis another smile. "I trust you will both be okay?" she continued, flashing Pela a pointed look.

Pela rolled her eyes, but when Genevieve did not look away, she nodded her ascent.

"Yes, yes, of course!" Lewis said, none the wiser to their unspoken communication. "I can hardly feed myself, can I, looking after all these sorry souls! Would you bring back some mutton, Genevieve? The goat does not agree with my stomach."

"I'll see what I can do, Lewis," the huntress replied. "But the sheep live high up near the snowline, and they don't let me roam that far very often."

The Elder sighed, but then his eyes brightened. "I will

put in a request! If the game is there, I'm sure they will not refuse."

"Very good," Genevieve murmured. She stepped towards the door, then glanced back, her eyes catching on Pela. "Goodbye, then."

Pela swallowed, struggling to dislodge the lump that had suddenly formed in her throat. "Bye," she whispered.

Then the huntress was gone, leaving her alone with the Elder and his patients. For a moment he stood staring after Genevieve. He gave his head a shake, and was all business again.

"Very well, what do we have here, young…sorry, I don't believe I got your name?"

Pela blinked. "What?"

"Your name, ma'am, you do have one, don't you?" Lewis asked, more slowly this time, as though speaking to a simpleton. "I can hardly just call you 'girl.'"

"Pela," Pela whispered, before she could think better of it.

After so many days answering to "slave," as though she were no more than a tool to be used, her name felt strange in her mouth. It was good to speak it, to remind herself she truly existed, that she had a past—and might still have a future.

Only a second later did she realise it might have been a mistake, that she might be recognised as the same Pela who had escaped the Great Sacrifice all those weeks ago. But Lewis only smiled.

"Very good, young Pela," he said. "Now, if you'd be so good as to lie on your stomach, I can inspect that wound."

Pela obeyed, though the metal bench was cold and her clothes offered little insulation. A shiver went through her as the Elder prodded the wound in her hamstring. Clenching her teeth, she muffled a groan, but Lewis must have felt her tense, for he released her at once.

"This won't do," he muttered to himself. "Wait one minute."

He disappeared back through the door at the end of the room, returning a few minutes later with a glass in hand. Copper coloured liquid sloshed within, and when he put it in front of her face, Pela caught the scent of alcohol.

"I'm afraid I have nothing stronger than my own whiskey," he said with a smile, "but it'll at least take the edge off the pain."

In truth, every part of Pela ached. Her leg was just one more pain added to her collection, but she wasn't about to refuse his offer. Taking the glass from his hands, she swallowed its contents in a single gulp—then coughed as the fiery liquid burned its way down her throat. Lewis chuckled and patted her on the back until she recovered. Then she lay back down, and he began his inspection anew.

"Not so deep," he muttered, and Pela felt his fingers prodding the wound again, "stones and dirt though…have to be cleaned…risk infection…painful."

Pela swallowed, her eyes watering despite the whiskey. She breathed a sigh of relief when he stood up. They shared a glance, and she glimpsed sadness in his eyes.

"You were the only one in the collapse?" he asked softly.

Grief closed over Pela's throat as she remembered Siden, trapped or dead beneath all that rock. Wordlessly, she shook her head.

"I'm sorry," Lewis whispered, placing a hand on her shoulder. "I wish I could help more, with your kind. I do not know what crimes you committed to find yourself here, but you are still human. I fear my people forget our own humanity sometimes, that we drift too far from the path of the Saviour. We need more overseers like this Ruebyn of yours."

Stunned by his words, Pela could only manage a nod as Lewis returned to the back room. What he'd said made no sense. In Malevolent Cove, dozens of his fellow Elders had watched in ecstasy as Pela and her mother were tied to the mast of a ship and set alight as part of their Great Sacrifice. Only Genevieve's intervention had saved them.

But she saw none of that same fervour in Lewis. She watched him with fresh eyes as he returned, wondering what kind of man he truly was, to speak of kindness while wearing the robes of an Elder.

"This is going to hurt," Lewis said as he walked up. He held another glass of whiskey in one hand, a bottle of clear liquid and rag in the other. "You'd better take this."

Pela took the offered glass and swallowed it as quickly as the first. Her vision swam as she lay back down—she'd hardly drunk more than a sip of ale before today, and the spirits went straight to her head. This time when the Elder's fingers prodded her leg again, she giggled.

"Cold!" Pela gasped.

"I'll take that as a sign the whiskey is helping," Lewis replied.

Chuckling, he soaked the rag in the clear liquid from the bottle. Pela stilled as she caught the raw stench of alcohol, far stronger than before. She opened her mouth to ask what he was doing, but Lewis gripped her by the leg and wiped the cloth through her wound before she could sit up.

A gasp tore from Pela. It as though her leg had been aflame. She writhed against the bench, but the Elder's grip was like iron around her ankle and she could not tear her leg free. Panting, she clung to the steel table leg. Another scream escaped her before she snapped her mouth closed. Teeth clenched, she closed her eyes and endured.

Seemingly an eon later, Lewis stepped back with a grunt. "It's done!"

Relief washed through Pela. She opened her eyes and her vision spun, but when she looked down she saw he had spoken the truth. The dirt and stones were gone from her wound. Pushing down the nausea in her stomach, she sat up. Smiling, Lewis offered her another glass.

"Take your time with this one," he chuckled. "The worst is behind us."

Her hand trembling, Pela accepted his offering. She took a sip as he retrieved a tub of cream and bandages, and began to dress her wound.

"So how long have you been here, young Pela?" Lewis asked as he worked.

"Not long," she croaked, her eyes flickering closed. The cream was cool on her leg, smothering some of the fire from the cleaning. She took another sip, and found she quite enjoyed the taste of the whiskey. "A month?"

"You must have committed a great crime, to have ended up here so young?"

"Only the crime of being Plorsean," she replied offhandedly.

His hands froze on her leg. For a moment, Pela did not notice the change that had come over him, but when she finally looked down, he was crouched, staring up at her. She frowned.

"What?"

Lewis rose slowly to his feet, his face grave. "What do you mean, 'the crime of being Plorsean'?"

Pela's heart lodged in her throat. Why had she said that? She had seen slaves beaten for denying their crimes. Even

Ruebyn had threatened her just for telling him she had a name. For the briefest of seconds she had forgotten Lewis was the enemy, but his reaction now revealed his true allegiance.

"I…" She trailed off, unable to think of a lie that would convince him.

"Pela, if you are innocent…I can help you," he whispered.

"*What?*" The question burst from Pela in a rush.

Lewis rested a hand on her shoulder. "Tell me."

And despite herself, Pela did—everything that had happened to her since the Baronians had plucked her from the ocean. Of the time before that, she said only that her ship had gone down in a storm. She did not mention Genevieve, in case she was making a terrible mistake trusting Lewis. The liquor made the words come easily, though several times she stumbled over her own tongue in her rush to get the story out.

By the time she was finished, the hour was late and the sun was beginning to set through the windows. The red light hurt her eyes and she had to close them again, though a headache soon began in the back of her skull anyway.

"I am so sorry, young Pela," Lewis whispered.

He embraced her, and despite herself Pela hugged him back, though she had run out of tears long ago.

"I promise you," he said, pulling back finally, "I will get to the bottom of this."

"Thank you," she whispered, unable to express the depths of her gratitude.

"For now though, we must go on as though nothing has changed," he continued. "For if what you say is true, there will be those who wish to conceal the truth."

"You mean…?" Pela whispered, the hope crumbling in

her chest. She couldn't say the words, lest she make them true.

"I am afraid so," Lewis said gently. Taking her hand, he lifted her to her feet. "For now, young Pela, you must go back to your overseer. You must go back into the mine."

13

"Halt!"

A woman's voice echoed from the shadows of the guard booth nested in the walls of Chole, bringing Kryssa to a stop. Braidon staggered on for another half-moment, until her hand whipped out to catch him. That jerked him out of his stupor and he looked around, eyes widening beneath the shadow of his hood.

The awful dragon had deposited them in the foothills half a day's walk from Chole, and they'd spent the last six hours tramping across the jagged terrain in a desperate attempt to reach the city before nightfall. While they were no longer desert, the summer sun had still been hot on the plateau, sucking the moisture from the air and the strength from their tiring limbs. The scant cover provided by the occasional patch of trees had been welcome, as was the end of their journey. But night had fallen an hour ago, and Kryssa feared the guards would not grant them entrance. There were still dark things that lurked out on these plains.

"My friend is unwell," Kryssa called.

It was not a lie. Though his injuries were outwardly healed, they still sapped at Braidon's strength. Only by sheer determination had he made it this far, and no one who looked at him would deny his illness. He swayed on his feet, eyes distant again, and she knew his mind was elsewhere.

"Gates are closed," came the gruff reply from the guardhouse. "Come back in the morning."

Kryssa could not see the woman through the narrow slot in the stone, but she wasn't going to be deterred so easily. "Please, we need a doctor!"

Shadows shifted behind the stone window, then a lantern flickered into life. A man's face appeared, looking out at them.

"Lass is telling the truth, Nicoyl!" he cried.

"Like hell," the woman guard muttered.

Even so, after a moment there was a rattle of metal and a squeal of hinges as a smaller door set into the wooden gates swung open. A woman stepped through wearing chainmail and a scarlet cloak—the same kind worn by all Plorsean warriors in service to the crown. Kryssa swallowed at the memories it stirred—she had once been adorned in the same fashion, though her cloak had been marked with the golden embroidery of the King's Guard.

"Please," Kryssa said, spreading her empty hands, "it's just the two of us. We'll do no harm."

"Inns will all be closed at this hour," the woman replied coldly.

"Nonsense, Nicoyl," the second guard cut in as he followed her out the gate. He was far larger than his counterpart, and held his spear loosely at his side. Striding across to stand beside the woman, he grinned at Kryssa. "There'll be space at the Bolthole, probably the Foxglove as well."

"Quiet, Dominic," Nicoyl snapped. She flashed him a

glare and Kryssa couldn't help but smile, though it disappeared before the woman's eyes returned to her. "Now, what are the two of you doing, arriving in the city at such an hour?"

Kryssa patted Braidon on the back. "As I said, my friend here was injured. Hurt himself crossing the plateau and we fell behind schedule. Lucky we made it at all!"

The suspicion in the woman's eyes did not change. "These are hardly the times for casual trips across country. You came from the south, you said?"

"Oh, enough of this, Nicoyl!" the second guard interrupted. "Can't you see the man's dead on his feet? Looks like he's about to keel over. Come on, I know a doctor who'll take a look at you at this hour. You think you can hold down the fort while I'm gone, Nicoyl?"

The woman could only watch, stunned, as Dominic ushered them forward. He had them both halfway through the gate before the she managed to reply.

"Dominic, don't you dare leave me here alone again!" she screamed. Striding after them, she slammed the door closed and threw down the crossbar. "I swear by the Saviour I'll report you this time!"

Already halfway down the street with Braidon in tow, Dominic waved a hand. "Don't worry, I'll be back before you know it!"

Kryssa hurried after him, though she cast a quick look over her shoulder as she went, pitying the woman. But her misfortune was their benefit, and Kryssa breathed easier when they turned the corner and entered the maze that was Chole's winding streets.

"Sorry about Nicoyl," Dominic was saying when she caught up with him. "Stickler for the rules, that one. And a follower of the Order to boot. Been hearing some terrible rumours about their lot these last few weeks—glad there's not so many of her kind here in Chole. Can't handle the heat, them Knights of theirs."

"What *has* been going on?" Braidon panted as they turned another corner. "We've been on the road a while, and haven't had much news."

"I bet you haven't," the guard murmured, "Your Majesty."

And suddenly Dominic was down on one knee in front of Braidon, head bowed. For a second they both stood there gaping, then Kryssa grabbed the man by the shoulders and dragged him back to his feet.

"*Enough of that!*" she hissed, casting her eyes around for watchers, but they were alone in the narrow streets. During its years of drought, Chole had developed an unsavoury reputation, forcing its residents indoors after sunset. While it was now one of the safer cities in Plorsea, the habit remained ingrained in its citizens.

Dominic chuckled at their panic and started off again as though nothing out of the ordinary had happened.

"How did you know me?" Braidon asked a block later, when they were sure no one was following.

"Knew you both the second I looked out of the guardhouse!" Dominic exclaimed. "Though I'm not surprised you don't remember me, except maybe from notoriety. Had a problem with the drink, once upon a time. Can't blame ya, really, kicking me out of the recruits for ya Guard."

"Oh!" Kryssa said, surprised.

She studied his features more closely when they passed the next street lantern. His hair and beard were closely cropped, black but for where a few strands of white were beginning to show, and his eyes were a cool grey. He certainly carried more weight than anyone who had ever served with the King's Guard, but then, Dominic had not said how long it had been since his discharge.

She could not pick his face, but then that was not unusual. She had served alongside hundreds during her ten years with the Plorsean army, and could not remember every soldier she'd met.

"Well, if you can help me now, I'll see you have whatever position you desire!" Braidon said as the shadows pressed in around them.

Dominic only chuckled. "Helping a dead man, that'll be a new one. I guess the official story was a tad overblown," he said, then added, "But no, I deserved what I got. Best thing that ever happened to me, really. Quit the drink and made a new life here in Chole. Never looked back, well, not till I saw our rightful king standing outside my gate."

"Thank you," Braidon said, and from his tone he meant it. "It seems I don't have many friends left these days."

"And where *are* you taking us, Dominic?" Kryssa asked, her suspicions not so easily swayed.

They must have been passing through a sparsely populated section of the city, for the street lanterns were less frequent now, leaving many of the intersections unlit. Kryssa cast a glance over her shoulder, but the streets remained deserted. Most of the buildings were single story here, built of stone taken from the foothills of Golden Ridge. But those quarries had run dry long ago, and here and there she spotted newer houses, recognizable by the irregular volcanic stones that had been mortared together to form their walls. Heavy wooden shutters barred the windows, blacking out even the faintest hint of light from within.

"My house, of course!" Dominic replied. "We're not far now."

Kryssa loosened her sword in its scabbard. With Braidon barely on his feet, their defence would fall to her if Dominic betrayed them. The guard seemed to be no more than he appeared—a former soldier wanting to aid his king—but Kryssa had learned not to trust anyone when it came to protecting Braidon. Not even his wife, it seemed.

"Must be quite the story," Dominic was saying, "with the queen taking your throne and all. And the Lonian one at that! All some secret plan of yours, I guess?" He chuckled to himself. "Or perhaps not, lookin' at the state of ya."

"What was that about the queen?" Braidon said sharply.

"You really are out of touch!" Dominic exclaimed. "Your wife went straight to Lon after her victory over the Baronians that ah, apparently *didn't* murder you? Anyways, she spoke with the Lonian council, convinced them to make her queen there, too. To have been a fly on the wall during that conversation, ay?"

"That must have been after the Cove," Braidon croaked to Kryssa.

"And I bet I can guess how she managed to convince them," Kryssa said, pursing her lips. "It's even worse than we thought.

"Wait, what was that about the Baronians?" Braidon asked. "Devon said she went after them with my King's Guard, but they weren't with Marianne when…I saw her last."

"Oh!" Dominic fell silent then, his face becoming a mask of sadness. "You haven't heard about that either?"

Braidon's hand snapped out and caught the man by the wrist, dragging him to a stop. "*What?*" he hissed. "What did she do to them?"

Kryssa pressed closer, her heart palpitating in her chest. Though she had retired almost two decades ago, there was a kinship amongst the Guard, both past and present. They were the most elite fighting unit of Plorsea, the king's last defence against betrayal. The best of them competed in a tournament every three years, to test their skills and challenge for the right of King's Champion—the best of the best. While Kryssa herself had never attained that honour, she had been close on several occasions.

"They're gone," Dominic whispered, his eyes wide. "They died to the last, fighting the Baronians. The Queen's Guard finished off what was left of the scum, or so your wife tells it."

"No," Braidon gasped.

He staggered back, his legs collapsing beneath him. Kryssa moved quickly, catching him beneath the shoulder and hauling him back up, though she was reeling as well. Faces flashed before her mind, men and women she knew still served in the Guard—gone now forever.

It didn't seem possible—and yet now she realised it made perfect sense. Caledan had told her that Pela's safety had been entrusted to the King's Guard, when they'd set out on their hunt for the Baronians. And yet, a week later, her daughter had been tied to the mast alongside her. Kryssa had hardly spared a thought for her former comrades this past month, but she realised now they would never have surrendered Pela so long as a single Guard remained standing.

Finally Braidon managed to get his feet back underneath him. Releasing him, Kryssa took a step back. Teeth bared, Braidon straightened. In the poorly-lit streets, he was almost unrecognisable. Raw hatred was etched into every line of his face, and his eyes glowed with an unspeakable rage.

"Take us to your home, Dominic," he ordered, his voice showing no hint of weakness now. "We have a war to win."

14

Caledan woke with a start, aware something was wrong, but unable to quite recall what. He opened his eyes and found himself in a richly furnished room. Woollen carpets covered the floors and a massive tapestry took up an entire wall, depicting the view from a mountaintop, of a green land of forests and grasslands and rivers, stretching away to a distant lake. There was an island in the centre of the lake, the gold and marble spires of a city rising from its clifftops. It could only be Ardath. In the image, shadows stretched from the mountains across the entire land—everywhere except the great city, which seemed to glow with a light all of its own.

Allowing his gaze to roam, Caledan took in an empty hearth and a pair of glass doors leading out to a balcony. A small mahogany desk had been placed near the doorway. He started, finally noticing the woman seated there. Fountain pen in hand, Marianne's features were set, her attention concentrated on the papers lying scattered across the desk.

His mind working slowly, Caledan stared at the queen,

trying to recall how he had come to be there. Images flickered in his mind—his dagger thrusting for Marianne's heart, the sudden paralysis, then pain as a Guard struck him, and fear as the crowd bayed for his death.

Shuddering, Caledan made to rise—and only then discovered he'd been bound hand and foot to the chair. He growled, straining against his bindings, and the chair tilted wildly to the side. His anger turned to fright and he leaned the other way, trying desperately to balance himself. It was too little too late, and he toppled to the floor with a crash.

Laughter carried to Caledan's ears as he thrashed against his bonds. He swore loudly, then to his surprise, the ropes gave way. Tearing himself loose from the chair, he struggled to his feet and faced the queen.

A broad sofa lay between them, but she had not moved from the desk. Her eyes danced as she watched him, lips turned upwards in mirth. Roaring, he leapt across the sofa and dove at her…

…only to find himself flung into the sofa by an invisible force. His head whipped back, striking the wooden support behind the cushions. Light flashed across his vision as he slumped against the couch. Groaning, he tried to rise, but finding himself off-balance, toppled sideways instead.

"You should be more careful, sellsword," Marianne observed, leaning back in her chair. "My doctors inform me it is unhealthy to take so many blows to the head."

Caledan looked up from the sofa. The queen drummed her fingers against the desk, one eyebrow raised as though waiting for an answer. She showed no fear that he was free, though Caledan had seen no Guards—in fact, they seemed to be alone.

"What am I doing here?" he growled.

Marianne smiled. "You don't remember?" You tried to kill me in the Grand Plaza."

Rubbing his head, Caledan scowled at her. "I remember *that*," he said. "How did you stop me?"

"Practice and skill," Marianne replied, and for a second her eyes appeared to glow. "Your name is Caledan, no?"

"How…?"

"You have been out for hours—time enough for me to do some research. You are a sellsword, I am told?"

Caledan nodded, and clenched his teeth as the pain in the back of his skull redoubled. His stomach swirled and it took an effort of will not to throw up on the queen's sofa. Normally he might have elaborated with a few of his exploits, but the strangeness of the encounter had robbed him of words.

"And quite proficient, if the stories are true," Marianne added. "Well, just as you have spent your entire life honing your skills with the blade, so too have I spent the last eight years studying the secrets of the mind and body. Ever since I discovered what the Elders had uncovered."

"Magic, you mean?" Caledan asked.

The queen shrugged. "To your limited understanding, yes it would appear as such, though this power bears little resemblance to the gift passed to humanity by the False Gods."

Caledan only grunted. He had no idea what she was talking about.

Marianne smiled. "I can see the distinction does not interest a man of your profession." She stood and wandered around the desk. "So tell me, sellsword, why would a sellsword of your skill so debase himself, serving the cause of the beggar king?"

"Who says I work for Braidon?" Caledan snapped.

"The Saviour forgive me if I am mistaken, but did I not see you carrying away my *beloved* husband in Malevolent Cove?"

"Devon bade me protect him," Caledan scowled. "But I would never serve Braidon."

"I see." Marianne took a seat on her desk. "But Devon is dead. I made sure of it. Does that mean then, that you sought to kill me of your own accord?"

Caledan grinned despite himself. "Is that so surprising? It's only fair, isn't it, after *you* tried to kill *me?*"

To his surprise, Marianne threw back her head and howled with laughter. Clapping her hands, she hopped off the desk and threw herself down on the couch beside him. Caledan stared at the queen, wondering whether she was mad. She was so close to him now, he could have reached out and snapped her tiny neck.

Her eyes shone as she watched him though, and Caledan sensed he did not have the power to touch her. He relaxed into the sofa, deciding it was better to hear her out than to throw away whatever goodwill he seemed to have earned.

"It was you who killed Ikar, wasn't it?" she asked suddenly, the smile falling from her face. "He was my friend once, you know, before he became a Knight."

Caledan swallowed, his blood suddenly running cold. He sensed it would be a mistake to lie, and yet to tell the truth… "I did," he croaked. "To…save my friends."

"Ah yes, Kryssa and her daughter, Pela. I was saddened to involve the girl. Had I known my dear husband still lived, I would have moved mountains to find him, to have him take her place." Her eyes flashed. "I take it he is still alive?"

"He lives," Caledan agreed.

"I don't suppose you'd like to tell me where he's hiding?"

the queen asked. A shadow darkened her face and the fire appeared in her eyes again, burning with a terrible intensity.

Caledan swallowed, suddenly unable to look her in the eye. His ears popped, as though a great pressure were building in the room, but he forced himself to speak. "I would rather not. He's with…a friend."

"So others survived as well." The pressure vanished as quickly as it had appeared, and when Caledan looked at the queen she was just a woman again. "No matter," she said. "They will reveal themselves in time. But what of you then, sellsword? Why come here to murder me? Surely you could not have been so arrogant to think you would succeed?"

"I was close enough!" Caledan retorted, his pride dented by her words. He half rose from the couch, but a look from Marianne sat him back down.

The queen flicked a hand. "You are skilled, I grant you that. And I expended too much of my strength on the crowd. You must be strong-willed, to have resisted my influence. I had mastered *that* skill long before Malevolent Cove."

Caledan narrowed his eyes. "You took something from that Knight, from Ikar, didn't you?"

Marianne shrugged. "Ikar was a faithful servant once, but his allegiances had shifted. He served the Order, not me." She smiled. "And I needed his life force after I was thwarted by your friends."

"I didn't think there was a difference between you and the Order."

A *click* came from the outer door before the queen could answer. She rose from the sofa as a high-pitched voice called from outside:

"Mama!"

Caledan started as a young boy, no older than five, came

racing across the room. Marianne stepped around the couch and dropped to one knee to wrap him in her arms. His laughter echoed from the high ceilings as she ruffled his curly black hair, so like his father's.

"Calybe, what are you doing out of your lessons? Your teacher will be in a fit of worry!"

"I was bored, Mama!" the boy cried. "And…the other children, they said something bad had happened to you!"

"Did they?" Marianne's face shone as she held him out at arm's length. "And what do you think?"

The little boy frowned, his blue eyes becoming serious as he looked her up and down. A grin stretched his plump cheeks. "You're okay!"

"I am." Marianne hugged him again, and the boy giggled. "Now run along back to your classes, Calybe, before your teacher comes looking for you!"

"Okay, Mama!"

The boy darted from the room without a backwards glance, his tiny feet slapping loudly on the stone floors. Rising, Marianne turned towards Caledan again. The smile fell from her face, the light in her eyes turning dark.

"There are many things you do not understand, sellsword."

❧ 15 ❧

Three days passed before they found Siden's body. Pela stood in silence as the slaves carried his body from the rubble and dropped him unceremoniously to the ground. A cry tore from Pela at the sight, and dropping her pick, she shoved her way past them and fell to her knees beside him.

Taking his cold hand in hers, she held it to her chest, wishing she could go back, that she'd had the strength to carry him clear. She didn't understand why, but he was dead because of her. Ruebyn claimed there must have been a weakness in the rock, a natural impurity that had collapsed their supports, but she knew the truth. *Something* had happened while she'd meditated, before the tunnel had collapsed, but she was too afraid to reach for it again.

Now her last hope that Siden might still live had been crushed. His body lay before her, bruised and broken, his pale eyes open but unseeing. She closed them as gently as she could, sensing the accusation there, a reflection of her own guilt. There was no way of telling whether he had suffered. Remembering her own torment, lying trapped in the darkness, she prayed death had come quickly for her friend.

"Pela."

She flinched as a hand settled on her shoulder. Swallowing, she turned to Ruebyn, waiting for the reprimand, but for once it did not come. His eyes were sad as he looked at Siden's body.

"He was a wise man," he said, "and a good worker. He will be missed."

Anger touched Pela and she came to her feet. "His name was Siden," she snapped. "And he was more than just a *worker*. He was a *person*, a good man."

Ruebyn shrank before her rage, his eyes growing wide, but he quickly took control of himself. His shock turned to anger and he tore the whip from his belt, shaking its coiled loops in her face.

"You forget yourself, *slave*," he growled, "and his death changes nothing. He was still a slave. He surrendered his personhood when he committed his crimes. *Just like you.*"

"I didn't!" Pela screamed, shoving him. "I'm innocent!"

Staggering back from the blow, Ruebyn gaped, his eyes flickering between Pela's face and his chest as though she had stabbed him. Then the meaning of her words seeped in, and he bared his teeth.

"Innocent?" he asked, his voice dangerously quiet.

Pela's whole body shook with pent-up fury. For the last three days she had kept her silence, waiting on the hope that Lewis had offered. But as time trickled by, her hope had withered. The sight of Siden dead amidst the rubble had burned away the last of it, and she realised now that no one was coming to help her, that no one cared. No doubt the Elder had been playing some jest, toying with her innocence. What a fool she had been!

But no longer.

"I am Pela from Plorsea, and a free woman, by the laws of your land!" she snarled.

A violent *crack* came from Ruebyn's whip as it struck empty air, an unspoken threat. Pela flinched but stood her ground. She refused to be cowed any longer, to crouch and cower in the darkness and wait for someone else to save her. It was time for her to plead her own case, and be damned with the consequences.

"I'm innocent," she grated, baring her teeth.

Ruebyn stared her down, the leather whip clutched tightly in one hand. His shoulders rose and fell as he sucked in a great breath. Too late Pela realised he was preparing himself, gathering his courage to do what he must. The whip snapped out, catching Pela in the side of the head. Pain slashed through her ear, but momentum carried the whip on, and the length of leather wrapped taught around her throat.

She gasped and staggered back, only for the whip to bring her up short. Her ear throbbed, each beat of her heart sending agony burning through her skull. Only the metal collar had protected her throat from being torn.

Jerking his wrist, Ruebyn dragged her forward. Flickering lights obscured Pela's vision and her feet tripped over an unseen rock, sending her crashing to the ground. Ruebyn yanked again on the whip, and it slipped free of her collar. Jaw clenched, eyes wide and lip trembling, he readied himself for another blow.

"Overseer Ruebyn!"

A voice carried to them from further down the tunnel. Ruebyn swung around, his eyes widening as a slave strode up. The man paused in front of the overseer, his eyes flicking to Pela for half a second.

"Yes, slave?" Ruebyn snapped. He seemed impatient, but as Pela dragged herself to her knees, he curled the whip back in on itself and clipped it to his belt.

"Sir!" the slave said, clearing his throat. "I…err, believe we have found the cause of the collapse."

Ruebyn's eyes had returned to Pela, and he answered almost absently, "What is it?"

"Another cave, sir." The slave paused. "It's…you had better come take a look."

The entire side of Pela's face was aflame and hot blood was running from her ear. With a trembling hand, she tried to feel the damage, but the pain redoubled at her touch. She cried out again and found Ruebyn's eyes on her. His lips were parted and for a second, horror registered in his eyes.

Then he jerked his head around, returning his attention to the slave. "Show me."

The man nodded and they retreated down the tunnel, leaving Pela alone in the dirt. Sobbing to herself, Pela pulled herself up, determined not to be defeated. Even so, her strength almost failed, and Ruebyn was disappearing round the freshly excavated bend in the tunnel by the time she found her feet.

Standing in the shadows, Pela cursed the boy with every vile word she knew. Their whispers carried to her from around the bend, and with a start Pela realised she was alone. Her head whipped around, checking, but it was true. The rest of the slaves were down the tunnel with Ruebyn. Her heart began to race. The chain around her ankle that had connected her to the others was gone, broken in the collapse. Ruebyn was still waiting for a replacement. This was her chance!

She started up towards the surface, adrenaline giving her strength. The tunnel rose steeply here, winding around in a sharp spiral that only allowed her to see ten yards ahead. But before she had made it a dozen feet, the whisper of voices came from ahead, followed by the soft rattle of metal.

Pela froze, cursing beneath her breath. Quickly she scanned her mind for an excuse that would allow her to pass whoever was approaching. Her gaze was drawn back to where Siden's body still lay, forgotten by his former comrades. She swallowed. His death had left Ruebyn's team a slave down; perhaps Pela could convince them she had been sent to request a replacement.

It was a frail excuse, but it was all she had. An escape attempt had next to no hope of succeeding anyway, but she was tired of waiting. Gathering her nerves, Pela continued. The voices grew louder and she wondered who would be venturing into these dark depths, what they wanted.

Abruptly the tunnel straightened out. Pela searched the darkness for the owners of the voices. A lantern must have burnt out, for the tunnel was cast in shadow ahead, and for a moment she saw nothing. Then a distant light flickered on metal, and she saw who was approaching.

Ice filled Pela's stomach. Before she could think, she turned and fled back the way she'd come. A voice called after her, but she did not stop, though it was Lewis who had spoken. He walked at the head of two Knights, their armour shining like dull mirrors in the darkness. Despite the Elder's earlier kindness, Pela sensed the Knights did not come with good intentions.

A crash of metal sounded as the Knights started to run. In their heavy armour, they would not catch her, not even in her weakened state. But there was only one tunnel in this part of the mine, so deep beneath the surface, and it ended in rubble. She was trapped.

Then Pela remembered what her fellow slave had said—that they had uncovered a cave. Could there be another exit from the mine? It was her only hope, though Ruebyn and the rest of her chain gang were waiting there. At least they were not armed with broadswords; she might just be able to slip past, if she was quick.

She staggered down the tunnel at twice the rate she'd gone up, only slowing at the final bend when Siden's body came into view. Guilt touched her again, but there was no time to pause now, and she stumbled past. The shouts of the Knights had fallen quiet, but from ahead she could hear the voices of Ruebyn and the slaves.

Light flickered as they came into view. Pela's strength was at its end now and she slowed to a walk, hoping Ruebyn wouldn't notice anything out of place. He glanced up at her appearance, and she saw a spasm twist his face. His hands shook as he clenched them, then forced them down until his arms were rigid. He nodded as she walked up.

"Slave," he said, "glad you could finally join us."

Pela ignored him. Her eyes were fixed on the tunnel wall. Though two of the slaves held lanterns, there was a shadow on the rock, a great patch of darkness that seemed to resist the light. A shiver started in her scalp and raced down her spine as she crept closer, unable to tear her gaze away. It was only when Ruebyn held out his hand to bar her path that she understood what it was.

"Careful," he whispered, his hazel eyes catching hers. "We don't know how far down it goes."

A lump lodged in Pela's throat and she did not try to resist his tug. The slave had spoken the truth—there was a cave, but not like anything Pela had imagined. A few feet from where she stood, the floor of the tunnel gave way to emptiness. She knew now what her pickaxe had struck—a great emptiness beyond the seemingly solid rock, a cavern that extended who knew how far into the earth.

Absently, Pela bent and picked up a stone. Ruebyn watched in silence as she tossed it over the side. They waited a long time, but it was as though the rock had vanished into a void. She never heard it strike the bottom.

"Stop!"

Pela spun as a metallic voice came from up the tunnel. The two Knights rattled into view, broadswords in hand. A vice closed around her chest as they approached, slowing now that they could see she was trapped. Movement came from behind them as Lewis came into view, his robes now dirt-streaked and his face ashen. When he saw her standing between Ruebyn and the other slaves, his eyes widened and sadness twisted his features. Panting, he stumbled to a stop.

In that moment, Pela realised he had not betrayed her after all. She had done this to herself. She had spoken about her past, and now her crimes against the Order had finally caught up with her. Not even Lewis could save her now. Meeting his gaze, she nodded her thanks.

"Pela of Skystead," the Knight in the lead growled. "You're to come with us."

Pela tensed her fists, readying herself for one last battle. She would not let them take her again, would not let them make her a spectacle for their followers. No, better she die here, in the darkness, than to suffer their cruelty a second longer.

"What's this all about?" Ruebyn said, stepping between her and the Knights.

Shocked, Pela gaped at him. The Knights were not so impressed. "Out of the way, fool," the leader spat.

Ruebyn's eyes widened at the insult and he drew himself up. "Excuse me?" he snapped. "I would have expected more manners from a Knight. Now, the girl is in my possession. She will go nowhere without my permission."

The Knights stopped before him, their faces concealed by cold steel. "You dare stand in the path of the Saviour's justice, boy?"

"The Saviour's justice?" Doubt crept into Ruebyn's eyes. "What are you talking about? She has already been sentenced—is that not why she's here?"

"This Plorsean brat murdered an Elder in cold blood," the first of the Knights growled. "Only death can pay for such a crime, so that her life may serve the *Saviour*."

The colour fled Ruebyn's face. He stood there in stunned silence, looking from the newcomers to Pela, his mouth hanging open. "Wh-what?" he finally managed.

"Enough of this!" the second of the Knights roared. "Let the traitor share the same fate as the Plorsean traitor."

Pushing past his comrade, he swung the broadsword at Ruebyn. Pela cried out as the blade flashed and Ruebyn staggered back, clutching at his chest. Without thinking she caught him before he fell. He sagged in her arms, his weight almost dragging Pela from her feet. The slaves leapt away and the lantern light danced across the tunnel. By its light she saw blood on Ruebyn's fingers.

Stones crunched as the Knight advanced, sword raised. Pela stumbled back, trying to keep the distance between them.

"She protects him!" the Knight snarled. "The coward has betrayed us for his consort!"

"Filthy beast," the second agreed. He moved to bar any escape up the tunnel. Beyond, Lewis still stood, one hand against the wall as though his legs alone could not keep him upright. Cackling, the Knight went on, "Your wisdom saw through their act, Watkyn. The honour of their cleansing is yours."

"Gladly," the Knight facing them growled.

"Get back!" Pela shrieked, struggling beneath Ruebyn's weight.

She should have dropped him. She was at the end of her strength, and her ear still throbbed where the whip had struck her. But she could not bring herself to abandon him. However misguided they might have been, the Knights had struck him down because of her. She could not bear another life on her conscience—not even Ruebyn's.

He groaned in her arms, hand clenched tight against his chest to stem the bleeding. She dragged him with her, though there was nowhere to go. Her stomach churned as she glanced over her shoulder. The darkness loomed. Dust swirled down from above, burning gold in the flickering light, so that it almost seemed that the opening to nowhere were magic. But beyond the light, the void beckoned.

A terrible cold touched Pela as she stepped up to the edge. Stones tumbled down into the cavern, rattling from its sides, then…*nothing*. The Knight cackled, the crunch of his footsteps approaching. He knew they had nowhere to go. Pela flinched as he darted forward with his sword, teetering on the edge. But it was only a feint. Laughter rattled from the ceiling, hammering at Pela. Her body a mess of pain, she swayed on her feet.

The Knights had her cornered, beaten. Ruebyn panted into her chest, his weight hard on her shoulder. Pela could not see how bad his injuries were, but his blood had stained her clothes. She feared he might perish at any moment.

"Come, little girl," the Knight taunted. "Give yourself up, and we may spare your lover's life—if my blade has not already killed him."

"The Elders will be pleased to have you," the second Knight said. "You caused our Order great shame at the Cove. That must be put right."

Anger gave Pela strength, and she scooped up a rock. "Screw your Elders!" she screamed, hurling the rock with all her strength.

The first Knight ducked, but there was a satisfying *clang* as it struck the second in the helmet. Despite the heavy armour, the blow staggered him. Roaring his rage, the first leapt, mailed fist extended. Pela's stomach twisted and instinctively she leapt back with Ruebyn—into nothing!

Suddenly there was no ground beneath her feet. She fell through the icy darkness, the void rising to swallow her up. A desperate hand clutched at her clothes—and she realised the Knight had followed her over the side. Her scream echoed off unseen walls, then with a great *crash*, she struck water.

$\approx$ 16 $\approx$

Braidon and Kryssa spent the next week hidden in the house of Dominic. Braidon grew more restless with each passing day, frustrated by his continued weakness, and increasingly worried by the rumours arriving from across Plorsea. Travellers spoke of Knights hunting down the followers of the Old Gods—even to the capital itself.

Despite what he'd seen with his own eyes, Braidon still struggled to understand how Marianne could have unleashed such evil against her adoptive nation. But then, she'd happily slaughtered the King's Guard for her cause, though they had dedicated themselves to protecting both their lives.

Fortunately, while Chole had a Castle of its own dedicated to the Order, its followers were not numerous in the city and so far its Knights had kept to themselves. But it would only be a matter of time before they too joined the cause.

Braidon had taken to rousing early each morning to exercise, seeking desperately to regain his former strength.

Dominic's house boasted a large open courtyard with a fountain in its centre, and Braidon would spend an hour before dawn practicing the sword patterns his grandmother had taught him in his youth. His wound still pained him, a dull ache that would not go away, but he could rest no longer, not with Marianne out there, hell-bent on destroying his nation.

Stopping her had become an obsession for Braidon. Caledan had bade him to fix his own mistakes, and he intended to do just that. No longer would he look to others to protect him, to make the hard decisions. He had been betrayed too many times, and his friends had paid the price.

As he trained, he imagined each of his fallen comrades. Devon was first, his face pale as Marianne struck him down. Then Genevieve and Pela, disappearing beneath the waves of Malevolent Cove, and his Guards, Rylle and Salver and Aldyn and so many others, cut down by Marianne's treachery.

With each face his anger grew. He wanted to scream, to shout and rage at his wife, to demand to know how she could have thrown away everything they had built.

And at his core, there was that terrible fear: that she had their son. Calybe had been the light of their lives, but Braidon doubted even that memory now. Marianne had casually murdered hundreds—what did she care for the life of one child, even her own?

He shuddered to think what she might do. And so the fear and rage drove him on, pushing him through the weakness. He was resolved to do everything in his power to stop her. Each morning the rising sun found him a little stronger than the day before.

A week after their arrival, it found him in the courtyard cutting wood. The summers were short in Chole and the wood rounds needed to be chopped and sorted before the first winter snowfall. The exercise was painstaking and difficult, but there was an art to it, one Devon had shown him long ago. He'd been just a boy then, caught up in a battle between the greats, but Devon had always treated him as an equal.

Sadness touched Braidon and he paused for breath, remember the smiling hammerman and his penchant for calling all he met "sonny." That had been Devon's way, he supposed. It didn't matter who you were—sailor or scholar or soldier—he treated all the same.

It was difficult to believe the hammerman was truly gone. Any moment, Braidon expected the giant warrior to come walking into the courtyard, a broad grin on his bearded face. Surely not even death could keep Devon from a fight.

But after so many years of battling, of striving against impossible odds, it seemed right that Devon could finally rest. Braidon just prayed he had the strength to finish the fight Devon had started.

Clouds darkened the sky as the morning grew later. Soon a light rain began to fall and Braidon decided he'd done enough for the day. He buried his axe in a wood round and headed inside. At the door he paused at a small shrine to the Three Gods, little more than a wooden platform with three candles. Dominic's wife, Janylle, must have lit them while Braidon was outside. Closing his eyes, Braidon sent a brief prayer to the long-departed deities.

The action turned Braidon's mind to his sister. These past weeks he had found himself missing Alana more than he had in years. *She* would not have spent weeks sulking in the forest, hiding from her responsibilities. Alana had never backed down from a fight; she would not be daunted by the frightening new power Marianne had discovered.

"What should I do, sis?" he whispered to himself.

Angrily, he shook his head. Already his resolve was faltering, giving way to the self-doubt that had crippled him his entire life. He straightened his shoulders and turned his back on the shrine. This was his fight and he would find his own way to win. He had to.

Braidon wiped his feet on the doormat and followed the scent of spiced eggs into the kitchen. Kryssa was sitting at the small table, while Janylle stood at the bench chopping carrots. Dominic was already on duty at the city gates, not due back until the afternoon. Janylle smiled as Braidon approached the woodstove and lifted the lid on the frying pan. The smell of turmeric and paprika wafted in his nostrils, making his eyes water, and he quickly replaced the lid.

"Take a seat, Braidon," Janylle insisted, waving him away. "You're on dishes, remember?"

Chuckling, Braidon obeyed. He'd tried to cook them a meal only once, and had been banished from using the stove ever since.

Kryssa raised an eyebrow as he sat. "How goes the training?"

"Well enough," Braidon sighed, "but it needs to be more. *I* need to do more."

"Have you thought any more on what happened in the Cove?" Kryssa asked, sitting forward in her chair.

Braidon waved a hand. "Of course. All I can figure is that Marianne stole the life force from Ikar as he lay dying. There were Magickers once who did the same thing with magic. My father, for one," he finished bitterly.

"Marianne mentioned the Tsar!" Kryssa exclaimed. "When she gave us the necklaces."

"It's not a pleasant thought," Braidon said with a shake of his head, "stealing another's life force to grant yourself power. Marianne could be ruthless, but I never guessed…"

"She fooled everyone, Braidon," Kryssa offered.

He only shrugged. "Anyway, even if our theory is right, it takes us no closer to a way to match her."

"No," Kryssa sighed, the excitement leaving her face.

"Breakfast time!" Janylle interrupted, placing a steaming mug and plate in front of Kryssa.

She had scrambled the eggs with tomatoes and spices, giving them a rich red colouring, while the hot drink smelt of cardamom and ginger. Milky brown in colour, it was known by the locals as *chai* and had a rich spiced flavour.

"What, still no coffee?" Kryssa asked mournfully.

Braidon accepted his breakfast with a grin. Kryssa had been asking the same question all week. Coming from Skystead, she was used to coffee being cheap and easily accessible, but Chole was a long way from the main trade route south, and only the rich could afford it here. Fortunately for Braidon, he had never developed a taste for the bitter drink.

Janylle offered an apologetic smile. "Afraid it can't be had for any amount of money just now," she said, "with the troubles we've been having since your friend here decided to abdicate."

Braidon winced, though it was a timely reminder of his responsibilities. He took a sip of chai and began to eat. His thoughts turned back to what Kryssa had said, about Marianne taking inspiration from his father. Braidon could not reveal himself until he knew exactly what they were up against in Marianne and her allies.

It was the Knights of Alana he most feared. He wished

he'd never let them gain a foothold in Plorsea. But he had underestimated the void left when the Gods had fallen. Without magic, without Antonia, Jurrien and Darius to unite them, the world had fallen into disarray.

The Order had taken full advantage, offering their followers a new purpose—to aid Alana in her eternal battle against the False Gods. Once revered across the land, the Three Gods had become the enemy, tyrants who had enslaved the world with their magic.

And Braidon's own sister, once feared for her role as the Tsar's enforcer, had become their holy Saviour, the one who had freed the world from the False Gods. According to the Elders, she fought for them still, keeping the Gods at bay. And she needed her followers to be strong, so that their strength became her strength, to keep the horror of magic from returning.

It was a worthy tale, Braidon couldn't help but think, but he had been present when the Gods had fallen, when his sister had lost her life. He knew the truth. The Elders had spun the stories to suit themselves, to forge a new power, to bring their Order to life.

But amidst the falsehood, they had obviously discovered one truth: Marianne could not have found her new power alone. It was linked to the Elders and their awful rituals, he sensed. And while their new power did not have the same bite as old magic, it remained dangerous. Marianne had taken something from Ikar and used it to *command* them. She had even altered her rapier, somehow allowing it to cut through Devon's hammer.

Braidon wondered if he might do the same. The thought made his heart quicken. There had been a time when he could conjure illusions so perfect none could tell truth from reality. His grandmother, one of the most powerful Magickers of the age, had trained him to master his emotions, and by extension, his magic. In the end, his power had helped he and his sister to defeat their father.

But that was thirty years ago now, those powers long gone. And while Braidon still longed for the thrill, for the rush of magic burning in his veins, he knew it would never return.

"Where will you go, Janylle, if there is fighting?" Kryssa asked.

Braidon jerked back to the present at the sound of his friend's voice. Finishing his last bite, he rose and carried his dishes to the cast-iron sink. He filled it with hot water from a pot on the stove and began on the dishes, while Janylle answered Kryssa's question.

"Where *can* we go?" Janylle whispered. "Trola is barred to all. Lonia is the source of our problems, though they're quickly spreading across Plorsea. If it comes to it, I would go to Northland, but…I fear now that Dominic has found you, Braidon, he will want to fight."

Braidon sighed. "I wish I could refuse him, Janylle. But I am desperate. Plorsea needs every fighter we can find."

"Do not worry, *My King*," Janylle said, her voice lacking its usual warmth. "I'm sure you'll find plenty still willing to die for your crown."

"I didn't mean…" Braidon started, but when he turned to face her, the woman had already left the room.

Kryssa met his gaze instead. "That was tactful."

Braidon scowled. "It's the truth. Marianne has every advantage—an army, followers, a secret power. We have nothing! No one!"

"And yet Janylle freely opened her door to you, though it would be worth her life if the queen found us here. Now you're asking for her husband's life as well. It's too much."

"*Nothing* is too much!" Braidon exclaimed, slamming a fist into the counter. "Don't you understand? Marianne will destroy everything with her greed! Or have you not been listening to the stories? Her Knights are pillaging the countryside, slaughtering innocents for no reason other than who they send their prayers to. What else would you have me do?"

Kryssa could not match the fire in Braidon's eyes and she looked away. "I don't know, Braidon," she murmured. "Remember what we talked about in the forest? About a perfect world? Maybe I believe in that vision more than I realised. I know we cannot turn away from this fight—though every fibre of my being screams for me to abandon you to search for Gen and Pela. But even I cannot bring myself to ask the same of others."

A sigh slipped from Braidon and the anger went from him in a rush. He lowered himself into the seat alongside Kryssa. "I'm sorry," he said, "it is easy…to forget. I pray to whatever remains of the Gods for both our families. But their fate is bound to Plorsea, and we can cling to childish notions of peace no longer. We must fight if we ever want to see our loved ones again."

Their eyes met across the table and for a moment it seemed Kryssa might argue further. Then a *click* came from the front door. They were both on their feet in an instant, hands on sword hilts. They shared another glance, and then Kryssa slipped silently from the kitchen into the corridor. She returned a second later, Dominic following behind her.

He still wore his guard uniform, and a glance out the window revealed it was not yet even midday. The rain had grown heavier and water was beginning to pool in the street. Braidon frowned at the man, his blood running cold. Dominic was puffing and his face was red, as though he had run all the way from the gatehouse. Stumbling into the kitchen, he bent in two for a moment, catching his breath.

"Dominic, what is it?" Braidon cried finally, unable to take the waiting. Had something happened?

Dominic straightened, sweat dripping from his forehead. "It's the Knights," he gasped. "A new squad just rode in, from Lonia. They say they've come to cleanse the followers of the Old Gods. They're marching on the Temple of Antonia—now!"

17

Kryssa's heart beat faster as she followed Braidon through the winding streets of Chole. The rain was falling hard now, the sky dark overhead. Dominic led the way, reminding her of his wife's fear, that he would lose his life following Braidon's cause. But he was their only chance of reaching the temple in time. Chole was a maze, and while she occasionally caught a glimpse of the triple spires of the Earth Temple rising above the rooftops, they could have never found it without him.

At least it was within the city. Unlike Skystead, many in Chole still openly worshipped the Three Gods, even maintaining the Temple of the Earth. Though all knew the Gods and their magic had departed from the world, their memory was ingrained in the very stones of Chole. Magic might have once doomed the city, but it had been magic too that saved it, restoring the rains and returning life to the desert.

Perhaps that was why the Knights of Alana had not acted until now. While they had followers in the city, they were not numerous, and the dozen Knights who garrisoned their Castle would have been badly outnumbered if they'd acted against the temple. But according to Dominic, another twenty had arrived in the city not an hour ago— enough to cow a crowd of unarmed civilians.

"Braidon, what are we going to do?" she asked as they rushed through the narrow streets.

"I have a plan," Braidon replied shortly. He did not look back, and she almost missed his added, "I think."

She cursed inwardly. What could Braidon do against so many? He might have recovered much of his strength, but twenty Knights against the three of them was impossible odds, even for her father.

Thunder crashed above as Kryssa caught the first cry of voices from ahead. Rain lashed down and the streets were beginning to flood,. Water gushed around Kryssa's boots as the gutters overfilled. Movement came from nearby door-ways as people stepped out into the streets with arms outstretched. Kryssa only cursed. Rain was a rare blessing for the citizens of Chole, but it made their progress difficult.

They were soaked to the skin by the time they turned the last corner and found themselves standing before the Earth Temple. Dedicated to the Goddess Antonia, its triple spires rose high above their heads, while below, a long series of steps led up to the oaken gates. Marble pillars lined the way, beckoning the faithful to their worship.

Today though, the temple's visitors did not come to meditate. The Knights of Alana stood like statues facing the steps, rain streaming in rivulets down their armour. Lightning flashed overhead, and for a second Kryssa wondered if the Storm God, Jurrien, would return to strike them down. The boom of thunder followed before fading away, leaving the Knights untouched. She knew then they were alone, that it was up to them to stop these men.

"What are they waiting for?" she cried over the roar of the storm.

They stood in the narrow street, still unnoticed by the Knights, but it could not last.

Dominic pointed at the doorway to temple. "Them."

Kryssa followed his finger and saw with a start that the Knights were opposed. A dozen men and women stood at top of the marble stairs, arms linked to bar their enemies' passage. Many wore the green robes of Earth Priests, others the clothes of citizens. Terror shone from the faces of all. There was not a weapon amongst them, but still they stood unwavering against the steel of the Knights. Kryssa's heart swelled at their bravery.

Then fear touched her as a Knight's voice rose above the pouring rain. "Step aside, blasphemers," he cried. "We do not come for you today, only to destroy the lair of the Goddess, so that this city might be free of her taint."

"Not this time," Braidon hissed, starting across the street towards them.

Kryssa cursed, afraid Braidon's anger was going to get them all killed. They had no plan, no way to fight twenty Knights by themselves. But it was too late to argue. Dominic was already at the king's side, and loosening her sword in its sheath, Kryssa hurried to catch up.

"Turn back, foul Knights!" a faint voice carried from above.

Laughter came from the Knights as one lifted his sword. "If you will not flee, you will burn with your Goddess."

"You hold no power in Chole!" the voice spoke again. "Turn back, or may the Gods strike you down!"

"Our Saviour banished your Gods long ago," came the

laughing reply. "Now we have come to drive your kind from these lands." There was a crash of metal as they started up the stairs.

"Stop!" Braidon bellowed, his voice ringing from the walls of the temple.

Kryssa's stomach tied itself in knots as the Knights looked back and saw the three figures challenging them. The sight gave them pause, but only for a moment—then the laughter returned, rattling strangely from the iron helmets.

"What have we here?" a Knight called. "The champions of the Gods?"

"A champion of the people," Braidon shouted. He threw back his hood and the rain washed down his face. "I am Braidon, the rightful king of Plorsea!"

Kryssa cursed beneath her breath and edged closer to Braidon. If it came down to a fight, they could not allow the Knights to separate them, or they would be cut down in seconds. Not that they stood a chance regardless. Kryssa gripped the hilt of her sword tight, wishing she'd followed her instincts and gone seeking her daughter. She didn't want to throw away her life, not after fighting so hard to win it back.

Silence answered Braidon's declaration. Coming from Lonia, the Knights did not recognise Braidon, and in the thread-worn tunic and pants, he looked nothing like a king. After a moment the laughter came again, though this time there was no warmth in the sound. Slowly the Knights started back down the steps.

"King Braidon is dead," their leader said, "and should stay that way. You are obviously mad, poor man, and a blasphemer to stand with these sorry souls. But fear not, we will cleanse you of that evil. Along with this foul temple."

Steel rasped on leather as twenty swords emerged into the gloom. Lightning flickered again and Kryssa held her breath, calling upon Jurrien to strike them down, but still there was no answer. She sighed, a self-disparaging smile touching her lips. She knew better than anyone that the Gods were dead—her own adopted mother had witnessed that sad day.

Yet Kryssa couldn't help but look to them for guidance in her darkest moments. It was a childish habit, born from her days as a street urchin, when the Gods had been her only source of hope. Even now it gave her comfort, to think they might still exist somewhere, beyond knowing, beyond life. That they heard her prayers, and sympathised.

"The temple of Antonia has stood here for a thousand years," Braidon retorted. "The Three Gods are welcome in Plorsea. You are not."

"The False Gods are sacrilege," the leader of the Knights screamed over a boom of thunder. "It is our duty to wipe them from the Three Nations, on behalf of the Saviour."

"You do not speak for my sister," Braidon hissed, his voice was taut with rage. "I have heard enough. Begone from my nation, foul Knights."

The Knights exchanged glances, but the three of them stood alone against their twenty. Steel thumped on stone as they started forward as one. Kryssa cursed and drew her sword. Her hair was tied back, but water streamed down her face, obscuring her vision. She wiped it away with her free hand, wondering how the Knights were coping in their helmets and breastplates.

"Aim for their armpits, groin and throat," she said to Dominic. "That's where their armour is weakest."

Still wearing the uniform of the city guard, Dominic

nodded and hefted his spear. She could see his face beneath the half-helm, sensed his fear. But at least his weapon had reach—Kryssa would have to avoid their broadswords to get within striking range. She still wielded Derryn's—Pela's—short sword, and while it was light to hand, it could not pierce the heavy plate mail.

Then Braidon stepped in front of them, one hand raised to stay them. "No," he growled, though whether it was to the Knights or his comrades, Kryssa could not have said.

Either way, she was too shocked to disobey. Kryssa and Dominic stood staring after the king as he strode towards the Knights, his sword still in its sheath. The hairs lifted on Kryssa's neck as the rain swirled about Braidon. Wind came howling down the street, buffeting them so hard that she stumbled, but the king walked on.

Reaching the bottom of the stairs, the Knights paused at the sight of the lone man approaching. Kryssa read the confusion in their hesitation. She felt it too. What madness had possessed Braidon? Slowly the Knights spread out in a semicircle to surround him, ready to strike. Above them on the steps of the temple, the priests and citizens guarding them temple watched on.

Kryssa stared at Braidon, willing him to draw his sword, but he stood with his eyes closed, as though he were no more bothered by the Knights than a passing cloud. Swearing beneath her breath, Kryssa lifted her sword, preparing to go to his aid. Whatever madness he was attempting had obviously failed. She started towards him…

Boom.

A cry tore from Kryssa as lightning arced from the sky and struck the king. The air itself shook with the crashing of thunder. She staggered back, tossing her sword aside in terror that she would be next. Behind her, Dominic screamed and threw himself on the ground, his spear going skittering across the cobbled street. She stumbled towards the guard, unwilling to look back, to see what awful fate had befallen Braidon.

Screams came from the direction of the temple and she imagined the Knights scattering in terror. She had prayed to Jurrien for lightning, but the storm had missed its mark, had struck the king instead. The air hissed and crackled with the terrible energy. Kryssa hoped at least some of the Knights had been killed as well.

She had to know. Gathering her courage, Kryssa glanced back. Her heart lurched in her chest at the sight that met her. She stumbled to a stop, unable to believe, to understand. Braidon still stood where he had before, seemingly untouched by the storm. Lightning flickered in the street, its brilliant light dancing across the king's arms, gathering in his palms.

The Knights fell back, unmanned by the appearance of this new magic. Their screams were echoed by others nearby, as those who had heard the confrontation fled back to their homes. Even Dominic scrambled to his feet and took off running down the street. Decades had passed since anyone had witnessed such a sight, enough time for magic to become the unknown, something to be feared.

Kryssa could only stare in disbelief. Where had Braidon found such power? They had spoken of Marianne's powers, but this was far greater than what the queen had revealed in Malevolent Cove. Hope swelled in her chest, that maybe they could succeed after all, maybe they could win.

The Knights had realised it too, and they fell back as one, as though fearing the Gods themselves had returned to smite them. Even their leader fled, but one alone stood his ground. Kryssa thought he was too afraid to flee. Then he lifted his blade and pointed it at Braidon.

"You are truly Braidon?" the Knight gasped, as though fighting just to breathe.

Braidon laughed. The lightning in his hands flashed and thunder rolled from the stone walls. Screams came from the nearby buildings and the rest of the Knights hurled aside their blades and scrambled back.

"I am!" Braidon's voice rose above the thunder.

"Good," the Knight hissed. He seemed to resolve something in his mind, and straightening, he took a step towards the king. "Then this is nothing but illusion!"

The breath caught in Kryssa's throat. The Knight was right! She had only been a young girl during the days of magic, but Braidon had admitted it to her himself, that his power had only ever been to construction illusion. However Braidon had managed to recover his magic, the Knight had seen through his trick.

Hearing the man's words, the other Knights hesitated, though none dared return to support him. The sight of Braidon's power was too strange, too unknown for them to confront. Instead, they waited to learn what would happen.

Braidon refused to back down. A smile twisted his lips as he pointed a finger at the Knight. The blue fire lit his face, casting it in light and shadow.

"Are you sure, sir Knight?" he asked.

Drawing himself up, the man pointed his sword. "I am Sir Harrison, and I am sure!" He roared—and charged.

A finger of lightning leapt to meet him. Crackling and hissing, it swallowed the Knight up in its light, a brilliant glow that forced all but the bravest to look away. A deafening *boom* crashed over the street. Kryssa stared into the conflagration, thinking the Knight had been right, that Braidon's bluff had been called.

Then an awful scream pierced the thunder, a shriek of agony that went on and on. The lightning flickered, returning to Braidon's hands with another *boom*. Shadows danced across Kryssa's vision and for a second she could not see what had become of the Knight. Then her sight returned and a gasp slipped from her throat.

Braidon's lightning had left the Knight's armour aglow, the steel plating turned molten in its intensity. Kryssa slapped a hand to her mouth as a muffled cry came from behind the scarlet visor. It turned to a gurgle, fading to nothing as the life was seared from the unknown Knight.

The cold eyes of the king turned on the other Knights, aglow with power, the lightning still flickering in his hands.

"Go from here," he roared, "or die like your fellow!"

The Knights did not need to be told twice. They fled, racing down the street as fast as their heavy armour would allow. Braidon waited until they vanished around a corner before turning and striding up the steps towards the temple.

Still in shock, Kryssa took several moments to go after him. He was moving quickly, but as he neared the top of the steps she saw him stagger. At the entrance to the temple he paused, and the priests and citizens parted to allow him entrance. Kryssa caught him there. Dominic still had not returned, but at least he was safe. Together they stepped into the shelter of the temple.

Only then did Kryssa catch the king by the shoulder. "Braidon!" she said, then words failed her; all she could manage was a single: "*How?*"

Braidon turned towards her, and she gasped—his face had lost all colour. The king was as grey as he'd been when she'd dragged him from the waters of Malevolent Cove. It was as though the very life had been drained from him. Swaying on his feet, he offered a fleeting grin.

"Told you I had a plan," he said.

Then his eyes rolled back into his skull and he crumpled to the stone floor.

$\approx$ 18 $\approx$

Darkness. Water all around. Ruebyn's weight dragging her down. An icy cold seeping into her bones…

Pela jerked as an iron hand grasped her by the ankle. A scream burst from her lips, bubbling in the silent depths. She kicked out in desperation, feeling herself sinking, desperate to free herself of the Knight. Her boot connected with something solid, and the pressure was gone. Distantly she heard a reverberation, of a panicked man falling forever into the darkness.

But she'd lost her grip on Ruebyn. She could not leave him behind, not after failing Siden. Pela waved her arms and connected with his shirt. She grabbed him and kicked out for the surface. Her lungs burned and her strength was all but gone. Desperation drove her on, the awful craving for oxygen.

All around her was pitch black. There was no telling how far they had sunk, no way of knowing they were even rising. The surface could be a hundred yards above, or one, and she would never know. But growing up in Skystead,

Pela had never been far from the water. She was a strong swimmer. All she could do was keep on, keep kicking, and pray to all the Gods…

A splash marked the sudden return of sound as Pela broke the surface. Gulping in great lungfuls of air, she hauled Ruebyn up and turned him on his back. He was cold as ice and for all she knew he'd already bled to death. There was no way of telling. She spun around and around, searching for light, but could not even see the tunnel above.

How far had they fallen? And where were they now? She needed to get out of the water. Her body was already shaking, and soon the water would suck the last of the warmth from her. Pela strained her eyes, seeking out some glimmer that might offer hope, a way out. But there was nothing, only the impenetrable black—

There!

It was just a glimpse, the slightest spark, so faint she might have imagined it. But there were no other options. She struck out through the water, dragging Ruebyn with her. Her strength, already robbed by the battle above, faded every second, leached away by the icy cold. She could sense the abyss lurking below, the infinite depths waiting to claim them both. Fully clothed in steel, the Knight had never stood a chance, but they might, if only she could find the edge. But her every gasp, every desperate splash, seemed to be swallowed up by the void, as though the chamber might stretch out forever.

But that was impossible. They were under a mountain.

It has to end somewhere.

Pela tried to reassure herself, but in the icy darkness, despair clung to her and she found her mind drifting. What would it be like to sink beneath the surface and know no more? Would her soul be able to escape this place, or would even her spirit be trapped here, forever?

The fear built in her chest, a primal, animal thing that screamed for her to run and never stop. She picked up speed, desperate to escape the pool. She even considered releasing Ruebyn and letting him sink into the depths. What did she care for him? She owed him nothing, after how he had treated her. He was probably already dead, his weight a burden she did not need to carry. And yet she kept on with him, unable to let go.

When she finally found the bank, it came as such a surprise that Pela shouted out loud—then cursed and started to sink. She'd blindly slammed her free hand into a rock and now she could barely keep them both afloat. Ruebyn started to slip from her grasp and she had to claw desperately at the rock to keep them both from slipping beneath the surface.

Fortunately, the lip of rock was not high, and half-dragging, half-crawling, she managed to pull herself and Ruebyn from the water. There she collapsed to the ground, gasping and sobbing while her entire body shook, barely able to believe she'd survived, that she'd escaped.

The air was still cold, but at least it was better than the water. Lifting herself up, she put a hand to Ruebyn. Her heart sank at the ruddy cold of his skin, but she would not give him up for dead yet. She reached for him, accidentally hit him in the face, then moved her fingers down to his chest. She was sure she would find a great gaping wound, but after a long moment of searching, she could only find a narrow cut that ran across his ribs.

Breath hissed between her teeth as she sat back on her haunches. The Knight's blade had barely nicked him. The impact with the water must have knocked him out, but the wound was certainly not mortal. Moving her fingers to his neck, she reassured herself that he still had a pulse.

She smiled despite herself. At least his life was not on her conscience. And poor though his company might be, she was not alone.

Lying down on the stone, she wrapped her arms around her chest in a vain effort to keep warm. A shiver wracked her and she cursed. The darkness pressed in, impenetrable, and unable to take it any longer, she closed her eyes.

The fear came creeping back, that she would be trapped down there forever. If she could not find a way out, how long would it take to perish in this place? Days? Weeks? Months?

Weariness pressed on her, the exertion of the past few hours catching up. Though she was damp and freezing, she could not resist the call of sleep. Her mind drifted into dreams of summer skies and open mountain fields…

Pela woke sometime later, unable to tell how much time had passed. The darkness was unchanged. Silence still enveloped the cavern. She was warmer though—she'd rolled up against Ruebyn in her sleep. With a start, she shoved him away, and he woke.

"What the…where…*what the hell?*" his voice shouted in the darkness, followed by a *crack* as he struck some unseen projection of rock. A string of curses followed.

"Ruebyn, calm down!" she hissed, reaching out a hand to him. There was no telling whether anyone was still listening for life in the tunnel.

"Slave, what have you done?" he growled. His fist struck her hand and she flinched back.

"Nothing!" she snapped. "This was your precious Knights, *remember?*"

There was a long pause, and she hoped he *did* remember what had happened above.

"That…that was a dream, surely?" he murmured. She heard him patting himself down. "I dreamt they murdered me…No, you've done something—treacherous witch!"

"It was barely a scratch," Pela said, her voice dripping scorn. "And the only thing I did was save your stupid life. More than you deserve, after what you did to me."

"After…" Ruebyn trailed off. Unable to see his face, she could not tell his reaction, but after a moment, he continued in a sullen tone, "You defied—"

Pela struck him in the face. She barely connected, her blow glancing off his chin, but even so she heard him scramble back.

"You attacked me!" he gasped. "That's a death sentence."

Pela would have hit him again, but he was too far away now. She laughed in his face instead. "I'm already under a death sentence. Weren't you listening up there? The Order wants me dead."

"A mistake, surely…" Ruebyn murmured. "Stupid thugs. You don't even weigh ten stone, how could *you* have killed an Elder?"

His disdain for her ability stung. Pela drew herself up. "It wasn't hard," she hissed. "I stabbed the bastard in the back, and he died like anyone else. And if you don't shut up, you'll be next!"

Ruebyn fell silent at that, and after a moment Pela sighed, thinking she'd frightened him. "I—"

"*You killed an Elder!*" he shrieked, his voice taut with rage. "They'll burn you for that!"

Pela's anger rose in answer to his. "They already tried,"

she sneered. "Besides, if I burn, you're going to burn with me now! Or didn't you hear? They think we're lovers."

"Fools," Ruebyn gasped. "I'll take you back and explain…"

"Like hell," Pela snarled. "I'm not going anywhere with you."

A stunned silence answered her declaration, then: "But…you have to!"

Pela's laughter floated up into the darkness. "I don't have to do anything. I'm free now, and I'm not giving that up for anyone. You can do what you want, but I'm not going back."

As she spoke, Pela felt a pang of guilt. She had left Genevieve behind, to suffer alone. But she had spoken the truth—she would never return to the torments of the mine. She would rather die.

"But…I can't go back without you! They'll…" He trailed off, as though unable to speak the words.

"Kill you. Torture you. Send you to the mines?" Pela snapped.

Ruebyn said nothing, and in the silence she sensed his despair. Guilt touched her then. With all his learning and his noble upbringing, it was easy to forget the overseer was little more than a boy. He was as naïve to the world as she had been just a few short months ago.

Pela sighed. "I'm sorry I dragged you into this, Ruebyn, I am. I didn't mean too. But you're right: you can't go back."

It was a long time before Ruebyn answered. "Then what do you propose we do?"

"Find a way out of this cavern, for starters," Pela replied. Tentatively she reached out and patted him on the shoulder. "Come on, we're in this together now. Take care, there's a big pool of water back there, I've only just started to get dry. I'm sure I saw light this way." She tugged him in the direction she was indicating.

"Thank the Saviour," Ruebyn whispered.

"I doubt Alana had anything to do with it," Pela muttered.

"What would you know about the great Alana, murderer?"

Pela whirled at him. "Me? Oh, I don't know. How about the fact my uncle was *Devon,* someone who actually *knew* her!"

There was a stunned silence, then: "Your uncle is the *Consort of Alana?*"

"Was," Pela said sharply. She started off again, taking care with each footstep to ensure there was earth in front of her. In the pitch-black, it would be easy to fall into a pit they could never climb back out of. "Your precious queen killed him."

"I don't understand any of this," Ruebyn whispered after a while. "Marianne is your queen as much as ours."

Pela snorted. "*That* was what confused you? She only took the crown by trying to have her husband murdered."

"None of this makes any sense," Ruebyn groaned.

"Then don't worry your pretty little head about it," Pela snapped. "Now keep it down, I'm trying to concentrate."

To her surprise, he obeyed. They continued through the cavern, their boots squelching with each step. Pela's had been close to falling apart before going into the water; they were disintegrating beneath her now. She prayed they would hold together a little while longer, at least until she could get safely away.

Ahead, the light seemed to grow, but as they neared, Pela began to suspect it was not the surface at all. She slowed, suddenly fearing they were heading back towards part of the mine, and Ruebyn walked straight into her back. She cursed and stumbled forward—but the ground was not where it should have been.

Pela started to fall, only for her boots to strike rock several feet down. The surface was slippery, taking her feet straight out from underneath her, and she fell painfully on her backside. Then water was gushing around her and she was sliding down the smooth stone, picking up speed.

Ruebyn's cries chased after her and she realised he had fallen as well. There was nothing she could do for him. She dug in her heels but the rock was slick and she raced on towards some unknown end.

The slide ended in an abrupt *splash*. Pela gasped as the icy water embraced her, though this time it was no deeper than her knees. A cry came from behind her, followed by a second splash as Ruebyn tumbled into the shallow pool. He thrashed about, still shouting at the top of his voice, before finally realising he wasn't sinking. Stilling, he whipped his head around, eyes wide.

"Gah!" He spat out water.

At the same moment, Pela realised she could *see* him. She swung around, heart suddenly racing as she raised her fists. If they were back in the mine…

A gasp whispered from her lips. She'd been right about the light not coming from the surface, but it wasn't manmade either. Overhead, a thousand pinpricks glowed on the low ceiling, each like a tiny star in the night sky. If she hadn't known they were underground, she might have thought it *was* the sky.

"What are they?" she whispered, still staring at the lights.

They filled the whole cavern, leading away into the dark

depths, following the path of an underground stream. Each was so faint it could not have illuminated even a finger, but together, the thousand tiny stars cast enough light to reveal the cavern around them. The cascade down which they'd fallen stretched up behind them, its waters dancing over milky white rock. The creek ran from an opening above, beyond which the cavern was like a black hole in the night sky.

"They're glow worms," Ruebyn answered quietly. "They live in the darkness, near water. They use their glowing tails to attract insects."

"Magic," Pela whispered

"No—" he started, but she waved him to silence.

From where they stood, the stream continued through a canyon of silver rock. Stalagmites rose from the earth like daggers, reaching for the ceiling where their opposites hung. The magic lights continued around a bend in the cavern and out of sight.

They stood together in silence for a while longer, taking in the glory, the wonder. Pela wondered if they were the first humans to have ever set eyes on this place. Then she thought of the awful, ugly coal mines somewhere above, and decided it was a blessing that this secret place remained untouched.

Finally Pela stirred, realising the cold was slowing draining the feeling from her legs. Rousing herself, she turned to her unwilling companion.

"Come on, Ruebyn" she murmured. "Let's see if this stream leads us outside."

Caledan gritted his teeth and strained against the chains binding his wrists. The shackles cut into his flesh and the bolt attaching the chain to the wall wobbled slightly, but did not come loose. Finally he slumped panting against the stone, though the wrist chains kept him from sitting. He had stood there for more than a day so bound, and now his whole body ached.

The dungeon was far beneath the citadel and the air was like ice, his breath misting before his face. The steel shackles burned his skin and he still wore the same clothes he'd been taken in, more suited to the summer heat. Marianne had disposed of him here after her questioning, and he had no idea how long she planned to keep him. Would she leave him forgotten in the tiny cell to rot? Or would she drag him back out one day soon, to be executed in a display to her followers?

Either way, he had no doubts about his fate. Even if he could escape the shackles, the heavy iron door to his cell would not be opened by anything but the key. Silence seemed to permeate the very air; not a whisper or scream reached him from outside. His offence had earned him a place of honour in the dungeons and he was alone on this level, far below where they kept the common criminals.

His only light came from a candle in the corner. He watched the tiny flame as it flickered, the candlestick growing shorter with every drip that ran down its side. It was burning low now.

Movement came from the corner as a rat emerged from its hiding place. It crept across the cell towards Caledan—until he shouted and stomped his feet. The vermin vanished back into its bolthole—only to return a few minutes later.

Caledan shuddered as he imagined the tiny teeth feasting on his wasting flesh. Did Marianne plan to feed him? Since she had left him here, no one had come, and his stomach roiled with hunger. How long would it take for starvation to kill him?

The candle flickered again. The stub was burning just above the pool of wax in the plate. He swallowed, wondering what would become of him in the darkness, what mad creature the queen would find when they finally hauled him out.

The meeting with the queen was his only source of hope. The strangeness of the encounter, her talk of his motives, and Braidon, had left him confused. And there had been no fear in her eyes, no worry that he was a threat to her. Why, then, had she brought him to her apartments? And why had she then sent him here, like a toy she was suddenly tired of?

She had certainly seemed a different woman than the Marianne he had met on the sands of Malevolent Cove. There she had been indomitable, crushing any enemy who stood before her, equal parts hatred and rage in her eyes. Yet in front of her son she had been kind, maybe even shown love.

Clang.

Caledan's head snapped up as something sounded from the corridor outside. The breath caught in his throat. Had the time for his execution already come? Or had they finally decided to feed him?

Footsteps sounded beyond his iron door and light shone from the crack beneath. He strained against his bindings one last time, desperate to free himself, to give himself a chance. But the chains held him fast.

A *bang* came from his door as the locking mechanism was opened, followed by the squeal of rusty hinges. The brilliant light of a lantern spilled inside, momentarily blinding Caledan, and he was forced to look away as four silhouettes stepped into his cell.

"So this is the assassin?" a man asked, his voice echoing loudly in the stone confines.

"The sellsword," Marianne answered.

Caledan's heart quickened as he saw Marianne standing nearby, a familiar face at her side. It was the young Elder from Townirwin, though Caledan had never learned the man's name. He had also been in Malevolent Cove, so must have some standing within the Order's hierarchy. A Knight stood at the man's shoulder, while one of the Queen's Guard shadowed Marianne.

"Doesn't look like much," the Elder murmured.

With a grin, he drove a fist into Caledan's midriff. Unable to pull away, Caledan tensed, but the weight behind the Elder's blow still forced the breath from his lungs. Gasping, Caledan lost his footing and fell sideways. The chains rattled as they caught him and held him up, tearing at his flesh.

Stifling a groan, Caledan straightened. "You punch like a child," he spat.

The Elder did not rise to the bait. "There is strength in this one. I will enjoy taking his life force."

"He was sent by Braidon, Servo," Marianne murmured, her tone reprimanding. "Though you insist the man is no threat, he continues to interfere."

Servo waved a hand. "It matters not. The sellsword failed, didn't he? This only shows Braidon's weakness, that he must resort to such underhanded dealings."

"He is the rightful ruler of Plorsea, whatever we might claim. So long as Braidon lives, he remains a threat."

"To you," Servo murmured.

"To all of us," Marianne snapped. "Or do you think Braidon would forgive the Order so easily, should he rise again?

"To all of us, of course," Servo agreed. "Though Braidon would find that what we have unleashed is difficult to undo."

Marianne's lips twisted into a scowl. "Yes, though I must say, I find your methods distasteful, Servo," she said, folding her arms. "Perhaps you could educate me, but I cannot see what point these cleansings serve, not when so many take place without an Elder present. Such waste! Or have you shared the secret knowledge with your Knights now?"

"Of course not!" Servo hissed. "That knowledge is sacred."

Marianne rolled her eyes. "Then why the killings? I thought you were a logical man, Servo. What point do they serve, other than to turn the people against us?"

"The blasphemous must be cleansed to serve the Saviour!"

"Truly?" Marianne's voice took on an awed tone. "These cleansings are to aid Alana in her eternal battle?"

"So it is writ—"

Marianne threw back her head and howled. "Please, spare me, Servo. You do not expect me to still believe that tosh? I was married to the woman's brother. There was nothing special about him—quite the opposite. Why would it be different for the sister? No, the Order gave me comfort when I was a child, but I am a woman now. Do not spout your stories to me."

Servo's face had grown dark as Marianne spoke. Now he stepped in close, casting her in shadow. "Careful, My Queen," he growled. "I have stood for years with my brothers on the side of the light, casting back the darkness of the False Gods. It is time for your adopted peoples to join that fight—or perish. No longer can Plorsea enjoy the privilege of freedom without the sacrifice. The Saviour demands they have a hand in these cleansings, so that all are bound to our cause, so that they may never return to their False Gods."

"I see," Marianne smiled. "And if I forbid it?"

"That would be a very bad idea, *My Queen*," Servo said, his voice barely a whisper.

"These deaths do not serve my purpose," Marianne insisted.

"They serve *mine*," the Elder growled.

"Then you had best do what you promised," the queen snapped. "I want Braidon dead, not sending assassins to my city!"

Servo laughed. "Then you should have done it yourself. Perhaps it is your resolve that must be questioned. After all, you had him in your power. So many years as his wife… maybe you grew to love him?"

"I am no one's wife," Marianne replied sharply. "Not now, and never again."

"My apologies," Servo replied, though the smile on his face suggested otherwise. He took a step closer, so that he towered over the tiny queen. "Though *never* is a long time."

Marianne's ice-cold eyes did not flinch away, and when she spoke, her voice barely rose above a whisper. "Does that trouble you, Elder?"

"Not overly much," Servo said simply. "I am sure your mind will change one day, when confronted with the *right* suitor."

The queen did not move so much as a finger, but suddenly Servo folded in two, as though struck by a blow to the stomach. He staggered backwards and crumpled to the ground. Steel hissed on leather as swords flew from their sheaths. The Knight and Queen's Guard stepped between Marianne and Servo, their blades pointed at the queen's throat.

Caledan stared, shocked by the turn of events. Marianne did not seem surprised, though her eyes burned with rage. "Kildren," she said, looking at her Guard, who still pointed his sword at her. "You're dismissed."

The man only smiled. "The Saviour was ever my master, Marianne. You cannot—"

He broke off as Marianne waved a hand. A sharp *crack* came from the man's neck. The colour drained from his face and he crumpled to the floor without a sound. He lay there unmoving, eyes fixed on the ceiling, forever unseeing.

Silence followed, then Servo began to laugh. Groaning, he lifted himself from where he'd fallen and stepped over the dead man.

"Such fire!" he gasped, waving his Knight back.

A scowl twisted Marianne's face and she raised her hand again, but this time something gave her pause.

The Elder smirked. "That's right, My Queen," he hissed. "You might have collected some small degree of power in Malevolent Cove, but do not forget who offered you that gift."

"Oh, I do not forget," Marianne snarled. "But I refuse to be manipulated any longer. Isybelle told me what you did before she died, about the role the Order played in arranging my marriage to Braidon."

Servo studied her for a long time, as though contemplating a fly trapped between his fingers. His hazel eyes shone in the lantern light. The tension built, an almost palpable pressure that hung over the room, as if a silent battle were being fought between them. Caledan could sense something gathering, a swirling power that throbbed at his temples.

Finally it was Servo who broke, his eyes flicking away, though he did not seem overly perturbed. Still smiling, he wandered to where Caledan hung from his chains. Keeping his gaze averted from Marianne, he spoke in a calm voice:

"You have gathered more power than I had thought." His eyes were dark as they looked on Caledan. "Perhaps I made a mistake, offering you our knowledge."

"I swore revenge on all those who had a hand in my marriage," Marianne replied. "My father, the council, you and your Elders, you took an innocent girl and made her your puppet. You robbed me of my life—why should I spare you?"

"I'll admit, we did not expect you to act against the Lonian council." Servo faced the queen. "That was a bold stroke, proclaiming yourself queen of both nations."

"They had outlived their usefulness. As, it seems, have you."

Marianne clenched her hand into a fist and Servo staggered, clutching at his chest. Faster than Caledan would have believed possible, the Knight leapt at Marianne, broadsword raised to strike her down. She spun, redirecting her attack, and the Knight slammed to a halt, his blade just inches from her face. Her blue eyes bored into the man and his plate mail groaned—then caved inwards as though struck an awful blow.

A wheezing groan whispered from behind the iron visor. Steel rattled on stone as the sword slipped from the Knight's hands. Then his feet went out from underneath him and he crashed to the ground. Marianne stood staring down at him for a moment, then returned her attention to Servo.

The Elder had regained his feet. He stood alone now, but remained unperturbed.

"You must tell me, Marianne, where you found such power," he murmured. "We gave you only one life in Malevolent Cove, but you have stolen far more than that."

Marianne smirked. "Your way is not the only way, Servo," she said. "But I will tell you nothing. Are you ready to meet your precious Saviour?"

To Caledan's surprise, Servo laughed. "Oh, it would be a delight, but alas, I do not think today shall be the day."

"Oh?" Marianne hissed.

"No." Servo's voice took on a steely tone as his gaze roamed the cell, pausing on each of his fallen men. "It is a shame to lose such worthy followers. I shall pray that the Saviour welcomes them into her sacred army. But I have many more servants, while you stand alone." He paused, his eyes returning to Marianne. "Tell me, how goes little Calybe's lessons, My Queen?"

Caledan's heart lurched at the man's words, recalling the innocent boy that had come running into Marianne's apartment. For a second, Marianne wavered, her eyes betraying her fear. Then the mask settled back into place.

"Leave him out of this, Servo," she growled.

The Elder straightened, clutching his arms behind his back. "Oh, the boy will remain safe enough—so long as you behave, *My Queen*," he replied, his voice cold now. "But should you ever forget your *duty* again, well…I cannot make any promises. Now, I think we are done here, yes?"

He watched Marianne for a second, then laughed and walked past her out into the corridor, taking the lantern with him. His footsteps faded away, until finally there was silence.

The breath left Marianne in a rush and she sank to her knees. Head bowed, she sucked in great mouthfuls of air, as though she had just run a great race. Time stretched out, the only sound the soft whispers of the queen's sobs.

Caledan stared at her, lips parted as though to speak, but he was unable to put words to what he'd just witnessed. Seeing the rawness of her grief, he found himself wanting to go to her, though they were bitter enemies.

Finally the queen grew silent, and lifting a hand to her face, she wiped away the tears. Rising, she turned to look at Caledan. The grief was gone, her face a perfect mask of composure once more, though he could see the rage burning in her crystal eyes.

"Now you understand?" she whispered.

20

It was night when Pela and Ruebyn finally stumbled from the cave back into the world, and at first Pela did not even realise they'd escaped their rocky tomb. The tall cliffs of a canyon rose to either side of them and the night was clear, the pinpricks of stars so similar to the glow worms that her exhausted mind did not recognise the change.

Then Ruebyn grabbed her, his face alive with excitement. "We're free!" he exclaimed, hugging her in his excitement.

Blinking, Pela struggled to understand what he was saying. "We did it?" she asked, then finally noticed the brilliance of the full moon shining above. Her mouth fell open, then: "We did it!" Despite herself, she hugged Ruebyn back, unable to believe it was true.

Then she released him and sank to the ground, weeping at the joy of it. *She was free!* No one in the mine knew she was alive, no one was coming after her. She could have howled her triumph from the mountaintops—if she'd had the strength to manage more than a slow shuffle.

"What is it?" Ruebyn asked, uncertainty replacing his happiness.

Seeing his confusion, Pela wondered how he could not know, how he could not realise what this meant for her, to be free of the darkness, to have her life back. But then Ruebyn understood little but what his books and teachers had taught him—nothing of the real world. She shook her head.

"Nothing," she said, rising. "And everything. I'm free."

The smile slipped from his face at her words and he took a step back. That Pela could understand. She was free, but her victory had cost the boy everything. The distance restored between them, he swallowed. She knew what he was going to say before he said it.

"I should take you back, and beg for their forgiveness."

Pela smiled, good-humoured despite his words. Nothing could take away her happiness now—certainly not Ruebyn. "I can see three problems with your plan." She started off along the narrow canyon before he could reply.

"What?" he shouted, running to catch up with her.

"One," Pela said, counting on her fingers, "I won't go willingly, and I doubt you have the strength to carry me."

She glanced over her shoulder at him, waiting for a reply, but he said nothing, and she went on.

"Two—you don't know how to get back to the mines."

"I could find my way," he snapped.

"Really?" Pela asked, raising one eyebrow. "Where do you think we are?"

He paused, his eyes flickering across the night sky. Then he pointed at one of the cliffs. "That way is east."

Pela was impressed, though she kept her face carefully neutral. "Well and good, but have you ever travelled in the mountains? Do you know which gullies are passable, which are dead ends? What would you eat, and how will you stay warm at night?"

"It's summer," Ruebyn retorted. "How hard can it be?" But even as he spoke, a cold breeze blew through the canyon. Their clothes were still damp from the stream and he quickly wrapped his arms around his chest.

Pela chuckled. "It's the *end* of summer. Or is it autumn already?"

"See, you don't know any better than me!"

"I lost track of time down there," Pela snapped. "And I grew up in Skystead." When Ruebyn only offered a blank look, she sighed and explained. "It's a small town in Plorsea, wedged between the mountains and a fjord. My mother and grandmother and I spent many nights camped in the mountains when I was young. I even went by myself a few times, when I was older and our inn was empty."

"Your family ran an inn?" Ruebyn sounded surprised.

"Yes," Pela said gruffly, "but that's besides the point. You'd starve or freeze to death long before you found your way out of these mountains.

Ruebyn fell silent at that and they continued, the only sound the crunching of stones beneath their boots. Pela surveyed their surroundings as they walked. The overseer wasn't the only one who could read the stars, and it seemed the canyon was winding north. Better than east, though she would have to find a pass west over the mountains eventually. Without any means of removing her collar, she could not return to Lonia without being recognized as a slave, though that was the fastest way home to Skystead.

Her only other option was to seek refuge in Trola—but that too might prove fatal. The nation's borders had been closed for decades and they did not take kindly to interlopers. Once Trola had been the jewel of the Three Nations, but their army and many of their cities had been crushed by the Tsar. Impoverished as they were, surely they would not turn Pela away, not when they learned of her plight.

"What was the third reason?"

Pela started and almost fell, her foot slipping in the loose gravel. They were still following the stream that had led them from the cave, its babbling waters winding slowly through the narrow gorge. She frowned at Ruebyn, not understanding, and he rephrased his question.

"You said there were three problems with my plan."

It still took her a moment to recall what he meant. She chuckled. "Your Knights are many things, but forgiving is not one of them. It might have been an accident, but you still helped cause the death of one of them. They would kill you for that alone."

Ruebyn scowled. "What would you know, slave?"

His words struck Pela like a blow and she staggered to a stop. Slowly she turned to face him, a terrible rage building within her. She wanted to hit him, to beat him as he had beaten her. Her ear still ached where his whip had struck. Unconsciously she lifted a hand to it, then flinched away as she touched the swollen flesh.

"My name is Pela," she snarled, "and if you ever call me a slave again…" She took a step towards him, leaving the threat unfinished.

Ruebyn scrambled back, and losing his footing, crashed to the ground. His mouth hung open in a great O and he lay staring up at her, shocked by the outburst. Pela leaned in close, fists clenched so tight she felt the nails cutting into her palms.

"And I'm never going back, not for anyone."

But even as she spoke the words, Genevieve's face flashed into her mind. Quickly she turned away before

Ruebyn saw the panic in her eyes. She had not told Lewis about the huntress…but what if Lewis or the surviving Knight figured out their connection? For a moment, Pela wavered.

Then memories of her time beneath the earth came rushing back, the constant cold, the dust and dirt and danger, the darkness. Her gaze lifted to the clifftops at the thought, seeking to reassure herself. There was a distant glow to the sky and she realised the dawn must be nearing. She sucked in a breath, watching the light, and grew calm once more.

No, she could not go back, not even for Genevieve. The huntress could look after herself. Pela started off again, her mind turning to the future. For the first time in an age, she wondered who else had survived the Cove. She could not imagine Caledan succumbing to the currents, but Braidon had been in a terrible way when the boat capsized. As for Kryssa…Pela could not bear to think of her mother's fate. And if she had survived, Pela would have to tell her about Genevieve. The thought was not a pleasant one, and she quickly forced her mind back to the present.

Boots crunched on stone as Ruebyn started to follow her again. Pela turned to scream at him to go away, but the words died on her lips. The boy's face was a picture of abject misery, his eyes downcast and his cheeks lined with sorrow. She sighed. He might know how to read directions from the stars, but he was helpless out in these mountains.

"What is it like, where you're from?" she asked, wanting to understand him better.

"Loud, busy," he answered immediately. "The streets are always packed, people are always going somewhere. I hated it. But my teachers always came to our house. The court-yard was my favourite place to study at this time of year."

His voice took on a dreamy tone. "We have a fountain that runs in the summer. At sunset the light turns its waters red —a trick the architects designed when they were building the house. Though it only works for a month."

Pela snorted. "What a waste of time."

"Yes, I imagine someone as uncultured as yourself would think so," Ruebyn replied in a haughty tone.

Laughing, Pela climbed over a cluster of boulders blocking their passage. The stream threaded its way beneath them and emerged on the other side, making the climb down difficult. Pela managed it, but a splash came from behind her as Ruebyn landed one boot in the water. He cursed, and she giggled despite herself.

"So why did you come to the mines then?" she asked. "If you enjoyed your little courtyard so much?"

Ruebyn's face grew tight. "Duty. The Order is a rising power in Lonia, especially now, with our new queen ruling from Plorsea. My parents sent me to the mines to court their favour. I'm to be a Knight one day…" He trailed off, and swallowed visibly before continuing. "Though now…my family will surely disown me, or our name will forever be tarnished."

His voice was thick with despair and Pela sighed. "Maybe you'll get lucky?" she offered. "Braidon could win. Then you'd be a hero, for rescuing me."

"Your king is dead," Ruebyn replied. "Surely even *you* must have heard that?"

Pela rolled her eyes. "Were you not listening to anything I said back there?" When Ruebyn only gave a blank look, she scowled. "I said Marianne *tried* to kill her husband. But she failed. Braidon is alive, or at least I pray to the Gods he's still alive. He was with my mother, and she's…full of surprises."

There was a long, disbelieving silence. "You truly are mad," Ruebyn said finally.

Pela ground her teeth, but it was obvious the conversation was going nowhere and she let the topic drop. They pressed on for another hour as the sun brightened the horizon, only stopping once when they crossed a set of animal tracks. There were only a few, in a patch of sand near the stream, imprints of a giant paw. The sight made Pela's blood run cold and they quickly moved on, eager to leave the creature's territory behind.

Pela's legs were aching by the time the canyon finally opened out into a broad gulley. The stream raced ahead, merging with a larger river threading its way down the mountain. Large gravels covered the entire three hundred feet width of the valley. In places the river split around islands of patchy vegetation, forming half a dozen channels that would make a crossing difficult.

A second cliff on the other side rose even higher than the canyon from which they'd just emerged, leaving them only two paths to choose from. Pela looked upriver, finally seeing the challenge that lay ahead. Sunlight touched the western mountains, turning their snow-capped peaks a fiery red and causing her eyes to water. They rose ten thousand feet overhead or more, impassable to all but the most experienced of climbers. But there would be a pass, some way through—she had only to find it.

Pain lanced through her temples and Pela was forced to look away. Her eyes were burning and she cursed, remembering the debilitating pain of her last trip to the surface. The light was growing rapidly now and she could barely keep her eyes open. She started upriver, desperate to find shelter before it became too bright for her to see. Ruebyn followed her in silence.

Thankfully, clouds rolled in with the break of day and Pela managed another hour before she could go no further. Finding a narrow opening in the cliff, she crept inside and settled in the shadows, hardly caring if Ruebyn followed. Stars swirled cross her vision and the headache was a constant now.

Jagged stones filled the crevice and Pela cursed as one tore through her boots. She sank to the ground anyway, wracked by pain and so exhausted she could not take another step. The rocks were cold but with the heat growing outside, she savoured their touch against her skin. Laying her head against her arm, she stayed there for a while, catching her breath.

Finally the aching from her boots became too great and she sat back up. Removing the offending items, she tossed them aside and sank her head onto her arms again. Rock crunched as nearby, Ruebyn tried to make himself comfortable.

It didn't take long for the heat Pela had built up during the walk to dissipate. Her clothes remained damp despite the morning's warmth, and after half an hour she was shivering. Ruebyn crouched nearby, his eyes distant, as though pondering some puzzle in his mind. Every so often a tremor would wrack him, though to his credit he did not complain.

Pela gritted her teeth, wondering whether they should continue. But just a glance outside made her eyes burn. The clouds had lifted and the gravel outside their tiny cave was aglow with sunlight. It was so bright it hurt to look in the direction of the entrance, even with her eyes closed. She would be as blind and helpless as a newborn kitten outside their measly shelter.

Cursing, she turned away. They were horribly unprepared for a trip through the mountains, even in summer.

Still weak from starvation and poorly clothed, they would be lucky to survive another night.

"So…" Pela jumped as Ruebyn spoke into the silence. She swung to look at him and he froze, mouth hanging open. But when she said nothing, he managed to swallow his fear and continued, "Pela…did you really kill an Elder?"

She sighed. Outside the wind howled down the valley and fingers of ice seeped into their cave, making her shiver. The cold of night clung to the stone and she longed to crawl outside and bathe in the sun's heat. But she remained, fearful of its intensity. She turned Ruebyn's question over in her mind.

"Yes, Rueben," she said finally. "Though he was the only person I have ever killed."

"Why?" he whispered, his face twisted by a frown.

Pela laughed. His face was an open book, and she knew he truly could not imagine why someone would commit such a deed.

"Because he was trying to murder my mother," she replied. "For worshiping the Three Gods."

"False Gods," Ruebyn corrected, though there was no force behind it. His eyebrows knitted together and he added, "There are some in the Order who believe such…cleansings are necessary."

"My mother and her friends never hurt anyone," Pela murmured. "They only went to pay their respects. They were happy—*I* was happy. Then your Elders and their Knights came, with their swords and their hatred, and changed everything. You think I am the monster, for killing one of your precious Elders, but I never wanted any part of this. I am only what they forced me to become."

Ruebyn had no answer to that. He sat rolling a rock between his fingers, eyes downcast, lips pursed. After a while

Pela realised he was not going to respond at all. She lay back down, exhaustion weighing on her like an anchor. It was still up for debate whether she could trust the former overseer, but nor could she remain awake for another second. Her eyes fluttered closed, and she slept…

When she woke, Pela was glad to find that her clothes had dried and the sun was dipping towards the distant horizon. Finding her eyes were coping a little better, she allowed herself to hope they could adjust to the real world again.

Ruebyn lay asleep nearby, mouth hanging open and giving the occasional grunt. A smile touched her lips. Like this, she could almost imagine him as an innocent young man, rather than the young noble that had called her a slave. It was a shame she had to wake him.

Pela replaced her crumbling boots and kicked him lightly in the shins. He woke with a start, eyes swinging wildly in his skull as he raised his fists. Seeing her standing over him, the fright faded.

"What is it?" he grumbled, rubbing sleep from his eyes.

"Time to go," she murmured, gesturing outside. "If you're lucky I might find us something to eat."

It would be tough at this time of year, but she had spotted some brambles amongst the vegetation dotting the gulley, and hoped there might still be some late berries. It was too warm to find trout in the streams, but if they were lucky the salmon might still be running.

The thought reminded her of the paw print they'd spotted earlier and she left Ruebyn to get ready, wanting to scout out the way ahead. The Mountain Felines near Skystead rarely approached humans, but the Sandstone Peaks were wild and few people ever set foot here. The creatures might not be possessed of the same fear. Outside, she saw no sign of a large animal, but that meant little with such a creature. One might be lurking a few feet away, concealed by its camouflage, and she would not know until it was upon her.

"Where *are* we going?" Ruebyn asked as he joined her outside.

"Someplace safe," Pela murmured, not wanting to delve into her plan. It would be hard enough to make the journey to Trola without Ruebyn knowing their destination. Given that their odds in the western nation weren't a lot better than in Lonia, she thought it best to keep the former overseer in the dark for as long as possible.

Ruebyn said nothing. Pela took his silence as anger and faced him, but the boy was not looking at her. Her heart lurched as she followed his gaze downriver and saw movement. Quickly she grabbed Ruebyn and dragged him back against the cliff-face.

"How did they find us?" she hissed.

"The Elders have their ways," Ruebyn said miserably.

Braidon woke to a pounding in his head and pain shooting through every inch of his body. It began in the base of his skull and radiated outwards, lighting his entire being aflame. His stomach lurched and before he could stop himself, he rolled onto his side and vomited.

Laughter greeted him, but when he tried to open his eyes, the light burned directly into the back of his skull. He quickly closed them again. Groaning, he lay his head back down. There was cold stone beneath him and he sighed as it took some of the fire from his skull.

"Where am I?" he asked, knuckling his temples.

"Inside the Earth Temple," Kryssa replied. "After you passed out, I thought it was probably best if the whole city didn't see you incapacitated."

"Did it work?" he asked.

His mind was hazy, his memory of what had happened outside the temple little more than a blur. He recalled the Knight's challenge, his sudden fear at being called out, then cold anger, the determination to do the impossible. After that, nothing.

"By 'work', do you mean burn the Knight to death?" Kryssa asked, her normally cool tone touched with awe. "If so, then yes, it worked."

Braidon tried opening his eyes again. This time he found it slightly more bearable. Carefully he pushed himself up—then cried out as pain sliced his forearms. His strength gave out and he collapsed back onto the stone bench. He lay staring up at the blue sky, struggling to catch his breath. It was a moment before he realised the strangeness of where he was.

They weren't quite as inside the temple as Kryssa had led him to believe. Around them was a garden of soft green plants and blooming flowers, orchids and roses and a dozen other varieties he did not know. A bird chirped from the branches of a nearby tree and the air carried the rich, earthly scent of the forest. It was warmer too, as though they were cut off from the world, in some hidden refuge.

Sitting up more carefully this time, he massaged the muscles in his arms. With the better vantage point he saw they were in a broad courtyard enclosed on all sides by marble walls. Windows dotted the stone, and he glimpsed men and women wandering past them in the green robes of Earth Priests. The three spires of the temple stabbed skywards in a triangle overhead, and from the position of the sun, Braidon guessed it was nearing noon.

He frowned. What had happened to the storm? And had it not been afternoon when they'd come? He turned to Kryssa, his heart beating faster.

"How long was I asleep?" he asked.

"A day," Kryssa replied. "Don't worry, no one knows.

The priests are good at keeping secrets. Though word of your feat outside has definitely gotten out."

"Why do you say that?"

"Oh, you'll see," Kryssa said ominously.

Braidon was feeling a little better now, though in truth he was surprised he was alive at all. He'd pushed himself too far, though it had been impossible to know before he attempted it. At least he'd started small, or he would already be dead.

Kryssa sat on another bench opposite Braidon, her gaze fixed on where he sat. His vomit had fallen amongst the roses and he felt a touch of embarrassment. Then his anger returned, that he'd been forced to go so far, to take such a risk. He pushed himself to his feet, but his legs were not ready and he staggered several steps before Kryssa caught him.

Lowering him to the bench alongside her, she leaned close, as though she might learn his secrets in the depths of his eyes.

"How did you do it?" she whispered finally, sitting back.

Braidon felt a thrill as he recalled what he had discovered, the power he'd tapped. It had been so simple, in the end, little different than accessing the magic he'd once wielded. Though what he'd done had been a forbidden thing then, so dangerous only the desperate or foolish would consider it.

"The same way Marianne found her power," he replied, "only without using someone else's life force."

Kryssa frowned, pondering his response. It took a moment for his words to seep in, but finally her eyes widened with understanding.

"You used your *own* life force?" she whispered. "Isn't that…"

"Dangerous?" Braidon croaked. "Extremely. Could I have some water?"

Rising, Kryssa waved to a passing priest. Words whispered between them and he disappeared, returning a minute later with a jug and plate of dried fruits. Braidon downed the entire thing in one gulp, then placed it beside him with a sigh. The food quickly followed. The water cooled his throat and eased the pounding in his head, while the sustenance cleared his mind.

"It…was still a better option than using another's life force." He shuddered at the thought.

"Agreed!" Kryssa replied. "Though…I still don't understand, how could you create true lightning, if with all your power as a Magicker, you could only make illusions?

Braidon smiled. "My *magic* came from the Light Element. It allowed me manipulate energies to create illusions. But it was not my *magic* that summoned the lightning. My own life force created it, not some gift from the Gods. Though, I'll admit, it *was* an illusion until the Knight challenged me."

"Oh?" Kryssa asked.

"My life force is like a candle before a forest fire compared to the magic I had before. Its energy is limited, and I wanted to avoid exhausting myself. So I created the illusion of lightning. But when the Knight called me out, I was forced to make it real. And that almost killed me. I should not have used so much energy…but it is a new skill. I didn't realize it would drain me so quickly."

"Wait…" Kryssa murmured, "but if this was possible all along, why did no one ever think of it?"

"Because we were taught *never* to use our life force as power," Braidon replied. "Another second back there, and I would have killed myself with the lightning."

"But then…" Kryssa's eyes became great circles in her face. "That must mean anyone could do the same as you?"

"Yes," Braidon replied. "With practice and meditation, this is a power everyone could use. Though I fear those who are not careful, who lack discipline, may end up destroying themselves with the effort."

"A gift for all," Kryssa whispered.

"Ay, and one the Elders have sought to keep from their own people. So much for the world being equal beneath the Saviour."

Kryssa snorted and started to turn away, then swung back again. "That must be why they hate us!" she gasped.

Braidon frowned. "Sorry?"

"You said this new power requires meditation. Followers of the Three Gods still practice the old ways. Sooner or later, someone was bound to stumble upon this discovery."

"You're right," Braidon exclaimed, then: "And while they were hunting down believers, they were also finding a way around their own limitations. By stealing another's life force in the moment of their death, they could cast as many spells as they wanted without costing themselves anything."

The smile slipped from Kryssa's face. "And that means we're still not powerful enough to face the queen. With their Knights loose across Plorsea, who knows how many innocents they've murdered and turned into power?"

"Yes, we must be careful. Now, what is happening outside?"

Kryssa smiled at that. "You'd better come see," she said, rising and offering Braidon her hand.

He took it and she led him from the courtyard into the corridors of the temple. Several priests were walking past, but they stopped when they saw him, their mouths falling open. Braidon nodded and followed Kryssa, their whispers chasing after him.

Movement came from ahead and Dominic appeared from around a corner. The man had obviously returned home to refresh himself, for his chainmail was shining as though recently polished and he appeared well-rested. He snapped a salute at their approach.

Braidon chuckled and clapped him on the shoulder. "None of that, Dominic," he said. "You helped me when I had no one…err, almost no one. I won't forget it."

Nodding, Dominic fell in with them. "Thank you, sir," he blurted out, then: "They're waiting for you, sir!"

"Who?"

The man looked confused. "Everyone, sir."

That's going to get wearing, Braidon thought with a sigh, before realizing what the guard had said. He looked at Kryssa to demand an answer, but she laughed before he could get the question out.

"Relax!" she gasped. "Come on."

She shoved him ahead, where two priests were just pushing open the doors of the temple. The hinges moved without a whisper and sunlight burst into the corridor. Braidon's heart started to race. Not knowing what waited outside, he paused on the threshold, but another gesture from Kryssa sent him forward.

A roar greeted him and Braidon reached for his sword, thinking they were under attack. Then he realised he was alone at the top of the temple steps. The sound came from below. A crowd packed the narrow street so tightly they could barely move.

Braidon stumbled forward another step, his legs still weak, and a sudden silence fell. The hairs on his neck stood on end and he realised every eye in the street was upon him.

Marble columns lined the stairwell, leading down to where the crowd waited—waited for him to speak!

He sucked in a great breath and stepped up to the top of the steps. Opening his mouth, he searched for words to offer them, but they refused to come. Then his eyes were drawn out over the surrounding rooftops, across the city to where another building rose from the dust of Chole.

The stone walls of the Order's Castle lurked like a shadow on the horizon, a distant threat, a promise of violence. He had won the first battle, but within those walls waited the Elders and their Knights. They would know what power he had used, knew he'd been bluffing. If a second Knight had challenged him, Braidon would have failed.

His heart beat faster as he turned to the crowd. The Order would come for him soon and he did not have the strength to stop them. But those below did. They were the army he had prayed for, the strength he needed to topple Marianne. He clenched his fists, thinking of how she had dismissed him, the contempt in her eyes as she'd looked at him. But he would show her, would take back what was his, would make the world right again.

And it would start with Chole.

"My people!" he cried, his voice echoing down the street. "Your king has returned!"

Whispers rose to greet his announcement and Braidon smiled. He let their confusion go on for a while longer, and then raised his hands. The silence was instant.

"I know you have questions. Fear not, they will be answered in time. But know this—my wife is a traitor. Marianne tried to have me murdered, so that she might take my throne. Now she sells us to her Lonian masters, would let their Knights march into your great city and burn your temple. She would take away our heritage, our history and beliefs. I will not allow it!"

A roar met his words as the crowd lifted their arms in salute. Braidon stood poised on the edge of the steps, listening to their shouts, allowing them to build themselves into a frenzy. Then he spoke again.

"The Order demands your obedience, demands you bow down to their Saviour. They would rob us of our freedom, would cast down the Gods that served us faithfully for so many centuries and replace them with a lie. Well I say, we will not stand for it! Follow me, good people of Chole, and we will cast down their Castle and drive their foul Knights back from whence they came!"

The voices of the crowd were deafening now, rumbling up from the street like an earthquake. Braidon's heart soared. He had his army. Together they would march on the Castle and drive the Knights from Chole, make the city safe from their evil. Then let Marianne try and stop him. An army could starve on the arid plains around Chole, and while the walls were old, they were solid, rebuilt during his father's reign.

Braidon dragged his sword from its sheath and thrust it into the air. "Follow me, for Plorsea!"

❧ 22 ❧

Pela and Ruebyn walked all night, the way lit only by the stars and the soft glow of the moon, but there was no losing their pursuers. The flicker of their torches was a constant presence, far below but always there, always threatening. Pela had no idea how they'd been found so quickly, how they even knew she was alive. All she understood was the sickly feeling of despair in her gut, the fear of being caught again, of being dragged back into the dark.

She'd been surprised when Ruebyn continued with her. There had been a moment when she'd thought he would betray her, but in the end his sense of self-preservation was greater than duty, and they'd set off upriver in silence.

Pela led them up the gulley for hours, following the whispering waters of the river. She was afraid to leave the open ground, for while they might lose their pursuers in one of the narrow canyons that opened in the cliffs every few hundred feet, they might just as easily meet a dead end and be trapped. Even in the broad gulley they had trouble. Several times they were forced to cross one of the smaller river channels when their way was barred by a cluster of boulders or a high bank of earth. The lack of light slowed their progress, but there was no help for that.

As the night progressed, Pela sensed their pursuers drawing closer. She was sure they hadn't been spotted yet, but when daylight came it would only be a matter of time before they were caught. If they continued in the light—*if* she could continue—they would be seen. Then their pursuers would know exactly how close they were, and hunt them all the more desperately. In Pela's exhausted state, they would be overhauled within hours.

But nor could they find a place to hide, for the hunters were following their tracks.

Their only hope were the winding mountain paths. That meant leaving the broad gulley and entering the maze of canyons.

Ruebyn stumbled along beside her now, his face a mask of misery, arms wrapped around his chest. It was colder this night, and no matter how hard they trekked, the icy air leached the warmth from them. The wind howled down from the mountain peaks, carrying with it the promise of winter. Out on the riverbed there was no shelter and each blast was like a thousand tiny needles striking Pela's skin.

As the moon closed on midnight and the torches remained stubbornly on their trail, Pela finally made the decision. A dark opening in the cliffs beckoned ahead, and she altered their course. They forded a narrow stream, not even bothering to remove their boots, and tramped up to the canyon.

Pela studied the entrance as they approached. It spanned twenty yards and appeared to narrow further inside. Enough to keep the worst of the wind from them. The cliffs on either side were not so much vertical as steeply sloping—in daylight she might have even been able to climb them. Below, the ground was dark and she could see little but the sheen of water against the far cliff.

"We're going in?" Ruebyn asked.

"We don't have a choice," Pela replied. "We have to lose them before daylight."

"How far does it go?"

"How would I know?" Pela snapped.

She moved inside without looking back. Gravel crunched beneath her feet, but in several places it turned suddenly to sand, sinking her boots to the ankle. She swore. They would need to be more careful not to leave tracks, or they'd never lose the hunters.

"It could end in a hundred yards, or several miles," Pela explained a few minutes later, feeling guilty for yelling. "There's no way to tell."

"Oh," Ruebyn replied, his voice taut. She could tell he was trying to mask his fear. "Do you really think we can outrun them?"

Pela glanced back. Ruebyn was watching her with a mixture of hope and awe, that she might be able to lead them to safety. A smile touched her lips.

"I may have…overstated my abilities slightly, earlier," she admitted, "but so long as we're alive, we have a chance. My grandmother always said that."

Ruebyn offered a grunt that might have been agreement, and she laughed. "She was a very positive person. Something about the Goddess Antonia saving her life when she was younger?"

"The…that's blasphemy!" Stones rattled as Ruebyn staggered to a stop.

She glanced over her shoulder and raised an eyebrow. "It's the truth. Devon was there, and Braidon—your precious Saviour too, actually. Maybe if we survive, you could ask Braidon the truth about his sister, and what happened that day."

"I have nothing to say to your king, even were he actually alive," Ruebyn grated. "Thanks to him, Lonia is a poor shadow of its former glory. His father's taxes drove our farmers off their land, leaving their crops to rot while our people starved."

"Braidon is not the Tsar," Pela replied, "and don't forget, it was *his* sister that freed us all from their father's grasp."

"Why do you think the Order of Alana was born in Lonia?" Ruebyn shot back. "We do not forget. Alana's sacrifice redeemed her past, freeing us from the Tsar and the False Gods both. But her brother never paid for his crimes."

Pela sighed, realising there would be no changing his mind. "And what about Marianne?"

There was a pause before Ruebyn answered. "She is loved by the people, like her father before her, but my own family is somewhat less trusting. They fear the Plorseans have corrupted her, that she might be a snake in devil's clothing."

"On that at least, we can agree," Pela chuckled.

They let the conversation fall quiet for a while then, concentrating on the way ahead. The canyon walls grew narrow around them and the ground sloped upwards, making the going difficult. Several times they stumbled into the blackberry brambles Pela had spotted the night before. The thorns tore at their clothes and skin, but at least they were able to collect berries as they walked. The fruit was dried by the long summer, but it was the first food they'd found since emerging from the cave.

Another hour passed and Pela started to wonder at

something Ruebyn had said earlier, about differing philosophies within the Order. But hundreds had come to Malevolent Cove to witness the Great Sacrifice—surely such an event could not have gone unnoticed by others, even by someone as sheltered as Ruebyn.

"Ruebyn, what do you know of the Great Sacrifice?" she asked finally.

A frown creased her companion's forehead. "It has occurred on the night of the solstice, every ten years since Alana's sacrifice. But it is a secret of our Order—how do you know of it?"

Pela snorted. "Because I *was* it," she said, her heart sinking. Ruebyn had claimed to disbelieve the more violent tendencies of the Order, but his actions said otherwise. "They tried to burn my mother and me alive, to please your *dear* Saviour."

"What?" Ruebyn gaped. "That's…not possible. The Great Sacrifice is not a person, but an act, a gathering of the faithful to send our strength to the Saviour. Only the most faithful, the most devout, are allowed to attend."

Coming to a stop, Pela turned to stare at him. He seemed earnest, but then perhaps that was all part of the lie. The Order would protect its secrets at all costs, and she could not dismiss the thought Ruebyn was lying.

Then the face of the Elder Lewis flickered into her mind. He'd been rigid in his own way, but he'd believed her, and had condemned the Order's cruelty. Perhaps she could give Ruebyn the benefit of the doubt as well.

They continued, the ground rising steeply now, and each footstep grew more difficult than the last. They had lost altitude in the caverns, but Pela sensed they had already made that up—and then some. Her lungs burned and no matter how deeply she inhaled, she could not seem to catch her breath. A pounding began in her head as they twisted their way up the canyon, taking turns at random whenever the way ahead split.

At times the stream vanished, its waters disappearing into hidden holes in the earth—then reappearing seemingly from nothing, bubbling up between the stones to continue its inevitable journey from mountains to ocean. They paused more often now, as the air grew colder and Pela's headache became a constant. Ruebyn said nothing, just kept on with his head down, eyes on the treacherous path.

Eventually they staggered to a stop. Ruebyn slumped against a boulder and slid to the ground, his head falling to his knees. A groan whispered from his chest as he toppled sideways.

Frowning, Pela stumbled across to where he lay. A tingle of concern passed down her spine as she gripped him by the shoulder and found him cold to the touch. He moaned again as she turned his head to study his face.

"I'm okay," he croaked. "Just...so...cold." His teeth began to chatter and a great shiver wracked him.

Pela cursed. They hadn't made it half as far into the maze as she wanted. And she was sure they'd left enough tracks for even a passable hunter to follow. But it was clear Ruebyn was in no state to go on. She stood and moved back down the path, scanning their backtrail. The canyon remained dark—no sign of their followers yet. Perhaps they'd missed where Pela and Ruebyn had left the river. She could only hope.

Returning to Ruebyn, she studied him a moment. He lay huddled on the ground with his arms wrapped around his chest. Every so often a shudder shook him and his teeth would chatter again. She might have left him there and continued alone, but after coming so far, Pela could not even contemplate the thought.

There was no help for it. Lying down beside him, she held out her arms.

"What…are you…doing?" he stammered, the cold making his speech difficult.

"It's the only way to warm you," she snapped, suddenly angry.

Why was she doing this? The boy was only slowing her down, putting her at risk of being captured. He was so cold she began to shiver herself. It only fed her anger. Why hadn't he said something sooner?

They lay there in the darkness as the minutes ticked by. Wedged between the boulder and the canyon wall, they were protected from the wind, and sharing one another's heat, they began to warm. Slowly the anger left Pela. Ruebyn had no idea what he was doing out here, had never even been in the mountains. It was a miracle he'd made it this far without exposure and the altitude striking him down.

Eventually Ruebyn ceased shaking and his eyes slid closed. Knowing she could not afford to do the same, Pela studied their surroundings. The walls of the canyon were steeper now, falling from above in shelves rather than a slope. Ledges had been formed in the sandstone, creating vertical steps every thirty feet.

An idea came to her. The rough sandstone would not be difficult to climb, even for a novice. With the ledges they could rest and recover between sections of cliff. She gauged the distance. It was maybe two hundred feet to the top. A tough climb, but if they could escape the canyon without leaving trace of their passage, they would leave their hunters clueless.

Deciding they'd rested enough, Pela rose and approached the wall for a better look. There was no question it would be dangerous. Despite the shelves, a single slip might still send them tumbling the entire way to the bottom. They could not afford mistakes. She didn't need to ask Ruebyn to know he'd never climbed a cliff before.

Even so, she continued her inspection. The ledges ran horizontal to one another, but looking back the way they'd come, she realised they were not in line with the valley floor. The ground fell away steeply from where she stood, so that the height of each ledge grew greater relative to the path.

Her heart lifted as a new plan came to her. Maybe they didn't need to climb all the way to the top. Each ledge was only a few feet wide, but it was enough to negotiate if they were careful. They might be able to backtrack down the canyon using one of the ledges, while their hunters passed unknowing below.

Ruebyn was just waking when Pela walked back to where he lay. A smile touched his lips when he saw her, but it quickly vanished when she explained her plan.

"You can't be serious?"

❦   23   ❦

"We can't outrun them," Pela snapped at Ruebyn, "not before daybreak."

She didn't like the plan any more than he did. Heights were not one of her many fears, but she had no desire to die falling from one of those fragile ledges. But she could see no other alternatives. There were only a few hours of darkness left. Even in the shadows of the canyon, she would not last long in the day, if it proved as bright as yesterday.

The stone would leave no trace of their passage, but once they were further down the canyon, they would have to be as silent as mice. If their pursuers heard them, Pela and Ruebyn would have nowhere left to go.

"Come on," Pela said quickly, before she lost her nerve. "If we can get to the third shelf, I think we'll be okay. It looks the widest. You go first, and I'll help your feet find the holds from below."

Ruebyn's wide eyes stared at her, but the time for hesitation was over. At least the moon was bright enough for them to see. He approached the wall as though it were his mortal enemy and took hold of the rock. The thirty feet to the first ledge were the easiest, the cliff sloping slightly away from them, so they barely had to use their arms to make the climb. It still cost precious time though, as they had to take care not to leave any scuffs or broken rocks that might give them away.

Reaching the first ledge, they took a moment to gather their strength. But with time in short supply, they soon pressed on. Here the wall was steeper, but the sandstone was well-worn, offering plenty of holds if you knew where to look for them. Unfortunately, they might as well have been invisible to Ruebyn. Pela was no expert herself, but she did her best to direct him to each new perch. She could do nothing to help with his hands, but she braced his feet with her palms each time he moved, ensuring his boots did not slip.

Even so, Ruebyn was panting hard by the time they reached the second ledge. One look at his pale face and Pela knew he would not make it to the third. He was too exhausted, too inexperienced. If they attempted it, he would fall.

She glanced down the canyon, but in the gloom there was no telling whether they were high enough to pass unnoticed by their pursuers. It would depend on how many torches the hunters had, whether they looked up.

It was going to be a mighty gamble.

"Come on," she murmured, drawing Ruebyn carefully to his feet. "This will have to do."

Ruebyn nodded, though he knew she'd been hoping to make the third shelf. Pela took the lead, heading back the way they'd come but now some sixty feet above the canyon floor. The ledge was narrower than the one above and she had to take care with each step, lest her crumbling boots slip from the sandstone. Ahead she glimpsed the distant flicker of torchlight. She was terrified of knocking loose a rock at the wrong moment.

They followed the ledge through the darkness, their way lit only by the cold light of the moon. It hung in the sky like a silver shield, their only hope of safely navigating the tiny shelf. But as the orange glow of flames drew nearer, Pela realised it might also be their doom. They were some hundred feet above the ground now, but if anyone looked up the two climbers would be clearly visible in the moonlight.

A glance at the cliff-face above revealed it was just as sheer in this section of the canyon. She could probably have managed it, but not Ruebyn. Only closer to where they had entered the canyon had the rain and wind eroded the rock enough that they might both climb it. They needed to wait for their pursuers to pass below before they could get that far.

She could do nothing to help Ruebyn now, for the ledge was too narrow for her to turn around. Pela had told him to place his feet where she did, but it would only take one mistake to send him plunging to the canyon floor.

Fear touched Pela as the brilliance of a torch appeared around the next bend in the canyon. Her heart jilted to a stop and she gripped the cliff-face with one hand, waving for Ruebyn to stop. His eyes were glued to his feet and he did not notice the gesture. Their pursuers were just fifty yards away now—any movement would be sure to draw their attention.

"*Stop!*" Pela hissed as quietly as she could.

Ruebyn's head jerked up, his eyes widening as he finally saw the orange glow. He froze, his hand shooting out to grasp at the cliff-face. But the rocks here were slick and the ledge narrow, and he missed by an inch. Panicked, he staggered another step, trying to catch his balance. Pela held her breath as his foot slid perilously close to the edge, but the Gods or his Saviour must have blessed them, and Ruebyn managed to finally catch himself.

The breath whistled between Pela's teeth as she crouched, gesturing for Ruebyn to do the same. The moon still shone in all its brilliance; there was not a cloud in the sky. They must be as small as possible, and hope their pursuers did not look up.

Ruebyn offered a shaky smile and crouched where he stood, not daring to move any closer to the cliff-face in case he slipped. Pela was glad. If he fell, it would be over for both of them.

The flickering glow marched steadily up the canyon. Squinting against the glare, Pela made out a dozen shadows beneath half as many torches. Too many to stand a chance against, even if they'd been armed and in any shape for a fight. Only their wits could save them from so many. Pela closed her eyes and prayed to whatever deity remained to watch over them.

The soft *crunch* of boots on stone echoed from the cliffs as their pursuers neared. Voices whispered in the darkness, though she could not make out what was being said. Pela guessed none of them were too pleased to be in the mountains at night, with all the perils that entailed. There weren't many Baronians in these parts, but she still hadn't forgotten the animal tracks they'd crossed earlier.

They belonged to a Feline, or maybe a Raptor—either could tear a man in two. Even those below would struggle to defeat such a beast, let alone herself and the unskilled Ruebyn. She doubted he'd ever even held a sword—not that she'd been any better before starting this journey.

Then again, maybe his noble parents had trained him in the martial arts. Pela knew next to nothing about his youth, other than his story about the courtyard. Was there anything else to know? Sadness touched her at the thought of such a closeted existence. She'd roamed the walls and hillslopes of Skystead at will. A life spent surrounded by walls must have been almost as much a prison as the one she'd just escaped.

Well…not quite.

Flames glinted off steel armour as the hunters passed below. There was no doubt now—it was the Knight that had come for her in the mines. She could not understand how they'd been tracked so easily. Was that another skill the Lonians had developed with their strange engineers? She swallowed, the collar pressing hard against her throat, and she touched a finger to it. Could it be helping them to find her? She prayed not, for she'd already tried to crack it open with a rock—to no avail.

Pela held her breath as the group passed below, but not a soul looked up. Slowly the hunters continued through the canyon past them. Letting out a heavy sigh, Pela was about to stand, when a sharp *crack* rang from the rockface. She swung around in time to watch cracks spiderweb outwards from where Ruebyn crouched.

There was another *crack*, then abruptly the ledge gave way. Ruebyn leapt for the wall but in the darkness his fingers missed the holds, and crying out, he tumbled back. It seemed he would fall all the way to the bottom—but at the last moment his hand flashed out, catching a jagged edge. A scream tore the night as the rocks sliced his flesh, but he did not let go.

Pela stood frozen, too shocked to act. Shout echoed around them, followed by the crash of boots against gravel.

Their pursuers were returning, racing down the gorge towards them. There was no way they would miss Pela standing on the ledge this time, nor the young man clinging to the cliff-face for dear life.

With an effort Pela would not have thought him capable of, Ruebyn almost managed to haul himself back up to safety. But at the last moment his strength gave in and he slumped back, only an elbow propped over the lip holding him in place. His terrified eyes searched the darkness, finding Pela standing across the gap the landslide had left.

"Pela!" he gasped.

A tremor shook her. She looked from him to the cliff-face above their heads. It would be an easy climb for her. She could be over the top before the Knight and his followers reached them. Without Ruebyn to slow her down, she might just get away. She gathered herself, trying to summon the courage to make the leap.

Ruebyn must have seen the look on her face. His mouth fell open, as though to beg her not to leave him. But no words came out, and after a second he pressed his lips tight together again. Tears shone in his eyes as he glanced down.

Pela followed his gaze. Shouts echoed up from below. The hackles rose on her neck as she caught the pungent scent of their oil lanterns. The light hurt her eyes, but she could see the frantic gestures the hunters made as they reached the bottom of the cliff. Even if she saved him, there was no way they could both get away.

Their eyes met and Ruebyn clenched his jaw. "Go," he said. "I'll say you held me against my will."

Pela didn't need to point out the absurdity of the idea. She had no weapons and in her half-starved state, Ruebyn had a good forty pounds on her. And even if she had beat him in a fight, there was no way she could have forced him to come.

"*Go!*" he said again.

Another tremor shook Pela. She put a hand to the cliff-face, readying herself for the climb. The shouts grew louder, the glow brightening to illuminate the scarlet of the sandstone. Within minutes they would scale the cliff and take him. Then Ruebyn's life would be worth less than the lowliest of slaves. They would not let him die easily, not so long as she was free.

The breath left her in a rush. Without giving Ruebyn a chance to object, she leapt across the gap in the ledge. His mouth dropped as she landed beside him, but wisely he said nothing. Grasping him by the back of his shirt, Pela mustered her strength and heaved. With much scrambling of boots and puffing, she hauled him up, until they were both crouched on the ledge again.

"Why did you do that?" Ruebyn gasped. "Now they're—"

"Don't say it," Pela croaked, closing her eyes.

Her chest swelled as she drew in a breath. She struggled to keep the terror from her face, but her legs were shaking so badly that if she stood, Pela was sure she would have tumbled over the edge.

The scuffing of shoes on stone whispered from below as the hunters began to climb. A shudder raced down Pela's spine as she imagined their knives, the pain they would inflict for her defiance. She had killed an Elder—and a Knight—and they would ensure her death was a long time coming. Or maybe they would simply lock her up as a slave again, with a new overseer to inflict his daily cruelty, for the lack of food and strength and light to slowly waste her away.

Pela stood suddenly, teetering on the edge. A shrill

keening came from her throat, her every hair standing on end. She would not go back, not now or ever. What madness had made her go back for Ruebyn? Now it was too late to flee. She could see the hunters, just a few feet below, their eyes aglow in the light of their lanterns. Even if Pela ran, in her weakened state, she would be overhauled within a mile.

"Pela, what are you doing?" Ruebyn gasped.

Ignoring him, Pela stared down at the sheer drop. The first of the hunters were drawing close. Thickly-muscled and dressed in leather armour, the man was no Knight, but then he didn't need to be to doom Pela. He was climbing away to their right, so that they could not keep him from gaining the ledge. Others were just a few feet behind, moving to cut them off from either direction.

Another shudder shook Pela as she fixed her gaze on the canyon floor. Dotted with boulders, it was some hundred feet below. A dozen watchers looked back at her, and she closed her eyes. It was high enough to kill her, if she…

Pela swallowed, not wanting to finish the thought, to think about what she was about to do. Letting out her breath, she released the wall, and swayed on the edge.

"Pela!" a voice carried from below.

Her eyes snapped open and she stared down at the silhouetted figures, searching, seeking…

Genevieve's face appeared amongst the hunters, lantern held high. Her eyes were wide, pleading.

"Stop!"

※ 24 ※

Caledan shivered as he stepped into the queen's apartments, the cold of the dungeons still clinging to him. Rubbing his wrists, he crossed the room and stepped out onto the marble balcony. Sunlight greeted him and he closed his eyes, savouring the feeling of the sun on his face. It was almost enough to banish the creeping horror he'd felt below. Almost.

Footsteps came from behind him as Marianne stepped out into the light. She joined him, leaning against the marble baluster and looking out across the city. The granite and marble rooftops of Ardath spread out below. Many of the mansions still sported the gold and silver enamelling from ages past, when the wealth of Trolan and Lonian trade had flowed through Plorsea's borders. For others, time and neglect had left the marble tarnished, and the precious furnishings had long since been pawned off to see their owners through the hard times.

Yet despite such efforts, many buildings now stood empty, their doors and windows boarded up, the owners fled in search of greener pastures. For Caledan, the sight of Ardath's degradation was yet another reminder of Braidon's failures.

"I still don't understand," he said finally, turning to the queen. "What do you want from me?"

Marianne's eyes were fixed on some distant point, far out beyond the walls of Ardath and across the great lake, but at his voice she blinked, slowly focusing on him.

"Servo spoke the truth—I am alone here," she murmured. "I knew before the…event in the dungeons that the Elders had betrayed me, but I needed to know the extent of their duplicity. I cannot trust my Queen's Guard, cannot trust anyone—not with the life of my son. So I would have you serve me."

It took a moment for the woman's words to sink in. Caledan blinked, then started to laugh. "You think you can trust *me*? After I tried to kill you?"

The queen's cheeks crinkled as she shared a conspiring smile. "I am not mad, I promise you!"

Caledan's laughter faded as he realised she was serious. "Why would I serve you?"

Marianne shrugged. Returning to the apartment, she pulled a bell beside her desk. A servant appeared as she faced Caledan. "You must be hungry?"

Caledan's stomach gave an audible rumble. He hadn't eaten for more than a day. The queen laughed and waved for the servant to bring food and drink. As the man departed, she wandered across to the sofa and seated herself. She patted the cushion beside her, but occupied by his hunger, Caledan ignored the gesture.

"I believe you are a simple man, Caledan," Marianne said then. "Despite your claims of friends and loyalty, you have abandoned Braidon, in what is surely his time of greatest need. In the end you are still a sellsword, your loyalty given to whoever offers the most gold. And I would pay handsomely indeed."

Caledan's head jerked up. He stared at the queen, turning her words over in his mind. Perhaps what she'd said had once been true, though even in his youth that one overarching goal had driven his every decision. He had accumulated wealth and skills, a reputation as a formidable foe, but always he was plotting to achieve his own ends. If not for the peace treaty between Lonia and Plorsea, he might have gotten close to Braidon and had his revenge long ago. Without a war to fight, a sellsword had had little chance of coming within a hundred yards of Braidon.

"You're wrong," he said finally. "My motives have never been simple."

"Oh?" Marianne gave a knowing smile. "Pray tell me, I am intrigued."

"It was a means to an end," he admitted. Taking the seat beside her, he looked her in the eye. "You are not the only one with a grudge against the *good* King Braidon."

Marianne arched one thin eyebrow, but when she said nothing, Caledan continued:

"I have loathed him for thirty years, since the day his sister stole the magic from this world, and doomed my mother to death. Alana destroyed my family, while her brother inherited a kingdom." He found himself staring into Marianne's sapphire eyes, seeking to pierce the carefully constructed veil she held about herself. "I made it my life's undertaking to set the balance right."

"A noble cause, revenge." Marianne pursed her lips. "Perhaps you are a more complicated man than I first thought. But why then do you align yourself against me?

Why save Braidon's life, when I could have taken revenge for both of us?"

A spark lit in her eyes as she spoke of her husband, and for just a moment Caledan saw her hatred, a mirror of his own. He swallowed, but before he could respond, the door cracked open and the servant reappeared, a silver platter in hand. Crossing the room, he set it down on the coffee table beside the sofa, bowed, and vanished back outside.

Another rumble came from Caledan's stomach as he eyed the spread laid out on the platter. There were a half a dozen different cheeses—some streaked with blue veins, others soft and creamy, and still more dotted with nuts and sliced fruits. Saltines and olives and pickled peppers had been laid around the edge of the board. A second plate held enough cakes to satisfy even the worst sweet tooth.

Chuckling, Marianne lifted the pot of tea and poured them each a cup, then gestured to Caledan. "Help yourself, sellsword," she said. "I hope it might balance my lack of hospitality earlier. I wanted your imprisonment to be convincing."

It was convincing enough for me, Caledan thought with a shudder, remembering the rat watching him from the shadows.

But he said nothing and did as she bid, combining a piece of blue with one of the fruit cheeses. Caledan would have preferred a steak, but he was too hungry to be fussy, and the rich flavours of the cheeses were pleasant enough. The hot tea finally helped to banish the last of the cold from the dungeons.

"So, you were about to explain why my husband still lives?" Marianne said when he finally sat back, the worst of his hunger sated.

Caledan sighed. "Because Devon bade me protect him."

"Despite your hatred for the man?"

Caledan looked away. "Ay. Despite everything. But Devon was my friend. I could not refuse him."

"A true friend would not have asked such a thing of you."

"He believed Braidon was a good man, that he could stop you—and the Order—from taking over Plorsea."

Marianne's laughter peeled like a bell. "Then the hammerman was more a fool than I thought." Her eyes narrowed. "But what do you believe, Caledan? You have travelled with Braidon, fought beside him, saved him from my blade. What do you think of the man?"

This queen's words recalled memories of Dragon Country, and Caledan saw again Braidon on his knees, begging for Caledan to end his suffering. Just thinking of the fallen king filled Caledan with disgust. How had he ever thought Braidon a worthy enemy? The man was a worm, and Caledan should have put him down there and then, before his incompetence brought more misery to the Three Nations.

"He does not deserve to live," Marianne murmured. Edging closer to him on the sofa, she placed a hand on Caledan's knee. "You know that is the truth."

Caledan sighed. "On that, at least, we agree." He glanced at the queen, his lips tightening. "But I cannot go against Devon's final wishes."

"Devon was wrong. Perhaps Braidon was noble once, but he lost his way long ago."

"And what about you?" Caledan hissed, leaning away from her. "Whatever evil Braidon did against you, however much you hate him for your arranged marriage, you cannot say the same for Devon. He was a good man, who lived his life in the light. You killed him for it."

To his surprise, Marianne could not meet his gaze. "You cannot understand how long I had waited for that moment in the Cove," she whispered. "To cast off the role of loyal wife, of obedient daughter. How I hated my father for sending me away, and Braidon for taking me. Then, in my moment of triumph, the *hero* sought to stand in my way."

"You tried to murder his daughter, his *granddaughter*, everyone he ever loved."

Marianne stood suddenly at that. She walked to the desk and leaned against it. Her hands turned white, she clutched the wood so tightly. "I told you I regretted that decision, but it had to be made. The Elders wanted their Great Sacrifice, and you have seen how little control I have over them. Besides, I needed that power to free myself from their control."

"Even at the expense of innocent lives?" Caledan asked. He rose and approached her, their eyes meeting across the desk.

"What are a few innocent lives to the future of our nations?" Marianne asked, though there was a haunted look to her face.

"*Everything*," Caledan whispered, remembering Devon's conversation with Braidon, how the hammerman had pleaded for the king to help save his daughter. At least there was one honourable deed in Braidon's murky past.

Marianne slumped into her chair. "What would you have had me do?" she whispered. "I could not save them, once Servo and his fellows took them. I would only have succeeded in making myself powerless, ensured I was never more than a pawn in someone else's game."

"You are still a pawn," Caledan snapped. "You cannot even stop their Knights from slaughtering your citizens."

"Then *help* me!" Marianne hissed, coming to her feet.

The scent of her filled his nostrils and she stepped in close, eyes aglow. "Help me stand against Servo. Help me free this city from his Knights." She hesitated, her eyes softening. "Help me protect my son."

Caledan stared down at the woman, wondering again why he was there, why he had been spared while so many others had been doomed. Even now he might have reached out and throttled the life from her. Almost unbidden, his hand rose, but she made no move to stop him now, only stood in silence as he wrapped his fingers around her pale throat.

She swallowed, the slightest shimmer of fear appearing in her eyes, but still she did not oppose him. Perhaps her powers had been spent in the conflict with Servo. Caledan did not know, but he sensed in that moment she was in his power, that this was his opportunity to free Plorsea from her evil.

Then he thought again of Servo, of his words in the dungeons. If Marianne died, who would take her place? Did Braidon have the steel to take control of Plorsea again? It was a foolish thought, immediately dismissed. So who then?

It would be the boy, their son. The Elders would lift him to the kingship and rule in his place. Then there would be no one to stand against their vile plans. All Caledan would succeed in doing was to replace one evil with something far worse.

Letting out a long sigh, he released Marianne.

"Well, sellsword?" she whispered. "Will you be the Queen's Champion?"

A shiver lifted the hairs on Caledan's neck. His mother's words whispered from the past, telling him of their family's history, of an ancestor who had once stood beside the

Plorsean King. He was said to have been the greatest swordsman ever seen, had served as the King's Champion for nigh a decade. But the coming of the Tsar had cast their family low, and by Caledan's time, the story was just that—a fiction of the past, an imagination, for all he knew.

Yet as a child, he had dreamed of following in his ancestor's footsteps, of lifting his family back into the ranks of nobility. Those dreams had died with his mother, but now they rose unbidden, resurrected by the queen's words—if only he had the courage to take what Marianne offered.

He dropped to one knee before her, bowing his head. "I will be your Champion, My Queen."

Stepping in close, Marianne traced her fingers across his stumbled chin, lifting him back to his feet. "You need never kneel before me, Caledan."

He stood there in silence as her sapphire eyes inspected him, as though only now wondering whether he could truly be trusted. Then her face softened and the queen smiled, the mask falling away to reveal the woman beneath the façade.

"Thank you," she whispered.

25

R ed seared across Pela's vision as the steel boot descended, catching her in the side of the head and sending her tumbling across the jagged stones. A cry tore from Pela's lips as her tormentor laughed, then came after her, driving another blow into her ribcage.

The breath exploded between Pela's teeth and she collapsed, choking, to the ground. A groan rattled from her throat. She dug her fingers into the stones and tried to drag herself away, but there was no escape. Her scream echoed from the cliffs as the Knight grabbed her by the hair and pulled her up.

"Filthy witch!" he snarled.

Pela lashed out with a fist, but the blow bounced harmlessly off of the Knight's armour. He laughed in her face.

"You thought I would let you escape?" he growled. "That after you murdered my brother, I would not stop until I had your cold, dead body lying at my feet?

He didn't wait for Pela to reply. Instead, he hurled her at a nearby boulder. Pela's hands windmilled but there was nothing to slow her flight, and she struck the rock with an awful *thud*. Something tore inside her, agony stealing away her breath. She managed only the faintest moan as she slid to the ground.

Struggling to her knees, Pela looked for her attacker, but the Knight had found another victim. She flinched as Ruebyn's voice echoed her earlier scream. She could see no sign of Genevieve, but the woman was here, somewhere.

Why had the huntress stopped Pela from jumping? She could have been free of this torment, free of everything. All she'd needed to do was hurl herself from that ledge…but instead Gen's voice had brought her fear rushing back, and Pela had stood frozen as the hunters climbed, submitting meekly with Ruebyn when they reached the ledge.

Pela prayed Genevieve had a plan; otherwise she was doomed. Her mind whirled, wondering at her fate. Would they sacrifice her to the altar of Alana, or sentence her to toil again in the darkness for weeks or months or years? The thought made Pela shake with fear and her eyes flashed around the canyon, seeking out the huntress.

Ruebyn's screams broke off as the Knight hammered an iron fist into his face. He fell to the stones like a dead weight. The Knight towered over him, his shoulders heaving from the exertion, while Ruebyn lay still. Pela's heart lurched and for a moment she thought the boy was dead, that she had gone back for nothing. Then his chest moved and his eyelids flickered, and she realised he was only unconscious.

Pela quickly lowered her eyes, not wanting to draw the Knight's attention, but she was too late. Metallic laughter rattled from the helmet as he approached and crouched alongside her.

"I should slay you now," he murmured, "but the Elders

have marked you for the Saviour. You and your mother. Where is she?"

"I don't know," Pela croaked truthfully. She stared into the hateful helmet, wondering who hid behind it. The Knights never removed them amongst strangers, but she could just make out the beady eyes beyond the visor. The sight offered no hope though, and she swallowed. "We were separated in the Cove."

"Pity," the Knight replied, straightening. "I would have been richly rewarded. No matter; the witch will come for her daughter."

Pela's stomach churned at the thought of her mother walking into a trap. She cursed herself again, and Genevieve too. If only she'd chosen to escape, or fallen to her death, Pela could have at least spared Kryssa. The Knight was right—her mother would come the second she heard Pela was held by the Order.

"Slave!" the Knight bellowed. A figure stepped from the crowd. Pela's stomach twisted into knots. It was Genevieve. "Secure them. The rest of you, set the camp. We'll rest here until midday. I am tired of walking."

"Yes, sir," Genevieve said meekly, her head bowed.

The rest of the party moved quickly, hauling off their packs and dragging out canvas tents to pitch. The slope was uneven and the stones jagged, a poor place for a camp, but not a soul objected to the Knight's command. He alone wore the steel armour of the Order—the rest were mere followers, squires in training and retainers, waiting for their chance to ascend the holy ranks.

Stones were swept from the flattest section of the valley floor and a larger tent set using ropes and metal poles. The Knight sat watching from a boulder until it was ready, then rose and disappeared within.

Genevieve approached them, her face a careful mask, and took a loop of rope from her shoulder. "Hold out your arms," she said, her voice as blank as her face.

Pela swallowed, but did as she was told. As Genevieve went to work binding their arms and legs, she stared into the woman's eyes, wondering what game the huntress was playing.

"How did you find us?" Pela asked finally, when she was sure the others were occupied. Despite her efforts, she could not keep the anger from her voice. "I thought we were free."

The slightest flicker in Genevieve's eyes revealed her irritation. "You left tracks any imbecile could follow." She scowled. "You didn't think they'd check the cavern? Once we found where you'd left the pool, they could have followed you, even without me. Don't worry though, I'll think of something."

Pela's heart lurched. "*What?*" she hissed, struggling to keep her voice low.

Genevieve's eyes widened at Pela's anger. "I said I'll think of something to save you."

Pela couldn't believe her ears—Genevieve didn't have a plan at all. Now *she* would suffer for it, would be beaten and tortured and slaughtered like an animal, all because she'd put her trust in this woman. There would be no escaping this place. Even without their bindings, they were surrounded by the Knight's loyal followers. The anger bubbled up inside her as she stared at Gen, all the rage and frustration of the past weeks, the hopelessness.

"I knew I should not have trusted you," she said coldly. "I don't know what my mother sees in you. It must be that you're both such great liars. I never even suspected you were her lover."

Gen rocked back on her haunches as though struck. Her

mouth hung open but no words came out. Pela spoke into the silence.

"Lesson learned. Go away, Genevieve. We don't need you. We never did."

For a moment it seemed the huntress would refuse. She crouched, staring at Pela, eyes shining, lips curled downwards in agonised indecision. Then her eyes slid closed, and she turned away.

Pela watched Genevieve walk away, immediately regretting what she'd said. But she could not bring herself to call the woman back, to apologise. After all, her words had been the truth. The woman had spent weeks in Pela's company without ever mentioning her relationship with Kryssa.

Even so, her heart ached with the sudden loneliness. For a second, Genevieve's presence had been a comfort, the last hope to which she could cling. But Pela could not afford such fantasies now, not with the cold reality of the Knight looming over them.

Ruebyn still lay unconscious beside her, but Genevieve had bound him as securely as Pela. She felt a pang of guilt for having dragged him with her, for convincing him of her mountaineering skills, then failing so gravely. Now he would die alongside her, or perhaps sooner, once the Knight realised he did not need to keep Ruebyn alive.

Crouching beside her companion, Pela turned him on his side, wishing he would wake. As though bidden by her thoughts, Ruebyn's eyelids flickered and he groaned.

"Quiet," Pela hissed, putting her lips to his ear. "Don't draw any attention to us."

"What's happening?" Ruebyn croaked.

"I failed," Pela whispered, unable to keep the despair from her voice. "I'm sorry I brought you into this mess, Ruebyn, truly I am."

Ruebyn must have been terrified, but to his credit, it did not show. He glanced around before sitting up. "Where's the Knight?" he asked.

"In his tent."

Nodding, Ruebyn rubbed his jaw where the man had struck him. "So what do we do now?"

The other hunters had set up makeshift shelters of their own, though theirs were only pieces of canvas tied to boulders or the cliff-face. They would provide some semblance of protection against the elements, although not in the face of a storm. Unfortunately, the sky remained clear. A guard had been set to watch either end of the canyon.

Stones crunched as a man approached them. Pela shrank away, but he said nothing, only sat on a nearby boulder. Eyes fixed on the two prisoners, he pulled out a knife and whetstone, and started sharpening the weapon.

Pela shuffled back against the boulder. They were in the centre of the camp—no chance of sneaking away with the three guards.

"Nothing," she finally said in answer to Ruebyn's question. A tremor slid down her spine as the wind whistled through the canyon. It had changed direction and now seemed to be funnelling directly between the cliffs. "I'm cold, come here," she added without thinking.

Ruebyn obeyed, shuffling closer until their arms pressed together. Pela shivered again, though this time it was at his touch, from his warmth. Suddenly she was glad he was there. She didn't want to face what came next alone.

They sat there together, watching the guard watch them, the shrill grinding of steel on whetstone setting their nerves on end. Pela longed for her father's sword, if only to die with it in hand, but it had been lost in Malevolent Cove.

Despair touched her. Who was she kidding? She

couldn't have even taken on the single watchman. After all, who was she but an inexperienced child? Who had she ever beaten in a fair fight?

She sobbed as the pain from her beating redoubled. Pulling her legs to her chest, she sank her head into her knees to keep Ruebyn from seeing the tears. He noticed anyway, awkwardly giving her shoulder a squeeze. She was relieved he did not speak. His words could offer no solace. She had doomed them both.

The night grew late, the first rays of sunlight catching on the distant peaks. Her eyes began to water, but the pain was not half as bad as the day before. She stared at the orange glow, willing her eyes to adjust. She did not want to miss a single second of the sunrise, not if she was doomed to return to the darkness. The collar grew tight around her throat. Pela wished she'd at least been able to remove it. It chafed her skin with every movement, a constant reminder of her fate.

Ruebyn's breathing deepened as he drifted into sleep, but exhausted as she was, Pela resisted the call. Snuggling closer to his warmth, her gaze roamed the canyon. The twisted cliffs turned a brilliant scarlet as the sun rose higher, and the soft gurgling of the stream mingled with the whistling of the wind. The rest of the camp slept. Pela could almost imagine the two of them alone on the mountainside, the rest of the world a distant memory.

A flicker of movement from the cliffs drew her attention, but she could see nothing against the red rock. She frowned, scanning the ledges, sure it had been *something*. Perhaps a bird or a rodent come to investigate the smells of the camp.

Nothing.

Pela was about to look away when the flicker came again. Her heart lurched in her chest—then crashed to an abrupt halt as she saw the shadow amidst the rocks. Her mouth opened but terror robbed her of voice. Lifting one trembling hand, she pointed a finger.

The guard saw and cast a quick glance back, but he could not see the camouflaged beast. Scowling, he faced her.

"What are you doing?" he snarled.

Pela's mouth opened and closed, but still no sound came out. Ruebyn had slumped alongside her but now he stirred, his eyes flickering open. A smile touched his lips, but seeing her outstretched arm, his gaze followed to where she pointed.

"Feline!" The word exploded from him.

The scream broke the spell. They staggered to their feet, but the bindings on their ankles and hands almost sent them crashing down again. Panicked voices came from around the camp as others heard Ruebyn's scream, but the guard would not be fooled. He took a step towards them, dagger raised.

"You little ba—"

An almighty *roar* cut him off. It echoed through the canyon like an avalanche, silencing even the loudest screams. Pela watched with detached horror as the Feline leapt from its ledge, the enormous body rippling with sheer muscle. The scarlet fur shifted, changing from red to yellow like quicksilver.

One of the camp followers had just emerged from his makeshift shelter when the beast landed beside him. He barely had time to scream before it was on him. One swat of a giant paw smashed the man to the ground. Groaning, his leg twisted at a terrible angle, he scrambled desperately for the hilt of his sword. The Feline lunged, its awful jaws stretching wide to close around his head.

There followed a sickening *crunch*, like a melon splitting on the rocks—then silence. A rotten stench filled the canyon and the man lay still, but the beast was not satisfied. It swung around, yellow eyes aglow in the morning sun, seeking out a fresh victim. Pela cried out as the twin globes fell on her. She tried to stumble back, but her bindings caught on a rock and sent her crashing to the dirt.

Screams came from across the camp as two retainers drew their swords and charged. Distracted, the Feline turned to meet them. Moving faster than thought, it leapt. One second the men were racing towards it, the next, a yellowed blur smashed the leader from his feet. A scream pierced the air as fangs sank into flesh, followed by the sharp *crack* of breaking bones.

Horrified, the second warrior staggered back, sword clutched before him. The Feline tore another chunk from its victim, then spun as the man's foot knocked loose a rock. The golden eyes followed the stone as it tumbled down the canyon, then flicked back to the man. He cried out, thrusting at it with his blade. The Feline batted aside his blows, then tore out his throat with a single swipe of its claws.

Blood gushed down the man's chest as he stumbled away, clutching at the wound. His eyes were wide, filled with fear, but he did not have long to live. With a roar, the Feline was upon him, jaws descending, blood and bone and flesh devoured.

Pela watched the events unfold in horror, unable to think, to move. This was a creature of death, a beast from the days of Archon, that even powerful Magickers had once feared to battle. What chance did any of them have against such a creature?

"Quickly!" A cry drew Pela's attention back to her

surroundings. Genevieve had appeared beside their guard, longbow in hand. She grabbed their guard by the shoulder and thrust him at the beast. "While it's distracted!"

The huntress nocked an arrow as the guard glanced back, terrified. The sight of the longbow seemed to reassure him though, and turning, he rushed at the beast. Other attendants were also converging on the creature now, but their leather armour meant little before its ferocity.

As soon as the man turned away, Genevieve dropped her bow and drew a knife from her boot. She slashed Pela's bindings, then Ruebyn's. Retrieving her weapon, she glanced at the Feline. Another retainer lay dead already, his face replaced by a mangled caricature of a man.

"Come on," Gen hissed, tossing a pack down beside them. "*Quickly!*"

"Gen!" Pela gasped, lost for words. She stared at the woman, mouth hanging open, wanting to say so many things, to grab her and hug her and repent her horrible words. But there was no time for any of that, and swallowing her fear, she managed only, "*Thank you!*"

Gen's jaw clenched and she nodded, though Pela could still see the hurt in the woman's eyes. She prayed there would be time for apologies later. Sweeping up the pack, she pushed Ruebyn ahead of her.

"Where?" he cried, his face white with fear.

"Up the canyon," Genevieve snapped. "Now, before…"

She didn't need to finish the sentence. Not ten yards from where they stood a desperate battle was taking place between beast and man. Whether the Feline emerged victorious, or the hunters, neither would hold any qualms about finishing off Pela and her friends.

A roar came from the Knight's tent as he emerged fully armoured, broadsword in hand. The Feline swatted aside another retainer and turned to watch him come, yellow eyes aglow. Its jaws opened wide and its roar sent men stumbling backwards. It leapt to meet the Knight.

Pela turned away as a crash echoed up the valley, Knight and beast coming together. A dead man lay nearby and her eyes caught on his sword. She swept it up and immediately felt better with the weapon in hand. Genevieve was already moving off, arrow still nocked to her bow, and they hurried to keep up. The guard at the top of the camp had abandoned his post to fight the beast, and the three of them passed by unnoticed.

Another roar came from behind. Pela looked back and saw the Knight go down, Feline atop him. Its claws raked his chest with a squeal of metal, but could not pierce the heavy steel. His fist came up, still clutching the broadsword, and drove the blade through the beast's chest. An awful scream echoed up the canyon but the Feline did not fall. It renewed its attack, rending and tearing with claw and tooth.

Pela looked away and sent up a prayer to the Three Gods that the two would kill one another. She could not imagine the Knight surviving such an encounter, but nor did she savour the thought of the Feline stalking them through the mountains. The sounds of battle followed them up the narrow canyon.

Only when they were a mile from the camp did silence finally return to the dawn.

26

Pela, Genevieve and Ruebyn walked for the rest of the day in silence, each too exhausted, too shocked by the violence of the morning to speak. Pela's mind kept returning to the slaughter, repeating again and again the image of a man's chest being torn open, the *crunch* of his skull as those awful jaws closed around it. In her exhausted state, she imagined the beast stalking them, a dark presence brooding in the back of her mind that would not go away.

She thanked the Gods for Genevieve, for acting so quickly, for scooping up a discarded pack and spiriting them away. If not for the huntress, they would all have been dead by now. Pela had seen the fierce intelligence in the eyes of the Feline, its hunger, its hatred. It would have slaughtered them all.

All the worse then, what Pela had said to the woman. In her anger and despair she had lashed out, and now she could not take back the words. There was a chasm between herself and Genevieve now, a distance created by hurt and mistrust, one Pela did not know how to heal.

Ruebyn said little either. Pela wondered what he thought of this fresh turn of events. He trudged along beside her, eyes fixed to the ground, uncomplaining though he must have been at the end of his strength.

In the aftermath of the slaughter, Pela had at least one thing to celebrate. The sun now hung bright above the clifftops, and while her eyes were aching, the pain was bearable. She could see! The relief was so great she might have cried, if she had not spent so many of the last few days in tears.

For hours they followed Genevieve through the winding canyon. She seemed to have a six sense when it came to the myriad of corridors, unerringly choosing the turns as they came to them. Not once did they encounter a dead end, and finally they emerged back out into the open, finding themselves in another broad valley bounded by rocky cliffs.

A braided river threaded its way across the plain, its path broken and twisted by the giant boulders littering the valley floor. A few yards downriver, an enormous mound of earth spanned the gulley, barring half the rivers path and diverting several of the channels down the canyon from which they'd emerged. They stood on a gentle slope, though behind them the pitch increased, eventually becoming a cliff-face that stretched five hundred feet above their heads.

"It's a glacial valley," Ruebyn said suddenly. When they only stared at him blankly, he smiled guiltily and went on. "My teachers say great rivers of ice once flowed through these mountains. Their weight carved broad avenues through the rock, then later when the glaciers retreated, they left these valleys."

"And how does this help us?" Gen snapped.

Ruebyn's mouth opened and closed, before he managed to stammer. "It…doesn't?"

Genevieve snorted. Her eyes turned on Pela. "And where were we going?"

Pela swallowed. "I…Trola," she said shortly.

"Terrible plan," Genevieve replied. Ruebyn looked like he was going to agree, but the huntress went on. "But probably the best we've got at this point."

Without offering another word, she set off up the valley. Pela offered Ruebyn an apologetic glance. She had created this problem; now she needed to fix it. Squaring her shoulders, she chased after Gen, leaving Ruebyn to catch up.

"Gen," she said, drawing alongside the huntress. "I… I'm sorry, okay? I didn't mean what I said."

"You did," Gen replied sharply, her eyes fixed on the path ahead. The gravels were larger here, shifting unexpectedly beneath their weight, and they had to take care where they stepped the unstable ground send them tumbling into the river.

Pela sighed. "I suppose I did, in a way," she murmured, "but my anger wasn't meant for you. It's…my mother kept so much from me! How my father died, that they were both members of the King's Guard, *you*. And in Malevolent Cove…I never had a chance to yell at her."

"So you yelled at me," Genevieve sighed, finally glancing at Pela. "You were right to be angry. Kryssa kept her secrets close."

"You too," Pela said, though this time a smile touched her lips. "All those weeks, and I never guessed you were dating my mother!"

"Am I?" Genevieve asked, eyes wide with innocence. Pela raised an eyebrow and the huntress chuckled. "Okay, I suppose I am."

"You didn't think to tell me that, back when we set off from Skystead?"

Genevieve wore a knowing smile now. "It wasn't my story to tell. It never sat right with me, but you are Kryssa's daughter, it was her decision to make."

Pela snorted. "I don't suppose you have any thoughts on why she kept it from me?"

"At first…well, we weren't sure *what* it was between us. I've always enjoyed my own company, but with Kryssa…" They shared a glance, and Pela was surprised to see the hint of a blush on Gen's cheeks. "She's…special," the huntress finished.

"How did you meet?" Pela asked, smiling despite herself.

"We were just friends…at first, taking coffee together, walking the mountain paths. A few times Kryssa joined me for a day hunt, when the inn was quiet and you were out roaming the town. At some point…we realised something had grown between us. Then we became—"

"Okay!" Pela gasped. "That's enough, I don't need the details!"

A grin tugged at Genevieve's lips. "I am sorry I kept it from you. Kryssa is a very private person."

"So I've discovered! Did *you* know she served in the King's Guard?"

Genevieve laughed. "No, that was as much of a surprise for me as it was for you. Though, she was always good with a blade. I once saw her strike a hare with her knife from twenty paces away. I couldn't have matched that shot if I practiced for a year."

Pela smiled, recognising the warmth in Gen's voice. It was good to finally speak about her mother. For so long in the darkness, she'd barely had the strength to worry for herself. Now that she was finally free, might finally have a future, her thoughts returned to the fate of those she loved.

Then she remembered Townirwin, and the pain of

thinking her mother had been killed. Her heart throbbed as she realised Genevieve had suffered that agony alone.

"You should have said something," Pela murmured, placing a hand on Genevieve's shoulder. "It can't have been easy, fearing for Mum all that time, and not being able to speak of it."

"I've been alone most of my life," Genevieve replied. "I'm used to it."

Sadness touched Pela, as she saw Gen with fresh eyes. "But you're not alone now. You have me, and Kryssa and…" She trailed off, remembering Devon's death, the uncertain fate of her mother and the others. A lump lodged in her throat. "Do you think…they survived?"

"I don't know," Gen replied. "I hope so, though…" Her eyes were drawn to some point over Pela's shoulder.

Pela glanced around. A smattering of vegetation grew amongst the branches of the river, some just a few feet from where they walked. Pela's heart beat faster as she glimpsed movement within the shadows. She reached for her sword, but before she could draw it the creature burst from the bushes.

A shrill cry echoed from the cliffs as the young deer bounded nimbly up the river and ducked behind a cluster of boulders. An arrow flashed from the rocks a second after it vanished. Genevieve swore and nocked another, but the creature was already gone. After a moment she returned the arrow to its quiver.

"Wishful thinking," the huntress murmured.

Pela's stomach gave an answering growl. "I'd settle for a rabbit, let alone a deer!" she agreed.

"That was a tahr," Ruebyn said as he caught them, then flicked an apologetic glance at Genevieve.

This time the huntress only smiled. "You're right; a young one, too. Keep an eye out, there might be more."

Ruebyn cast an uneasy glance behind them. "We should keep going," he said, shuddering visibly. "That Knight won't give up until his brother is avenged."

Genevieve waved a hand. "That Knight is *dead*, and good riddance. Hopefully he managed to do one good deed and take that cursed beast with him."

A frown twisted Ruebyn's lips. "I don't think so. Monstrous as it was, the Feline couldn't get through his armour."

Pela was surprised. She'd sensed Ruebyn's fear as they walked, but had thought it was the beast that frightened him. It certainly terrified her. But she'd hardly given the Knight another thought since their escape.

Silence had fallen at his words, but finally Pela shook her head, determined to put the fear from her mind. "The beast had him, we all saw it. Even if he managed to survive, they won't be in any condition to come after us…surely." Pela said the words with conviction, but somehow she failed to convince even herself.

Neither of her companions replied, but after a brief rest for water, they set off once more. Exhaustion weighed on Pela and eventually she traded the pack to Ruebyn—though he looked little better than she felt. She had checked its contents earlier and had been relieved to find a fur-lined jacket, a block of flint, some kindling, and a waterskin. No food, though.

Her stomach rumbled again, and she looked ahead, alert for fresh prey. Genevieve was better prepared than either of them, having her own pack and jacket, along with the bow and quiver.

They walked on until the sun began to set. By then, Pela

was so tired she could do nothing but put one foot in front of the other. Her eyes ached and the pain of her body had driven all thought of deer and rabbits from her mind. There was only the next step, the next boulder to climb, the next stream to ford.

Here and there banks of soil formed along the edges of the valley, allowing vegetation to take root. Where they could they walked through these areas, finding the way easier on dirt than the gravels that constantly shifted beneath their boots.

Slowly the twilight slipped away, the light of the sun giving way to the faint glow of the rising moon. It seemed an age had passed since they'd emerged from the caves, but the brilliance of the near-to-full moon proved it had only been a few days.

Still they kept on, pressing themselves to the ends of their endurance. Ruebyn's words about the Knight became a promise, a threat that ate at the back of their minds, refusing to rest. Pela watched the moon as they walked, wondering if her mother still looked upon the silver orb each night. The Knight had not thought Kryssa captured, but then they had not realised Pela's identity either. Could the same have happened to Kryssa?

No, Pela insisted to herself. *Mum is free, and the king, and Caledan. They have to be.*

How Pela longed to find a way back to them. But with every step she took they drew further away, leaving behind the lands of the east, marching into the unknown. No one knew what had become of Trola since the fall of the Tsar— no one was *allowed* to know. Under normal circumstances it meant death to cross the border, but surely the Trolans would understand? They were desperate, could not survive much longer in these harsh mountains, even with the new supplies.

Trola was their only hope.

Finally they reached a break in the valley. Another great mound of earth lay across their path, rising almost two hundred feet above their heads. Twisted trees sprouted from the slope, while away to their right the river roared over a cascade of interlocked boulders to crash upon the rocks below. Thankfully the way was not sheer, but it would still make for an exhausting climb.

"It's a moraine," Ruebyn said unhelpfully, "sediment left behind when the glaciers melted."

"Let's just reach the top and make camp," Genevieve said.

They started up, eager for a view of what they would face on the morrow, and to finally rest. Pela's stomach rumbled as they climbed, and she prayed Genevieve's pack might have a little food. Despite her trepidation, the going was easy, the trees providing plenty of holds with which to pull themselves up. Even Ruebyn was able to make the climb unaided.

Only towards the top did the way become more perilous. The stones were loose in the soil and there were fewer trees. Pela and Ruebyn slowed, forced to take care with each foot and handhold, while Genevieve forged ahead, disappearing into the darkness. Pela hoped she'd gone ahead to set camp, but a few minutes later a cry carried to them from above.

Heart racing, Pela picked up the pace and soon the huntress reappeared. She was still on her feet, but moving slowly now, and her right foot no longer appeared able to take her weight.

"Twisted my ankle," Gen explained with a curse as Pela drew level. "Bloody rock shifted under me."

"Almost there," Pela said, giving her a reassuring pat on the shoulder.

The huntress offered a wan smile. She made it the last few dozen feet at a limp, and though she kept her complaints to herself, Pela could see the pain in the lines of her face.

Finally they emerged from the sparse trees onto an open flat at the top of the moraine. There, Genevieve sat herself on the ground and stretched out her leg, a scowl on her lips.

"That was stupid," she muttered to herself. Her eyes flickered around them, and the anger faded. "Least the view was worth it."

Only then did Pela look up. A gasp slipped from her as she saw the way ahead. Below, the ground dropped a hundred feet to a lake. Its crystal waters stretched up the valley as far as they could see, the stark snow-capped peaks rising all around. In the moonlight, the water seemed aglow, as though it had absorbed the day's sun and now cast it back at them. Barren slopes surrounded the lake, rising a thousand feet in every direction—except one tiny notch Pela glimpsed in the far distance. There, the ground rose only fifty feet before falling away to who knew what. Pela glimpsed stars beyond, and hoped it meant they might have finally found a pass through to Trola.

But they would have to navigate the lake first. It was massive, at least fifteen miles long and three hundred feet wide, filling the whole valley with its alien glow. The going would be tough on the steep slopes, especially with Gen's injured ankle.

A cold wind blew across the waters, reminding Pela of

her aching eyes. Shivering, she turned her attention to Genevieve.

"Let's get this elevated," she said. "No more walking tonight, or you'll struggle tomorrow."

Genevieve smiled grimly. "I'll do my best. Can you manage a fire?"

Pela grunted. "I'm not entirely useless. Do you think it's wise though?"

"Depends if either of our enemies survived," Gen replied. "It could be useful, if that beast is stalking us, but if it's the Knight—"

"I don't think we should," Ruebyn croaked, moving up beside them.

Pela caught the heavy tang of fear on his voice. The hackles on her neck rose as she looked back the way they'd come, out across the scraggly trees, to the shadows of the glacial valley. A long way off, a single light glinted amongst the darkness.

"It wasn't the Feline that survived," Ruebyn whispered.

27

The crowd pressed against Kryssa as they marched through the winding streets of Chole, their voices echoing loudly against the narrow walls. Many carried makeshift weapons they had collected along the way—clubs and hatchets and pitchforks, whatever came to hand. But while they must outnumber the enemy twenty to one, she was apprehensive for the coming confrontation. The Knights had the advantage with their plate mail and broadswords, to say nothing of the Castle walls they could hide behind.

In contrast, Braidon's forces were woefully unprepared for a battle. But his call to arms had caught her off-guard and the king had been lost amongst the crowd before Kryssa could reach him. Now as she struggled to catch up, she wondered what madness had taken Braidon. The Knights would see them coming a mile off. What would his ragtag army do when they found the Castle gates barred?

Shoving bodies from her path, she threaded her way to the side of the street, and the press lessened. Her sword slapped against her leg and she had to take care not to trip in the chaos. Braidon was somewhere ahead, leading the mob. She needed to reach him before this went any further.

Amongst the lighter crowds, Kryssa moved faster, dodging in and out of the slow-moving citizens. Even so, the walls of the Castle were looming overhead by the time she finally reached the king. Dominic marched alongside him, a broad grin on his bearded face. As she approached, he faced the crowd and roared, his spear pointing to the way ahead.

"Braidon!" Kryssa gasped, slipping past Dominic and grabbing the king by the arm.

"There you are!" Braidon grinned when he saw her. "You finally decided to join the party?"

"I'm not sure I'd call this a party," she muttered. "How are you planning on getting inside?"

They had just turned the final corner before the Castle. It rose above the single-storey buildings lining the street, its granite walls topped by thick crenulations. Just as she'd suspected, the gates were barred and armoured men stood atop the ramparts, crossbows in hand. Kryssa shuddered at the sight, remembering the damage they had wrought against the Red Dragons. She feared to think what the weapons would do to a human.

"We're just here to talk," Braidon replied lightly. He seemed to be enjoying his sudden turn of fate. The only sign left of his exhaustion were the shadows beneath his eyes.

"Are you sure *they* know that?" Kryssa asked, gesturing at the mob.

Braidon shrugged but he did not reply. They continued their march down the street until a voice bellowed from the ramparts.

"Come no closer!" A man in flowing green robes appeared atop the ramparts, arms outstretched. He called again, his voice like thunder in the street. "Or we will be forced to defend ourselves."

"Halt!" Braidon shouted, raising his arms to his followers.

The men and women at the front obeyed, but those further back continued forward, and it took several minutes for the king to calm the chaos. Even then they were not cowed, and Kryssa could sense the tension building amidst the mob. Braidon had stoked their anger at the Knights and their Order. Now hundreds were crowded into the narrow street, cramped and jostling one another, stocking their rage. Braidon needed to act fast if he wanted to avoid a riot.

She shared a glance with the king and he nodded his understanding. They strode forward together, Dominic one step behind, until they stood halfway between the Castle and the mob. A cold wind blew across the street, sending a tremor down Kryssa's spine. She felt a foreboding, as some sixth sense screamed that they should turn back. But it was already too late for that.

"Come out, Elder!" Braidon called, his voice as loud as the man in the Castle. "I must speak with you."

A strained silence hung over the street, though the whispers of the crowd were rising. The man atop the wall did not move, but after a moment his words carried down to them.

"And who are you to command an Elder of the Order?"

"I am Braidon, rightful King of Plorsea!" he bellowed.

"I see no king," came the Elder's reply. "Only a violent mob intent on murder."

"These are faithful of the Three, loyal citizens all," Braidon replied. "They will do you no harm, Elder. You have my word."

There was a long pause. "Very well," the Elder said finally.

He disappeared from the crenulations. A few minutes later the gates of the Castle cracked open and the man stepped out. Kryssa and Braidon shared an astonished look, while Dominic edged up to the king's other side. The crowd fell silent as the Elder approached. His face was lined with age and his robes were faded, though there was a strength in his gaze as he came to a stop before them.

"Very well, you who claim to be king," he said softly, his tone resigned. "What would you say to me?"

For a moment Braidon looked lost for words, but he shook himself and straightened. "Your Knights attacked the Temple of Antonia, threatened innocent citizens. Your kind are no longer welcome in my city."

"I have lived in this city ten years," the Elder snapped, but then his face softened. "That deed was not by command. Those Knights came from Lonia."

"And yet they have taken refuge within your walls."

"They were attacked, but by your own magic, if I'm not mistaken," the Elder snapped. "And they are not the only ones who have taken refuge within my walls. *My kind* are afraid. Can peace not prevail here? Already a Knight lies dead, his soul forever joined with the Saviour—"

"My sister be damned," Braidon snarled, taking a step towards the man. "The man came to my city intent on murder. I'll not grieve him, nor will I stop until his fellows are held to account."

"I have already stripped them of their ra—"

"*I* will be their judge," Braidon interrupted. "They broke the king's peace; now they must answer to my justice. Open up your gates so the guilty can be judged."

"This is a sanctuary," the Elder replied. "As I said, many

have come to us these last hours, fearing the rumours, fearing for their lives. I will not allow any harm to come to them."

"My friends and I won't be leaving without the guilty," Braidon retorted.

"And who are the guilty?" the Elder hissed. "There are those who would hold *you* to account, My King, for killing a man with magic. A man who had no means to defend himself against such an attack."

"The Knight put himself in my path," Braidon said. "I gave him fair warning. Had he left my people alone, there would have been no need for his death."

"Is that what you intend for all of us then?" the Elder asked. "To burn all you find within these walls, because they sought refuge in their faith?"

"No!" Braidon gasped, seeming taken aback by the Elder's words. "I only want those responsible. Your Knights will be imprisoned, and banished back to Lonia when the battle is won. All others will go unharmed, you have my word."

"But only the Lonian Knights were present at the temple."

"Perhaps," Braidon murmured, "but how could we know? Their helmets covered their faces."

"I will bring the ones who attacked you," the Elder insisted.

For moment Braidon seemed to consider it, but finally he shook his head. "I am sorry," he said, sounding genuine. "I cannot take the risk. There is a war coming and I cannot allow your Knights to stand against me."

The Elder's face hardened and Kryssa thought he was about to refuse the king's demands. But then his shoulders slumped and his eyes fell to the cobbles.

"Very well," he whispered.

His chest rose as he sucked in a breath, then stepped forward and lifted a hand. Kryssa tensed, reaching for her sword hilt—but the hand was empty. On Braidon's other side, Dominic did not hesitate. His spear flashed down, bringing the Elder up short.

"Halt!" he snapped.

The Elder stumbled back, unharmed but taken by surprise. Braidon frowned and turned on the guard, a scowl on his face. Atop the wall, a shout came from Knights gathered there, followed by a sharp *twang*. The hackles on Kryssa's neck rose and without thinking, she hurled herself at Braidon. They slammed together and crashed to the ground.

Pain slashed her arm as the crossbow bolt tore past and buried itself in the cobbles. Collapsing alongside Braidon, Kryssa stared at the thing. It stood quivering beside them, the steel point embedded an entire inch into a cobblestone.

Her head snapped up as a roar came from down the street. The mob surged forwards, weapons raised as they rushed to avenge their fallen king. Kryssa stared in horror as the Elder fled, while atop the walls the Knights turned their weapons on the crowd. Screams pierced the air as bolts tore through flesh and bone, but they could not stop the mob.

Men and women raced around Kryssa and streamed after the Elder. He moved faster than Kryssa would have thought the old man capable, but he still only reached the gates with mere moments to spare. He slipped inside and the heavy wood slammed closed. A second later the hatchets of the mob were hammering at the door.

Beside her, Braidon groaned. There was blood on his shirt and for a second Kryssa thought he'd been struck after all. He shook his head as though to answer her unspoken question.

"Opened my wound," he murmured, hauling himself to his feet. "Thank you, though. That was too close." He offered his hand.

Kryssa accepted it and rose beside him. Her heart sank as she watched the chaos unfolding beneath the walls of the Castle. Dozens had already fallen to the Knight's weapons, their blood staining the granite cobbles. Most of the mob had passed them now, and Kryssa saw a young woman lying nearby, pinned to the cobbles by one of the great bolts. She was clawing at the arrow as though to pull it free.

A lump lodged in Kryssa's throat and she staggered over to help. A great shudder shook the woman, air hissed from her throat, and then she lay still. Kryssa stopped and stood over the dead woman. She was barely older than Pela. Tears stung Kryssa's eyes as she forced herself to look away.

Her gaze travelled up the street, taking in the carnage. Everywhere men and women lay dying, while above, the Knights still fired into the milling crowd. The fight was already going from Braidon's followers, though those at the front continued to hammer at the timbers of the gate.

Kryssa swallowed. "We have to stop this."

"We have to stop *them*," Braidon said. He stepped past her, eyes aflame. "We have to end this."

❦ 28 ❦

A child's laughter echoed from an open doorway in the hallway ahead, and Caledan slowed his approach, wondering for the thousandth time if he was doing the right thing. But it too late to change his mind now; the opportunity to dispose of the mad queen had passed. Swallowing his hesitation, he stepped through the entrance to Marianne's apartment.

The queen was out, and he closed the panelled doors behind him. They were thin and would not hold longer than a few seconds, but at least they would warn of an enemy's approach. In the centre of the room, the boy Calybe looked up. Caledan wore a light chainmail vest and his sword at his side, and the boy's eyes widened at the sight.

"Who are you?" he asked.

He sat on a rug at the foot of Marianne's bed, a cube of some sort in his hands. Caledan crossed to the double doors leading out onto a balcony. He checked it was unoccupied before returning and addressing the boy's question.

"Your mother sent me to look after you."

A youthful frown wrinkled the boy's forehead. "I saw you," he murmured. "With my mother, when she was working."

Caledan nodded. "She and I are friends."

The announcement bought a smile to the child's face. "That is good! She doesn't have many friends…not now… Father is gone."

"I was sorry to hear about your father," Caledan said, and seeing the sadness in the boy's eyes, was surprised to find he meant it. Whatever his opinion of Braidon, it was obvious the man was loved by his son. "And I am glad to be your mother's friend."

The boy smiled and turned his attention back to the strange cube. Each side sported nine squares painted in different colours, but they moved as the boy twisted the object, shifting the colours into rows.

"What have you got there?" Caledan asked finally, squatting beside the boy for a better look.

Calybe held the toy up to the lantern light. One side was now all the same colour, but the others remained mismatched.

"You can make them all the same," he explained, his lips twisted in a frown, "but this is as far as I can get," he finished sadly.

Caledan smiled. "Perhaps it is a trick, and it is not possible at all?"

"No," Calybe replied, "my mother showed me, but she would not tell me the trick! She said it was for me to figure out."

"Your mother is very wise—" Caledan started, but a sudden *boom* cut him off. The floor shook as an answering explosion followed.

The boy's eyes widened and Caledan rose and went

back to the balcony. Leaning out over the banister, he looked across the sloping rooftops of the citadel. Smoke rose from where he guessed was the throne room, thick acrid stuff that stained the pale sky. He closed the doors and strode to where Calybe still sat.

"What was that?" the boy asked.

Caledan said nothing. His mind was in the throne room, wondering what fate had become Marianne. She claimed to have mastered the strange power wielded by the Elders, to have enough strength to force Servo from her city. Now she had finally taken the battle against the Elder and his followers.

But the queen's magic was limited. She could not be everywhere at once, could not trust anyone with the protection of her son. Only him.

And so here he was, his sword the only thing standing between an innocent boy and the Knights of Alana. The thought did not fill him with confidence.

"I think we'd better be going," he said. The plan had been to stay and wait for Marianne's victory, but she had entrusted Calybe's safety to him. And the more he thought about it, better they run than stay and fight. "Let's take a trip down to the lake," he finished.

The boy stared at him and then rose with a nod. He took Caledan's offered hand, but as they started for the door, something heavy slammed against it from outside, splintering the wood. A great *crack* followed as a second blow struck, and an axeblade appeared through the thin panelling.

"Under the bed!" Caledan hissed, spinning and shoving Calybe away from him. "*Quickly!*"

The boy obeyed without question this time. Caledan faced the door in time to see the latch disintegrate under a third blow. The doors crashed open and two Knights stepped inside, three of the Queen's Guard close behind. Seeing Caledan they hesitated, confusion in their eyes.

"Who are you?" the leader bellowed. "Where is the boy?"

"I am your death," Caledan hissed, drawing his sword. "And the boy is gone."

The Knight scanned the room, his eyes settling on Calybe's hiding place. "Under the bed." Sword already drawn, he started towards the young prince, ignoring Caledan.

Irritated by the show of disrespect, Caledan leapt, his boot flashing out to catch the Knight in the side of the head. The blow staggered the man and he stumbled back into the arms of his comrades. Snarling, the Knight recovered. The group spread out in a half-circle, arranged against him.

"That's better," Caledan laughed. "Come and meet your Saviour, boys."

Shifting his feet, he drew a heavy hunting knife from his belt and waited, sword raised high, knife low. His foes were wary now, unsure of this strange warrior who stood against them. Another *boom* echoed from below. The sound seemed to spur them into action, and with a roar, the leader charged.

Caledan leapt to the side and the Knight's broadsword cut empty air. Driving his hunting knife low, he thrust it at the gap between the Knight's backplate and steel leggings. His aim was true and the blade sank to the hilt, severing the man's spine. An awful scream rent the air as he fell forward, dragging the knife from Caledan's grasp.

Taking a double-handed grip of his sword, Caledan thrust up to block a swing from the second Knight. Sparks flashed as the Knight's broadsword ricocheted sideways, almost slamming into the shoulder of the Guard coming up beside him. Unable to drag back his sword in time for a blow, Caledan drove his shoulder into the Knight's breastplate.

Off-balance, the man hurtled backwards into another of the Queen's Guard. The two went down with a crash of metal. Before the other Guards could close on him, Caledan spun and retrieved his knife. The fallen Knight screamed as he tore the blade loose, but made no move to stand. His sobs echoed pitifully from the marble walls as Caledan leapt at the two Queen's Guard still on their feet.

Wearing only chainmail, the Guards moved quickly, though it was clear their confidence had been sapped by the fall of their leader. They retreated before his blows, until a bellow from the remaining Knight brought them up short. Behind them, the two fallen men struggled back to their feet.

Screaming an obscenity, one of the Guards leapt at Caledan, but his comrade hung back, waiting for the others to re-join the fight. At the last moment, Caledan's foe realised he was alone and tried to pull back, but it was already too late for him. Caledan's short sword took him in the throat, the razor-sharp blade tearing through the thin steel of his gorget.

Grinning, Caledan started for the remaining three, but a sharp pain tore through his leg, bringing him up short. He glanced down and cursed, surprised to find a dagger protruding from his thigh. Releasing his blade, the Knight on the floor collapsed, the last of his energy spent.

Caledan gasped as the strength went from his leg. He almost fell, but with an effort of will forced himself to remain upright. Raising dagger and sword, he looked at his three remaining opponents, and laughed.

"Ready, boys?" he asked with false bravado.

They came at him in silence. Unable to match their speed, Caledan let them approach. The two remaining Guards reached him first, one of their blades hacking for Caledan's head. But it was a clumsy blow and Caledan's sword flicked up, turning aside the attack and then lancing at his foe's helmet. The Guard's helmet lacked the full visor of the Knights', and Caledan's blade slid through the eye slot with a sickening *crunch*.

Screaming, the Guard dropped his blade and stumbled away, blood pouring from his helmet. Caledan leapt to finish him, but pain seared through his injured leg and instead he found himself retreating. Ignoring their injured comrade, his remaining foes parted and came at him from either side, seeking to divide his attention.

Caledan lunged at the Guard, his blade feinting for the man's helmet, then spun to deflect a blow from the Knight. The man shouted in surprise, almost losing his grip on his sword when their weapons connected, but he leapt back before Caledan could counter.

Stepping after him, Caledan's leg almost gave way. He cursed, tried to straighten, and heard the tread of the Guard approaching. Spinning, he thrust his sword up in a block—but this time the man had put all his weight behind the blow. Their swords came together with a screech of metal, then the weapon was jarred from Caledan's hand.

He dove to retrieve it, but a painful *thump* from the Guard's broadsword hammered into his ribs, bringing him up short. Caledan staged back as something went *crack* in his chest. His vision spun, but he sensed the chainmail had done its job. The power in the blow had broken bones, but the blade had not penetrated.

The Guard laughed and stepped in close, readying himself for the final blow. Baring his teeth, Caledan stepped in to meet him, driving his hunting knife up into the man's armpit. The laughter ceased as the blade sank deep into unprotected flesh, replaced by a terrible gurgling as blood gushed into the man's lungs.

An answering scream came from the last Knight as he charged. Caledan tried to face his foe, but a wave of pain overwhelmed him and he could not raise his dagger in time. A sword speared for his chest, and this time the chainmail could not withstand the blow. The metal links shrieked as they snapped, and the blade sank deep into Caledan's chest.

A gasp tore from Caledan as he slumped against the cold steel. Suddenly he felt as though he were drowning. His mouth opened and closed as he tried to breathe, but the air did not seem to reach his lungs. Blood bubbled on his lips and he slumped to his knees.

With a wrench, the Knight tore his blade loose. Caledan toppled forward, but the Knight caught him by the shoulder and held him there.

"Foul blasphemer," he spat. "It is an honour to cleanse your kind from our world. Your life, and the lives of my brothers, now serve the Saviour. As will the boy, in his death."

A great weakness was sweeping over Caledan, a yearning to sleep, to embrace the darkness, to flee the pain. But with the man's final words he saw again the fear in Marianne's eyes, the innocence on Calybe's face. The black mask of the Knight's helmet watched him and Caledan opened his mouth, struggling to find words.

"What's that, blasphemer?" the Knight cackled, leaning closer. "Do you still plea for your Gods to save you?"

Caledan could barely lift his head, but as the Knight neared, he thrust up with the dagger. The blade slid low, catching the gap in the armour near the man's groin, and sank to the hilt. The pressure on Caledan's shoulder tightened momentarily, then vanished as the Knight fell back.

Gasping, the man within the iron shell clambered to his feet. Blood pumped down his leg to pool on the tile floor, but by an effort of will he stumbled towards the bed. A roar echoed from the darkness of his helmet. He hurled the bed aside. A scream rent the air…

Caledan did not see what happened next. He found himself suddenly on his side, the cold stone pressing into his face, numbness spreading through his body. The light faded from his vision and he imagined himself back in the dungeons, his only light a candle in the darkness.

As he watched, it flickered low…

✣ 29 ✣

Pela and Ruebyn stood atop the moraine, watching the distant torchlight. It was still miles off, back where they'd first left the canyon, she guessed, but there was no mistaking it, no avoiding the truth. Someone had survived the Feline. Someone was coming after them. And they were still at least a day's march from Trola. Exhausted, injured, at the end of their endurance, they could never make it in time.

"Go," Genevieve said, sitting up.

"We can't," Pela wailed. "Your leg!"

"No, *you* go," Genevieve hissed.

She pushed herself up and hobbled to a boulder on the edge of the moraine. Taking a seat, she swung her bow from her shoulders and laid her quiver alongside her.

"What are you doing?" Pela asked, taking a hesitant step towards her.

"She's going to fight," Ruebyn whispered, his eyes wide.

"*No*," Pela snapped. She held out a hand to Gen, as though to pull her back from the edge.

Gen only smiled. "There's some beef jerky in my pack. You'd better take it." Her eyes turned to the distant light. "I'll do my best to stop them. There can't be many left. They'll be out in the open climbing this slope—I should be able to pick off a few."

Pela straightened her shoulders. "Then we should stay," she announced, dropping a hand to her sword. "We can help."

"No," Genevieve said. "You have to go, in case I…fail. If I can deal with them, I'll catch up."

A lump lodged in Pela's throat as she caught Genevieve's eye and saw the truth there. Her quiver had only six arrows. If even half the Knight's entourage had been slain by the Feline, she would have to make every shot. Then there was the Knights' armour. Gen had only hunting arrows—the wooden points could not pierce solid steel.

Pela swallowed, struggling to find the words. "We…we can help you."

"No, Pela," Genevieve said, offering a sad smile. "Kryssa can't lose us both. And she would never forgive me if I let something happen to you."

"I told you, I can look after myself!" Pela insisted. She knelt beside her friend and took Genevieve's hand in hers. "Please don't do this."

Genevieve touched her other hand to Pela's head. "It's already done," she whispered. "Now *go*." Her eyes flickered to the sky behind Pela. "Before the storm arrives."

Twisting where she crouched, Pela saw that Genevieve spoke the truth. Lightning flashed above the distant peaks and the sky had darkened, the stars vanishing behind unseen clouds. Even as she stood, the rumble of thunder carried to their lonely perch.

Pela closed her eyes, unable to bear the thought of

leaving her friend behind. But she had already faced this choice, had already opted to stay rather than allow Ruebyn to fall to his death. Remembering the awful fear, the despair of her capture, she knew she could not do it again, not for anyone. Genevieve had offered her a way out, and for better or worse, Pela had to take it.

Exhaling, she stood. They shared another glance, she and Gen, but there was nothing left to be said. They were all exhausted, weary beyond belief, but they had to push on, had to continue or be lost.

Biting her lip, Pela nodded to Genevieve and turned away before the tears could spill. Walking past Ruebyn, she took his hand and drew him away, stopping only to collect her pack and take the food from Genevieve's. There was a thin animal trail along the edge of the lake and she started along it without looking back. Pela prayed it would lead them to safety.

The darkness pressed down as they began the long journey around the lake. Soon the clouds overtook the moon, but the midnight waters still glowed with that unearthly light and they continued unhindered. The lake became a presence of its own, a strange, haunting thing. There was a sadness about the place, as though a great tragedy had taken place here in ages past.

Pela imagined the glow must come from the souls of the long dead, trapped within the icy waters, forever longing for freedom. She wondered if that was to be their fate, to die upon these windswept slopes, their lives stolen by the unforgiven mountains—or the Knight that pursued them.

Jagged gullies crisscrossed their path and as they climbed the broken slope, and the ground to their right fell away, becoming a cliff that plummeted down to the lakeshore.

Soon Pela's legs began to shake. Every movement became an effort of will, her knees so weak they threatened to collapse with every step. In all her life, Pela had never pressed herself so hard, had never come so close to utter exhaustion.

On they marched, clambering over boulders and shuffling along narrow ledges, the way lit by the flickering glow from far below. Several times they were forced to rest, clinging to each other in their desperation to keep warm. The winds grew stronger, howling across the lake with a terrible fury, while a threatening darkness stole the sky.

The weather closed in, the icy gales slicing through their thin cloaks. They took turns wearing the jacket from the pack, until Ruebyn's face lost all colour and Pela left it with him. Boulders dotted the slope, offering scarce shelter. An ache began in the base of Pela's skull, and despite the extra layer of clothing, Ruebyn started to lag, forcing her to slow.

Lungs burning, they continued, for without shelter they could not stop. Then with a roar, the skies opened, and sleet fell down to lash the mountainside. Pela gasped as it struck like a frozen wave. She was drenched within moments, so cold the breath was stolen from her lungs. No matter how hard they walked, they would never warm themselves now.

They could go no further. They would freeze on the shores of this lake if they did not find shelter. There were no trees here, only stark stone and water, but surely there must be a cave, something, anything that might protect them. They had enough kindling for a small fire, but it would never light in these conditions.

Her eyes caught on a dark patch above, set back in the cliffs. It might have been nothing, a twist in the rock or darker stone, but there was no choice. They staggered towards it, ice seeping into their bones, their strength fading with every step. Pela knew if she was wrong, they would die.

By the time they reached the cliffs, the sleet was so thick that Pela could barely see a foot in front of her. The cold stung her eyes and she had lost all feeling in her face. Ice-laden water rushed across the ground, soaking their boots. A deep ache had begun in her hands and feet, and she feared frostbite would soon follow.

For a second, Pela could see only blank stone. Blood pounded in her skull as she stumbled up to the cliff-face and placed her hands to the rock, feeling for what she had seen so easily just moments before. Could her instincts have been wrong?

She almost fell as the cliff gave way suddenly to a cave. Turning, she grasped Ruebyn by the arm and dragged them both inside. The cave hardly went ten yards into the mountain, but the respite from the wind and sleet was instant. Pela's relief was so great that she almost fell to her knees. But there was no time to rest, not yet.

Tearing off her pack, she dragged out the pile of kindling. It was barely enough for an hour of fire, but it might still prove the difference between life and death. She dumped it in a pile while Ruebyn stood dumbly in the entrance, his face so pale he might have passed for a ghost himself.

"Stack the wood!" Pela cried, her teeth chattering.

The ache in her extremities was growing worse. A tremor shook her and she cursed as the pack slipped from her frozen fingers. Ruebyn staggered over and started sorting through the wood, doing his best to prepare it for a fire.

It took long minutes for Pela to find the flint. By then Ruebyn was ready, though she had to rearrange several pieces of wood to give the fire room to breathe. Her hands were shaking so badly she could barely strike the flint. It took several attempts before she produced even a single spark. The flames died quickly on the damp earth, but she persisted until finally a soft glow caught amongst the tinder she'd placed in the centre of the wood.

Pela fanned the tiny flame, only sitting back when she was sure it would not go out. Another tremor ran from her scalp to her toes. They'd lit the fire right at the back of the cave, where the stone would reflect its heat back at them. Even so, she could barely feel its warmth against the icy storm.

Water from her hair tricked down her back. Pela cursed. They would die of hypothermia in their drenched clothes before the tiny flame did anything to help them. She dragged the jacket from her back and slung it across a nearby rock to dry. Ruebyn stared as her pants and shirt followed, until she wore only her filthy underclothes.

"What are you doing?" he cried.

"Take off your clothes," she snapped, unable to muster the energy to explain. "Before you freeze."

Ruebyn hesitated, but with a glare from her, he obeyed. The oilskin jacket they'd shared was soaked through and he laid it alongside hers. He removed his shirt next, revealing the pale skin of his chest. There he hesitated, casting a glance in her direction.

"Pants too," she said, unable to keep the grin from her lips. "They're soaked."

Understanding showed in his eyes and Pela couldn't help but giggle at his naivety. He laid his pants as near to the fire as he dared then stood in his underwear, hands extended to the flames. A shiver rippled through him, the hairs on his arms standing on end.

"I'm *freezing!*" he gasped.

"Be thankful we found the cave," Pela replied, "or we'd already be dead."

Ruebyn nodded. Seating himself alongside her, he wrapped his arms around his chest. "Do you think your friend is okay?"

Pela swallowed. For half a second she'd forgotten Genevieve in their own desperate fight to survive. What would she do with this storm approaching? But then, she was better clothed than them, and there were trees on the moraine that could provide shelter.

"Gen used to hunt in the mountains of Golden Ridge," Pela answered finally. "She knows what to do in a storm."

"I hope she can stop them," Ruebyn said.

Remembering the last look Genevieve had given her, Pela did not answer. A cold breeze whistled through the cave, sending the firelight flickering across the stones. Pela shuddered, though whether it was from the cold or dread, she could not have said. Her chest ached with an awful loneliness, with the realisation she had lost her last connection with Skystead. She edged closer to the fire, basking in its heat, but it did nothing for the hole in her heart.

"Come here," she said suddenly to Ruebyn. "I'm cold as well."

"What?"

"Just come here," she gasped.

Her teeth were chattering, the awful emptiness swelled within her chest. A shrill keening began in the back of her throat and she felt as though she must explode, that the terror and despair and desolation must all come bursting from her, must tear her apart.

Then Ruebyn was there. She shivered as his arms went around her waist. He was as cold as she was but he held her tight, and the pressure within lessened, if only a touch. She closed her eyes, relaxing into his embrace. Her heartbeat slowed, her mind drifting.

How had it come to this, the two of them alone against the Knights of Alana? Just a week ago she had loathed Ruebyn, could not have even tolerated his touch. His cold indifference had been anathema to her, his rigid subservience to the rules a cold cruelty she could not bear.

Absently, Pela touched a hand to her cheek, tracing the thin line of the scar Ruebyn's whip had left on his first day. It was only one of many, and yet it was everything, a cold reminder of their reality. She started to pull away from him, then flinched as his hand touched hers. Her eyes snapped open to find him watching her.

"I'm so sorry, Pela," he whispered. His hazel eyes shone in the firelight.

Pela stared at Ruebyn, wondering whether she could trust him. For the first time since their escape, she really looked at him, seeing how his face had changed. The plumpness had melted from his cheeks and there was no fear in his eyes now, no uncertainty. The last few days had changed him utterly, burning away the child she had met in the mines. She wondered who he was now.

Almost without realising it, Pela entwined her fingers in his and leaned her head against his shoulder. She moved his hand to her ear. It still ached from the blow he had struck before their escape, the flesh torn and broken.

"What about this?" she murmured.

He shivered, cupping the side of her face. His fingers were cool and she sighed as they stole away some of the pain. Pela burrowed her head into his chest, catching the rich, earthy scent of him. After so long with the awful dust and the stench of burning coal, his smell was surprisingly pleasant.

"So, so sorry," he croaked. Pela was surprised to hear his voice break.

She lifted her head and watched the tears spill down his cheeks. She wiped them away.

"No more tears," she said.

He swallowed, his head bobbing up and down. "I wish I could take it back."

"You can't," Pela whispered.

"What can I do?"

"I'm still cold," she replied.

She took his head between her hands then, turning her face to the side. For once, Ruebyn knew what to do. A tingle ran down Pela's spine as he pressed his lips to her ear, a shudder that went right through her. He pulled her closer, his chest a burning warmth against her flesh.

Turning again, she stared into his eyes, then drew him to her cheek. His lips caressed the line of her scar and her eyes fluttered closed, her breath quickening. Her hand slid down his back, savouring the softness of his skin, so unlike her own, made rough by the long days in the sun, beaten by the torture of the mines.

Finally Pela could wait no longer. With the hand still on his cheek, she turned his head so their lips brushed gently together. Then they were kissing, his body pressing hard against hers, drawing her down. And suddenly the cave was no longer quite so cold, quite so lonely.

※ 30 ※

Kryssa watched as Braidon pushed his way through the crowd and lifted a hand. The gates gave way with a horrible *crack* and Braidon staggered, but the mob was already surging through the opening. She gave Braidon her shoulder and they stumbled after them, weapons in hand.

The *twang* of crossbows greeted them as they stepped through the gates into a courtyard. Ahead, a dozen of Braidon's followers went down. Those still on their feet charged at the enemy.

The Knights of Alana tossed aside their crossbows and drew swords. They stood barring the entrance to the inner keep, a large doorway closed at their backs. Shouts came from overhead as those still atop the wall fired down into the courtyard.

Braidon shouted at those crowding around him, gesturing to a nearby staircase that led up to the ramparts. Part of the mob split off, weapons at the ready, and a minute later the sound of fighting carried down from above.

Kryssa and Braidon turned their attention to the more immediate threat. The mob was hurling themselves at the line of Knights, but their makeshift weapons were little use against steel armour and heavy broadswords. Even as she watched, a club bounced from a Knight's breastplate before its wielder was cut down.

A growl hissed from Braidon as he straightened and shrugged off her aid. Hefting his sword, he leapt to join the melee. Kryssa cursed and raced after him. The king still had not recovered from the confrontation at the temple, and who knew how much energy he had used busting open the Castle gates.

Ahead, the tide was already turning in the Knights' favour. Using their weight, they pushed the crowd back, swords rising and falling in bloody fashion. Fear showed in the faces nearest Kryssa. If they broke, it would be a massacre.

A gap opened in the press of bodies facing the Knights. Braidon leapt to fill it, his sword flashing at the first Knight to stand against him. Steel grated on steel as his blade struck the man's armour, but Braidon dragged it upwards so that the point slammed into the gorget protecting his opponent's throat. The thin iron crumbled beneath the blow and the Knight staggered away, dropping his sword.

Another iron-clad warrior stepped up to take his place. Braidon ducked a blow from his sword and Kryssa joined the fray, her blade slamming into the Knight's wrist. Steel crunched and the broadsword tumbled harmlessly to the ground. Seeing the man was unarmed, another of Braidon's followers leapt on him and bore him to the ground. Others piled on, clubs and axes hammering at the man's armour. Inevitably, they found their mark.

Roaring at their comrade's death, the Knights attacked with renewed fury. Braidon parried a blow, but the Knight's momentum carried him on. He slammed into the king, hurling Braidon from his feet. Kryssa charged to intercept the silver warriors before they could strike a mortal blow, her sword flashing furiously to keep them back.

Then Braidon was up again. Joining Kryssa, he attacked with a cold fury, struggling to hold back the iron tide. Lacking the skill and arms, those around them died by the dozens. Only Braidon and Kryssa could hold their own, while Dominic had disappeared in the first minutes of the siege. Kryssa could sense the mood of Braidon's followers turning, their rage giving way to fear. If something didn't tip the scales…

Bellowing, Braidon leapt at the nearest Knight. His shoulder caught the man in the chest and hurled him from his feet. But now Braidon stood alone, isolated from his allies. Two Knights moved to intercept him, their swords held at the ready.

Braidon's lips twisted in a snarl and he roared again. Kryssa struggled to go to his aid, but a third Knight attacked, forcing her to defend herself. The king's blade lanced out to meet the first of his foes. Their weapons came together with a *shriek*, but instead of deflecting the blow, Braidon's sword carved straight through the Knight's. A shriek came from the ironclad warrior as the king's blade continued its path, slicing through his breastplate like a knife through cheese.

Dragging back his weapon, Braidon spun to meet the second Knight, but the man had frozen at the fate of his comrade. Braidon cut him down before he could recover. Others fell back as well, fearful of the king's power. Armies and mobs these men could face without a hint of fear, but the sight of magic unnerved them above all else.

Braidon strode forward, and with a cry of terror, one of the Knights dropped his sword and turned to flee. Seeing their opportunity, the mob chased after him. One hurled a club that slammed into the Knight's knee, sending him crashing to the ground. Then they were upon him.

Kryssa looked away in time to see the other Knights turning to run. The battle suddenly became a rout, the terrified Knights fleeing for their lives—only to be brought up short by the barred doors of the inner keep. Her heart thudded painfully in her chest as she staggered over to Braidon.

"Are you okay?" she croaked. His face was hard, but she could see the exhaustion behind his eyes. She wondered how much of his own life force he had used in the past few minutes.

"I'll manage," he replied, then gestured to the giant oak doors. "Let's get these open."

"Do we need to?" Kryssa asked as men and women leapt to obey. She gestured at the dead lying around the cobbled courtyard. "Wasn't this enough?"

Axes crashed into the wood, sending splinters across the yard. She could still hear the sound of fighting from the ramparts, but there had only been a few Knights atop the wall by the time the gates had fallen. Even so, she spied a crossbow lying nearby and swept it up. Taking a quiver of bolts from a dead Knight, she loaded the weapon and then eyed the battlements, in case anyone attempted another attack on the king.

"There could still be Knights inside," Braidon murmured. He leaned against the courtyard wall, looking wan. "I want to be sure."

"What about what the Elder said? There could be inno-cent people hiding inside."

"What choice do we have, Kryssa?" Braidon asked. "If we leave them, it's only a matter of time before they're rein-forced. Then they'll strike again. We need to put an end to this plague while they're still weak."

A chill blew across Kryssa's neck, but she said nothing. There was no more time to argue. A great *crack* came from the timbers of the door and then those too were crashing open. Braidon bellowed an order and the crowd parted for him. Kryssa followed the king as he led the way inside.

Within, the hallways were unlit. Braidon shouted for torches to be brought. No one wanted to be stumbling around in darkness, with the crossbows the Knights wielded. A calm fell over the crowd as burning brands were lit and passed around. Many had taken swords and armour from the fallen Knights, and a few like Kryssa now wielded the heavy crossbows.

Silence hung over the Castle as they crept through the dark corridors. Kryssa scanned the shadows, seeking out danger, wondering if all the Knights had fallen on the doorstep.

It wasn't long before she was proven wrong. They came screaming from a side corridor, attacking the group from the flanks. Braidon spun to meet them, sword in hand. A crossbow discharged, sending a bolt straight through the breastplate of a Knight and stopping him dead. He fell back against his comrades, slowing their charge, and Braidon's followers fell upon them.

Kryssa watched in shock as the carnage played out. There had been only five Knights in this group; they were horribly outnumbered. With the impetus of their charge ruined, they didn't stand a chance, and they fell within minutes. Braidon led the crowd down the corridor from which they'd emerged, leaving Kryssa alone in the dark.

Swallowing, she made to go after them, but something gave her pause. The last attack did not sit right with her. Braidon still had over a hundred followers with him—the five Knights could not have possibly thought to win. Why had they thrown their lives away?

It had to be a distraction. Drawing her sword, Kryssa continued down the corridor in the direction they'd originally been heading. She did not know what to expect, but she encountered no one in the long hallways, not a soul in any of the rooms branching off the main corridor. After a while she began to think she'd been wrong, but still she did not turn back. Finally she turned a corner and realised where she'd been heading.

In Townirwin, there had been a holy pantheon in the centre of the Castle, a great chamber dedicated to the sacrifice of the Saviour. The corridor ahead was painted with the same murals as the ones outside that Caste. Kryssa hesitated. If the Elder had spoken the truth, if innocents had taken refuge inside the Castle walls, she would find them here.

She started towards the twin iron doors that waited at the end of the corridor. Shadows clung to the floor, the only light coming from the open windows high above. When she was halfway to the end, movement came from ahead. Kryssa acted instantly, the crossbow coming up, but she hesitated when a lantern was unshuttered.

The Elder who had spoken with them outside the gates stood barring her path.

"Put down your weapon, sister," he murmured.

Kryssa tightened her grip on the crossbow. "Step aside, Elder. I have no wish to harm an unarmed man."

She started towards the man, but the air grew dense, until it was as though she were wading through thick mud. Within a couple of steps Kryssa found she could not move forward at all. An invisible barrier stood between her and the Elder.

"I need no weapon but my mind," he murmured, "but I wish no harm to you either."

Kryssa took a step back and the pressure eased. "You have power."

"I do."

"You cannot stop us all," Kryssa replied. "Braidon told me how your new magic works. You are limited by the strength of your own life force."

"I fear I have power enough to stop you all," the Elder replied sadly. "I have drunk the lives of the sacrificed, as have all the Elders of the Order. It is a strength I am loathe to use, but I will not hesitate to protect my people."

Kryssa's stomach churned. "What sacrifices?"

"You know very well, Kryssa. You may have escaped my brothers, but you were not the first to go beneath their blades. I left that darkness behind when I came to Plorsea, but all these years the power I collected has lain dormant."

"You're a murderer," Kryssa whispered, her hands shaking.

"I am," the Elder replied, bowing his head.

Anger boiled up within Kryssa. She started towards him again, but the barrier brought her up short. Her fist slammed against it. "You took me from my home!" she snarled. "You tried to burn my daughter alive!"

"I took no part in your Great Sacrifice," the Elder replied. His voice was barely a whisper now. "But to my shame, I once performed cleansings, once believed our two kinds could not live side by side."

Kryssa ignored him. "So you lied! It *was* you who sent those Knights out into the city, to slaughter our priests and burn our temple." Teeth bared, she pointed the crossbow and fired.

The bolt slashed the air, but it only managed a few feet before it slowed to nothing and clattered harmlessly to the floor. Growling, she tore another from the quiver and reloaded the weapon.

"I did not lie!" the Elder tried, but Kryssa barely heard him.

She turned her mind inwards, anger driving her to action. Three times now she had seen Braidon tap into that unknown power. Recalling their discussion, Kryssa sought to do the same. Drawing in a deep breath, she stared at the Elder, but she no longer really saw him.

Her consciousness was elsewhere, plunging inwards with each inhalation, following the passage of breath to her core. She needed no schooling in meditation. Kryssa had been practicing since the first day Selina had taken her off the streets of Ardath. It was a skill valued by the followers of the Old Gods, a way to control their emotions and themselves.

The practice helped to cool her anger and calm Kryssa's racing heart. But she knew now Braidon had been right. This man had confirmed as much. The Elders had a terrible advantage with the power they had collected. They needed to be stopped, to pay for what they had done to her and Pela and so many others. Kryssa would make them regret choosing her for their Great Sacrifice. She was a helpless prisoner no longer. She intended to show this Elder as much.

Slowly the rest of the world dissolved away, until only darkness remained, the empty void of her inner mind. This was where Magickers had once found their power, but now that infinite black was empty. She had never encountered the power Braidon had discovered before, but then, she had not been looking for it, had not needed it.

Now she did.

Kryssa searched the void, seeking the flickering of power, but finding only darkness. Drifting through nothingness, she wondered what she was doing wrong, why the power would not come. Braidon had said this new magic belonged to all…so why, then, could she not reach it?

Cursing, her control slipped. Her mind retreated, but as the darkness faded she caught a flicker of light in her spirit eyes. Hope touched her and drawing another breath, she centred herself. The void returned—and the glow vanished.

What am I doing wrong?

She could not understand it. The power was her own life force, it should be here, it was part of her…

A part of me!

In a rush, Kryssa spun in the dark, turning her eyes upon herself, and saw the brilliance at her centre. Braidon had been right—the power *was* her, but she'd been so concentrated on finding some outside force, she'd missed it.

Fear touched her now. The flame was a tiny, pale thing, surrounded by an infinite void. Surely it could not hold the power she needed, not enough to stand against the Elder. He had claimed the lives of so many—what could her little candle do against him?

But perhaps she could catch him by surprise. Kryssa's resolve tightened, and gripping the flame with her spirit fingers, she opened her eyes. Power surged through her but she held it in check, not yet ready to act. The crossbow was heavy in her hand. She started to wind back the crank.

"You cannot pass, Kryssa," the Elder said sadly. "You cannot harm me."

"Like hell," Kryssa snarled.

"I understand your hate," the Elder continued, "but I will not let you harm those inside."

"I don't care about the people inside, it's you I want!" Kryssa snapped.

She took hold of her power and sent it questing out beyond her. There was a strange, disorientating sensation, as though her mind had separated from her body, and then she *was* beyond her body. Drifting between herself and the Elder, suddenly the barrier became visible, flickering before her like a wall of mist.

Time slowed to a crawl as she examined the swirling white. At first it seemed impenetrable, but as the fog flowed, she began to see gaps, weaker points through which she caught glimpses of the Elder beyond. She focused her energies on one of these, tugging and pulling with her mind, feeling the energy draining from her with each touch. Braidon had been right about their limits. Working against her was the strength of who knew how many innocent lives.

The thought restored her anger, and baring her teeth, Kryssa kept on. Finally, with a cry of triumph, she stabbed through. An answering cry came from the Elder as an inch-wide hole opened in the mists. In her mind's eye she saw him stagger, then thrust out his hands. Power streamed from him, burning and churning reality, but Kryssa's arm was already sweeping up.

The crossbow *thumped* backwards in her grip as she fired. The bolt hissed down the corridor, passing freely through the hole in the barrier, and buried itself in the Elder's chest. His eyes widened and his mouth fell open. The barrier blinked out as though it had never been.

Then the power he had summoned slammed into Kryssa, picking her up and driving her into the wall. Her head smashed against the marble and she collapsed to the floor. Stars danced across her vision and she had to close her eyes to keep herself from throwing up.

When she finally opened them again, the Elder was gone.

❧ 31 ❧

Pela woke to the warmth of sunlight on her face. Her eyes flickered open. For a second, she was surprised to find herself lying naked in Ruebyn's arms. Then her memories of the night came rushing back and her cheeks grew hot. In the grips of the storm, she had not been cold.

She sat up quickly, disentangling herself from Ruebyn. He gave a quiet moan and rolled over, his arms curling around her waist. Still drowsy from lack of sleep, Pela examined their little cave in the daylight. The fire had burned out long ago but the storm had broken, and now light streamed in from the crooked entrance…

Cursing, Pela leapt to her feet. Her heart was suddenly racing. For the sun to reach them here, it must already be well above the mountain peaks. They had slept too long!

"Wake up!" she gasped, grabbing Ruebyn by the shoulders and shaking him. "We have to go."

"Wha…?" he groaned, blinking in confusion. A frown touched his forehead as he saw her standing over him. Then a handsome smile crossed his lips. "Good morning."

Pela paused, her cheeks warming as she recalled the night…before her sense of urgency came rushing back. She threw off his arm.

"We can…discuss what happened later!" she said. "The sun's up. We have to go. Unless you want that Knight to catch us."

At the mention of their foe, Ruebyn's senses returned. He leapt to his feet and they scrambled for their clothes, mostly dried from the fire's heat, tugged them on, and gathered their gear. Ruebyn swung the pack onto his back while Pela strapped the sword to her waist, and together they stumbled outside.

Pela's gaze was drawn down to the slopes behind them. She searched the dark rocks surrounding the lake, looking for their pursuers, but there was no sign of movement. She let out a long sigh and turned to continue their march.

"Good morning, young lovers."

The words froze them in their tracks. Pela's mouth fell open as she saw the Knight sitting alone on a boulder, sword resting across his iron legs. Sunlight danced from his visor as he rose, his armour squealing with the movement. An arrow protruded from his shoulder, where it had torn through a joint in the steel, and the Feline had left great gashes across his breastplate. Even his sword was nicked and twisted, as though some weight had put it under great strain.

"You led a merry chase," he growled, taking a step towards them. The blade was in his left hand, though he had wielded it right-handed against the beast. "But it is over now."

Pela struggled to breathe. Panic rose to choke her, but there was no time to lose control. She scanned the slopes around them, but there was no sign of anyone else. The Knight was alone.

"Where is Genevieve?" she growled, returning her gaze to the Knight.

The Knight laughed, the sound echoing awfully from his helmet. "The slave fought well, but I killed her all the same. Her strength now serves the Saviour."

The news staggered Pela, and if not for Ruebyn's hand on her back, she would have fallen. She thought she'd accepted Gen's death the night before, but now she realised that that had been a lie. Somehow, she'd still expected the wily huntress to win. Now the truth stood before them, cold and implacable, and there was nowhere left to run.

But there was no time to mourn now. The Knight might have been injured, but with his broadsword and armour, they were still outmatched. She dragged the sword from her belt.

"I'm glad she took your friends with her," Ruebyn spat. He swung the bag from his back and dragged out a dagger.

Their foe only laughed. "My retainers wait for me below. This is Trolan land, and it means death to be caught here. A sacrifice I alone am willing to make, to ensure there is justice for my brother's murder."

He swung a practice blow with his sword. It was twice the length of Pela's blade. He would cut her down before she could get anywhere near him. Ruebyn edged closer to her, dagger in hand.

"I hope you know how to use that," she muttered as the Knight started forward.

Ruebyn flashed a regretful smile. "I think you know the answer to that, Pela."

Pela sighed, but there was no changing things now. "Keep away from his sword. Aim for the joints in his armour, if you can."

She slid sideways across the slope, seeking to draw the

Knight after her. Her feet spread instinctively into the fighting stance Caledan had taught her, improving her balance on the uneven surface. Dotted with rocks and loose gravel, the slope ran fifty feet towards the lake before plunging over the cliff, down another hundred feet to the water.

The Knight's armour squealed as he followed her. He had seen them back in the canyon, and must have known that Ruebyn was no threat. All the better—maybe Ruebyn would have a chance to attack him from behind. If he had the courage.

"Come on then," Pela hissed, brandishing the short sword, trying to raise him to anger. "Come die like your brother."

Her words had the desired effect, as with a roar, the Knight lunged. He moved faster than Pela had expected, given his injuries, and she barely managed to avoid the first swing of his sword. The blade hissed dangerously close to her throat as she staggered back, only the weeks of Caledan's training keeping her upright.

The man obviously wasn't going to take prisoners this time. That was fine with Pela—she didn't intend to be taken alive anyway. Setting her shoulders, she thrust the sword out in front of her and waited for the next attack.

This time when it came, she was ready. His sword flashed down in an overhanded blow. Pela skipped to the side and the blade carried past, striking rock and jarring violently sideways. Seeing the opening, she stepped in, her blade flashing for his midriff. But her blow was off and she missed the fine gap between the armour under his arm. The point of her sword scraped off solid steel, leaving a long scratch in the metal.

He felt the blow though, and roaring, he swung out his

injured arm, catching Pela in the shoulder. There wasn't much power in the blow, but it knocked her back. Recovering her balance, she retreated another step as the deadly broadsword carved an arc where she had stood.

Beyond the Knight, Ruebyn darted to and fro, his face an agony of uncertainty. He didn't know how to help, how to find the weak spots in the Knight's armour. In a sudden premonition, Pela realised he could only get himself killed in this fight.

"Stay back, Ruebyn!" she screamed, then leapt at the Knight again.

His sword rose to meet her, but it was an awkward blow and she easily caught it with the hilt of her sword, sending his blade slamming into the ground. Then she stabbed out, aiming for his throat. The point of her sword slashed his gorget, but he turned aside and the blow only dented the lighter steel.

Pela retreated a step, drawing back her sword, and the Knight's gorget fell loose. She had sliced through its bindings and now his throat was exposed. A smile crossed her lips as she faced her iron foe. He must be growing weary by now, his energy sapped by the forced march to catch them —whereas sleep had restored some of Pela's strength. And he was clearly not skilled with his left hand.

She sent up thanks to Genevieve for her final act, and a prayer for the Old Gods to bless the huntress. Genevieve had suffered so much for Pela and her mother—she deserved to rest now.

Tightening her grip on the sword, Pela beckoned the Knight forward.

Stones crunched as he came for her. Ruebyn hung back and Pela hoped he would listen, would not interfere. She could not stand to see him die for nothing, to be left alone on this stark mountainside. Snarling, she hurled herself at the Knight.

His sword rose to meet her, but he was lagging now, weighed down by pain and exhaustion. In a fair fight they could never have matched this armoured man, but Genevieve had given them a chance, and Pela was more than happy to take advantage.

Their weapons came together with a crash, but as she swung again the Knight slipped in the loose stones, and her sword drove beneath his guard. The blade crunched into his wrist, leaving a dent in the steel and forcing him back. Tasting victory, Pela chased after him—but his wound was not as bad as she'd thought, and his broadsword flashed for her face.

Only instinct saved her. Stones scattered in all directions as she threw herself at the ground. The hackles rose on her neck as the blade passed overhead, but before could regain her feet, the Knight's foot flashed for her face. She rolled desperately and the steel-shod boot collided with her shoulder. A cry tore from her lips as she flung herself back, sword raised to defend herself.

Their weapons came together with a crash, but the impact tore the blade from Pela's hands. Her foe gave a cry of triumph as Pela's weapon skittered across the ground and struck a rock, snapping in two. The broken blade flew off down the slope, disappearing over the cliff, leaving the hilt discarded amongst the gravel.

Fear froze Pela in place. Lifting her chin, she looked at the Knight, waiting for the end to come. He raised his sword, so close Pela could not avoid the blow. Then roar came from above them, and Ruebyn charged. He was on the Knight before their foe could react, slamming into his armoured back and hurling them both from their feet. Their weapons went flying as they crashed down the slope, coming to rest several feet below.

Groaning, Ruebyn struggled to his hands and knees. But the Knight had been protected by his armour, and was the faster to recover. With a shriek of twisted steel, he tackled the young overseer, slamming him into the ground. Pinning Ruebyn beneath his weight, the Knight reached with iron hands for his throat.

"No!"

Sweeping up the broken sword hilt, Pela came to her feet and hurtled down the slope. The stones shifted beneath her weight, almost toppling her, but she recovered and leapt again. Ruebyn was beating at the iron arms but he could do nothing to dislodge his tormentor. His face was turning pale, suffocated by the unyielding strength of their foe.

Fixated on Ruebyn, the Knight did not see Pela coming. She slammed into him with the force of a small avalanche, tearing him loose from the overseer. Her momentum carried them on, and out of control, she and the Knight flew down the slope. Each time they struck the ground, sharp gravel flew in all directions. Pela cried out as stones sliced her flesh.

Clutching a hand to her face, she glimpsed the lake—and the cliff rising quickly to meet them. It was a hundred foot drop into the icy waters. Even if she somehow survived the fall, the cold would kill her before she found a way out.

She slammed into the mountainside again, driving the last of the air from her lungs, but this time she lashed out, stabbing the broken end of her sword into the earth. There was only an inch of blade left and she prayed it would not break. Steel shrieked on stone as she clung to the hilt, her weight almost dragging her arms from their sockets.

Stones rained down around Pela as she slowed, then ground to a stop. Gasping, she slumped against the dirt. Her shoulders shrieked, the muscles torn and bruised from the effort it had taken to stop her downwards plunge.

She could not rest yet, not until she knew they were safe. Gathering her strength, Pela pulled herself to her hands and knees, an awful groan slipping from her in a sigh.

But as she made to stand, a hard weight struck her, driving her backwards into the gravel. The broken dagger spun from her hands. Stars flashed across her vision as her head was slammed into a rock. Her groan turned to a scream as she found the mottled face of the Knight just an inch from her own.

He must have lost his helmet in the fall, for now she saw him in all his terrible truth. His nose had been crushed sometime in the past, leaving it flattened and purple with broken blood vessels. Bloody eyes bulged from their sockets as he bared his teeth and clasped his iron fingers around her throat, silencing Pela's scream.

She gasped as the iron collar was crushed against her windpipe. Only the slightest whisper of air made it to her lungs. Then not even that was possible as he leaned closer. She beat at his twisted breastplate, but all she achieved were bruises on her knuckles. Changing tact, she searched for the gap in his armour.

Finding a crack, she shoved her hand through, stabbing at his flesh with her nails, pinching, scratching, whatever she could do to hurt him. His face twisted and momentarily his grip loosened. She sucked in a desperate breath, and the darkness retreated slightly. He twisted, one hand still gripping her throat, the other knocking aside her questing fingers.

Then he lifted her up and slammed her head back down

into the rocks. The strength left Pela in a rush. She slumped against the ground, watching as a grin warped that awful face. He crouched over her, both hands at her throat again.

"May the Saviour condemn you to a fiery pit," he snarled, goblets of spit spraying her face.

Pela's lungs screamed for air. Her whole body throbbed, her skull pounding like a drum. A great weariness crept over her. She felt the darkness calling, an open void crying out for her. In her mind's eye, she turned towards it, saw something flicker, reached for it.

The light was only the tiniest of candles amidst the dark. A strong breeze would blow it out, but when Pela touched it she felt a rush to her spirit, a renewed will to live. The flame flickered, shrinking, as though the act of restoring her will had lessoned it. Fear touched Pela, an understanding that the light was her, that she was the light.

If it died, so did she.

But it was not yet extinguished. She had strength enough for one last, desperate act. She touched the light again.

Back on the mountainside, her eyes snapped open. The Knight's face loomed above. His laughter rang distantly in her ears and there was a joy in his eyes, a sickly ecstasy at his power over life and death. It fed her desperation, and drawing on the light, she willed him to release her, to fall back, to fly.

It was as though some invisible power struck the Knight. Little more than a tap, but his position was unstable on the mountainside, and it was enough to push him back from her. He reared up, his feet slipping on the loose stones, arms windmilling. But he could not regain his balance, and with a cry he tumbled backwards. His armour added momentum to the fall and he bounced twice on the treacherous slope.

That was all it took.

One second the Knight was there, the next he was over the cliff, disappearing as though he had never been.

Pela stared at the space where he had vanished for a long second, and then fell back against the gravel. Her eyes fluttered closed. She was suddenly so weary she lacked the strength to move. In her mind's eye, the candle was reduced to an ember, its glow surrounded by the frigid void.

"Pela!"

Warm fingers touched her cheek. Her eyes cracked open to find Ruebyn crouched beside her.

"Hey," she croaked.

"You did it!" he gasped. "You beat him."

Pela smiled, but could not find the strength to reply. Her eyes slid closed again. "So…tired."

"Hey, stay with me, okay?" Ruebyn cried.

His arms went around her as he lifted her up. She gasped, feeling then the damage the Knight had dealt to the back of her skull, the pain in her shoulder, in her entire body. He shifted her carefully, resting her head against his shoulder.

"I've got you!" he cried.

Pela did not reply. Her head shrieked with every step they took. Several times Ruebyn staggered, and she gasped, but each time he managed to recover and continue. She would never know where he found the strength, but somehow he carried her all the way up the long slope to their cave.

She let out a long breath as he laid her down, feeling the sun's warmth shining down. She wanted desperately to open her eyes and look upon the lake in daylight, to see its beauty, but could not find the will. Ruebyn's arms were warm around her and she sighed, secure in the knowledge she was finally safe, that they had defeated all their enemies.

That she could rest.

❧ 32 ❧

Braidon found Kryssa sitting slumped on the floor outside the pantheon. He and his followers had encountered several more groups of Knights throughout the Castle, and had only realised she was missing half an hour earlier. His gaze caught on the pool of blood staining the floor nearby her. Thinking she was badly injured, he rushed to her side. Her head lifted at the sound of movement and seeing his approach, she rose unsteadily to her feet.

"Are you okay?" he asked, offering his hand.

His men gathered behind him in the corridor, Dominic at their head. He'd lost the guard in the melee outside the gates, but he'd reappeared not long after they'd entered the Castle. Braidon planned to have words with the man later, but for now he was just happy to have another trained sword at his side.

"I'm fine," she replied. "The Elder got away."

Braidon breathed out a sigh when he saw her clothes were unstained, though a large bruise now marked her forehead. His eyes returned to the blood.

"His?"

She nodded. "I thought the wound was mortal, but obviously not."

"Our people have secured the exits. He won't get far." He hesitated. "Though if he has power, it had better be me who confronts him."

"I'll come," Kryssa said, straightening. Their eyes met. "Though he's stronger than both of us."

Braidon clenched his jaw, understanding her meaning. He looked from the blood to the corridors leading off the main hallway. It didn't take long to find what he was looking for. In his haste to flee, the Elder had left a trail of blood leading away from the pantheon.

"Let's go find him," he said grimly.

"Wait," Kryssa said, "what about his people?"

"What?" Braidon asked, his chest tightening.

"Inside the pantheon," Kryssa said wearily.

Her feet still slightly unsteady, she strode to the giant double doors and pushed them open. Braidon followed her inside and was met by a hundred pairs of eyes watching from the shadows of the hall. Men and women shoved children behind them at the sight of Braidon. They had stacked the wooden pews between themselves and the door, but it was little barrier against attack. Their eyes were filled with fear, and too late Braidon realised his clothes were covered in blood. He must have appeared a fearsome sight. But there was not a weapon between the crowd, and letting out a long breath, Braidon retreated into the corridor, Kryssa a step behind. They closed the doors and shared a glance.

"So he was telling the truth," Braidon murmured.

"About some things," she replied, her eyes shining. "He also spoke of cleansings and the Great Sacrifice."

Braidon nodded grimly and faced Dominic and the

others. They had come to form the core of his fighting force since entering the Castle, but there were still other groups roaming the hallway. If any of them stumbled upon the pantheon, Braidon feared what they might do in their righteous anger. The innocents within needed to be protected.

"Dominic," he said. The man could be trusted with guard duty, at least. "You and the others stay here. Make sure no one leaves or enters this room. I trust you can take care of these people?"

Dominic looked from the iron doors to Braidon. "Are you sure, Your Majesty? What of the Elder?"

"We will take care of him," Braidon replied curtly. "I leave this responsibility to you."

With that, Braidon turned away, drawing Kryssa with him. They followed the trail of blood their quarry had left through the twisting corridors, then up a spiral staircase to the upper floors of the Castle. Braidon had not yet explored these parts, and now they slowed, fearful of ambush. Kryssa and Braidon were both nearing the end of their strength, worn down by injuries and the expenditure of energy, but they could not rest while the task remained unfinished.

Braidon scanned the way ahead, cautious for any sudden attack. Kryssa's warning about the Elder's power rang in his ears. He still wasn't sure how they could counter the man if he had stolen the lifeforce of others.

At least Kryssa had injured him. She still carried the crossbow—maybe they could get off another lucky shot.

Sunlight lit the upper levels of the Castle, streaming in through broad windows and half-raised shutters. Marching down another corridor, Braidon caught glimpses of the courtyard outside and heard the distant cries of his followers. Worry touched him as he leaned out a window and saw them waving torches. If someone was careless, they might burn the whole place to the ground.

Movement came from ahead. Braidon spun as the Elder stepped from an alcove. Blood stained his satin robes and he seemed to have aged since their meeting outside the gates, his face even more lined, his skin sallow.

"Braidon, Kryssa," he greeted them calmly, as though they were two passing visitors and not his mortal enemies.

Braidon gripped his sword tightly in one hand. "Surrender, Elder," he said. "Kryssa told me about your past. You too must answer for your crimes."

The Elder's eyes fell on Braidon's blade. "You will not need that, King," he murmured. "I am no threat to you. Your faithful servant saw to that."

Kryssa scowled. "I am no one's servant," she snapped, gesturing with the crossbow. "Now, are you going to surrender peacefully, or do I need to put another bolt in you?"

"Surrender?" the Elder asked, his voice sad. "So you can slaughter me like my faithful Knights? Or will it be prison, a comfortable cell to wile away my final days? Which is it, my dear king, that you would doom me to for a past I left behind long ago?"

"Your choice," Braidon snapped, hefting his sword. "I will not allow your kind to rule us."

"My brothers and I said the same about Magickers, long before the Saviour freed us of their curse. Why do you think we worked so hard to keep the secret knowledge from this world? Why we sought to squash the practice of meditation?"

"Because you wanted the power for yourselves!" Braidon snapped.

The Elder sighed. "I fear it has become so. Too many of

my brother Elders have given themselves to conceit, allowed avarice to outweigh the greater good. I had thought my efforts here in Chole might bring balance, might begin the Order anew, but alas, it has all been in vain."

"You speak in riddles, but your guilt is clear. You attacked Kryssa with your power."

The Elder's head bowed lower. "In my fear, I lashed out," he whispered. His chin came up and he caught Kryssa's eye. "I am glad you are okay."

"I thought I killed you," Kryssa said coldly.

A smile creased the Elder's face. "You struck me a mortal blow." His face fell. "Coward that I am, I used the last of my power to heal it."

"I don't believe—"

A great boom came from behind them, cutting Braidon off. Braidon spun towards the window as screams came from the courtyard. His people were fleeing towards the open gates. He spun back to the Elder.

"What treachery is this?" he cried. "You were biding your time, distracting us from the last of your Knights!"

"No—"

As the Elder opened his mouth, Braidon lunged, seeking to strike him down before he brought his power to bear. The Elder's hand came up and Braidon felt a moment's resistance. Summoning his own strength, the king forged on, concentrating that energy into the point of his blade, cutting through the Elder's assault. A cry tore from his enemy and Braidon glimpsed despair in the old man's eyes—then his blade plunged home.

A sigh whispered from the Elder's lips as he slumped against the blow. Eyes wide, he stared at Braidon, mouth opening and closing. Blood bubbled from his nostrils as he struggled to speak.

"Please…" came his whisper. "The…pantheon."

There was a long hiss of expelling air as his lungs emptied, and then he was dead.

Braidon carefully lowered the man to the floor and retrieved his blade. Standing over the lifeless body, he felt inexplicably sad, as though lessened by the man's death. The quiet *drip-drip* of blood from his sword sounded loudly in the corridor. He scrunched his eyes closed.

"*Braidon!*" Kryssa screamed.

He leapt back, expecting to see the Elder rising again, but instead saw Kryssa at the window, a hand to her mouth. Braidon quickly crossed to where she stood, his heart beating hard in his chest. Smoke was pouring from the rooftops of the citadel, the first tongues of flame just beginning to appear through the slate tiles.

"The pantheon," she whispered.

To his horror, Braidon saw she was right.

They ran the whole way, but it made no difference. It was already too late.

Gasping, Braidon staggered up to the great iron door. Dominic still stood at his post, his face impassive as he watched Braidon's approach. He did not seem to notice the smoke pouring from beneath the doors, nor the distant crackling of flames, the fading screams. His other companions wore identical expressions.

"*What are you doing?*" Braidon screamed.

Dominic blinked. "We took care of them, Your Majesty," he said simply.

Braidon blanked, his stomach spasming in horror. He shoved Dominic aside and staggered forward, hauling at the locking bar set across the pantheon's entrance. Heat radiated from the steel doors, burning his face, but he would not retreat. The bar slid free and he reached for the knob.

With a roar, the doors flew open, unleashing a wave of heat that struck Braidon in the chest and hurled him back. He screamed as his beard caught flame, the fire searing at his skin. Holding up a hand to shelter his face, he squinted through the inferno, desperate to reach the pantheon, to do something, anything to help those trapped within. A desperate wail rose above the crackling, though Braidon could no longer tell whether it was real or imagined, the souls within or his own, or Kryssa's, the long dead Gods or his own sister, crying out for the innocent.

He sank to his knees and slammed a fist into the stone tiles. His scream shook the walls, filled with the torment of regret, of pain and guilt and the awful knowledge that he had done this. It had been his words that had stoked the crowd, that had given them their rage, fed their hatred.

Braidon scrunched his eyes closed against the heat, unwilling to retreat, to turn away. His mind reached out towards the flames, but there was nothing he could do to extinguish them. Such a feat was beyond his feeble power.

But as his mind quested out, Braidon sensed something else, something terrible and remarkable and brilliant. In his mind's eye, the pantheon was aglow—not with the inferno, but a swirling, shining whirlpool of energy. It hung in the air before him, almost tangible in its power, as though he might reach out and touch it like the currents of a river.

The hairs on Braidon's scalp stood on end as he realised this was the power released by the dead within the pantheon. Fire and smoke had stolen their lives, casting their spirits into the void and releasing their life force into the world.

It hung before him, a burning, raging force that none could stand against. Braidon's heartbeat quickened as he realized it was everything he'd prayed for, everything he needed to stand against Marianne, to free his people from the tyranny of the Knights of Alana.

Could he truly do such a thing? But what was the alternative? If he let this opportunity pass, he would face Marianne unarmed, his feeble life force a shade before her own power. He would lose, and Plorsea would be left to suffer her wrath…

No.

Whatever the consequences, Marianne must be defeated. It was too late to save those within, to protect them as he should have. But he could ensure their lives were not wasted. Their deaths might still help restore peace to the Three Nation, if only Braidon had the courage to grasp the opportunity.

And so Braidon reached for the shimmering vortex, and drew the power to him.

❧ 33 ❧

"Caledan, wake up!"

Light flashed across the darkness. Caledan cried out as the agony of his body suddenly came rushing back. He gasped, fresh air filling his lungs, and a fiery warmth swept through him. Glowing lights swirled across his vision as he opened his eyes. Panicked, he tried to sit up, but his limbs refused to obey and he slumped back to the floor.

"What…?" he croaked.

"You're alive!"

This time Caledan recognised Marianne's voice. Drums hammered at his skull, making it difficult to think. The queen's face swirled overhead. He could feel her hands on his chest. Slowly the spinning slowed and he saw she was smiling—then the image split in two and it was all Caledan could do to keep from throwing up. He closed his eyes again and it helped…somewhat.

"What happened?" he asked when the sensation had passed. "Is the boy okay?"

"He's safe," Marianne replied, though her voice was faint. "Thanks to you."

"And the Elders?"

"Gone!" she gasped. Her fingers tightened on his chest as she continued. "Though I barely…had the strength…"

Caledan's eyes snapped open as her voice faded away. Her head thumped into his chest. His arms went around her before she slid to the floor. Forcing himself up, he held Marianne in place. Fading light streamed in from the balcony and he realised it was already sunset. Marianne was still awake, though exhaustion hung heavy in her sapphire eyes.

Only then did he remember his own injuries. He placed a hand to his chest, feeling the tear in his shirt, the blood soaking his tunic—but the skin beneath was whole. He stared at the queen.

"What did you do?"

A smile creased her cheeks. "Could…hardly let you… die," she murmured. Her eyes slid closed as she continued. "You saved…Calybe."

"What's wrong with you?" he asked.

"Used…too much energy…against Servo," she croaked. "Had to use…my own life force…for you."

"Why would you do that?"

"Why not?" she whispered. "Think…I'm going to sleep…awhile now."

Caledan smiled despite himself. Lifting her in his arms, he stood and carried her to the bed. Calybe lay asleep beneath the covers. He laid her down beside her son, then sat on the edge of the bed and took Marianne's pulse, reassuring himself she would live.

Then he stood as realisation came to him. Servo and his Knights were gone. The city was free. And now the evil queen lay sleeping, defenceless. He stared at her, remembering that night in Malevolent Cove, how she had struck down Devon and tried to burn Kryssa and Pela alive.

This was the opportunity he had come to Ardath for, to rid the Three Nations of Marianne's evil, to avenge Devon's death. Without the Order pulling the strings of the capital, someone true could be lifted to the kingship, until Calybe came of age.

Beside Marianne, the boy stirred. Reaching out in his sleep, Calybe pulled himself closer to his mother. Caledan's heart hammered in his chest as he watched them sleep. His hand drifted to his chest, feeling again the smooth skin where the Knight had torn him open. He'd been dying, would already be dead if not for Marianne. She had given the last of her strength to save him.

Recalling the cold, calculating woman of Malevolent Cove, the hate-filled monster that had come for Braidon, he could not reconcile the two. There was no reason for Marianne to have healed him. She had won her battle, her son was safe—why then take such a risk, weakening herself at the moment of her victory?

He could not understand it.

Finally he let out a long sigh and sank onto the bed. The boy's eyes flickered open at the movement. Seeing Caledan sitting beside them, he smiled and hugged his mother tight.

"Thank you for helping us," he whispered. Then he looked at his mother, a frown touching his forehead. "Is Mum okay?"

"She's fine," Caledan murmured. "She's just tired."

A smile lit the boy's face. "I'll keep her safe!" he said, cuddling beneath his mother's chin.

Caledan smiled as the boy closed his eyes. A knock came from the door. Rising, he collected his sword from where it had fallen. The Knights and Queens Guard still lay where they had died. Crossing the room, he found the ruined doors half-propped up in the frame. He hauled them open, weapon at the ready.

A frightened man jumped back, hands raised in surrender. "Please, no!" he yelped.

Caledan hesitated. "What do you want?"

"Sir, the queen, I have news for her?"

"The queen is currently indisposed," Caledan growled, then wondered at the man's words. "I speak for her, at this moment. What is the news?"

The messenger hesitated, trying to see into the room, but Caledan barred the way. The man's shoulders slumped and he shrugged. "What does it matter? It will be common knowledge within the hour."

"Out with it then, man!" Caledan barked.

"It's the king!" the messenger gasped, then seeming to realise the statement needed more explanation: "King Braidon has risen from the dead. He has proclaimed Queen Marianne a traitor and led an uprising in Chole, claiming the city for his own."

Caledan stared at the man, stunned. "Truly?"

"Of cou—"

The sellsword slammed the broken door in the messenger's face. Half the panelling fell out with the movement, but taking the hint, the man turned and scuttled off down the corridor.

Caledan stood staring at the wood. He could not believe it. Braidon, leading an uprising? Thinking of the miserable mess he had left behind in Dragon Country, it was inconceivable. How had this happened?

Returning to the bed, Caledan sank onto the mattress alongside Marianne. This changed everything. This meant he had to choose a side—the rightful king, the man Devon had begged him to protect, or the woman who had usurped his crown. The woman who had murdered his friend.

Marianne stirred beside him, her eyes sliding open again. "What was that about?" she whispered.

"Braidon lives," Caledan murmured. "He has taken Chole."

He watched her, trying to gauge her reaction, but she only smiled. "Of course he has."

"I'm serious."

The queen pushed herself up on one elbow, though he could see it took her an effort of will. "So am I," she said. "My dear husband comes from a line of heroes—and villains. No doubt he hates me now as much as I him. He has nothing left but that, and so he will not stop, not until I lie dead at his feet."

Caledan's chest tightened. "I should have done my duty in Dragon Country," he said. "He begged me to do it then."

"The mistake is made, my Champion," Marianne replied. Her hands found his wrist, squeezed. "And so the question becomes: will you do your duty now, even against your rightful king, even against your friends? Will you kill Braidon for me?"

Caledan stared into the queen's sapphire eyes. Her face was a mask of beauty, untouched by flaws, her auburn hair tumbling around her shoulders, as perfect as though she had just bathed. She was the most beautiful woman he had ever seen, more intelligent than Servo and all the Order's scheming, more powerful than Braidon, a Magicker of old. Who else could rule Plorsea, but this woman before him? He let out a long breath.

"I will, My Queen."

EPILOGUE

Servo's horse was breathing hard by the time he galloped through the gates of Sheffield. He had ridden all day and night to reach the southernmost bastion of Lonia, a retinue of Knights and retainers stretched out far behind him. Yet even with their support, he could not be sure of his safety.

How far did the queen's power truly extend? She had taken the Lonian capital without a fight, cowing the council with her power. And despite Servo's efforts, Ardath had fallen into her hands. The news would travel the land within days.

Marianne was now the undisputed queen of two nations.

He could not understand where she had found the power. How many souls had the woman slaughtered without his knowing, to wield such strength against the Order? A dozen Knights had died in the throne room—and a dozen more of Servo's loyal Queen's Guard—and still he had barely escaped with his life.

It was inconceivable. Servo had spent the better part of ten years collecting power, ever since he'd discovered the secrets of the Elders and joined their ranks. He had manipulated kings and councils and even his fellow Elders, all to achieve one end—to make the Order supreme ruler across the Three Nations.

But Marianne had picked his plans apart, piece by piece, until they lay unravelled for the world to see.

He would not stand for it.

"Sir?"

With an effort of will, Servo returned his thoughts to the present. They had reached the central plaza of Sheffield and his escort had drawn up around him. They numbered some fifty Knights and twice as many retainers—enough for what he planned. Darkness still clung to the dusty streets of the mining town and there was no one else in sight.

"Take the town hall, empty the guard barracks, wake the citizens of Sheffield. They are to be the first to hear the new words of the Saviour."

Within an hour, it was done. Sheffield was a small town, without walls or a standing army, but it would do for now as his safehold. First though, he had to be sure of its citizen's loyalty. He could no longer afford mercy—the blasphemous must be uncovered and cleansed, lest their treachery wake the Gods from their slumber.

No, with the sunrise, a new day would dawn. Let Marianne think him defeated, but the Order would rise again, and soon. His Knights had planted their seeds across Plorsea—Braidon's people could not turn from it now. They had murdered their neighbours in the name of the Saviour and seen the truth.

Close to a thousand men and women had been packed into the town square, many still in their bedclothes, so hurriedly had they been forced from their homes. Servo sneered at their weakness. Sheep—that was all they were, these people, livestock to be used and discarded at their master's will. Had they the strength, they might have fought off the Knights. Instead they cowered, defeated before the fight had ever begun.

Exhaustion weighed heavily on Servo's shoulders. He had wasted too much power in his battle with the queen. But it mattered little now, with the sheep gathered. He had only to sort the loyal from the blasphemous—and he still had power enough for that.

"My people!" he bellowed. He stood in the centre of the square, surrounded by Knights, but his voice carried out over the heads of the crowd. "She who would be our queen has betrayed us!"

Whispers spread through the crowd. Servo let them grow for a moment and then clapped his hands. Thunder boomed across the square—a simple illusion—and silence returned.

"Marianne serves not the Order, nor our mighty Lonia. She cares only for power, and has made a deal with the False Gods to raise herself above her fellow mortals. She intends to enslave us all with their magic."

Now there was terror in the voices in the crowd. They jostled back and forth, as though the False Gods walked amongst them even now, preparing to strike them down.

"But fear not, my people!" Servo bellowed, enhancing his voice with a touch of power. "The Saviour has armed her Elders with weapons of our own." He threw out his arms, and with a *whoosh* fire leapt from his hands. Gasps came from the crowd at the illusion, and Servo suppressed a smile.

"The Knights of Alana will stand against the dark

queen, but we cannot stand alone. So I ask you, my people, are you with us?" His voice dropped to a whisper. "Or are you against us?"

As he spoke, Servo released a wave of power. The day was proving costly, but he still had enough—or so he prayed. He should have done this long ago, but the other Elders were old, limited by the past. They had forbidden such uses of power, for fear of what might follow.

But Servo would no longer be constrained. He knew what was needed. In one stroke, he would restore his power and destroy his enemies amongst the crowd.

A collective cry rang out as Servo's power touched each of the gathered townsfolk. A thousand fists lifted skyward— but not all. As one, a hundred men and women fell to their knees. Their voices no longer lifted in agreement, but dissent.

"No! Never! No!"

His power had given their true nature voice—their rejection of the Order, of the Saviour, of Servo.

Still smiling, Servo let the power ebb. Horror contorted the faces of the blasphemous as they realised what had happened. Servo wanted them to know, to realise the consequences of their failure.

"The blasphemous lie revealed before us," he called. "Let us cleanse them in the name of the Saviour!"

He did not even need his power now. A roar rose from the crowd as they fell upon the traitors. With foot and fist his loyal soldiers knocked their enemies to the ground and tore away their lives, one by one. Servo wandered amongst the slaughter, hands—and mind—extended, drawing the departing souls to him. His heart raced with the thrill of it, with the intoxicating power of their life force.

He should have done this long ago, should have walked

amongst the cities of Lonia, through the streets of Ardath, culling the blasphemous. Instead he had bided his time, given people time to change their ways, to join the Order of their own free will. He had put up with Ashoka and his mechanisms, with Braidon's resistance to his own sister's call, with the Trolan blockade.

But no more.

From this day forth, he could afford no weakness. He would gather the faithful and destroy all who stood against him. None could conceal their treachery from him now.

The sun lit the distant peaks by the time the slaughter was done. By then, Servo felt better than he had in weeks, his power restored. He might have moved against the queen immediately, but without knowing the true source of her strength, he dared not act so recklessly. He would take no chances this time. When the time came he would attack with overwhelming force, and Marianne would be swept away like a leaf before the storm.

"Elder!"

Servo turned as a voice called from the back of the crowd. A group of several men and a woman stood there, their clothes tattered and torn, faces dirt-streaked and hair unkept. It looked like they had just spent a week in the wilderness. They must have just arrived in Sheffield, and missed his ceremony.

Unwilling to take any chances, Servo sent a sliver of power through the group, demanding their loyalty. None wavered, but for the woman. She cried out and fell to her knees. The men took a collective step back from her, surprised by her cry.

"What have we here?" Servo asked as he approached. Closer, he saw that the woman wore the collar of a slave. Little wonder she was unfaithful.

"An escaped slave," one of the group said, stepping forward to address Servo. "One of two who escaped the mines this past week. The other crossed the border into Trola, but she won't get far. She killed a Knight—and apparently an Elder. Sir Isyc went after her alone. He won't stop until she's dead."

A scream came from the ground. Leaping to her feet, the woman charged the speaker. Servo flicked a hand and she staggered to a stop. Eyes wild, she clawed at her throat, mouth opening and closing like a fish out of water.

Chuckling, Servo stepped in close. "Feisty, isn't she? You said she was a slave? Best not kill her too quickly then. An example must be made for the others. What was the punishment for a runaway slave again?" He paused for effect. "Oh, of course!"

He snapped his fingers and a sharp *crack* came from the slave's legs. At the same time, he released the power from her throat. Screaming, she fell to the ground clutching her ruined shinbones. Servo stood over her, savouring the screams, before finally making to turn away. But something her captors had said gave him pause.

"What did you say of the other slave? That she had killed an Elder?" he asked.

The leader nodded quickly. "Yes, sir. In Townirwin—at least that's what Sir Isyc claimed."

It couldn't be.

"What was the girl's name?" Servo asked quickly.

"Pela, sir!"

It was! One of those who had caused so much chaos in Malevolent Cove. And she'd escaped with this woman. He looked at the slave again. Her face was contorted in agony and she no longer seemed to know where she was, what was happening. He studied her features, but it was not the mother. But he recalled there had been another woman in the amphitheatre.

"I know you," he murmured. "You were with the sellsword, and the king. What was it they called you?"

The woman only moaned, writhing in the dirt, clutching her ruined legs. One bone had broken so badly it now stabbed through her flesh. Servo sighed. He would get nothing from her in this state. Touching a finger to her forehead, he took the pain from her—if only for the moment.

She collapsed sobbing to the ground, incoherent words tumbling from her mouth. Impatient, Servo grasped her by the hair and pulled her head up.

"I asked you a question," he snarled.

Her pupils constricted as they concentrated on Servo, seeing him for the first time. "I know you."

Servo struck her hard across the face. "And I you," he snapped. "What is your name, woman?"

"Genevieve!" she gasped.

Servo smiled. "Was that so ha—?" He broke off, staring at the woman.

She scowled, locking eyes with him. "What, lost your tongue, butcher?"

"It can't be," he murmured, ignoring the taunt.

He grasped the woman by the chin thrust her head to the side, exposing the iron collar. She tried to fight him, but a trickle of power was all it took for Servo to hold her. He had taken the pain from her legs, but she still could not stand. There was nowhere she could go, no way she could escape him.

Staring at the collar, Servo struggled to believe what he was seeing. So this was why Marianne had gone to Lon. He should have realised the experiments had not truly failed. That had been the last news he'd received from the engineers in the capital, that a mechanism to synthon a victim's life force from afar was impossible to create.

But here was the truth laid bare. A jet-black jewel had been set into the centre of the iron collar, a channel through which the woman's life force would be conveyed upon her death. Sure, a slave's life force might have dwindled by the time of their death, but there were thousands of them working in the mountains and fields of Lonia. More than enough power for one woman.

Rage touched Servo, that Marianne had realised this opportunity while he had been blind. No wonder she'd wanted to halt the Order's cleansings. She no longer needed them. The woman could sit on her throne and gather enough power to conquer the Three Nations, without ever getting a drop of blood on her hands.

Growling, Servo gripped the collar between his fingers. A sharp *shriek* followed as the iron cracked in two and fell to the ground. He raised a fist, readying himself to strike the woman dead, but something gave him pause.

This woman had been with the sellsword Marianne had recruited to her cause. She knew the man, had travelled with him—King Braidon and the woman Kryssa as well. All had proven to be wily foes, but this Genevieve could be a weapon against them.

Perhaps the slave might yet prove useful.

———

HERE ENDS BOOK TWO
OF
THE KNIGHTS OF ALANA
The adventure continues with…
Crown of Chaos

AARON HODGES

CROWN OF CHAOS

THE KNIGHTS OF ALANA: BOOK THREE

PROLOGUE

The first hints of dawn had just touched the horizon when Braidon stepped into the courtyard of the Castle. Walking slowly, he crossed to the old stone stairwell and started up. It was some thirty feet before he reached the ramparts of the defensive wall. A fresh breeze greeted him, but even there the tang of smoke clung to the air.

It had taken them most of the night to gain control of the fire. In the end, half the Castle had been gutted, but that was nothing compared to the loss of lives. A lump lodged in Braidon's throat as he recalled the men, women, and children who had been trapped in the pantheon. They had never stood a chance, not after Dominic and his men had lit the fire, after they'd barred the doors to trap them inside…

Braidon's stomach twisted and it took an effort of will to keep from throwing up. The fire had burned so hot that there had been little left by the end. Where just hours before there had been a hundred souls, filled with life and love and hope, only ash remained. Dead because of Braidon's folly.

Silently, Braidon slammed his fist down on the granite crenulations. Why had he trusted Dominic? He should have realised the man's evil, should have seen the darkness in his heart. But Dominic had been there in the moment of Braidon's greatest weakness. And so the king had put his faith in the man.

Braidon would regret that decision for the rest of his life.

Shuddering, Braidon turned his eyes inwards, to that void that was his inner mind. Once his magic had burned there, a gift granted to him by the Gods. But that power was long gone, departed with their death some thirty years ago. And for thirty years the void had been empty, an infinite darkness at his core.

Now though, a fresh power burned there, the multi-coloured glow of a hundred lives. A shiver slid down Braidon's spine as his mind touched the energies. They lit his veins aflame, filling him with renewed vigour, giving him confidence that he could take on the world. He shuddered at the sensation, at the strangeness of it all.

In an instant of despair, Braidon had reached for the flames and tried to extinguish them with the power of his own life force. It had been a futile act. The strength of one man, however brave or noble, could not quench such an inferno.

But in doing so, Braidon had sensed something else—the energies of the dead, the power of the departing souls. He had seen an opportunity then, a chance to make something of their loss. Here was the power he had prayed for, the strength he needed to defeat his vile wife. So he had gathered the power to him, had drawn in the life forces of the dying members of the Order, and made them his own.

The light was growing now, the sun creeping up over the rooftops of Chole. The Dying City stretched out all around him, the outer walls a half-mile away at their nearest point. They were strong walls of granite and iron, walls that had never fallen, not even to the Dark Magicker Archon. They would serve him well in the coming war. He might not yet have the strength in arms to carry the fight to Marianne, but neither did she have the numbers to attack him here.

And even should she take the walls, the city would fight her to its dying breath. They had seen the darkness of the Order of Alana, the cult that had lifted Marianne to queen. Their Knights had threatened to burn the Temple of the Earth, to purge the city of those they deemed blasphemers. Only Braidon's interference had kept the temple and its priests safe.

Now he had taken their Castle, the centre of the Order's power in Chole. With Marianne's followers purged from the city, he would make their fortress his own. There was nowhere else stronger in Chole. He would be safe here, protected until the time came to face his wife. It would buy him time to plan the revolt, to train his army and plot the queen's eventual downfall.

Boom.

Braidon's thoughts were interrupted as the doors to the keep swung open in the courtyard. Shaking himself free of thoughts of the future, he looked down at the new arrivals. Men and women emerged from the keep in twos and threes, heads down, their whispers carrying up to where Braidon stood unnoticed.

Yesterday, Braidon had offered all who'd followed him a position in his army. Though their losses had been heavy and even the survivors were battered and bruised, most had accepted. Afterwards there had been some celebration, but most of his new recruits had been muted, still processing the violence and raw grief of battle. Soon they had taken to their beds—lying down wherever they could find space in the parts of the castle untouched by the fire.

He had bid them return to the courtyard at first light, and now it looked that most were gathered below.

All but Dominic and those men who had joined him in burning the pantheon.

As though summoned by his thought, the doors of the keep creaked open again, and the betrayers filed out one by one, their arms bound behind their backs and mouths gagged with cloth. Two guards led the way across the courtyard, forcing the crowd to part before them, while his King's Guard, Kryssa, brought up the rear with a third soldier.

Their eyes met as Braidon started back down the staircase. Kryssa's face was gaunt, her eyes dark with shadow. She had taken the loss in the pantheon even harder than Braidon, after driving off the Elder that had been protecting them. It had been the right thing to do—the man had slain hundreds to grant himself power—but there was little Braidon could say to sage her guilt.

They met in the centre of the courtyard. Kryssa stood a few inches below Braidon's own five feet and nine inches. She'd retired from his King's Guard over a decade ago, but with the rest of his Guard decimated by Marianne's treachery, Kryssa had been forced out of retirement. Fortunately for Braidon, she had lost none of her edge. She was now his most steadfast lieutenant—though he knew she longed to go in search of her missing daughter, Pela.

The thought reminded Braidon of his own son, Calybe, taken hostage by his wife in Ardath. He could not attack the city so long as Marianne held the boy, though such thoughts were a long way off yet. First he needed an army.

Transferring his gaze to the condemned men, Braidon was touched by doubt. He could not afford to lose a single loyal soldier, not with the war to come. And Dominic had proven his loyalty without question. He and the others had made a terrible mistake, but…

Swallowing, Braidon caught Kryssa's eyes on him, and knew he could not turn back now. The energies of a hundred innocent lives flowed in his veins, lost because of the hatred in the hearts of these men. However desperate his cause, Braidon must hold to the laws of the land.

He nodded to Kryssa, and as one they turned to the makeshift gibbet that sat in the corner of the courtyard. Six nooses had been tied and hung from wooden poles over-hanging the courtyard, while matching barrels waited beneath. Kryssa and her guards led Dominic and his fellows across the courtyard and forced them onto the barrels at sword point, then looped the nooses around their necks.

Whispers spread around Braidon as his followers realised what was happening. Several cast angry glances in the king's direction, but most watched in silence, though he did not miss the sorrow in their eyes. Braidon felt it too. There had already been so much loss, so much destruction —and for what? To fight for a crown he had never wanted, to defend a nation that had rejected him time and time again?

For a second he was tempted to turn and walk away from it all, to leave his crown and Chole and Plorsea behind.

It will all be yours one day, son, his father's voice whispered from the depths of his memory. *It has been my life's goal to make this land safe for you and our people.*

Braidon shuddered. The Tsar had been evil at the end, but once he had loved his children, had cared for his people. It had been his ambition to free the Three Nations of magic, to bring balance to the world. That had been

Braidon's destiny, to usher in the peace his father had always dreamed of.

Instead, his rule had invited only chaos. But he knew the reason now. His wife, Marianne, had been scheming behind his back all along, plotting his downfall. Now she wished to rule, to hold herself up as the rightful queen.

No, he could not walk away now, could not leave the world to chaos. Marianne was mad, would plunge Plorsea into another war and allow her Knights to roam freely, hunting the faithful of the Old Gods. Braidon had no choice—Marianne must be destroyed for what she had done to his nation.

For what she had done to *him.*

Shivering, Braidon forced himself back to the present. Dominic and his five fellows stood awaiting their fate and the whispers of the crowd were growing. The mood was muted, the ecstasy of their victory lost with the morning's gloom. It was time to end this, and fast.

"The six of you have been found guilty of mass murder," Braidon called, stepping up before the condemned men.

Of them all, he knew only Dominic. The former guard had risked his life to protect Braidon, had sheltered him at great risk. Braidon had promised Dominic the world for his aid, but now he stood staring down at his king in terror, and he would receive only death.

"The act was witnessed and admitted," Braidon continued at last, "and so I am left with no choice—"

"My liege!"

Braidon spun as a woman's voice called from across the courtyard. There was a commotion amidst the crowd before Dominic's wife, Janylle, pushed her way to the fore. Her eyes were wide and stained red, and there was a panicked look on her face. She stumbled up to Braidon, tears streaming down her cheeks. Several men made to stop her, but Braidon waved them back.

"Please, don't do this!" Janylle gasped. "Dominic gave up everything to serve you. Please, you are the king! Grant him pardon, and he will be your loyal soldier until the end of his days."

A shiver ran down Braidon's spine as he looked at Janylle, remembering the conversation that had passed between them just a day before. She had feared losing her husband in Braidon's war, that he would die fighting in some distant battle. But she could never have suspected *this*, that her husband would meet his end by Braidon's own hand.

But then, no one could have predicted what would happen next.

"He murdered innocent men and women, Janylle," he croaked, his voice close to breaking. "He murdered *children*. I cannot pardon that."

He made to turn away, but Janylle lurched forward and grabbed his arm. "Bastard!" she screamed. Braidon tried to break free, but there was no hiding from her words. "So this is how you repay loyalty? We sheltered you, protected you! Now you turn your back, defend the lives of those devils from the Order over your own people?"

"I'm sorry, Janylle—"

"Damn your sorries," she spat. "Those so-called innocents were followers of Alana. They would have betrayed you to their precious queen the second she reached our gates. My husband did you a favour, ridding you of them. But you were never strong enough to make the tough choices. Now he pays the price for your weakness."

Braidon scowled. He'd heard enough of the woman's

ramblings. At his gesture, several of his newly appointed guards dragged Janylle away. Her screams continued long after she was gone though, ringing in his ears, in his thoughts, and Braidon couldn't help but wonder at their truth.

Shivering, he looked up at Dominic. The fear had vanished from the man's eyes, and now his face was screwed up, contorted by a terrible rage. Braidon swallowed and cast a glance over his shoulder, but Janylle was long gone.

Gritting his teeth, he lifted a hand and six guards took their places behind the condemned. Ice spread through Braidon's stomach as they looked to him for the final signal. He wanted to be anywhere but the shadowed courtyard, but he was as trapped in his fate as Dominic was his own. There could be no going back.

Braidon dropped his hand, and the barrels were kicked out from beneath the prisoners' feet.

I

An entire day passed after their fight with the Knight before Pela found the strength to walk again. Even then, her entire body ached, making every step an agony. It hurt just to speak, let alone eat or drink, and so she and Ruebyn passed the time in silence. Yet with the Knight's companions still somewhere in the mountains, neither dared wait long, and as the sun dawned on the second day, they started off around the lake.

At her stumbling pace, it took long hours to traverse the steep slopes and reach the pass leading down into Trola. Only when she stood between the towering mountain peaks and looked down into Trola did Pela finally feel relief, that they had truly escaped their pursuers. She wouldn't let herself think about what lay ahead, about the fate that awaited if the Trolans found them.

By the time they reached the foothills, the last of their food was gone and they were forced to scavenge for whatever scraps they could find. Thankfully the western slopes of the Sandstone Mountains were covered by lush forest, and they were able to forage for late berries and tubers dug from the roots of trees.

Without a bow, they could not bring down any of the game they spotted amidst the undergrowth. But a dozen streams crisscrossed the landscape, and in one isolated pool, Pela found a fat trout trapped by the falling autumn currents.

The contrast to Lonia was a welcome change. On the other side of the mountains, the land had been dry, the earth parched but for a few glacier-fed rivers, and the vegetation had been thin and unwelcoming. Now as they reached the lower slopes, tall saplings of pine and firs rose around them, providing shelter from the mountain winds.

"A hundred years ago, great forests covered most of Trola," Ruebyn explained one morning as they made their way down a steeply sloping hillside. "But they were almost all cut down—or burned—to make way for farmland. These trees are young, though. I guess their new king is allowing the forests to regrow."

Pela wasn't particularly interested in Trola's history with forests and farming, but she nodded anyway and offered a smile to show she had heard. With nothing else to add though, the conversation quickly petered out, turning to an uncomfortable silence.

A distance had grown between them in the last few days. Pela had been unable to recover the closeness they'd shared the night of the storm. They hadn't spoken about what had happened between them that night, and now she felt too much time had passed, that she no longer knew what it had meant.

So instead, she focused her thoughts on what lay before them. For decades, Trola's borders had been closed to Lonia and Plorsea, entrance forbidden on penalty of death.

Desperation had forced her westward, but now Pela was no longer sure she'd made the right choice.

The iron collar around her throat was a constant presence, the dull black gem at its centre an ugly reminder of her time in the darkness, her captivity. It was the collar that had forced her down this path. It marked her as a slave. Any Lonian citizen who saw her would know what she was. There was only one punishment for an escaped slave —death.

Trola had been her only choice for freedom, but Ruebyn could have chosen another path. He had been her overseer in the mines, and while their hunters thought him culpable for her escape, he had no collar to mark him as a fugitive. He could have returned to Lonia unrecognised, could have lived out his life in peace.

Five days after their desperate battle with the Knight, they finally emerged from the fledgling forest into open farmland. There the going became gentler, the rolling hills giving way easily to their worn-down boots.

That day they saw no sign of any other living soul, except when Pela noticed a flock of sheep in the distance. They'd diverted from their course in case the shepherd was nearby, and when darkness fell, they'd lit no fire.

The next morning Pela woke before the sunrise, feeling strangely alert, ready to begin the day. Ruebyn still lay asleep nearby, his eyelids fluttering in the grips of some dream. His brown hair, once cropped short, was now long enough to hang across his face. Several twigs and leaves had taken up residence in it during the night. She found herself smiling at the sight, and she gently brushed them away.

A groan sounded from Ruebyn's throat and he twisted on the ground, his brow creasing with a frown. Then his eyes snapped open and she saw a look of panic there. He flinched away from her and half-scrambled to his feet.

"The Knight!" he gasped, spinning around as though he expected the steel-clad warrior to come upon them at any moment. Then his senses finally seemed to return. Staggering to a stop, he cast a sheepish glance at Pela. "Sorry, bad dream."

Pela shivered, remembering her own nightmares, how the Knight still hunted her there. So many terrible things had happened since their escape, but the image of his mottled face as he leaned over her, the twisted nose and bulging veins and loathing in his eyes…she would never forget that face as long as she lived.

"It's okay," she said softly, even as her hand drifted unconsciously to her throat, where the Knight had tried to throttle the life from her. "He'd dead. We never have to worry about that monster again."

Ruebyn stared at her for a long moment before sinking back to the ground. "Ay," he whispered. "Thank the Saviour he lost his footing and fell."

Pela frowned at his wording. "What are you talking about?" she asked, arching an eyebrow.

They had said nothing about that brief, violent battle in the past few days. Neither of them wanted to relive those frantic moments, those brief seconds during which they had been mere inches from death.

"You must have missed it, you were barely conscious. I was trying to reach you, but he was too quick. He had you by the throat, but the stones were loose, and he stumbled backwards, went over the edge before he could recover."

Pela's frown deepened and she shook her head. "That's…not how it happened."

In those last moments as the Knight tried to strangle

her, Pela had found a final spark of strength within her. Pinned beneath his weight, she had been unable to fight against him, but in her desperation Pela had taken that last ounce of energy and hurled it at the Knight with her mind.

"I…threw him from me," she murmured, her eyes on the ground. "I don't know how. It was like I could use my own life force against him, as if I could project my strength beyond my own body." She looked up at Ruebyn as she finished, unable to offer a better explanation.

He raised one bushy eyebrow. "That's not possible."

"Why not?"

"Because what you're describing would be magic," he replied, wearing a slightly bemused grin. "And magic died with the…Old Gods."

Pela scowled. "It wasn't magic, it was…a part of me."

Ruebyn sighed. "Pela, you were barely alive when I reached you," he said. "Is it possible you imagined it?"

He held out a consoling hand, but she slapped it away and leapt to her feet. "No, it's not."

"Fine, then show me," Ruebyn replied, sounding weary.

"What?"

"Show me this power of yours," he said patiently. "If you could use it on the edge of death, it should be easy to summon now."

Pela flashed him a glare, but after a moment's hesitation, she closed her eyes and turned her back on him. Drawing in a breath, she tried to squash her irritation. She had felt the power flickering within her the last few days, burning hotter as she recovered her strength, but she had not tried to reach for it.

Now she drew on her mother's teaching, seeking to sink into the meditative trance where she had first noticed the strange power. Her mother, Kryssa, had taught it to her as a child, passing down the knowledge from her own adopted mother, Selina. As she had grown older, Pela hadn't given the technique much thought, though she'd continued to practice during their weekly visits to the old temple.

Pela cursed inwardly as she realised her mind had become distracted. Letting out a sharp exhalation, she focused again on her task. Meditation was meant to calm, to bring clarity of thought, but Pela was unused to being watched while she practiced. She could hear the heavy breathing of Ruebyn behind her, could sense his impatience, and it tugged at her concentration.

Finally, she swore and swung around. "Damn you!" she snapped.

He leapt away, eyes wide and hands raised in front of him, but Pela ignored him. Sweeping her scant belongings into the worn backpack and clipping their only dagger to her belt, she started off across the hillside. She was too angry to look back and check whether Ruebyn followed.

It was so like him to disbelieve, to question her words. He believed in nothing but what his damned teachers back in Lon had taught him. Even his precious Saviour preached the importance of the physical, the need to push back against the magic the Three Gods had once instilled in the land. The spiritual was anathema to the Order of Alana and their followers.

Yet Pela knew what she had felt—just as she knew that even without the Gods, there were other powers at large in the land. On the shores of Malevolent Cove, the queen had wielded some strange new magic against Pela and her friends, *commanding* them. Only her uncle Devon had been able to resist—and he had died for it.

She couldn't help but think it was all connected. Another memory flickered into her mind, of her pickaxe plunging through sheer rock, back in the mines beneath the Lonian mountains. She had been meditating then as well; had she unwittingly tapped into her own power? The thought twisted her stomach into knots—her friend Siden had been killed in the landslide that followed. If that was true, his blood was on her hands.

Suddenly cold, Pela forced her attention to the path ahead. They were still moving through hilly country, though with the forest behind them, it was easy to see the way now. Taking her bearings against the sun, she continued southward. If they were lucky, they could keep to these back-country trails and avoid the Trolan people entirely. The Brunei pass was somewhere to the south—it would take them to Plorsea, and safety.

"Where is everybody?" Ruebyn asked after they had been walking for an hour.

Pela's head jerked up. She had not looked at him since their fight, but now she slowed, allowing him to catch up. He offered a sheepish grin as they drew level, as if to admit he had been a fool earlier.

"What do you mean?" she asked, deciding it best to let the issue of her power drop.

"Look around," he said, indicating their surroundings. "This is good land, but these fields are untended. See here." He pointed to where a cluster of saplings grew near the trail. "The forest is returning, even here. Why would they let that happen?"

Pela shrugged. "Maybe they prefer the trees." Then she started to laugh. "Besides, we should be thankful! We're not meant to be here, remember?"

Ruebyn shook his head. "It's weird, I'm telling you."

"Ruebyn, you worry too much," she said, flicking him a sidelong glance. But when he only frowned and said nothing, she let out a sigh. "Look, we're still a long way from the coast, right? Weren't most of Trola's cities close to the ocean?"

"Yeah but there were still *people* in the countryside, surely?"

Realising he would not be convinced, Pela suppressed a sigh and they settled back into silence. She couldn't help but feel as though something had been lost between them these last few days. Gone was the closeness they had found in the mountain cave. She longed for the warmth of his company, the heat that had burned in her chest at his embrace, and yet…

Cheeks flushed, Pela shook her head to dislodge the memories. The day was quickly growing warm and while it was a welcome relief after the chill nights in the mountains, she unbuttoned her coat to cool herself. The ground was soft beneath her feet and for a time she was forced to concentrate on each footstep, lest her already crumbling boots disintegrate altogether.

But eventually her thoughts drifted once more. Despite herself, Ruebyn's earlier words still irked Pela. In her mind, somewhere in that awful fight with the Knight, she had been changed. Just a few short months ago, she would never have even thought about challenging such a warrior. Yet somehow she had found the courage and ability to stand against him. And this time there had been no hero to come to her rescue, no Devon or Caledan or her own mother to save her.

And she had won. Through magic or skill or sheer determination, she had bested him. It had changed her in ways she still could not comprehend.

And yet in a few short words, Ruebyn had denied her that victory.

"There!"

Pela jerked to a stop as Ruebyn suddenly let out a shout. Swinging around, she saw him pointing to the way ahead. Her gaze followed his finger, out across the rolling fields. A shiver passed through Pela as she saw the village lying in their path, nestled at the top of a nearby hill. Slate rooftops shone in the noonday sun, sloping down to brick walls that stood to either side of a dirt road.

She glanced at Ruebyn. "I hope you're happy," she muttered.

But Ruebyn wasn't smiling. His eyes were still fixed on the distant town. A frown wrinkled his face and without saying anything, he started forward again.

"Hey!" she cried, snatching his arm and dragging him back. "What are you doing?"

His hazel eyes turned to look at her. "I don't think anyone's home."

❧ 2 ❧

"**D**amnit!"

The scream greeted Caledan as he stepped into Marianne's apartment. He ducked as a bottle of wine went hurtling past him to shatter in the corridor. Quickly he closed the door behind him before anyone else noticed the queen's outburst. Whatever had brought about Marianne's sudden change of mood, the whole citadel didn't need to be alerted to her distress.

The queen herself stood before her desk, the contents of which were scattered about the room in various states of destruction. The sofa had been flipped on its side and the wooden chair to which he'd once been bound lay in pieces against the far wall. It looked as though a small tornado had swept through the apartment.

"Something the matter?" he asked, struggling to conceal his surprise. Marianne was usually so controlled. He hadn't seen her in such a state since…Malevolent Cove. He shuddered at the memory and quickly cast it aside.

Marianne spun at his voice. Surprise showed on her face

at the sight of him standing amidst the wreckage. Her auburn hair was frizzed and shadows of fatigue hung beneath her sapphire eyes. Clenching her fists, she took a step towards him.

"What?" she snapped.

Caledan raised an eyebrow. "That was a Lonian red, if I'm not mistaken," he said, gesturing to the shattered bottle that lay behind the closed doors. "Your favourite, and hard to come by nowadays."

The breath hissed between Marianne's teeth as she exhaled, her eyes flickering closed. Caledan waited as the queen gathered herself, and was not surprised to see that her rage had vanished when she looked at him again.

"I apologise, my Champion," she said formally. "You should not have had to bear witness to such an…outburst."

Composed once more, she gestured at the sofa. As though gripped by the hands of a giant, it rose from the ground and righted itself. Marianne took a seat and nodded for him to join her. Used to her displays of magic by now, Caledan said nothing. But after her earlier rage, he still hesitated.

"I have had a…setback," Marianne admitted.

Letting out a breath, Caledan crossed to the couch and sat. No sooner had he done so did Marianne leap back to her feet. He watched in confusion as she paced back and forth in front of the sofa.

"What…was the setback?" he asked.

"Servo has taken Lon!" the queen exclaimed, swinging on him. "I don't understand how. The council and the Lonian army are loyal to *me*. Not all the Knights in the land could have retaken the capital for the Order!"

"Perhaps it is a falsehood?" Caledan mused. "How did you receive this news?"

Marianne strode to her desk and searched amongst the papers that had fallen alongside it until she came up with the one she wanted. She thrust the letter at him as though it were poison. He took it and set it aside without reading.

"Tell me," he said quietly.

Marianne stared at him, nostrils flaring, eyes wild. Her calm demeanour had cracked again, and he sensed this was about more than just the Lonian capital. He had never seen the queen so flustered, not even when Servo himself had threatened her son. In the two weeks since they'd driven the Elder from the citadel, Caledan had all but forgotten the man. Their attention had been focused on Braidon, on how to deal with the former king's uprising in Chole.

"It doesn't say much," Marianne said, slumping down beside him. Her eyes took on a haunted look. "And what it does say makes no sense. The Lonian army turned on itself. It was open war on the streets of Lon. Servo arrived amidst the chaos with several thousand militants—untrained civilians mostly—along with his Knights. After that, Lon fell within a day. Now they cheer his name in the streets."

"What does it matter if they cheer for that monster?" Caledan asked. "The people of Plorsea love you."

"Ay, I bought their love with peace," Marianne said, looking away, "but what will become of their love when a Lonian army marches south? When Servo burns their villages and pillages their crops? I will become like my damned husband, loathed for my failures."

"You will never become like Braidon," Caledan replied with a smile. "The man is a coward, but you have the power to stop this war before it ever begins. When the time comes, we will sweep Servo from the streets of Lon, just as you did for Ardath."

Marianne sighed. "There is more."

"What?"

Her eyes shimmered as she stared into the distance. "You asked me once where my power came from."

"You never gave a straight answer," he murmured, "but…I surmised that the Elders had found a way to feed their magic with death."

"That is…the essentials of the exchange," Marianne agreed, the faintest of smiles touching her cheeks. "Though Servo and his ilk think of it as a gift from the Saviour, a way of cleansing the unfaithful from this world, of using their lives to fight against the return of the False Gods." She snorted. "Garbage, I now realise. The Elders, like all men, were greedy for power."

Caledan frowned. "But you stopped the cleansing. And I have never seen you take a life, except…" *For Devon*, he thought, though he left the sentence unfinished.

The queen's eyes fell to the floor. "Yes, that was my first taste, my initiation into the circle of Elders—though I had learned to use my own life force to perform small miracles before that."

"Then how…do you perform your magic now? Surely the power you took in Malevolent Cove…"

"Was consumed long ago," Marianne agreed. "Thankfully, I have more imagination than all the Elders combined. When I first learned of their powers, I had my engineers in Lon begin work on a secret project, one that would allow me to harness the energies of many, from all across Lonia."

"I see," Caledan commented, though her explanation had not told him much.

Marianne gave a throaty laugh. "I can see the specifics do not interest you overly much, My Champion," she said. "So I will get to the point. My engineers and I created new collars for the Lonian slaves, ones that would capture their life force upon their deaths and channel them back to me, through this." She pulled back the sleeve of her silk dress, revealing the silver bracelet on her wrist.

"But how does this have anything to do with Servo?" Caledan asked.

"Not only has Servo taken Lon, he has taken my power with it. He must have gotten the truth from the council, and had their engineers tune the collars to him."

Now Caledan saw the fear in the queen's eyes, realised what she was saying. Servo had stolen the source of her power, would use it now for himself. And with the power of Lonia at his back…

"But…you were using your power just now," he said as the thought came to him.

"Yes, and I was fool to do so," Marianne cursed. "The energies of all those who died before Servo stole control of the collars still rest within me. But there will be no more, not unless I resume the cleansings, and I will not countenance any more bloodshed. Not after risking so much to free ourselves of that evil."

"I'm glad to hear it," Caledan replied with feeling. He rose and strode past her desk onto the marble balcony. Footsteps followed as Marianne joined him, and he gestured out over the glistening rooftops. "As will they."

The queen said nothing, only slumped against the banister. Her eyes were fixed on some distant point, and he wondered if she were already regretting her declaration. Marianne was a woman driven, and she had already shown her willingness to do whatever it took to have victory. If that meant sacrificing a few more lives…

"From now on I must conserve my power for the confrontation with Servo," she said, then swore. "I knew it was a mistake to let him slip through my grasp. Had I gone after him, there would only be Braidon to deal with."

"Had you gone after him, both myself and your son would be dead," Caledan reminded her softly, placing a hand on her shoulder.

It had been Caledan's task to protect the boy while Marianne confronted the Elder Servo. But he had been alone against five armed men. In the end, he had slain four of his foes, but the last had mortally wounded him. Marianne had arrived just in time to stop the Knight and heal Caledan's injuries with her magic.

"You're right, I know you're right," she whispered, and he saw the shiver go through her, saw the haunted look in her eyes. "I am forever in your debt for that day."

"You paid that debt when you brought me back from the brink of death."

It was true. There in that room, waking from what he'd thought to be the sleep of death, Caledan had truly become Marianne's champion. She had given up the last of her strength to save him, had slipped into unconsciousness even. He would never forget her sacrifice. Not even the news of Braidon's uprising could shake his loyalty. Braidon had had his chance to rule, and had failed on every front. Marianne's day had dawned now.

The queen smiled at his words. "Don't be absurd. You gave your life in service to me. The debt remains, My Champion." She moved closer on the balcony, so that her body pressed up against his. "You have only to ask, and it will be repaid."

Caledan shivered at the offer in the queen's sapphire eyes, suddenly unsure of himself. He was not a stranger to strong woman, but Marianne was beyond anything he had ever imagined—powerful, elegant, beautiful. She could crush him at a whim, or lift him up to heights unimagined.

He swallowed, thinking again of her fear, the challenges to come. Servo was a threat they could not ignore, and unlike Braidon, he was likely to act sooner rather than later. Caledan needed to be alert. He had seen men who became entangled in thoughts of love. They inevitably died, their senses distracted, their decisions compromised. Without her power, Marianne was vulnerable.

Nodding his thanks, Caledan stepped away from her slightly and returned his gaze to the city. The distant waters of the lake shone in the setting sun. Laughter came from the queen as she reclined against the bannister, though Caledan sensed a note of disappointment beneath her mirth.

"So, My Champion," she said, "how shall we defeat my enemies?"

❧ 3 ❧

The *thuds* of swords striking shields met Kryssa's ears as she left the Castle and entered the courtyard. A week had passed since the burning, but the air within the stone walls still stank of smoke, a constant reminder of the evil that had taken place there. So it was with relief that she felt the sunshine on her face, breathed the fresh air. Unfortunately, the sight that greeted her did little to lift her mood.

Over five hundred men and women filled the courtyard. For the last week, she and Braidon had chosen sergeants from amongst their ranks, and grouped the remaining soldiers into regiments of fifty. Each sergeant was to command a regiment when the war finally came, though Kryssa remained doubtful of many. There were a few veterans from the civil war, but for the most part they were young souls, eager but inexperienced in battle.

But they were still better than the majority of Braidon's recruits. Most of those gathered had hardly seen a sword before this week, and no more than a handful showed any real promise. Given six months, Kryssa might have forged them into a half-decent force, but they didn't have months. They didn't even have weeks. A Lonian army was marching south, and word from the capital was that Marianne would soon ride out to meet them.

And now Braidon needed her for something else, some secret quest that would take them from the city for at least a night. In truth, the thought of leaving Chole—and the Castle—was a relief. It might have been the strongest fortress in the city, but there was hostility about the place, as though the very stones screamed out against their presence. Or perhaps that was just her own guilt.

Yet despite her relief, Kryssa couldn't help but think she was needed more in the city. Morale was already low amongst the recruits after the hanging, and to leave them in the hands of the untrained sergeants was to invite disaster. Even as she watched the chaotic training taking place in the yard, one of the recruits slipped and fell. Within seconds a sergeant was at his side, screaming for him to get back up.

Irritated, Kryssa started towards them, ready to give the sergeant a few choice words about leadership, but at that moment the clatter of horse hooves carried from across the courtyard. She looked around as the king emerged from the stables leading two horses.

"Kryssa!" he called, and she was forced to turn her back on the beleaguered recruit.

She watched as he approached, her mind turning again to this secret mission. What could possibly be so important that they needed to leave Chole now, when so much relied on their holding the city? What if Marianne stole a march on them while they were away? Or worse, the Order?

"So where are we heading?" Kryssa asked when he joined her.

Braidon only grinned and offered her a set of reins. "I'll

tell you at the city gates," was all he said before mounting up.

Cursing inwardly, Kryssa leapt into the saddle and directed her horse after him. At least the king looked to be in a better mood today. The strain of the past week had taken its toll on the man, adding a stoop to his shoulders and leaching the life from his face. Despite their success at taking the city, he knew they still stood little chance against the forces Marianne could muster. The army marching from Lonia had been a terrible blow for Braidon. This was the first time she'd seen him smile since receiving the news.

They passed quickly through the city, Braidon taking the lead through the broader avenues that would take them to the southern gates. They stopped only once as they passed the central plaza, where a demonstration was just beginning.

Braidon dragged his horse to a halt as the voices echoed from the stone walls.

"Murderer…traitor…coward…king…"

A vice clenched around Kryssa's chest as she realised they were talking about Braidon. She glanced at the king, seeing the smile vanish from his lips, his fists tightening around the leather reins. As he was dressed in nondescript clothing, the crowd had not noticed the king's presence. Even so, Kryssa edged her mount forward, placing herself between Braidon and the protest.

"Ignore them," she hissed under her breath.

"It's Janylle," Braidon replied, his voice cold.

Kryssa twisted in the saddle, her gaze sweeping out across the square to where the crowd had gathered around the silent fountain. A woman stood above them beside a statue of King Thomas, the man that had saved Chole from Archon's army. A shiver passed through her as the woman threw back her hood, revealing the wife of Dominic.

"The king had betrayed us!" Her voice carried over the jeers of the crowd, her face twisted with hatred. "He says he will protect us from his queen, but it is a lie. When she comes, our king will greet her with open arms! Then our temple will burn, and the Knights of Alana will take us…"

A roar rose from her followers, and Kryssa did not hear what else she had to say. She didn't need to. Glancing at Braidon, she saw the rage in his eyes, and the hurt that lurked beneath. Janylle had been their friend, but that had been before…

"Come on," she said, urging her horse forward. "Let her rage, they are only words."

Braidon did not reply, but after a moment he obeyed, turning his horse and riding from the plaza.

The sun was still low on the horizon when they finally reached the gates. They found them open and the first few wagons already trundling into the city, overseen by the fresh faces of the day guards.

"Okay," Kryssa said as they passed beneath the heavy blocks of stone and out onto the plains of Chole. "Speak."

"What?" Braidon asked, sounding distant. Then he shook himself and his eyes focused on her. "Oh, you want to know where we're going?"

"It's easier to protect you when I know what's coming."

The king let out a long sigh. "Sorry," he said. "After Marianne…its difficult to trust anyone."

"What about your talented new sergeants?" Kryssa asked, her voice dripping sarcasm.

"Not the most promising of recruits, are they?" Braidon asked, but despite the words, his voice gained some humour.

"Not to worry—if my plan comes to fruition, they won't matter come tomorrow."

"Oh?" Kryssa said as they started off across the open plains.

Braidon grinned. "Just you wait and see," he replied, and before she could ask any more questions, he kicked his horse into a gallop.

They alternated between trotting and walking their horses through the rest of the morning, and all the while Kryssa grew more irritated by Braidon's silence. They had left the road hours ago and the land around them was rugged, the bush untouched by man's axes. Twisted trees dotted the landscape, offering scant shade against the sun. While they'd seen the end of summer, the days were still hot on the plains, the air still.

Only as the sun started its inevitable journey towards the western horizon did Braidon finally break the silence.

"It's good to be on the road again," he said, eyes on the snow-capped peaks rising to the west. "Sometimes…sometimes I wish this could be my life again. Some of my best memories are from traveling the backroads of Onslow Forest with Devon." His voice cracked at the mention of her father. "If only…"

Kryssa said nothing. She and Derryn had made much the same decision when they'd first discovered she was pregnant, retiring from the King's Guard and moving to Skystead. But the decision had not been difficult for either of them. They'd known someone else would step up to take their place.

Braidon did not have that luxury. If he abandoned his duties, there would be no one left to stand against Marianne, no one to oppose the darkness of the Order.

"If only…" Braidon said again into her silence. "But

then who would avenge Devon and my King's Guard? Who would rally Plorsea against Marianne and her Lonian allies? Who would protect the people against the Knights of Alana?"

Kryssa sighed. "I don't envy you, Braidon."

Braidon chuckled. "Forgive me my self-pity, Kryssa," he said, offering a sad smile. "It gets the better of me sometimes, when I see people like Janylle, when I remember how my decisions have hurt people. But I've always known this was my fate, to rule Plorsea. Still, sometimes it's nice to dream."

"Of course," she replied with a grin. "So is that the purpose of this trip, then? A quick ride down memory lane, before you lead the forces of good against the dark queen?"

Now Braidon really laughed, his mirth echoing out through the browning trees. "Sadly, no," he replied, looking more relaxed than he had in weeks. "There is reason behind my madness, I'm afraid. We're out here looking for the tribes of Chole. They aided me in the last war, against Lonia. I'm hoping they will do the same again."

"And how do you expect to find them out here?" Kryssa asked, her good humour evaporating. The tribes were an unknown quality, and while they might have once allied with Braidon, there was no guarantee they would do so again. "These plains stretch for a hundred miles in every direction."

"Don't worry, we're on the right track," Braidon said, though he did not look her in the eye. "I've been experimenting with this new power. I found their trail yesterday. We must be drawing near by now."

Kryssa's heartbeat doubled as her eyes flicked to their surroundings. Silently, she cursed Braidon for a fool. The people he sought were nomadic and wild, and many tales considered them little better than the Baronians from whom they were said to have descended. She still remembered their mounted units from the war, how they had carved through the Lonian foot soldiers. It would be a mistake to cross them, and by trespassing on their land uninvited, Braidon risked doing just that.

The scrub had grown up around them now, alternating between thick bushes spotted with long thorns and open patches of grass. Movement came from nearby and she spun in the saddle, her hand dropping to the dagger on her belt. A cow lifted its head to stare at the passing horses, before returning to its meal.

Braidon chuckled. "You worry too much, Kryssa."

She snorted and loosened her sword in its scabbard. "That's my job as your King's Guard," she said. "You should have told me about this sooner."

"You would only have argued against it."

"I would have suggested you bring more soldiers," she snapped.

"As I said, I don't trust them. I can't have word getting back to Marianne of my plans," he argued. "And anyway, how many would you have brought? A dozen? A hundred? The tribes number in the thousands, too many, however many of our recruits stood with us. No, it's better just the two of us. At least now they will not see us as a threat."

Kryssa ground her teeth. "You still should have told me."

"Fine," Braidon surrendered. "Next time I go wandering into the dragon's den, I'll give you fair warning."

"Don't get me started on those beasts," Kryssa remarked with a shudder. She still hadn't gotten over the trauma of their flight from Dragon Country.

Braidon grinned. They were riding through another

patch of scrub and Kryssa scanned the way ahead. The light was fading now and she could see little in the shadows beneath the wiry trees. The sound of breaking branches came from nearby, followed by movement. Kryssa's sword leapt into her hand, but it was only another cow. It pushed through the bushes, the thorns unable to pierce its thick hide, and stumbled into the narrow track they were following.

"This is ridiculous," Kryssa snapped as they were forced to stop, their way barred by the beast. "What are cattle doing in this sort of country—"

She broke off as the answer came to her, and sword still in hand she kicked her horse forward into Braidon's. A hiss came followed as an arrow slashed the air where she had been. Her horse screamed as a second rushed from the bushes and struck its hide, and then it was rearing up beneath her, feet lashing the air.

Kryssa tumbled from the saddle and crashed to the earth. She rolled to the side as the horse slammed back down, its hooves mere inches from her face. Before she could regain her feet, the beast fled back the way they had come, its screams echoing in her ears.

Scrambling for her sword, Kryssa leapt to her feet and swung around, searching for the enemy. Braidon was still trying to recover control of his own mount. The beast bucked beneath him, its screams echoing through the fading light and making him an easy target. Cursing, she staggered forward to help him.

Laughter brought her up short as men and women appeared from the shrub with bows bent. A dozen steel-tipped arrows pointed at Kryssa's chest. She froze, raising her hands, while the cries from Braidon's horse faded as he got the beast back under control. A curse exploded from the king as he finally noticed their assailants.

Teeth clenched, Kryssa edged towards Braidon, seeking to shelter the king from their arrows. If he was lucky, the mount might carry him clear and back to Chole. She, however…

Movement came from amongst the hunters as an older woman pushed her way to the fore. White streaked her brown hair and her face was wrinkled, but she still moved with the confidence of youth, as though unconcerned by her advancing years.

"Put down the sword, girl," she said. Her teeth flashed in a wild grin as she looked from Braidon to Kryssa. "Unless you have a desire to become a human pincushion."

Kryssa risked a glance at Braidon. He gave the slightest nod. Exhaling loudly through her nostrils, Kryssa lowered the blade and the woman laughed again.

"So the man is in charge. How quaint. What foolish desires have brought you to our lands, vagabond?" the woman asked.

"These are *my* lands," Braidon grunted. "Unless you have forgotten your treaty with the Plorsean crown, Loyla?"

It took a moment for the significance of Braidon's words to sink in. Frowning, the woman took a step closer, her pale eyes sweeping Braidon up and down before widening in recognition.

"King Braidon," she murmured. "Death does not suit you, *Your Majesty;* you look…poorly."

Braidon scowled and gestured at his horse, requesting permission to dismount. The woman he'd named Loyla nodded and signalled her warriors to lower their weapons. Kryssa breathed a sigh of relief as the steel points were put away. With a scuffling of leather, Braidon leapt from the saddle and approached the nomadic leader.

"Can't say I've missed your honesty, Loyla," he said, wearing a grim smile, "nor your hospitality. I don't suppose some of your people would be so good as to chase down my Guard's horse?"

Loyla chuckled. "It'll be halfway back to Chole by now." Her gaze turned to Kryssa. "My apologies…?"

"Kryssa."

"Kryssa," Loyla confirmed with a nod. "I will have my people provide you another horse." Her attention switched back to Braidon. "Our camp is not far. I assume you wish to talk, unless Your Majesty has taken to enjoying long rides in the countryside?"

Braidon scowled. "I *was* rather enjoying it, until your people showed up." Then he laughed. "What happened to giving a warning shot?"

"Since men in iron suits began waging war against our people, we've become somewhat less forgiving of interlopers," Loyla replied.

"When did this begin?" the king asked.

"A little over a year ago. They started crossing our country, taking the mountain paths towards Dragon Country. Didn't take well to company. They killed several of our hunting parties before we learned to avoid them—or kill them on sight."

A cursed exploded from the king. "That news would have been useful a year ago."

"You think I did not send word to Ardath?" Loyla replied mildly, though Kryssa caught the shimmering in her eyes, the silent rage. "I never received a response. I assumed you were too busy with that pretty wife of yours to concern yourself with such a trivial matter."

"Marianne," Braidon muttered under his breath, then louder: "My apologies, Loyla. I would have acted, had your letter ever reached me. I fear there is much you do not know."

"I can imagine," Loyla said dryly, glancing from Braidon to Kryssa. "But night is approaching. Let us continue this conversation in our camp. We have not seen the Knights for several months now, but there are still dark creatures that stalk these plains at night."

$$\maltese \quad 4 \quad \maltese$$

"There's no smoke," Ruebyn whispered.

Pela frowned, looking at the town again—though it could hardly be called that. There were no more than a dozen of the stone buildings, clustered around a hilltop that would give the occupants clear views in all directions. Squinting, she saw that Ruebyn was right about the smoke.

"It's barely autumn," Pela shot back, though even as she said it, she wondered about the cooking fires or iron stones that would surely be burning at this time.

She drew in a breath, seeking the telltale scents of humanity—smoke and dust and cooking meat, the musk of animals kept in close quarters. But all she could smell was the crispness of the crushed grass beneath their feet.

A breeze blew down the valley, whistling through the rooftops of the village. The hackles lifted on her neck as she realised the buildings were utterly silent. From where they stood, surely they would hear sounds of civilisation, the buzz of voices and the hammering of tools, the squeal of wagon wheels or the screaming of a child.

But there was nothing.

Suddenly uneasy, she glanced at Ruebyn again. "I think you're right."

He nodded, but his face remained grim. "What do we do?"

"I don't know."

Pela shivered, thinking again of Ruebyn's earlier words. Trola's borders had been closed for decades. The rest of the world had assumed it was to rebuild after their liberation from the Tsar…but after so much time, anything might have happened.

"I say we go in," Ruebyn whispered, as though afraid now they might be overhead.

Fear touched Pela, and unconsciously she dropped a hand to the hilt of her dagger. "Why?"

"We have to find out what's going on," he replied.

He straightened his shoulders and glanced at her, but when she said nothing, he started along the path again. After a moment's hesitation, Pela followed, though she was still unsure if they were making the right choice.

By the time they reached the village, there was no longer any doubt that the place had been empty for a long time. Abandoned by their former owners, many of the houses were showing signs of dilapidation. While the stone walls still stood, roofing tiles now lay scattered across the dirt street or in piles amongst the ruins.

The first door they encountered was slumped in its frame, and fell backwards at a touch. Pela coughed as dust swept up around them, but shielding her eyes, she stepped inside. Light spilled in from a hole in the ceiling to illuminate the room. The house's occupants had obviously departed in a hurry, for their belongings had been left behind—pots and pans and furniture, half-rotten books and children's toys. A fine layer of dust covered everything and there was a heavy stench of decay. It was clear the place had gone untouched by human hands for years.

Pela retreated into the street. "What happened here?" she whispered to Ruebyn.

There were no bodies, but she couldn't shake the feeling that something terrible had happened. The whole village felt like a tomb, a place for the dead.

"What happened to Trola?" Ruebyn countered.

Pela scowled, rebelling against her earlier thoughts. "One village is not a nation."

"We've seen no sign of life since we crossed the mountains," he argued. His gaze travelled eastward, where the hills still stretched up to snow-capped peaks. "I don't like it. I think…maybe we should go back."

"Back?" Pela felt as though he had struck her. "*Back?*"

"There's something wrong here, Pe—"

"I can't go back!" she shrieked, lifting her chin to emphasise the slave collar. "Or had you forgotten *this?* Have you forgotten what they'll do to me?" She stalked towards him until they stood face-to-face. "Remind me, overseer," she hissed, her voice like ice. "Remind me the fate your precious handbook sets out for runaway slaves."

"I…I…" he stammered, then shook his head.

"*Tell me!*" she shrieked, grabbing him by the shirt and shaking him.

Ruebyn's eyes were wide as he stared at her, but finally he bowed his head. His answer came in a whisper. "They would break your legs and leave you in the mountains for the scavengers to find."

Pulling him closer, Pela placed her lips at his ear. "*I'm never going back,*" she hissed, then pushed him away from her.

He staggered several steps before righting himself. "I

didn't mean it like that," he said, looking hurt. "I…there are people that would help us, even in Lonia. You told me Elder Lewis tried—"

"And failed," Pela spoke over the top of him. "Do whatever you like, Ruebyn. I don't care. I'm staying right here. Whatever surprises Trola holds, they can't be worse than your Godsforsaken nation."

She was shaking now, her mind racing over every hurt, every awful thing that had happened to her over the last few months. She thought again of Genevieve, dying alone in the snowstorm so that they could escape. How could Ruebyn even think about returning after that? Suddenly she couldn't believe she'd ever slept with the foolish boy, had ever considered him anything more than a useless coward.

Turning her back, she marched down the street, intending to leave Ruebyn behind with whatever ghosts still haunted the awful village.

But as she neared the edge of the stone houses, a distant thunder carried to her ears. She paused, glancing at the sky, but there was hardly a cloud overhead. Frowning, she looked back at Ruebyn, but he only shot her a look of utter confusion.

Pela rushed to the edge of the village. A beaten dirt road stretched away to the south, what must have been left of this part of the Gods Road from ages past. She followed its winding path down the valley, through the overgrown fields and patches of trees. In the distance, sunlight flashed, reflecting off metal.

Her heart raced as she finally saw the horsemen. They were approaching from the south, riding at a steady trot that would see them reach the village in minutes. A cloud of dust rose obscured any details, but Pela made out flashes of Trolan blue. Whirling, she rushed back into the village.

"Hide!" she snapped at Ruebyn, and ducked into the nearest building.

Darkness embraced her, along with the icy cold of a space that had been untouched by fire or sunlight in years. Stones crunched beneath her boots—the roof here remained intact, but parts of the ceiling had begun to crumble, leaving a fine layer of dust and mortar on the ground.

Glancing back, Pela searched for Ruebyn and realised too late he had not followed her. He still stood frozen in the middle of the street. There was a frown on his face, as though he was still trying to work out how he could have been wrong about Trola's fate. She cursed beneath her breath and ducked back to the empty doorframe. The rattle of hooves grew louder as she leaned out—the riders would be upon them at any moment.

"Ruebyn!" she screamed. "Get out of the street!"

His eyes widened and he swung to look at her, then back at the houses on the other side of the street. Those houses were closer, and without further hesitation he ducked into one of them, vanishing from view.

A second later the rumble of hooves grew to a roar as the riders entered the single lane through the village. Pela shrank back from the doorway, seeking to disappear amongst the darkness. Her heart hammered against her ribcage, so loud in her ears she was sure the riders must hear it. A terrible fear touched her then, that the men had already seen them, that they had come to this village to hunt them down.

Standing in the darkness, Pela waited for the shouts of discovery to come. Her breath came in ragged gasps as she watched the door. The thunder of horse hooves slowed, then came to a stop outside. The whisper of voices followed, carried in from the street by a breath of wind. But standing in the corridor deep within the house, she could not see what they were doing.

Unable to take the suspense, Pela slipped into a room on her right, hoping for a view onto the street. When outside, she'd noticed that every window in the town had its shutters drawn. She should be able to spy on the street through the gaps without the horsemen noticing—or so she prayed.

The room in which she found herself was plain and unadorned, its simple furnishings covered by the same fine layer of dust as the rest of the house. A shiver passed through Pela as she saw the small bed tucked into a corner. The covers were still made, while on the floor a toy carriage lovingly carved from wood lay abandoned by whatever child had once lived there.

Shivering at the memories locked within the room, Pela skirted the toys and crept to the window. A shadow passed across the shutters and she ducked midstride, breath held. Through the cracks she saw a mounted man ride past.

"Men, dismount!"

The voice was so loud it seemed to rattle the shutters. Pela pressed herself up against the wall, suddenly terrified of being seen. It was clear from the man's tone that these were military men—soldiers, possibly sent to patrol the border against trespassers. Thankfully, her room was entirely in shadow, and it would have been all but impossible for them to glimpse her through the tiny cracks in the shutters.

The thump of boots against dirt came from outside, followed by groaning and the distant buzz of conversation. Pela let out a long breath and edged up alongside the window. Silently, she pressed her eye to the shutters.

Her heart sank. Finally she had a clear view of what they faced. At least a dozen men stood in the street. There was no question now that they were soldiers. Each wore plate mail armour and full-faced helmets, the steel stained dark blue, and all were armed with longswords. Kite-shaped shields hung from the saddles of their horses.

"Ten minutes break, then we continue," the last man to dismount shouted as he stepped down onto the street.

Sighs of relief came from the other soldiers as they removed their helmets. Several rummaged in their saddlebags, coming up with strips of jerky and honey cakes. The food was handed out, along with skins of water. Pela's stomach rumbled as she watched, and she struggled to suppress her hunger. She and Ruebyn had found little to eat since leaving the forest.

When the food was done, the men drifted apart. Their casual manner had eased Pela's fears, but now her chest constricted as several soldiers wandered close to her hiding place. Their leader stretched his arms above his head and yawned. As they drew closer, she noticed the intricate patterns inscribed into the breastplates, accentuated with several jet-black gems. Matching stones had been inset into the hilts of the blades they wore on their waists.

They were drawing closer to her hiding place now, close enough they might glimpse her through the blinds. She edged back, taking care not to move too suddenly and draw their attention. But as she placed her foot down, it landed on the wooden wagon. The toy slipped beneath her boot, throwing her off-balance.

Pela bit back a cry as she stumbled sideways, her arms windmilling in a desperate attempt to keep upright. Thankfully there was nothing else to trip over, and in two steps she recovered her balance. Freezing in place, she stared at the shuttered windows, blood pounding in her ears.

"Wha' was that?"

Her stomach twisted in a knot as the voice carried in from the street. A shadow flickered beyond the shutters as a soldier approach. His shape filled the window as he pressed an eye to a crack. Pela hardly dared to breathe. Scrunching her eyes closed, she willed herself to disappear, to vanish from the sight of her enemies.

"Can't see nothin'," the voice spoke again in the thick accent of the west. It was shockingly loud in the tiny room, and Pela had to keep herself from flinching. "Prob'ly some damn cat."

Pela's breath hissed between her teeth as the man stepped back. Her legs trembling, she sank to the floor, hardly able to believe her luck. These men truly were confident they were alone—or they would have searched the building.

"*Hey!*" Pela's heart dropped into her stomach as a familiar voice carried through the blinds. "Whatchu idiots doing in my place?"

No, no, no!

It was Ruebyn, making some terrible attempt at a Trolan accent. Leaping to her feet, she rushed to the window in time to see the soldiers forming up. Steel flashed as they drew their blades and advanced on the solitary figure standing on the other side of the street. Ruebyn yelped and tried to retreat, but they had him surrounded in seconds, swords extended, ready to impale him.

"Wait!" he gasped, raising his hands. "Don't, I'm unarmed."

Pela closed her eyes and repressed a moan. What was he thinking? He had already dropped the horrible accent. It was clear as day to anyone who heard him speak that he came from an eastern nation. Her hand dropped to the hilt of her dagger, but she could not fight so many. She swallowed, the collar pressing hard against her throat.

"What are you doing here?" the captain of the soldiers snapped, advancing until the tip of his sword rested on Ruebyn's chest.

"I…I…I seek asylum!"

"Asylum?" the man asked, and his voice revealed his disbelief.

"Yes. I am hunted…"

A stunned silence answered Ruebyn's words, before laughter broke out across the street. Ruebyn leapt back in fright, but the leader kept pace, his sword pressing forward, and now it drew blood. A scream came from Ruebyn as he tripped and went crashing to the ground. Pela snapped a hand to her mouth to keep from crying out as outside the captain raised a hand. The laughter died as quickly as it had begun.

"I would say you are caught, Lonian," the captain said, a cruel grin on his face. "Tell me, have they forgotten our laws in the east? I would not have thought it needed reminding that our nation is closed to foreign scum!"

Ruebyn's mouth opened and closed, but no words came out and the soldiers laughed again. Pela swallowed, a tremor running down her spine. They were going to kill Ruebyn and there was nothing she could do to stop them. And once he was dead, they would search the village to make sure he was alone.

Slowly she drew the dagger from its sheath. Her hand shook as she rose and stepped back into the hallway. Light beckoned from the front door, drawing her back out into the street. Focused on her friend, the soldiers didn't notice her approach until she was just a few steps away.

"Hey!" a man shouted as he glanced back and finally saw her.

The others responded instantly, whirling to face her with weapons raised.

"Leave him alone," she said quietly, raising the dagger.

The men stared at her for half a moment, before their laughter rolled out across the street again. A cold fury lit in Pela's chest. Instinctively, she reached within herself, seeking her calm centre, the burning flame at her core. This time it came easily, flaring to life in her mind's eyes, filling her with warmth, with power. She bared her teeth.

"I said *leave him alone!*" she cried, putting all her anger and energy into the words.

A tremor went through the men. Steel rattled as they wavered, then one by one stepped to the side, swords dropping to their sides. Pela stood gaping as Ruebyn sat up, a frown creasing his face. Her heart beating hard against her chest, Pela rushed forward and dragged him to his feet. She glanced at the men, but they made no move to stop them.

"Wha…what?" Ruebyn mumbled, looking groggy. Blood stained his tunic where the soldier had sliced his chest.

Pela shook her head, and stars danced across her vision. Blinking them away, she tried to walk back down the row of men, to draw Ruebyn away from them, but her legs felt suddenly weak. She gasped as they gave way and she sank to one knee. A collective cry came from around them as the soldiers returned to life.

"So." The captain's voice was cold now as he advanced on them. "The people of the east have discovered power. No matter." He lifted his sword above her head. "It will not save you from the *morbus*."

"Please," Pela gasped, scrambling back, "where is your mercy?"

The captain drew back his lips, revealing sickly yellow teeth. "To set foot in Trolan lands is death," he said cruelly. "*This* is our mercy—now hold them!"

Men leapt forward at his command. Pela lashed out with the dagger, but the blade scraped uselessly against a steel breastplate before it was knocked from her grasp. Iron hands pinned her arm behind her back and pressed her face into the dirt. She could no longer see Ruebyn, but from the sounds of his struggles, he wasn't faring any better.

The thump of boots approached, and screaming, Pela tried again to break free. But her assailant bore down on her, his weight unmoveable, and she slumped back to the ground gasping. Desperately, she reached for that unspoken power, but in her terror, she could not find it.

"Ready them," the captain growled.

"Bastards!" Pela shrieked as a rough hand pulled her silver hair to the side, exposing her neck. "Cowards!"

A cry came from overhead and Pela closed her eyes, expecting the end.

"What is this?" the captain whispered.

She shuddered as a hand touched the back of her neck. Looking up, she found the captain leaning in close, his eyes on the back of her head—no, *on her collar*. There was a frown on his face, as though he were seeing something he could not quite believe.

Then Pela noticed her dagger, lying forgotten on the ground, just a foot from her face. She stretched out her arm, slowly so as not to draw attention, though her heart was racing and she knew at any second the captain must return to his task.

Her fingers were just on the hilt when the captain cried

out as though bitten. Suddenly his hands were in her hair and he was dragging her up, spinning her around. She gasped, shocked at the violence, and threw out her fist. But the blow was poorly aimed and her hand careened from his breastplate.

"Who is your master?" the captain snapped, ignoring her attack. When Pela only stared at him blankly, he grasped her by the collar and shook her: "*Who is your master?*"

"What are you talking about?" Pela gasped, fighting to break his hold.

Releasing Pela's collar, he kicked her legs out from under her, sending her crumbling to the ground. Red flashed across her vision as her head struck the earth. Groaning, she crawled several paces away from the captain before turning to stare at him. Ruebyn lay nearby, still pinned by one of the soldiers. The others stood watching on, amused grins on their faces.

"You're monsters!" she cried.

"Ay," the captain replied, then turned to his men. "Mercy will have to wait. Bind them. Our lord must see what we have found."

⚜ 5 ⚜

Sitting with his legs crossed beneath him, Braidon looked at Loyla and wondered what he needed to do to win the woman's support. It was dim inside the tent, lit only by a single lantern, while the swirling smoke from the incense burning in each corner made the air thick and difficult to breathe.

It galled Braidon to think that Loyla's call for aid had gone unnoticed. Had Marianne kept the message from him, or had it been someone else in the capital, some aide who thought the plight of the nomadic people unworthy of his attention? He might never know, but it was unworthy of the crown to have ignored them after everything they had done in the war against Lonia.

Even so, that did not excuse Loyla's treatment of him. She had said nothing to him since reaching the camp, and now sat making conversation with Kryssa. The two were talking about the sword his Guard wore, how it had been her husband's, apparently, before passing to her daughter and then finally to her. Kryssa still planned to give it back to Pela one day.

"Loyla," Braidon said suddenly, unable to keep the impatience from his voice. Despite the touching nature of the story, he was in no mood to be ignored, particularly not after being set upon earlier. "I am sorry, but time is short. Already I have been gone too long from Chole."

Kryssa chuckled dryly at that, until a glance from Braidon silenced her. Calming himself, he looked again at the nomadic leader.

"I came in person to ask for your aid, as a matter of respect," he murmured. "Had I known you would get along with Kryssa so well, I might have reconsidered the use of my time."

"Prickly, isn't he?" Loyla said to Kryssa with a smile, before addressing Braidon: "Forgive me, Your Majesty, and thank you for honouring us so. Now, on behalf of what fresh squabble do you wish my people to spill their blood? I had heard your wife now sits on the Plorsean throne—can I take it this involves something of a lover's quarrel?"

Braidon scowled. "Marianne is the reason the Knights have been harrying your people."

"Is that so?" Loyla mused, her eyebrows lifting into her fringe. "Yet the Knights have not bothered us for some time, and rumours from the capital speak of the queen driving them from the city."

"Don't be fooled; Marianne is good at manipulating the truth," Braidon snapped. "Make no mistake, it was she who invited the Knights into our lands."

"Braidon speaks the truth," Kryssa offered. "The queen stood with the Order in Malevolent Cove. She used their profane rituals to grant herself power. If she has driven the

Knights of Alana from Ardath, it is for her own ends, not yours or our own."

Loyla stared at Kryssa for a long while before turning back to Braidon. "You have a loyal ally in this one," she said softly. "You speak of your wife's evil, but what is it *you* want, Your Majesty?"

Braidon frowned. "I want peace for my nation."

"Perhaps," the woman murmured, "or perhaps you only want power for yourself."

"What?" Braidon started. "I have dedicated my entire life to Plorsea, to righting the wrongs of my father. I have done nothing but fight for this nation these last thirty years. Through war and betrayal, I have done my duty. And still you question my motives?"

Loyla's eyes drilled into him. "I do."

Braidon could hardly believe what he was hearing. He wanted to shout at the woman, to scream at her for her accusations, for spitting in the face of his honour—but he sensed that was what she was waiting for. Instead, he sucked in a breath and slowly exhaled.

"Under Marianne's brief reign as queen, the Knights of Alana have marched unchecked in the streets of our cities, slaughtering hundreds on the altar of their Saviour. A Lonian army marches on our nation, and she waves the flag of greeting. Make no mistake, Loyla, there is a darkness coming. And like my grandmother, Enala, before me, I am the only one left to stand against it."

Silence answered his words. Kryssa sat beside him, looking from the nomadic leader to Braidon, her brow creased with concern. Braidon ignored her, his whole attention fixed on Loyla, as though by willpower alone he might force her to agree, to do her duty to her king and nation.

"Perhaps you are right," Loyla said finally, her words so

soft they could barely be heard. "Perhaps there is a darkness that must be opposed. But are you the man to lead us, Braidon? I had faith in you once, in younger days, when you fought against Ashoka to keep us free. But now…the years have lessened you, Braidon."

"What must I do to prove myself to you?" Braidon asked, his tone rising in notches. He was exhausted, so tired of fighting for a nation, a people, that did not care. Recalling his conversation earlier in the day with Kryssa, he wondered again whether he should just walk away, if he should turn his back and ride off into the mountains.

A smile crossed the woman's face as she rose. "Come," she said, gesturing towards the tent flap.

Braidon let out a heavy sigh and followed her into the night with Kryssa. A thousand stars shone down from overhead, while in the distance the crescent moon was just peeking above the horizon. They were camped out on the plains, away from the tangled scrub they had been traversing earlier. Braidon's horse was tethered nearby, alongside a new mount for Kryssa, but Loyla did not lead them there.

Instead, she made her way through the cow-skin tents towards a distant whispering. Turning his gaze ahead, Braidon sought the source of the voices and saw the glow of flames. Silhouettes moved in the darkness as they stepped from the tents out into the open, where a bonfire was burning brightly.

Men and women packed the space, but they retreated at the sight of Braidon, forming a wide circle around the bonfire.

Frowning, Braidon turned to Loyla. "What is this all about?"

She smiled. "You asked what you must do to prove yourself. So I will tell you. Prove you are still the Braidon of old, that the flame of your ancestors still burns in your heart. My champion awaits."

With the words, she gestured at the fire. A shadow stepped from behind the bonfire, a hulking presence in the twilight. Braidon swallowed as he looked the warrior up and down, taking in the barrel chest and trunk-like arms. He was at least as big as Devon had been in his prime, and almost a foot taller.

"This is him?" A grin twisted the giant's face as he appraised Braidon. "He does not look like much of a king, mother."

Braidon turned back to Loyla. "You would have me fight your own son?"

Loyla chuckled. "Are you afraid, Your Majesty?"

Scowling, Braidon faced the giant and drew his short sword. Steel rasped against leather as his opponent removed a massive scimitar from a sheath on his back. Firelight glittered on the curved blade and Braidon widened his stance, readying himself for the power the giant would put behind his strikes. Suddenly he was glad for the sparring sessions he'd had with Kryssa back in Dragon Country.

"Loyla, are you sure this is necessary?" Kryssa asked, advancing half a step to put herself between Braidon and the giant.

"Get out of the way, Kryssa," Braidon snarled.

Taking his sword in both hands, he reached for the power burning in his core. Braidon was done playing Loyla's games, done with the disrespect, with the constant questioning of his every decision. He was the rightful King of Plorsea, damnit. He'd never wanted it, never asked for it, but the kingship had been thrust upon him all the same. No one had ever acknowledged that sacrifice.

His every muscle was lit aflame as the energies of those lost in the pantheon leapt to his summons, feeding him fresh strength. Lifting his blade, Braidon saluted the giant. He would not kill the man—to do so was guaranteed to lose Loyla's support—but he would show the woman exactly who she was dealing with, that he would not be questioned.

Still grinning, the giant started towards him, scimitar raised in preparation to strike. Still feeding the power to his arms and legs, to his ears and eyes, Braidon let him approach. When the first blow finally came, it seemed to Braidon as though his foe moved in slow motion, the giant blade lifting high and swiping ponderously for his skull.

Ducking low, Braidon easily avoided the blow. The blade hissed over his head, rippling the parting of Braidon's hair, before he straightened and smiled at the giant. His foe stumbled forward a step and then leapt backwards out of range—though Braidon had not so much as lifted his blade. A frown touched the man's face as he struggled to comprehend exactly how the king had bested him.

Braidon smiled and spread his hands. "What happened, sir? Are you having trouble with your balance?"

The giant scowled. Hefting his blade, he approached again—though cautiously this time. Still Braidon let him come on unchallenged. Holding his short sword casually at his side, he adopted a bored expression. Enraged, the giant stabbed at Braidon's chest with a roar.

Braidon skipped sideways to avoid the blow. His sword flashed up then down, connecting with the giant's blade close to the hilt. Sparks flashed as the impact drove the scimitar from the giant's hands and sent it skittering across the stony ground.

"Clumsy, clumsy," Braidon *tsk*ed, kicking the blade back

to the giant. "Did your mother not teach you how to hold a sword?"

The giant swore and swept up his weapon. "How did you do that?" he hissed.

Braidon grinned. The man's bulk dwarfed him and the power behind his blows would have been enough to cut Braidon in two. But after two encounters, the advantage was entirely Braidon's. There was fear on the giant's face now, as he came to the realisation Braidon's skill might be beyond his abilities.

Then the man's face set, his fear vanishing behind an iron mask, and he started forward again. Braidon was impressed—this was a man unused to being challenged. Yet now, when faced with certain defeat, he did not skulk or turn away.

But it would change nothing. This time as the giant rushed forward, Braidon leapt to meet him. The shift in tactic caught his foe by surprise, and the man's eyes widened to find Braidon suddenly within range of his blade. Howling, he swung down with all his might. Braidon's short sword slashed up, catching the narrow blade of the scimitar with a shriek of grating metal.

Despite the power surging through his veins, Braidon grunted at the weight behind the blow. Under normal circumstances, his blade might have shattered, leaving the giant's scimitar embedded in his skull. But as the weapons came together, Braidon fed his energies into the blade, reinforcing the steel and adding strength to his own arm.

And so the giant's blow was stopped dead, caught upon the hilt of Braidon's short sword. The man gaped down at the king, unable to believe his own eyes. Smiling, Braidon took full advantage.

Twisting his sword sideways, Braidon caught the scimitar's hilt and sent it crashing to the ground. The giant staggered back emptyhanded, still stunned from the sudden turn of events, and Braidon leapt after him. His short sword slashed out, opening a cut in the giant's chest and igniting cries of fear from the crowd.

Lashing out with his boot, Braidon caught his foe in the chest, hurling him from his feet. Blood pounded in his skull as he advanced on the man, short sword gripped tightly in one hand. The giant lay crumpled on the ground, a hissing noise coming from his throat as he struggled to breathe. Fear showed in his eyes as he saw Braidon approaching. Still winded, he scrambled back, one arm raised as though to fend off a blow.

Braidon slammed his foot down onto the man's chest, pinning him to the ground. Another cry came from the audience as Braidon lifted his blade, pointing it at the giant's heart. He hardly heard their fear over the roaring in his ears, the fire burning in his core.

"Wait!"

A voice cut through the screams. Braidon looked up, finding Loyla standing nearby. He stared at her coldly, sword still poised to strike.

"You would have me show mercy?" he asked quietly. "I thought you had need of a strong king? One with the power to face Marianne? *She* certainly will have no mercy, when she comes for you."

"You have shown us your power, Your Majesty," she said quietly. "There is no need to prove your cruelty. Let my boy go."

The giant was still squirming beneath Braidon's boot, but despite his bulk he could not dislodge the king's weight.

Braidon tasted disgust as he glanced at the man, that he had allowed Loyla to shame him so, to fight for her loyalty.

He still clutched the short sword tightly in one hand, its leather grip digging into his flesh. The tip trembled as he shifted it to the warrior's throat. The man stilled at the touch of cold steel, and he could not keep the terror from his eyes now.

Smiling, Braidon returned the blade to its sheath and faced Loyla. The giant warrior scrambled back to his feet and fled to his mother's side.

"You are satisfied?" Braidon asked in a whisper.

"Ay, I have seen enough," she replied softly. "You will get no aid from us, Braidon."

"*What?*" Braidon exploded, so stunned he could only stand and stare at the woman.

"Loyla, please," Kryssa put in, extending a hand in entreaty. "You cannot—"

"I will not ally myself with one who has drunken the lives of others," Loyla hissed, her eyes shining in the light of the bonfire.

"What are you talking about?" his King's Guard asked. A frown creased her forehead as she looked from the woman to her king. "Braidon, what is she saying?"

Feeling inexplicably ashamed, Braidon allowed his gaze to fall to the ground—before his rage came rushing back. His head snapped up. "They did not die by my hand, nor by my orders," he said to Loyla, before glancing at Kryssa. "I did what I had to…when the fire was raging."

The colour drained from Kryssa's face at his words. "The pantheon?" she whispered. "You took their life force, when they died? You couldn't have…"

"They were already gone, Kryssa," Braidon said, then

swung on Loyla. The woman had pushed and prodded him, had sought to test his resolve, but now it was she who shirked her duties.

"I am your rightful king," he growled. "It is your duty to answer my call, to march beneath my banner."

"Ay," Loyla replied, "and yet still I refuse you."

And with that, she turned and walked away into the night. One by one her people followed, their silhouettes fading into the darkness, even as the bonfire raged on behind Braidon.

Braidon stood staring after them, too stunned to intervene, to call her back. How could she do this to him? He had proven his strength, shown that his will was the equal of Marianne's. And still she abandoned him.

Finally there was no one left but Kryssa. Their eyes met and for the merest of seconds he saw the horror there, the disgust at what he had done. It was gone in a second, replaced by a mask of polished silver.

"I am sorry, Your Majesty," she said in a wooden voice, barely audible above the crackling of flames. "Shall we return to Chole?"

Sadness touched Braidon as he felt the distance between them. Gone was the camaraderie they had shared since Dragon Country, the openness. The last of his anger faded, replaced by despair, and he nodded silently. Together they returned to their horses and climbed into the saddles.

They rode from the camp in silence. Braidon was still reeling from his rejection, from the utter failure of his mission. He might still have gone after Loyla, might have argued and fought and forced her to accept his authority, but there was little point. Her people would fight him at every turn if he tried.

Only as the darkness of the night embraced them did Braidon finally see the truth. If he was to defeat Marianne and free his nation from the grips of the Order, he must do it himself. There was no one left in the world he could trust, not even Kryssa.

He was alone.

$$\mathbf{\text{\textbxi}} \quad 6 \quad \mathbf{\text{\textbxi}}$$

The rain was falling hard in camp by the time Caledan lifted the canvas flap to Marianne's command tent. The journey downriver from Ardath had been long and fraught with difficulties, the vast array of fishing vessels and ferries struggling to keep together on the swiftly flowing currents. The rain had not helped, as the river swelled to the point of topping its banks. The brown waters had surged around the vessels, promising death to any who fell overboard, and Caledan was thankful none had been lost on the journey.

Most of the king's galleys had been destroyed along with the King's Guard and the only real ship left now was the strange vessel Marianne had used to sail from Malevolent Cove. But she had sent that ship south with her son, Calybe, in case the worst happened in the coming battle.

So their whole force of two thousand had been ferried downriver in a host of trading galleys and fishing ship, barges, and anything else that could survive the journey. The fleet had set out at sunrise, taking the better part of a day to travel downriver through the foothills that surrounded Lake Ardath.

Finally reaching the plains of Plorsea, they had set ashore on the eastern banks of the Jurrien River. Word had already reached them of Servo's army—his force was said to be some five thousand strong. Gladly, they had yet to cross the Jurrien, and Caledan had sent scouts ranging west to ensure they were not come upon unawares.

He could do less about the sheer size of the Elder's force. Not for the first time, Caledan found himself cursing Braidon. The former king had gutted Plorsea's standing army, reducing it to little more than his King's Guard and a handful of militias dotted around the nation. There was no true fighting force left in Plorsea, and Caledan had struggled just to gather their two thousand. Most were raw recruits with little fighting experience, more to make up numbers than of any real use. If it came to open battle, he would rely mostly on a core force of some five hundred veterans and sellswords to hold the army together.

Their one advantage was the Jurrien River. Further downstream, the Forest of Sitton blocked passage of ships from Lonia. Servo could have taken his force the long way down the eastern coast and up the River Lane, but instead had opted to march overland. No doubt he'd expected them to wait for him in Ardath, safe in the city fortress while his army ravaged the land.

But with Marianne's power source in his control, the Elder's power would only grow with time. Marianne had had no choice but to confront him. Now he would be forced to ford the Jurrien and face her in battle, or risk their army cutting off his supply lines and harrying him from the rear.

It was a bold plan and might have been enough to win the war, if not for Servo's overwhelming numbers. They might hold the banks of the Jurrien against the bulk of his force, but Servo had enough men to send forces up and downriver. There they could cross unopposed and circle back to attack the Plorsean army from the rear.

"Come in, My Champion," Marianne's voice called from inside the tent. "You're letting in a breeze."

Shaking off his worries, Caledan let the canvas flap fall closed behind him. Inside, the tent was lit by several lanterns, though Marianne was the only one present at that hour. Once they might have found an inn on the banks of the Jurrien, but they had long since closed with the loss of the river's trading route.

Outside, the rain poured down and despite the coal brazier in the corner, the air was cold in the tent. Marianne did not seem bothered though. She sat on the other side of the room in a wooden folding chair, a glass of wine in one hand and a smile on her lips. Over the last week she had pushed herself hard to ready her nation for war, organising supplies and speaking to the people, rallying their morale when word reached the capital of the approaching army.

Caledan had barely slept since the day Marianne had told him of her power, and even less after she had named him as her general. He was a sellsword and had fought in many battles, but he was no strategist. Marianne had given him the command because there was no one else she could trust, but he did not know how to win this battle.

Since their departure though, a sense of peace seemed to have come over the queen, as though the last week had removed a great burden from her shoulders, rather than adding to it. Tomorrow would determine not only the fate of her queenship, but that of her own life and her son. Yet she sat in her chair as though she held not a care in the world.

"Take a seat, and a glass, Caledan," she said, nodding to the bottle on the table beside her. "You look as though you could use the rest."

"There is still much to do, Marianne," he murmured. He did not sit, but he took her lead in dropping the formalities. "We need to decide a strategy, some way of defeating Servo."

Marianne leaned back in the chair, her sapphire eyes appraising him. "His forces are on the opposite banks of the river," she said finally. "They have commandeered several barges that are used to ferry goods along this strip of the river. Tomorrow, when the flood waters have receded, they will try to cross. We will do our best to stop them. Now, will you join me for a drink, Caledan?"

He stood staring at her for a long moment, unable to understand how she had received such intelligence before his scouts had returned. In the end, he decided it was best to let the subject drop. Exhaling, he poured himself a glass, and placing a chair close to the brazier, sat.

"Stopping them will be easier said than done," he said finally. "Servo has more men, and if he has gathered enough power…"

Almost unconsciously, Marianne lifted a hand to the bracelet on her wrist, before dropping it back to her side. "Relax, Caledan," she replied, though her voice had tightened. Drawing in a breath, she continued in a calmer tone: "We have done all we can. Tomorrow, we will find out if it was enough."

"Very well," Caledan consented, though there were still half a hundred things he wanted to discuss. Instead, he sipped at his wine, then made a face. "Whiskey would have been better."

"I'm afraid it was all destroyed after my husband's… departure," Marianne said with a grin.

"I take it you'd rather not discuss how you're going to deal with him, either?"

The queen chuckled. "You are persistent, sellsword."

Caledan took another sip. It was a red from the vineyards of northern Lonia, something of a taboo he would have thought, considering who they were going to fight tomorrow. But he supposed Lonia was still Marianne's home, whatever her adopted nation. Perhaps that was why she did not want to talk about the morning.

"Do you still miss it?" he asked, then when she only raised her eyebrows, elaborated: "Lonia? I can't imagine what it must be like, marching against the people who raised you."

Marianne did not look up from her glass, but he saw her eyebrows lift in reaction to his question. "You know, you're far more astute than I would have given you credit for, sellsword."

"Understanding one's foe is half the battle," Caledan replied.

"Are we still foes then, Caledan?" Marianne murmured, glancing at him now. The hint of a smile touched her lips. "I had hoped for more loyalty from my Champion."

"You know I am yours, Marianne," Caledan said. He locked eyes with her until the queen was forced to look away, then laughed. "But I doubt my behaviour surprises you as much as you would like me to believe."

"Oh?" the queen asked, arching one eyebrow.

"You've always been one step ahead of everyone else, Marianne," he answered. "You would not have chosen me to protect Calybe unless you had seen something more in me, something beyond a mere sellsword."

"You've caught me," Marianne laughed. "After our… encounter in Malevolent Cove, I had my people enquire about all of those who had escaped. You kept your secret well, but there were those who knew of your hatred for Braidon. Yet you had carried the man to safety from the amphitheatre. It was a puzzle I could not solve until you sat here before me, and told me of the hammerman's request. I knew then you were the man I needed."

"I am flattered, My Queen," Caledan said with a smile, "but you are diverting from the conversation."

Rich laughter pealed through the tent. "So I am!" she replied. "Very well, Caledan, you have seen me. I do not long for our battle on the morrow. I love my people, for it was never them who betrayed me. Servo has misled them, claiming I am an enemy of the Order, of Lonia. But it is he who has corrupted the teachings of the Saviour, who would so callously throw away their lives, all for his own gains."

"He must be stopped," Caledan murmured, "or his corruption can only spread."

"He must," Marianne agreed. She took another sip of wine, then gave a sharp shake of her head, as though she had tasted something sour. "But why must it always be *my* people who bleed? When the Tsar ruled the Three Nations, it was Lonian soldiers who formed his vanguard, though they were as much enslaved to his power as the Trolans they faced. Even in ages past, it was Lonia who bore the brunt of Archon's wrath. Now they will bleed again, following a leader who cares naught for them."

"I do not know what to tell you, Marianne," Caledan replied, "only that I believe in you. And that tomorrow I will stand at your side and do my best to keep you safe."

"I am glad," Marianne said quietly, then sighed. "I am sorry for my melancholy, Caledan. I told you we should not discuss such matters tonight." She rose to her feet and stepped around the brazier, stumbling slightly as she did so. Caledan's eyes were drawn to the bottle of wine, and he realised she had drunk most of it before his arrival. She knelt awkwardly beside where he sat and placed a hand on his knee. "But I will reward you for your service, my Champion."

Caledan swallowed at the queen's proximity. Her eyes were wide, her face flushed red, and for a second he was struck by a desire to take her in his arms and kiss her, to tell her everything would be okay. Almost as quickly the thought was gone, replaced by a wave of doubt.

Would things be okay? Tomorrow they would face bloody battle on the waters of the Jurrien. With her powers limited, Marianne would be relying on him to protect her from harm while she faced off against Servo. He could not afford any distractions.

So again he pulled away from her. Carefully her removed her slim hand from his lap. "I am sorry, Marianne," he croaked, his mouth suddenly dry. "I cannot accept…such a gift…not with the battle on the morrow…"

"What?" For the merest of seconds, shock showed in Marianne's eyes. It was gone in an instant, and suddenly she was standing, her face a mask once more. "I did not mean that kind of gift," she growled, her voice like ice.

Caledan's mouth dropped open, but no words came out. Mortified, he stared at the queen, wishing he could sink into the floor.

"Your sword," she snapped, holding out her hand. "Give it to me."

"I…" Caledan closed his eyes, unable to face her rage.

He had failed her. Now he must face the consequences. He stood and unclipped his sword belt before handing her the weapon. She took the sheathed blade without a word and drew it into the lantern light. He did not flinch away as she held it in her hand.

But Marianne made no move to strike him down. Instead, a calm settled over her face as she closed her eyes. Her hand began to glow, as though she held some multi-coloured light between her fingers, and slowly that light danced its way up the blade. Swirling and flickering, it spread until the whole blade was aglow.

Then slowly, reluctantly, the light seeped into the sword, until nothing remained of the power Marianne had summoned. Wordlessly, she sheathed the blade and handed it back to Caledan.

"Carry the blade into battle tomorrow, sellsword," she said coldly. "If you are truly faithful, perhaps it will offer you some small measure of protection."

Stunned, Caledan looked from the sword to Marianne. "I…thank you—"

"That will be all, sellsword," Marianne spoke over him. "Leave me now, I have much to think about."

At that she turned away, dismissing him with a glance. Caledan stared at her back, then swinging the belt around his waist, he started for the tent flaps. But at the entrance he hesitated, glancing back. Marianne stood beside the brazier, her eyes on the coals. For a second he was struck again by the impulse to go to her, to wrap her in his arms and pull her close.

Then she glanced back and saw him still standing there. Flames appeared in her eyes, a silent rage that promised retribution. Spinning, Caledan fled the tent in silence.

$\mathfrak{K}$ 7 $\mathfrak{K}$

The ride to Kalgan took three days, during which Pela and Ruebyn were watched day and night. The soldiers had freed up two packhorses to carry them, though without proper stirrups, riding the beasts was impossibly uncomfortable. Their hands had also been bound, and with the horses being led by the soldiers, they'd no control over the pace at which they rode. By the first night, Pela had felt as though her entire body was one giant bruise.

The following days had not improved from there. Pela had soon come to realise that Ruebyn had been right—Trola was empty. For three days they saw only empty fields and ghost towns, a land abandoned by its people. Even as the road had widened and the way grew clearer, the countryside remained bare.

Only as they neared the capital had people finally appeared. The first had been a lonely vagabond, wandering slowly down the side of the road. His eyes had been fixed to the ground and he did not look up as the soldiers rode past. The next was the same, while a third carried a hand wagon loaded with dishevelled-looking onions. They'd overtaken him just an hour before the city, and the soldiers had been unhappy by the delayed caused while he shifted his wagon from the centre of the road.

In the silence on the road, she and Ruebyn had not been able to talk about what had happened in the village. But that had not stopped her anger from brewing. She still could not believe he had acted so foolishly, had revealed himself, and for what? Some half thought out plan to save her?

Her anger was made all the worse now she knew they could easily have avoided detection in the Trolan country-side. Their path would have been clear, if only Ruebyn had not given them away.

Now they were at the end of their journey, Pela wondered what fate awaited them in the ancient city. Kalgan had stood as the capital of Trola for a thousand years—even during the reign of the Tsar, when he had razed it to the ground. Its walls rose before them like moun-tain cliffs, so high she could hardly believe they had ever been taken. Guards stood at the gate, dressed in the same blue armour as their captors, and Pela and Ruebyn were ushered through without delay.

The city itself was a strange place, its buildings squat and unadorned, as though their creators had feared to make them beautiful lest the Tsar return again to burn them. A heavy silence hung over the place, and for the first few minutes Pela feared the city as dead as the rest of Trola. But as their party progressed through the grid-like streets, she saw hints of life—a wagon rumbling by the next intersec-tion, a flicker of movement in a nearby building. The door to one house stood open, and peering inside, Pela saw stairs leading down.

She remembered then a tale her uncle had told her

once, that after the Tsar's invasion Kalgan had built down, rather than up. Beneath the streets were half a hundred tunnels and chambers, a civilisation hidden from the world above. Who knew how many souls still survived beneath their feet?

Nearing the city centre, Kalgan's streets finally began to fill, though its people still walked with their heads bowed, avoiding eye contact with the soldiers. Those who could went hurriedly about their business, while the beggars and occasional street vendor did their best to avert their gazes from the armed men. Most wore little better than rags, the fabric worn and dirt-streaked, though despite their obvious poverty they all displayed at least one piece of jewellery—bracelets or necklaces, or for many, a plain circlet of brass or copper. Each was inset with the same black gems sported by the armour and weapons of the soldiers.

But it was their eyes that haunted Pela most. Though they were quick to look away, she could not miss their despair, the misery of all they passed. Trola had suffered during the Tsar's reign, but with his fall they had been free to prosper. What then had happened, that Trola's crops went untended while its people starved?

"Look," Ruebyn whispered as they turned a corner.

Pela would have stumbled to a stop if she'd had the ability. Instead, her horse continued its slow plodding towards the glimmering marble walls at the end of the street. They rose some hundred and fifty feet above their head—the towers beyond even higher—a stunning citadel of marble and gold, utterly out of place amidst the squat buildings of Kalgan.

"They really rebuilt it," Ruebyn whispered.

Pela could only nod as she carefully closed her mouth. Before the Tsar had invaded, all of Kalgan must have looked like the citadel. It was said to have been badly damaged by the dragon fire that had ravaged the city, but its renewal had been one of Trola's first projects after they'd won their freedom, to restore the pride of a broken nation. But that had been before the borders had closed, and no one in the east knew whether the work had been finished.

Without magic, Pela could hardly imagine how such a feat was possible. The marble blocks must have weighed tonnes, and the spiral towers looked so delicate that a strong breeze should have blown them down. Built of marble and granite and gold, it was a glorious and terrifying foil to the poverty that surrounded them, a reminder of all Trola had once been—and had since lost.

"It looks just like the history books," Ruebyn said as they approached.

Finally shaking free of her shock, Pela flashed him a glare. "I wouldn't know."

"It's said the original citadel predated the False Gods," he went on, unaware of her anger, "that ancient powers were imbued into its very walls." He fell silent, glancing at their captors, but now that they were close to the end of their journey, the soldiers seemed to have relaxed. "The Sword of Light, from your own legends, hung in its gardens before anyone learned how it could be used."

Pela lifted her head at that. He was right—she knew that tale. "The Trolan King, Thomas, came for it when Archon's forces first invaded the Three Nations," she murmured, then frowned. "No, that cannot be right—he was fighting on the frontlines, and the war only ever made it as far as Plorsea."

Ruebyn offered a telling smile. "You're right," he replied. "The stories say King Thomas led the final battle in Chole, but that The Way transported him to the citadel in time to defeat the Dark Magicker."

"The Way?" Pela frowned. Her grandmother had told the story many times when she'd been a child, but that was long ago, and the details were fuzzy.

"It was said to be a magical portal between Plorsea and Trola, left over from the Great Wars. Supposedly it was a place of safety, used for peace negotiations, but it became corrupted during the time of Archon." Ruebyn chuckled. "Personally, I've always thought it proof that the stories are no more than that. Magic was never powerful enough for such a feat."

Rolling her eyes, Pela tried to rub the circulation back into her wrists where the cords had cut deep. "I thought you might have learned to open your eyes by now," she said. "There are powers not even your engineers can explain, Ruebyn. Or do you think the soldiers stood aside willingly when I came to rescue you?"

Ruebyn fell silent at that, though Pela sensed he was far from convinced. Even so, she let the subject drop as they moved into the shadow of the citadel walls. Oaken gates groaned as they swung open and darkness embraced Pela as the horses carried them into the gate tunnel. A shiver passed through her as she sensed a change in the air. Frowning, she studied the ancient stones, but they looked no different than the outside. A moment later they were returned to the light, and the world was normal again…

…if what greeted them on the other side could be called normal. In place of the slums they had left behind, a brilliant lawn of lush grass spread out before them. Gardens of gold and red and violet flowers grew here and there, while vines and creepers covered the inner walls of the keep.

There were people too, merchants and nobles it seemed, from the cut of their clothes. They wandered amongst the gardens in pairs, arm in arm as they spoke in soft voices, their lives as disconnected from the poverty outside as a desert cat from the ocean.

Pela could only stare as they rode past. After her time in the mines beneath Lonia, she knew well the pain of the poor, the agony of working until her hands bled and still not earning enough food to sustain herself. Those outside might not have been slaves, but they were still trapped by their poverty, made servants to the rich who wandered these gardens.

Anger touched her then, a wild rage at everything she had suffered, born of her frustration, of the days of silence.

"What is wrong with you?" she shouted, tugging hard at her bindings, trying to redirect her horse at the nearest couple. "How can you just stand here talking while there are people outside starving?"

The nearest couple looked around at the commotion. Their eyebrows lifted half an inch when they saw her, as though surprised that an outsider had spoken to them. They stared at Pela for a long moment, the slightest of frowns denting their brows. Then a look of disinterest came over their faces, their eyes turning blank, and they turned their backs and wandered away.

"Bastards!" Pela screamed after them. "You don't even care!"

She had expected the soldiers to react, but the man holding her reins merely edged his horse onwards, drawing her along with him. Pela swung on him, using every curse word she'd learned in the mines, but he remained impassive. The mood of the soldiers had grown sombre upon entering the citadel and even the captain rode with his eyes fixed straight ahead.

Finally the soldiers reached the inner keep and dismounted. The captain himself cut Pela's bindings loose.

She stepped down clumsily, but her legs numb from the morning's ride and she would have fallen had he not caught her by the collar. Dragging her up, he brandished a knife.

"You will be silent before the king," he hissed, "or I'll remove your tongue before our little appointment."

Pela swallowed an angry retort when she saw the darkness in his eyes. Instead, she nodded and clamped her jaw shut. The captain smiled grimly and led her inside, while the man she had come to know as his second-in-command brought Ruebyn. The others remained outside with the horses. Pela saw no guards here—had seen none since entering the citadel, in fact. She supposed they weren't needed. Everyone the nobles might fear was kept outside by the massive walls.

They walked quickly through the marble corridors, their way lit by the warm glow of lanterns. Great tapestries covered the walls, though these surely could not have been the originals. Those would have been destroyed when the Tsar's Red Dragons had burned the city.

A shiver ran through Pela as she noticed the tapestries hanging at the end of the hall. One depicted a narrow canyon, bordered by snow-capped peaks. A great battle was taking place between the cliffs, as soldiers of red and blue hurled themselves at one another. In the centre of the red-caped soldiers, one man stood shrouded in darkness, a terrifying warhammer held high above his head. Yellow eyes glowed in the shadow of his face, as though the warrior were possessed by the devil himself.

On the other wall was a matching tapestry, this time of the rolling hills in northern Trola. Here the red-cloaked army swarmed up towards a last bastion of resistance—an army of blue and green, led by the golden figure of the Northland Queen and the man Betran, who would later become the Trolan King, at least before the borders had closed. And there again was the hammerman, though now a pure light shone upon him.

Devon.

Pela had once been ignorant of her uncle's past, but no longer. The tapestries depicted the two battles that had marked his great life—the first where he had led the Tsar's forces to victory against the Trolans, the second years later, when he had stood with the resistance and put right the mistakes of his past.

Boom.

She jumped as a crash echoed down the corridors, but it was only a set of iron doors opening ahead. The captain and his second gestured them onward, and Pela fell into step beside Ruebyn. Servants pressed their shoulders to the doors as the four of them passed inside, and a second *boom* followed as they were sealed inside.

Coming to a stop, Pela was surprised to find herself in a sparsely furnished room. Gone were the grand tapestries and golden fittings. Even the walls were looking worn, the stone stained with moisture. At the opposite end of the room several men and women sat speaking at a wooden table, their whispers echoing from the high ceilings. The voices died away as a dozen eyes turned to face the entrance.

"Captain Shand," an old man at the head of the table rasped, coming slowly to his feet. Pela started as she saw the copper crown upon his brow, inset by a single black gem. "What brings you to the citadel? I had thought you stationed in the northern regions."

The captain released Pela and stepped forward, bowing low. "We were, Your Majesty," he said as he straightened, "but we found these two wandering in a village in the foothills."

"Ah, such beautiful country," the king murmured, settling himself back into his seat. "I have not visited in many years, hardly once since the great battle. I must plan a return…one day…" He trailed off, his eyes taking on a distant look.

There was a moment's pause as the captain waited for him to continue. When the king remained silent, he cleared his throat. "Your Majesty?"

"What?" The king sat up suddenly, shaking his head. "Oh yes, my apologies, Shand. You found them where? I thought all the villages in those parts had been decimated."

"They are not Trolan," Shand announced. "They crossed the border from Lonia."

A collective gasp came from the table as the men and women there turned to one another, speaking quickly. Pela's heart pounded hard in her chest as she watched them, wondering what they would say, how they would pass judgement.

Finally she could bear it no longer. The captain had left her unattended, and gathering herself, she leapt past him. "We seek asylum—" she shouted, before something hard slammed into her from behind.

Stars flashed across her vision as she struck the ground, the weight of the captain driving the breath from her lungs. Gasping, she tried to roll away, but then his hands were in her hair, forcing her face into the cold marble tiles.

"Stay down, you little witch," he snarled.

Straining to breathe with his weight on her back, Pela replied in a series of hissing sounds that might have been agreement. The pressure relented a little, and after a few more gasping mouthfuls, she managed to draw a full breath.

She turned her head as a muffled cry came from across the room, and saw Ruebyn struggling with the second soldier.

"Pela!" he managed, before the captain's second cuffed him in the side of the head and he slumped into his captor's arms.

"Shand!" the king's voice echoed from the ceiling, louder now but still seemingly frail. The soldiers froze, looking up as the monarch continued. "What is the meaning of this violence?"

"Forgive me, Your Majesty," Shand grunted. Taking hold of Pela's hair, he stood, dragging her up with him. "As I was saying, these two came from beyond the mountains. We do not know who sent them, but I believe they could be a threat."

"Release them—now," the king said, his voice taking on a dangerous tone.

The captain obeyed immediately, releasing Pela so quickly she almost fell and dropping to one knee.

"Forgive me, Your Majesty," he replied. "I only meant to protect you."

"I will have no violence in my throne room, Captain Shand," the king murmured, his voice so low now he could hardly be heard.

Pela shuddered at the look he gave the captain, but seeing her opportunity, she gathered her courage and faced the king.

"Your Majesty," she said, bowing low. "As I was saying, we come seeking asylum."

"Asylum?" he asked, then waited until Pela nodded before continuing. His eyes were sad as he looked at her, as though her fate were already sealed. "I see. Did you not know it is forbidden to enter Trola—on pain of death?"

"Y…yes, sir," Pela stuttered, put off by the man's

demeanour. Would he so easily condemn them without ever hearing their story? "But…we were desperate!"

"There are many desperate souls in our world," the king said, his eyes turning distant once more. "So much war, so much death and destruction. Oh, how my people have suffered these past fifty years." Then his eyes focused on her once more. "Tell me, girl, do you know my name?"

Pela shook her head, not daring to speak, though she prayed to the Gods this was the man who had once fought beside her uncle.

A smile crossed his face. "I am called Betran, he who fought alongside the Northland Queen in the battle for our freedom." There was a touch of pride in his voice, though it hardly seemed to lift him from his melancholy. "It fell upon my shoulders to lead Trola from the ruin left by the Tsar's reign."

"Betran?" Pela whispered. Her heart soared and she was hardly able to believe her luck. "My name is Pela, and this is Ruebyn. You knew my uncle, Devon!"

Now it was the king's turn to show surprise. A spark lit in his eyes as he looked at her, burning through the sadness. "You are related to the hammerman?" he whispered. "I thought him long dead. Perhaps there are heroes yet in this world."

"I am sorry," Pela said, and watched the spark fade, "he died not long ago." She forced a smile, and when she spoke the words were strained. "But his memory lives on in all of us."

The king made a gesture, as though to dismiss her words. "I am sorry for your loss, my dear," he said. "Though I am more sorry you have so carelessly thrown away your own lives."

"What?" Pela hissed, the blood pounding in her ears.

She took a step towards the king, one hand extended in entreaty. "Please, surely you can make an exception, after everything Devon did for your land."

"An exception?" the king asked. He stared at her for a long while, then slowly he shook his head. "You do not know, do you?"

"Know what?" Pela asked. When the king still said nothing, her voice rose to a shout. "*Know what?*"

"I suppose word did not reach your lands," he replied. His eyes drilled into Pela. "Closing our borders was an act of desperation. It was the only way to stop the *morbus*."

"What is the *morbus?*" she asked, though in her heart she already knew.

"A plague, my dear. One unlike any the Three Nations has ever seen."

8

Kryssa and Braidon rode all night to reach Chole just as the sun began to stain the horizon red. In all that time, they'd said not a word. Kryssa was still reeling from the revelation in the camp, that Braidon had taken the energies of the dying as the pantheon burned. She knew that the king had had nothing to do with the slaughter, and yet…just the thought of what he'd done made her skin crawl.

The guards were just pushing the gates open to admit the first travellers of the morning as the two rode up. Kryssa was flagging, her strength consumed by her preoccupation with Braidon's new power, by the endless ride, and a desperate lack of sleep. Yet the king still seemed fresh, as though such trivial matters no longer affected him. Indeed, they might not, with the life forces he had gathered…

"Sir!" one of the guards called as Braidon edged his horse forward, sounding surprised. "Your Majesty—your sergeants, they've been looking for you!"

A look of irritation crossed Braidon's face at being recognised, but was quickly concealed. "I was called away

715

on an urgent matter," he replied from the saddle. "Was there a message?"

"Ah…" The guard trailed off, glancing at his companion before continuing. "No, but…I imagine it was to do with the riots, sir!"

"Riots?" Kryssa asked, concerned. She edged her horse up alongside Braidon. "What's happened?"

"Well, maybe not riots," the guard replied. "There was a protest, outside the…err, *your* Castle, sir. They refused to leave. There was some…confusion about what to do about them."

"And what *did* my illustrious sergeants decide?" Braidon asked coldly.

"They…they led a few regiments out the gates and sent them packing."

Braidon swore. Giving his horse a kick, he set off at a gallop. Kryssa followed just a few feet behind, her heart racing. What had Braidon's men been thinking? They needed the city on their side, not on the verge of an up rise. How could such a disaster have unfolded in just a few days?

The streets were empty as they raced through the city, and there was no sign of Janylle or her followers. A shiver ran down Kryssa's spine as she wondered whether the woman had been involved in the protest. Her eyes fixed on Braidon's back and she wondered what he would do.

There was no sign of disturbance in the streets outside the Castle either, but as they approached, men appeared atop the ramparts. Kryssa pulled back on her reins as several crossbows were pointed in their direction.

"Halt!" a voice bellowed down. "Who goes there?"

"Your king," Braidon snapped. Unlike Kryssa, he had not slowed his approach. "Now open the bloody gates."

There was a moment of confusion atop the walls, until

someone apparently recognised Braidon. The rattling of chains was followed by the creaking of steel hinges, and the wooden gates cracked open. Braidon rode through without so much as a glance back, and Kryssa hurried after him before the recruits locked her out.

Inside the walls, she was surprised to find a regiment standing at arms. Braidon had already dismounted and was now striding through their ranks, bellowing for his sergeants. Her heart racing, Kryssa looked around for an attendant or stablehand, but there were none in sight. The gates slammed closed behind her, and cursing, she leapt from the saddle and ran after the king.

"Braidon!" Kryssa gasped, but the king did not turn back.

She didn't catch him until the inner corridors of the Castle. Even then he did not spare her a glance, and they strode down the hallways in silence, making for the room Braidon had designated as his war chambers. An aide met them as they approached the final corner, puffing hard. He had been a minor noble before, working as a tax collector. In need of every spare hand he could get, Braidon had raised the man up to help with the organisation of the Castle.

"Sir," the man gasped. "Where have you been?"

"Gather my sergeants," Braidon snapped, ignoring the question. "I want them in the war chambers, now."

The aide recoiled at Braidon's abrupt tone. The king was always polite with his assistants, but he was gripped by a terrible rage now, one that brooked no argument. After a second's hesitation the aide nodded and raced off down the corridor.

A few minutes later, Kryssa found herself alone in the war chamber with Braidon. Though the name sparked images of grandeur, of a space filled with maps and strategy papers, the room itself was nothing of the sort. Containing only a long wooden table and a dozen chairs, it had been someone's sleeping chambers before Braidon's occupation. The bed had been removed and the windows shuttered to keep unwanted intruders from entering, but otherwise the space hadn't been changed.

Finally able to catch her breath, Kryssa sank into one of the chairs. Braidon's aide still had not returned and the space was unlit, the gloom casting shadows into the corners of the room. Winter was a long way off, but a chill clung to the stones of the Castle, as though the ghosts of the dead still haunted its passageways. Kryssa cast a glance at Braidon, wondering what it must be like to hold the lives of so many innocents within him.

Shuddering, Kryssa quickly returned to her feet. There was a wood stove in the corner, probably used by its previous occupant for heating during the winter, and she crossed to it. Pulling open the iron door, she was pleased to find a small stack of wood already in place. She lit the stove with her flint and returned to her chair.

All the while, Braidon paced back and forth across the room, his jaw clamped closed. She watched him from the corner of her eye, still wondering what he would do, what had happened. The king could not afford such unrest in his city, not with Marianne due to join with the Lonian forces in a matter of days. With an army beneath her command, it would only be a matter of time before they stood outside Chole's gates.

One by one, the various men and women Braidon had elected as his sergeants filed in. Each cast one glance from the pacing king to Kryssa, then took their seats in silence. Kryssa nodded to a few, but taking her cue from Braidon, she said nothing. The only sounds were the padding of the king's boots, the gentle crackling of the fire.

"How many died?" Braidon announced when all ten of his sergeants had gathered, his eyes sweeping over them. When no one replied, he strode to the head of the table. "I asked: *how many died?*"

Several of his sergeants flinched as the king's shout echoed from the walls. Kryssa held her breath, waiting to see which of her fellows would take the lead. Movement finally came from the end of the table as a woman climbed to her feet. Kryssa thought she recognised the face, but she'd not yet taken the time to memorise all of their sergeant's names.

"Two recruits, Your Majesty," the woman murmured, her eyes fixed to the tabletop. "Of the crowd…we aren't sure. The dead and wounded were dragged away by their fellow protestors."

"Estimate," Braidon grated.

The woman swallowed visibly. "Ten? Twenty? No more than that, we believe."

"And was it you, Sergeant Macy, who gave the order to attack unarmed civilians?" Braidon asked, his voice like ice.

The sergeant drew herself up. "No, sir," she replied in a wooden voice. "It was decided amongst all of us, in your absence."

Kryssa winced. There was no missing the rebuke in the woman's words, the implication that Braidon had failed his people in their moment of need. The king stared at the sergeant, his eyes hard, and when he spoke, his voice was like granite:

"Sit down, Sergeant Macy." Wood grated against stone as the woman practically fell into her chair. Teeth bared, Braidon continued. "From now on, no action is to be taken against the population of this city without direct orders from myself or Lieutenant Kryssa." He let out a long breath, seeming to calm somewhat. "Make no mistake, what happened is a tragedy, but we must press on. Any day now, Marianne will meet with the Lonian army. We must be ready when they come. How goes the training of our recruits?"

The sergeants exchanged nervous glances. Several looked to Macy again, but apparently the woman had decided she'd said enough. Finally one of the men rose. "There have been…setbacks, Your Majesty."

For the merest of seconds, Braidon's eyes slid closed. "Yes?" he asked, as though he already knew what was coming.

"A number of the recruits have…quit. The rest continue their training, but morale is low, especially after yesterday. Some are questioning…" He trailed off, glancing at his companions as though seeking their support before continuing. "Questioning your commitment to destroy the Order."

Placing his palms against the table, Braidon leaned forward, his gaze locked on his subordinate. "And what do you think, Sergeant?"

"I believe Your Majesty knows best!" the man shouted.

"And what about the rest of you?" Braidon snarled, swinging on the table. Not one of them could meet his gaze, and after a moment the king turned away. Arms clasped behind his back, his next words barely rose above a whisper. "Get out, all of you."

The sergeants went. Only Kryssa remained in her seat, waiting until the rest had gone before rising and approaching the king. Her heart was still palpitating in her chest, and she couldn't help but question whether Braidon had done enough. A dozen civilians were dead, and he'd given his sergeants little more than a reprimand…

"Braidon…?" she whispered, rising to her feet.

"What?" he snapped.

She recoiled at the fire in his eyes, but Braidon made no move towards her, and after a moment the flames faded. His shoulders slumped and he stumbled to the table. Sinking into a chair, he laid his head in his hands. Kryssa stood staring at him for a long while, then crossed and took the seat beside him.

"What am I going to do, Kryssa?" Braidon croaked, lifting his head to look at her. "It's all falling apart."

Despite her disgust at what he'd done, Kryssa felt pity for the king as she saw the despair he had been trying so hard to conceal. For a moment out on the plains, Braidon had been himself again, free of responsibility and the burden of leadership, but now its weight hung heavy on his shoulders. Drawing in a breath, she reached out and gripped him by the shoulder.

"We keep fighting," she said, making a conscious effort to squash her own qualms. "We struggle on, for what's right, for our freedom."

"What's the point?" Braidon asked bitterly. He made a gesture, as though to include the whole city. "They've all abandoned me. Why should I fight for them now? Why *shouldn't* I just abandon them to Marianne's tender care?"

"Because you're their king," Kryssa whispered. "Because the blood of heroes flows in your veins. Because you're all we have, Braidon."

A sad smile twisted the king's lips. "Now that's a depressing thought." Groaning, he pushed himself up. Shadows lined his face and red streaked his eyes. The exhaustion of the road seemed to have finally caught up with him. "I'm sorry I didn't tell you," he murmured. "About the…pantheon."

Swallowing, Kryssa supressed a shudder. "Get some sleep, Braidon," was all she said.

The king waved a hand. "I'll sleep when I'm dead." Even so, he closed his eyes for half a moment, as though to gather himself. "Come on then, there's much to do if we're to save these fools from my dear wife."

Kryssa rose and made to follow him, but the king only managed two steps before a new arrival stepped into the doorway. Movement came from the corridor as other figures pressed forward, and Kryssa frowned, wondering who wanted to speak with the king now.

"Who—" Braidon started, coming to a stop, but before he could finish the figure threw back her hood.

Janylle stood in the doorway, her face a mask of hatred. She clutched a dagger in one pale fist.

"I said you'd pay, Braidon!"

❦ *9* ❦

Pela sat in silence at the dining table. Her eyes were on the servants carefully carving a haunch of ham nearby, but her thoughts were far away, her mind occupied with that one, terrifying word.

Plague.

The word had hardly been spoken in living memory, but since the demise of magic, it had become an unspoken fear amongst the peoples of Lonia and Plorsea. In the past, healers from the Earth Temple had used their magic freely in times of illness. But without magic…there was only the knowledge of doctors to defend against disease.

The morbus.

That was what they had called it, the reason why the fields and villages of Trola stood empty. It had swept the living from the land, had decimated the already crumbling nation. No wonder they had closed their borders, why they had not dared send a single rider to carry word to the east.

She and Ruebyn had stumbled right into the middle of it, had more than likely exposed themselves when they'd entered the village. The king had not seen how the sickness spread, but...Pela had seen their doom in his eyes. There was a burning sensation beginning in the back of her throat, and she wondered if that might be the first symptom.

But no one had told them anything more, only bustled them from the throne room to a private chamber where they'd been ordered to bathe and change clothes. Pela had scrubbed herself until her skin was raw, but she feared it would do her no good. Then they had sat, alone on their single beds, and waited to be summoned for they knew not what.

Now she could only stare as the servants placed a steaming plate of roast ham and vegetables before her. She had hardly eaten anything in days—the soldiers had fed them the barest of rations—but she was not hungry now. Her stomach was a churning mess of emotion, and she was on the verge of throwing up.

Ruebyn sat beside her, his eyes just as distant. He hadn't spoken a word as they waited for the king's summons, hadn't even looked at her. She could sense his anger, knew what he was thinking—that this was all her fault. If only she had listened to him, if they had turned back when he'd sounded his warning, they might have never come to Trola.

But despite her fear, despite the king's words, Pela was not ready to surrender. Surely there had to be a cure—how else had people survived, however few?

The king himself sat at the head of the table, fingers steepled as he watched the servants prepare the last plate and set it before him. Another man sat to the king's left. They still had not been introduced, but it seemed to Pela that the man was watching her from beneath his long black hair.

Finally the servants were finished, and with quick bows

to the king, they turned and departed through a pair of mahogany doors.

"Very well," the king announced, turning to them. "Thank you for joining us for a meal, young Pela and Ruebyn. This is Rayan, my son. I must apologise for my earlier melancholy. You can understand, the pain I have felt, watching my nation suffer so." He let out a sigh, before a smile broke across his face. "But we must make good on the gifts we are given. It pains me to hear of Devon's fate, but I am honoured to welcome his niece to my halls. Now, let us eat!"

So saying, he picked up his knife and fork and began to cut the tender meat. Pela could only stare, unable to comprehend the strangeness of it all. Just a few hours ago, this man had proclaimed them both doomed; now he sat eating with them, as though this were any normal supper. A tremor shook Pela as she watched him lift a morsel of ham to his mouth.

"No!" The cry tore from her without thought.

Steel rattled on porcelain as the king's fork slipped from his fingers and fell back to the plate. Mouth still open, he turned to stare at her, followed by the gazes of the others. She stared back, her own lips parted, unable to believe what she'd done. But there was no taking the word back now.

"I…" She swallowed, flicking a glance at Ruebyn before continuing. "Please, we need to know, what's going to happen to us?"

A smile returned to the king's face as he picked up the piece of ham that had fallen on the table and placed it in his mouth. He chewed it slowly, his eyes boring into hers.

"I had thought you might enjoy some food before speaking of such grim tidings," he said finally, after he swallowed. "You spoke of some strife, before you reached Trola. Are you not hungry?"

"Please!" It was Ruebyn's turn to burst out. His hands were gripping the table so hard they'd turned white. "Please tell us!"

The king offered a sigh. "Very well," he said, knitting his fingers together. "It seems I may have spoken too hastily when I announced your fate earlier."

A warm tingling sensation spread across Pela's skull. There was hope! She wanted to scream for joy, to demand to know what had changed, but she found that words had quite abandoned her.

"What do you mean?" Ruebyn asked, his voice tight with expectation.

The king turned to his son. "Rayan, would you be so kind as to check, before their hope grows too great?" He turned back to them as his son rose. "Rayan is one of our chief engineers in the citadel," he explained.

Pela felt as though she'd been punched in the gut. The king's words had left her in utter confusion, and she could only watch as Rayan walked around the table and knelt beside her. He was older than her own eighteen years, closer to thirty than twenty. But he wore a kindly smile as he gestured to her neck.

"May I?" he asked in a quiet voice.

Blinking, she looked from him to the king. "What?"

"Your necklace," Rayan continued. "May I see it?"

"My…necklace?" Pela asked. Then the warmth fled her face as she realised what he meant. "It's…not a necklace," she whispered. "It's a slaver's collar."

"Oh!" he said, pulling back slightly. A frown creased his brow. "I'm sorry, we did not know."

"It's okay," she said, swallowing her mortification. "I… what did you want to know about it?"

"I'm not sure yet," Rayan replied.

He made another gesture, and she nodded that he could take a closer look. A shiver ran down her spine as his long fingers stroked the steel, turning the collar back and forth. Absently, he brushed a lock of black hair from his face, and she saw now that his eyes were the darkest green, almost as dark as his hair. His eyes narrowed as he came across the black gem set into her collar, before he finally rose and returned to his seat.

"Well?" the king asked.

A hesitant smile appeared on Rayan's face as he looked at her. "It is a primitive design, but it contains the right elements."

"What does that mean?" Pela croaked.

"The *morbus* has no cure," the king replied. "But working with our doctors, the citadel's engineers did find a way to defend against the infection."

"A long time ago, we realised that not all of the Gods' magic died with them," Rayan continued for the king. "Some crystals have retained the magic of the Earth Goddess. Black opals in particular have the power to heal. Captain Shand recognised the crystal on your collar when you were found. That is why they did not…" He trailed off, then abruptly returned to his earlier train of thought. "The crystal is the same as what we have worn these past decades to protect against the plague's spread."

At that, Rayan pulled an amulet out from beneath his shirt. Hung from a chain of steel links, it held a black gem far larger than the others Pela had seen, but now she looked at it closely, she realised it was true. It was the same as the one set into her slave collar. Relief swept through her—

followed by a terrible despair as she realised what this meant for Ruebyn.

She turned and stretched out a hand to him, trying to relay her remorse, but he flinched away from her. His eyes fixed on Rayan, and when he spoke, his voice was like iron.

"What does this mean for me?"

The king and his son exchanged a glance. "Yes…" Rayan said finally, drawing a fine silver chain from his pocket. "You may wear this," he said, sliding it across the table, "it may save you yet."

Pela watched as Ruebyn scooped the chain into his palm. "Its power comes from the Goddess?" he croaked.

"That is our belief," Rayan replied.

"Ruebyn…" Pela whispered. The Saviour forbid the use of magic to enhance oneself, but surely in times of such desperation…

Ruebyn scrunched his fist into a ball around the necklace, and she could see the pain in his face. Finally he exhaled, and with a nod, he slid it over his head. He seemed to relax somewhat, his shoulders straightening almost imperceptibly.

"I pray the opal works," Rayan murmured, "but I fear it is already too late."

"Surely not?" Ruebyn whispered, the fear returning to his face. "We have seen none of the infected since we arrived here. Even a plague needs a means of dissemination."

A smile touched Rayan's face. "You are a learned man, Ruebyn," he said, "but I fear your people have never seen anything like the *morbus*. Our doctors believe it spreads through the very air, that it can survive in a room for decades undisturbed. Every soul in the village you entered fell to the plague. Just by stepping foot in their houses, you likely doomed yourself."

Ice ran down Pela's spine as she looked at Ruebyn. His face had turned a deathly pale and his whole body was shaking.

"I'm so sorry, Ruebyn," she whispered.

His eyes flicked in her direction and she saw the accusation there, the reminder that this was all her fault, for refusing to listen when he'd said they should turn back, that something was wrong. But after a moment, Ruebyn's eyes returned to his plate. Woodenly, he picked up the utensils and began to eat, ignoring the rest of them.

A long silence stretched out, during which the king and his son started on their food as well. Pela did not so much as touch her fork. Her entire insides were churning, so tangled up she couldn't even stomach the idea of food. What had she done, leading them here? She had been so confident they could face whatever they found in Trola, but she had never expected this…

"And what of our eastern neighbours?" the king spoke finally, adapting an overly cheerful tone. "What has become of Plorsea and Lonia after all this time?"

"War," Pela said after a long while. "After you closed the borders, a decade-long war broke out between Lonia and Plorsea. It only ended eight years ago, when a peace treaty was brokered between King Ashoka and Braidon."

"Braidon!" the king exclaimed. "I met him during the revolution—charming young man. Shame about his sister, though I never got to meet her. Must have been quite the woman, to have old Devon traipsing across the Three Nations looking for her." He paused, a look of sadness crossing his face as he glanced at Rayan, then back to Pela.

"I don't suppose you would tell me how the hammerman died?"

"I'm sure the girl does not want to recount her uncle's death, Father," Rayan interjected, a scowl marking his forehead.

Pela swallowed. It was true; Devon's death was still too raw, too recent. But the icy silence coming from Ruebyn was worse. She would do anything to break it, to distract herself from the reminder of her failure.

"It…was a few months ago," she began softly. "On the beach of Malevolent Cove. My mother and I had been taken by…" She glanced at Ruebyn before continuing. "By the Order of Alana."

"Oh!" The king's face showed his surprise. "That must be quite the story in itself."

Nodding, Pela went on with Devon's story. "A woman… I'm not sure what to call her, Braidon's estranged wife? Though she calls herself Queen of Plorsea and Lonia now. She was with the Order, wanted to kill us. Devon…delayed her while the rest of us escaped."

"And so ends the life of one of our greatest heroes," Betran murmured, his voice returning to its usual melancholy. "Alas, it seems that all the greats have now passed from this world."

"Not all," Pela replied. "Braidon lives because of Devon's sacrifice. He will stand against Marianne and the Order."

"So it seems another war is brooding," the king murmured. He had abandoned his food and was staring into the distance again. "The Three Nations remain divided. It will never end."

"It has ended for Trola," Rayan offered. His eyes were soft as he turned to Pela. "If your people knew the pain my nation has suffered, perhaps they would not be so quick to throw away their lives in such petty struggles."

"Then why the soldiers?" Ruebyn cut in sharply, dropping his cutlery onto the plate. The sound rang into the sudden silence as he scanned the table. "Your men certainly didn't seem fond of peace when they tried to execute us, nor when we were brought before you in the throne room."

"I am sorry for that," the king replied, "but we do what we must to ensure our nation's safety. Anyone in our land found without the protection of a black opal is to be executed, to protect against further…upheaval."

"That's barbaric," Ruebyn replied.

"It is mercy," Rayan said sadly. "You do not yet know… the pain of the infected."

"That is their choice!" Ruebyn spat back. "Who are you to take it from them?"

"I am their king!" Betran snapped suddenly. He half rose from his seat, but went no further. Drawing in a deep breath, he lowered himself back down. His eyes shone as he looked at Ruebyn. "I do what I must, to protect the ones I love. Without the black opals, our people would have ceased to be."

"So you raised an army to ensure no one could question your power." Braidon snorted. "That doesn't sound like peace to me."

"It was not just for the opals," Rayan murmured. "After the plague, much of Trola became a lawless place. Without soldiers, without guards, bandits ruled the land. There was no safety for the survivors. Soldiers such as Captain Shand are helping us to reclaim our lands, so that we might prosper once more."

"Nor do I forget the lessons of our history," the king added. "That is why I built the fortress across the Brunei

Pass, to ensure our fate will never again be controlled by a foreign Tsar."

Uncomfortable with Ruebyn's accusations, Pela flicked him a warning glance, but he only glared back at her. She swallowed, and felt the cold of her collar pressing against her throat. A shiver passed through her. The thing might have saved her life, and yet…

"I…" she started, then trailed off, thinking of Ruebyn's likely fate. But it was too much, the constant reminder of her torment, her bondage to the mines. "Do you…do you have any way to remove my collar?" she whispered.

A smile appeared on Rayan's face and her heart lifted. "Of course," he said. "A blacksmith can come in the morning. I believe I have an opal necklace that would serve as a replacement against the *morbus*."

"Thank you!" Pela gasped. Her eyes teared up at the thought of finally being rid of the thing. She touched a finger to the cold steel, hardly daring to believe. "Thank you so much."

"Had we known, I would have had it removed immediately," the king said with a laugh. "How unfortunate that it is not some new fashion trend in the east, or we might have finally been safe to open our borders."

"Or perhaps they already know about the opals," Rayan mused.

Ruebyn snorted. "Unlikely—none of my teachers ever mentioned them. Though I cannot imagine why they gave such precious things to *slaves*." His voice was bitter as he looked at Pela, and she looked away, unable to face his rage. "I—" he tried to continue, but was interrupted by a hacking cough.

Pela spun back as Ruebyn bent in two over his dinner plate, palms pressed tight to the table. Another coughing fit shook him, an awful wheezing that rose from the depths of his chest. Specks of red splattered the porcelain plate as he coughed on and on, until finally, gasping, he collapsed back in his chair. Air rattled in his throat as he struggled to catch his breath. There was terror in his eyes when he looked at her.

"Pela!" he gasped.

$$\text{❈}\quad 10 \quad\text{❈}$$

"I said you'd pay, Braidon," Janylle snarled.

"Janylle, don't!" Kryssa shouted.

But the woman was already drawing back her hand, the dagger shimmering in the lantern light. Abandoning any hope of reasoning with her, Kryssa kicked her chair, sending it skating backwards across the room. Braidon stood frozen, eyes wide, too shocked to react to Janylle's threat.

Kryssa cried out as the blade hissed across the room, throwing out an arm. Instinctively, she reached within for the power at her core. Her life force leapt to her aid and went from her in a rush, surging out to meet the blade. There was a shriek of twisting metal, then the blade went hurtling sideways to bury itself in the back of a chair.

Relief swept through Kryssa a second before the exhaustion. Her energy spent by the spell, she sagged against the table. Across the room, Janylle and her supporters stood frozen, but their shock did not last long. One of those behind Janylle lifted a sword and roared.

Gathering herself, Kryssa straightened and dragged her sword from its sheath.

Face pale, Braidon still stood staring at Janylle as though she were some ghost from his past. Snarling, Kryssa shoved him aside and leapt to meet his foes. Steel rang out as her blade met the swordsman's, then spinning, she twisted her weapon and drove it into the man's stomach. Caught off-guard, he crumpled in two as the death blow struck.

Satisfied, Kryssa tried to tear her sword loose, but the man collapsed to the floor, dragging her weapon with him. She cursed and leapt back as Janylle's other followers entered the fray, dodging a clumsy blow that had been aimed at her head.

"Kill the witch too," Janylle snarled, picking up the sword of her fallen follower. "She's no better than her master."

Kryssa raised her hands and started to back away. She did not dare glance around to see what Braidon was doing. Unarmed and badly outnumbered, she scanned her foes, trying to figure which would attack first.

"Janylle, don't do this," she said, trying to stall. "Think about what you're doing. Dominic—"

"*Don't you dare say his name!*" Janylle screamed, waving her blade wildly in Kryssa's direction.

The rest of her followers filed in from the corridor. They were five in all, and she and Braidon didn't have a blade between them. They were hopelessly outmatched, and from the look on Janylle's face, the woman knew it too.

"How could you do it?" Janylle whispered, edging forward. "After everything we did to help you, how could you string him up like that?" A tremor shook the woman as she raised her sword. "I would expect such cruelty from a man like Braidon, but you, Kryssa? How could you help him do such a thing to a fellow soldier?"

Kryssa's stomach twisted at the accusation in her words, but she did not back down. "You know what he did—"

"Be damned!" Janylle screamed over the top of her. Baring her teeth, she thrust out with her blade, forcing Kryssa back. "You'll die slow for what you did to my sweet—"

"Enough!"

Kryssa jumped as Braidon's voice thundered inside the room. Janylle and her men took a collective step back, their faces showing shock. Braidon advanced, his eyes aglow. The hackles on Kryssa's neck prickled as she sensed the power radiating from Braidon, and now she remembered the energies he had collected. The assassins outnumbered him five to one, yet within Braidon carried the power of a hundred lives.

But Janylle did not know that.

"How dare you command me?" the woman spat, her face now a mottled shade of red. She raised her sword and pointed it at Braidon's chest like a spear.

"Tonight you have betrayed your nation, Janylle," Braidon continued, ignoring her threat, "but all of you have not yet thrown away your lives. Put down your arms and surrender to the king's justice, and you might yet keep them."

Janylle laughed. "Your words are dirt, King, nothing but lies. You would hang us before the day is done. No, you are unarmed and outnumbered. So I think we'll finish what we came here to do."

Raising the sword, she started forward, the others at her side. Fists clenched, Kryssa made to step up alongside Braidon, but instead felt an invisible presence holding her back. She lashed out at the barrier, screaming at the king, but he did not seem to notice. His eyes were fixed on the assassins, though he seemed no more concerned by them than a cat by a mouse.

Only when his foes came within striking range did Braidon move. As the first assassin rushed him, the king raised his hand. The man ran on, stabbing low for Braidon's stomach—but as the point flashed down there came a hideous *shriek*, and the blade shattered as though it had struck solid rock. The shards flashed backwards as though propelled by a catapult, impaling the assassin's chest.

Braidon watched calmly as the man staggered to a stop. His eyes fell to the terrible wounds, the slivers of steel embedded in his flesh. A groan rattled from his throat, ending in an awful gurgling. The strength fled his legs and he slumped to his knees. Pale-faced, he raised an arm as though to beg for mercy. Instead, blood burst from his lips and with one last, despairing cry he crumpled to the ground and lay still.

Behind the king, Kryssa gaped. The man's death inspired the same reaction amongst Janylle and her remaining followers, as they stumbled to a stop beside their fallen comrade. They had all heard of Braidon's feat at the temple, his power during the battle for the Castle, but to witness it first-hand…

Kryssa looked back at the king, as disbelieving as the others. Braidon had used the power he'd taken from the victims in the pantheon. She had not realised its potential until now, the deadly nature of the energies he'd stolen. Now having seen it, she was all the more terrified for what he had done.

Janylle's face could have been etched from stone. She stood staring at Braidon, lips drawn back in a snarl, teeth clenched, her eyes burning with such hatred Kryssa recoiled. It was the look of one who knew she was doomed but would fight on anyway. Taking a firmer hold of her sword, Janylle stepped over the body of her companion.

"I see what you are," she spat, waving the sword in front of her as though it might fend off Braidon's next attack. "You pretend to stand on the side of the Gods, but you are naught but a servant, a creature of your wife, your sister. You only claim to serve us so that we will open our doors to their evil."

Braidon said not a word as she approached, only stood watching, listening to her hateful words.

"But you have already betrayed yourself," Janylle cried. "You sent your soldiers to murder the faithful of the Three Gods, to butcher our people in the streets. Now they will rise against you, against your Order, against your *queen!*"

With the last words, Janylle lunged, driving her blade for Braidon's throat. At the last possible moment the king twisted, his hand flashing up to catch the woman by the wrist. He slammed his other arm into her elbow, and the blade clattered harmlessly to the ground.

Janylle screamed and kicked at him, but her blows could not seem to find their mark. Braidon waited in silence as she raged, trying her best to destroy him, but unable to even free her wrist. Lacking the courage to intervene, her followers stood in silence beyond.

Finally Janylle slumped in Braidon's grasp and stared up at him, defeat in her eyes. "Do it then!" she spat, her voice dripping with loathing. "Kill me, and stoke the flames of your doom! The faithful of the Gods will see who you truly are, King. They will not be blinded by your words."

Braidon shook his head, and when he spoke, his voice

was cold as ice. "I am sorry for your husband," he said. "I can see now the mistake I made. I will not make it again."

Sensing what he was about to do, Kryssa opened her mouth to cry out, but Braidon was faster still. A sharp *crack* came from Janylle's spine as he twisted his hand and the energies went rushing from him. A second later, Janylle's lifeless body struck the ground with a *thud*.

Screams came from the other assassins as they turned to flee, but Braidon was already lifting his arms. The assassins stumbled to a stop and raised their swords. For a moment Kryssa thought they would make another attempt on the king—but then they launched themselves at one another, their blades hacking and slashing until all lay dead on the floor of the war chamber.

Silence fell as Braidon lowered his hands. Kryssa could only stare in shock at the carnage he had unleashed, unable to summon any words. Blood seeped slowly across the floor towards her, shimmering in the lanternlight. Not one of the assassins still breathed. With her own life no longer in danger, Kryssa saw now that they were young men and women, barely out of adolescence. Slowly her eyes were drawn back to the king.

Braidon stood in the middle of the carnage, his eyes dark and face pale, and for a second she thought it was not Braidon at all who stood there. Then he let out a long breath and his shoulders slumped, his eyes flickering closed for a half moment. Concern creased the king's forehead as his blue eyes found hers.

"Are you okay?" he asked.

She nodded, still struck dumb by his display of power, by the bloody nature of their assassins' ends. With a shudder, she broke from the trance. Finding the invisible barrier vanished, she moved forward to stand beside him.

"I'll…find someone," she croaked.

"No," Braidon whispered, his eyes on the body of Janylle.

"What?" Kryssa hissed.

The king's head came up. "You heard what she said, Kryssa," he murmured. "She *wanted* me to kill her, to become a martyr for her followers. If word of this reaches the people, there'll be open rebellion in the streets."

"But…" Kryssa trailed off. "What…what will we tell them?"

"The Order has made an attempt on my life," Braidon said. Kryssa shivered as his eyes bored into hers. Unable to hold his gaze, she looked away, and he went on matter-of-factly: "No one can know Janylle was ever involved in this."

"There will be people who knew her, Braidon, people who will ask questions."

"But they will not *know*," he hissed. He drew in a breath, as though summoning the will to do what was necessary, before facing her. "Leave me, Kryssa. I will deal with the bodies."

Kryssa's mouth fell open as she looked at the king. She might have argued, but his eyes were lit with a terrible rage, and the words died in her throat. Clenching her jaw closed, Kryssa spun on her heel. Retrieving her sword from the man she had killed, she fled for the door.

"Kryssa." Braidon's voice brought her up short as she reached the entranceway. She turned back, an icy fear sliding suddenly down her spine. Their eyes met from across the room. "Speak not a word of this, to anyone," he murmured.

Nodding, Kryssa practically fled into the corridor and swung the door closed behind her. She staggered several steps and slumped against the wall. Only then did she let the tears fall. She had only known Janylle for a brief time, but the woman had been kindly, welcoming. She deserved a better fate than this, and yet…what else could any of them have done? From the moment Dominic had lit the pantheon ablaze, had murdered all those innocent souls, their path had been set.

Gathering herself, Kryssa straightened. Whatever had happened, it was over now. All they could do was make the best of it. She may not entirely agree with Braidon's plan, but—

Her thoughts were interrupted as the softest of whispers carried down the corridor. Kryssa froze where she stood, the hairs on her neck lifting in sudden intuition. Holding her breath, she waited, and the sound came again. Her eyes settled on a nearby closet. Dropping a hand to her sword hilt, she crept to the door and threw it open.

A cry came from within the closet as a shadow leapt away from the light. Kryssa's sword leapt into her hand and she raised it to strike down the final assassin—but at the last moment she paused. Something made her hesitant, a wrongness to the shadow. Carefully, Kryssa pulled the door open wider, revealing a young woman crouched on the floor, barely Pela's age.

Terror shone from the girl's amber eyes and a short sword lay on the floor beside her, but she made no move to grasp it. Instead, her arms were wrapped around her knees. Staring out from beneath long locks of brown hair, she looked ready to burst into tears.

Shocked to her core, Kryssa stared down at the girl. Time stretched out as she thought of her own daughter, lost in the currents of Malevolent Cove. Kryssa had failed Pela, failed to protect her, to prepare her for the darkness of this world. Now here was another young woman, led astray by Janylle's words, brought to her doom.

It was Kryssa's duty to show the girl to Braidon. She had been part of Janylle's group, of that there was no question. She must face the king's justice. And yet…Kryssa knew what Braidon would do with her. He could not afford to have his lie exposed, not with the fate of Plorsea resting on his shoulders. At best the girl would be thrown into a dungeon to live out the rest of her miserable days, at worst…

Kryssa shuddered, the image of the dead assassins lying not twenty feet away all too fresh in her mind.

The girl had not moved. She still crouched on the floor of the closet, staring at Kryssa as though she expected to be struck down at any moment. A shudder ran down Kryssa's spine, and suddenly she was stepping back, leaving the door unguarded.

"Go," she hissed, pointing with her sword, "and never come here again!"

The boat rocked wildly beneath Caledan as the captain pushed off into the swirling currents. He quickly sat himself on the narrow wooden bench. Marianne was already there, but she said nothing as he took his place. Her eyes were fixed on the opposite bank of the Jurrien, where the Lonian army awaited. They stood rank upon rank, their green cloaks and shining spears forming a forest of armoured men.

The rains had cleared during the night but the river remained swollen. Silt-laden waters rushed around their tiny vessel as the captain and another sailor set their backs to the oars. It would only take one mistake to hurl them all overboard, where the powerful currents would drag them straight to the bottom. Caledan had no fondness for boats, but he would rather be aboard the tiny vessel than facing the currents unprotected.

Across the river, a second boat was just pushing off from the banks. Caledan strained his eyes, counting four within the vessel, the same number as their own. Reassured that the Lonians were obeying the terms of truce, Caledan's eyes were drawn to their destination—a tiny island in the centre of the river.

Word had come from Servo in the night requesting a parlay before the battle began. Sensing a trap, Caledan had argued against such a meeting. There was no reason for the Elder to negotiate. He had the superior force, and it was only a matter of time before his power surpassed Marianne's—if it hadn't already. The parlay could only be a trap.

But perhaps Servo knew of Marianne's weakness, that she still cared for the Lonian people. She could not pass up an opportunity to spare their lives, though not even she believed the Elder would surrender so easily.

Caledan shook his head. This was a fool's errand, but at least she had allowed him to accompany her. After his folly during the night, he would not have been surprised if Marianne had ordered him to the front lines.

His hand drifted to his sword hilt as their boat approached the island. He was determined to do his duty. Turning his eyes to the other boat again, he watched as it bobbed and twisted on the currents, and sent up a prayer to the Storm God to drag it down into the river's murky depths.

But fate was not on their side, and both ships made it safely to the island. Standing on opposite shores, the two parties watched each other across the open ground. Though still high, the river had fallen during the night, leaving the earth damp beneath their feet. Twisted trees grew on the island further upriver, but where they stood was little more than slick mud and long grass pressed flat by the flood waters.

All this Caledan took in at a glance—but his attention

never left Servo and his followers. They had not moved from where they had disembarked, their tiny boat tied to the trunk of one of the twisted trees, straining against its bindings. Two of Servo's companions appeared to be sailors, without swords or armour. They carried a third person between them, but as they stepped from the boat, they let their burden fall to the mud.

Caledan frowned, staring at the fallen figure. It took him a moment to realise it was a woman, for her hair had been hacked short and her face was so bruised as to be barely recognisable. A cry carried across the mudflat as she fell, her legs bent at a strange angle and obviously badly broken. Even so, she somehow found the strength to drag herself up and try to crawl away. One of the sailors put an end to her efforts by driving a boot into her side, flipping the woman on her back.

Only then did Caledan recognise Genevieve. His mouth fell open and unconsciously he took a step forward. A cackle answered his actions, and his gaze snapped back to Servo. Distracted, he had not seen the Elder advance to the centre of the island.

"I see you recognise my new friend," Servo said, wearing the slick grin Caledan remembered all too well from his time in the dungeons beneath Ardath. "I'm afraid she's a little worse for wear than the last time you saw her. Found herself a slave in one of your dear queen's mines, it seems."

"Set her free," Caledan snarled. His sword leapt into his hand and he started towards the man, but Marianne's arm snapped out, bringing him up short.

"Stop," she hissed, "before you get all of us killed."

Enraged, Caledan swung on the queen, but one glance at her face was enough to suck the rage from him. Teeth bared, her eyes did not flicker from Servo. Her jaw was clenched, and the muscles in her neck were bulging as though she held the weight of the world on her shoulders. Across the muddy ground, Servo stood seemingly relaxed, but as Caledan looked closer, he saw the Elder's eyes were aglow.

A silent war was taking place between the two, a battle of wills that Caledan could only imagine.

Then the Elder threw back his head and laughed. He made a gesture, and the glow faded from his eyes. A long, drawn-out hiss came from Marianne as she exhaled through her teeth. Her throat contracted as she swallowed; then flicking an angry glance at Caledan, she strode forward to confront her foe.

"My apologies, Marianne," Servo said lightly. "Though you cannot blame me for trying, can you?"

"What do you want, Servo?" Marianne growled. "I defeated you once, I would have thought you'd had enough."

The Elder spread his arms. "I did not seek this confrontation," he said, "but my people have placed this burden upon me, demanded I bring their message to the queen that claims to rule them."

"Oh really?" Marianne said dryly. "And what message would that be?"

"They demand Lonia be returned to the rule of the council, that the Order be free to practice its beliefs." A grin twisted his face. "And that you, Marianne, submit to their judgement for crimes committed against your homeland."

"The followers of the Order are free to follow the original message of the Saviour," she replied. "Of personal growth, of inner strength, and individuals standing together to protect the collective." Her face hardened and her eyes flashed as she looked at Servo. "But there will be no more of your vile cleansings. I am done with the bloodshed. As for your other…requests, I do not believe for a moment these few you have gathered represent the whole of my kingdom."

Servo chuckled. "You call my methods vile, but your hands are no cleaner than mine, gathering power from the deaths of slaves. We are the same, my dear—lions amongst the sheep. I do not judge you for it."

"My way did not require a single life to be taken before it was due," Marianne growled.

"Ay, such an inefficient use of your creation. Your slaves barely have a spark of power left when death comes for them." He nudged Genevieve with his boot as he spoke, a disgusted look crossing his face. "But enough of this. Surrender, woman, or I will destroy everything and everyone you ever held dear."

"My son is far from here, and out of your reach, Servo," the queen answered coldly. "And why would I surrender when we are so evenly matched?" A sly smile crossed her face. "But you are right; let this end now, between the two of us."

"Ha! You think I am such a fool to surrender my advantage?" Servo cried, throwing out his arms. Caledan tensed, readying himself for whatever trap the Elder was about to spring, but after a moment Servo lowered his arms again. "Besides, once battle is joined, your fate is sealed."

"Oh?" Marianne asked, edging forward.

Servo flicked an imaginary speck of dust from his cuffs. "As I was saying, your collars were ingenious, but I have unlocked their true potential." He made a gesture at the two sailors standing behind him. "Do you not recognise your own creation, Marianne?" he asked, and Caledan saw now that each man wore an iron collar around his throat. "I took your invention, and gave it to my people. Now their every sacrifice will add to my own power. So even should you somehow defeat my army, even if you slay every one of my followers, still you will lose."

Beside Caledan, Marianne had gone pale at the Elder's words. She said nothing as he took another step towards them, eyes flashing in the dawn light.

"So bring your army, bring your swords and arrows and spears, Marianne. Kill them all, but in the end, I will come for you. I will burn your feeble champion to ash, enslave you to my will. Then, my dear Marianne, you will take me to your son, and you will watch as he dies by my hand."

Caledan gripped the hilt of his sword, his entire body trembling with rage. Servo towered over Marianne now, and she wilted before his threats. More than anything Caledan wanted to draw his blade and drive it through the Elder's heart, but instead he stood frozen, listening to the awful words.

"In the end, Marianne, you will sit beside me as queen, obedient to my every whim. Just as you once were for Braidon. But this time, there will be no scheming, no secret plots. You will be mine, body and soul, a slave to my power."

"You would sacrifice a thousand lives for the sake of a crown?" Marianne croaked, her voice barely a whisper.

"I would sacrifice ten thousand to destroy the witch who shamed me," Servo snarled.

"Please," the queen rasped. "This fight is between us. Let us settle it, the two of us. There is no need for anyone else to die."

Caledan's heart thundered in his ears at the queen's words. Her whole body was shaking; she was practically begging the Elder now. He recalled their conversation so many nights ago, about how she had suffered, trapped in her unwanted marriage, been forced to bear Braidon's child. Servo threatened to do far worse: to enslave her entirely to his will. There could be no fate more awful for Marianne, no greater fear.

Servo laughed in her face. "You think to negotiate? Who do you think you are, witch? You were nothing more than the daughter of a pig farmer before we raised you up. And yet you thought to destroy me, to rule in my stead. Such arrogance! No, I will not negotiate with the likes of you. There is only one way to save yourself. Kneel in the mud like your precious pigs, or I will send my army. A thousand might die before I have power enough, but the end will be the same. You will kneel."

Silence fell across the island at the Elder's words, punctuated only by the roar of the river as it raced around the little patch of mud. It rolled over them like the distant rumble of thunder, like the howling of wind through tree branches, or a thousand voices raised in anger…

Caledan frowned, his gaze drifting past Servo, across to the opposite bank of the river where the Lonian forces waited. Except they were no longer standing still, but rioting up and down the riverbanks, their weapons raised to the sky. Even as Caledan watched, the roar of their rage grew louder, rolling out across the turbulent waters to where their leader stood.

"*Trait…basta…kill him.*"

The individual words could not be heard, but their meaning was clear, the subject of their anger indisputable: Servo.

Caledan stared at the queen in disbelief. "What did you do?"

A smile touched the queen's lips as the fear fell from her face. "Nothing at all," she said, straightening. "I only shared the Elder's words with his own people. It seems they are none too happy with his plans to sacrifice them for his own power."

A desperate snarl crossed Servo's face as he looked from his rioting army to the queen. "You little witch!" he screamed, lifting a fist. "I'll tear you limb from li—"

"Ah, ah, ah," Marianne interrupted, wagging a finger at the Elder. Her smile spread, and Caledan realised everything had played out exactly as she had planned. "We are evenly matched, remember. But don't worry, I'll wait for you to send a few of your men to their deaths. Off you go, it looks like they're excited to receive you!"

Servo looked ready to explode. His jaw was clenched so hard Caledan could almost hear his teeth grinding. Eyes wild, he dragged his sword from its sheath. Genevieve still lay at his feet. He pointed the blade at her throat.

"I'll kill her!" Servo screamed.

The huntress did not move—did not even seem aware of anything that was happening around her, in fact.

"Now, now, there's no need for that," Marianne replied, showing little concern for Genevieve's life. Indeed, the woman had been Marianne's enemy when last they'd met— there was no reason for her to care. But Caledan's heart beat faster at the thought of the huntress's peril.

"My offer still stands, Servo," Marianne continued. "A fight to the death, sword against sword, without powers. Let the Saviour's hand guide the victor."

The Elder stared at Marianne, looking half-mad with rage. His hands shook and the tip of his blade was mere inches from Genevieve's throat. Caledan held his breath, though he wasn't sure what he was hoping for. What was

Marianne thinking, offering a duel now? She was decent with a bow, and she had shown some proficiency with a rapier in Malevolent Cove, but she was far from a master. Servo was almost twice her size—that alone gave him a terrible advantage in a sword fight.

The same realisation seemed to have occurred to Servo. A wild grin spread across his face. "I accept!" he screamed, stepping away from Genevieve. "A final gambit then, to decide the fate of our nations." He pointed his blade at Marianne. "Are you ready, witch?"

Marianne's eyes widened in feigned surprise. "Me?" she gasped. "Why, Servo, I am a queen! It would be unseemly for me to participate in such a competition. As you said earlier, Caledan is my champion. He will stand on my behalf." She inclined her head and Caledan's eyebrows lifted in surprise at her announcement. "You may, of course, select a champion of your own, should you fear the skills of a mere sellsword."

Servo bared his teeth as fresh rage twisted his face, but he had little choice now. With his army in open rebellion, he had only one chance to snatch back the initiative. His eyes narrowed as they focused on Caledan. Caledan stared back, his heart suddenly racing.

"Very well, Marianne," Servo snapped. "You had best bid farewell to your favourite sellsword."

Letting out a long breath, Caledan looked from Servo to his queen. What game was she playing? Had she planned this as well, as punishment for his insolence? Without any power of his own, Caledan could not counter Servo's magic if the Elder tried to cheat. And with such high stakes, there would be no room for mistakes.

Marianne only smiled, her sapphire eyes glinting as they met Caledan's gaze. "Fight well, my Champion."

❧ 12 ❧

S tanding on the ramparts of his Castle, Braidon looked out over the rooftops of Chole and wondered where he had gone wrong. Just a short few weeks ago, Janylle had been serving them breakfast in her house with Dominic. Now they were both dead—and by his hand.

Regret touched him as he thought again of Dominic's fate. Why had he acted so rashly, sentencing his own men to death for slaying some followers of the Order? It had forced a wedge between himself and the people of Chole, when they should have stood united against the Knights of Alana. And it had created an enemy in Janylle.

At least she'd made her assassination attempt in private. Had she attacked him publicly, forced him to take her life in front of others, how many more of Braidon's followers might have abandoned the cause? As it was, he had managed to spin things in his favour, to make a lie of Janylle's final words.

If only unrest in Chole had been his sole problem. With Loyla's rejection, his last hope of matching Marianne in the field lay in ruins. His five hundred recruits could not even hope to defend the city walls, let alone meet the queen in open battle. As things stood, Marianne would take the city within a day, and power or no, there was little Braidon could do to stop her.

Rage bubbled up within him, burning in his veins. Marianne's betrayal still cut deep, and every rejection and failure since had only added to the wound, feeding his pain, his hatred. His mind was a mess of self-loathing, that despite all his efforts, all his planning, he was still no closer to reclaiming his crown than he had been while lying half-dead on the shores of Malevolent Cove.

Well, maybe a little closer.

Braidon shivered as he turned his mind inwards and felt the power respond. It was his only comfort, the only reminder he was not entirely helpless against the forces that opposed him. He had spent precious energy defeating Janylle, but it had almost been worth it to feel the rush of his power.

It was *soldiers* he needed, though, men and women who could stand against the Knights of Alana, and whatever other allies Marianne had found. His spies claimed her army numbered some two thousand, the Lonians more than five. Even if he could match Marianne's magical abilities, Braidon could not create several thousand warriors from nothing.

Silently he cursed Loyla a fool, for refusing him, for shaming him with her outrageous challenge. Could she not see what was coming for them, that if they did not stand together, Plorsea would fall? What then for her people?

Grinding his teeth, Braidon looked again at the city and wondered how many of Janylle's followers survived. The crowd that had gathered while he'd been outside the city had numbered in the hundreds. How many were still plotting against him? Janylle had said the followers of the Three Gods stood with her, but Braidon was not so gullible as to believe her words. He had *saved* the Temple of the Earth, its priests would never think to betray him…

But then, he had once thought his wife beyond suspicion. So he had taken precautions, placing the temple under watch. If only he could trust the watchers. His sergeants had proven themselves worse than useless, ordering the attack on the crowd. How he missed his King's Guard now, their utter loyalty, their dependability. His chest ached as he recalled the familiar faces that had once stood alongside him. All dead now, the first casualties of his wife's so-called vengeance.

Balling his fists, Braidon ground his knuckles against the stone crenulations. He was again thinking of events he could not change. The past was fixed, his friends dead, his family stolen away. He had to find a new way, new powers to counter the forces Marianne would bring against him.

They didn't have long now. The queen's army could be at their gates in a week and his recruits remained untrained, unprepared for a major battle. At least they had weapons enough, with the stockade they had taken from the Castle—armour and swords and dozens of the deadly crossbows the Knights had brought from Lonia. He had blacksmiths around the city trying to replicate them, but so far they were having little success creating steel that could bend and flex as the Lonian weapons did.

Braidon needed something more, something to restore the confidence of his people, something to silence his doubters and restore the city's morale. Something to convince them all of his power.

A smile touched Braidon's lips as an idea came to him.

But was it possible? Dragon Country was a long way off, far beyond normal calling distance. Perhaps with his new power…who knew what his limits were?

Closing his eyes, Braidon focused on his breathing, sinking slowly into the meditative trance. Light flickered in the darkness, blue and red and green and a hundred other colours, leaping and dancing in place, the life forces of the souls lost in the pantheon.

He drew the light to him, feeling the surging power as it touched his consciousness, feeding confidence to his wasting soul. For a moment he lost sight of his plan, felt only the rush of energy, but with a wrench he refocused. Opening his inner eyes, he sent his soul soaring.

Out across the plains of Chole he flew, as he once had as a true Magicker, across the scrublands and pastures, up the steep slopes of the volcanic range, between the twisted snow-capped peaks, until far below him were the wild forests of Dragon Country.

Nidryt!

He called the dragon's name in his mind, sending his voice rumbling out across the bowl-shaped land, to ring from the peaks, to whisper through the twisting branches below, to seek out its owner.

King?

Nidryt's voice sounded surprised, and back on the ramparts of the Castle, Braidon smiled.

Did you think I was dead, dragon?

Laughter sounded in his mind. *You humans are sickly creatures,* the dragon's voice rumbled. *Your fate must have changed, to have power enough to reach so far.*

Ay, Chole is mine, Braidon replied. *Though enemies still assail me on all sides.*

Such is the fate of kings, the dragon growled.

I would have your help to destroy them.

You ask much of us, came Nidryt's reply, *for a man yet to fulfil a single promise.*

Braidon's stomach twisted as he recalled the oath he'd made with the dragons—that he would grant them fresh territory, gift them broad swaths of Plorsea in exchange for their aid.

I can offer you nothing until Plorsea is won, he replied, hoping the beast would accept his excuse.

Laughter was the answer. *Ay, we would have that promise too,* Nidryt reverberated, *but I speak of your pledge to drive the Knights from our land.*

They left, did they not? Braidon asked, surprised.

They have returned, the dragon replied.

Images flashed into Braidon's mind's eye, almost too quick to follow. They revealed a great encampment rising from the cliffs of Malevolent Cove. The amphitheatre that had once stood on the sands had vanished, but now great walls of sandstone rose from the blackened clifftops. They were only a few feet tall, but out in the cove, a dozen ships bobbed at anchor. They must have been ferrying supplies from Lon—Braidon knew it was only a matter of time before the walls would be finished.

They build anew, some foul structure from your stinking cities. We will stand for their desecration no longer. My people have pledged to drive them from our lands forever, though it may cost every one of our lives.

No! Braidon cried out, his voice ringing with power as he reached for the beast's mind.

A wrenching sensation followed, and suddenly he *felt* the dragon, the rippling of its muscles, the bulk of its wings, the power in its terrible jaws. Fear touched his mind as he sensed the beast's uncertainty—then a terrible rage as it realised what the king had done. Walls of fire encircled Braidon and he cried out, hurling his power at the flames. An opening appeared and he darted through, returning instantly to his disembodied state.

Now though, he found his spirit drifting before the dragon itself. Nidryt's scarlet head swung around, its one good eye swivelling in search of its attacker.

Where are you, King? the dragon growled, its voice now so loud Braidon felt his soul shiver. *Why do you seek to control me?*

My apologies, Nidryt, Braidon said, adopting a consoling tone. *I am still…new to this power.*

The growl increased in pitch, but after a moment the dragon gave up its search. Lowering its head, it spoke once more into Braidon's mind:

You once bade my people fight. Why do you now demand our cowardice?

Because I need you, Braidon replied. *If you throw your lives away against the Order, my last ally will be lost.*

What do we care for your fate, King, the dragon snarled, *when iron men trespass in our lands?*

Back in Chole, Braidon ground his teeth. He needed the Red Dragons desperately, but how could he convince Nidryt the true fight was with him? If Marianne could be defeated, the Knights that had set up camp in Malevolent Cove would be quick to follow, cut off from their supporters back in Lonia. But he sensed the dragon did not care for logic or strategy, that it was determined to end their strife now, whatever the consequences might be.

There was only one option left. Braidon could not convince the dragons to join him, so he must give them reason. He turned again to the power curling around his soul, the burning heat of a hundred lives. Would it be enough? Whatever Knights the Order had sent to build their new Castle, they would not be alone. They were bound to have at least one Elder with them, someone with power to protect the fledgling fortress. Would Braidon have the strength to match them?

It was a risk he would have to take.

Because I will help you, Nidryt, Braidon said at last. *Allow me to fulfil my part of our bargain. If we are to be allies, the Knights must learn to fear us. Where better to start than their most sacred of places?*

The golden eye of the dragon swivelled, seeming to stare straight at Braidon's spirit form. *Your power can stretch so far?*

Braidon frowned. It was doubtful—he was already beginning to feel the strain of reaching this far, and he was only using his energy to communicate, not to fight. If he was to go up against an Elder, he could not afford such waste. Finally he shook his head, though the beast could not see him.

No, he murmured into the dragon's mind. *I will need your aid, Nidryt. Come to Chole, my friend. Carry me back to Dragon Country, and together we will watch our enemies burn.*

"**A**re you ready to meet the Saviour, sellsword?"

Caledan did not rise to his foe's bait. Servo was younger than most of the Elders he had seen, closer to Caledan's thirty-three years. His shoulders were muscular and he moved with confidence on the slick ground—though the way Servo held his blade suggested he had not spent much time practicing with the weapon. His guard was too low, leaving his throat open to a sudden attack.

But Caledan could not forget the other energies Servo had at his command. Marianne had said this was a battle of blades, but Caledan was not about to trust his life to the word of the treacherous Elder.

"Very well," Servo said when it became obvious that Caledan would not reply. "Send my regards when you see her. I hope she condemns you to the darkest pits of hell for your blasphemy."

Caledan smiled at that. "Are you afraid, Servo?"

A scowl twisted the man's face and he leapt forward with a roar. Aware of the slick mud beneath his feet, Caledan moved carefully, his sword flashing up to deflect an overhand blow. Spinning sideways, he tracked Servo's movement as the Elder followed him, holding back his attack. Caledan knew from years of practice that a reckless attack would open him to a riposte. A master swordsman must bide his time, studying his opponent for weaknesses, before launching his assault.

Servo had no such patience. A growl rumbled from his throat as he came at Caledan again, moving faster than the sellsword would have thought possible. Slowed by the mud, Caledan would have struggled to deflect the blows if not for Servo's habit of dropping his shoulder before each attack, warning Caledan just in time.

Turning aside a third blow, Caledan twisted on his heel and lashed out with his free hand. The blow crashed into the side of Servo's face, sending him reeling back. With his opponent bent in two, Caledan saw his opportunity and moved in for the kill—but at the last moment he pulled back, sensing a wrongness to Servo's stance.

Quick as lightning, Servo leapt, his blade slashing through the space where Caledan would have stood if he'd continued the attack. A snarl crossed the Elder's face as he realised his deception had failed. Caledan laughed in his face.

"Enjoy your last breaths, sellsword," the Elder snapped. "Soon you will drown in your own blood!"

With the words, Servo made a gesture. Caledan gasped as he suddenly found himself unable to breathe. A metallic taste filled his mouth as a desperate gurgling came from his throat. For a second, he was back in Marianne's apartment, dying on the tile floor with the Knight's blade embedded in his chest.

A fiery warmth ignited in his palm, and the sensation

vanished, returning him to the muddy island. He blinked, glancing at his sword, before a scream returned his attention to Servo. The man's blade arced for Caledan's face and he leapt back—but not fast enough. The razor-sharp edge slashed through his shirt, opening a shallow cut across his chest.

Cursing, Caledan slipped in the mud and went down on one knee. Instinctively he thrust his sword above his head and the shriek of clashing steel followed as Servo's blade connected, almost jarring the weapon from Caledan's hands. Clinging to the hilt, Caledan threw himself to the side, rolling smoothly and coming back to his feet.

"Afraid, sellsword?" Servo laughed, blood now dripping from his sword tip. "You should be. The Saviour will torment your soul for a thousand years. Your agony will be the fuel in her eternal battle against the False Gods."

"You talk too much," Caledan snapped.

It was time to end the subterfuge, to finish the Elder before he had a chance to use his power again. Taking a two-handed grip of his sword, Caledan edged forward, eyes on the man's feet, waiting.

The second Servo lifted a boot, Caledan leapt. His sword drawn back for a strike, the Elder's eyes widened in shock. Caledan aimed high, taking advantage of the gap in the Elder's guard. But to his surprise, Servo's blade moved faster than thought, flashing upwards to catch Caledan's blade on its razor edge. Steel shrieked as the impact left chinks in both blades, but Caledan was already twisting, his boot coming up to catch his foe in the chest.

Servo staggered back from the blow, the breath hissing between his teeth as he struggled to inhale. Caledan followed, his blade arcing for the Elder's exposed neck.

Servo threw himself sideways, crashing face-first into the mud, and Caledan's attack missed by inches.

Unwilling to surrender his advantage, Caledan pressed the attack. Servo was still struggling to regain his feet and made a clumsy swing at Caledan's legs as he approached. Caledan deflected the Elder's blade into the ground. A scream tore from Servo as his fist collided with a stray rock, knocking the sword from his hand. Caledan quickly kicked out, catching the hilt with his boot and sending the weapon hurtling away.

"No!" Servo screamed.

Suddenly the Elder was back on his feet, eyes wild, face red. Realising what Servo was about to do, Caledan leapt, bringing up his sword to stab for the man's heart. The blade arced out, its aim true, but with a cry Servo threw out his arms.

A brilliant red leapt from the Elder's outstretched hands, a terrible, burning glow that seemed to light the very air aflame. It rushed at Caledan, coalescing into an inferno that could not be avoided. A cry came from Marianne, but she was too far away, too slow to save him. Grim-faced, Caledan lifted his blade and screamed into the firestorm.

Heat seared at his face, searing, burning. He smelt the faint stench of burning hair—then the fire was upon him, so hot he no longer felt anything, no longer knew anything but the brilliant, burning white. Eyes clenched shut, Caledan thrust out with his blade, determined to kill the Elder before he took his last breath, to do this one last thing for his queen.

The blade shook in his hand, vibrating as though the very metal had come alive, as though the flames were about to hurl it back in his face. Teeth clenched, flesh searing, Caledan screamed into the inferno.

Then as quickly as it had appeared, the light was gone, leaving Caledan standing unexpectedly on a patch of scorched earth, blade still outstretched. A second later the pain struck him, a wave of agony that drove him to his knees. The sword slipped from his fingers as he toppled to the earth.

Lying there, he waited for death to find him, for the cold release of the afterlife. Instead, the sounds of the world came rushing back, and he became aware of someone groaning, the gurgling of liquid in lungs, the gasps of a dying man. He thought they must be his own desperate, dying cries, but as he drew in a breath, he tasted only fresh air in his throat.

Caledan's eyes snapped open. Light blinded him, then the world resolved, and he found himself looking across seared earth to where Servo lay nearby. The Elder's hands were clutched at his chest, where Caledan's sword was now lodged. The wound should have killed him instantly, but Servo was still trying to tear it loose, even as blood bubbled from his purpling lips.

Beyond the Elder, his sailors stood transfixed, either unwilling or unable to help their master. Groaning, Caledan turned his gaze on himself, and was surprised to find his clothes only singed, his flesh untouched by the fire.

The crunch of footsteps on burnt ground sounded as Marianne strode past, her sapphire eyes on the dying Elder.

"Oh my dear Servo," she murmured. "Do not waste your precious life force trying to remove it. I invested enough of my power into the blade that your magic cannot affect it." She knelt beside the man, drawing his head into her lap. His hands were bloody from trying to grip the blade, and now he turned them on the queen. He fumbled weakly at Marianne's arms, leaving red streaks on her pale skin. She laughed. "Relax, my dear Elder," she whispered. "It will all soon be over. The Saviour awaits, remember? I trust you will send my blessings?"

With her words, Marianne drew a dagger from her waistband. A desperate, drowning cry came from Servo as he tried to fend her off, but the queen swatted his hands aside and drove the blade through his eye. She held the blade there as Servo's legs drummed against the earth for a few seconds more, then yanked it clear when he finally grew still.

"Yesss," moaned Marianne as her eyes flickered closed.

Sitting up on his elbow, Caledan struggled to comprehend the sudden turn of events. The queen's hands were on the Elder's chest. Multicoloured sparks leapt from Servo's corpse into Marianne, lighting her skin aglow, until with a final flash, all sign of power vanished from sight.

"Ah, but that is better," Marianne murmured, opening her eyes again. They settled on her foe, and she reached down to remove a bracelet from his arm. "And this ensures my victory," she added, removing her own bangle and replacing it with Servo's.

"What did you do?" Caledan asked, staggering to his feet.

"Reclaimed my power," Marianne replied.

Before Caledan could enquire further, a moan came from nearby. His eyes lit on Genevieve, still collapsed in the mud on the other side of the island. Servo's sailors stood nearby, but at a look from him, they raised their hands and backed away. Ignoring them, Caledan staggered to his friend's side and knelt beside her. She flinched away at his touch, another moan rasping from her throat.

"Genevieve, it's okay," he whispered. "It's me, Caledan."

Her eyelids flickered, but her eyes were so swollen he

doubted she could see him. She didn't react the next time he touched her, though. Her skin was burning and her lips were cracked and dry, sure signs of dehydration. This close to her, he realised Genevieve was far worse off that he'd first thought. Every part of her was bruised and there were gashes on her arms and legs, many still seeping blood and worse. Both legs were twisted at a terrible angle, no doubt broken in a dozen places.

"Gods, what has he done to you?" Caledan whispered.

"Caledan," came Marianne's voice from nearby. "Come, we must move quickly, before Servo's army breaks up."

Caledan looked around, surprised at the coldness of the queen's tone. "What are you saying?" he hissed, gesturing at Genevieve. "She needs my help!"

Her brow creased and she did not reply, but after a moment she flashed a glare at Servo's soldiers. They seemed to freeze in place, and with a nod, she joined Caledan. Crouching beside him, she stretched out a hand to Genevieve. The huntress must have been unconscious after all, for she did not pull away from the woman who had tried to kill her the last time they'd met.

Marianne's eyes narrowed, but after only a few seconds she withdrew her hand.

"Her fever is well advanced. Her body cannot last much longer." She offered Caledan an apologetic look. "I am sorry, my Champion. She is not long for this world."

"Can't you heal her?" he asked. "Like you did for me?"

"I…" She hesitated. "This is…different. Her wounds are physical, but the infection now stretches all throughout her body. It would take a tremendous amount of energy…"

Caledan caught the hesitation in her words. "But you *can* do it?" he insisted.

Her lips tightened. "She is my enemy, Caledan."

"She is my *friend*," Caledan snapped.

He bowed his head until it touched Genevieve's brow, remembering how the huntress had stood strong in Malevolent Cove, how she had rescued Kryssa and Pela when all others had failed. The whisper of Genevieve's breath touched his cheek, and he heard the crackling from her throat, as though the very act of breathing was becoming difficult.

"Please, Marianne," he said, looking again at the queen. "You told me once how you regretted your actions in Malevolent Cove. This is the partner of Kryssa, the woman you tried to sacrifice. You owe her this!"

Marianne's eyes shimmered and for a moment Caledan thought she would refuse. Then the light faded and her eyes slid closed, her face falling. She gave the slightest of nods, then pushing Caledan aside, she placed her hands on Genevieve's chest. A groan came from the huntress as rainbow light seeped from the queen's palms. Her hands came up, fumbling at Marianne's wrists.

"Hold her down," the queen ground through clenched teeth. Her eyes did not so much as flicker from her patient. "This is hard enough as it is."

Obeying, Caledan took the huntress's wrists in his hands and pulled them away from Marianne. Genevieve was so weak that it took little effort, though she still managed to dig her nails into his flesh before he got a good grip. Grimacing, he glanced at the queen, then back to the huntress.

Genevieve's face contorted as the light spilling from Marianne intensified, her mouth opening in a silent scream. Her back arched as she strained against his grip. He held her tight, but it was a full minute before she collapsed back to the earth. Marianne kept on, her face tight as she concentrated, the multicoloured light flickering from her hands. A trickle of sweat ran down her face and dripped onto Genevieve's cheek.

Caledan wondered if he was doing the right thing, asking this of the queen. An army still waited on the other side of the river. What if one of Servo's fellow Elders managed to take command and attack while they sat here unawares? What if healing Genevieve drained too much of her strength? What if the huntress died anyway?

He swallowed, his throat suddenly parched, but he pushed his fear back down. Whatever trials Genevieve had suffered these past few weeks, she deserved a chance at life, whatever the cost. Besides, after Servo's little speech, Caledan doubted if a single Lonian soldier remained loyal to the Elders.

Time stretched out, and Caledan began to wonder whether Marianne would fail after all. Genevieve lay unmoving, her breath faint, her skin so pale she might have already passed to the other side. Then Caledan began to notice changes coming over the huntress—a touch of colour returning to her cheeks, the slight easing of her breathing, the agony slipping from her face. Half an hour passed before Caledan finally believed Marianne might truly save her.

Finally the queen sat back with a gasp, though her hands remained on Genevieve's chest. She swayed where she sat and her eyes flickered open, though it was a long time before they focused on Caledan.

"Water!" she croaked.

Caledan rushed back to their boat, where the sailors still stood waiting. They handed him a waterskin and he returned to the queen, holding it out for her.

"You…do it," she said. "I cannot stop until every trace of infection is burnt from her body."

With that, she bent her head back and opened her mouth. Caledan hesitated, then removed the steel cap and awkwardly shifted the bulging skin into place. He did his best to pour just a splash, but the thing was large and unwieldy, and he managed to spill a small torrent over the queen's face.

By the time Marianne had finished coughing and spluttering up the extra water, Caledan had regained control of the skin. He opened his mouth to apologise, but to his surprise, the queen only laughed.

"I guess that will have to do," she said, returning to her patient.

Now she moved her hands to and fro along Genevieve's body. Wherever the rainbow light fell, bruises faded and gashes knitted themselves back together, leaving hardly a mark.

Caledan swallowed, finally seeing the true power in the queen's fingertips, her control over life and death. If she could do this to save his friend, what else might she be capable of? The inferno Servo had summoned had been awful, but this…this was something else, a power at once miraculous and terrifying.

Finally Marianne moved onto Genevieve's legs, where the worst of Servo's cruelty had been inflicted. Here she paused, glancing at Caledan with worry in her eyes.

"Her legs are broken in a dozen places," the queen whispered. "I must move them back into alignment. You will need to hold her tight now."

Caledan grimaced and got a better hold on the huntress. The queen gripped Genevieve's leg tightly enough that her nails left marks, then slowly straightened the limb.

A hair-raising shriek clawed its way up from Genevieve's throat as she began to thrash. If Caledan had not been warned, she would have torn herself free. As it was, he hung on grimly, using his weight to pin her down, his hands fixed like shackles around her wrists. But he could not block out the screaming. The sound seemed to come from her very soul, as though her flesh were being peeled back from her bones.

Marianne moved as quickly as she could, struggling against Genevieve's thrashing to straighten each leg, and all the while light poured from her fingertips. The queen's face was pale now, her brow soaked with sweat, but still she kept on.

By the time she reached the second leg, Genevieve had ceased her thrashing. Her screams had died away too, but a dull keening still came from the back of her throat. Her face was screwed up tight, her eyelids flickering as though she were trapped in a nightmare from which she could not wake. Caledan held her close, whispering to her beneath his breath, doing whatever he could to reassure her.

Finally Marianne let out a gasp and sat back. The light died in her hands as she released the huntress, and swaying on her haunches, her eyes flickered closed. Caledan released Genevieve and placed a hand on the queen's shoulder, supporting her in case she fell.

Marianne's eyes snapped open at his touch. She looked from him to Genevieve, exhaustion writ across her face. Then leaning across Genevieve's body, the queen tapped her on the forehead. A long breath whispered from his friend as she relaxed, as though passing from nightmare into a dreamless sleep.

"There," Marianne said, drawing back. "It is done. Your little friend is healed."

"Thank you, Marianne," Caledan whispered, giving her shoulder a squeeze. "I don't know how I can ever repay you."

Marianne smiled at that. "It was but a small thing," she murmured, though the exhaustion etched into her face said otherwise. "More than earned. Now," she continued, standing and offering him her hand, "it is time I spoke with my new army. I would have my Champion beside me, should he still want the role."

"I do." Caledan smiled, and taking her hand, he stood. Then he frowned as he realised the significance of her words. "But why do you think they will follow you?"

"Revenge," Marianne replied, her eyes drifting out across the waters. "They might love me because I freed them, but they will follow me because their hearts still scream for justice. Lonia has but one enemy left—the son of the Tsar." She grinned, and light spilled from her eyes. "Let Braidon try and stop me now."

❧ 14 ☙

Pela paced up and down the room, fists clenched, her entire body shaking. After Ruebyn had collapsed at dinner, Rayan had helped her carry him back to their room. The place was sparsely furnished, containing only a pair of beds and a washroom where they had cleaned themselves earlier. The stone walls were unadorned and even the blankets on the beds were an unattractive grey.

Another tremor ran down her spine and she looked at the unlit brazier, wishing they'd at least been left fuel for a fire. Night had fallen an hour ago and the temperature in the windowless room was falling quickly.

Ruebyn himself lay in one of the beds, the covers tucked up to his chin, eyes fixed on the ceiling. His face had lost all colour and every so often another bout of coughing would overcome him. Each time Pela would race to his side, though there was nothing she could do but watch as he doubled up beneath the sheets in agony. Every spell seemed to last a little longer, to take more from him.

She returned to his side as another bout started. Specks

of blood stained the sheets as he gasped into the pillow. She stretched out a hand and stroked his hair. Her eyes stung, but she refused to cry. To cry was to accept his fate, to accept that there was nothing she could do to save him. And Pela would rather die than surrender.

Finally Ruebyn's coughing faded and he relaxed back into the pillow. His eyes fluttered closed and his breathing eased.

Silently, Pela resumed her pacing. Rayan and the king had said there was nothing they could do for Ruebyn now. The *morbus* was almost always fatal, and while water and warmth might help ease his suffering, there was little that could be done to save someone once infected. Ruebyn was doomed: she had seen it in the eyes of the king, in the grim-faced look Rayan had offered.

Doomed, unless she did something, unless she found a way to save him.

"Pela."

She jumped as Ruebyn's voice carried across the room. Bracing herself, she turned to face him.

"What?" she whispered.

She could hardly bear to look at him. His eyes were like sunken pits, his face so pale he might have already been a ghost. How had the life left him so quickly?

"Come here," he breathed, so softly she barely heard.

Pela went without thinking, dropping down beside the bed and hugging him tight. Whatever her own doubts, she could not deny him that small comfort now. Sitting back, she ran a hand across his forehead and shivered. He was burning up.

A sigh slipped from his lips as his face twisted in pain. "I'm sorry," he whispered just as she thought he'd fallen asleep. "It's not your fault, you know."

Steel jaws closed around Pela's chest and she had to force the words out. "Of course it is. You wouldn't be here if not for me. I should have listened when you said to go back."

"No." He shook his head weakly. "I made my own choices. Truth is, I wanted to follow you. You're…nothing about you makes sense, you know." A smile touched his lips. "I still can't figure out how you made the soldiers obey you."

Pela laughed. "Magic, silly," she croaked, and now the tears did spill across her cheeks.

Ruebyn chuckled, but the action quickly turned into more coughing. By the time they left him, Ruebyn's strength had gone, and he lay back in the bed with his eyes closed. Pela sat beside him, gently stroking his brow. She longed to do something, but in the face of the *morbus*, her newfound confidence had evaporated. She'd been a fool to think her victory over the Knight had ever meant anything, that she would ever be good enough to make a difference.

"I'm so sorry," she gasped, burying her head in Ruebyn's chest.

Why was this happening? Was this her fate, to watch everyone she'd ever loved die? First it had been Devon, then Genevieve. Now Ruebyn seemed destined to follow them.

His breathing had deepened now, its rhythm steadier, and he did not respond to her words. She watched him sleep, fighting the urge to flee. She could do nothing here, nothing but wait for her friend to die—then whatever she felt for him would be meaningless. There would be only pain.

Shivering, she ran her fingers across the curve of Ruebyn's face. Their night in the cave flickered into her mind and she flushed. In the danger and creeping cold, there had been no time to think, to pollute her mind with doubts and reservations. Perhaps that had been a good thing. The Gods only knew, she had been overwhelmed by those doubts ever since.

Meditation helps to regulate our emotions.

Pela shivered as her mother's voice whispered from the past. Letting out a long breath, she focused her mind on the action of breathing. In the rush of the last week, in the excitement of her discovery, she'd forgotten why she had first learnt the mindfulness technique. Meditation was more than power or magic; it was a pathway to peace, to tranquillity of spirit.

In, out. Think of nothing else.

Simple in theory, something altogether more difficult in practice. Ruebyn's forehead was still hot beneath her fingers, and she could not block out his breathing, could not help but hear his every agonised inhalation. Pain radiated from him in waves, so powerful she could almost *feel* it, could sense it calling to her, twisting the fabric of her mind.

Pela started, her eyes snapping open as she returned to the room. What had *that* been? For a moment, she had felt separated from her body—at once herself, but also something else, able to view the world around her in an entirely different way.

Looking at Ruebyn, she remembered the agony she had sensed, a violent, almost tangible thing that seeped from him like an outgoing tide. There was nothing now. It had only been her imagination, surely?

The hackles on her neck stood on end. What if it wasn't? What if she had unwittingly tapped into her own power, if she had reached out for him subconsciously?

A lump lodged in her throat as an idea came to her. Swallowing, she wondered if it was possible, if she might actually have a chance of helping him.

A candle flickered into life in her mind's eye—her life force, burning bright in the darkness. But was it enough for what she planned? Or would she fail, as she had in the village, in Malevolent Cove, on the Queen's ship?

Pela shivered, but she could not submit to her fear. If she did nothing, Ruebyn's fate was sealed. She had to try.

Closing her eyes, Pela focused on the trance, following her breathing inwards, on the light in her mind, before reaching out for her friend.

This time the transition was jarring, a sudden tearing sensation that left her suddenly hanging in the air, staring down at her own body. Fear touched her, a sudden terror that she was actually dead. Then she saw the slight movement of her chest. Opening the fingers of her spirit hand, she saw the tiny flame burning in her palm, felt its warmth.

Steeling herself, she turned her attention on Ruebyn. An angry red glow radiated from his body, an inaudible agony only she could see. It seemed to come from every part of him, and Pela trembled as she realised the scale of the task before her.

But she could not waver now. Drifting closer, she reached out a spirit hand and touched it to Ruebyn's chest. Her vision spun, and then it was as though his whole body was all around her. She saw at once every intricate part of him, every bone and muscle and organ, felt his life force, diminished but still burning, still fighting. She felt his pain as well, an agony that she grasped in her hands, and followed deeper into his core.

Pela shuddered as she found herself in his lungs and finally saw the damage there. The pink flesh was bleeding, seared by the angry red flames burning in his core. Her courage was shaken by the sight, but she held on, gathering herself in preparation for what must be done.

Ruebyn was burning up, his entire chest aflame. Focusing her mind, Pela imagined the cooling touch of water, then drew on her own energies to bring the thought to life. A swirling wave of blue swept from her, an icy breath that immediately lessened the angry glow filling Ruebyn's lungs. She kept on, willing the flames of his agony away. With a touch of surprise, she watched the flickering red crumble to embers.

Elated, Pela retreated from Ruebyn and looked at him again. He still slept, but his breathing seemed lighter now. The angry glow still burned elsewhere though, and returning to his body, she followed the light to his heart.

Its rhythmic pounding filled her ears as she surveyed the damage. Here the glow was green rather than red, forming sickly vines that weaved their way around the pounding muscle, forming a strangling cage about his heart. Wherever they touched, his tissue sickened, turning to black.

Her stomach swirling, Pela summoned flames and hurled them at the vile things. To her delight, they fled from her spirit, burning in the face of the inferno.

Her confidence growing, Pela continued through Ruebyn, destroying the *morbus* in all its forms, using her power to chase the illness from his frail body. It surprised her, how little energy it consumed, as though his healing took no effort at all. The sickness might have overwhelmed Ruebyn's life force, but it could not stand against hers.

Finally she turned her attention to Ruebyn's mind. Here the sickness was worse, clinging to his brain, creating a fever that would destroy him if she did not stop it. Pela poured herself into the effort now, turning back the heat, cooling it, taking the pain from her friend.

When that was finally done, she retreated from Ruebyn, hopeful she'd defeated the awful virus. Drifting in her bodiless state, she gave an inner smile at the sight of Ruebyn sleeping peacefully in his bed. The angry colours had vanished, revealing the soothing blue of his true aura…

Pela frowned as a spot of red appeared amidst the blue. Fear touched her as it began to spread, growing from the tiny seed, spreading rapidly to encompass his chest. A racking cough struck Ruebyn as his breathing became strained again.

No, no, no!

Desperate, Pela returned to Ruebyn's body. She poured all her energies into the effort now, determined to burn every last trace of the *morbus*. Swirling through him like a hurricane, she tore the illness from its roots everywhere she found it.

Outside their bodies, time ticked slowly past. Exhaustion crept over Pela as her life force flickered, lessened by her exertions, but she kept on, determined to succeed.

But as she destroyed the sickness in Ruebyn's lungs, more appeared in his heart, then brain. She attacked each of these in turn, only to find new vines had taken root elsewhere. However fast her efforts, the *morbus* sprang up again each time she turned away, its spread unstoppable.

A moan rasped from Pela's throat as she retreated to her body and felt the weight of her exhaustion. She slumped against the bed, gasping for breath as though she'd just run ten miles. An ache had begun in the back of her skull and she sensed her entire body would be hurting by morning.

Ruebyn still lay asleep in the bed. His breathing was better, but a touch to his forehead confirmed his fever burned on. Despite her efforts, the *morbus* was winning.

In despair she turned her eyes inwards and watched the red slowly spreading through Ruebyn's body. She felt drained, as though she had poured her life force down a bottomless hole rather than into Ruebyn. He was coughing again, and there was blood on his lips. She wiped it away, but a second later it was back, gurgling up from the depths of his chest.

How much longer could he last like this?

Pela shivered and forced the thought from her mind. She drew in a breath, battling with despair, and sent her spirit soaring again. The process came easily now, almost instinctively.

The last of Ruebyn's blue was already succumbing to the red. She drifted closer to her friend, still searching desperately for something she could do, some way to help him. Perhaps a single, overwhelming wave of energy was needed, to burn the illness from him all at once?

Did she even have enough energy left for such an attempt? A shiver passed through her as she looked at the dwindling flame of her life force, then back at Ruebyn. It was their only hope. Drawing on her power, she readied herself...

...then frowned, suddenly aware of a strangeness to Ruebyn's aura. The red aura swirled about his body, but not in a random manner as she had first thought. There was a pattern, a spiral that led inwards to his chest. She watched in curiosity as the aura continued to flicker. The blue was almost gone now, draining away through that strange spiral.

Then she noticed something else, something utterly out of place. The finest of threads twisted from Ruebyn's chest, so thin she had not noticed it until now. The silver string hung in the air before her, and without thinking, she followed it across the room. It disappeared through the wall, but that was no obstacle to her spirit, and she drifted after the silver glow. Something was terribly wrong here, and Pela intended to find out what.

Unseen, her spirit traversed the citadel, passing down corridors and kitchens and dining rooms, through closed doors, until Pela no longer knew where she was, how long she had been gone from her body.

Then Pela realised the thread she followed was not alone, that she had entered a room where a thousand trails of light converged on one another. They crisscrossed the room like the web of a spider, all directed to the centre, where a ball of multi-coloured light shone so brightly Pela could hardly see.

Though she was only present in spirit, Pela couldn't help but tremble at the energies burning in the room. Fist clenched tight about the flame of her own life force, she drifted closer. Her whole being vibrated as she passed through the webs, straining to discover what lay at their centre.

Confusion touched Pela as she found herself floating over a canopy bed, looking down upon the aged face of the king. She looked again at the shining threads and finally realised what they were—slivers of life force, gathered from across the city, maybe even the nation. Every one of them must be connected to a soul like Ruebyn, but why…

No, no, no.

A scream built in Pela's throat as her gaze was drawn back to the king. Each of the threads had been drawn to this place, to this man, igniting a brilliant light in his chest. Betran was connected to all of his subjects, was somehow drawing on all their energies at once.

The king was stealing the lives of his people. Surely it could not be true, not after the man had been so generous with them, after his people had suffered so much, not unless…

Pela groaned as she realised the terrible, horrible truth.

There had never been a *morbus*—only a terrible deception. Ruebyn did not have the plague. He had not gotten sick until he'd worn the opal necklace. The illness had only ever been an excuse to force the Trolan people to wear the black opals. The king only need draw slowly on their life forces to make him stronger than any living soul, and ensure his deception was never discovered. But Ruebyn though…with his apparent exposure, there'd been no reason to use constraint.

Staring at the monster lying in his bed, Pela thought of all the empty pastures stretching across Trola, of the despair in the eyes of his people, the lifeless looks of even the nobles. She thought of all the innocent lives this man had destroyed, the pain and misery he had unleashed upon his own people.

Rage wrapped its fiery fingers around Pela's heart. She drifted closer, her whole spirit trembling. King Betran lay unawares. Despite the power that burned in his core, there was no barrier to keep her away, nothing to stop her. All she had to do was use her own life force against him, to channel all her rage, all her grief into a single killing blow.

Pela's life force burnt hot in her fist. Slowly she reached out, then afraid he might suddenly wake, went forward in a rush. Thrusting her fist at the king's skull, she readied herself…

A gasp tore from Pela as her spirit was spun around, surrounded suddenly by a cacophony of light. Images jarred her vision, memories that were not hers. She found herself looking out across a great expanse, a land of giant forests and lush pastures. People moved across the land with joy on their faces, and at the centre of it all stood their king.

Then a darkness crept into the land, and soon the people were fleeing, falling to their knees before a shadow they could not resist. Blood flowed freely in the streets as the scenes progressed. Pela saw a father clutching a child to his chest, watched a mother trying desperately to wake her baby, heard the screams, smelt the decay.

A scream tore from Pela's throat as the creature appeared amongst the dying, a monster clothed in shadow. Its outstretched arms reached into the souls of all it encountered, tearing the life from them. Their energies disappeared into a void at the creature's centre, consumed by an insatiable hunger. Some tried to stand against it, but with a flick of a finger the strength was drained from them.

Before long there was no one left to fight. The only option left for the Trolans was to run, and Pela watched as they fled into the wilderness, into the mountains and forests, but even there they could not escape. Drawn to its power, men with black hearts and blue armour joined with the monster. They rode after their former comrades, rounding up the innocent and driving them back to Kalgan, back to the creature's embrace.

The king had not lied when he spoke of a plague that had swept across the land. It had not come from any illness, but from a creature of darkness. A word sprang into Pela's mind, one that had not been spoken since the time of the Gods.

Demon!

✵ 15 ✵

The days passed quickly after Caledon's defeat of Servo. The confrontation with the Lonian army had played out just as Marianne had predicted. She'd won their hearts by revealing Servo's true nature, but it had been revenge that finally motivated them to join her. For decades, Lonia had suffered beneath the yoke of Braidon's father—then at Braidon's own hand, during the ten-year-long war between the north and south. Now Marianne offered them retribution, a chance to unleash their fury against the man who represented every hurt, every injustice they had ever suffered.

They had shouted her name to the skies.

And so Marianne's newly enlarged army had taken to the Gods' Road. Now two days later, they were already nearing Chole. Caledan expected to come within sight of the city walls by the morning. Reinforced by the Lonian army, he did not doubt their victory would quickly follow.

Even so, his mind remained heavy. Marianne had thrown herself into organising the army's march, becoming more withdrawn with each passing day. Caledan was saddened to see her retreat into herself, and as the final battle approached, he noticed her smiles becoming less frequent. Her eyes would often take on a distant look, as though she were already imagining her confrontation with Braidon.

Then there was Genevieve. The huntress still had not woken from her sleep, and while Caledan had ensured she was well cared for, he was beginning to fear Marianne's healing had not taken. He longed to ask the queen what was wrong, but she already had too many worries on her shoulders.

Instead, as the sun set on the makeshift camp that Marianne's forces had erected for the night, Caledan found himself carrying a bowl of broth to the tent that had been set aside for the injured. Other than Genevieve, there were only a couple of occupants, those who had sprained ankles on the march or injured themselves while training.

He ignored them as he entered, crossing directly to the corner where the huntress lay sleeping. As Caledan approached, he saw her eyes flicker. His heart began to race as he quickly knelt beside her.

"Gen—"

Before he could finish, Genevieve surged up and her fist careened into his chin. The broth went flying as Caledan tumbled backwards, the huntress crashing down atop him. He cried out as she raised her fist again, and now he saw a glint of steel there.

"Genevieve, wait!" he cried. "It's me, Caledan!"

For a second it seemed she had not heard him—then her eyes widened and the dagger tumbled from her fingers.

"Caledan!" she gasped, sitting back suddenly. "What are you doing here?"

"That's…a long story," Caledan replied with a grimace, still smarting from the hot stew that had spilled on his lap. "But…you're safe."

Genevieve swallowed visibly. "Servo?"

"Dead," Caledan said. "Marianne made sure of that."

"Marianne?" Genevieve croaked, the panic returning to her voice. "The queen is here?"

"She is."

"You're working for that witch?" Genevieve whispered, her eyes flicking around the tent as though expecting the queen to appear at any moment.

"I am," Caledan replied.

Despite himself, he felt hurt as Genevieve pulled away from him. But then, the huntress would not have forgotten Devon's death at Marianne's hand. A part of Caledan still felt shame, that he now served the hammerman's killer.

"I don't understand," the huntress whispered. "She tried to kill us all. How could you betray your friends like this?"

"If not for her, you would be dead," Caledan shot back, anger touching him now. "She healed you, though it cost her dearly."

"That doesn't make any sense."

Caledan sighed. "There is much for you to catch up on. Where have you been? How did you survive Malevolent Cove, after we capsized?"

Genevieve scowled and sat back on her haunches. "Well, while you were making friends with the enemy, Pela and I were taken by Baronians."

"Pela?" Caledan asked, his heart quickening. The girl hadn't been amongst Servo's people.

"She's alive," Genevieve replied. "Last I saw her, she was fleeing into Trola."

"*What?*" Caledan gasped.

"She didn't have much choice," Genevieve growled. "It was that, or be sent back to your queen's precious mines."

"You were *slaves?*"

Genevieve nodded, and for the merest of seconds, Caledan glimpsed the terror in her eyes. She swallowed visibly before adding, "Pela...she had it the worst. I didn't know what had happened to her, the first few weeks. When I found her...she was in poor shape. But she is Kryssa's daughter. In the end, it was Pela who found a way to escape." She hesitated, drawing in a deep breath. "And... what of Kryssa?"

Caledan looked away. "She lives," he said softly.

"What is it, Caledan?" Genevieve asked.

"She's with Braidon in Chole," Caledan replied, forcing himself to look at the huntress. "A day's march from us. Marianne intends to put an end to the king's little rebellion. She's going to storm the city."

"*What?*" Genevieve gasped, staggering to her feet.

Caledan rose with her, gripping Genevieve's hands to keep her from doing anything rash. "*Calm down,*" he hissed. Glancing around, he looked for listeners, but the other injured didn't seem to be paying them any attention. "Do not forget where you are," he added with a glare.

"In the camp of my enemy," Genevieve said coldly. "The prisoner of a traitor."

"You are not a prisoner," Caledan snapped. "And I'm no traitor—Braidon was never my king."

"Yes, I remember," Genevieve growled. "You would have killed him and let Kryssa die, had I not intervened."

"I wouldn't..." Caledan couldn't finish the sentence. He looked away again. "We saved her in the end, didn't we?"

"From your queen, Gods damnit!" Genevieve snarled. "And now you seem determined to correct the error. Did

Devon die for nothing, that you spit in the face of his sacrifice?"

"I saved the bastard King!" Caledan hissed, raising a fist. Genevieve did not so much as flinch. "I half-drowned myself, dragging Braidon from the waters of Malevolent Cove. My obligation ended there," he finished, though now his words lacked conviction.

"And now you're actively trying to kill him." Genevieve shook her head. "She must be a fantastic lover."

"She is my queen!" Caledan lashed out, then sucked in a breath, seeking calm. "Don't you see, Braidon cares only for himself, for his own power. Otherwise, he would have marched against Servo, instead of sitting in his fortress while the Elder led a Lonian army into our lands. He did *nothing,* while Marianne did what he never could—brought peace between our two nations, with hardly a drop of blood spilt."

"Ay," Genevieve murmured, "and in doing so, she earned the loyalty of the Lonians, and tripled the size of her army."

Caledan's stomach twisted as he stared at Genevieve. He could see the fervour in her eyes, knew she would never listen, not while her lover stood with the other side.

"She is a better ruler than Braidon could ever hope to be," he breathed finally. "*That* is why I support her."

"Very well," Genevieve said. "In that case, I would like to see her for myself."

The huntress darted suddenly forward. Ducking past Caledan, she was across the tent in two strides. He cried out and leapt after her, but she had already disappeared through the flaps. By the time he found her, she was already a dozen yards away, darting through the men and women still trying to set their tents for the night. In the distance, the gold-tinged pavilion of the queen's tent rose above the surrounding camp.

Cursing, Caledan set off after her, keeping pace as she weaved through the workers, but slowed by the press of bodies, he was unable to catch her. Only at the entrance to the queen's tent did Genevieve stop, her path barred by two of the Queen's Guard.

"Genevieve," he gasped, taking her by the shoulder before she got herself killed. "You can't just go running up to the queen's quarters."

"Be damned," Genevieve snapped, shrugging him off. She spun on him, eyes aflame. "Your *queen* tried to murder the woman I love. She killed Devon, and…" Genevieve's voice trailed off, and she took a deep breath before continuing. "And her people put a collar around my neck and made me a slave. *You* may have forgotten what kind of woman this queen of yours is, Caledan, but *I* have not."

"I—"

"Caledan," came the queen's voice, interrupting whatever argument he'd been about to make. The two of them spun, surprised to find Marianne standing between her guards. A smile touched her lips at the sight of the huntress. "Enough, my Champion. I will see her. Why don't the two of you join me for a drink?" She disappeared into her tent without a backwards glance.

Steel rattled as the guards stepped aside, granting them passage. Caledan exchanged a glance with Genevieve, but whatever doubt the queen's words might have given the huntress, it quickly vanished as she spun and stepped through the canvas flaps. Letting out a long breath, Caledan followed her inside.

Within, he found Marianne standing at her war table, already pouring wine into three glasses. She might have had any number of retainers do such a menial task, but she generally preferred to serve herself when it was practical.

Genevieve still stood in the entrance, her courage lost now that she had crossed the threshold into Marianne's lair. Caledan hesitated beside the huntress, but after a moment's hesitation, moved to join his queen.

"Welcome back, my Champion," Marianne said with a smile, offering him a glass of wine.

Caledan took it reluctantly, still mindful of his duty to defend her. Taking a sip, he stepped aside and placed it on the table. Chuckling, Marianne turned her eyes on the huntress and held out a glass. Genevieve had her hands clenched at her side, but drawing in a breath, she accepted the offered wine.

"So, you're awake," Marianne murmured as she picked up the final glass and took a seat at the table. "I am glad all my hard work did not go to waste."

"What do you mean?" Genevieve asked. She did not sit, and held her glass out in front of her as though it were a snake about to strike her.

"Caledan begged me to save you," the queen explained, reclining in her chair. "So I used my power to mend your broken bones and cleanse your body of fever."

"Why?"

"Because Caledan did me a great favour, not too long ago," Marianne said simply. "I owed him a debt."

"Even if it meant healing your enemy?" Genevieve questioned.

Marianne shrugged. "Caledan was also once my enemy. Now he stands as my Champion. Perhaps it will be the same with you."

Genevieve slammed her glass down on the table so hard

that the wine sloshed over the sides. "You tried to kill the woman I love," she hissed. "I will *never* be your ally."

"So be it." The queen did not flinch from the woman's anger. "You have every reason to hate me. But I will say this: I regret what took place in the cove. Braidon was my enemy, not Kryssa or her daughter. I let thoughts of power corrupt me." She hesitated, and Caledan thought he glimpsed doubt on her face. Her eyes flickered to the bracelet on her wrist, then back to Genevieve. "I will not let it happen again."

Caledan held his breath, waiting for the huntress's response, but Genevieve seemed at a loss for words. She swallowed visibly, glancing at Caledan, before finally managing to croak, "So you have changed?"

Marianne spread her hands. "I am doing my best."

A sneer twisted Genevieve's face. "Pretty words, but your actions prove them a lie."

"Oh?"

"You say you regret the blood that was spilt in Malevolent Cove, but here you are again, expecting others to bleed to settle your grievance with Braidon."

Marianne's sapphire eyes stared up at Genevieve. "I did not seek this fight," she said. "It was Braidon who attacked Chole. I cannot stand by while he still claims to be king."

"Yet he speaks the truth. He is the rightful king of Plorsea."

"By what right?" Marianne asked mildly. "By the right of his father, who enslaved the Three Nations for decades? Or do you claim that his years as king were prosperous, that he is a fit ruler for Plorsea?"

"Braidon was never perfect," Genevieve shot back, "but at least he didn't condon coldblooded murder."

"No?" Marianne asked mildly. "Then you have not heard the news. Under his command, the Castle in Chole was stormed by his followers. Innocent believers had gathered there, seeking protection from the riots he had stirred up in the city. Braidon's people murdered them all—locked them in the pantheon and burned them alive."

"No," Genevieve whispered. Her face had lost all its colour. "Braidon would not…"

"It's true," Caledan said quietly. "I read the reports myself."

All the fight seemed to go from Genevieve as she slumped into a chair. Her glass still sat before her, and almost unconsciously she reached for it and downed the wine in a single gulp. Marianne picked up the bottle and refilled her glass before continuing the story.

"If it helps, I do not believe murder was Braidon's intent," she said. "Just more of his general incompetence."

A shudder passed through Genevieve as she looked at the queen. "What is wrong with you people?" she whispered. "You play with our lives, hold our fate in your hands, but do any of you even care?"

"I care," Marianne replied softly, her eyes taking on a distant look. "With Caledan's help, I have put an end to the faction within the Order who were intent on murder. The cleansings ended with Servo's death. And the Great Sacrifice will return to what it once was—a celebration of strength, of devotion to the Saviour, to mankind's future. I would have peace."

"Peace?" Genevieve gave a hollow laugh. "You just have to fight one little war first, right? Why is it always so? All of you powerful men and women, you all claim to want peace. But somehow it's always one war away." She shook her head. "No, don't tell me you want peace, woman. Blood, revenge, power, any of that I would believe, but peace?" Genevieve laughed again and finished her second glass.

A strained silence followed her words. The queen said nothing, only sat swirling the wine in her glass. Every so often she took a sip, her face pensive. Still standing at her side, Caledan held his breath, wondering how Marianne would react to Genevieve's challenge. What game was the huntress playing at here? Surely she must see there was no other way, that Marianne must take the fight to Braidon now, or risk the fallen king drawing the nation into a bloody civil war.

Finally the queen sighed and placed her glass aside. Steepling her fingers, she fixed her eyes on the huntress. "And what would you have me do, Genevieve?" she murmured. "Braidon took my childhood, my innocence. I cannot turn my back on our past—nor the threat he poses to myself and my son. I do not want a war, but neither will I give up my crown to a man who again and again has proven himself unworthy of the title."

Genevieve stared back at the queen, eyes angry, defiant. "I would have you find another way."

❧ 16 ❧

Wind tugged at Braidon's hair as Nidryt circled the cove. Each stroke of the beast's massive wings sent them soaring upwards, only to drift slowly down again, the constant beat holding them aloft as he studied the terrain.

The dragon had caused a panic in Chole as it swooped down to his Castle. By then, Braidon had gathered his sword and warmer clothing from his quarters and was waiting on the battlements. The beast had dropped in low, settling only long enough for Braidon to leap upon its back. Shouts had chased after them and a solitary figure with silver hair had come running into the courtyard, but Nidryt was gone before Kryssa had a chance to call them back.

Braidon had not told her of his plan. This was something he had to do alone, to prove he was still worthy of being king, that he was not destined to fail in this as he had in everything else. That, and a part of him knew he was alone now, had been alone since the day he'd gathered the energies of the dying in the pantheon.

Now high above Malevolent Cove, Braidon looked

down on his enemy. They were little more than ants from the height at which Nidryt soared. Braidon wanted to be sure they went unnoticed until he was ready for the attack.

The scene below was exactly as the dragon had shown him back in Chole. Scorched timbers lay scattered across the cove, where the Red Dragons had destroyed the amphitheatre abandoned by the Knights. Now though, a new structure stood atop the cliffs, the makings of a Castle, its sandstone walls cast red in the setting sun.

Braidon smiled, determined to make the scarlet display a foul omen for the Order. At least a hundred were camped around the structure, nestled within a wooden stockade they had been raised to protect them from the dark creatures lurking in the jungles of Dragon Country.

Of course, wooden walls could not stop the Red Dragons, but that was not their only protection. Hidden behind each wall and atop the cliffs were dozens of sleek steel catapults, their arms already loaded with the familiar barrels. Braidon knew from experience that within each was an explosive black powder that could tear through stone and steel alike. The catapults had been a match for the dragons the last time they'd attacked the Knights, though they'd still managed to wreak havoc before their defeat.

Braidon had not been awake to see that though, having been half-dead and drowning in the cove himself. Now though, an army of Red Dragons swirled around him, the five that Nidryt had chosen to take part in their attack. But if all went as Braidon planned, they would not even need five to defeat the Knights.

Letting out a long breath, Braidon closed his eyes and sent his spirit soaring. The process came easily to him even now, thirty years after his grandmother had first taught him the ability. Drifting free of his body, he gathered the power of the dead around him like a cloak. He shivered as the energies formed a protective shield, his spirit tingling at their touch, then shot down towards the fortress.

Braidon slowed his flight as he neared, reaching out with his senses for the enemy. Still new to his powers, he had no idea what tricks the Elders might be capable of, what traps they might have set for wandering souls.

While the weapons of the Order were formidable, the Elders themselves were Braidon's greatest fear. Only they could sense his flight through the camp, and had the power to threaten his spirit. It was the Elders of the Order who performed the ritual cleansings, drawing power from the innocents they murdered. Braidon knew at least one must be in the camp, but there was no way of knowing yet how powerful his foe would be.

But their sacrilege would at least reveal them to Braidon's spirit gaze. Every man and woman within the camp glowed with a unique aura, the essence of their life force. But the Elders would be different, their aura warped, marked by the multicoloured hue of those lives they had taken.

The camp was massive, occupied by more than a hundred men and women now, each there with the sole purpose of raising a new Castle on behalf of the Order. It took long minutes for Braidon to sense his target, as the Elder's tent was much like the others—its only difference were the two Knights stationed outside. That, and the brilliant glow of the man's aura within.

Slipping unseen past the guards, Braidon hesitated on the threshold. The interior of the tent shone with the Elder's aura, so bright it sent a shiver through Braidon's soul. How many lives had this man stolen to become so powerful?

Doubt touched him then. Did he have enough power to go up against such a man? And even if he did, the energies he'd taken from the lost were finite—if he used his power here, what would be left to him when Marianne finally came with her army?

Reaching for his own power, Braidon felt reassured as it surged through his spirit, reinforcing his courage. What was the point of having such strength if he was too afraid to use it? Power or no, he could not defeat Marianne without allies, and there were none more powerful than the Red Dragons. Even should he use all the energy he had collected from the pantheon, it would be worth the sacrifice to have the beasts at his side.

Then an idea came to him. Perhaps there was a way to have both—to destroy the Elder and the camp, and to still preserve his own power.

Gathering his nerve, Braidon drifted closer, studying the Elder's aura. The man was asleep, his consciousness trapped in the depths of his dreams. What was to stop him from attacking now, while the man lay unaware? Braidon could kill the Elder before he ever realised his danger.

Energy crackled through Braidon's spirit as his excitement rose. He scanned the room one last time for traps the Elder might have set, but there was nothing. Why would there be? The man was far from any threats, in the centre of his own encampment. The dragons might pose a risk, but they were not magical creatures; they could not harm him here.

Braidon smiled at his enemy's arrogance. Nowhere was safe now, and Braidon made a mental note to find some way of protecting himself while he slept. He would learn from the Elder's mistake—even as he took full advantage.

Hovering over the Elder, Braidon wondered how best to

dispose of the man. With the energy held at his disposal, the Elder would be a fearsome enemy should he wake. Fire or suffocation might be effective, but they could also alert the man to Braidon's presence. In those few seconds before death took him, the Elder might have time to lash out, to save himself.

But what of his own body? The man was old, and despite the power he wielded, frail. Braidon drifted down, allowing himself to merge with the Elder's body—though he took care not use too much power, lest he wake his foe.

A dull, unsteady pounding carried to Braidon's ears, the rattling whistle of breath, the hiss of blood through veins. It was a strange sensation, being cocooned inside another man's body, listening to the sounds of his life—a life Braidon was about to snuff out. For a moment he considered what he was about to do—to kill a man as he lay unawares—but this was the only way. Allowing him the chance to fight back would risk everything. Braidon could not afford to take that risk.

Thump, thump, thump.

Inevitably, Braidon's attention was drawn to a distant thumping. The pounding muscle of the Elder's heart rushed into focus, covered by a chrysalis of brown and yellow, sickly strips of fat clinging to flesh. Such a simple thing, little different from the great pumps used to ventilate a blacksmith's forge. Yet it meant the difference between life and death.

Looking at the twisted organ, it was clear the man was already in poor health, his heart practically decaying in his chest. With his power, Braidon might have healed him, burned away the fat and restored the dying tissues. He had not realised such a feat was possible until that very instant.

With his own life force, it would have been exhausting, but with the power Braidon had collected…

But he had not come here to heal his enemies.

Reaching out with his mind, Braidon wrapped the Elder's heart in his power. He steadied himself, drawing on more energy to shield his soul in case he failed. Then with a gesture of his spirit, he sent fire rushing into the man's heart.

At its touch, a single cry tore from the Elder, a scream of horror quickly cut off. The man lurched upright, mouth open wide, and for a second Braidon thought he had miscalculated. He threw up his arms, summoning all his strength in preparation for battle—but there was no need.

A long, drawn-out sigh whispered from the Elder, his life's breath leaving his body, and he slumped back onto the bed. Shouts came from outside, and behind Braidon the tent flaps were yanked aside, admitting the Knights as they came racing to their Elder's aid.

But it was already too late.

Braidon watched in fascination as the energy left his foe's body, his life force and all those others the man had stolen cut loose from the ties of the flesh. Here was an opportunity Braidon had not expected, but he did not hesitate now. Quickly, he drew those fresh energies to himself, gathering the swirling colours like a cloak around his spirit.

He gasped as power surged into him, almost overwhelmed by this new force. Bending in two, Braidon was momentarily unaware of the Knights crouched over the Elder's body, of the sobs that rattled from their helmets as they tried to wake the man. All he felt was the power, the surging energies of so many fresh lives.

When Braidon's senses finally returned, he found the tent empty again, the Knights departed for he knew not where. Now the Elder lay covered by a sheet. Braidon stole a moment to look at the body, wondering if the man had known in his last moments what had killed him. Then a smile touched Braidon's lips.

"Thank you for your sacrifice," he whispered to the night. "It might not have reached your precious Saviour, but her brother appreciates it."

King?

Braidon jerked as the voice of Nidryt shook his spirit. His gaze was drawn upwards, though the dragon could not have been seen from the ground, even had he stood outside. Elation swept through Braidon as he rejoiced in his victory.

I live, dragon! he replied. *You have only to wait a few minutes more, then revenge will be yours.*

The dragon did not reply, but Braidon sensed a rush of emotion from the beast, its lust for blood, to tear and rend and burn those who had dared to invade its homeland. Laughing in the darkness, Braidon returned to the night, ready to complete his part of the plan.

With the Elder dead, there was no one to stop him now, no supernatural force to oppose him, and he walked freely through the camp. He started with the catapults, quietly burning away the hinges that drew the firing arm back. Now if the Knights tried to operate them, the catapults would tear themselves apart rather than fire.

Next, he searched out the deadly crossbows. There were many more of these, but he did not need to destroy them all, only enough that they could not drive off the dragons. One by one, he made his way through the camp, slicing wire strings and bending firing arms, whatever he could do to sabotage the Knight's last defence against the scarlet beasts.

A wave of exhaustion touched Braidon as he returned

to his body. He swayed on the dragon's back, eyes closed, trying to readjust to the sudden weight of his flesh, the hardness of the scales beneath him, the wind in his hair.

Then the full force of the power he had gathered struck him, burning through his veins. His eyes snapped open and he gasped, heart suddenly racing. In an instant his gaze fixed on the camp far below, on the unsuspecting souls he was about to sweep away.

"It's time," he said.

What of their weapons? the dragon asked.

Braidon laughed, the sound carrying across the sky so that every one of the beasts heard his next words.

"Their weapons are destroyed. The camp lies unguarded."

Nidryt rumbled beneath him, and throwing back its head, the dragon unleashed a blood-curdling roar. Answering cries rose from the other dragons and their flames lit the sky. Braidon crouched low on Nidryt's back as the beast folded its wings and dove towards the enemy.

The bellowing of horns greeted their approach as watchmen sounded the alarm. Braidon grinned as the ground came rushing up towards him, bemused at the desperation of his enemies. They had been so confident, so assured of their own power. Now they would pay for their arrogance.

The night had passed unnoticed while he had haunted the camp, and now the rising sun marked the horizon. Its brilliant light shimmered on the armour of the Knights as they rushed for their weapons. In moments, a dozen cross-bows were aimed at the sky, while others leapt to the cata-pults, swinging them to face the new threat.

Braidon had to admit, the camp was better prepared than he had expected. Within seconds, the full might of the

Knights was trained on the dragons, ready to tear them from the skies. The *clack-clacking* of catapult arms being drawn back whispered up from below, and Braidon sensed the sudden hesitation in Nidryt, the faltering of the dragon's wings.

"Fly!" Braidon bellowed, pointing to their enemies. "Let the Order feel the wrath of the Red Dragons!"

The beasts roared around him and he sensed their fear evaporating, replaced with a terrible resolve to burn their enemies from the earth. They flew on, the camp rushing up at frightening rate now, until it seemed they must surely crash into the unforgiving ground.

At the last second, Nidryt spread its wings. A sharp *crack* followed as they caught the air, bringing them to a halt so suddenly Braidon was almost torn from the beast's back. He clung to its scales with all his strength, even as his eyes fell on the camp below.

With the dragons in range, the Knights were desperately seeking to ready the catapults. The *clack-clacking* was like thunder in Braidon's ears, but as the arm of the first device neared its apex, there came a *crack*—then men were falling back as the catapult disintegrated, the great arm tearing from the base and hurling shards of wood in all directions. Screams filled the dawn as the other catapults followed suit.

Now silence fell across the camp, as a terrible realisation came over the Knights, that their most deadly weapons had been rendered useless. Without them, they had no defence against the Red Dragons. With that realisation came terror, and suddenly the followers of the Order were fleeing, tripping over one another in their desperation to escape.

But penned in by their own fortifications, there was nowhere left to run, and with a roar, the Red Dragons set upon them. An inferno fell from the sky, the rage of the beasts unleashed. The wooden stockade burst into life, becoming a boiling wall of flame that none could pass. Trapped within the camp, one by one the Knights of Alana burned.

And atop the back of Nidryt, Braidon reached out as each Knight perished, and plucked the life force from their burning bodies.

"**R**uebyn!" Pela screamed as she found herself back in her body.

Gasping, she flailed about in the darkness, trying to find Ruebyn's bed. The lantern must have burnt out while she was trying to heal him. She swore as her hand struck a wall, but she followed it until she finally found Ruebyn's hand. Dragging herself up, she threw herself across him and fumbled at his shirt.

"Wha…Pela…" Ruebyn's voice was faint.

Ignoring him, Pela cried out as she found the necklace Rayan had given him. She yanked it with all her strength and felt a satisfying *clink* as the chain tore. The thing burned hot in her hand, and crying out, she tossed it to the floor then brought her boot down on it. There was a satisfying *crack* as the opal shattered.

"What…have you…done?" Ruebyn gasped.

Movement came from the bed as he tried to sit up, and she imagined him reaching for the necklace. She threw her arms around him and hugged him tight, ignoring his cries of protest. Finally she released him and sat back, switching to her spirit eye to see him in the darkness. Already his aura was returning to a steady blue. Shivering, she sent up her thanks to the Gods.

"It was killing you," she said shortly when Ruebyn tried to sit up again.

She rose and stumbled her way to the lantern. They had been left a spare, and after several minutes struggling in the darkness, she had it lit. Holding it up, she returned to Ruebyn's side. There was no time to waste now. She did not think the demon had sensed her questing about the king's memories, but they could take no chances.

"That's…insane."

Moving faster than she'd thought him capable of in his current state, Ruebyn tumbled from the bed and scrambled for the necklace. She quickly kicked the remains out of reach and moved to bar his path. Growling, he clutched at the bed and tried to haul himself to his feet.

"It's the truth!" Pela snapped, her irritation returning now that she could see he was no longer in mortal danger.

Grinding her teeth, she took him by the shoulder and pushed him back onto the bed. Though he had already regained some of his colour, his strength had not returned so quickly, and he succumbed with hardly any effort on Pela's part. Tears streaked his cheeks as he collapsed on his back and lay there panting.

"Please, Pela," he whispered. "You have to give it back. I don't want to die."

"You're not going to die," she grated. Seating herself beside him, she took his hand in hers. "I promise."

Pela wished she could make him see, that he would

understand. Almost unconsciously she reached for the flicker of her life force. Ruebyn gasped as heat rushed down her arm and into him, and his eyes lost their focus. A tremor shook his body, followed by a desperate moan. Terrified of what she'd done, Pela snatched back her arm.

A scream hissed from Ruebyn's throat until she lurched forward and slapped a hand over his mouth.

"Don't!" she gasped. "You'll wake it!"

His eyes widened and she saw the terror there. She knew then what her power had done, that it had revealed to Ruebyn the vision she'd had at the king's bedside. After a moment, he nodded, and warily, Pela released him.

"We have to get out of here," he whispered.

"Finally you're talking some sense," Pela muttered, struggling not to roll her eyes.

Her mind was already far ahead, thinking of the dawn. They would need to be a long way from the city when the sun rose, or they would never escape the demon's grasp. She swallowed, feeling again the collar's iron embrace. The Gods must have been looking over her after all, that the hateful thing already had a black opal in place. She didn't understand why, but the demon must only have a connection with its own devices, or she would have been in the same state as Ruebyn by now.

Then realisation struck her like a blow. It could not be a coincidence that the slave collars were inset with the same black opals the demon used to drain the energy from its subjects. She shivered as memories rushed before her eyes, and she found herself back on the deck of the queen's ship.

The Elders discovered long ago there was a power in death. They just lacked the creativity to use it efficiently.

"*No,*" she whispered as another piece fell into place.

"What?" Ruebyn croaked, his head whipping around to stare at her.

Queen Marianne had said that long ago in Malevolent Cove, as she'd slipped the necklaces over her and Kryssa's heads. Those had had black gems set into them as well. And on the shore of Malevolent Cove, the queen had crouched beside the body of Ikar and had spoken of death and power again. Only then had she revealed the strange magic that had held them in her thrall.

Rayan had called her collar a primitive design. Indeed, it had never made her sick as Ruebyn's necklace had. But Pela recalled now how it had warmed when she'd been close to death, as though preparing to steal the life from Pela the second her soul departed.

Shuddering, Pela stood. "Do you remember the way out?"

"Wait," Ruebyn murmured, shaking his head as though to clear a fog from his eyes. "How...how did you show me that?"

Pela stared down at Ruebyn, one eyebrow raised. "Magic."

He stared back at her for a long moment, then a grin broke across his face, and suddenly he was laughing. Climbing ponderously to his feet, he wrapped her in a bear hug.

"I'm sorry I ever doubted you," he croaked, still pale but looking a thousand times better than a few hours earlier. "You're...incredible, Pela."

Pela found herself smiling back. "Thanks, Ruebyn," she replied, her cheeks growing warm. "But I'll be even more thankful if you remember how we got here?"

The citadel was huge and she had hardly seen a fraction

of it. What she had seen, she could barely remember for all the winding back and forth they had done to get to this room. Coming from tiny Skystead, she was unused to large buildings, and she would never find her way out alone, not by dawn.

"I think so," Ruebyn replied, his face turning serious.

He made to step towards the door and his legs almost gave way. She was at his side in an instant, lending him a shoulder, though she was by no means at her best either. Her earlier efforts had left her drained and she wasn't sure how much strength she had left, how long she would last.

"We'll need food, supplies," Ruebyn rasped, "and water, or we'll never reach Plorsea. Come on, there was a kitchen attached to the dining hall."

"How will we get past the guards?" Pela hissed as they staggered for the door. They had no possessions but the clothes on their backs. At least she was free of the rags she'd worn in the mines.

"I don't know," Ruebyn whispered. "We'll think of something, somehow."

Pela wasn't convinced. "We should kill the king," she croaked, though just the words sent ice shooting through her veins.

The idea was suicide. They had seen the king's memories, the ease with which the demon had destroyed its opposition. Not a man or woman could stand against it. And yet...

"If we don't, one day it will come for us," she added.

"If it could be done, someone would have already done it," Ruebyn replied. They were staggering through the corridors now. With the late hour the halls were thankfully empty, though Pela kept glancing back, expecting someone to discover their absence at any moment. "Come on," Ruebyn continued, tugging at her arm. "We're close."

Pela fell into step beside him, though his words had not convinced her. She was thinking again of her uncle. The legends told how Devon had stood alone against the Tsar— a mortal against the all-powerful Magicker. People had said the same then, that the Tsar was immortal, that he could not be defeated. Yet still Devon had defied him, and with Alana and Braidon's help, they had cast him down.

In the kitchens they found cured sausages and cheeses, fruits and a wine skin that could be emptied and used to carry water when they were on the road. Ruebyn managed to fashion a canvas sack into a bindle that he could loop over his shoulder. He was recovering well from his sickness, though he could still move no faster than a hobble.

"Come on," he murmured when they had collected all they needed. "The gate to the city is this way."

Pela did not respond. Her eyes had fallen upon a carving knife that had been left on the steel bench. Gingerly she picked it up, watching as the razor edge glinted in the lanternlight. Clutching it to her side, she followed Ruebyn to the door and found him in the corridor outside, his eyes flicking back and forth as he searched for enemies. Watching him, she felt her heart swell, and she allowed a smile to touch her face.

"You go," she whispered. "I can't leave, not yet."

"What?" Ruebyn hissed. "You can't kill him, it's suicide!"

"I know," she replied, trying to keep the terror from her voice, "but I still have to try. It's what my uncle would have done if he were here."

"Devon had the Saviour on his side," Ruebyn croaked,

stepping forward and taking her hand in his. "Here, now, there is only the two of us against that demon."

Holding back tears, Pela nodded. "All the more reason for me to try. At least I have my power."

"Pela," Ruebyn gasped, his eyes shining, "I…I believe in you, but…whatever power you have discovered…it's no match for that thing. It has harvested thousands of lives."

"Even so."

Releasing her, Ruebyn scrunched his eyes closed. Knuckling his forehead, he turned away, and for a moment Pela thought he would do as she bid and leave. The breath caught in her throat and her heart pounded at the thought of facing the demon alone.

"Okay, Pela," he whispered, turning again to face her. "Lead the way."

She stood staring at him for a long moment, hardly daring to believe she'd heard him right. Then she spun on her heel and set off down the corridor. Silence clung to the citadel as they made their way through the night, following as best they could the path Pela had taken in her spirit state. Thankfully, the king's apartments had not been far, and whenever Pela was unsure of the way, she had only to open her inner eye to see the threads hanging in the air.

Finally they stood before a door, the way barred to them. There had been no guards as they walked the citadel, and Pela now knew why. Nothing could threaten the demon, with an entire nation in its thrall. Nothing, until now.

The door swung open with a push—it had not even been locked—and they advanced into the king's chambers. Pela held the carving knife clenched tightly at her side. Ruebyn had claimed a knife of his own, though he still had the bag of supplies looped over his shoulder. A lantern had been left partly shuttered in the corner, casting a sliver of light that illuminated a sofa and meeting table. They slipped through the shadows, searching for danger, but there was no sign of the demon.

Breathing a sigh of relief, Pela crossed the room to where a second door led to the king's private chambers. Her mind was fixed on what waited beyond, on what must be done. Reaching out, she placed a hand on the panelled wood, readying herself.

"I would not do that, were I you."

Pela's heart almost leapt from her skin as a voice spoke from behind them. Stifling a cry, she spun and raised the carving knife. But no attack came, and staring into the darkness, she found a man standing in the doorway to the corridor. It was Rayan.

There was sadness in his eyes as he looked at them. "You cannot kill it."

A lump lodged in Pela's throat as she struggled to reply. Ruebyn found his voice first. "You know what it is?"

"How could I not?" Rayan whispered. "The day my father changed…but I could not let him go, could not believe what he had become. I looked for a way to save him, but I waited too long, and then…" He made a gesture, as though the creature beyond the door needed no explanation. "The creature was starving. It took to the land, and wherever it walked, death followed. There were some who believed the story, that it was a plague, but I knew the truth. With every life the demon stole, its power grew, until all of us were faced with a choice. Submit, or perish."

"Then why are you here?" Pela gasped finally, unable to believe Rayan would willingly help such a monster.

The king's son bowed his head. "I will not let you suffer the same fate as my people," he whispered. "I came to your room to remove the necklace and help you escape, but you were not there." He looked up then, his emerald eyes glinting in the darkness. "My father spoke of Devon often. I knew there was only one thing his niece could do, should she discover the truth."

Pela swallowed, her heart swelling at his praise. Shuddering, she took a firmer hold of the knife. "We have to stop it."

"You cannot," Rayan repeated. "The second you open that door, the demon will wake and destroy you."

Pela froze. Her hand was already halfway to the knob. A tremor shook her as she stared at the copper handle, and somewhere within a voice screamed for her to grasp it, to try anyway, though it would surely cost her life. Then she saw again the eyes of the demon, the dark depths that would tear her soul from her body and cast it into the void, and with a shudder she turned away.

"What can we do?" she croaked to Rayan.

The muscles in his jaw tightened. "Live," he whispered. "Bring word to your nations of what happened here. Maybe this King Braidon or Queen Marianne of yours can find a way to defeat him."

"They are already paving the way for his victory," Pela replied, gesturing to her collar. "The queen created these to channel the life forces of her slaves from all across Lonia."

A frown passed across Rayan's face. "Truly?" But shaking his head, he pressed on. "All the more reason for you to return, to warn them of their folly."

"Will you help us?" Ruebyn whispered.

Rayan's eyes drifted to the king's door, as though he feared even now the demon would burst forth and destroy them all. But lips tight, he nodded. "I will," he said grimly, turning and gesturing towards the corridor. "Come, I know a secret passage through the walls. I will show you."

He disappeared into the corridor. Ruebyn followed, Pela just a step behind. Only in the doorway did she hesitate. Glancing back at the darkened room, she wondered whether they were making the right decision. But there was no more time for second guesses, and swallowing her doubt, she followed the others out into the corridors of the citadel.

❧ 18 ❧

"**G**uard up!" Kryssa shouted a second before she leapt, and watched with displeasure as the recruit clumsily raised the wooden practice sword above his head.

For a second she was tempted to take her frustrations out on the young man, to deliver a beating he would not soon forget and hope it hammered in the lesson. But the morale of Braidon's makeshift army was already low enough. Kryssa had told the populace that the king was enlisting the Red Dragons to their cause, but that had been two days ago now. With their scouts placing Marianne's army at little more than a day's march from the city, many were openly suggesting surrender.

So as she faced the recruit, Kryssa forced her practice blade to slow, and only tapped him lightly on the wrist.

"There goes your arm," she said, then stepped back and turned to the other recruits who had gathered in a circle around them.

Irritation touched her as she saw the doubt in their eyes, the fear that they had been abandoned. What had Braidon been thinking, leaving on the back of a Red Dragon? And why had he not told her of his plans? Yet again she had been left behind, blindsided, forced into a corner by the king's reckless actions.

"Drop your guard on the battlefield, and you're dead," Kryssa announced. "Since none of you seem able to remember that, we will return to the shield drills. Partner up with one shield and sword between you. Take turns with each, drills three and six."

Eager to avoid being partnered with her, the recruits rushed to obey, grabbing practice blades and shields from the piles of equipment. Kryssa claimed a shield of her own as she watched the men and women retreating into two lines. Taking her place in the centre, she gestured to the young man she had beaten earlier. He held only a shield now, and his eyes were on the ground. His defeat had left him shamed, and now he needed to regain his confidence.

Lifting her sword, Kryssa saluted him. "Defend yourself!"

His eyes widened as she leapt. The time for patience was over and she attacked quickly this time, her wooden stave flashing for his face. Instinctively, he raised the shield, catching her blow on the steel rim.

"Better," Kryssa said, stepping back.

The man's mouth hung open, as though he could hardly believe he'd blocked the attack. Polite clapping came from the other recruits and Kryssa suppressed a sigh. He might have deflected her blow, but he had overcompensated with the shield, lifting it so high his stomach had been left exposed. Had it been a real battle...

"What are you all standing there for?" she bellowed. "I said drills three and six!"

Flinching at the volume of her voice, the recruits leapt

to obey and the rattle of swords on shields followed. Leaving her partner to pair up with another recruit, Kryssa marched up and down the line.

'Drills' were perhaps too strong of a word to describe the exercises she had assigned. With only a few weeks to prepare, the sergeants had only taught the recruits the most basic of blocks and strikes. The first she had assigned was a simple stab to the chest by the attacker, countered by a thrust of the defender's shield, the second a high strike and block combination.

Striding through the ranks of men and women, she corrected several pairs on their stances and technique, then gestured for her sergeants. Marching forward, they snapped her a quick salute and then looked to the recruits.

"Take them through the drills for another hour," Kryssa commanded. "Then break for lunch. If a battle is coming, I want them fresh."

"Yes, sir!" the sergeants bellowed and then spread out amongst the lines of recruits.

Kryssa watched them for a while longer, a weight settling in her stomach. Marianne had joined with the Lonians, as expected, and now marched with a force of almost seven thousand. She outnumbered Braidon's fledgling army seven to one. Even with the walls of Chole, those were impossible odds. And if the king did not return soon to lead them…

With an effort of will, Kryssa forced the worry from her mind. Braidon would return—he had to. It was his duty, his destiny. Yet even as she thought it, Kryssa recalled their conversation on the plains of Chole, how he had talked of leaving it all behind.

No, he wouldn't…

Kryssa was lost. It seemed there would be no choice but

to surrender when Marianne came…but what would that mean for Plorsea's future? The queen had already shown her true colours in Malevolent Cove, when she'd coldly attempted to sacrifice Kryssa and Pela to her precious Saviour. Kryssa couldn't just step aside and let the woman enforce her twisted religion on the rest of the nation.

Yet if Kryssa stood against the woman, she would be dooming herself and everyone in Chole. Maybe if there was some slim possibility of victory…but Kryssa had been a soldier most of her adult life. She knew a lost cause when she saw one. Not even her father and all his heroics could have turned the odds in their favour.

Turning her eyes upward, Kryssa wondered again at Braidon's fate. Had the Red Dragon come in peace, or to seek revenge for the king's broken promises? The sky was clear overhead, the blue heavens stretching all the way to the distant volcanic peaks.

A frown touched Kryssa's brow as she glimpsed movement above the mountains. Squinting, she made out several specks on the horizon. Unsure of what she was seeing, Kryssa watched as they flickered in the light of the sun, waiting. Her heart started to race as they grew larger, swelling as they approached, becoming scarlet blobs drifting between the snow-capped peaks.

Dragons.

A cold sweat dripped down Kryssa's back as the sounds of clashing weapons fell away, others now noticing the coming creatures. Whispers spread through the recruits, of fear, of excitement. They knew the king had gone with the beasts, but in a thousand years of history, the Red Dragons had always been the enemy of man.

They might still be, for all Kryssa knew. After all, the beasts had promised to wage war on humanity should

Braidon fail them. Had that time finally come? Had the beasts grown tired of the king's excuses and murdered him? Did they now come to burn his cities to the ground?

Kryssa knew what needed to be done. She needed to take command, to order her soldiers to the walls, to arm the catapults, to protect the city. Yet all she could do was watch as the dragons approached, frozen by her memories from Dragon Country. This was an enemy she could not fight, no matter how skilled she might be with a blade. The tiny flame of her life force might offer some resistance, but against a Red Dragon…what was she but an insect to such a beast?

Minutes raced by as the dragons swept on towards the helpless city. As they neared, the blobs resolved themselves into individual creatures. There were five in all, a terrifying, unstoppable force of nature. Mount Chole might as well have erupted again, for all Kryssa could do to save the city and its people.

Finally the beasts were directly overhead, over the Castle. Their broad wings cast the courtyard in shade, sending fear rippling through the gathered recruits. A hundred eyes turned to Kryssa, looking for guidance, but she could do nothing as a single creature spiralled down.

A mighty *thump* came from the ramparts as the dragon landed atop the walls. Shuddering, Kryssa forced herself to face the creature. A wave of exhaustion swept through her as she found the beast's eyes on her. She had worked so hard these past days to prepare Braidon's recruits, but now none of it would matter. In an instant, she would be gone, and all her aspirations with her. Kryssa almost felt relieved, that she might finally rest.

"My people!"

Kryssa started as a voice called down from the ramparts.

A figure leapt from the dragon's back, one arm raised high in greeting. Braidon's sapphire eyes swept over the courtyard as he spoke: "I have returned with new allies!"

There was a moment's silence—then a ragged cheer rose from the recruits as they thrust their blades skywards. Their cries rang from the walls, becoming a roar of triumph, of renewed hope for the cause they had sworn their lives to. Wearing a satisfied grin, Braidon moved to the edge of the crenulations and raised his arms, basking in the love of his people.

Yet looking up at the king, Kryssa could not find the same joy, the same cause for celebration. All she could think of was how Braidon had abandoned her. He had expected her to be here, to make up for his absence, yet he had not even warned her of his mad quest.

"The dark queen comes to take our freedom!" Braidon was saying, but Kryssa was no longer listening.

Feeling sick, she turned away, even as the dragon threw back its head and unleashed a roar. Heat washed over the courtyard and Kryssa saw the flames flickering in the corner of her eye. The recruits screamed their enthusiasm, but Kryssa felt nothing but a dull emptiness as she moved through their ranks.

The king might have returned with fresh hope for their cause, but once again he had betrayed her. While she had suffered here alone, worrying and wondering, Braidon had been off on his own quest, plotting his own victory.

The cries of the crowd faded as Kryssa left the court-yard. The darkness of the Castle engulfed her and she smelt again the acrid tang of smoke, the constant reminder of her failure. She went quickly through the corridors, finally emerging before the gates to the city. The guards saluted as she strode past, well used to her comings and goings—

though this time she had no plan, no destination, only the sense she must get away.

Mindlessly, she wandered through the twisting alleyways of Chole, her thoughts drifting to other times, other places. She thought she'd left this all behind long ago, when she'd first quit the King's Guard and retired to Skystead. Tired of war and death, she and Derryn had been ready to begin life anew.

Yet now Kryssa had somehow found herself in the centre of a new war. Once she had railed against her father for returning again and again to battle, but now Kryssa realised she was little better. She had been all too quick to encourage Braidon to take up the fight against Marianne, to retake his crown. And all the while, Kryssa's own daughter had been missing, lost in the darkness of Malevolent Cove. She should have left in search of Pela long ago, rather than staying to fight for the ungrateful king.

And now it was too late.

Kryssa didn't known where she was heading until she turned a corner and found the triple spires rising from the street ahead. Realising her feet had unwittingly led her to the Temple of the Earth, she crossed the road and strode up the long marble staircase to the entrance. There she was met by several men and women in the long emerald robes of priests.

"Daughter of the Earth," they greeted her. "How might we help you?"

"My mind is clouded," Kryssa said truthfully. "I've come to meditate."

"Then welcome," came the reply.

A sense of peace fell over Kryssa as she entered and breathed in the earthen incense they burned to honour Antonia, Goddess of the Earth. Candles flickered in the entrance hall, guiding her through marble columns to the inner sanctum. Here, she carefully removed her boots and put them aside, before following the priests across the velvet carpets to the altar.

She had spent a day here while Braidon lay unconscious after his battle on the steps outside, but had not been back since. There had been too much to do, too many fears and threats, to take the time for herself.

The temple was almost empty, and Kryssa knelt in silence, thinking how wrong it felt to be practicing her worship so openly. Even in Skystead, her belief had been a hidden thing, not forbidden, but something people preferred not to think about. But then, that was the people of Skystead with most things—kind, but hard, welcoming, but closed off.

In Chole though, all forms of worship had been celebrated openly—at least until the Knights of Alana had ridden into the city two weeks ago, threatening to burn down the temple. If Braidon had not intervened, they would have succeeded.

Shivering at the reminder, Kryssa closed her eyes and began the gentle *in-out* of breath that she had learned from her mother, Selina. Meditation had been an escape for Kryssa as a child, a way to rise above the nightmares when they'd come, to free herself of the fear that sometimes still plagued her even now. She had begun her life on the streets, and if not for Selina, she might have lost it there as well. She still thanked the Three Gods every night for the old woman's kindness.

She missed them both more than ever now, Selina and Devon, her adopted parents. At least with her mother she'd had more time. They'd known the end was coming for a long time. With Devon though…Kryssa had hardly spoken to him in years, not since he'd left for war with her husband, and returned only with his body.

But Devon had never stopped being her father, not even from afar. She had not been surprised when he'd come to rescue her—but his death had shocked Kryssa to her core. As a child, she'd been terrified of the giant hammerman. From the start, he'd made it clear she was not part of his plans, that she was not his daughter. But as she'd grown and had shown her affinity with the blade, Devon had finally warmed to her, had even taken her under his wing as a warrior.

The day she'd been named amongst the ranks of the King's Guard, she'd seen the pride in his eyes, felt the love in his hug, even if he had never spoken the words.

Tears stung Kryssa's eyes. They flickered open and she looked to the panelled ceiling.

"You are distracted, my daughter," a priest murmured from nearby.

Kryssa shuddered as a sob tore from her throat. "I don't know what I'm doing anymore," she said, sitting up and angrily rubbing away the tears. "I thought helping Braidon was the only way to get my family back, but I'm no closer to finding my daughter than I was when we started."

"And now we stand on the brink of a new war," the priest added sadly. He seated himself across from her and crossed his legs. "You were with the king, when he came and stood against the Knights who would have destroyed our temple."

Nodding, Kryssa swallowed the lump that had lodged in her throat. A sad smile crossed the man's face.

"A dark day for my Order," he said. "To see so many led astray from the path of the Goddess."

"What?" Kryssa asked with a frown.

"The death of the Knight was regretful, but he came here with hate in his heart. It was a noble act, for the king to stand against him." The priest drew in a breath. "Less so, when he led a mob against the Castle."

"They were sheltering the Knights who attacked you."

"Ay, and many more innocents." His eyes bored into Kryssa's, as though daring her to refute his words. "Now they are dead, their power given over to your king."

Kryssa shivered. "That was an accident."

"It was inevitable from the moment the king broke down the gates of the Castle."

Frowning, Kryssa was about to respond when she realised the significance of his earlier words. "Wait," she gasped, her head jerking up. "How did you know what the king did in the pantheon?"

The priest's eyes fell to the floor. "We have always known of the potential within each of us—and the risk for its abuse."

"He did not kill them," Kryssa insisted. "I was with him. It was his followers…"

"And it was Braidon who led them there, who fed the anger in their hearts, when we would have preached forgiveness. Why do you think *we* did not strike against the Knights when they came for us?"

"What do you mean?"

"We were not helpless." As the priest spoke, he lifted a hand and turned it palm up. A flame leapt to life, dancing across his flesh until he closed his fist, snuffing it out once more. "We could have done as Braidon did, could have struck down those men in their steel armour. But their deaths would only have stoked the Order's hatred—then more would have come seeking blood. Peace would be impossible."

"You would have died rather than defend yourselves?"

A smile touched the priest's lips. "Evil must be opposed wherever it is found, my daughter. But it does not always take a sharp blade or magic to stand against the darkness. Sometimes mercy is all it takes to change a man's heart."

As he finished, footsteps came from behind Kryssa. Suddenly fearing deception, she spun and reached for her sword, but there was only a young woman standing nearby. Kryssa's heart lurched as she recognised the assassin she had spared. Her amber eyes were wide with terror, but she made no move to flee as Kryssa drew her blade.

"So Janylle spoke the truth," Kryssa croaked, her legs trembling as she faced the priest. "The temple *was* behind the assassination attempt of Braidon."

"No," the priest whispered as he came slowly to his feet. "We only offered the girl shelter and forgiveness, after her anger led her astray."

"Why should I believe you?" Kryssa snapped.

"Have we not kept Braidon's secret?" the priest murmured. "Are the streets buzzing with word of Janylle's death by the king's hand? Or of the mercy you showed his would-be-assassin?"

The anger drained from Kryssa in a rush. She swallowed. "I betrayed him, letting her go," she said, her eyes fixed to the ground.

"She is naught but a child," the priest replied. "Surely it is no crime for the king's lieutenant to spare such an innocent."

The sword shook in Kryssa's hand. Maybe the king did know of her betrayal. Was *that* why he had not told her about the dragons? Why else would he have left so precipitously, without a single word of warning?

"I trust this secret will not leave these walls," Kryssa said finally.

The priest nodded. "The girl will remain in our protection until the war has ended."

"Very well," Kryssa said, turning away.

Looking around the temple, she thought about returning to her meditation, but it was an impossible task now. She was too distracted, too fractured, to centre herself. A sigh slipped from her lips and she was about to sheathe her sword when the doors at the back of the hall banged open.

She swung around as two men raced into the temple, both armed with short swords and shields. She recognised them as two of the recruits she'd been training that morning. Sliding her sword back into its sheath, she strode across the hall to greet them before their boots tramped dirt into the fine carpets.

"Lieutenant Kryssa!" one gasped as she strode up. "The king sent us to find you."

"And so you have," Kryssa said, inclining her head. "What does Braidon require of me?"

"It's the queen!" the second recruit burst out before the other could answer. "Her army is at the gates!"

19

Braidon stared across the packed earth at Marianne. He could barely believe she was actually there, standing boldly outside the gates of his city as though she were there under invitation. So many months had passed now since Malevolent Cove, since her betrayal, that she had almost become a caricature in his mind, a dark and demonic woman who sought only to destroy everything he had ever built.

Now though, he was forced to face the reality his hatred had allowed him to forget—that she was still the woman he had loved for the better part of a decade, who had lain beside him for nights uncounted, who had listened to his private fears, who had born him a son. For half a moment, Braidon found himself wondering whether they might turn back the clock, if he could restore their lives, if they could be together once more.

Then an image flickered into his mind—of Marianne towering over him in Malevolent Cove, of the hatred that had twisted her face, and all his hope withered away. Marianne had never loved him. All that time the woman had claimed to be his queen, she had been scheming behind his back. It had been *her* plan to invite the Knights of Alana into his nation, her reign that had seen the streets of his capital run thick with the blood of innocents.

No, there could be no turning back for either of them now, no redemption. The past as he remembered it, the love and shared companionship, it had never been anything more than a construct, an act to manipulate him.

Grinding his teeth, Braidon flicked his gaze to the man standing alongside his wife, and now he could not keep the rage from his face. Caledan stood there, one hand resting on the hilt of his sword. The sellsword wore a casual smile, as though he were exactly where he belonged.

They had come together in neutral territory midway between the city gates and the grounds upon which Marianne's army was setting camp. Both had a dozen soldiers at their back and a champion at their side. With Caledan standing beside Marianne, Braidon had been relieved when Kryssa joined him in time for the meeting.

Although Braidon was still surprised he'd received the call for a truce at all. Marianne's forces greatly outnumbered his own. Word of the Red Dragons must have reached her, or…perhaps she now sensed the power reverberating in Braidon's core, and feared it.

The thought put a smile on his face, though it faded when a quick check of the queen's aura revealed that she too had been busy collecting lives.

"So, here we all are," Marianne said finally, opening her hands in a gesture of peace. "I am glad you agreed to see me, Braidon. It is my hope that we can settle our…disagreement without bloodshed."

Braidon gaped at his wife, stunned by her words. She

had tried to kill him twice already, had stolen his son, slaughtered his King's Guard. Now she spoke of avoiding bloodshed, of peace. If he hadn't already suspected some trap before, he was certain of it now.

Rage touched Braidon as he realised she thought him a fool, that he would fall for her sweet words. She still wore that smug grin, as though she alone ruled the world, and everyone else on the field were beneath her. He fought an overwhelming desire to reach out and throttle her, to wipe the grin from her face. Let the sham continue; eventually Marianne would show her true colours, would betray herself. Then the whole world would see her for the monster she truly was.

"So, this is how you repay Devon's loyalty, sellsword?" Braidon spoke finally, ignoring his wife. "I thought you were his friend, yet now you stand beside his murderer."

"Devon *was* my friend."

Braidon laughed. "Then I am glad you do not count me amongst your friends."

Caledan stared back, his brown eyes cold as ice. "I stand with the side I believe in," he growled. "You have failed Plorsea one time too many, Braidon. It is time for you to step aside."

"I am the rightful king," Braidon snapped, "and when your queen lies dead at my feet, I will—"

"*Enough!*" Marianne snarled, speaking over him.

She took a step forward, and from behind Braidon came the rattling of steel as his soldiers reached for their blades. Braidon raised a hand, bidding them to wait.

"You should be thanking Caledan," Marianne continued, her voice returning to a calm tone. "His council is the only reason I am not already knocking down your gates."

Braidon sneered. "You think you could take Chole so easily?" he asked. "Not even Archon could breach its walls."

"You have less than a thousand soldiers, husband," Marianne said. "Not even enough to man the walls of which you boast so loudly." She took another step forward. "But let us not quarrel over the trivial. I have come to talk of peace."

"Peace?" The word slipped from Braidon before he could stop himself. "You want to talk about peace?"

When Marianne only nodded, Braidon started to laugh. "Very well then, my beloved!" he gasped. "What are the terms of your surrender?"

Marianne clasped her hands behind her back, her smile unchanged. "I see your failures these last few months have not dented your arrogance, husband," she murmured. "The only surrender which interests me is yours."

"Ha!" Braidon cried. "And what would your terms be? Last I knew, you wanted to watch me bleed to death on the shores of Malevolent Cove." He shook his head. "No, I will not be surrendering to the likes of you, Marianne. You say you care about peace? Well it was you who broke it in the first place. If you wish to repair the damage you have wrought, kneel before me and I might consider sparing your life."

"I did what I had to for my freedom!" Marianne snarled. The smile finally slipped from her lips as rage twisted her face. "I wouldn't expect you to understand. I'm sure you would have been happy to have me in your bed until I withered away to nothing."

"I wouldn't touch your corruption with a ten-foot pole," Braidon shot back.

"Ah, so finally you know how I felt all those years, forced to lie in the arms of a vile old man," Marianne spat. Then she took a breath, and when she looked at Braidon again, the mask of calm had been restored. "You know, everyone else who had a hand in our marriage is dead now. My father, the Lonian senators, the Elders. Only *you* have not suffered, my dear husband."

"You think I have not suffered?" Braidon asked, his voice dropping to a whisper. "After being betrayed by the woman I loved? After you stabbed me in the heart, murdered my friends, and turned my people against me? No, it is *you* who have not suffered for your evil. But then, I would not expect you to see that, Marianne. You care only for yourself."

Silence fell across the plains as Marianne stared at him. She said nothing, but there was a distant look to her eyes, as though she were weighing the truth of his words. Finally though, she shook her head.

"That is not true," she replied, then gestured with a hand.

The soldiers behind her parted and Braidon tensed, preparing for treachery. Instead, he stood frozen in place as a woman appeared through the ranks of Marianne's followers. A gasp came from beside him, then in a blur of movement, Kryssa threw herself forward.

"Gen!" she cried.

Braidon watched in disbelief as Kryssa and Genevieve came together. Clasping desperately at one another, they kissed. He hadn't seen Genevieve since the disaster in Malevolent Cove, though he'd sent out messages asking after her and Pela when he'd won Chole. In truth, he'd thought them both long dead. It beggared belief to see the huntress here now.

Finally the two broke off their kiss, but they did not

separate, only pressed their foreheads together, eyes closed as their tears flowed freely.

"You see?" Marianne said quietly, drawing Braidon's attention back to the queen.

His heart raced as he realised he'd been distracted. With Kryssa's attention elsewhere, Marianne might have struck at him, overwhelming his defences and destroying him before he knew what was happening. But she had not moved from where she stood, only looked at him with sadness in her eyes.

"The Elder Servo had her," Marianne continued, "when we met on the River Jurrien. He had been using power to manipulate the Lonian army, but Caledan destroyed him. Genevieve was amongst his prisoners. She was on the verge of death, but I saved her, at great cost to my own power."

"Why should we believe you?" Braidon hissed.

"It's true," Genevieve interrupted. Breaking away from Kryssa, she stepped between the two monarchs. "It was Servo who was intent on eradicating the followers of the Three Gods."

"Ay, the entire Order is corrupt," Braidon snapped. "Whether they are led by Servo or Marianne, there is no changing that. If she killed the Elder, I have no doubt it was only because he stood in her way."

"Perhaps that is true," Genevieve frowned, glancing at the queen. "I only know that she freed and healed me. But...I want to believe she is telling the truth when she claims to want peace."

"It's true, Braidon," Marianne said. "I do not want war. I only want what's best for my people, to finally bring peace and prosperity to this land." Then her face hardened. "And for you to pay for what you did to me."

"Me?" Braidon growled.

He clenched his fists and the energies within him went crackling to his fingertips. For a second he was tempted to launch an attack, to destroy Marianne before she could defend herself. But he swallowed back the urge and lashed out with his tongue instead.

"What of your crimes, dear wife? It was not by my command that Knights were allowed free rein in our lands, not my rule that saw innocents stolen from their families and sacrificed in the name of the Saviour." He shook his head. "No, if that if your idea of peace, I want no part of it. So bring your foreign army and your Knights; they will break on the walls of Chole, as every invader since the Great Wars has done."

A ragged cheer came from the recruits behind him, but Braidon did not glance back. His eyes were fixed on Marianne, sensing the anger radiating from her, a mirror of his own. Any second now she would lash out, would try to strike him down, but this time he would be ready for her. When the attack came…

"Very well, dear husband," Marianne said, a sigh whispering from her lips. He was surprised to hear sadness in her voice. "You will have your war. But when the prairies are stained with the blood of our people, do not forget: it was you who asked for this."

"I will fight until my dying breath to protect my people," Braidon hissed.

"Ay, and they will bleed for it," Marianne said sadly. She turned to go, then hesitated, her sapphire eyes lingering on Genevieve. "You may stay, Genevieve," she said at last. "As I told you, you are not a prisoner. Enjoy your lover's embrace while you can. Tomorrow, we will be at the gates."

20

Pela let out a long breath as they emerged from a side door into the gardens of the citadel. Moonlight bathed the world, casting everything in black and white, and she paused to stare at the scene, remembering the vibrant colours of the flowers, hidden now by darkness.

Shuddering, she shook off her dread and followed Ruebyn down the steps. Rayan was just ahead, moving down a narrow path between the rosebushes. Their scent touched Pela's nostrils as she stepped onto the path, but now they seemed overly sweet, setting her stomach to roiling.

Pela moved quickly between the rows of bushes. The beauty of the garden had been nothing more than a thin veneer, an act to conceal the true corruption at Trola's core. The demon's greed, its hatred, had infected everything.

How could they stop such a monster? An awful sorrow gripped Pela as she hurried after the others, a sickly sense of despair. The Gods had truly abandoned them if such evil could take root in the land. They were all alone now, each and every one of them, their lives but candles before the vastness of the world. And the demon was the storm that would snuff them all out.

Ahead, Rayan left the path and cut across the lawns towards the outer walls of the citadel. Following him across the uneven grounds, Pela stumbled against something. She paused to check what had tripped her in the otherwise perfectly manicured lawn. A block of slate the size of a small table lay in the grass, smooth and unadorned, though amidst the grey, tiny specks of crystal shone in the moonlight.

She remembered then what Ruebyn had said, about how the Sword of Light had once been kept in these gardens, before Alastair and King Thomas had passed through The Way and claimed its power. Tears sprang to her eyes as she thought of those ancient heroes. How easy it must have been in those days, knowing the Three Gods were on their side.

Now Pela stood in the very spot those ancient powers had once gathered, alone and defeated, fleeing the dark creature that had taken residence at the heart of Trola. But what else could she do? What was her fleeting power against such darkness?

Her shoulders heavy, Pela crossed the lawn to where Ruebyn and Rayan waited in the shadow of the wall. The king's son gave her a quick glance before pressing a small stone in the wall with his thumb. Then he put his shoulder to a larger block and heaved.

To Pela's surprise, the stone swung easily inwards, revealing a hollow. Rayan continued pushing until the entire opening was unearthed before stepping back. The block had been the size of a small person, though the space revealed was low to the ground. They would have to crawl to enter.

Then Rayan cursed. "Did either of you bring a lantern?"

"We left it behind," Ruebyn whispered.

Pela swallowed, looking from the tunnel to the sky. The eastern horizon was just beginning to brighten. There was no time left.

"What is inside?" she whispered. "Maybe we can manage in the dark."

Rayan looked uncertainly at the tunnel. "After a few feet, you can stand," he said. "From there, you follow the wall to the right. Eventually you will come to a turn that leads down a series of steps, into a tunnel ends in an abandoned building."

"We'll be blind," Ruebyn croaked. His strength was fading fast. He looked almost as bad as he had at dinner.

"We'll manage," Pela replied.

"I must leave you here," Rayan said, looking gaunt now. "I will try to delay your discovery as long as possible, but…"

He trailed off. Pela knew what he meant, though. Their newfound friend could do little against the demon. Silently she nodded her thanks, and without anything else to say, she dropped to her hands and knees and started into the darkness. The knife she had taken from the kitchen she tucked into her waistband, though it would do little good against those that would come after them. Shuffling came from behind her as Ruebyn followed, and then a grinding noise echoed in the dark as Rayan sealed the door behind them.

Pela suppressed a scream as the faint light from outside vanished and the darkness swallowed them up. For a moment, all she could do was kneel there in terror. The black was so absolute it was like a physical thing, so thick Pela felt she could hardly breathe. Suddenly she was back in the mines, the collar cold around her throat, the weight of a mountain pressing down from above. A moan built in her chest as she sucked in a lungful of air.

"Pela?" Ruebyn's voice came from behind her. A second later his hand touched her leg. "Are you okay?"

No!

Pela wanted to scream, to thrash and scramble back to the light, but they were trapped now in the dark, just as she had been in the mines. She had escaped her servitude, had vowed she would never go back, but now…

"Just breathe," Ruebyn whispered. "What was that exercise your mother taught you? Meditation?"

"Yes," she managed to croak.

"In, out, right?" he said, and she could almost see him smiling.

Despite herself, Pela laughed. "Well, when you put it like that."

She closed her eyes all the same, focusing on her breathing, allowing everything else to fade away. She sank into the darkness of her mind, but this was a familiar darkness, a part of her, and slowly she began to relax. Her life force flickered into her mind's eye, and she let out a sigh, reassured by its presence.

Edging forward, Pela felt above her head and found she could stand. Carefully, she pulled herself to her feet and then reached down to help Ruebyn to do the same.

"By the Saviour, I wish we could see *something*," he muttered. She heard his boots scuffing on stone as he shifted on his feet.

"Reminds me far too much of where we first met," Pela agreed.

Working by instinct, she closed her eyes and reached within for her life force. Then she held her hand out before her, imagining the energies gathering in her palm, and a tiny flame flickered into life. She grinned as a glow appeared against her eyelids, but before she could open her eyes, Ruebyn's scream thundered in the tunnel.

Panicking, Pela stumbled backwards and reached for her knife. Before she could draw it, a hand jabbed at her back. She spun, expecting to see Ruebyn, but he was standing across from her, his face a mask of horror. His hand lifted to point across her shoulder.

Pela cried out as she saw their assailant. He stared back at her, eyes wide, his face a mask that mirrored her own terror. Leaping back, she placed the knife between them, expecting him to give chase.

But he did nothing, only stood fixed in place, almost statue-like for his stillness. The blood pounded in Pela's ears as more figures took shape beyond the man. Dozens— no, hundreds—of men and women hid in the hollow beneath the wall, their faces showing looks of rage and terror.

Pela retreated another step, gesturing for Ruebyn to follow her, but he did not move. His eyes were on the watchers, his face so pale he could have been a ghost.

A shiver ran down Pela's spine as she faced the man who had attacked her. He had not moved an inch, had not even changed expression. It was as though…

Breath held, Pela took a trembling step forward, then another. The light grew in her hand, illuminating the glassy sheen in the man's eyes, the wax-like tone of his skin. Pela's scalp crawled as her eyes darted from face to face, but not one of them moved.

A scream built in Pela's throat as she realised what she was seeing—mummified corpses, frozen in their final moments by some spell and hidden here. This could only be the demon's work. Pela slapped a hand over her mouth to silence her scream and looked at Ruebyn. Why had Rayan brought them here?

Laughter echoed through the cavern as movement came from amongst the corpses. For a moment she thought they had returned to life, but then footsteps echoed loudly in the narrow passage, and a figure emerged from the shadows.

"Welcome to the hall of the damned," Rayan said quietly.

"What?" Pela whispered. She stared at the man, though as he approached she found herself retreating, until Ruebyn brought her up short. "What are you doing here?"

"*My* hall of the damned, should I say," Rayan said with a laugh.

"No," Pela hissed as realisation struck her. She shook her head. "No, that's not possible. It was the king, I saw!"

Rayan only smiled. "Anything is possible, with power." He waved a hand, and a single golden thread appeared, winding its way into the amulet that hung about his chest. "A simple deception, though only necessary in my early days, when I was still weak and feared discovery. Long since redundant—or so I had thought."

Pela stood frozen in place as Rayan approached, clinging to Ruebyn as though her life depended on it. She could feel him shaking, could see the terror in his eyes as he watched the creature come for them. Fear gripped Pela's mind, robbing her of reason, even as she tried to find a way out.

"What did you do to Betran?" Ruebyn's voice rang suddenly from the walls, thin and trembling, but it cut through Pela's fear like a dagger, bringing her back to the present.

Rayan waved a hand. "My father, like most of my vassals, has come to believe his own lies. To them, the *morbus* is real, a dark shadow hanging over our lands." His smile grew and Pela watched as the colour seeped from his eyes, turning them to the deepest black. "But then, my power does not allow them to think otherwise."

"Why did you bring us here?" Pela rasped. Drawing on every ounce of her courage, she stood hand in hand with Ruebyn against the monster.

"Your collar, of course," Rayan replied. "When I saw it through my soldier's eyes, I feared the rise of a rival in the east." He laughed. "But it seems your queen is still far beneath me. When I come, she will bow to my power, or perish like all the rest."

Pela's entire body was trembling now. Ruebyn must have felt it, for he hugged her tight. She shivered at his embrace, and for a second almost felt better.

"Everything's going to be alright, Pela," he whispered before pulling away.

"How?" she gasped, staring up at him.

"Because I believe in you." He smiled. "You'll find a way."

"I'm afraid your friend is overly optimistic," Rayan interrupted. He spread his arms, as though to encompass the rows of mummified corpses. "Or do you not yet understand the reason for my collection?"

A shudder passed through Pela as she looked at the host standing behind Rayan. "They're still alive…" The words left her mouth before she knew what she was saying.

The creature's laughter rose to a fever pitch. "They are my crowning achievement," Rayan whispered. "The strongest of those who opposed me, frozen forever by my magic, for me to feast upon whenever the hunger takes me."

As Rayan walked, he drove his boot down on the foot of one of his collection. Pela's stomach tied itself into knots as a distant scream rasped from the desiccated body, a dry, far away thing that spoke of untold horror. Her every hair stood on end as they stumbled back.

"No, no, no," Pela whispered, her tone rising to a scream. She gripped Ruebyn's hand tight enough to break bones.

The demon continued towards them, a dull light seeping from its fingers. "The people of this sweet nation no longer prosper." The voice was Rayan's, but it was darker now, cold like steel. "The light in their souls is a dull, dwindling thing. I have not tasted lives as sweet as yours in decades. Such a delight cannot be wasted." A smile morphed his face into something awful. "It must be savoured."

Rayan made a gesture, and a sharp *shriek* came from Pela's collar. She cried out, thinking it would snap closed around her throat, but instead it cracked apart and crashed to the ground with a heavy *thunk*.

"Now you are *mine*," the creature cackled, throwing out its arms.

"Pela!" Ruebyn cried as a wave of darkness swirled towards them. "Use your power!"

"How?" she screamed back, clutching at him.

There was nothing she could do, not against Rayan, but at Ruebyn's cry she reached for her life force all the same. She could have sobbed as the light appeared, little more than a drop before the ocean of darkness that rushed for them. She had wasted so much this night, and now she stood on the brink of exhaustion. One push was all it would take to drain the last of her strength, to hurl her into the void.

"Find The Way!" Ruebyn was screaming nonsense in her ears now, his voice barely audible above the pounding in her ears, the cries of the demon. "You can open it, I believe in you!"

But there was no way out of this. There was no escape for them, not unless some miracle of the Gods blessed them…

The Way!

Her heart lurched as she realised the meaning in Ruebyn's words, that they stood at the entrance to the fabled gateway from Kalgan to Plorsea. But that was just a story, a figment of her people's collective imagination—Ruebyn had said so himself. Even if it existed, only magic could open such a gateway, only the Gods themselves, surely.

Instead, there was just her. She turned to look at Rayan, at the darkness pouring from the demon's hands. His eyes glowed with all the lives he had collected, and Pela's confidence wilted. She was weak and small, untrained, a useless girl who thought to stand against an eternal beast. She could not do it, could not see the way, could not even grasp the light of her own feeble life force.

"Pela!" Ruebyn cried again. Then his hands were on her face, turning her from the beast, so that all she could see was him, all she knew were the depths of his hazel eyes. "Pela," he repeated. "You can do it. You can do anything."

Pela swallowed. She could feel the darkness pressing down, the weight of the demon's power. For a second, all she could think about were those terrible mummies, about being trapped in this place for eternity, unable to move, only wait for the awful creature to come and feed…

Ruebyn's fingers tightened on Pela's arm and finally she heard him. Blinking, she found herself back in the cavern beneath the wall, but now she looked out not with her own eyes, but those of the spirit. A thousand golden threads filled the cavern, spiralling inwards, with the beast at the centre of it all. A shiver shook her soul as she saw finally the corroded black of Rayan's aura. She could sense his elation, his arrogance that victory was assured, that they could not escape.

But perhaps he was wrong, perhaps there *was* a way.

Grasping the candle of her life force, Pela used its power to send tendrils of herself out into the night, questing, seeking something different, something unlike anything else in the ancient citadel…

…and to her shock, she found something respond. Deep beneath their feet, a power stirred at her presence, a rumbling giant that had lain dormant for a hundred years, now waking. She gasped as the ground itself rocked beneath them, as the air suddenly shimmered, changed. An unworldly light filled the cavern around them.

"What are you doing?" the demon roared, its eyes burning with sudden rage.

Pela did not respond. Her mind was still turned inwards, fixed on the dwindling flame of her life force. Whatever she had done, it was consuming her. Weakness spread through her body and she slumped into Ruebyn, still clinging to the flame, even as it crumbled to embers. She groaned as her spirit slammed back into her body, the weight returning to her soul.

"Hold on!" Ruebyn cried out and she clung to him, too weak to even open her eyes.

An explosion of colour burst through her eyelids, and then they were falling, spinning, hurtling through some unseen vortex, and Pela felt the last traces of her consciousness slipping away, the darkness rising up to embrace her.

áé

21

"I still can't believe it," Kryssa murmured, cupping Genevieve's cheek in her hands. Her vision blurred as tears stung her eyes. "I can't."

They were back in Chole, back in her room in the Castle. Now though, the place no longer seemed so dark. It was as though someone had just lit a candle, and she'd discovered the monsters she'd feared had all been in her imagination. Even with Marianne's threats, even with the battle to come on the morrow, Kryssa was not afraid.

Because Genevieve was here. Because Pela lived.

Genevieve had just finished telling her about their ordeal in the Lonian mines, and of their escape. Kryssa could hardly believe the things Pela had done, the challenges her daughter had risen above. She knew now that whatever came to pass tomorrow, Pela would be okay.

And after hearing the truth about Lonia, of the awful cruelty of their overseers, the horror in their mines, Kryssa also knew that Braidon had been right. They could never surrender to Marianne, could not give up their sovereignty to such callous masters.

"I'm here," Genevieve whispered, leaning in and pressing her lips to Kryssa's. Their tongues met, and Kryssa savoured the familiar cinnamon taste of her lover. She moaned as Genevieve pulled away with a whisper: "Believe it."

Smiling, Kryssa ran a hand through the huntress's hair. "Thank you," she whispered. "For everything you did for Pela."

They were sitting together on the sofa in Kryssa's room. She had one arm around Genevieve's shoulders, while her other traced slow circle's over the huntress's leggings.

"She is her mother's daughter," Genevieve chuckled. "She hardly needed my help to send those Lonians fleeing."

"And yet you were willing to sacrifice your life to protect her."

Genevieve looked away at that, and Kryssa felt the tremor in her lover's body. She pulled the huntress closer, holding her tight. Genevieve had spoken only briefly of her capture. She had fought the Knight that had pursued them, almost defeating him before the man managed to disarm her. He had gone on alone, yet with a storm bearing down and an arrow through his shoulder, he could not have gotten far.

But Genevieve had been left in the tender care of the Knight's attendants. They had carried her back to Lonian lands, where they had met the Elder Servo. There was no mistaking the fear in Genevieve's voice when she had spoken of the man, how he had tormented her, taking sick pleasure from her screams.

Kryssa could only imagine how long the torture might

have lasted if not for Marianne, and despite her misgivings, she found herself thankful for the queen's mercy.

A shiver ran down Kryssa's spine and she quickly shook off the thought.

Remember, Marianne is a masterful manipulator. She killed your father!

Recalling that night in Malevolent Cove, anger touched Kryssa. How could Caledan have given his oath to such a woman. The sellsword had travelled with Devon for weeks, had fought alongside him against the Order's evil. Yet now he stood beside the hammerman's killer. She could not understand such a betrayal.

"What of Pela and this boy?" she murmured after a time. "Do you truly think they will be safe in Trola?" Her greatest fear was that Pela might have escaped from one danger, only to step straight into the path of another.

"As safe as anywhere right now," Genevieve said wryly. She rubbed her hand across Kryssa's back. "Your daughter is smart. So is the boy, for that matter. They've probably already made it south and crossed back into Plorsea. They could be safer than either of us right now, for all we know."

"I pray you're right."

"I am," Genevieve replied with a smile.

Kryssa shivered as her partner's fingers moved to her neck and gently began to massage the stress from her muscles. A long sigh whispered from her lips and she relaxed into the huntress, her eyes flickering closed.

"I missed you so much," Kryssa whispered, thinking of the endless days and nights since they'd last been together, of all despair and grief and guilt she'd felt since that fateful day in Skystead. "I can't believe you're really here."

"You already said that," Genevieve chuckled, her lips nuzzling Kryssa's ear.

Opening her eyes, Kryssa looked up at the huntress. "I mean it."

Still smiling, Genevieve leaned down and kissed her. This time it was no soft thing, but hard and urgent, and Kryssa gasped as the huntress's fingers tightened in her hair. They fell sideways together onto the cushioned sofa. Heat lit Kryssa's stomach, and growling, she ran her hands over Genevieve's chest, fingers plucking free the buttons of her lover's shirt.

"Kryssa," Genevieve whispered.

A tremor shook the huntress as Kryssa's fingers slid inside her shirt. Wearing a wicked grin, Kryssa moved her lips to Genevieve's neck, enjoying the soft moans as her lover responded. Then Genevieve was tugging at her own tunic. Kryssa gasped as the buttons gave way and Genevieve's lips traced fiery paths across her breasts and stomach.

She slid her fingers through Genevieve's hair, savouring her lover's touch, pulling her down. An answering moan came from Genevieve and the huntress's head lifted an inch, their eyes meeting across her naked body.

"I missed you too," Genevieve whispered, her emerald eyes alight with desire.

Afterwards, Kryssa lay dozing in Genevieve's arms, her mind adrift. Memories of the past weeks and months and years danced across her thoughts, of her father and daughter, her husband and the king, and a million other things both important and insignificant. They had moved from the couch to her bed, and now lay curled together beneath the blankets, insulated from the frigid air that hung about the Castle.

"You truly think Pela will return?" Kryssa murmured when Genevieve stirred.

The huntress's eyes flickered open, shining emerald in the faint light. "I do," she said, propping herself up on one elbow. "Like I said, she is her mother's daughter. Whether you wanted her to be or not."

Her words made Kryssa shudder as she recalled the day Devon had returned with her husband Derryn's body. She had been so angry at her father then, so determined to prevent her newborn daughter from following the warrior's path. And so Kryssa had locked away her sword, turned her back on that life.

Somehow, it had found her daughter anyway, and now Kryssa found herself regretting her decision. If only she'd been more open, Pela might have been prepared for what the world had thrown at her these last months. Maybe then they would not have lost each other in the cove, maybe they would have all been together…

Grinding her teeth, Kryssa forced her mind back to the present. There was no changing the past and whatever her feelings, there was nothing she could do for Pela now. She had to have faith, had to believe the girl could fight her way back to Plorsea.

"Then we'd better make sure there's something for her to return to," Kryssa said finally, smiling at Genevieve from her pillow. "Marianne will come tomorrow. You've seen her army up close—did you notice anything that might help us?"

Genevieve sighed, her eyes turning distant. "I don't know, Krys," she said. Then her eyes flickered back into focus and she looked down at Kryssa. "Are you sure we're fighting on the right side? Caledan…he told me what happened here, about the civilians in the pantheon. Is it…is it true?"

Kryssa swallowed as her guilt came rushing back, and

she lowered her eyes, suddenly unable to meet her lover's gaze. "It's true," she whispered. "Though it was not by any order. Braidon wanted them protected, but he was betrayed by his followers. Those responsible were hung for their crime…but it was I who failed. I promised to protect them."

"Promised who?"

"The Elder who served this Castle," Kryssa croaked. "He had power, admitted to performing their vile cleansings. He claimed to want only peace, but I didn't care, not after everything I had lost. I drove him from the pantheon— from the people he was protecting. We hunted him down, saw him killed. And while we were occupied…" She broke off as her grief spilled over, choking her throat.

Warm arms wrapped Kryssa in their embrace. She folded into the huntress and sobbed onto her shoulder until the tears finally dried. Then Kryssa sat back, wiping the tears from her cheeks.

"It's not your fault, Krys," Genevieve said, lifting her chin so their eyes met. "You could not have known."

"I should have."

"It's done, Krys," Genevieve insisted. "You can't change it, so you must find a way to live with it. To make things better."

Kryssa swallowed and said nothing, but when Genevieve refused to look away, finally she nodded. A long breath whispered from her throat. "Okay, Gen."

Genevieve kissed her brow. "Good," she said. "Now, it's your turn to tell a story. I've only heard up to where Caledan left you. Tell me the rest, my love."

So Kryssa did, starting from Braidon's fight with Caledan, how it had woken the king from his stupor and put him on the path of vengeance. How they had bartered with the Red Dragon, then ridden the beast to Chole. How

Dominic had recognised them, had sheltered them in his home, and led them to the Temple of the Earth. How Braidon had stood alone against the Knights of Alana and used the power of his own life force to defeat them. How Kryssa herself had used the same power against the Elder, when the mob stormed the Castle.

And how Dominic had murdered all those innocent souls who had taken refuge in the pantheon.

She finished the last parts in a croaky whisper—about the execution and the assassination attempt, the tribal leader's rejection of Braidon's kingship, and of the Red Dragons' arrival in the city.

"You've had quite the adventure yourself," Genevieve said when Kryssa finished, gently running a hand across her cheek. "I wish I could have seen you in action," she added, kissing her on the cheek.

Kryssa smiled and kissed Genevieve back. "I should never have stayed," she replied. "I should have followed my instincts and left, gone looking for the two of you."

"As single-minded as you can be, my love, I don't think even you could have plucked us from the depths of that mine," Genevieve replied gently. "It was better you were here, protecting the king." Her eyes darted sideways for a half a second, before returning to Kryssa. "You are sure about him?"

A lump lodged in Kryssa's throat as all her doubts came rushing to the fore. Braidon had never stopped fighting for the side of good, had sacrificed so much for Plorsea, and yet…

No, she insisted to herself. *My father believed in Braidon.*

How she missed Devon now. He had always been so calm, so reassured. Even in the face of battle the hammerman had been undaunted, giving courage to those who stood around him. If only she could hear his voice, to know they were on the right path.

But there was only her own voice, her own conscience now, and drawing in a great breath, she nodded.

"I'm sure," she whispered, then: "He's all we have."

A smile touched Genevieve's lips. "Then I will stand."

❧ 22 ☙

P ela woke to the warmth of light against her face. Blinking, she pushed herself up, then suppressed a groan as her entire body screamed out in protest. Sinking back to the cold earth, she placed a hand across her face to shield herself from the sun. Her heart was racing as though she'd just run a great distance, but she could not recall why.

Cracking open her eyes, she took a moment to look around, trying to remember what she'd done the night before. She'd had such strange dreams…but they must still be on the road to Kalgan, for now she found herself in a narrow canyon with tall cliffs stretching up towards a red sky. The earth was hard beneath her and after a moment she tried sitting up again. This time it was slightly more bearable.

Her eyes alighted on Ruebyn, lying nearby, but there was no sign of the Trolan soldiers. She frowned—they had never been left unattended before, nor did she recognise the land around them. She looked upwards again. The sun must have still be rising for the sky to be so red…and yet she could not find its orange glow anywhere.

She crawled across to Ruebyn on screaming arms and shook him. He gave a groan, and then his eyes flickered. He frowned, then suddenly snapped bold upright.

"Where is it?" he gasped, struggling to his feet.

Pela groaned as he tried to drag her up, her muscles protesting. "Where is what?"

"Rayan!" Ruebyn cried. "The demon!"

The demon!

His words set off an explosion in her mind. A scream built in her throat as memory of Kalgan and Rayan came rushing back. She saw again the smiling king, the armies marching across the land, the desiccated bodies and Rayan stalking towards them, his eyes changing to the pitch-black of a demon…

Coming to her feet, she clasped desperately at Ruebyn. They swung around, searching for their foe, but there was only the narrow canyon, only the warmth from above.

Pela frowned, her sense of wrongness growing. She stared at the scarlet sky, realising it had not changed since her waking, that there was not a cloud or sun or moon in sight. A shiver went through her as a desperate, terrifying thought came to her…

"The Way," Ruebyn whispered. "It's actually real."

A lump lodged in Pela's throat, but she swallowed it back down. They stood there for a long moment, struggling to comprehend what had happened, where they were. The land around them was barren, without any sign of life—not even a blade of grass grew between the cracks in the cliffs.

"Can it follow us?" Pela whispered at last.

"I…" Ruebyn frowned. "Like I said before…The Way

was a meeting place during the Great Wars. Only one party could enter from either end, so there could be no treachery. If that's true, no, it cannot come after us so long as we're inside."

Relief struck Pela like a blow. She slumped against Ruebyn, sobbing great gasps of joy. They had escaped, they were safe! Somehow, inexplicably, they had eluded Rayan and all his power. Clutching at Ruebyn, she remembered those last, desperate moments, how his words had steadied her, how he had found his courage in the face of the demon's darkness.

Pulling away slightly, she found him staring at her, just as he had back in the tomb. His eyes shone with unspoken emotion and she swallowed.

"How?" she whispered, feeling safe in his arms. "How did you know it could be done?"

"I didn't," he replied, "but I knew *you* could do it." With the words, he leaned in close and pressed his forehead to hers.

"Why?" she croaked.

"Why not?" he chuckled. "After everything I've seen you do, what was one more miracle? If anyone was going to open an imaginary doorway to another world, it would be you." He smiled as he said it, taking any sting from his words.

Pela cupped his cheek, seeing again the man she had found in the mountains, his kindness, his courage. "I've been so terrible to you," she croaked, scrunching her eyes closed to keep the tears from falling. One escaped anyway, the hot liquid streaking her cheek. "I should have trusted you, should have gone back when you said something was wrong with Trola."

Chuckling, Ruebyn wiped away the tear. "No," he

replied. "I was the fool, for not believing you about your magic."

Laughter bubbled up from Pela's throat. "You are a fool," she said with a smile. Then standing on her tiptoes, she kissed him on the lips. "But you're my fool."

Ruebyn chuckled as he kissed her back and then they were falling to the ground. Pela's heart raced as their kisses slowed, their tongues dancing against one another to a music of their own making. The smoky taste of him filled her mouth, and she shivered as his hands traced patterns across her back.

Desire burned in her chest, a need for them to be together, to celebrate their very existence. They were alive, had escaped, were safe! She plucked at the buttons of Ruebyn's shirt, suddenly regretting all the cold nights they had spent separate.

They broke apart and Ruebyn's lips moved to her neck, raising goosebumps wherever they touched. By then she had his shirt undone. He shivered as she slid her hands over his chest, enjoying the warmth of his skin, the fire in his body. Suddenly she could hardly feel her own aches, could barely remember the fear that had so filled her just a short while ago. Beneath that strange, sunless sky, there was nothing but herself and Ruebyn, only his body and hers.

A moan built in her chest as Ruebyn's kisses moved to the small of her throat. Impatient, she sat up, and taking the hint, Ruebyn helped to pull the shirt over her head. Before it was even completely gone, he was back at work. Flames lit in Pela's stomach as his tongue traced circles around the mounds of her breasts.

Growling, she slid her fingers through his hair, directing his mouth where she wanted it to go. A gasp escaped her as he obeyed, the heat in her centre swelling to a roar. Blood pounded in her ears as she tugged the shirt from his shoulders, as her fingers trailed down his stomach, plucked at his belt…

Afterwards, Pela lay nestled against Ruebyn's chest as he snored softly, the flames at her core finally sated. She could hardly believe it had happened, but she knew now there would be no more doubts, no more hesitation. Whatever happened, wherever this strange land took them, she wanted Ruebyn at her side.

Ruebyn twitched in his sleep and his eyes flickered open. He smiled when he saw her awake, and reaching, he stroked a hand through her silver hair. She smiled, moving her body closer to his.

"What are you thinking about?" he whispered in her ear.

"Oh, everything," she replied, "and nothing."

He grunted. "They're not our worries anymore."

"Aren't they?" She tried to give him a stern look, but the innocent glint in his eyes made her smile. "And why is that?" she whispered, kissing him on the cheek.

To her disappointment, Ruebyn sat up. She felt so at peace entwined around him, she never wanted to let go. She remained on the ground as he stood, her naked body inviting him to return to her arms. Flashing her a grin, he nudged her with his foot, and with a dramatic sigh, she joined him. Looping a hand around her waist, he pulled her close.

"We're in a whole other world," he said, "a whole other place. Even time is said to move differently here. The demon can no longer touch us, nor the Knights or the queen or anyone else. Why don't we just stay?"

"Stay?" Pela's eyes widened at the thought. "We can't stay!"

"Why not?"

"I…" She trailed off, then managed: "It's a wasteland, we would starve."

Her stomach rumbled at the words and casting her eyes around, she found their bag of food nearby. Rummaging inside, she pulled out the sausage and sat on a rock. Ruebyn raised an eyebrow as she tore a chunk off the salami with her teeth, and grinning, she held it out to him.

Taking it with a nod, he joined her on the rock. "It doesn't look like a wasteland anymore," he said as he ate.

Pela frowned, but as she turned to the rocky canyon, she saw what he meant. All around them, The Way had changed as they slept—was still changing. Where before there had been barren rock and broken gravels, bare cliffs and a blood-red sky, now life sprang unbidden amongst the stones. Grass grew from the earth and here and there around them, daisies blossomed, bright yellow beneath a now violet sky. Vines twisted their way up the cliffs, swirling and changing, red and yellow and blue roses appearing amidst the thorny tendrils.

"What is happening?" Pela whispered.

"A better question would be why?" Ruebyn replied.

She sighed as he ran his hand through her hair again, her eyes fluttering closed. "Why?" she whispered absently.

"Because of us? Because of you?"

Pela shook her head, her eyes still closed. Now she could smell the scent of the flowers, taste the freshness on the air, as though it had just been raining. Shivering, she opened her eyes to look at Ruebyn, wondering at his words.

"This was a tormented place once," he explained. "Cursed by the Gods or by Archon, the tales differ. But all say it had become the domain of a demon."

Fear shot up Pela's spine at his words and she tried to pull away, to grab for her clothes, but Ruebyn held her tight.

"Relax, that demon was destroyed long ago!" he gasped, a grin on his face. "Now, where was I? Oh, yes. Some of the earliest tales have it that The Way was a beautiful place before its corruption, a place of peace. But even though that demon is gone, the balance was never restored. *Life* was never restored."

"I still don't understand," she said.

Ruebyn slid his fingers under her chin and lifted her head to kiss her. She shivered as he held her close, enjoying the feel of his body against hers.

"Maybe I'm just a romantic," Ruebyn said finally as they broke apart, "but I wonder at this place. It is strange, different to anything in the Three Nations. If we follow your legends, it was Archon's hatred that corrupted this place." He swallowed, locking eyes with her. "Perhaps…perhaps our love is restoring that balance."

Pela stared at him for a long moment, then burst into laughter. Bending in two, she let her mirth ring from the canyon walls. It was a long time before she recovered, and all the while Ruebyn sat alongside her, a sheepish look on his face. Finally she straightened, and catching her breath, offered an apologetic grin.

"Sorry," she murmured, leaning forward to kiss his cheek, before adding: "I love you too, Ruebyn." Her laughter burst out again. "But you really are too much sometimes!" She danced away as he tried to grab her.

Leaping to his feet, Ruebyn snatched her back and kissed her. A soft *oh* slipped from her lips as she sank into his embrace.

"So what do you think?" he asked finally, resting his temple against hers.

"About staying?" she whispered, eyes closed, breathing in the scent of him.

The thought sent a tremor down to her very soul, and for a moment she truly considered it. Perhaps they *could* stay here, away from the darkness, away from the war and strife that had gripped the Three Nations for a thousand years. The demon could not reach them, and no one else in Plorsea even knew The Way still existed. They would be safe…

…But her mother would not be. She and Ruebyn might have escaped the demon, but eventually Rayan would come for the east. How long before he marched with his armies? In the vision she had seen, the blue-armoured soldiers had been legion—ten thousand men just as cruel as the patrol that had taken them. Divided, the east would not stand a chance.

Not in two hundred years had the Three Nations seen such a threat, not since the days of Archon.

And no one even knew it was coming.

What would Devon think if Pela did nothing? What would her uncle say, if he knew Pela had turned her back on those she loved?

Letting out a long breath, she pulled away. Her vision blurred as she looked up at Ruebyn. "I'm sorry," she croaked. "I can't. I have to go back. I have to warn them, Ruebyn."

He stared at her for so long Pela began to think he had not heard her, that she had only imagined speaking the words, that this had all been some hallucination in her mind, and she was truly back in the cavern beneath the wall, trapped in the webs of the demon's spell.

With a smile, Ruebyn suddenly hugged her tight. "I expected no less," he said softly. Looking around, his eyes settled on their clothes. "Come on then," he added, "we'd best get going. If time really does move differently here, who knows what's happened back in the real world."

Watching him move way, it was Pela's turn to smile. Quickly, she stepped up behind him and slid her arms around his waist.

"Not just yet," she murmured in his ear. "I think we still have a few minutes to spare."

❦   2 3   ❦

Standing outside the gates of Chole, Caledan looked up at the ancient walls. They stretched high above, the giant blocks of granite shining in the rising sun. No army had ever taken them, and without scaling ladders they would be impossible to climb. But that mattered little against what Marianne and her forces would hurl against them. The explosive powder had already been loaded into the catapults. The gates would fall within the hour.

If the information Marianne's spies had provided was correct, the battle would not last much longer. Braidon had less than a thousand fighters inside the walls, plus a handful of Red Dragons. The beasts concerned Caledan, but Marianne was confident she had power enough to handle the creatures should they try to intervene.

Caledan had stationed their army well back from the walls, well outside the range of the defender's longbows. The seven thousand-odd men and women of Marianne's army waited behind him, their eyes fixed on the distant ramparts. A squadron of veterans and Knights who had joined Marianne's side waited around him, the backbone of the army. They would be the first through when the gates fell, to face whatever threat waited on the other side.

Marianne did not have the numbers to completely encircle the city—not without thinning her army enough to be vulnerable—so they had chosen to launch a frontal assault, relying on their superior numbers and weaponry to sweep away the defenders.

The king must have guessed their strategy though, for a glance at the walls revealed only a few dozen defenders on the ramparts. Braidon had seen first-hand in Malevolent Cove the power of Lonia's black powder. He knew the walls could not be defended against such a weapon. The bulk of his forces had no doubt been stationed beyond the gates, ready to defend the inevitable breach.

A horn sounded behind Caledan, back amongst the ranks where Marianne waited. It was the order to begin the attack, and Caledan swallowed, casting one glance back. He had argued his place was at the queen's side, but she had insisted he lead the assault, that no one else could be trusted. She was protected by her Queen's Guard, yet even so...

No, it was too late to second-guess their plan now. Casting one last glance at the sky, Caledan pointed his sword at the gates.

"Set distance!" he bellowed.

At his command, two catapults lurched against the hard earth, their arms springing forward to hurl rocks at the distant walls. Each had been carefully measured to weigh the same as the barrels of black powder. The engineers watched the projectiles closely as they arched high and then plunged back down towards the enemy. There was a dull *thud* as they struck empty earth a dozen yards short of the gates.

"Adjust!" Caledan shouted. The engineers leapt to obey, resetting their machines with the new distance. When they were done and Caledan received the confirmation, he pointed again. "Fire!"

Another set of rocks arced upwards, and this time they fell true, slamming into the gates with a double *crack*. The heavy timbers shook on their hinges but held tight.

Caledan stared at the walls of Chole, waiting, praying that Braidon would signal the surrender. The king had to know what would come next. The gates could not withstand the black powder, and once they were gone…no force within the city would stop the invaders. Anything could happen then, and while Marianne had given strict orders for the citizens to remain unharmed…Caledan did not trust the Lonian forces to obey. Bitterness ran deep amongst the Lonian soldiers, an anger embedded by the decades their nation had been enslaved beneath the rule of the Plorsean Tsar.

Beneath Braidon's father.

Now their time for revenge had finally come, it was difficult to see them holding back. Caledan could not blame them for their anger, but he would do everything in his power to see his queen's orders obeyed. If only he could spare Kryssa and Genevieve…but his friends were warriors. They would go wherever the fighting was thickest. There was nothing Caledan could do for them.

"*Fire!*" he bellowed finally when it became obvious the surrender would not come.

Two barrels arched into the sky, a thin cloud of smoke trailing out behind them from the fuses. If the engineers had been successful, the powder would ignite at just the right moment–

Boom.

Caledan staggered as a tower of flame erupted from the gates. A cry went up from the Plorsean veterans gathered around him—they had never seen this new weapon in action—while the Knights of Alana only stood in silence, watching as the black powder devoured their enemies.

The column of flame engulfed the gates and rushed upwards, the power of the explosion slamming into the stone ramparts above. For a moment it seemed the ancient walls would resist the terrible inferno—they had survived beasts and dragons and Archon himself, after all. But then the stones itself seemed to lift. Time seemed to slow as Caledan watched the enormous granite blocks surrounding the gate begin to crumble.

The inferno surged on, swallowing wood and stone and human flesh in an instant, then dying back to embers as its fuel was spent. Then there was only a thick column of smoke left where Chole's gate had been, only rubble where once an impenetrable wall had barred their path.

It was time.

"Ready?" Caledan bellowed, raising his sword and pointing the way. "Charge!"

The Knights and veterans gave an answering roar, and then they were racing across the two hundred yards to the rubble-strewn breach. Chole's walls still stood to either side, but the remaining defenders were scattered and broken, their morale shattered. A few recovered their bows and began to fire down at the oncoming army, but Caledan had Lonian crossbow men stationed on either flank, and they began to fire back, their steel bolts peppering the ramparts. With their superior range, the steel weapons took a terrible toll, and the defenders soon ducked back behind the crenulations.

Reassured Braidon's archers were occupied, Caledan risked another glance at the sky, but there was still no sign of the Red Dragons. He had held back several catapults, loaded with barrels of the black powder and steel shrapnel. Detonated mid-air, they would tear the dragons from the sky should they decide to attack. But perhaps the beasts had already seen the futility of the king's cause, and abandoned the fight?

Several of the veterans had drawn ahead of Caledan, their eagerness to reach the fight overcoming their training. He bellowed an order and all but one slowed, reforming into their ranks as they approached the smoking ruin that had been the gates. The wall might already have fallen, but Braidon's forces still waited within. A man alone would quickly be cut down.

They slowed again as the wind sent smoke swirling around them. On either side of Caledan he glimpsed the ruin of the walls, the battlements warped and broken by the explosion, even where they still stood. Giant blocks of stone lay scattered all around, impeding their advance.

Caledan tried to organise his men into tighter ranks, but shouts came from behind them as the less disciplined of Marianne's followers caught up with the vanguard. Cursing, Caledan found himself wishing he'd ordered the rest of the army to hold back.

But the way ahead was clear. All they needed to do was pass through the rubble and the city belonged to Marianne. Bellowing above the voices coming from behind, Caledan urged his force onward. The smoke swallowed them up, acrid and tasting faintly of sulphur, thick enough that Caledan's eyes were soon watering.

Forcing himself through the press of bodies, Caledan strained to reach the front ranks and take command. Braidon was no strategist, but neither was the king a coward. He would not be hiding in his Castle, and it was only a matter of time before he launched a counterattack. Caledan intended to be ready when it came.

The ruined walls lingered like shadows amidst the smoke to either side of Caledan as he neared the front ranks. Just a few more yards and the battle would begin in earnest—unless Braidon attacked before Marianne's forces escaped the rubble. The thought gave Caledan pause and he strained to see through the smoke. It was finally beginning to thin. He watched as buildings took shape, the red slate roofs of the city, rippling and shining in the sun.

Caledan frowned. Something wasn't right…

Then an awful roar thundered in the breach, and all hell broke loose. Suddenly men were screaming and throwing down their weapons, fighting against one another in their desperation to retreat. For a moment Caledan could only stare in disbelief and confusion—and then the last of the smoke blew away, and finally he saw the truth.

A dragon sat crouched behind the breach, its scarlet scales shining in the morning sun. Staring into the maw of the beast, Caledan had only a moment to appreciate the brilliance of Braidon's plan. The king had known Marianne could thwart any outright attack the Red Dragons might launch.

But he had also known the gates would fall, and that Marianne's forces would quickly storm the breach. He'd left just enough soldiers atop the walls to assuage their suspicions, so that they would not realise the dragon waited beyond the gates.

A brilliant glow appeared in the throat of the dragon as

its jaws stretched wide. Men were streaming past Caledan now, shrieking and scrambling over one another, becoming a stampede. But Caledan had seen a dragon's flames first-hand in Malevolent Cove. There would be no escape, not for any of them.

With another roar, scarlet flames belched from the beast and rushed across the killing ground into which they had been lured. The first ranks of soldiers vanished into the inferno, Knights and veterans incinerated in an instant.

Caledan closed his eyes, and lifting his blade, he waited for the end to come. A wall of heat swept over him, and the screams of his comrades fell abruptly silent. His arms shook as his flesh began to sear, but an answering vibration began in his sword, and the heat lessoned.

His eyes snapped open. They immediately began to water, as the flames bore down on him—but somehow, he wasn't burning. The inferno was all around him now, but it came no closer, held back by the rainbow glow of the sword in his hands.

Then a sharp screech came from the blade, and the multi-coloured light flickered. Caledan watched in horror as a crack spread through the steel. Whatever spell Marianne had cast was fading beneath the dragon's onslaught. Shuddering, Caledan started to back away, even as he felt the heat returning.

But the firestorm was dissipating as well, the roar of the dragon fading away. Caledan choked as the flames suddenly flickered out, to be replaced by the stench of burning flesh. Now he saw the bodies lying around him, the blackened remnants of his Plorsean comrades, the twisted scraps of metal that had been the Knights.

The roar of human voices carried over the crackling of flames still burning amidst the ruins. Caledan's head jerked up as a great gust swept away the smoke, revealing the soldiers charging from the city. They rushed across the blackened ground, swords and shields held high, screaming their triumph.

And at their head was a man in shining armour, his sword lit from within by a brilliant white, a golden crown upon his brow.

Braidon.

Caledan watched as his lifelong enemy rushed towards him. For a moment he was filled with a desire to meet the man with sword in hand, to finally take his revenge. But Marianne's army was in disarray, her vanguard destroyed. If someone did not take control, the battle would be lost.

Gritting his teeth, Caledan turned and fled. Not one other soul who had entered the breach had survived the dragon fire, and as he leapt from the rubble, Caledan found the ranks that had come after them in disarray. Men and woman stumbled across the parched earth, many sporting burns, while others had lost their weapons in the chaos. With the best of Marianne's fighters already dead, the army was on the brink of collapse.

"Soldiers, on me!" Caledan bellowed.

Several faces turned in his direction, but their eyes showed only shock and few seemed to understand what he was saying. Cursing, Caledan grabbed the nearest man and spun him to face the enemy.

"Swords up!" he screamed, and finally the man seemed to understand.

Caledan continued the process, until more than two dozen men and women stood with him, weapons held at the ready. The sight seemed to bring order to the rest of Marianne's forces, and for a moment calm returned to their ranks.

Then the king emerged from the smoke, walking slowly now. Two women appeared behind him, and Caledan's heart fell as he recognised Kryssa and Genevieve, both decked now in the scarlet and golden uniform of the King's Guard. More soldiers followed, hundreds of them marching in line.

At their front, Braidon lifted his sword, and the white light flashed out across the battlefield.

"This is your last chance, traitors!" His words crashed across the plains like thunder. "Surrender, and I will spare your lives!"

A tremor swept through the ranks around Caledan and he cursed, sensing their fear. The king was still badly outnumbered, but Marianne's soldiers had already seen the best of their comrades obliterated before their eyes. Now the King of Plorsea stood before them with a magic sword offering survival…

"*Enough!*"

Caledan swung around as Marianne's voice carried over the battlefield, an equal to Braidon's command. Stillness fell as every soul held his breath. Ripples spread through the ranks of soldiers behind him, and then the queen herself appeared. She strode through her followers, her scarlet dress swirling with each step and lightning crackling at her fingertips.

"Enough of the bloodshed, Braidon," she cried. "It's time this ended."

The king and his soldiers had frozen at Marianne's appearance, and now they waited as she emerged into the open. Caledan shivered as she glanced back at her army, seeing the silent resolve, her determination to end this battle once and for all. Her gaze seemed to focus on him, and for a second her mask cracked, and he saw the joy in her face, the relief he had survived. A smile touched her lips, then her attention returned to the enemy.

"Marianne," Braidon said softly. He stepped from the ranks of his soldiers, arms spread. In his silver armour and with shining sword in hand, he looked for all the world like the battle king of his early days. "Your army is sundered," he continued, "your power proven naught but illusion. Now you stand here begging for leniency?"

"I would face you myself."

Braidon laughed in her face. "You, or your champion?" He grinned. "Did you think I would not hear the tale?" His eyes flickered to Caledan, then back to Marianne. "No, Marianne, I will not fight you. But I offer the same bargain you extended to me. Surrender now, and your people will go free. Only you need suffer for your crimes."

"I spent eight long years suffering you, sweet husband," Marianne spat. "I have no intention of returning to my bonds." Then she smiled. "And I wasn't asking your permission."

At that the queen threw out her arms. An awful *boom* rang from the walls as lightning leapt from her hands. Braidon recoiled and raised his sword as though to defend himself, but the blade became a lightning rod, and with a *crack*, the blue fire exploded through the steel.

Blazing light lit the plain and Caledan was forced to cover his eyes, even as the shriek of rending metal tore at his ears. He clenched his teeth and waited for the brilliance to dim, then spun to face the enemy again.

Smoke clung to where Braidon had been, but now a breeze blew across the battlefield. The air cleared, revealing the king standing untouched—though his apparently magic sword now lay in the dirt, a mess of molten steel. Rage twisted Braidon's face as he looked at Marianne.

"Oh my dear wife," he whispered, "how I have waited for this moment."

His hands flashed up, though no lighting or fire emerged from the king. For a moment it seemed his magic had failed —then a dozen yards away, Marianne gasped. Her hands clasped desperately at her throat, though not a mark showed on her flesh.

Sneering, Braidon stalked closer, one hand outstretched as though to throttle her. Behind him, Kryssa and Genevieve watched on from the ranks of soldiers, their faces pale.

"I am not powerless anymore," the king hissed. "Your disciples gave me power when they died in my Castle, and on the shore of Malevolent Cove. Enough to match your hateful curses."

He was closing in now, barely ten yards from the queen. Caledan's heart throbbed in his chest as he watched the silent battle, sword still clutched tightly in one hand. It was ruined, the steel cracked and broken, the spell probably destroyed. But he was still the Queen's Champion. He could not stand by while Braidon murdered her.

Silently he slipped closer. The two armies had drawn close together now, almost forming a ring around the two monarchs, but the soldiers were watching the silent battle and did not notice the sellswords movements. Dull gasping noises came from Marianne as she clutched at her neck, as though she were trying to breathe through a reed pipe.

Caledan's hands shook and his heart beat faster. He was as close as he could get, at the very edge of the crowd. Another step and Braidon was sure to see him. There was no other choice. Gradually, he drew back his arm, then with sudden speed, he hurled his sword.

The blade hissed as it slashed the air, flashing for

Braidon's chest. Caledan saw the surprise flash across Kryssa's face, but Braidon had left his King's Guard behind and now they were too far away to intervene. Caledan's aim was true—but at the last second a flicker crossed Braidon's face, and suddenly he was spinning, his arm coming up…

Boom.

Caledan staggered as an explosion rang out over the plains. The earth rippled beneath him like a wave, as though Braidon's magic had turned it to water, and he was forced to one knee. Gasping, Marianne staggered back and fell to her knees as the king's spell broke. Across the battlefield, the soldiers did the same.

Looking to the king, Caledan wondered what new power Braidon had unleashed. But the man seemed similarly perplexed. Caledan's sword had shattered as it struck Braidon's outstretched hands, but the king's attention was already elsewhere, his eyes on the distant city. A frown marked the king's forehead, while on the ground nearby Marianne gulped in great mouthfuls of air, momentarily forgotten by her enemy.

Following Braidon's gaze, Caledan gaped as the walls of Chole seemed to come alive, the stone warping and twisting, becoming a shimmering, boiling cacophony of colour. Another *boom* followed, as of a door blowing open, and the light exploded outwards. A blazing spiral spun over heads of the gathered armies and came to land not far from where Marianne and Braidon had been fighting. Men and women leapt aside as it crashed to the earth, still spinning and swirling, mesmerising in its brilliance. If Caledan had been able to stand, he might have gone to it, such was its call, but all he could do was watch as the silhouette of two humans took shape within the vortex.

Now the brilliance began to fade. Caledan could not

begin to comprehend what was happening, but he knew in his heart one thing—this was true magic, unlike anything that had been seen in the last thirty years.

With one final flash, the light vanished. A young man and woman were left standing in its place, the earth scorched beneath their feet. The man sported short brown hair and hazel eyes that seemed equal parts terrified and amazed by what had just happened, while the woman… recognition shot down Caledan's spine, but before he could call her name, another voice cried over the heads of the army, a cry filled with joy and terror and love.

"Pela!"

$$\text{❦} \quad 2\,4 \quad \text{❦}$$

"**P**ela!"

The cry had left Kryssa's lips before she could think better of it. She stared across the battlefield, the sword heavy in her hand, unable to believe what she was seeing. Surely this was some dream. She must be still lying in her bed back in Chole, enfolded in Genevieve's embrace. This could not be real…

Yet here she was, Genevieve at her side and the king nearby, surrounded by death and destruction, the very earth scorched by the ferocity of the battle.

And there was her daughter, standing with the strange boy, midway between the opposing forces. She guessed the boy was the overseer Genevieve had spoken of. He looked almost as shocked as Kryssa felt. Horror appeared on his face as he saw the destruction, the burnt bodies lying amidst the rubble nearby. He blanched and turned away, dry retching.

In contrast, Pela stood straight, her sapphire eyes shining as she surveyed her surroundings. They took in the ranks of soldiers, lingering on the king and then flickering to the queen. Marianne was just getting to her feet, and fast as lightning, Pela swept up a fallen blade and stepped between the young man and the woman.

A smile touched Kryssa's lips at her daughter's fierceness. She cast a glance at Braidon, but the king was as shocked as anyone. All across the battlefield, the soldiers of both sides stood staring at the newcomers. No one spoke, and heart beating hard in her chest, Kryssa started towards them.

Pela spun at the sound of approaching footsteps, her sword coming up. Her eyes widened as they settled on Kryssa, her mouth falling open.

"*Mum!*" she screamed.

Then they were both running, and Kryssa was throwing open her arms, drawing Pela into her embrace. A sob tore from her chest as they clung to each other. Hardly daring to believe this was real, she drew in a breath, savouring the scent of her daughter's hair, the feel of her arms around her waist.

"Mum, what are you doing here?" Pela gasped finally. Tears streaked her cheek as she pulled away.

Kryssa offered a faint smile. "I could ask you the same thing, missie."

The hint of a grin touched her daughter's cheeks. "That's...a very long story." Her eyes drifted away, then widened in surprise. In an instant she had released Kryssa and dodged around her. "Gen!" she cried, her voice lifted in joy.

Genevieve's laughter carried over the plains as Pela tackled her. The huntress staggered several steps before recovering her balance and hugging Pela back. Kryssa watched the surreal moment in bemusement, the surrounding armies momentarily forgotten.

"I see you two have bonded," she said after a moment, laughing softly. Then remembering the young man still standing awkwardly nearby, she held out her hand. "Kryssa," she said in greeting. "I hear you are a friend of my daughter's?"

The boy's cheeks grew red and he coughed and spluttered in such a way that Kryssa's was left with no doubt he was more than just Pela's friend.

"Ruebyn!" he managed finally, accepting her hand.

Shaking her head, Kryssa turned back to her daughter.

"I thought you were dead," Pela was saying as she danced hand-in-hand with Genevieve. "The Knight said he'd killed you!"

Pain flickered across Genevieve's face at the memory, but she forced a smile. "He decided I was more valuable as a prisoner." She swallowed, her eyes drawn to where Marianne stood. "I…would still be a prisoner if not for the queen."

"*What?*" Pela gasped.

Glancing around, Kryssa's senses finally came rushing back. The four of them stood in the middle of a battlefield, and while the magical conflagration had brought about a temporary truce, the battle could resume at any moment. She drew herself up and stepped between her daughter and the queen.

"She is still the enemy," Braidon said as he joined them.

Genevieve said nothing and Kryssa glanced at her, remembering their midnight conversation. But Braidon was right. They had managed a great victory, but the battle was not over yet. Marianne was still a threat. After everything she'd done, all the evil she'd wrought across the Three Nations, she could not go unopposed—

"No!" Pela's voice lifted above the others.

Kryssa spun as her daughter strode forward, placing herself between the king and queen. Braidon's forehead creased into a frown, while beyond Marianne had resumed her usual self-assured smile. Kryssa could not understand the woman's confidence, not with her army in tatters, and her magic so clearly outmatched by Braidon's. But Caledan had joined her now, the slick swordsman like a second shadow; perhaps his presence gave her strength.

"Pela, what are you doing?" Genevieve asked, stepping up beside Kryssa.

"It doesn't matter," Braidon answered. Energy crackled in his hands as he faced Marianne. "She must be stopped."

"*No!*" Pela said again, holding out her hands. She looked from Braidon to the queen, her jaw hard, eyes wide with fear. "Please, you have to listen. This fighting, it has to stop, before you destroy us all!"

"I say we listen to the girl, sweet husband," Marianne chuckled. She strode forward and halted a few paces from Pela. "Unless you're too afraid of losing your advantage?"

Braidon bared his teeth. "I'll not fall for your tricks, woman," he snapped, raising a hand.

"*Enough!*" Pela screamed, and now her voice was thunder, ringing out to crash upon the walls of Chole.

Kryssa staggered, shocked to realise her daughter had learned how to tap into her life force. Neither Pela nor Ruebyn seemed surprised by the effect, but Braidon's eyes also showed his amazement at her use of power. It gave him pause, and Pela spoke into the silence.

"I know you hate one another," Pela continued, her voice low now, though it still carried to the ears of every soldier on the battlefield. "But whatever our grievances, whatever our allegiances, they no longer matter. We have been to Trola. There is a darkness there, a demon that will consume us all if we do not stand together."

"What nonsense are you talking about?" Braidon snapped. "No one is allowed to enter Trola."

"We took refuge there, fleeing *her* Knights," Pela replied, swinging on Marianne. "We escaped from your mines and entered Trola through the mountains. We expected to find salvation, but there is only death there now."

"What are you saying, Pela?" Marianne whispered, her eyes shimmering. "What death do you talk of?"

"They said it was a plague." A shiver went through Kryssa at the mention, but her daughter went on: "Perhaps it *was* a plague of sorts, but it came from no disease. The creature needed to feed, to sate its hunger with the life force of innocents. Trola is a dead place now. Only a few remain, slaves to the demon's magic, their lives preserved so that it might feed."

Silence fell as Pela finished. Kryssa watched on, wondering what madness had overcome her daughter. How could a demon have taken Trola without anyone being the wiser? It couldn't be possible…but then, there had been no communication with the western nation in more than a decade…

Her eyes fell on Braidon, seeing the doubt in his face, the sudden indecision. If the demon truly existed, then Pela was right—this petty war meant nothing, and every death was only another soul lost to the fight against the darkness.

But only if Pela spoke the truth.

"You are exhausted, child," Marianne said softly, approaching Pela. "Whatever magic you used to come to this place was powerful. Perhaps you saw a vision of this demon, but I do not believe it to be a true one. Ardath received communication from Trola only recently, speaking of a reopening…"

"Lies!" Pela shrieked. "The king is a puppet to the demon's will. It has an army, soldiers loyal only to its strength, and power enough to destroy us all. You cannot fight them alone, cannot fight *it*. We only stand a chance together."

"I will *never* work with her," Braidon snarled, stepping past Kryssa and approaching Pela. "Maybe what you say is true, Pela, but Marianne is as bad as any demon. We cannot trust her. The second she sees an advantage, she will betray us."

"But—"

"I'm sorry, young Pela," Marianne murmured. She no longer looked at the girl, but stood staring at Braidon. "My dear husband is right in one thing at least—we can never work together." She raised a fist and light spilled between her clenched fingers.

A rainbow swirled around Braidon. "Get away, Pela," he growled. "If there truly is a demon, I will stand against it— once I have dealt with *her!*" He pointed a finger, and the light strengthened to the point of blinding…

"*No!*" Pela screamed, and now it was her turn to throw out her arms.

A shimmering yellow glow rushed from Pela, encasing all who stood nearby—Braidon and Marianne and Caledan, Kryssa and Genevieve and Ruebyn. The king cried out, throwing up his arms to defend himself, while the queen staggered, her eyes widening in surprise. But neither could be harmed by the light, not by the power of only a single life.

But they could be shown.

A scream sounded in Kryssa's mind, of a thousand voices crying out as one, and suddenly she was in another place, another time. She watched as darkness swept from the walls of a great city, spreading across the land, swallowing all in its path. Then she was on the streets of a town, watching a figure stride the cobbled paths. Men and women fell dying before it, their skin shrivelling to wrinkled husks, their screams falling silent.

In desperation, parents told their children to flee before turning to face the demon. With swords and bows and rocks, they attacked the creature with all they had, but nothing could slow the monster. One by one they fell, their lives sucked away, and still the darkness came on. Horror tore from Kryssa's throat as the children were overtaken and their lives were sucked away by the demon's greed.

Finally the image faded, and Kryssa found herself again on the battlefield. She staggered as her eyes caught on the blackened body of a man. Bile burned her throat as she saw the death all around with fresh eyes, as she realised the atrocities her own people had committed upon one another.

So much pain, so much waste, and for what? So a king and queen could decide which would rule them? What did it matter? Life was so short, so precious; how could they have thrown it away so wilfully? What did any of it matter, when such a darkness approached, if they were all to be enslaved by the demon?

Shivering, she looked at Braidon and Marianne, and knew they had seen the same as her. She held her breath, waiting for what would come next.

The spell had taken the strength from Pela, and now she crouched on one knee, her face pale and panting, her eyes on the monarchs. Ruebyn moved to her side and knelt beside her, offering his reassurance. Kryssa shivered and searched for Genevieve. Finding the huntress nearby, she reached out and entwined her fingers with those of her lover.

Braidon's face was pale, his hands trembling. The queen was in a similar state, and as Kryssa watched, a single tear streaked her cheek. She swallowed visibly, then with one trembling hand, reached up and wiped the tear away.

"Well, that was something," Marianne murmured.

A tremor shook the king as he scrunched his eyes closed, as though he were fighting some great internal battle. His hands opened and closed, and Kryssa could sense the power radiating from him.

Finally his eyes snapped open. "We have to stop it," he whispered. Another convulsion shook, his eyes shimmering. "But how can I trust you, Marianne?"

The queen stared back at him, her jaw clenched hard. She said nothing, but at her side Caledan took a tentative step forward.

"That was truly Trola, Pela?" he whispered.

Pela nodded. "He will come for us next."

Caledan swung back to the others. "Then you must find a way, Braidon, or all is lost."

"If only it were so simple!" Braidon shouted, turning on the sellsword. "You I would trust, Caledan. Though you are my enemy, you have never pretended to be anything different. But her…" He faced Marianne now, pointing one trembling finger at her chest. "*Her…*" His voice cracked. "She spent years pretending to love me…fathered my son, and still she betrayed me!"

"Calybe is safe," Marianne whispered. "Servo wanted him dead, but Caledan defended him. *That* is why I served the Elders, why I destroyed them when it was finally within my power."

Braidon laughed, and the sound was filled with anger and self-loathing. "Ay, and I suppose that explains as well why you pretended to love me."

Marianne could not meet his eyes. "I…" Her voice faded and she swallowed. "I convinced myself you knew my feelings, that you didn't care. I grew to loathe you for it, and then…then anything could be justified, if only it meant I could have my revenge for the years that you took from me."

"That *I* took from *you?*" Braidon snarled. "All that time I loved you, wasted, and for what? So you could steal the throne out from under me, so you could murder my Guards, my *friends*, so you could rule us all?"

Marianne's eyes flashed. "I did what I had to do to protect myself," she snapped, but her fury faded as quickly as it had appeared. "To protect my son."

"Oh yes, I'm sure that's what you tell yourself, how you sleep at night. But I see through you, Marianne, even if no one else does. You did it for the power, and nothing else. You were raised to rule, and when they sought to take that from you, you did whatever was necessary to steal it back."

"Are you any different, Braidon?" she whispered. "Were you not raised to rule as well? Were you not destined to be king?"

"Perhaps," Braidon whispered, "but I did not commit murder for my crown."

Marianne chuckled. "No one but your own father."

Braidon said nothing, only stared at her, his eyes hard. The smile slipped from Marianne's lips and she let out a sigh.

"So what are we to do, my dear husband?" she asked, extending her arms. "Darkness threatens the Three Nations, one far greater than our own petty grievances. You saw that creature, felt its power. Alone, we will fail. Will you stand with me against it?"

A strained silence fell as Kryssa looked from the queen to the king. She knew Braidon hated Marianne more than anything else. He had spent the last months nursing that hatred, feeding his rage, all with the goal of destroying her. But now, surely, Braidon must do his duty for his people, must—

"I can't," Braidon croaked, and tears streaked his cheeks. Kryssa's heart lurched in her chest as he continued: "After everything you've done, after all your betrayals, I cannot do it. Perhaps your offer is sincere, but I cannot know, cannot believe you will not stab me in the back the first chance you have."

Marianne's face twisted as she stared back at him, and for a moment Kryssa thought she might lash out at the king, might try to destroy him then and there. Instead, her eyes slid closed and she let out a long sigh.

"My mistakes have returned to punish me," she whispered, "and yet I cannot stand by while this creature takes our world. For my son, for my people, I will not let it destroy us." She paused, her eyes flickering open. She looked at Braidon through her eyelashes as Kryssa and the world stood waiting.

"Promise to spare my life, Braidon," she whispered, "and I will give you my power."

❧ 25 ❧

Braidon stood gaping at Marianne, frozen to the spot. He half-expected the queen to throw back her head and laugh in his face at her own joke. Instead, she only waited before him, arms hanging at her side, shoulders slumped in defeat.

This had to be a trick. After all they'd been through, all the death and battling for power, she could not simply be giving up. It was not in Marianne's character to surrender, to give in or allow herself to be dominated…and yet there she was…

"What are you doing?" he croaked.

"I will not let this creature destroy our world. It has to be stopped. If you cannot trust me, then…I must trust you." She lifted her hand to him, where a silver bracelet shone. Sliding it from her wrist, she tossed it to the ground between them. "That is the source of my power. It channels the lives of Lonia's slaves to the wielder."

Frowning, Braidon stared down at the device. He sensed no traps about the thing, no power at all, in fact. But Mari-

881

anne's words made sense, given all he knew of the woman's ingenuity, and the engineers at Lonia's disposal. After a moment's hesitation, he picked it up and slipped it onto his wrist, but felt no change.

"There's nothing," he murmured, glaring at Marianne. "Is this some trick?"

She lowered her head. "No, Braidon," she sighed, "no more tricks."

"Then where is your power?"

Her eyes came back up and she lifted a hand to her breast. "The bracelet does not store power, only channels it. The life forces of those that have already departed lie within me."

"Then you *are* trying to trick me," he snarled. "You are holding back your power, to strike me down when I turn my back."

"No, Braidon," she whispered, "I would not, not with Calybe's life—"

"Do not say his name," Braidon roared, his heart pounding with sudden anger. "Not after hiding him from me, not after trying to murder his father."

"I did everything I could to keep him safe," Marianne replied. "And for what it's worth, I am sorry for taking him from you."

"Enough of your lies," Braidon snapped, clenching his fists. "What trick are you playing, woman? I'm done talking."

Stones crunched as Marianne took a step toward him. He started to retreat, but she only shook her head. "No tricks, Braidon," she whispered, falling to her knees. She spread her arms in supplication. "My power is yours."

Braidon could only stare in disbelief. This was the woman he had loved, who had betrayed him, had stolen everything from him. Now she was on kneeling before him, offering the world. And all he had to do was reach out and take it.

Yet still he hesitated. Braidon knew in his heart it could not be this easy. Around him the others watched on—Caledan and Pela and Genevieve and Kryssa and the strange young man. None of them made any move to intervene.

Braidon swallowed, returning his gaze to Marianne. He had already proven he was the stronger, that the lives he'd accumulated were greater than her power. But she might still do him harm, might still defeat him with some under-handed blow.

Gathering his power, Braidon drew it about himself in a brilliant suit of armour, a shield against any attack she might hurl. He sensed the tension growing in Caledan as the sellsword took a step closer, but a look from Marianne sent him back. The others wavered, unsure of Braidon's intentions, but no one else moved to intervene.

"Do it," Marianne whispered.

Sapphire eyes stared up at him, eyes he had loved, eyes he had loathed. Gritting his teeth, Braidon did as she said. His power whipped out, catching her in its swirling rainbow light. She stiffened against the magic, but made no move to defend herself, and after a second Braidon sensed her barriers retreating. Silently he left his body, soaring out in spirit to look upon his wife.

Power danced within Marianne, more brilliant than he had ever expected, and suddenly he wondered whether her earlier distress had been an act, if she'd been holding back in their brief battle. Fear shook his spirit, that perhaps this was a trap after all, that she might still lash out at him. But she still appeared unguarded, unprotected. If Braidon wished it, he might have reached out and stopped her heart.

No, this was no trap. Finally convinced, Braidon latched his power to the swirling light at Marianne's core. A whimper slipped from the queen's lips, but he could not be stopped now, and slowly Braidon drew the energies to him. Feeling the queen tense, he readied himself for resistance, but instead her eyes slid closed as she relinquished control to him.

Braidon smiled and drew more power from the queen's frail body. A gasp of his own escaped as the energy touched him, a burning, swirling cacophony of light that set his blood to boiling. His whole body shook, as though it were true fire burning within him. In that instant, he felt as though he might leap the walls of Chole itself, that he had the power to fly and soar, to face any enemy, to conquer the world if he wished it.

His breath came in ragged gasps as the raw power continued to flow, the glow within the queen dwindling by the second, even as his own strength redoubled. Braidon clenched his fists, his teeth rattling as his entire being shook.

Finally the last of Marianne's power dwindled, the multicoloured light fading to a single candle of blue—her own life force. It flickered alone at her core, its glow radiating throughout her body. Such a tiny, feeble thing, the difference between life and death. He could snuff it out with a pinch of his fingers.

A shudder ran through Braidon at the thought. Withdrawing, he looked at Marianne with his spirit eyes. She had given him everything, and all she'd asked in exchange was her life. And yet…

Marianne's will was unquenchable. So long as she lived, she would not give up her claim to the throne. Whatever setbacks she suffered, she would recover, and her wrath would return the pain a thousand-fold. She might have surrendered her magic, but that could be regathered. Then one day, she would come for him. He would never stop looking over his shoulder.

Unless…

Braidon swallowed, staring at the woman who had lain beside him all these years, who had born his son. Shadows now haunted her face, and her skin was pale beneath the blazing sun. Her eyes were closed, but as he watched they flickered open.

Now he saw not his lost love, but the woman he loathed, who had betrayed him. And he realised his love was long dead, that it had been burned away by her betrayal, and his compassion lost with it. After everything Marianne had done, after the murders and devastation she'd wrought, why should he leave her with her life? She did not deserve a second chance, did not deserve to go free.

Silently, Braidon reached out again with his mind, and wrapped his power around the flickering blue candle. Marianne's eyes widened as she felt his touch and her lips parted as though to cry out, but it was already too late. Braidon had possession of her body, her soul, and there was nothing she could do to protect herself now.

Nothing but stare at him with those crystal blue eyes.

A smile touched Braidon's lips as he saw her fear. Slowly he began to draw her life away, savouring in her pain, in this final retribution for all the hurt she had caused him. Once she had held him in her power, and done her best to destroy him. Now he would do the same.

Only he would not fail.

"Braidon!" a voice called, though it was faint, as though spoken from a great distance. He looked up to see Caledan approaching, a sword clenched in his fist. "Marianne, are you okay?"

Braidon made a gesture and a wave of power caught the sellsword in the chest. The blow sent Caledan tumbling backwards across the plain, only coming to a stop several yards away. He did not lie still, but instead pushed himself back to his hands and knees. Anger touched Braidon at the man's defiance, and he raised his hand, preparing to strike the traitor down.

"Braidon!"

Irritated, the king swung in search of the fresh disturbance. Marianne was still held in his thrall, her life his to do with as he pleased. She could not escape him now, no matter who tried to intervene, but still the interruption had enraged him. He collected his power, ready to strike this new enemy down.

He paused as his gaze found Genevieve. The huntress had her bow drawn, an arrow pointed at Braidon's chest. Her eyes were wide, her fingers shaking on the drawstring. Kryssa stood nearby, hand on her sword hilt, though Braidon could not tell whether it was to defend her king, or her lover.

"Please, Braidon. Stop this," Genevieve begged, her voice taut with pain.

"You would betray me, huntress, after I saved your life?" Braidon asked.

"*She* saved me," Genevieve whispered. Her voice cracked and the arrow dropped half an inch before she restored her aim. "I won't let you kill her, not like this."

"You don't understand," Braidon hissed. "She is too treacherous to live. I am sorry, huntress. I only do what I must."

He turned and lifted his hand, ready to draw the last

flickers of life from the queen. A sharp *twang* came from behind him, and lighting fast, Braidon spun back in time to see the arrow flash from Genevieve's bow.

Rage boiled through Braidon as he watched the arrow come. Were they all so blind? Could none of them see the truth, that Marianne was playing them all like puppets, turning them upon each other? But they could not stop him, not now, not when he was so close to his victory. With a roar, Braidon threw out his hand.

A wave of energy surged from him, more than he could ever need to deal with mere mortals. It raced to meet the arrow, catching it mid-air and turning it aside, hurling it backwards…

…until Genevieve's breast brought it to an abrupt halt.

For a second, no one seemed to realise what had happened—not even the huntress. She stared at Braidon, eyes wide and mouth open, as though unsure why her arrow had not found its mark. Slowly, she lowered her bow, and her gaze was drawn downwards. A frown marked her forehead as she found the arrow lodged there.

Staggering, Genevieve looked back at Braidon, and now there was panic in the woman's eyes. Her mouth opened as though to speak, but instead blood burst from her lips. The fear grew on her face as the strength left her legs and she crumpled to the ground.

"*Gen!*" Screaming, Kryssa threw herself down beside her partner. "Gen, no!"

She grabbed the fallen huntress and turned her over. The fall had driven the arrow deeper and now blood stained Genevieve's red and gold tunic. Her head lolled as Kryssa cradled her.

"Kryssa?" Genevieve whispered, her eyelids fluttering but unable to open.

"It's okay, I'm here," Kryssa whispered, before her head whipped up, her eyes fixing on Braidon. "Help her!" she screamed.

Movement came from alongside Braidon. He glanced around as Marianne staggered back from him, only now realising she had broken free while he'd been distracted. There was open fear in her eyes, and it was clear that she could barely hold herself up. He smiled and would have finished her then had Caledan not pulled her into his arms.

"Braidon, please!"

Kryssa's screams drew him back to the dying huntress. He frowned as he looked at the two, then let out a sigh and strode across to where they lay. A quick glimpse through the eyes of his spirit confirmed what he already knew. The arrow had sliced open the arteries in the huntress's heart. Even as he watched, her life force dwindled to nothing.

"I am sorry, Kryssa," he murmured. "She is already gone. She should not have gotten in my way."

An awful sob tore from his King's Guard as Genevieve's eyes closed a final time, the dull rattle of her last breath whispering from her lips.

"No, no, no," Kryssa gasped, burying her head in her lover's chest. "Not like this, not again."

Braidon watched them for a moment, feeling he should be sad but not quite sure why. Genevieve had gone against him, had betrayed him as he stood on the verge of victory. Now she had paid the price. Shaking his head, he searched again for Marianne.

Boom!

Braidon staggered as the strange light in which Pela had arrived exploded once more from the walls of Chole. Ice took hold of his heart as the whirlwind of colours billowed across the plains, rushing over the head so the splintered armies, flickering here and there as though in search of a place to land.

This time it settled much further out on the plains, far beyond either army. There it slammed into the earth with a clap of thunder. Colours rushed out in all directions, then back inwards as though sucked into a vacuum.

In its wake, an army was revealed, thousands of men and women garbed in dark blue armour. They stood row upon row in perfect unison, spears held in one hand, shields in the other, swords sheathed at their waists. Black gems shone from their armour and weapons, leaving no doubt about where this army had appeared from, who they served.

Death.

26

Pela watched as the swirling light flickered, listened to the dying *booms* of thunder, smelt the distant decay as The Way faded, revealing the army now standing on the plains. She couldn't move, couldn't think, only stare as the last trace of magic vanished and the world finally saw what had come.

Ten thousand soldiers in shining armour, no raw recruits but professionals in the practice of death, well-trained and armed with deadly steel. It only took a glimpse to know they outnumbered the combined forces of the king and queen. They would cut through the ragtag armies of Lonia and Plorsea like a wave against the sand, sweeping all away before them.

And every death, every life stolen, would feed the demon's power.

Pela shuddered, scanned the ranks of blue-armoured soldiers. Ice slid down her spine as movement came from the army and Rayan came striding forward. The shadows clung to his form like a cloak, billowing as though caught in a great wind. Tendrils of darkness reached out before him, sliding through the grass and twisted shrubs, bringing death to all they touched.

Coming to a stop at the fore of his army, Rayan's gaze swept his tattered collection of enemies. The black eyes lingered on Braidon and Marianne, before finally alighting on Pela. Her heart dropped into the pit of her stomach as a sickly smile crossed the demon's face.

"Pela," he said in a whisper, and while he stood some hundred yards away, his words carried to the ears of every watcher. "Thank you for leading me to The Way. To think, it lay hidden beneath my feet all these years." The demon spread his arms. "You have granted me a great gift." His grin spread, and a tingle of warning shot through Pela, a voice screaming for her to flee. "In exchange, I grant you the gift of life."

Pela stood frozen as Rayan lifted a hand. Only at the last moment did she realise what he was about to do, the significance of his words—but she found her muscles were unable to move, her whole body petrified with terror. This was her fault, her doing—if only she and Ruebyn had remained in Kalgan, the creature would never have found the secret way into Plorsea.

Darkness rushed from the demon, just as it had beneath the walls of Kalgan, a swirling cloud that at a touch would entomb Pela's soul forever, trap her in her own flesh, to be feasted upon at the demon's pleasure. Watching it come, she thought of all she still wanted to do, that she would never get to go home, to show Ruebyn her quiet town, to climb the mountains or swim the fiord.

A voice shouted out from nearby, and suddenly someone was tackling Pela, pushing her from the path of the magic. She gasped as she struck the ground, her head whipping around to see who had hit her. She had the merest of seconds to glimpse the surprise on Ruebyn's face, as though he could hardly believe what he'd done.

Then the darkness collided with him and his mouth fell open in the beginnings of a scream. Only the shrillest of whistles emerged, like hot steam escaping a kettle. His skin hardened before Pela's eyes, taking on the shiny look of polished wax.

"*No!*" Pela screamed.

She scrambled to her feet as the darkness receded, reaching for him, but his skin was like leather beneath her hands. Only his eyes remained the same, frozen open in his face, staring out with such desperation that Pela could almost hear his silent cries.

"No, Ruebyn, why?" she gasped, clinging to his mummified figure. "Why would you do this?"

But he could not reply, could not do anything but stand fixed to the spot as the demon's voice carried across the plain.

"Your man is brave, girl," Rayan chuckled. "If foolish. He has bought you no more than a few seconds. Enjoy your last breaths."

"Enough, demon!" Braidon howled. Leaping past them, he extended a hand towards the creature. "Your darkness ends now."

"Ah, the king!" Rayan cackled as its attention turned to Braidon. "Though your kingdom looks to have fallen into disrepair. Are these here truly the best Plorsea has to offer?"

Ignoring the demon's taunts, Braidon threw out an arm. Lightning crackled between his fingers and then leapt at Rayan, crackling as it went. The demon only raised a hand. The blue fire struck with a *boom*, but as Rayan closed his fist, it was quickly snuffed out. Braidon staggered at the sight, his face paling a shade, and the demon laughed.

"So, you too have taken the power of the living?" Rayan murmured. "Tell me, does it burn you, King?"

Panic appeared in Braidon's eyes, before his face hardened into a mask and he turned his gaze skyward. "Nidryt, to me!"

For a second, Pela thought Braidon had gone mad—then an answering roar came from the city behind them, and a red streak shot up from beyond the walls. The air *cracked* as giant wings beat down, carrying the beast overhead. The Red Dragon circled the king once and then spiralled down to land between Braidon and the demon with a crash. A dull growl rumbled from its throat as it looked from the king to Rayan.

"What have we here?" Rayan sounded almost bemused by the beast's appearance. Folding his arms, he took a few steps forward. "Do the Red Dragons now bow to mortal masters?"

The dragon threw back its head and roared at the demon's words. Warmth washed over Pela as the great jaws swung around, revealing row upon row of dagger-like teeth and the burning glow in the depths of its throat.

Your enemies spring from this earth like rabbits, King.

Braidon scowled. "The demon comes to destroy us all, Nidryt," he replied, holding out a hand. "Help me to defeat the creature, before it's too late."

A rumble came again from the dragon as it looked upon Braidon, eyes aglow, before it turned back to the demon. Rayan had not moved, only stood watching them, that sly smile on his sickly face.

"Come then, dragon," he murmured, spreading his arms. "Do your master's bidding."

A roar sounded from across the battlefield, not only from Nidryt, but also from above. Flames lit the sky and Pela found herself shrinking as more of the Red Dragons appeared. The demon's laughter rose over the cacophony of the beasts.

"Or perhaps you would return to your true purpose, to follow your noble desires, rather than obey the whims of this mortal. Perhaps you would help me to burn the scourge of humanity from these lands."

The dragon's head whipped around at the demon's words, the giant globe of its single eye aflame. Beside it, Braidon seemed ignorant to its sudden change in mood.

"False promises will not sway our alliance," Braidon said dismissively. "Come, Nidryt, let us destroy this foul creature."

Another rumble came from the dragon's throat, though this time it reminded Pela of laughter. The beast turned its head to look down at Braidon.

You have made an enemy beyond your powers, King, Nidryt's voice growled into their minds. *We are not so foolish as our extinct cousins, to throw away our lives. Our arrangement is at an end. Humanity is once again the enemy of my people!*

The dragon's mouth spread into a wicked grin, and Pela glimpsed the flames building at the back of its throat. The hackles on her neck lifted as she threw herself to the ground, dragging Ruebyn's mummified body down with her, but the demon's voice came again before the flames could emerge.

"Wait, my eager new friend," Rayan said as he stepped up beside the dragon and put a hand on its massive forearm. Still smiling, he looked at Braidon, then past the king to the gathered soldiers. "They have brought together so many lives for me, I can hardly wait to break my fast." He laughed. "But I need be prudent. The fruits of the Three Nations must be made to last, lest I find myself starving once more for sustenance."

"I…I will stand…" Braidon started, but the demon waved a hand, and words seemed to fail the king.

"People of the east!" Now Rayan's voice rang out over the heads of the broken armies. "Your world is at an end. Your beasts have abandoned you, your king stands helpless before me. But fear not, for I have come to free you from the bonds of chaos. Surrender to my rule, and you will live long and peaceful lives." His voice hardened. "Resist, and I will turn all who stand against me to dust. I give you until the morrow to decide your fate."

With that, Rayan turned his back on Braidon and the armies of Plorsea and Lonia, as though they were of no more consequence than fleas to the Feline. Indeed, with the dragon standing between them, there was nothing anyone but Braidon could have done. And the king stood defeated, his eyes locked to the ground, his courage fled in the face of the demon's power.

Finally the dragon lifted its head and unleashed a plume of flame into the sky. Pela and the others flinched back as heat washed over them, and with a single bound, the dragon leapt into the air.

Then there was only the silent army, the row upon row of blue-armoured men staring across the plains at them. The demon had vanished, but the army remained, a promise of the death that would find them come morning.

But in that moment, Pela did not care. She crouched beside Ruebyn's helpless body. His eyes were still frozen in terror, his mouth open in that silent scream. Throwing her arms around him, she sobbed into his shoulder. But it was like hugging a mannequin, and after only a moment she drew back, her chest in agony.

"Let me help you with him."

It was her mother, her eyes red with grief. Pela swallowed the lump in her throat and nodded, and Kryssa moved forward to take a hold of Ruebyn's petrified arms. Stones crunched and Pela saw Braidon approaching.

"Here—" he started, holding out an arm.

Kryssa's head snapped up at the sound of his voice. Releasing Ruebyn, she drew her sword. "Get away from us!" she shrieked, pointing the blade at Braidon's chest.

The king threw up his hands, a frown touching his forehead. "Surely we must—"

"*I said, get away!*" Kryssa screamed, leaping at him and swinging the blade.

Braidon jumped backwards out of range, his frown turning to a scowl, but he made no move to strike at Kryssa. For a moment, they stood facing off against one another, until finally Braidon let out a sigh.

"I am so—"

"Don't you dare apologise to me," Kryssa raged, taking another step and thrusting out with her sword again. "Don't you dare say another word, or I swear by the Gods I'll kill you where you stand."

A bemused smile crossed Braidon's face and he raised his hands, though he might have been mocking her now.

"Come now, Kryssa," he murmured. "We must work together, if we are to defeat that creature."

The sword shook in Kryssa's hands as she shook her head. "No, Braidon," she whispered. "I will never stand with you." Her voice was breaking now. "For the first time, I am glad my father is no longer here. It would have broken his heart to see the monster you have become. Now go! Leave us! You are my king no longer."

Braidon reeled back at her words, his eyes wide with shock. But a second later, his faced closed over and when he spoke his words were like ice.

"Very well, Kryssa," he grated. "I will return to Chole. But know this." His voice rose in volume, carrying now to the entire army. "Any who wish to swear their fealty to me will find shelter in the city. But all who stand against me will remain outside my walls. Now I bid you farewell."

With that he turned and disappeared into the fading light. Movement came from around them as his men followed. A minute passed, punctuated only by the crunch of boots on dirt. Then the first of Marianne's soldiers broke rank and set off for Chole—a few at first, then as though a dam broke, hundreds more followed.

By the end, only a few thousand remained on the fields outside the city, those who had seen what Braidon had done to their queen, who still held their love for her close in their hearts. They would not abandon her now, whatever darkness came against them.

And amongst them all stood Pela and Kryssa, alone now with the bodies of Genevieve and Ruebyn, alone with their love, and with their grief.

🙣 27 🙥

Caledan stalked back and forth across the campsite, his arms clasped tightly behind him. Though just over a thousand men and women remained with Marianne, the night was silent but for whispers. Not a soul had the courage to raise their voice, to rage or fight on this night—the last night.

Turning, Caledan made another loop of their campsite, studying his companions as he did so—Pela and Kryssa and his queen. Enemies not long ago, now united in their grief, in their desperation. Before the sun had set, they had started a fire from the timbers of a broken wagon, none of them wanting to face the darkness without light. Yet its glow cast his companions in shadow, so it seemed each were already halfway to death.

A shiver passed down Caledan's spine as his eyes were drawn beyond the circle of light, where Genevieve and the petrified boy lay. The first of their party to fall. They would not be the last.

Catching Marianne's eyes on him, he stalked across to

her. "We have to fight," he hissed. "I'll kill them all, Braidon and the dragons and the damned demon itself, if that's what it takes."

He knew it was an empty threat, his rage futile in the face of what would come for them on the morrow. Always before, his skill with a blade had been enough. But now magic and darkness had returned to the world, and he found himself powerless to protect his queen. The demon was too powerful, its army to great.

A smile crossed Marianne's face as she rose and took his hands in hers. "Calm yourself, my Champion," she whispered. Though Braidon had taken her powers—and almost her life—she seemed remarkably calm. "Now is not the time for anger."

Caledan shuddered, but he knew she was right. He dragged in a breath, seeking to calm his racing heart. "There must be something we can do," he whispered, looking from the queen to their companions.

Pela and Kryssa did not respond, only sat staring into the campfire, each lost in her own private grief. Marianne spoke in their stead. "You cannot feel his power. Even with the energies I gave to Braidon, it is not enough. My soul shudders at the lives the creature must have stolen, the souls that screamed out beneath his blade." Her eyes slid closed at the words, as though she could truly see all those lost innocents.

"It cannot end like this," Caledan insisted. He tried to return to his pacing, but her arms drew him back. He resisted for a moment before submitting. "What are we going to do?" he croaked.

"I have a plan for tomorrow," Marianne murmured, "though I do not know whether it can succeed. So for now, we are going to live, my Champion." With her words, Marianne took his hand in hers and drew him away. "Come, the night is beautiful, let us not waste it."

Caledan cast one last glance back at their unlikely companions, but neither seemed interested in their departure, and finally he allowed himself to be led. The stars burned overhead, and the half-moon shone down on them, lighting the way. Several times they had to detour around sleeping soldiers, but soon they left even those behind, and found themselves walking alone across the open fields.

Inevitably, Caledan's eyes were drawn back to the city. Chole was brightly lit, as though its citizens thought the light might protect them, might keep the demon from their doors. The thought brought Caledan's rage rushing back, as he recalled how the king had tricked them with his dragon, how he had tried to steal the life from the woman Caledan loved.

He shivered at the thought, glancing sidelong at Marianne. He realised in that moment it was true. They had grown close these past weeks, and he'd come to see the woman who hid behind the mask, her steely determination, her courage to do what was necessary for herself and her people.

As though reading his mind, Marianne's glanced up to catch his gaze upon her. She smiled, her sapphire eyes dancing in the moonlight.

"What are you thinking about, my Champion?" she whispered, her hand sliding into his.

"How beautiful you are," he croaked, surprised at his own boldness.

Her eyebrows lifted, but she said nothing, and they continued their midnight walk. The whispers of their loyal soldiers had fallen far behind them now, and silence ruled the night. A flash of light from nearby drew Caledan's attention, but it was only two fireflies, dancing in the dark.

Finally Marianne let out a long breath and came to a stop. Seating herself in the long grass, she bid Caledan join her. In the moonlight her face seemed softer than he had ever seen it, or perhaps that was only the loss of her power, the removal of the illusions she had used to hide herself away from the world.

"You know, as a child, I never dreamed of any of this," she murmured, then smiled wryly. "Well, that's not quite true. I knew one day I would be queen, but I thought only of Lonia, of lifting my people from the generations of poverty that had beset them since the time of the Tsar. What did I care for Plorsea?"

"But then your father led an invasion against us."

"He was desperate. His senators convinced him it was the only way, that Plorsea owed us for the crimes of their Tsar. And because of him, because of them…" She shivered, shook her head. "No, I will not hold this hatred in my heart any longer. The past is done. I refuse to let it stain this last night."

"And yet it pains you still," Caledan murmured. He took her hand in his, squeezing her fingers.

She shivered at his touch and her eyes found his once more. Her throat contracted as she swallowed.

"They were lonely years," she whispered. "Until Calybe came. And even then, to bear that man's son…" She shuddered. "In all that time, I did my duty to my father and my nation, but…it was never more than that, a task I needed to complete." The breath caught in Caledan's throat as she lifted a hand to his cheek. "I am curious to know if there is more, my Champion."

Caledan swallowed as he looked into his queen's eyes

and saw her vulnerability, the fear that he would spurn her once more, that he would turn away. Thinking of her anger before, he realised now his mistake, how he had misread her. It had been Marianne's way of protecting herself, of concealing her pain at his rejection. She was a woman used to getting what she wanted, but now all she could do was wait, was hope.

Staring into the depths of her eyes, Caledan leaned down and pressed his lips to hers. A tremor shook the queen as his arms went around her waist, and for the briefest of seconds he thought he'd been wrong. Then her lips were pushing back against his and her arms were looping over his head, her fingers sliding through his hair. A moan hissed from her throat as he hugged her close, kissing her again, tasting the rosemary of their last meal on her tongue.

They broke apart for a moment, panting softly in the moonlight. There was a wicked grin on Marianne's lips now, a sly look in her eyes. Her fingers traced a pattern over Caledan's shirt, making him tremble wherever they touched.

"I have nothing left now, you know," she said softly. "No crown, no army, no magic."

"You have me," he responded.

"Ay, I have my loyal sellsword." Again the smile, that crafty glint. "But…I fear I no longer have the coin to pay you, my Champion." Her eyes travelled down as she started flicking open the buttons of his shirt, sliding down until they were playing with the hairs on his belly. "I am afraid I have nothing left to offer you," she continued, "but myself."

A growl rumbled from Caledan's throat as he took her in his arms. He kissed her hard now, and she seemed to dissolve into him, her body clinging to his, her fingers still dancing around his midriff. Despite the burning in his chest, he drew back, sliding a hand up her leg. She still wore her scarlet dress from earlier, the silk fabric hugging her silver skin.

"That was all I ever wanted," he whispered.

Slowly, he slid his hands up her thighs, lifting the hem of her dress. She shivered at the intimacy of his touch, but made no move to stop him. His hands slipped around her thighs, raising the dress as they went. Obediently she stretched up her arms, then the dress was gone, exposing Marianne to the night's breeze.

Tossing the clothing aside, Caledan sat back on his haunches, drinking her in in the moonlight. Naked, Marianne no longer appeared a queen or Magicker, only a woman, a human with the same hopes and fears as anyone else. Her sapphire eyes stared up at him, and he saw the fear there, the sudden worry he would find her wanting.

Smiling, Caledan slowly removed his shirt and pants, until he was as naked as his queen. Then he drew her close and kissed her. His hands trailed gently over her stomach, cupping her breasts, toying with her.

A moan hissed from the back of the queen's throat and suddenly it was Marianne who was pushing him down. Now it was his turn to acquiesce, and he shivered as her hands slid across his body, as her mouth kissed and explored his flesh, touching and tasting.

Only then did Caledan realise what he was doing, who he was doing it with. It was by no means his first time, but never before had he been with someone so powerful, with a woman who could destroy him in a single word. Whatever Marianne said, she was still queen to the thousands camped out on the plains. If he hurt her…

Laughter whispered from Marianne as she sat up. "You just realised what you're doing, didn't you?" she asked.

Caledan's eyes widened. "You can read my mind?"

"No!" Marianne cried, her face alight with amusement. "But a fool could have seen it in your eyes." Her smile grew as she leaned closer. "Do I scare you, sellsword?"

A growl rumbled from Caledan's throat as he took the queen in his arms. "Nothing scares me."

❧ 28 ☙

The fire had burned low when Kryssa finally stood. Numb from kneeling so long beside Genevieve's body, her feet were unsteady beneath her and she stumbled several steps before righting herself. Then she straightened, her hand dropping to her sword hilt.

For hours she had sat in the darkness, wondering what she could have done differently, how she might have changed things. She had been blind to Braidon's evil. His greed for power had been there for all to see. It was behind all their troubles. Marianne might have been little better, but in the end the queen had at least been willing to sacrifice her power to save the Three Nations.

A shiver shook Kryssa as she looked at Chole. The gates still lay broken, destroyed by Marianne's black powder. Without thinking, she started towards them, before uncertainty brought her up short. She glanced back to where Pela lay sleeping beside Ruebyn. She claimed the mummified boy still lived, and while Kryssa had her doubts, she was proud of her daughter's courage that day.

Her gaze fell to the sword on her belt. Derryn's sword. She should have given it to Pela long ago, but instead Devon had been the one to pass the blade to her daughter. Thinking back, Kryssa could hardly believe how naïve she'd been, how she could have ever hoped to keep Pela from this world. Darkness would always rule, and the only way to fight it was with cold, hard steel.

From tonight on, Pela would be alone. Kryssa could hardly bear the thought, yet neither could she turn away from her fate. She had helped to raise Braidon up—now she must hold him accountable for his crimes. If not for his greed, they might have stood united against the demon. Instead, their forces had been sundered, and Marianne's followers abandoned on the indefensible plains to die.

She had to put things right, but she would not leave Pela defenceless. Silently, Kryssa unstrapped her sword belt and laid it beside her daughter, returning it as she had promised to do all those months ago.

Then she rose. She retrieved a spare blade from a nearby wagon and started again towards Chole. Movement came from the shadows before she made it more than a few feet, and she dropped her hand to the hilt of her new sword.

Pela stepped from the darkness ahead to bar her path. "You can't leave," she said, her voice breaking. "Not again."

Tears stung Kryssa's eyes and her heart ached, but all she could do was shake her head. "I must, Pela," she whispered. "I have to stop him. Everyone out here is doomed unless they find shelter inside the city."

"Then we swear loyalty to him!" Pela hissed. "What does it matter, when tomorrow the demon comes for us?"

A lump lodged in Kryssa's throat, but she swallowed it down, even as her mind replayed the king's disastrous attempt to ally with the nomads out on the plains. The woman Loyla had seen what Braidon was, even then. Her eyes slid closed.

"He has lost himself," she whispered. "We cannot stand with him, or we risk trading one monster with another. They both must be destroyed."

Pela stared up at her, eyes wide, fists clenched at her side. But despite her anger, Pela said nothing, only waited.

Kryssa smiled, placing a hand on her daughter's shoulder. "Your father would have been proud of you, you know," she whispered. "You are stronger than we ever were. You do not seek war."

Her eyes dropped to the sword Pela now wore, her father's blade. She let out a sigh and released her daughter. "But sometimes war is necessary," she continued. "I supported Braidon, lifted him up, though disaster followed wherever we went. I should have realised the truth after the Castle, but I was blinded by my hatred for Marianne." Her gaze returned to the city. "I have to put things right."

"You are still blind," Pela whispered. "Please don't do this."

"I'm sorry, Pela," Kryssa croaked.

She was already moving away, eyes fixed on the terrible gash Marianne's weapons had left in Chole's fortifications. Only as she neared the first bodies did she glance back. Illuminated by the moonlight, Pela still stood where she had left her. Kryssa's heart lurched in her chest and she almost turned back. Then she saw again Genevieve falling by Braidon's hand, and steeling herself, she walked into the awful city.

It was not hard to gain entrance to Chole now. Braidon's forces had erected a makeshift barricade beyond the rubble of the gate, but one look at her face, and the regiments guarding the entrance allowed her to pass.

Apparently, the king had not thought to pass on word of her betrayal.

Threading her way through the city, Kryssa found her path drawn away from the Castle. She did not stand a chance against Braidon, not alone. First, she needed to find allies.

The Temple of the Earth was full to bursting when she stepped through the great doors into the entrance hall. Priests wearing the green robes of the Goddess rushed to and fro amidst the crowds packing their chambers, offering aid wherever it was needed. Food and water were passed out amongst the healthy, while those trained in the healing arts attended to citizens that had been injured in the explosion Marianne had unleashed upon the city.

"And so you return, my daughter."

Kryssa found the same priest she had met on her last visit standing beside her. A sigh slipped from her lips as she bowed her head.

"You were right," she whispered. "The king is consumed. He must be stopped, before he destroys us all."

The softest of chuckles came from the priest. "Perhaps I was right, perhaps wrong. I know only that tomorrow the world could end, and I am tired of our wars."

"The queen's army is outside the walls. If we stand together, we might yet repel the demon. But Braidon can no longer see reason. The power has driven him mad."

"It was always a forbidden art, even before the fall of the Gods," the priest whispered. "The taking of a life force." His gaze alighted on her. "But none of that is why you wish to see the king's end."

Kryssa opened her mouth to argue, but instead a sob tore from her throat and suddenly her strength was gone.

Sinking to her knees, she looked up at the priest, her vision blurring.

"He took her from me," she gasped. "He has to pay!"

"Oh, my daughter," the priest replied, kneeling alongside her and drawing her into his arms. "I am sorry for your loss. This is a cruel, hard world. But you must let go of your hatred."

"I can't!" Kryssa cried, pulling back from him. Angrily she wiped her eyes and clambered back to her feet. "It is all that keeps me going," she grated. "All I have left."

The priest remained on his knees, and there was sadness in his eyes as he looked at her. "I am sorry to hear that, my daughter," he whispered.

Kryssa shuddered as another wave of grief threatened to engulf her. "The king must be stopped," she said. "But I cannot do it alone. Will you help me?"

"You would use our strength to fight the king?"

"I would."

"Then you still do not understand," the priest replied. "The energy of our souls is a pure, sacred thing. I would not ask any here to use that power to kill. To commit such an act is to invite corruption, to lessen yourself, your spirit."

"Even so," Kryssa whispered, "This must be done. And you must help me to do it."

The priest stared at her for a long time, his eyes boring into hers, as though he could see through to her very soul. Knowing what was in her heart, Kryssa thought he would refuse her, that she would be forced to stand against Braidon alone.

Finally he bowed his head, the wrinkles of his face deepening. "Very well, my daughter," he said. "We will put our fate in your hands. But I pray to the Gods you find another way."

$\mathscr{H}$ 29 $\mathscr{H}$

Standing atop the walls of Chole, Braidon watched as the sun crept above the line of the horizon. His heart lifted as the darkness retreated, the shadows that had clung to his mind throughout the night falling away. The time had come and there could be no going back now. He would stand against the demon, would end it here on the plains of Chole, or he would die, and Plorsea with him.

It was almost a relief now, to see the path clear ahead of him. There would be no more doubts, no more confusion. Braidon alone had the power to stop the demon, and he would not shirk from his duty.

Slowly the daylight grew, revealing the armies aligned on the plains below. The ragtag remnants of Marianne's forces had aligned themselves near the breach in Chole's walls, as though they thought they might still retreat to the city before the demon's army came. But they had made their choice. They might have been his people once, fellow Plorseans, but they had surrendered their right to his protection when they'd pledged their loyalty to Marianne.

Braidon shivered as he fixed his attention on the true enemy. The blue-armoured soldiers had hardly moved from where the portal had deposited them. They must have possessed some supernatural resilience, to stand in perfect stillness all through the night. The thought sent ice down Braidon's spine, and he checked them again through his spirit eyes, reassuring himself they were still mortals, that they could die.

There was no sign of the demon himself, nor Nidryt and the other Red Dragons. Anger touched Braidon as he recalled their treachery. With the beasts' aid, he might have driven the demon back, but now he must wait, must bide his time and gather his strength.

Drawing himself up, Braidon took stock of his own forces. His army had swelled with the queen's defections, which he had integrated amongst his own regiments. That would ensure their loyalty, at least until the day was done. If they survived until the morrow, Braidon would have all the time in the world to judge their true allegiance.

Not that any of them could hurt him, not with his power. It burned inside him even now, setting his veins alight, feeding confidence to his soul. The demon thought him conquered, but the creature had not seen a fraction of Braidon's strength. And there was power yet to gather, once the battle outside the walls commenced.

"People of the east!" Despite himself, Braidon flinched as the demon's voice boomed down from some unknown point in the sky. "The time to decide your fate has come. Choose: life, or death."

A ripple went through the forces aligned below, and Braidon could sense the terror amidst the ranks of Marianne's soldiers, the sudden uncertainty. He smiled at their fear. With their queen's powers lost, they had no hope of victory. Even should the demon withhold its magic, those rallied beneath Marianne's banners were little more than farmhands and labourers, men and women who until a few weeks ago had not known a sword from a spear. Their ragged lines would be swept aside, their treasonous souls put to death.

But Braidon would ensure their deaths were not for nothing. With each life lost, he would be there, to gather the energies of the dying, to add to his own power. Then, when the demon finally turned its attention to Chole, Braidon would finally be strong enough to destroy it.

"Do not listen to its words, my friends." A single voice rose above the whispers of discontent as Marianne stepped to the front of her forces. She was garbed in chainmail and followed by several others, some in the silver armour of the Knights, others dressed in the attire of Elders. Braidon recognised Caledan standing at her side.

"The demon offers life, but promises only slavery," Braidon's wife continued. "I say to you, we will not submit willingly to the damned! Whatever our beliefs, whatever our loyalties, we must let go of our hatred, must stand together against the darkness." Then she glanced back, and Braidon shivered as her sapphire eyes flashed in his direction. "The king may have abandoned his people, but I will never surrender." She lifted her blade above her head. "For the Three Nations!"

A ragged cheer rose from her army, followed by the rattling of swords striking shields. The lines of the Plorsean soldiers straightened, gathering into a tight-knit square. Silence fell once more as they stood together, waiting for the enemy's reply.

The wind howled into the quiet, raising the hackles on Braidon's neck, and for an instant he longed to be with the army below, to stand with those he had once considered friends and family, facing the darkness together.

"So be it." The demon seemed unperturbed, as though the queen's declaration mattered naught to it. Its voice rose to thunder. "Then go, my soldiers. Bring me a feast!"

The rattle of steel echoed up to the city walls as the blue armoured soldiers lowered their spears, followed by the *thump-thump* of marching boots as they advanced. A ripple went through the queen's forces at the sight, but Marianne only lifted her sword and let out a shout of defiance. Then she was charging forward to meet the enemy, her Guard and army following, and the sounds of clashing weapons filled the air.

Braidon watched on, his arms clasped tightly behind his back. What did he care if Marianne mocked him? She would soon be dead, her life thrown away for a hopeless cause. She might have saved herself, might have bowed down to him as so many of her followers had done, but instead she had chosen oblivion. As had all the others below.

Closing his eyes, Braidon let his spirit soar out across the battlefield. With the armies joined, the deaths came quickly now. Drifting overhead, he waited for the first glow of life to be released into the world. The screams of the dying rang in his ears and he drifted closer, an ache beginning in his soul in anticipation of the fresh energy.

Then he frowned as he sensed that something was wrong. He watched as one of Marianne's soldiers leapt forward, only to be cut down. The man staggered, then crumpled to the ground, his aura flickering out. But there was no sudden release of energy, no life force for Braidon to absorb.

That's not possible.

In horror, Braidon saw a flash of light race up the blade of the demon's soldier. Only then did he realise what his foe had done. The black gems had not just been embedded into the blue-stained armour—they had been set into the blades of the enemy soldiers as well, so that every life they stole would feed their demon master.

There would be no energy for Braidon to absorb, no fresh power to use against the creature. Instead, every death would only make the demon greater, would only make Braidon's defeat all the more certain.

Braidon gasped as his soul slammed back into his body, and he slumped against the crenulations. He had made a terrible mistake, had all but guaranteed the demon's victory. Something had to be done, before it was too late…

Laughter sounded in his ears as darkness coalesced in the air beyond the ramparts. Braidon shuddered and drew himself up, the power in his core leaping to his defence. The demon materialised and hung before him, a wicked smile twisting its face.

"Greetings, brother King," it cackled. "Do you still think to stand against me?"

Fire burned through Braidon's muscles as he hurled a wave of light at the creature. The brilliant white billowed outward, pressing against the demon's darkness, forcing it back from the ramparts. Yet still the cackling sounded in Braidon's ears.

"Your last allies fall, King," the demon continued, its hand sweeping down to the battlefield. "Their power becomes mine. Ah…what a wonder it is, to feed on the living."

"Begone, demon!" Braidon bellowed.

He sent the light flashing at the creature again, but this time the beast raised a hand and the wave was cleaved in two, parting around the demon like it was a rock in the sand. Braidon fought back despair as the demon floated closer and landed on one of the crenulations. It stared down at him, the same awful smile on its face. Braidon retreated a step, while along the wall his soldiers tripped over themselves in their efforts to escape the monster.

"You cannot defeat me, brother," the demon murmured. "Your powers are naught but the playthings of a child beside mine." It bent its head to the side, as though it were inspecting him. "But of all these boorish creatures, you have at least offered some entertainment. I see the trinket on your wrist, the power you gather from across your nation. Perhaps we might learn from each other yet."

It stepped from the crenulations and landed softly on the stone ramparts. With nowhere left to go, Braidon gathered himself for one last desperate strike. But the demon only extended a hand.

"Join me, brother," it murmured. "Join me, and I will share the power of their lives. I know you long for it. I can sense the hunger growing within you, the need to feed your soul. Come; there is enough for both of us."

The demon's words struck Braidon like a physical blow. He wanted to scream and lash out at the monster, to denounce its words as the lies they were. But even as he opened his mouth to speak, he heard again the screams from below, and imagined the shimmering energies of the dying flowing into his mortal body. All he needed was a little more, a few more lives, and he would have the strength to defeat his enemy.

But the demon's instruments thwarted him, stealing the power before it ever left its owner's flesh. Now the creature offered the unthinkable, to share those energies, to stand side by side with Braidon. He shuddered at the thought of allying with such darkness, and yet…

What if he accepted, and betrayed the monster in turn? A wave of excitement swept through him, and his every hair stood on end as he faced the beast. Did he have the courage, the strength, to deceive a creature of darkness? He must, or all was lost!

Braidon drew himself up and was about to speak, when a roar came from the battlefield. The demon spun and leapt back to the crenulations.

"It seems there is some fight left in these fools yet." The demon glanced at Braidon. "Forgive me, brother. I shall return in but a moment."

Then the demon was gone, vanishing as though it had never been. Braidon staggered to the edge of the wall and searched for the source of the commotion. His heart lurched as he saw the dust cloud rising from a nearby hill, glimpsed the flashing of hooves and swords lifted high.

Screaming their fury, the cavalry force rushed down the hillside. A great crash echoed up from below as they struck the enemy flanks. Screams followed as the horsemen carved deep into the enemy ranks and then swung away.

Braidon could hardly believe his eyes. It was Loyla and her tribe. But how had they known to come?

Then he remembered that the woman had known of his power, and the lives he had absorbed. Loyla must have power of her own and had sensed the danger. But if she had come to save them, it would not be enough. The blue-garbed soldiers were already reforming, their flanks turning to face the new threat. There was still no sign of the demon or its Red Dragons, but even on horseback, Loyla's five hundred-odd riders could not turn the tides of this battle.

Instead, their deaths would only add to the demon's

power. Braidon's heart beat faster as darkness materialised above the heads of the enemy, the demon reappearing. Watching the beast, Braidon longed to lash out at it with all his might, but he knew it would not be enough. Below, men and women were dying by the score, and every second the demon grew stronger. He needed to act, find some fresh source of strength…

Braidon's breath caught in his throat as an idea came to him. Swallowing, he stepped back from the edge of the ramparts, his gaze turning the city. Through the eyes of his spirit, Chole was alive with light, its streets and buildings lit by the glow of ten thousand spirits. The energies of every citizen within the city walls washed over him, alive and vibrant. Only now did he realise their potential, that the power to destroy the demon had lain within his reach all along.

A shudder rippled through Braidon as he looked upon each soul. They would all die if the demon won. It would kill them all, would walk through the streets of Chole and drain the life from them one by one. And if he did nothing, the death would not stop there. If he failed, the demon's evil would continue on through the Three Nations, would carry to every town, every city, as the demon feasted on the lives of the free.

Only he could stop it. Only he could destroy the beast.

Turning his eyes inwards, Braidon reached out with his power.

❦ 30 ❦

Crouching atop the walls of Chole, Kryssa crept closer to where the king stood. The demon had just vanished, but she had heard its every word, had seen the look in Braidon's eyes. Whatever happened below, Kryssa knew now what she had to do.

The energy of a hundred souls burned in her veins, making it hard to think, and she found herself wondering how Braidon had born it so long. Madness would have claimed her if she'd been forced to contain such energy for more than a few minutes. But at least she could return it, could send it back to the Earth Temple, where the priests lay in their meditative trance.

Or she could use it.

Her ears hummed as she concentrated the power into her blade, creating a deadly point that would slice through whatever defences Braidon might raise to protect himself. All she needed was to get close enough to strike. The king had retreated from the battle and now stood looking out over the city. Kryssa sent up a quick prayer to Antonia, for the Goddess's hand to guide her sword.

Then raising her blade, she charged.

For a second it seemed she would be successful. Her boots made no sound as she sprinted the last few yards, sword held out before her to drive into Braidon's back. But just as it seemed her blow must fall, the king spun. His eyes widened as they took in Kryssa and the blade, and then he thrust out his hand.

Power rushed at Kryssa, just as it had with Genevieve, and her sword grated to a stop. Enraged, she channelled more energy into the weapon, determined to avenge her fallen lover. The blade shrieked as it struck the wall of power Braidon had summoned, and a brilliant light flashed from the steel. For a second it seemed she would fail, then with a *boom*, it cut through and plunged for the king's chest.

Braidon's eyes widened in sudden fear as he realised the danger. His other hand came up, energy crackling in his palm. Kryssa's blade was mere inches away now, and with a shriek of triumph she drove it forward, sure that it must find its mark…

…Only to find herself flung backwards across the ramparts, the sword torn from her grasp. The stone crenulations brought her to an abrupt stop, driving the air from her lungs. Gasping, she slumped on her side and clutched at her stomach. With his second attack, Braidon had ignored her weapon entirely, aiming the blow for her own unprotected body.

Boots slapped against stone as the king approached. Finally managing to inhale, Kryssa dove for her fallen sword, but a gesture from Braidon sent it skittering away. Despair swept through her as she dragged herself to her hands and knees and found the king staring down at her.

"Oh, Kryssa," Braidon murmured. "What are you doing? Can you not see past your petty rage? I am our only hope against the darkness!"

"You are the darkness," Kryssa croaked, staggering to her feet.

A scream tore from her throat as she leapt, dragging the dagger from her belt. The king did not move from where he stood, only flicked his hand. Kryssa drew on the power of the living priests once more, forming a shield around her, but Braidon's power shattered it like glass. She gasped as she found herself frozen in place, her body no longer hers to control.

"Everything I have ever done was for the good of my people," the king said calmly, as though she had not just tried to kill him. "Though they reject and betray and abandon me, though I now stand alone, still I fight for them."

"You could have stood with us!" Kryssa shrieked. "But you were too consumed by your hatred." The anger went from her in a rush and her shoulders slumped. "Instead, you stand here watching while your friends die. But what do you care? I heard you speaking with the demon. I saw your temptation. Truly, you are lost, Braidon."

"I am not lost, Kryssa," the king murmured. "I am the only one who sees the truth, the only one with the resolve to do what must be done."

An icy breath blew across Kryssa's neck with his words. "And what must be done, Braidon?"

Braidon walked past her, his eyes drifting out over the city. "I don't know why I didn't see it before," he said softly. "Perhaps I was too afraid—but now the haze has lifted. There is power enough here to destroy the demon, if only I have the courage to take it."

Kryssa's heart lurched in her chest as she followed his gaze and realised what he meant. "Braidon, no! You cannot—"

The words died in her throat as Braidon made a gesture and her mouth snapped forcibly closed. He made to step past her, but drawing on the power of the priests, Kryssa tore loose from his spell.

"The power has corrupted you!" she shrieked. "Braidon, this is not you, please—"

Kryssa broke off as Braidon swung around. This time when his power came, it was not ice that stole the words from her, but a terrible fire. Her plea turned into a scream as every nerve in her body was suddenly lit aflame. The strength went from her legs and she collapsed against the ramparts. She clawed desperately at the cold stones, desperate to relieve the searing, to free herself of the agony.

"And where did *you* discover such power, Kryssa?" Braidon growled, his eyes burning as he stepped closer. "You speak of *my* corruption, but your resistance reveals your own desperation. Tell me, my most loyal servant, whose life did you drink to gain such strength?"

"None!" Kryssa moaned, her back arching as she writhed against the stone. "It is only borrowed!"

A frown crossed Braidon's face. Kryssa gasped as the pain vanished as quickly as it had come, and she slumped against the ground, struggling to regain her composure. The lines on Braidon's brow deepened as his eyes took on a distant look, as though his mind was far away. Kryssa had the sense that she could have struck him down in that moment, but her body was frozen once more, and this time she could not find the strength to break free.

"The priests!" Braidon bellowed suddenly, staggering back from her. Rage twisted his face as he swung towards the city. "Traitors spring like maggots from my ranks." He raised a fist, as though to strike the whole city down.

"No," Kryssa whispered, but she did not have the strength to oppose the king, not even to stand. All she could do was watch as the flames gathered in the king's fist.

———

LOOKING THROUGH THE EYES OF HIS SPIRIT, BRAIDON stared at the threads of energy swirling about Kryssa, radiating up from the city, from the Temple of the Earth. The priest's treachery struck him like a blow, for he had given everything to save them when the Knights had come. To learn now that they had betrayed him…

A shiver passed through Braidon as the last of his doubt fell away. He knew now that his path was true. If even his most beloved subjects had turned from him, then none in Chole could be saved. The city was corrupt to its core and must be cleansed. But the lives of its citizens might at least serve the greater good, might still save the Three Nations from eternal servitude.

He raised a fist, preparing himself to snuff out the traitors huddling behind his walls. But reaching for his power, Braidon sensed a commotion from behind him, a surge of energy radiating from the battlefield. Fear touched him. The demon approached, but he was not yet ready!

His whole body shook as dark energies washed across the walls. Cursing, he spun and braced himself for the demon's attack. Light flashed in his inner eyes, coming from the battlefield. He walked past Kryssa and stepped up to the nearest crenulation. Almost absently he gestured for her to follow, and though she could not move, his power lifted her from the stones and drew her with him.

Below, Marianne's forces were being pushed back by the blue tide. The demon's darkness now hovered above the Trolan army, but it made no move to strike down its enemies. Perhaps the creature took some perverse pleasure in the chaos of battle.

If so, the entertainment would soon be at an end. Marianne's ragtag army had retreated almost to the breach in the city walls, while out on the plains, Loyla's cavalry was attempting to harry the enemy's rear. Even as Braidon watched, they spun and charged again. A great *crash* followed as the cavalry slammed into the enemy. Dozens of the blue-armoured soldiers went down, their life forces blinking out, then surging through the black gems to the demon.

Loyla's force began to retreat—but this time the demon had had enough. An awful *roar* came from above and then the Red Dragons were diving from the clouds, their jaws open wide, the flames building in the depths of their throats. Horses screamed as panic swept through Loyla's ranks, but the inferno was not for her people.

Instead, the dragons swept past them, and their flames fell upon the earth beyond the horses. For a moment, Braidon thought the beasts had changed allegiances again—until he saw what they had done. The fields all around Loyla's cavalry were burning. Smoke stained the air black as the firestorm raged, trapping the horses in a burning circle, driving them back towards the spears of the enemy.

Ice crept down Braidon's spine as he realised why the dragons had spared Loyla's people. The life forces of those killed by dragon fire would not be claimed by the black gems—so instead the Red Dragons were forcing the horsemen back onto the blades of the demon's soldiers.

Realising his time was short, Braidon was about to turn

away when he saw Loyla herself. She had dragged her horse to a stop and now stood in the centre of her people, sword raised to the heavens. The flames burned all around them, and the rest of her cavalry had come to a stop as well. As one they turned their eyes to Loyla.

"My people!" Her voice carried over the gathered armies, though she had done nothing to amplify her call. "Lend me your strength."

Braidon could have laughed at her desperation, but the sound died in his throat as a violet light sprung from her blade. Then the other riders were following suit, and each of their swords was set aglow with a different colour. The combined energies of the army rose above their heads, shining with a brilliant rainbow light, and flashed like an arrow for the darkness gathered over the Trolan forces.

Taken by surprised, the demon's energies recoiled on themselves. A cry rose from the blue army and their ranks wavered, gaps opening in their formations. With a roar, Loyla's cavalry lowered their swords and charged, and now they carved deep into the Trolan army.

Only Loyla herself remained behind. Standing alone, she still held the blade above her head. The multicoloured light had not retreated, and at her direction it rend and tore at the demon's darkness, forcing it back upon itself.

Another cry came from across the battlefield. Fear touched Braidon as he saw Marianne leap upon a stone block that had fallen in the destruction of the gate. Sword raised to the sky, she sent her strength streaming up to join the conflagration. But the power was more than anything her own life force could have summoned, and looking out through his spirit eyes, Braidon saw she had done the same as Kryssa and Loyla. Cords of power streamed from her soldiers all across the battlefield, adding their strength to hers, even as they fought and died against the blue-garbed Trolans.

The darkness flinched against this new attack, and for a second Braidon's heart lifted. Perhaps the demon truly could be defeated, if only they worked together. Silently he gathered his strength, readying himself to join the fight, to add his power to that of Loyla and Marianne…

…But at the last moment he hesitated, his eyes drawn again to his wife, to the power shining from her body. It was exactly as he had predicted, as he had foreseen and tried to stop. It had not taken her even a day to regain what she had lost. His eyes slid closed as the fear raged inside him.

"Braidon!" Kryssa was screaming at his side. "This is your chance, help them! Together—"

She broke off suddenly, and Braidon's eyes snapped open, aware something had changed on the battlefield. His gaze was drawn back to the demon's darkness, and he saw now the truth. The attacks had not lessened it, only pressed it back on itself. Now a *boom* swept across the battlefield as it tightened, forming a terrible knot of utter black. Then it shot outwards, not as an arrow or blade but an awful hammer of pure darkness. It smashed upon the rainbow powers of Marianne and Loyla and burst them asunder. Streams of light flashed outwards across the battlefield in all directions, dying to nothing.

And then there was only the darkness.

On the hillside, Loyla bent in two in her saddle, while Marianne crumpled to the stone and lay still. Even from a distance, Braidon could see they were finished, their strength and that of their people done. Already the blue soldiers were reforming, their shields slamming together as though they were of one mind. Seeing their danger, Loyla's riders dragged back on their reins, seeking to retreat before the armoured men could encircle them.

The Trolans were faster still. A great rattling rose from the battlefield as the soldiers drew back their spears and hurled them into the clustered cavalry.

The effect was devastating. Without any armour and caught in the moment they'd been turning to flee, Loyla's people were exposed. Braidon watched grimly as horses crumpled and warriors went toppling from their saddles. The blue-garbed warriors offered no chance for respite. They marched forward into the chaos, blades rising and falling.

And as the demon fed upon their deaths, the dark cloud grew larger.

"I offered them a chance to survive," Braidon said sadly, "but they spurned me."

"You can still help them!" Kryssa shouted.

Her eyes were wild as she fought against his bonds, but Kryssa could not break free of them now, could not hurt him any longer, and he only shook his head.

"They made their choice," he said. "Now they are lost, but the Three Nations might yet survive."

His gaze returned to Chole, to the thousand pinpricks of light adrift amidst the twisting streets. Gathering himself, he sent his power streaming through the city, spinning the energies at his command into a thousand invisible threads. Each one he sent swirling about a single soul, wrapping it tight, so that all it would take was a thought, a tug, and all life in the city would be drawn to him.

Excitement swept through his soul at the fresh strength that would soon flow in his veins. Not even the demon could stand against him then. But he must act quickly, before it destroyed the last of his enemies and came for him. He steeled himself for what must be done.

"Braidon, don't do it!" Kryssa's voice came from far away.

A sharp *popping* sounded in Braidon's ears as something in the air gave way. He spun in time to see the forces gathering within Kryssa once more. With a scream she tore loose from his bindings and dropped to the ramparts, her breath coming in ragged gasps. Braidon sighed, weary of her distractions. Silently he reached out to snuff the life from her.

But she was already unleashing her energies, and surprised, he threw up his defences. The attack was red-hot when it came, shooting at him as a fiery cone, a sword of flaming light. But though it forced him back a step, there was no chance it could touch him, just as there had been no chance for those gathered out on the fields of death. It was the last gasp of a desperate soul, and Braidon pitied her for it.

Only at the last minute did he sense a deception. His power brought the fiery blade to a halt, but there was no force in the blow, none of the strength he had expected. But a second wave swept on, a shimmering power invisible to the eye. He did not know how it had evaded his shield until it struck him, and he realised it had not been an attack against his body at all.

Braidon gasped as his spirit was forced from his body. In a rage, he reached for his power but found himself separated from it. Kryssa's power had formed a shimmering shield around his body, keeping him from the energy within.

Fear touched Braidon as he found himself vulnerable. It faded as he saw it was taking all of Kryssa's strength to keep the power locked inside him. Already it was roiling against her barriers, seeking to reach him, to join once more with its master.

Enough, Kryssa, he said, drifting close to whisper into the woman's mind. *You cannot win.*

A spasmed passed through Kryssa's face but she hung on, her sapphire eyes finding his spirit. "Look, Braidon, please!" she gasped. "For the love my father held for you, look at what you have become!"

Braidon recoiled at the mention of Devon, his soul suddenly heavy with grief. He had not realised how much he missed the hammerman, how he longed for his calming presence. The campaign had hardly allowed him a moment to relax these past months—indeed, he'd been afraid to, lest his courage fail him. Now though, free of his body, of his power, he found his thoughts becoming melancholy.

Unconsciously, his gaze was drawn down. A shiver passed through his spirit as he saw the shining cords that crisscrossed the city, binding the fates of the unwitting citizens to his own. All there was left to do was to tug…

"You promised to protect them," Kryssa whispered, her voice choked with the strain of holding him.

Then suddenly her spirit was alongside him. Her image flickered in and out, strained by the force it was taking to hold him. Even so, he could sense the grief radiating from her, the pain. A picture rushed into his mind, of Genevieve collapsing to the cold earth, an arrow sprouting from her breast.

Gasping, Braidon's spirit folded in two as the anguish of what he'd done washed over him. He had killed her, his friend, and for what? Because she had tried to stop him from murdering a helpless woman?

What have I done?

He turned to Kryssa, seeing her again for what she truly

was—his most loyal follower, the woman who had believed in him, even when he'd given up on himself. How he had made her pay for that loyalty.

A sob tore from Kryssa and he could see her spirit was fading, the last energies of the priests burning away.

So much, she whispered. *Now you must do one last thing!*

Then she flickered out, and back on the ramparts her body crumpled. With the last of her strength consumed, the spell keeping Braidon from his body dissolved. He gasped as he found himself flesh and bone once more, and the burning of his power came rushing back.

Groaning, Braidon sank to his knees, the certainty of just a few moments before vanished. Power surged in his veins and he felt again the temptation, the need to reach out and drain the energy from his subjects. Already the resolve he had found was fading, overwhelmed by hunger.

He clenched his eyes closed and a moan dragged from his throat. Beyond the wall, the demon's power was like a hurricane, its surface flashing as each new soul was added to the creature's strength. Seeing its power, the need grew within him, the desperation to do whatever it took to match his foe. All he needed was a few more lives, and he could save Plorsea, save the whole of the Three Nations.

What's the point of saving Plorsea, if I can't save my family?

The hairs on Braidon's scalp stood on end as he recalled Devon's words from so long ago. That night seemed but a distant memory now, words spoken in a different time, to a different Braidon. Yet still they rang true in his mind, carving through the temptation, granting his thoughts clarity.

He might not have any family left, but there was still Kryssa, still her daughter, and ten thousand other souls in

Chole. They were all relying on him, had put their faith in him to protect them. He could not fail them now.

Braidon forced his mind to the present, and sending his soul flying, he merged his mind with the cold stone of the wall, seeking to escape the dark desire that burned in his body. Electricity surged through him as he sensed suddenly another power amidst the ancient blocks, a strange, unknown magic…

And Braidon knew what he had to do.

$\text{❧} \quad 31 \quad \text{❧}$

B*ang.*
Pela cried out as an explosion erupted overhead, sending the rainbow conflagration shooting outwards in all directions. A shock wave followed, knocking Pela backwards from the blue-armoured soldiers they fought. A rough hand caught her collar before she fell and hauled her back.

"You good?" Caledan asked quickly, flashing her a glance.

Nodding, Pela swung around in search of Marianne. There was a lull in the fighting where they stood, as their allies pushed forward to confront the Trolans. The queen had been standing atop a fallen block of granite, but there was no sign of her now...

"There!" Pela shouted, glimpsing a slender arm hanging from the top of the granite block.

"With me," Caledan growled.

The clash of swords grew louder again as the Trolans surged forward. Pela hefted her father's sword and stepped up alongside Caledan, spearing out her blade to knock aside an enemy blow. The injured Lonian soldier who had been the intended target staggered back, clutching his shoulder. Their eyes met and he nodded his thanks, then retreated towards the city.

Pela drove herself into the space he'd left and blocked a second blow from her foe. Steel shrieked on steel and the soldier stepped back. She feinted for his chest, but as his sword came down, she twisted her wrist to change the attack, and her blade went crunching through her opponent's helmet. Screaming, he dropped his blade and crumpled to the ground. The black opal set into his breastplate flashed, and Pela retreated to Caledan's side.

He offered a grim nod, but she had only a second to celebrate the victory, as two more of the Trolan soldiers took their fallen comrade's place. The fighting was all around them now, their defensive line fracturing under the weight of the enemy. Pela fought desperately, her father's sword almost an extension of her now, while at her side Caledan's blade rose and fell with deadly accuracy.

And still the blue-armoured soldiers came on. As their comrades began to fall, Caledan and Pela were slowly forced back. Caledan angled their retreat towards where the queen had collapsed, though what they would do when they reached her, Pela was not sure. Beyond the rubble that had been Chole's gates, Braidon's forces lay in wait, and the king had already made it clear they would not be allowed to pass.

Another blue-armoured warrior leapt at Pela, his broadsword swinging down for her skull. She skipped sideways and the blow cut empty air. Thrown off-balance, the soldier staggered forward, bringing him within range of her short sword. Pela thrust out, driving the point of her blade hard into his groin. Steel crunched as it found a weakness between the steel plates and plunged home.

Beside her, Caledan threw himself forward as two men came at him. Their swords danced out, one high, the other low, and for a second Pela thought the sellsword would be cut in two. But he ducked and one soldier staggered past him, while his sword flashed down to block the second. Then Caledan's dagger was in his hand and he was surging back up.

Shocked by the speed of his recovery, the Trolans had no time to recover their guard. The first screamed as the sellsword's dagger punched through the joint beneath his armpit and found his heart, while the second crashed to the ground, blood pumping from his jugular where Caledan's sword had found its mark.

"To the queen!" Caledan shouted as he leapt away from the dying men.

Pela nodded, and keeping their swords to the enemy, they crept backwards, allowing others to take their place at the front. Screams came from around them as queen's army began to disintegrate. They had all lent their strength to the queen, to aid in the desperate battle that had been fought overhead. But the demon had proven its power greater than all of them, and now they had nothing left to give.

Heart racing, Pela glanced over her shoulder and saw Marianne was now crouching atop her chunk of granite. A dozen Plorseans stood in a ring around her position, but as Pela watched a unit of Trolans broke through the frontlines and rushed at her guard.

"Back!" she cried, grasping Caledan by the shoulder.

Alerted to the danger, Caledan leapt to intercept the Trolans. Pela rushed after him, and together they tackled the group of five blue-garbed soldiers. Three turned to meet their attack while the other two raced on, determined to reach the queen.

Gritting her teeth, Pela braced as her armoured opponent bore down on her. Her father's sword leapt to deflect a horizontal blow, and her whole arm vibrated as their blades came together. For a moment she was forced back, her feet moving quickly to keep her balance.

The Trolan soldier came after her but she stabbed upwards, aiming for his helmet. Steel rang out as her blow struck, but this time her blade did not find a gap in the heavy steel. Even so, her foe staggered back, his helmet twisted out of place. Roaring, he tore it loose and tossed it aside. Face twisted in rage, he started towards her once more.

Fear slipped its way into Pela's heart as the man approached, but she did not flinch from it. In her mind, she heard her uncle's words from so long ago.

Fear is a warrior's greatest weapon—and greatest weakness!

A smile touched her face as she raised her father's blade in mock salute. A snarl tore from the man as he charged her, but even in that moment of rage, Pela sensed the sudden doubt in her foe. His sword came up, but he hesitated, and she leapt into the opening with sword raised. With his helmet lost, there was nothing to stop her blade as it took him through the eye.

Dragging back her sword, she spun in search of Caledan. But the sellsword had already dispatched his foes and was making again for the queen. The remaining Trolans had been cut down by her Guard—though not without cost. Two of the Plorseans had fallen and now lay entangled with the men they had slain.

Pela raced after Caledan, and together they took their place in the ring of soldiers. Scuffing noises came from behind them, and then Marianne stepped up beside them with rapier in hand. Shadows hung beneath the queen's eyes and her face was stretched with exhaustion, but she smiled when she saw them gaping at her.

"Marianne!" Caledan gasped. "What are you doing? It's not safe…"

The queen's smile faded with his words. "Soon nowhere will be safe, my Champion," she murmured, lifting her blade. "And when there's nowhere left to hide, a woman must choose a place to stand. I choose here, Caledan, with you."

Pela gaped at the woman, stunned that she would place herself in such danger. But then she realised the truth of Marianne's words. This *was* the end. Their last gamble had failed, and now there was nothing left to do but wait for the Trolan swords to find them, for their life forces to be absorbed by the awful demon.

Sadness touched her as she looked at Marianne and Caledan together. If only her mother had not left, they might have stood together in their final moments. But instead Pela stood alone, and Kryssa lost to her hatred.

But Pela did her best to swallow her grief. At least she had escaped the fate Rayan had planned for her, to be trapped within her own body for eternity. Just the thought of Ruebyn, lying motionless in the camp behind them, his eyes staring forever into the distance…

A shudder passed through Pela—and then, as if bidden by her thoughts, the demon's laughter rang out across the battlefield. Ice slid down her spine as the dark storm descended in a swirling column. Men and women leapt back as it struck the earth near where Pela and her friends stood together. Slowly it drew inwards, coalescing into the body of Rayan.

"And so it comes to an end," he murmured. Smiling, he

started towards them. "It will be a pleasure to drink the life from ones of such courage."

A scream came from Caledan as he leapt to meet the beast. But while the creature still took the form of Rayan, this was no man, no mortal to be defeated by the blade. With a gesture, the sellsword was hurled aside and the demon walked on.

Rage built in Pela as she watched Rayan approach. This was the creature that had stolen Ruebyn from her, who threatened her friends, her entire world. Pressure built within her as she drew on her life force, as she fed all her anger and hatred and grief into a whirling ball of energy. With a scream, her power came to life, becoming a burning ball of flame. Its heat seared at her flesh as she sent it hurtling at the demon.

The inferno crackled as it flashed across the space between them but Rayan strode on, unconcerned. As the flame approached him, the darkness rippled out in a great wave, extinguishing the flames of her power at a touch.

Gasping, Pela sank to her knees as the strength went from her legs. Stones crunched as Marianne stepped between them, but another gesture from the demon and she fell alongside Caledan. The Queen's Guard shrank back before its power, unmanned by their terror.

Then Pela was all alone, staring up into the eyes of the beast.

"Oh, my poor, Pela," Rayan murmured. "You have suffered so, trying to survive in this unjust world. But fear not: the pain is almost at an end."

"Get away from me," Pela croaked.

Finding some flicker of strength within, she forced herself to her feet. Her father's blade was still in her hand, the sword her mother had carried all these months, that

Devon had first gifted her. Rayan wore only a richly woven tunic and leggings. There was no armour to turn aside her blade, but surely it could not be so simple. Her strength at an end, Pela gripped the weapon tight and thrust it at the demon's chest.

A bemused expression crossed Rayan's face as he caught the blade between his thumb and forefinger. Laughter whispered from his throat as he thrust it back, propelling Pela from her feet. Rolling across the scorched earth, she came to rest against the granite block that had once formed part of Chole's walls.

"Enough, young Pela," Rayan whispered as he closed the fresh distance between them and crouched beside her. "You need fight no longer. The time for your reward has finally come."

His hand snaked out and caught Pela by the wrist. Unable to tear herself loose, she cried out as something dark crossed between them, an awful, sickly presence. A cry built in her throat, but before Pela could let it loose, she found her mind retreating. Suddenly she was in the depths of her consciousness, in that empty void where her life force burnt.

Except it was no longer empty. The dark tendrils of the demon were all around her, swirling cords of infinite black just waiting to snare her, to hold her fast and trap her in this silent space. Terror filled Pela and she reached for her life force, for the last few drops of flame to protect herself, but the darkness was faster still.

Pela's fear turned to horror as the first black vine snapped fast to her leg. Her screams echoed through the void as she thrashed, but Pela had no strength left to resist, and soon another grasped her. Her arms were pinned fast, then her other leg. Her skin crawled as the darkness crept over her, engulfing her torso, then chest, slowly creeping towards her head.

Boom.

Light flashed across the void and suddenly the vines were retreating, as though some other force had torn them loose at the root. Pela cried out as she found herself suddenly back in the real world. Her whole body screamed in pain, but there was no time to dwell on it.

A blinding rainbow light swirled all around her, tearing at her hair, lifting her up, dragging her to her feet—no, not the light, but the demon's grasp on her arm. Screaming, she brought the hilt of her sword down on its wrist, desperate to break its hold, but Rayan clung on, his fingers like a vice. Another shriek tore from Pela as she was yanked up, her arm almost tearing from its socket.

Then the ground beneath her vanished and she found herself flying, spinning, and lurching through a rainbow of light, the world disappearing around her…

🦋 32 🦋

Boom.

An explosion on the battlefield tore Kryssa from unconsciousness. Gasping, she pushed herself upright and then promptly slumped back to the battlements as her entire body screamed out in agony. Distantly she felt her own pain reflected in the minds of the priests whose power she had drawn on—she'd used far too much of their energies, and now they would all suffer for it.

The last rumbles of the explosion were already dying away, but the air still hummed with power, filling her with a sense of urgency. Gritting her teeth, she forced herself to her hands and knees. Scanning the ramparts, she found Braidon crumpled nearby.

For a second, Kryssa thought he was dead, but then his chest moved half an inch, and a soft groan came from the depths of his throat. Agony wrapped around Kryssa's forearms as she clawed her way across the ground to him, but she swallowed her screams. Her heart pounded in her chest, and she sensed something of significance had happened while she'd been passed out, that Braidon had done something terrible.

Her stomach swirled as she remembered his plan—to drain the life from every soul in Chole. But she had gotten through to him, had forced him to see the truth with the last of her power. Surely, surely Braidon could not have committed such an atrocity.

The king's eyelids fluttered as Kryssa slumped beside him, and then sapphire eyes were looking up at her. Kryssa's breath caught in her throat as she saw the despair there. A sudden silence fell around them, as beyond the crenulations all went still.

"Kryssa," he croaked.

"What did you do?" Kryssa whispered.

She pushed herself to her knees to look between the stone crenulations. Beyond the walls, the battle had ceased, though there was no way of telling why. The Trolan soldiers stood frozen in their rows of blue-stained steel, while opposite them the forces of the free watched them with trepidation, clearly confused by the unexpected respite.

Then steel rattled as the blue-garbed soldiers began to disengage and pull back. The thud of marching boots carried to the walls as the Trolans retreated out onto the plains and regrouped. Marianne's army watched on, mystified by their enemy's actions, while Loyla's few remaining riders trotted their horses up to join them.

"I'm so sorry, Kryssa."

The hairs on Kryssa's neck stood on end at the tone of Braidon's voice. She spun on the king.

"*What did you do, Braidon?*" she repeated.

"I should never have tried to kill Marianne," the king continued as though he had not heard her. She leaned closer, but his eyes were fixed on some distant point, and she realised his mind was somewhere else. "Genevieve was right...to stop me. How I wish..." He trailed off, and now blinking, his eyes fixed on her. "I'm so sorry."

Anger flared in Kryssa's chest and she felt a longing to drive her dagger through his heart. She fought the desire, her soul weary of the hatred, of the rage that had driven her these last months. She could see the pain in Braidon's eyes, the guilt. She could not offer him her forgiveness, but she rested a hand on his shoulder all the same, trying to comfort him.

"Thank you for stopping me," Braidon rasped, his gaze still fixed on hers. "For saving me. I...could never have forgiven myself had I..." He scrunched his eyes closed. "I should have seen the way sooner."

"What way?" Kryssa asked, leaning closer, but Braidon was rambling again, his mind lost.

"The demon needed to be separated...from its power... but I could not do it...like you did with me. Too...well protected. Ah, but that I had acted sooner...such a price..."

Kryssa's heart was starting to race again as she sensed the meaning behind Braidon's words. He had done something to the demon, but something had gone wrong. Something terrible.

"*Braidon*," she said, gripping him by the shirt and shaking him. "Tell me what you did, or by the Gods, you'll wish the demon had killed you."

The king's head lolled on his shoulders but he did not resist her. When she released him, he slumped back to the ramparts like a ragdoll. Only his eyes moved, fixing again on her.

"It already has," he coughed.

As though bidden by his words, Braidon's face contorted and he cried out, his whole body going taut. A convulsion wracked him and for a second Kryssa though he would die without telling her a thing. But finally he slumped against the ground, his breath coming in ragged gasps. She leaned in close, straining to hear the words he spoke next.

"It…was so strong, I hardly had the strength. But I held it. I banished the demon, though it took all the energies I had stolen. If only I could have saved her as well."

"Saved who?" Kryssa barely dared to ask the question. She knew what Braidon would say before he ever spoke the name.

"Pela."

Kryssa reared back as though she had been struck by lightning. She couldn't breathe, couldn't see, couldn't think. There was a ringing in her ears, a horrible, awful burning in her heart. She clutched at her chest as her entire body shook.

"No," she gasped, as though her denial could take back Braidon's words. Leaning forward, she grabbed the king and shook him. "No, Braidon, tell me you didn't! Tell me you didn't take my daughter from me!"

But the king's eyes only fluttered closed. The tension fled his body, the last spark of his life force with it. Suddenly Kryssa was alone atop the ramparts, with only the company of the dead for comfort. A sob tore from her throat as she buried her face in Braidon's shirt.

"No, no, no," she groaned, then threw herself back from him.

Folding into herself, she slammed her fist into the stones. A sharp *crack* came from her knuckles and pain shot through her fist. She screamed and lashed out again, concentrating on the pain, the agony of her broken bones—anything but what she had lost.

Selina, Devon, Genevieve, Pela, Braidon. They were all

gone, everyone she had ever loved, had ever cared for. How could this have happened?

Kryssa lurched to her feet and stumbled to the edge of the ramparts. The battlefield stretched out below, and she saw now the piles of bodies, heard the distant groans of the dying. Marianne's survivors had gathered near the gates, but they were so few now. The dead outnumbered the living.

Slowly, her gaze travelled downwards and she stepped up to the top of the crenulations. It was a sixty-foot drop to the rocks below. Pain radiated from her hand, but it was nothing to the anguish in her heart. One step, and it would all be over.

Her eyes were drawn back to the huddle of survivors. It was impossible to say who remained, if Marianne or Caledan still lived. If both had fallen, who would take command now? Movement out on the plains drew her attention to the Trolan force. The men had retreated only a short distance from the city. Even without the demon, they badly outnumbered the defenders. And these men were men who had willingly served the beast. They could still prove a threat.

Swallowing her grief, Kryssa stepped back from the ledge. She could not give up. That was not the woman Selina and Devon had raised her to be. Whatever her pain, whatever her loss, she must go on. There were people who would need her before the day was done.

Absently, she started along the ramparts, making for the stairwell. Passing from the wall to the narrow alleyways of Chole, she made her way to the gates in a daze, to the barricade Braidon's soldiers had erected to guard the city. His solders were still there, though they were scattered and disorganised, their leaders long since fled.

"Lieutenant Kryssa!" one gasped when he saw her, hope alighting in his eyes. "What news from the king?"

Kryssa paused mid-stride, casting a glance in the man's direction. "The king is dead," she murmured. "Open the barricade. Let the queen's soldiers into the city."

She walked on as shouting broke out in her wake, uncaring whether they obeyed her orders or not. She wanted only to find the survivors, to see for herself the truth of Braidon's last words. Perhaps the king had been wrong, delirious in his final moments. Perhaps Pela had survived after all.

But Kryssa couldn't bring herself to believe it.

She climbed over the barricade and started across the blackened earth. Chunks of granite rose up around her, and it was not long before she came to the first of the bodies. The men and women who had followed Caledan into the breach lay all around, blackened and broken by dragon flame.

You did this.

Kryssa shuddered and lifted her eyes, unable to face that guilt today. Ahead, Marianne's forces had gathered in a tight group around their injured, still watching the distant Trolans. It seemed they did not believe the battle was done either.

"Does the queen live?" Kryssa called as she approached.

A dozen faces spun towards her. Several reached for their blades, but a man's voice rose above the whispers before any could attack:

"Let her pass!"

The slightest of hopes touched Kryssa's heart as she recognised Caledan's voice. The soldiers parted at her approach, and she made her way through their ranks to where a single block of granite lay. There she spied Caledan and the queen. They stood atop the block, their eyes on the enemy. At Kryssa's appearance they gestured for others to take their place, then stepped down to meet her.

"I'm so sorry, Kryssa," Caledan whispered, and the last pieces of her heart shattered. "The portal…it took her before I could…" He shook his head, leaving the sentence unfinished.

"It was Braidon," Kryssa said, her vision blurring. "But…I did not see. Please…how did it happen?"

"It was The Way," Marianne answered, "Braidon must have opened it with his power and directed it at the demon. But it already had Pela in its grasp. She was dragged in with it."

"They are in The Way?" Kryssa gasped. Her head snapped up, her heart missing a beat. "Then she is not dead!"

"No," Marianne replied, but there was such sadness in her voice that Kryssa felt the hope wither in her chest, "but it matters not. The demon's power came from its subjects. It could draw on their strength at will, from all its soldiers here —and in Trola. But The Way is another world, another place entirely. By banishing it there, Braidon cut the creature off from its source of power. But if the door were opened…"

"Its power would be restored," Kryssa croaked.

"And Pela would be its first victim, if it hasn't already…" Marianne trailed off, and Kryssa could see the sadness in the queen's eyes, the pity.

Kryssa turned away, head bowed. "Your people may enter the city," she whispered, unable to face them.

She had failed. Had failed her daughter, her lover, her king. All she had left now was her duty to her people.

"Will you join us?"

It was Caledan. He moved to stand beside her as around them the army started towards Chole. Kryssa looked up at the sellsword, wondering at his words, knowing he meant so much more than just entering the city. After all Plorsea had suffered, the nation would need rebuilding. As would Trola.

Looking back at Chole, Kryssa shuddered. So much had happened inside its walls, so much darkness. She had played her part in it, helped to feed the hatred that had consumed Braidon. How could she *not* return, to offer whatever aid she could to put right her wrongs?

And yet, hadn't that been Braidon's fate? He had returned again and again, always trying to right some past wrong, to correct his mistakes. In the end, he had succeeded at least in halting the demon's darkness, but…he had almost fallen to that same fate in the process. Kryssa had no desire to walk that line. And she had no desire to ever see the inside of Chole's walls again.

"No, Caledan," she whispered, watching as the soldiers streamed past them. "They don't need me. I will find my own path."

Caledan stared down at her for a long moment, his expression unreadable. Then abruptly, he dragged Kryssa into a hug. She hugged him back, struggling to keep the tears from falling. Her dignity was the only thing she had left, the last comfort to which she could cling. She felt a touch of pride when Caledan finally drew back and her eyes remained dry.

"I don't know what happened up there," Caledan murmured, his eyes drawn to the battlements. "But I have a feeling you had a hand in what happened. Thank you, for everything."

She dropped her head in acknowledgement but did not

speak, least the dam break. Then she was turning her back on him, moving through the ranks of soldiers, away from the cursed city. Still fearful of the blue-garbed army standing out on the plains, most of Marianne's soldiers were already through the breach, but several had stayed to help with the injured.

There were plenty of those after the last hour of battle, and Kryssa's mood soured further as she looked on the aftermath of the demon's plague. It might not have come from a disease, but her daughter had been right in that, at least. The violence, the hatred and greed that had beset the Three Nations these last thousand years was just as deadly as any sickness.

But Kryssa was done with sacrificing her own life, her own happiness, for the sake of others. She would not make the same mistake as Braidon.

"Kryssa?"

The hairs on her neck stood on end as a voice called her name. Kryssa's heart tumbled into her stomach as she swung around and saw the boy, Ruebyn, standing nearby. He was as pale as a ghost, as though all the blood had been drained from his veins, and he barely seemed able to keep his feet. He staggered towards her, and she darted forward to catch him before he fell.

"Easy," she whispered, holding him up, even as her heart split in two all over again.

She could not face this, could not bear to see any more pain, any more grief. Not when it so closely reflected her own…

"Where is Pela?"

The whisper was softly spoken, but it broke her as surely as any blade. Tears poured down her face as she hugged the boy, desperate to offer him some comfort, some words of hope, but unable to find them. Wet heat soaked into her shoulder as the boy cried with her.

She didn't have to say a word for Ruebyn to know the truth.

They clung together in the silence. It was all they could do now—comfort each other in their grief. Yet recalling the moment she had stood on the edge of the ramparts and contemplated ending it all, Kryssa felt relief that she had turned away. Her family might be gone, her whole world and agony, but she at least was no longer alone.

And nor was Ruebyn. Together, they would survive, and those they had lost would live on in their memories. Their names would be carved into fresh legends, and tales of their bravery passed down to inspire a new generation of heroes, to bring hope on the darkest nights.

And perhaps then the world would become a slightly brighter place.

EPILOGUE

Pela groaned as she woke alone amidst a broken forest. Shattered tree trunks lay strewn all around her, their roots torn up and leaves withered to a sickly brown. The earth beneath her feet was churned and broken, marked by the passage of a thousand men. She drew in a breath, then retched at the scent of rotting meat, though beneath it a faint trace of life still lingered. Overhead, the sky was a swirling purple.

The Way.

But how had she come to be there? Had the ancient magic drawn her back? No, that didn't seem right. She shivered, remembering the awful battle, the screams of the dying and the scent of blood. Compared with that, The Way remained tranquil, despite the damage the demon's forces had left during their passage.

The demon.

Suddenly alert, Pela dragged herself to her feet. She might be safe here, but the demon and its soldiers remained free. Her family and friends were still in danger

—she had to get back and help them, before it was too late. Closing her eyes, she reached for the power of her life force.

Before the walls of Chole, she'd had barely a spark of energy left, yet something about this other world seemed to restore her energies. Indeed, when Pela looked through the eyes of her spirit, she found a soft mist of white all around, seeming to concentrate around her and the other points of life that had survived the demon's passage.

Returning to her body, she gauged her strength. The flame of her soul remained weak, but it would be enough. She could not afford to linger in this place, not with its strange passage of time.

She was about to wake the magic of The Way when the hackles on her neck lifted in warning. Her father's sword leapt into her hand as she spun, scanning the battered undergrowth. Laugher carried to her ears as a figure appeared amidst the shadows, and then Rayan stepped into the light.

"Hello, sweet Pela."

A scream built in Pela's throat as she leapt back from him, the blade extended before her.

"Stay away from me," she gasped, though she knew there was nothing she could do to stop the demonic creature's approach.

"I must admit, your king had more power than I gave him credit for," Rayan continued. "If he survived this effort, I'll be sure to tear the life from him when I return."

"What made you so hateful, Rayan?" Pela rasped. Her vision blurred as the demon continued forward. She staggered, her feet threatening to give way beneath the weight of her terror. She was powerless before him. All she had left were her words. "Can't you see what it has cost you?" she continued. "Can't you see the truth? Look around, look at what your evil has done."

She made a gesture at the ruined forest, the broken, lifeless trees. When she had finally left this place with Ruebyn, it had no longer been the barren world they'd found upon their arrival, but a thriving jungle, its life restored by whatever magic their presence had brought.

"What do I care for this place?" Rayan spat. "It is imaginary, a construct of some ancient magic. It does not touch the real world." His head leaned to the side. "And it is you who cannot see. The Gods had it right when they ruled us, but they lacked the resolve to bring a lasting peace. They could not see it was your freedom that divided you, that drove your petty wars. I will not make the same mistake."

"You bring only death," Pela whispered. "Only hatred."

Drawing on the last ounce of her courage, she leapt at him, her father's sword flashing for his face. She put all her anger and rage into the blow, all the strength she could muster to strike the creature down—but as her blade slashed for Rayan's neck, the strength seemed to be drawn from Pela.

Crying out, Pela's knees buckled and she staggered sideways, barely able to keep her feet. Laughter sounded in her ears, rekindling her anger. Straightening, she found Rayan still standing in the centre of the clearing, the smug smile still pasted across his face. Teeth bared, Pela leapt at him again—but again the energy went from her as though sucked down a drain, and instead she found herself crashing face first into the broken earth.

"You know, my father was like you." The demon's voice seemed to circle her as she spat out a mouthful of dirt. "Always looking for the *right* way, always seeing the good in humanity. Even at the end, when he discovered what I had become, he sought to *save me from myself.*" Rayan cackled as though this were some grand joke. "The fool might have saved himself, had he been ruthless enough. But he proved as weak as all the others."

The demon's voice was close now, just above her head. Roaring, Pela drove her blade upwards, praying for the speed to strike her foe down. This time she summoned her own power as well, funnelling it into the blade, determined to slash through whatever defences the demon raised against her.

She might as well have poured her power into the infinite depths of the ocean. It went from her in a rush and then vanished, leaving the demon standing untouched. Pela staggered to her feet and backed away, the sword slipping from her fingers as the last resistance left her.

The air seemed to darken as the creature stalked after her, as though a little more life had left the world. The stench of rot was all around her now, so thick she could barely breathe, barely think. Suddenly her legs were giving way and Pela crashed to the ground.

Despair swept through her as she watched the demon approach. What was the point in fighting anymore? She could not defeat Rayan, could not slay the demon he had become. He was toying with her, stretching out the moment of her death, if only to savour her agony when she finally succumbed.

"Surrendering so easily, young Pela?" Rayan chuckled. A sharp *thwack* came as Pela's blade slammed into the ground beside her head. "There," he continued, "I thought you could use the help. Come on, don't give up yet. There is still so much fun to have!"

Rage fed fresh energy to Pela's limbs. Snatching her blade from the earth, she scrambled backwards. A wiry bush brought her up short but she crashed through it, barely managing to keep her feet. Glancing back, she watched the plant's last leaves wither and die, but Pela was too exhausted to care. She couldn't understand where her strength had gone. Just a few minutes before this world have been restoring her—now it seemed to have reversed. Rayan stood across from her, mocking her with his calm.

"Or maybe you prefer to flee?" Rayan rumbled. "Go on, I'll give you a head start. Run!"

Pela bared her teeth in a show of defiance. But in her mind, a tiny voice screamed for her to obey, to open the portal and hurl herself back into the real world. The Way had transformed back to a place for the dead, the life she and Ruebyn had born almost consumed now. Soon it would take her too, she sensed. She needed to escape…

But the demon would only follow. He was too powerful, could snuff out her life with hardly a thought. She was surprised Rayan had not already destroyed her. Surely he wished to return to his army, to resume his destruction of Marianne's army.

A frown touched Pela's brow as she faced the beast. Why *hadn't* Rayan finished her? On the battlefield, he had been on the brink of stealing her soul, but now he had not made single attack—only rebuffed her own efforts.

Or had he?

Closing her eyes, Pela looked out again with her spirit and finally saw what had changed. The white glow that had lit the world earlier was all but vanished, reduced to mere whiffs that clung to the last patches of life. Clouds of darkness swept out in the wake of the darkness—but they did not come from the demon.

The darkness came from her.

Pela turned her gaze on Rayan. The darkness swirled

about him, but there was no longer any light in his core, no glow from the thousands of souls he had stolen. And she remembered now how the demon's power had been channelled through the king—rather than stored within Rayan.

The Way had cut him off from that source.

Pela gasped as she returned to her body. Blood pounded in her ears as she looked on Rayan with fresh eyes. Without his subjects, without his soldiers, he was all but powerless here. The darkness was sustaining him as the light had done her, but it was not enough. She could see Rayan's hunger now, as though he were a Feline and she a helpless deer. Shuddering, she backed away.

"That's right, run," Rayan whispered as he stalked after her. "Flee back to your mother's skirts."

Pela staggered to a stop. Her heart hammered in her chest and she wanted desperately to obey the demon's command, but she could not. The second she opened the portal, Rayan's connection to his subjects would be restored. She would only be dooming herself and everyone else back in the real world.

The truth struck Pela like an arrow to the heart. She was trapped here, doomed to remain in this dying land, alone but for the awful demon. There was barely a glint of green left amongst the forest now, and the sky had darkened to bloodred.

Pela's whole body shook as she imagined spending the rest of her life beneath that sky. She sank to her knees, the blade slipping from her fingers.

"No," she whispered.

Tears streaked her cheeks as she grieved for the life she would never have, the friends and family she would never see again. Stones crunched as Rayan stepped closer. She could sense his hunger now, his greed. It was so strong it almost seemed real, a stench she tasted on the air, felt in her very bones.

"It doesn't have to be this way." His voice whispered in her ears. Pela shuddered but did not pull away. "You can still escape. I will spare you, spare your loved ones. You can still be together."

Temptation shot through Pela like a living thing, desperate, burning, but she fought it down. The demon spoke only lies—and even were it telling the truth, it could not offer life, only servitude. Despair rose to take its place and she fought to keep from screaming.

In, out. In, out.

Sucking in a deep breath, Pela sought to calm herself, to follow the words that had brought her through so much strife. Her heart slowed by half a beat. The hiss of Rayan's anger sounded from nearby, but he had no power here, and reaching calmly now for her life force, she erected a barrier around herself. She was almost surprised when The Way did not steal the energy, but she did not open her eyes, did not allow herself to be distracted. In each moment, there was only the cool breeze of her inhalation, the heat of each exhale.

Finally she found herself in the void of her inner mind. Only then did Pela allow other thoughts to intrude. Warmth touched her as she remembered her kindly grandmother, Selina, and her patience when Pela had first learned to meditate.

The image flickered, and now she saw Devon as he worked on their family inn, his hammer rising and falling, sealing the roof against the coming winter. Her mother stood nearby, an absent smile on her face as she watched the aging hammerman.

Pela's heart swelled as the image of her family faded.

Another rose to take its place, and she saw again Genevieve and Caledan on the deck of the *Seadragon*, their practice blades flashing as they sparred. It soon changed again, and Pela watched as the huntress lifted her from the darkness of the mines, as she stood alone in the pass to hold back their enemies, as she raised her bow that final time to defend the helpless queen.

Tears stung Pela's eyes as she watched her friend fall, but there was no anger now, only love for everything Genevieve had done, for everything she had offered the world.

And finally Pela saw herself in that cave far above the Lonian planes. Her heart ached as she watched Ruebyn take her in his arms, as they made love while the storm raged outside. How losing him hurt, how she hated Rayan for sacrificing himself, and yet…

The demon could not steal these memories from her, could not take the brief moments she and Ruebyn had shared. The warmth in her chest seeped slowly outwards, filling her every limb. Within, Pela felt her strength retuning. Without, time passed unnoticed, and The Way changed.

Finally, Pela cracked open her eyes. Wonder touched her as she looked upon a new world. Gone were the rotting trees and rotten stench, the absolute stillness of death. Life had returned to the forest and now noble firs and pines grew up all around her, their emerald branches stretching for the sapphire sky.

For a long while, Pela sat staring at the beauty of the place, her heart filled with joy at the miracle. But eventually, memories of the demon drew her mind back to the present. Letting out a breath, she turned to face her foe—and recoiled.

Rayan still wore his sickly grin, but it was his only feature that had not changed. While she had meditated, the flesh had peeled from his face, exposing the yellowed bones beneath. Empty eye sockets stared down at her, while atop his scalp the skin had retreated, and now long white hair hung around his shoulders. Even his clothes had rotted, the remnants revealing the jagged points of his ribs.

Hand clasped to her mouth, Pela stifled her horror. Letting out a long breath, she sent her thanks up to the Gods. Somehow, she had won, had outlasted—

Lurching suddenly, Rayan took a step towards her, his laughter returning. Now though it was a hollow, empty sound, like the distant scream of a man falling to his death. Pela scrambled to her feet as the skeletal remnants reached for her, a scream tearing from her throat.

"You thought me dead?" the demonic skeleton rasped. "Not without you, sweet Pela!"

Panic rose in Pela's chest and she felt an irresistible urge to flee. Instead, she steeled herself to face the demon. If this was the end, she would not retreat. Like her father, she would stand against the darkness with sword in hand. This creature could not be allowed to escape, to return its evil to the Three Nations.

But as the skeleton approached, a thought came to Pela. Fighting for calm, she straightened and sheathed her sword. "I think you are powerless," she said softly, staring into the empty eyes. "I think you have nothing left, Rayan. Only the magic of this place sustains you."

"Come, girl," the skeleton rattled, and it seemed that sparks of red appeared in its eye sockets, "and I will show you my power."

Pela shook her head. "I don't think I will," she whispered.

Even as she spoke, Pela was reaching for her life force. It leapt to her summons now, restored by the magic of this strange world, by her own love. With it, she reached out for the ancient magic of The Way, ready to open the portal. Sensing what Pela was doing, Rayan staggered to a stop. His skull's grin grew wider.

"Yessss," the demon hissed. "Open the doorway."

A rush of air struck Pela as the portal burst into life. The skeleton readied itself to leap, but Pela's sword flashed up, barring its path.

"Think twice, mighty demon," she murmured. She wore a smile of her own now. "Perhaps you should look to yourself first."

Rage twisted what remained of the skeleton's features as Rayan swung on her. "You will not stop me."

Pela spread her hands. "Why would I? You must realise there is nothing for you outside this place now?" Silence answered her words, and chuckling, she went on: "Look at yourself, Rayan. There is nothing left of you, no flesh or blood or heart. The Way sustains you, but all the power in the world cannot restore your body. The second you step from this place, your bones will collapse and your soul will flee to whatever awaits us after death."

The skeleton did not respond, did not even move. It was as though Pela's words had truly struck Rayan dead. Slowly she retreated towards the portal, sword still stretched before her. The empty eye sockets followed her, and she could sense the hatred there, but now the demon made no move to follow her.

Finally she stood at the edge of the portal. Its energies buffeted Pela as she looked back at what now passed for Rayan. He would be trapped here forever, unable to escape, yet unable as well to die. She could not imagine such a fate, yet he had made his choice. He could end it now, could leap through the portal and allow death to claim him. But despite all the lives he had stolen—or perhaps because of them—that was one fate Rayan could not accept.

"Farewell then," she said.

Then the portal was swallowing Pela up, and the swirling rainbow lights of The Way were all around her. The passage only seemed to last a moment this time, and with an earth-shaking *boom*, she found herself standing in the real world.

Relief swept through Pela as the portal vanished, quickly followed by joy. She was free, she was safe! The Three Nations were safe. Slumping to her knees, she sobbed into the dirt, uncaring who might see.

All around, the world was silent but for the wind through the trees. A frown touched Pela's forehead as her thoughts turned to the present. What had become of the battle? Had the forces of the free succeeded in defeating the Trolan army? Or had the blue-armoured soldiers surrendered when their demon master failed to reappear?

Coming to her feet, Pela finally took the time to examine her surroundings. The plains were overgrown where she had landed, the scraggly trees and bushes thick around her. Taking her father's sword, she hacked her way to a nearby tree that stood above the rest and scrambled up.

Pela's heart was hammering in her chest by the time she reached the top. But when she looked out across the land around her, the view was not what she had expected. There was forest all around her—there was nothing like it within a day's ride from Chole. What had gone wrong with the portal? It was meant to be connected to the city walls, yet the only landmark she could see was a nearby escarpment, its surface thick with vines.

Frowning, Pela stared at the cliffs. There was something wrong about them, but she could not quite tell what.

Returning to the ground, she set off towards them, using her blade to carve a path through the dense undergrowth.

She was panting hard by the time she reached the escarpment, but even there she did not stop. Blood pounded in her ears as she followed the base of the cliffs, studying the strange stones. What she was seeing could not be possible, surely. Ruebyn had said that time moved differently in the way, but even so…

Pela staggered to a stop as the cliffs came to an abrupt end. Fifty yards ahead, they resumed, but between there was only empty space, as though some giant had carved through the rock with his sword. Heart in her throat, Pela staggered into the gap between the cliffs—though she knew now that was not what they were—and the earth turned to cobbles beneath her feet.

Tears streamed down Pela's face as she stood in the breach in Chole's walls. A great sob tore from her throat as she stared at the ruins, long since abandoned by the hands of men. In a rage, she swung her blade at a sapling that had taken root amidst the rubble. But it was a futile gesture—the decades had long since claimed the city. There was nothing she could do to change her fate, to turn back time. It was already done, her life lost to the abyss. Now there was nothing left.

Turning her eyes to the empty heavens, Pela mourned for the world she had lost forever.

———

THAT'S IT FOR NOW! BUT BE SURE TO CHECK OUT MY OTHER fantasy world in **_Descendants of the Fall_**, and out what happens next in , and don't forget to **_leave a review_** if you enjoyed the story.

NOTE FROM THE AUTHOR

Wow, what a ride! And if you've made it this far, thank you for joining me on the journey! This series might have been a little different from my earlier books, and even what I originally intended, but sometimes the world and our lives have other plans. I finished the first draft of Daughter of Fate on the day of the Christchurch terror attacks, and after seeing the horrible outcome of such hate, I knew I needed to write something different this year, something that rejected that hate. I hope you enjoyed it :-)

Anyway, onto other business. With Pela now an unknown number of years in the future, there's obviously the possibility of more stories in the Three Nations, but for now I'm looking at another project to refresh myself. I hope to start working on something new in the next few weeks and all going well you might be seeing something brand new from me in February! In the meantime, if you'd like to hear more from me, please remember to join to my mailing list for updates, specials, and a free copy of my novels Stormwielder and Oathbreaker! I also send out lots of free deals and specials most months, so if you love fantasy you can't go too wrong.

And of course, remember to read on for free excerpts from my other works!

Descendants of the Fall

If you've enjoyed this book, you might want to check out another of my fantasy series!

Centuries ago, the world fell. From the ashes rose a terrible new species—the Tangata. Now they wage war against the kingdoms of man. And humanity is losing.

Book 4: Dreams of Fury

The Alfurian Chronicles

Book 1: Defiant

Book 2: Guardian

Book 3: Conquest

The Swords of Heaven and Hell

Book 1: Darkstrider

The Four Circles

Book 1: Help! My Wizard Mentor Had A Heart Attack And Now I'm Being Chased By A Horde Of Giant Spiders!

The Untamed Isles

The Path Awakens